Philip Boast is the a............................nten the
Deus, Resurrection, ... the
Ben London trilog.............*Child, London's
Millionaire* and *London's Daughter,* as well as *Gloria*
and, more recently, *The Foundling,* all of which are set
in London. He is also the author of *Watersmeet,* a West
Country saga, and *Pride,* an epic novel set in Australia
and England.

Philip Boast lives in Devon with his wife Rosalind
and three children, Harry, Zoe and Jamie.

Also by Philip Boast from Headline

London's Child
London's Millionaire
London's Daughter
Watersmeet
Pride
Gloria
City
The Foundling
Resurrection
Deus
Sion

Era

Philip Boast

HEADLINE

Copyright © 2000 Philip Boast

The right of Philip Boast to be identified as the Author
of the Work has been asserted by him in accordance with
the Copyright, Designs and Patents Act 1988.

First published in 2000
by HEADLINE BOOK PUBLISHING

First published in paperback in 2000
by HEADLINE BOOK PUBLISHING

10 9 8 7 6 5 4 3 2 1

All rights reserved. No part of this publication may be
reproduced, stored in a retrieval system, or transmitted,
in any form or by any means without the prior written
permission of the publisher, nor be otherwise circulated
in any form of binding or cover other than that in which
it is published and without a similar condition being
imposed on the subsequent purchaser.

All characters in this publication are fictitious
and any resemblance to real persons, living or dead,
is purely coincidental.

ISBN 0 7472 5961 5

Typeset by CBS, Martlesham Heath, Ipswich, Suffolk

Printed and bound in Great Britain by
Mackays of Chatham plc, Chatham, Kent

HEADLINE BOOK PUBLISHING
A division of Hodder Headline
338 Euston Road
London NW1 3BH

www.headline.co.uk
www.hodderheadline.com

For John and Susanna

There were giants in the earth in those days; and also after that, when the sons of God came in unto the daughters of men, and they bare children to them, the same became mighty men which were of old, men of renown.

Genesis 6:4

Prologue

Belize, Yucatán Peninsula, Central America

Prologue
Belize, Yucatán Peninsula, Central America

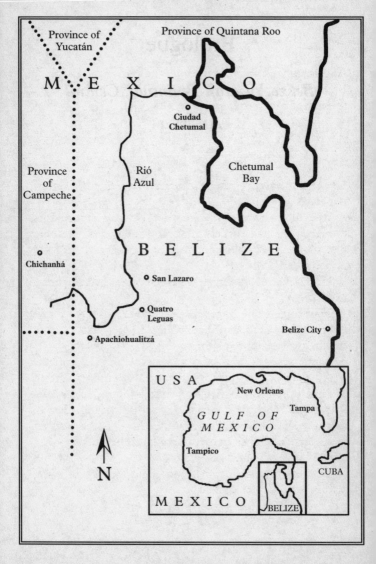

I

Angels sing.

A child's voice says: *I am Wotan, and I remember the moment of my conception.*

II

The present day
Deep in the Belize jungle, Yucatán Peninsula, Central America

A tree fell, and nobody heard. The rain stopped as though a tap had turned off, and nobody saw. Nothing had moved here for more than a thousand years, and nobody knew.

Heat. Silence. Ripe fruit clustered on the acotzintli trees, unpicked.

Four huge stone fingertips reached through the forest floor, slightly bent, as if beckoning. Blind. Deaf. Dumb. Waiting to be found. Come to me.

Come to me.

A brightly coloured tropical butterfly flutters among the treetops, pauses briefly on a moist budding leaf. Its fluttering wingtips send drops pattering down, multiplying as they fall, splashing through the tiers of leaves and branches below, spreading out, reaching the jungle floor as a fine hot mist.

Crashing sounds begin, as at the approach of some primitive mighty animal.

III

The same time
Room 43, Hotel Xunantunich, Ciudad Chetumal, Belize

A fly crawls on the ceiling, and the phone rings.

Beneath the slowly swishing blades of the ceiling fan Creole market cries echo into the shadowy room through the slatted balcony doors, and the phone rings, rings. A simple room: wicker chair, Mayan throw-rug, bedside table with the phone on top, double bed. On the bed lies a beautiful woman, blue-eyed, her blond hair spreading around her head on the grimy pillows like the sun's rays across a cloud, her right hand livid with a three-pointed scar on each side. The phone rings and rings. At last her hand unclenches, reaches out to the telephone with powerful elegant fingers, long, unadorned. Her fingernails have gouged four fresh agonised crescent moons of blood across her scarred palm.

Her hand lifts the black plastic receiver, drops it back, silences it.

It's baking hot in her room, and the fly buzzes.

Beneath the swishing ceiling fan she lies naked under the wrinkled white sheet that clings to her like sweat, sticks like a kiss to her sweating outspread arms and legs, not concealing but revealing her: her body made as explicit as pornography by the sheet's clinging caress, transparent, showing every cleft and curve, her heavy painful breasts, her engorged nipples trickling moisture through the weave, her armpits and crotch like murky triangles stamped through the damp linen, the straining mound of her belly rising up, a woman exposed in all her agony.

Whichever way she turns hurts worse than before. She sits up with low wrenching groans, the sheet slides from her breasts and belly and she stares down at her flesh, her almost unrecognisable flesh. She can't believe how much

4

her body has changed; she never can. Her breasts look embarrassingly huge, bloated with milk, blue-veined, her alluring cherry-red nipples swollen to these maternal dark brown teats hanging from bruised sensitive aureoles of the same colour. Her long slim legs now flabby and mottled, her ankles swollen, her once-flat tummy sagging low between her thighs, and her womb . . . her womb is a whole world of pain.

A knock on the door. The woman stops breathing. A child's high voice: '¿Señora Winona?'

Winona's eyelids squeeze closed, she gasps, then lies back groaning. She needs the toilet. Her baby needs to be born.

Again the Mayan bellboy's shy tapping knock on the door. 'Señora Winona, el teléphono.' She remembers the skinny boy in the lobby yesterday, Pepito, not nine years old, the face of a starving angel; struggling under Martin's cases to the queue of waiting Jeeps, bringing down the expedition members' backpacks piled in the ancient elevator, Gonzalez slapping him when one was dropped. She whispers, 'Go away. No telephone.'

'¿No esta bien?'

'I am well, Pepito. I feel good.' She bites her lip to the blood. 'Go away.'

Now the manager's voice arriving, taking charge, worried. Why does the señora not answer her telephone? Is there a problem? He puts his ear to the door, then his mouth. '¿Muy bien, Señora Winona? Are you better today?' He tries again. 'Perhaps el teléphono is your expedition calling with good news, eh?'

Inside the room Winona's vagina is splitting open. The pain is the worst she has ever experienced, as always. The scream rises in her and she clamps her hand over her mouth, then her hand over her hand, silent. *It's not my expedition, you fool! I was trying to stop them . . . To lead them in the wrong direction, at least*. Drenched in sweat, she waits for the sound of footsteps going away. No footsteps. Each side waits with held breath. She screams aloud, '¡*No me molestare*! Leave me alone!'

In the hallway the broad-faced Mayan manager jerked back from the door, rubbed his thinning hair, muttered to the bellboy, 'She got someone in there, eh? Gringo women, all the same, *Americanos*.' But Pepito whispered, 'She speaks perfect Spanish.' The manager shook his head, worldly-wise, 'Especially don't trust those ones.' Kneeling, he lifted with his bitten fingernail the Do Not Disturb sign hanging from the doorknob, placed his eye to the keyhole. She'd jammed the key inside, blocking his view. The manager pursed his lips, stared impotently at the door, then recovered his dignity by clipping the bellboy round the head. 'You, what are you doing still here? Obviously she have a man.' They listened to her groans. 'Two men.' The manager strode away down the hall shaking his head, gringo morals. But the child scampered back, pressed his ear eagerly to the door for what he could learn, listening to the woman's uninhibited cries. As he listened his face changed. Her cries were of such awful suffering through the thick wood that he stepped back shaken. He murmured in Spanish: 'It sounds like they are murdering her. If that's what love is like I swear I will never fall in love.' The manager uttered an angry call from the elevator, and he ran obediently.

Inside the room Winona, lying on her back, stares at the ceiling fan, at the turning blades flashing rhythmically in a slat of sunlight. The blood runs from her lips. The muscles gather inside her, pushing. The phone rings. The fly buzzes. The phone rings, rings.

The contraction releases her.

Winona reaches out her hand, picks up the phone. It slips in her sweat, swings from its cord. Martin's voice squeaks tinnily, no louder than a bat squeaking, coming

6

and going with the swinging phone. 'Winona? Dr Wotan? That you? Hi?'

Her muscles tighten. She swings the phone to her ear, speaks with her eyes squeezed closed, urgently. 'Give it up, Martin, you stupid bastard. You won't find anything. Give it up.'

Does he hear her? Jungle sounds, suddenly loud, the crack of machetes against undergrowth, a motor revving, the grunt of Martin's breath. She can hear his spittle as he speaks, his mobile pressed against his mouth. 'Winona? Thank God! Why didn't you answer?' He doesn't ask how she feels. 'If only you could be here with us, we're almost there! You were wrong about that little Indian, Cakchiquel. Eliot found it, Eliot walked straight into it where it stood—'

She interrupts, 'A building?'

'What? What? No, I—' The revving motor stops, Martin's voice comes clear. 'Building? What building? How could it be? This jungle's been growing up for fifteen hundred years – we're the first—'

She grips the phone tight to her ear, it slides in her sweat. 'What does Cakchiquel call it? Martin, listen. Listen to me. What do the Indians call the place?'

Laughter, Martin joking, someone pushing past him on the trail. then his voice comes back. 'It's Apachiohualitzá. Winona, we've found Apachiohualitzá. The place the natives call the Hand of God. There's more. That's what Eliot—'

'What?'

'Eliot dropped the torch inside – definitely something there—'

'Inside? There's an inside?'

Then Winona hears only her pain, drops the phone. She gives the scream that Pepito does not hear, no one hears; screaming inside herself, her clenched fist drags the phone cord from the wall. Her baby's birth can be resisted no longer, her back arches in agony. The ring of bicycle bells from the street, the clank of cranes, tooting horns, the cries of children playing and the buzzing of a fly mingle with her own anguished cries as her lifeblood spreads across the sheet.

IV

Apachiohualitzá, the temple of the Flood, Yucatán Peninsula
'Winona? Winona?'

Birds fly up shrieking from the treetops. The primitive mighty animal is Man, men and women, archaeologists, students, guides, guards, financial backers, a film crew with video backup, porters beating a path with machetes like silver teeth, winding forward like a serpent in the depth of the jungle, almost hidden from the air, hidden almost from each other.

'Winona? Oh, Christ!' Martin snaps the phone closed, grabs the rollbar as the Jeep rises up, plunges down into the flood-stream throwing a surge of brown water ahead, stalls. The two men sit stunned for a moment beneath the screams of birds and monkeys.

'I heard her. "Give it up, Martin, you stupid bastard."' Eliot grins white teeth in the jungle gloom, leans forward with his handsome hatchet face, guns the motor. 'Winona sure knows how to keep a man in his place. Soon to be the mother of your child, and already swearing at its father.'

Martin shouts, 'It's not my child, you jerk!' Somebody pushing through the fronds bordering the stream sees his angry face, calls, 'You cool, Professor Rendell?' Eliot says, 'Sure he's cool, daddy's got a bottle of champagne to celebrate the happy event – whenever it is.' Martin says, 'You jerks.' The others laugh, but they're glad to be free of Winona's formidable personality. She makes a man feel six inches tall. Someone says, 'That bitch. Better off without her.'

One of the students wading past mutters, 'Right, the bitch wanted the glory for herself, but she was *wrong*. We wasted a month and now I guess Apachiohualitzá's thirty miles north of where she reckoned.' Morale's hit rock bottom in Eliot's shoestring expedition, the half dozen whiskered crotch-itching foot-rotted deodorant-less mavericks who wasted twenty-nine days camping too far south, too hot, too cold, too wet, running out of time, striking pay dirt a day too late: now Martin and the whole shebang arrives from Salt Lake City and takes everything over.

But yesterday Eliot the loner got lost, got lucky. Saw *it* with his own eyes. Touched those great black basalt fingers with his own wondering hands. Pure luck.

Yesterday's a thousand years ago. Today Eliot's unique personal innocent moment of discovery and breathless wonder's gone, swept under the mass of people and Jeeps pushing forward from the overnight camp at Mennonite Settlement. 'I could've got tenure, Martin.'

'Guess you found the Hand too heavy to steal?'

'Winona's right, Martin. You are a bastard.' The two men have been like this since student days, equal but different, different sides of the same coin, fanatics competing since Saqqâra in Egypt, the early Christian monasteries in Sinai. Eliot with his legendary luck against Martin the theoretician. 'My entire budget's half what you'll spend today, Martin.' Eliot stirs the gearshift bitterly, clay showers from the trapped wheels as the revs rise. The Jeep twists sideways across the stream, jams over a fallen treetrunk. The winch burns out, Eliot throws up his hands, cuts the motor. '*Finito.*'

Martin says quietly, 'It's not my child, Eliot. I will never have children.'

'Sure you will, you're not gay.' Eliot stares. 'You? Not.'

'How long have we known each other?'

'I never knew.' Eliot wipes his lips hungrily, tempted, seeing all the possibilities at once. 'You've been a Mormon half your life. Those guys don't know, do they? Your saintly paymasters in Salt Lake City? They don't.'

'You could tell them, Eliot. Cut my throat. Finish my career.' Somewhere the helicopter drones above the treetops, the radios chatter, a chainsaw buzzes. 'Everything you despise that you want so badly. You could get it for yourself.'

'You're too honest, Martin.' Suddenly Eliot laughs. 'Shit, all this, and Tanya's horny for you too. The guys think you're screwing Winona and Tanya both, why else would they respect you?' He jumps cheerfully into the foaming clay-coloured stream, kicks the Jeep goodbye. 'So, Tanya's free, huh?'

'Why such a low opinion of human nature, Eliot?'

'Years of living with my own.' Eliot turns serious. 'Don't trust Gonzalez, don't trust the men with him. Whatever good you've been told about them, Martin, don't trust them.' His cocky grin returns. 'Anyway, Winona won't get credit for Apachiohualitzá if she's laid up with morning sickness. No presence, no credit, right?' He chucks a bundle of wet-weather gear to one of the students, the jungle's still dripping after the last downpour, it'll rain again before dark. He swings out the backpacks full of torches, the video, finally the satellite phone, tosses it to Martin. 'Just call her up. Goodbye. You don't need her.'

But Martin hesitates. Eliot should be leading the expedition, Winona should be leading it, anyone should be leading it but him. Leading from the front's not Martin's style. Half a dozen of them are almost as expert as he is in meso-American fieldwork: Jurgen, Colin, even Tanya directing the National Geographic camera crew. No one's more knowledgeable of pre-Colombian artifacts than Bernstein or Coles, or Winona for that matter. Martin feels threatened by the toothless Mayan scout Cakchiquel and Gonzalez's polyglot army of jungle guides and guards – the English latecomer Tallboy who joined at San Lazaro, and a Negro who walks in the steamy heat wearing a woollen hat, trenchcoat, dark glasses – any number of *mestizo* toughs with assault rifles and Uzis for 'protection', yet the expedition's fifteen miles from the nearest village, the nearest thief! But Martin knows this is the way it's done, always been done. The Belize Department of Culture official who strongly recommended Gonzalez talks only Spanish to the man from the Museum of Antiquities, and all of them ignore the blank-faced Mayan porters pushing past, docile but tough. Probably more used to escorting drugs than archaeologists. Gonzalez sees Martin, steps aside from Tallboy and Snowflake fording the stream, tips back his hat brim with his thumb, waits. Gonzalez's black eyes take in everything about the expedition, the pupils enlarged as if day were night; some of his own merchandise perhaps. He scratches the whiskers of his round sweating face with his fingernails, then as Martin and Eliot pass points his thumb towards the camera crew struggling beneath their equipment. 'Hollywood Angelenos to a man,' Gonzalez says, 'but look at that one.' He grins at Tanya, baseball cap and short shorts, white thighs, long black hair. 'I must walk with our director Ms Spielberg, as I call her. Warn her of jungle pitfalls.'

'You keep away from her, Gonzalez, and keep those guys of yours on the move,' Eliot warns, but Martin says, 'Pitfalls? What pitfalls?'

Gonzalez puts his face close to Eliot, too close, eyes unblinking. 'Man, did you really see it, Eliot? The Hand of God?'

'Just keep them away when we get there, Gonzalez. Your Negro, or your Englishman, I don't want to see them.' Eliot puts his hand on the pistol at his side. 'And you, Gonzalez, you make sure you keep a *long* way from me.'

Gonzalez smiles, perfect teeth gleaming in his corrupt sweating face. 'Thank you for your orders, *Señor* Eliot. However, you are not giving the orders.' He turns, looks Martin up and down: Professor Martin Rendell wearing his oatmeal safari suit still properly creased, hair combed, steel-rimmed spectacles, an intellectual out of his depth, the leader. Drops fall out of the leafy treetops into the gloom around the three men, impacting like slaps on their hats and shoulders.

'Rendell.' Gonzalez speaks calmly, face to face to Martin for the first time since leaving the drug-runners' trail at Quatro Leguas. 'Welcome to jungle, Rendell. I know jungle better than any other man alive. Snakes. Spiders. Death. I see death all over the world.' Gonzalez picks something wriggling from Martin's hat brim, squeezes the juice between his fingertips. 'Here in jungle everything is real, beyond civilisation, beyond culture. Beyond doubt. There is no God in jungle, no table manners, no beliefs, no illusions. Here everything is alive, even death is alive. Everything crawls and creeps and grows and multiplies. Thorns to pierce you, thorns to poison you, here is every disease under the sun, maggots beneath the skin, fevers, malaria, Chagas' disease, foul water. And this is only the start of jungle.' He touches the tip of his cigarette to his flesh, burning a maggot out of his skin. 'Jaguars and jaguar-poachers, even more dangerous. Looters of ancient ruins, looters of smashed helicopters, crashed planes. Drug-runners. Smugglers channelling crates of mummified heads from the Andes, sacrificed Inca children, a crate for Atlanta to London to Zürich containing two hundred and eight grisly items to my personal knowledge hijacked half a dozen times between gangs, like dogs fighting over bones. Criminals, DEA men, madmen, Customs officers, terrorists, informers, drug czars, murderers, defrocked priests, paedophiles, all hiding out. My dear university friends,' Gonzalez winks, hefting his rifle as he turns away, 'jungle's the least of the enemies you made when you came here.'

Eliot and Martin look at one another. Eliot says, 'You know these guys as well as you think?'

'Don't worry. They know how to oil the government wheels, get things done. Highly recommended.' Martin wades to shore, Eliot joins him spreading the map against a treetrunk, and both men try to forget Gonzalez, Winona, the slapping drops overflowing from the bromeliads high above, forget even the whine of mosquitoes. 'Here. We're here.' Eliot's forefinger jabs the site he found yesterday, less than an inch away on the map; covered by Martin's neat cross in red ink. Shakes his head in admiration. 'Exactly where you worked it out, Martin. We both found it, in our different ways.'

'Head of the three valleys. Good soil, watered, protected on three sides, cooled by the prevailing wind.' Martin shrugs, it's the obvious location for the builders of a city to choose, easy for an archaeological detective to find: just take local native myths about a flood in ancient times and add satellite mapping technology. 'Highest land for miles. The last place they'd expect a flood would reach in a Deluge.'

'There's no evidence for a Deluge here in the Isthmus in historical times.'

'When did history start? The Mayans didn't write their history down. Doesn't mean they didn't have any, one of the world's great ancient civilisations. Just shows us our ignorance not theirs.' He claps Eliot's shoulder, pushes him towards the jungle. 'You know the way. Lead on, Indy.'

Eliot makes a Harrison Ford face and the two men push forward behind the Mayans' flashing machetes. A path for thirty men and a film crew is altogether more than the wriggling animal trail Eliot crawled along yesterday, lost, pulling leeches off his face, ducking under treefalls, scrambling across the streams that plunge off the sides of the valley. The streams are smaller now, higher, and they see patches of daylight pierce the tree cover, glimpse the great green dome of jungle at the head of the three valleys.

'Apachiohualitzá!' Eliot runs, pushing through the thorns and fronds, feet sliding on the soft growing soil, climbing, clambering. He stumbles into the sunlit glade. Stands motionless.

Inhales. Exhales. It feels like nothing's moved here for centuries. He breaks the silence, calls without turning, 'Martin?'

'I'm here. My God. It looks like it's beckoning. Calling.' Martin walks forward reverently, reaches up on tiptoe, can almost touch the tip of the littlest finger. He steps back. The four great monoliths stand up out of the jungle floor like the fingers of a drowning man reaching towards the sun. Even through the thick green moss Martin discerns the shape of each fingernail faithfully carved. He walks forward between the stones, turns, tugs at the moss with his hands, reveals the giant creases of the finger-joints. Higher above his head the basalt is worked into giant whorls like ribs, each as thick as his wrist: fingerprints.

Martin whispers, 'It's the Hand of God.'

Shouts, running footsteps. Followers run into the glade. 'Wow!' Tanya guides the cameraman, Jerry, forward by his belt so he doesn't trip over the roots in the soft soil; he films the moment of discovery as it happens. Tanya backs in front of the camera, asks Martin journalist questions. 'What are your feelings right now, Professor Rendell? Are you amazed? Are you shocked? Are they what you expected to see? You've worked for this moment for years.'

Martin says, 'I don't know what I feel.'

Tanya speaks to camera. 'Here in front of our eyes is the proof that ancient Maya craftsmen, pagan, brutal, indulging in the blood sacrifice of their children and tearing out the beating hearts of their defeated enemies, nevertheless succeeded in producing the artwork of considerable power long known to local legend as the Hand of God. Is this the lost Mormon city?'

'God was unknown to these people,' Eliot mutters. 'They worshipped gods.' He moves behind her, embraces one of the fingers in the background of the shot. 'I name you tenure. God bless you.' The Englishman, Tallboy, skinny as a rake, ginger hair slicked back to his pinstriped shoulders, walks with long strides to the edge of the clearing, checks the perimeter then calls to Gonzalez, 'Clean as a whistle, chum.' Foliage moves, Gonzalez points. The toughs spread out, crouch.

'I believe it's too early to say, Tanya, but these figures may originally have been part of a statue.' Martin responds authoritatively to Tanya's breathless questions, then remembers Winona interrupting him, *A building?* He continues smoothly, 'We may even conjecture this as just one of a number of statues once decorating, for example, the rooftop of an important building.' Behind them Tallboy sweeps the Uzi smoothly from his back, points with two hands, clicks off the safety with a smooth action of his thumbs.

Eliot whispers in Martin's ear, 'Tanya's breathless for you, Martin.' But he watches the Englishman out of the corner of his eye. 'Martin? Is it Zarahemla?'

'A building,' Tanya asks, 'what building?'

'A temple,' Eliot interrupts. Tallboy moves the fronds aside with his gun barrel. It's only a spider monkey. Tallboy's trigger finger whitens but Gonzalez says, 'No, no noise.'

Tallboy turns away smoothly, long silent footsteps. 'Lucky monkey.' But he doesn't click the safety on, the gun's live.

Tanya steps closer to Martin, only the microphone between them. 'Tell us, professor, what did a Mayan temple look like?'

15

Martin says, 'A ziggurat.' Eliot explains for the cameras, 'Pyramids. But steeper, lots of steps. Could be hundreds of feet high.'

Martin says, 'We believe we've found the site of the temple to Apachiohualitzá, the Flood.'

The man from the Belize Department of Culture pushes forward. 'I claim this site as a treasure of national importance on behalf of my government.' Martin says, 'Don't worry, you'll get your money.' The representative of the administrator of antiquities interrupts promptly, 'All artifacts and artwork are the property of the Museum, and must be registered.' Martin soothes him, 'Everyone gets their cut.' He placates the observer from the regional office, flatters the valuer, defers to the Customs officer who will ensure nothing is removed from the site without official permission. Thunder growls above the distant hilltops.

'Gentlemen, gentlemen,' Martin says, 'I'll say again, we've found nothing of financial value yet.' He blinks in the failing light as cameras flash, students taking group shots posed by the gigantic fingers. 'And there may be nothing to find.'

Eliot calls over: 'Martin.' He takes the torch out of his backpack, crouches against one of the fingers. 'Look. Couldn't see down here yesterday.' He points the beam into a hole in the soft earth, originally dug by a wild animal perhaps. The torchlight follows the line of the finger down. Something gleams earthily.

Eliot says, 'Huge fingers, therefore a huge hand. I think that's part of the hand going down, buried under a thousand generations of leaves, rotting vegetation, soil. The earth's grown up over the statue. I reckon the statue may be standing almost complete beneath us.'

Martin nods. 'I concur. The fingers appear still connected to a palm.'

'An incredible moment, don't you agree, professor?'

Tanya puts forward the microphone.

'Absolutely incredible, Tanya.' Martin takes the torch from Eliot, but Gonzalez holds out a bigger one, brighter. Eliot kneels, pulls handfuls of dirt from the top of the hole, then slides his legs down against the finger, goes into the ground to his waist. 'Give.' He holds up his hand for Gonzalez's torch, ducks down. Martin lies peering, widens the hole with his hands when nothing happens, then someone brings a shovel.

Martin puts his head inside. 'Eliot?'

The torch beam shines up from below. 'I'm okay. It's good. I'm standing on the palm, no problem.' Eliot's voice muffles as he crouches. 'The palm's angled, but cupped. Maybe used for sacrifices.' His voice becomes clear as he looks up. 'This would be the highest place in the city, everyone would see the statue's hand symbolically reaching up towards the sky. Imagine what happened here, it's a gigantic receptacle for sacrificial blood. There must have been a way for the priests to climb up . . .' The torchbeam jerks, he frees it. 'Tree roots everywhere. Getting beneath them here. That's better.' The torchbeam stabs upwards, Eliot's voice echoes. 'Come on down. Plenty of room.'

Martin grips his torch, slides from the thundery glow of the clearing into darkness.

Eliot steadies him, soil trickles past them. 'Careful, there's more.' He points the torchbeam between his shoes, where the solid surface ends. 'We're standing on the semi-lunar bone of the palm. I think that's the wrist going down beneath us.'

'We're going to need a rope.'

Eliot calls up. Soil showers down as the hole's widened by shovels and eager hands, making a ramp. Gonzalez slides down with a rope. Eliot says, 'That's far enough, Gonzalez.' But Gonzalez grins. 'I know how to do these things, gentlemen. I know the knots.' He pushes the barrel of his rifle behind one of the fingers where it joins the

17

hand, levers a gap in the earth. 'Pass the rope through, Rendell. Quickly! Push it through. Good.' Gonzalez pulls the end out, loops it round the finger, ties it off.

He turns with his infuriating grin, stares into the barrel of Eliot's pistol. Eliot says steadily, 'That's as far as you come, Gonzalez. You won't try a single thing.'

'Me?' Gonzalez splays his hands. 'You know me, *Señor* Eliot. You know you can trust me.'

'I know how far I can trust you, Gonzalez. I want you up top with your men. Nobody comes down here.'

Gonzalez grins at the pistol. 'Sure, Eliot. Anything you say.'

Eliot holsters the pistol, slips his wrist through the thong of the torch. He leans out, tests the rope. Gonzalez says urgently, 'We worked together before. Want to keep it all for yourself this time?' Eliot grins a flash of white teeth, swings down.

Martin stares at the Spaniard. 'What's that about?' Gonzalez shrugs, hands on knees. 'Oh, it's true, Rendell. Eliot and I have known each other for years. Many years.' Face hidden by his hat brim, Gonzalez peers down into the dark.

Martin pushes in front, kneels. Down there the drop's not quite sheer, he can make out the stone arm outstretched up towards the hand at a realistic angle, modelled from life. The rope goes down like a thin bright line scratched against the black basalt. Eliot pushes off with his feet, the torch swinging from his wrist sending light flashing over his face and across the adamantine arm beneath him as he goes down. The elbow's slightly bent, and again Martin imagines it in his mind's eye: lifelike. Then the bony curve of the elbow hides Eliot but the rope keeps jerking. Down there Eliot's torchbeam shows, flashes up briefly, then down. 'I think I see the shoulder. Can you hear me?'

'I hear you.'

Eliot's shout comes up. 'Martin? You hear me?'

'I hear you, Eliot. You see anything?'

'There's something.'

Martin grips the rope, leans out trying to see. Gonzalez grips his shoulder. 'Don't worry, *señor*. I won't let you fall.'

Martin leans far out over the drop. Eliot's shout comes up from below, 'Godamnit!'

Martin shouts down, 'What is it?'

No answer.

Then Eliot calls up, 'It's something big.'

The rope jerks as Eliot lowers himself down towards the statue's gigantic head in the earth. Martin sees Eliot's stabbing torchbeam swing across part of an eye in the darkness below, a stone eye staring up, flaring Mayan nostrils, finally a huge stone face twisted upward beneath Eliot with stone lips parted in a scream of pagan sacrifice, worship exalted and given meaning by the ritual agony of death: a religion.

V

Her blood spreads through the sweaty sheet that clings to her body, outlines her spreading thighs in red. Her mouth opens in her agony, stretching wide, showing her teeth perfectly white, now clenching tight together and biting down on the twisted corner of sheet she holds between them in her lonely agony, her silent scream.

It's always this bad. Across the world a million women are giving birth this day; it's no different for Winona, no easier for her, no more delicate, no more or less explicit. Her breath gasps the same as theirs, first through her nose, then through her mouth, she thrusts her head and shoulders back into the pillow, pushes back with her feet, her fists clasp the heavy brass bedstead, her bottom rises off the bed with the force of her push, the brass rail creaks, groans, bends.

Alone. Always alone. There is never anyone to help her.

It will not come. She writhes, utters a low cry. It will not come.

'Jesus Christ help me!'

VI

'My God,' Eliot's voice comes from below. 'It's obscene. It's . . . grotesque.'

Martin swings on the rope. Above him someone calls for the folding aluminium ladders, but he bumps past the huge basalt elbow, slides through silhouetted tree roots and tubers and crumbling soil, sees Eliot standing on the huge face below him. Eliot reaches up for the rope, steadies it. Martin jumps down.

Martin crouches, touches the warm black stone of the statue's face. 'One of the gods? Quetzalcoatl?'

'No. It's different. More.' Eliot sounds shaken. His torchlight illuminates the face around them in flashes, an eyelid, sweat pores speckling the curve of the cheek, the agonised creases of the lips wide open around the mouth in its eternal scream of death. A faint warm draught rises out like exhaled breath. 'It's bad. Worse. Stinks.' Eliot shivers. 'It's a demon's face.' Martin turns round and round, illuminating with his torch the carved rock around the two men and below them, volcanic, black, locked in the earth for a thousand years or more, a face of such fierce aggression, pain and suffering that both stand silent, lost for words. Eliot puts out his hand suddenly, grips Martin's shoulder. 'Mind yourself, don't fall.' The mouth behind Martin gapes wide enough for a man to tumble inside, easily. The black frontal teeth are filed into incisor points in the grim Mayan fashion.

Martin sniffs the exhalation. 'What's that?'

'Smells like naphtha. Probably coal seams below, volatile oils. Don't strike a match.'

An aluminium ladder clatters, finds its angle. The ladder creaks as Gonzalez comes down, the red cummerbund that holds his fat belly showing beneath his open jacket as he steps off the ladder. 'I was worried for you, gentlemen.' He sweeps off his hat, looks into the mouth. 'An entrance. It goes down inside the statue. I thought so. That's how the priests got up, eh?'

Eliot shines the torch down. 'We know that, Gonzalez.'

'It's Gonthaleth.' The Spaniard touches Eliot's elbow lightly. 'Pay me at least the respect of saying my name properly.' He spits into the mouth. 'They came out of here, yes? Probably there are steps set into the upper surface of the arm, where we can't see them, where the worshippers far below wouldn't see. They would see only the priests rising from the mouth and walking up the arm like magic to make the blood sacrifice. This is worth millions.' He looks into the eyes of both men. 'You know it. Imagine this statue standing in Times Square. This immense totem of America. Real America. True America. Vast and ancient America.'

Eliot shakes him off. 'Get your hands off me, Gonzalez.'

'*Señor*, you know there are bound to be other artifacts below. Sacrificial cups, knives. Jade. Gold. All the usual detritus. A coffin like we found at Palenque, eh, inlaid with gold and jade?'

'I never knew any of this,' Martin says. Gonzalez grins his grin.

'Eliot knows.'

Eliot stares into the mouth. Martin says, 'Eliot?'

'The hell with you both.' Eliot ties the rope around one of the teeth, crouching, not looking at Martin. 'I've done things I'm not proud of. You wouldn't understand about that, Martin. You always get your way, don't you?' He swings down between the teeth, glances up. 'I don't run a department, hold tenure, publish papers. This is what I do.'

He slides from sight.

Martin lies on the lip of the mouth, peers down. 'Heights. I hate them.' But Gonzalez says, 'It's only the inside of an open mouth, a chamber.' They stare at Eliot's torchbeam turning below them as the rope untwists, illuminating a mouth of huge black teeth painstakingly carved, the ribbed palate, the tongue rising up to press against the front teeth of the lower jaw. Beyond the epiglottis the entrance to the throat is blocked by a thousand years of debris, roots, bones, soil.

Eliot stands on the debris carefully, looks up. 'Still stinks.'

Gonzalez calls, 'Sulphur. These rocks are rich in sulphur.'

'Smells like hell.' Eliot kicks a bone, something beneath the rubbish creaks. 'Careful. I don't think it's solid.'

Martin climbs down the rope, tests his weight on the floor before letting go. 'I agree. Wooden boards covering the throat or gullet below. That's how the priests must have climbed up. This was their robing room, sanctum, I don't know.'

'Shrine, maybe.'

'If it was it's empty now.'

Tanya's voice calls down eagerly, 'Hey, we see you guys! Wait. Zoom in. Look up, professors, smile.' Eliot smiles at her cleavage, which wobbles as she pushes Gonzalez forward. 'Down you go, Gonzalez, give the shot some story.' Gonzalez swings down, grunting, calling up apologies if his overweight figure is blocking the view. Meanwhile Martin ducks behind the epiglottis, as big as an automobile, and stands up inside the darkened nasal cavity. 'Can't see.' He clicks his fingers urgently for the torch, Eliot kneels and passes it through. The beam stabs upwards.

Martin whispers, 'Eliot. Look what I found.'

This is no nasal cavity; the skull is an empty dome.

Inside the dome on an altar of black rock stands an angel carved of the same black rock, black wings arched above its head, cupped hands reaching in fury or supplication up almost to the tips of its wings, its upturned face half screaming mouth.

'Eliot,' Martin whispers. 'It's a shrine. A hideous shrine.' There isn't room for the two men to stand: Eliot bends his head up awkwardly, kneeling. Martin whispers, 'That angel, it's the smaller image of this whole immense statue that contains it. An icon.'

'It's not an angel. The Maya had no concept of angels.'

'Eliot, this statue's got wings, I bet my life on it. We'll find angel's wings buried behind us in the earth. Immense wings.'

'That's not an angel.' Eliot crawls backwards. 'It's something horrible. Look at it. It's a corruption of something, look at that face. It looks like something that started off as an angel. I don't want to look at it. Let's get out of here. I'm getting out of here.'

Gonzalez takes his place. He looks up, takes off his hat, reaches up to the black angel. Margin grabs his grasping hand.

Gonzalez says: 'It's genuine, isn't it. I can see it is. Ten million dollars, Professor Rendell.'

Martin stares into Gonzalez's black eyes.

'Look. The Fallen Angel.' Gonzalez shrugs. 'That face. Those wings. A Mayan angel, in a culture with no tradition of angels – a tradition that Jesus Christ visited them as a plumed serpent, yes, but let's be serious now. An angel after its Fall from Heaven. This scream, total loss, total abandonment, total thrown-down desolation, this is the scream of an angel forsaken by God. Yes, ten million. Any modern museum will give every last dollar to own such an icon. Such a powerful symbol speaking to our age of suffering. Our search for belief. One true faith to cling to. One truth in this world of lies that can make sense of our lives. Something real.'

'It's hideous.'

'If he says ten million,' Eliot says, 'it's worth more.'

'Sure.' Gonzalez speaks in a low voice, the film crew are lowering the ladder. 'Gentlemen, we're close as spit to the borders, Mexico, Guatemala, take your choice. We can make these finds go either way, Rendell. I have contacts. The Mexican border by dawn, the cartel airstrip at Chichanhá at noon. Eliot already understands me.'

'I understand you too much,' Eliot says.

Martin says, 'He means looting, smuggling?'

'My dear Rendell,' Gonzalez says smoothly, 'I mean profit. You were a poor man who spent his life finding riches for others and nothing for himself. It was all a waste, Rendell. All vanity and pride. You thought you were important. You fed on scraps, you were just a label on a door, possessing nothing for yourself.' He chuckles. 'Rendell, it's just Mayan art. It's not like stealing a Picasso or anything important.'

Martin crouches, whispers, 'Eliot?'

Eliot digs through the rubbish without looking round. 'You know he's right, Martin.'

Gonzalez kneels, murmurs persuasively, 'Rendell, Martin, my friend, these ancient dignified things that you steal for nothing, the museum industry takes these things for itself and makes people pay to see them. Makes postcards of them, dishcloths of them, paperweights, desk ornaments, patterned toilet paper of them, changes these works of art into whatever trash can be made for a penny and sold for a dollar in museum shops and mail-order. And because you give your finds away to these thieves who pay you a pittance, you pretend it's not stealing.'

Martin says, 'These things belong in the earth.'

Gonzalez spreads his hands. 'Then what, my dear Rendell, are you doing here?'

'Maybe you're right. We shouldn't be here.'

But Gonzalez reaches up for the angel, grips it by the

wings with both hands, and this time Martin does not stop him. Gonzalez holds it out for Martin to touch. 'You in, Martin?' His eyes glitter with cunning. 'Or shall we put it back and go no further?'

Martin sighs. 'No.' That's all it takes.

'There!' Gonzalez beams. 'Now you are one of us.'

'It's not art, Martin, it's just an artifact,' Eliot says. 'It's called making a living. We all do it.' He taps the floor, gets a hollow sound. 'Hey, there's more—'

Wood creaks, snaps, Eliot sinks to his waist in bones and soil. 'Martin.' His torch flashes, swinging from its wrist-thong as he struggles. Martin grabs from the side as Eliot sinks down in the centre, he grabs Eliot's sweaty hand, it slips, the torch bangs Martin's head, the light blinds him. 'Gonzalez, quick.' Gonzalez holds the angel tight.

Eliot shrieks, 'Gonzalez!'

Gonzalez drops the angel behind the row of teeth, takes Eliot's hand in his own. The floor goes down in a burst of dust blowing upward, muck pours down over Eliot's head, his hand reaches out of the throat like a white claw grasping Gonzalez's fat white hand, then Eliot's head and eyes come out staring upwards as the last of the debris pours away past him.

Eliot looks up from the splintered wooden boards, his legs swinging over nothing below. Air blows up around him like breath.

'Gonzalez.'

The skin slides up Eliot's hand, his fingers stick up like a drowning man's as they slide down through Gonzalez's palm. Martin screams, 'Can't reach.' The film crew are useless, paralysed. The Englishman, Tallboy, slides down the ladder wedged across the inside of the mouth, braces his feet on the bottom rung, reaches out at arm's length. Not enough.

Gonzalez says: 'He's slipping.'

Tallboy changes grip, holds out the Uzi, Eliot grips the barrel. He dangles between the two men, then falls. The torchlight falls away in the darkness below and illuminates Eliot's flailing shrieking body as he falls, the torchlight flashing up the streaking ribbed walls as it falls with him, the light shrinking smaller in the dark, fading until it's no brighter than a star, a spark, something imagined in the dark.

'I couldn't hold him,' Martin says numbly in the silence. 'He fell.'

'None of us could hold him.' Gonzalez wipes his face in the crook of his elbow. 'Well done, Tallboy. You saint, you.'

Tallboy shines a torch unsentimentally into the darkness. 'That's the deepest bloody hole I ever saw, black as the devil's arsehole. Maybe it is the devil's arsehole. Looks like it goes down to the centre of the world.'

Martin tries to understand. 'Is he dead?'

The Germanic voice of the Negro, Snowflake, calls down into the mouth: 'The dead . . . they do not return in this world, Herr Rendell, not in the flesh. Not as they were.'

'He's a dead 'un if he ever reaches bottom, chum, that's for sure.' Tallboy scratches his face thoughtfully with long fingers, long nails. 'So how did those old priest geezers get up?' He braces himself across the hole on his long legs. 'Mr G? Here it is. Something here.' He points the torch at an angle.

'We must report what's happened,' Martin whispers. 'Not my fault. The police. Coroner. There will be an inquest, of course. Questions. I don't know if he had anyone who cared about him. Anyone who ought to know he's dead.'

Gonzalez turns Martin's shoulder. 'We will continue,' he says. 'It's what Eliot would have wanted.' Tanya's weeping echoes into the mouth, she saw it happen on film.

26

'Oh, Martin, Martin, I'm so sorry.' More voices, footsteps, others coming down the silvery web of ladders in the dark, gathering round looking down into the mouth. Their hair drips moisture on the people below, it's raining up top.

'This is it.' Tallboy bends down. 'Just common sense, if you think about it. Anatomy.' Tallboy puts his arm through the hole, pushes the barrel of the Uzi against the ribbed wall of the throat. 'Go on, old lad, swallow.' With a grinding sound something moves below and the epiglottis, counterbalanced, swings with a crash that makes the floor shake, closing the immense windpipe and revealing a second passage slanting downwards.

'The gullet.' Tallboy grins. 'Even angels got to eat.'

VII

Still it will not come.

The sweat slides on Winona's flesh, into her open mouth where she lies motionless on the bed, her chin between her breasts, her body a mass of straining muscles tightening, gathering, the veins standing out in her legs and neck like a weightlifter's, a strongman's, not lifting but pushing. Not taking, giving.

But it will not come.

She relaxes, slumps back dry-mouthed in the darkened room. Anything for a drink of water: always this thirst, always this pain. Pepito listens again beyond the thick panels of the door; she hears the whisper of breath in his nose, the beating of his heart, the steady wash of evening rain across the balcony, drips dropping from the railings into the darkness below. The bell rings in the lobby, Pepito doesn't hear. The bell again, impatiently, and his feet scamper down four floors to the murmur of people checking out, cases to be carried, the *ting* of a dollar tip into his palm.

So thirsty.

27

Winona reaches past the broken phone to the heavy crystal tumbler of water, lifts it to her lips, and her pain swells inside her again as if to burst her, to burst out of her. Her fingers squeeze, the thick tumbler shatters as though made of plastic, the bedside table goes over. Winona jerks up, sitting, her face a rictus of straining muscle like a mask, the mask of a beautiful woman stretching round her open mouth and staring eyes as she drags away the sheet, naked, stares down at the livid split between her legs, and a tiny head poking out. So tiny. Oh, oh. With her fingertips she touches the blond hairs plastered with her blood, cups the curve of her baby's head in her palm, strokes it wonderingly even while the lips of her flesh split in agony.

Her eyes yearn with love, her mouth cries out hoarsely, 'Winona, my love, Winona I love you, give him to me. Give me our son.'

VIII

'The belly of the beast,' Martin says.

Gonzalez shakes Martin's shoulder. 'Pull yourself together, professor.' Martin stumbles forward, the ribbed tube of the great gullet leading downwards making slippery steps for his feet. Voices gathering behind them, great excitement: student voices calling *Whooo* as if it's a theme park ride. And it *is* exciting: the passage going down beyond the reach of light, the bevy of torches swaying and flashing like bright eyes as they descend, Tanya beginning her commentary again. 'It must be raining hard on top, everyone's coming down soaking wet, everyone wants to share in the discovery, everyone wants to be out of the rain, everyone wants to be part of what we find!' Gonzalez runs behind Martin clutching the black angel to his chest, laughing; they're all running now, jumping from step to step going down.

Something moves below; a shadow, a flickering light. Martin calls, 'Eliot?'

Behind him Tallboy says, 'Not unless dead geezers jump back to life, prof.' They push through cobwebs into a larger space, past a boulder like a bolus as round and wide as the gullet, lying with a skeleton trapped beneath. Martin stops, then takes a step forward.

'We're further in than anybody's got now,' Gonzalez says.

Martin stands in an empty room lit by a flame in a stone bowl, the flame almost certainly burning since before Columbus discovered America. He touches the oil with his fingertip, sniffs. 'Naphtha. Burning naphtha.' The flame wavers, gusts in the draught as the people come down, pushing. 'Keep back. There's years of work here. Natural springs feeding conduits—'

'Treasures to be found.' Gonzalez heads past the flame to the far doorway, but Martin has the torch. 'After you, professor.'

Martin bows his head beneath the massive lintel, goes down cramped twisted corridors as though dragged forward by the beam of his torch. From time to time the camera lights fling his shadow ahead of him, a black man-shaped hole leading through the cobwebs and dust, glimmering along walls of stone blocks hewn with stelae of screaming faces, screaming angels, demons, spirits. Now Martin descends steps to an earlier level, to long inward-leaning narrow halls scrawled along the sides with Mayan rulers and gods. Tanya calls, 'Wow, aren't these great discoveries? We're making history.'

'This *is* history.' Martin peers through his torchbeam at a wall of carved figures intertwined in strange contortions. 'Yucatec glyphs. Writing. We can't read it. The monks accompanying the Spanish conquistadores could hardly translate even the basic sound language, so many Mayan vocalisations and glottals were alien to them.

There's a lifetime's study here.'

'Keep moving, professor.'

'See these star-shapes? Great astronomers, the Mayans. They divided the sky into the figures of a zodiac like the Babylonians and Egyptians; observed the movements of the Moon, Venus, Mars, Jupiter, more precisely than the Greeks. The Mayan calendar's the Long Count, it begins almost five thousand years ago with their creation story, the *Popul Vuh* . . . the gods created the earth from a watery void, made animals, plants, men, but when men became sinful they were wiped out by black rains and a great flood – all except Cocoxtli and his wife who had to build a great ark, which they beached on a mountaintop as the waters receded, and then the gods sent a dove to give Cocoxtli's children the gift of languages, a whole Babel-babble of languages.' The camera lights follow Martin's pallid torchbeam rippling across the stone. 'It's a temple complex, a centre of learning. Like Copán, Tikal, others, the temple of the Sun at Palenque, yet different . . . this is something different. Something doesn't add up. It's more. There's more, look . . .'

'Don't stop, prof.'

'These wall engravings – these diagonals represent the sky, Caan. This face engraved in a mass of volutes, clouds, long hair I guess, he's the sky god. Like the Greek sky god Ouranos and his wife Gaia, but of course these people knew nothing of the Greeks. The Maya fell under Teotihuacán domination in about AD 400, and this is later work than that. Late Classic, but it's more than that period as well . . . Some other influence embedded inside. I reckon the upper levels are a history of the slow assimilation, corruption, of earlier beliefs. Maybe that's the same everywhere, of course. The evolution of gods. As we go down we're coming closer to the original, the primal archetype.'

Tanya says, 'The primal truth?'

'Well, most primitive form of belief, anyway. The original myth. I believe your Fallen Angel, Gonzalez, built astride the highest, latest temple, was the decadent culmination of this society. Its end not its beginning.'

'Its final most glorious expression,' Gonzalez says, clutching the screaming angel tight. 'This is art, Rendell.'

'Look at this down here! Come further down. This smiling figure with outspread arms over the crowd, that's not Miraflores Culture.'

'Not smiling,' Gonzalez says. 'Screaming. It's screaming with horror. With horror at the loathsome crowd clutching and clawing below.'

Tanya says, 'Heck, Gonzalez, don't you know what a smile looks like?'

'Look, they're smiling,' Martin continues. 'See these smiling faces looking hopefully upwards. Not skulls, they're living faces, not mutilated, not sacrificed. They look like smiling children. Classic Period technical skill interpreting earlier beliefs. Yes, we're definitely going backwards in time as we go down, Tanya, it's like descending in a time machine. These temples are often built over earlier sites. I myself excavated the E-VII sub-pyramid at Uaxactún, found the original beautifully preserved beneath later structures.'

Tanya nods. 'Temples built on temples.'

'Just like the Christian Church taking over pagan temples and rites for its own ends. A religious site is holy for ever.' Martin touches the stones with reverence. 'This must be Early Classic, look at the decorative style. I'd guess this level to about AD 400, traces of Chicanel, here's Gujalhantón work, but this pyramid with the rising sun is definitely Teotihuacán style . . .' Martin slows at a ramp of steps slanting steeply downwards into the floor, the walls still white with limestone plaster slashed and gouged by weapons, even the hard stone at the top chipped, split, blackened by ancient fire.

31

'Keep on down, prof.'

Martin follows the step downwards, slipping. The roof lowers, the steps deliberately broken down and blocked long ago, now even the blockage broken down by time. 'We're going much earlier.'

He slides down the rubble, reaches bottom in a small room, looks up. 'At last! Mayan calendar wheel.' He holds the torch awkwardly between neck and shoulder to direct the beam, feels upwards on the wall, his fingers revealing what he can't see clearly among cobwebs and shadow.

'Got it, feel it. Coefficient twelve.' Probes with his fingertips. 'A skeletal jaw, the day sign, Eb. I can feel the numbers, Mayan dots and bars.' His face squeezes up with concentration. 'A bar, 5, with three dots, makes 8. Here we go. 8.14.3.1.12. It's a date.'

Gonzalez says hoarsely, 'What date?'

'AD 320.'

Tanya whispers, 'The Christian Church was just being born.'

Martin shrugs, flicks the torch round the high walls. 'Doesn't mean a thing. Rome and Jerusalem were seven thousand miles away. Other side of the universe to these people. Light years away. Christianity didn't get here for another thirteen hundred years. Then it wiped them out, mostly.'

The next opening is larger, high, but surrounded by walls of earth, as though once this open space stood in the sun. Near-darkness falls as Jerry cuts the floodlight, changes the film. Tanya shoves back the people trying to get down, giving him room to work. 'Okay?'

Jerry swings the camera to his shoulder, clicks the floodlamp on and holds up his thumb, okay.

Tanya says, 'What's through there, professor?' She nods at a doorway as high as the roof, flanked by two metal pillars.

Martin doesn't move. 'Look.'

'The pillars don't touch the roof? So what?'

'Can't be.' Martin walks forward through the dust and cobwebs.

Gonzalez calls, 'What is it, man?'

'Strange. It's strange.' Martin touches the fluted right-hand pillar, stares up. 'About twenty-five feet high, eighteen cubits, near enough. But made of copper, not brass . . .'

Tallboy calls down the steps, 'That's gold, right? Real gold? These people had gold coming out their arseholes, didn't they?'

'Sure, but copper was even more valuable, came by donkey from Mexico, what's now Mexico.' Martin murmurs, 'So they traded with the north even at this early date. The transport difficulties alone . . . These pillars were fantastically valuable and important to them, obviously.' He leans back. Each pillar is topped with a cobwebby copper brazier of frozen golden flame. 'That's pure gold.' Shakes his head. 'But what did the pillars mean to them? What do they represent? There's *nothing* in Mayan culture—' He stops. 'They're gateposts. But no gates . . .'

Tanya says breathlessly, scented, 'Go on, professor.'

'What, them flames is solid gold?' Tallboy comes down; the floodlamp gleams blue across the Uzi. 'Must weigh half a ton each.'

But Martin is crouching at the base of the left-hand pillar, his fingers brushing away the dust. 'Gateposts without gates.' He stares, whispers to himself. 'I know this . . .'

'Ton of gold altogether,' Tallboy says. 'How much a ton of gold fetch?'

Martin caresses the writing with his fingertips, the dense shapes making neither pictures nor letters. 'I know this text. It's Reformed Egyptian, a mix of Hebrew and Egyptian. Pharaoh's administrators bossed his conquered tribes using a "common" language the people would understand. Reformed's the hieratic, cursive form of

Egyptian hieroglyphic writing. Very rare, one undisputed fragment known from Arad in Israel, some from Coptic monasteries in the Sinai, others found and lost, maybe destroyed. A language of the people.' His fingers trace the line. '"And he set up the pillars in the porch of the temple: and he set up the left pillar, and called the name thereof Boaz." Boaz, one of the royal line of David.' Martin moves to the right-hand pillar, touches the marks beneath the dust. '"And he set up the right pillar, and called the name thereof Jachin". Jachin, one of the line of priests.' Martin bumps back on his haunches. 'Phew. King-priests.'

Tanya says, 'Boaz and Jachin, so what? Sounds like the Bible. Am I stupid or what?'

'The two pillars of the world.' Martin wipes his face with his fingers. 'No, you're not stupid, Tanya. One Kings, six or seven, I forget.'

Gonzalez laughs. 'I don't see the world on your pillars, Rendell! They don't go anywhere.'

'Headless pillars. Symbolic. Waiting to be' – Martin shrugs – 'given a purpose. Joined. A burden to carry. Unity, a Messiah, whatever you like.' He takes a long step between them as if crossing an invisible threshold. 'The original pillars were built by Hiram of Tyre, a coppersmith, to guard the entrance of King Solomon's Temple. Only the holy, the chosen, the pure, might enter between them.'

Gonzalez puts down the angel. 'This? This is not King Solomon's Temple!'

'Here's the pillars, there's the doorway. This is an exact replica of Solomon's Temple which was destroyed by the Babylonians six centuries before Jesus. I bet my reputation on it.'

'Martin, if that's true,' Tanya says, 'you've made the archaeological find of this century. Of any century since Christ.'

The camera follows Martin from the porch into a narrow side corridor, others crowding behind, the ones at the back following his progress on a video monitor. Martin demonstrates. 'Three floors high, yes, just as it should be. We should find a central hall surrounded on three sides by chambers connected by trapdoors.' He points to holes in the ceiling and floor, the trapdoors and wooden steps leading up and down long rotted away. 'This way.' Martin turns left, down stone steps. A vaulted stone room thirty feet by sixty opens up, massively buttressed against the weight of the structure above, but half its roof collapsed into an ancient rubble of broken pillars. Martin reaches up, touches a line of reformed text carved roughly, almost stabbed, despairingly perhaps, into the lintel. '"Every—"' shakes his head, wrong word. 'All, it's all. "All mankind are in a lost and in a fallen state."'

Tanya says: 'That's not in the Bible.' She remembers the camera. 'Close up, Jerry.'

Martin leaves them, picks his way carefully between the fallen stones, shattered columns. Nothing. Bare walls, no altar, no burial goods.

'There's nothing here,' Gonzalez says. 'It's empty. There's no treasure.'

Something touches the toe of Martin's boot. A finger of bone, a skull, a spine, now others, and as he turns round and round he sees the dusty floor is bone dust, bones everywhere, now a rusty sword, arrowheads, fragments of armour, bracelets, jewellery crunching in the bones beneath his soles with every step.

'They knew the battle was lost,' he whispers. 'They couldn't keep the victors out. So they sealed themselves inside. To die.'

The bones pile highest at the far end, by a doorway where most had chosen to wait for death.

Tanya comes forward, tracking shot. 'Martin?' Again she's forgotten to call him professor, it doesn't matter. 'Martin, where's that exit lead?'

'It isn't an exit.' Martin bends into the low doorway at

the far end. 'It's an entrance, probably once covered with a curtain woven by Temple virgins. A hymenal curtain veiling the ultimate mystery. Smoke. Incense. Terror. Worship. God. The mystery of life.' He shrugs. 'Only the hereditary High Priest of the Israelites, the Zadok, dared to pass through – and only once a year on the Day of Atonement, atoning for the sins of the priesthood and thus the whole people, though they got a scapegoat thrown them in addition. Death for anyone but the Zadok who tried to enter here.' The winding corridor beyond is so narrow it scrapes Martin's shoulders. 'The Zadok sacrificed, not himself, but a bull instead of himself, on the Temple porch. He himself, alone, carried the bowl of blood inside to the Holy of Holies, where God had His divine Presence in the "Ark" or Arch of the Covenant. The Arch, as well as all its other meanings to the priests, was also an archive . . . a memory. It contained the Law given by God to Moses in the mountain. On top, flanked with golden cherubs with outstretched wings, was a gold seat called the *kappōret*, the mercy-seat. The throne of God.' Martin's voice dies away, swells. 'The throne of God. When he at last reached the Holy of Holies the Zadok would sprinkle the *kappōret* with blood from the bull, meaning his own blood.' Silence.

Tanya calls, 'Martin, wait. Martin? Don't. It's frightening.'

'Booby traps don't work after two thousand years.' Martin's voice comes back. 'All right. This place is dead, Tanya. It's as dead as those dead bones.' Tanya whispers, 'But people don't change.' Then she turns in confusion as Martin's voice comes from one side then the other, apparently from the solid walls. 'It's a maze,' he calls. 'Even the Zadok couldn't approach God directly.'

Her girlish voice comes calling after him, 'How could they worship God at all in this dreadful place? Martin, please. This is Central America not Jerusalem. Martin, stop. Slow down.' His footsteps fade. She shouts, 'We're in America not the Holy Land—'

His shout echoes back, 'Millions of Americans believe America *is* the Holy Land. The land that was promised . . .'

'Martin, please. Please wait. Please be careful.'

Martin turns left, turns right, turns left. He'll be first, he can taste the adrenaline. 'The Zadok threaded his way through the maze carrying in his right hand the gold bowl of blood still steaming with life. At the end he came to the Holy of Holies, a cube thirty paces by thirty paces by thirty paces high, unlit except by the seven flames of the menorah he carried in his left hand, a room filled with smoke, the House of God roofed with gold, with walls of gold, floored with solid gold.' Martin turns left, almost running, certain. 'Left again—'

He turns left.

He stops. Wrong. A blank wall, a dead end.

Something flickers behind him. Martin turns slowly. His eyes fill with a golden glow.

He takes one step forward, then another, and the torch drops from his hand.

IX

'No, my love,' Winona whispers. She pulls gently, and her baby slips out of her agonized constricting body into her cupped hands with a fierce little cry of loss. She holds her child to her face, kissing away her blood from the lips, ears, eyelids, and her baby's eyes flick open fiercely blue, then close again.

Winona whispers: 'No, my love, not our son.'

With nail scissors Winona cuts the cord joining them, ties it off, leans back naked against the bent brass bedhead, holds her baby to her breast. No one knows the future, and that is sufficient blessing. This moment is hers. She smiles as her baby latches to her nipple, drinks thirstily.

'Not our son, my love. Our daughter.'

X

Martin drops the torch, but the darkness is not dark.

It's golden.

Martin steps forward into the golden light, the Holy of Holies. It's not what he expected; nothing like it; it's wonderful. At the centre seven naphtha flames burn in a seven-headed stone candlestick, the menorah, illuminating the gold floor. Beneath centuries of dust the floor is solid plates of gold, inches thick Mayan gold; his boots make no sound, no vibration whatsoever, he seems hardly to move, but he trails bright footsteps. Gold reflections spread up the skin of his hands and face as he stares around him at the stained patterns in the mould that covers the walls, stained human-sized shapes.

Martin reaches out his hand, sweeps the side of his hand across the mould like a man wiping condensation from his shaving-mirror, and his face stares back at him. No, not his face now, worn down by adulthood: his face as a child, making him smile.

Martin wipes again, and again. More faces, children's faces.

Children's faces, hundreds of them, staring upwards.

Martin reaches up. Touches the mould, and the mould falls away from his hand.

'Oh my God.' He stares up quietly. 'Oh my Lord.'

Tanya calling from the maze. 'Martin? What . . .'

Her footsteps coming to stand beside him. The two of them breathe in the same rhythm, staring upwards. 'My God,' Tanya breathes. 'Oh my God, sweet Jesus.'

Jesus Christ looks into their eyes. His smile is for each of them, the compassion in His wide brown eyes flows into each of them, both Martin and Tanya falling to their knees in the dust and their hands finding each other's and holding tight, and Jesus Christ holds out His arms wide over them and over His flock of Mayan children who jostle in the sunlight in front of Him and hold up their hands to Him to be picked up.

'Look,' Tanya whispers. 'It *is*, it's happening.'

'And we are. We're happening. We're part of it. It's here.' Martin's hand moves, swathing brilliant lines with his palm as the mould falls away from the view: in the distance behind the children and Jesus rises the great green dome of Apachiohualitzá, a cleared tonsure of jungle on its crown where the Temple of Solomon stands alone and sparkling in the tropical sun of the Isthmus. Priests wearing seamless white linen climb in procession on the Temple steps. Closer, brightly coloured parrots flutter in the bushes, and here a group of farmhands wearing white loinskirts, white cloths over their shoulders, are chopping down a tree. Martin smells their sweat, hears the harsh squawking of the parrots like human voices, and the heavy bluster of their wings blows his hair into his eyes. 'My God,' Tanya whispers. 'We *are*.'

Jesus Christ is speaking to the children, Martin can almost overhear His voice, can almost pick out His words. 'Tanya, listen. Listen!'

Tanya leans forward, peering. Older children are watching Him from between the acotzintli trees, groups of women watching Him from near and far. The groan of the falling tree, the satisfaction of the clean-shaven men leaning on their axes. She peers close at the Temple. 'It's perfect. Perfect in every detail.' A woman in her doorway beating out a rug, a laughing toddler wobbling unsteadily after a dog. A cat, tiny, no more than a few flecks of paint, perches on a fencepost licking its paws. Everything's alive. 'They even had cats.'

Behind them Gonzalez says, 'Who is it?' He points at Jesus. 'Who's that?'

Tanya turns towards him, her eyes adjusting to the dim light. 'What do you mean who is that, Gonzalez? You must be blind.'

Martin says, 'It's exactly what it appears to be, Gonzalez. The legends are true. Jesus came to the people of the Isthmus. Here's Jesus Christ in America.'

Gonzalez puts down the angel carefully, straightens. 'That's not true. He never did.'

Martin shrugs. See for yourself.

Gonzalez comes forward through the firelight and shadows, squinting as his face is illuminated with sunlight. 'It's a window. It's a trick.'

Martin says, 'It's a painting.'

Gonzalez reaches out, flattens his fingertips against the paint. 'Who of? Who do you say?'

Martin doesn't bother to answer. He turns, sweeps his hand across the second wall. A storm, the sea, a ragged ship with its sail in tatters, the crew of men and women screaming and sick with fear. A dragon's head rises from the sea, towers above them shedding spray, the prayers of the white-haired man in the bow and the strength of the strong man wrestling with the rudder will not prevail: and a man walks calmly towards the ship across the violent water and holds out His arms, hands, fingers, come to Me and fall down in worship of Me, and I will save you.

'It's a lie.' Gonzalez trembles. 'It's a lie.'

'Gonzalez.' Tanya turns him by the shoulder. 'He's Jesus Christ, you can see that.'

Gonzalez stops Martin's hand reaching out to the third wall. 'No, no more lies, Rendell.' But Martin's hand sweeps down, reveals another bright picture: Jesus Christ wearing a gown of seamless white linen, sandals of rope and wood, a wounded child hanging bloody in His arms, and all around Him stand armed men with eyes blackened for war and swords and bows raised, now falling back from Him, and the child lives.

'He's Jesus Christ,' Tanya whispers in Gonzalez's ear. 'He's still here.'

The magic breaks, the cold white glare of the camera floodlight freezes the firelight's flickering shadows. Jerry crouches, panning shot, whole room. 'Gee, hard to get focus.' The Mayan *mestizo* roughs from the barrios gather behind him, light glinting on the machetes stuck through their belts, faces broad, native, impassive.

Gonzalez stares at the camera's monitor. 'These are paintings of Jesus Christ? Fakes. Modern, obviously.'

Martin brushes the patina of the paint with his fingertips. 'The Holy of Holies had walls of cedarwood covered with gold leaf. Here the cedar and gold's been painted over. These paintings were made contemporary with the events they portray.'

Tanya murmurs to the camera. 'We believe these incredible works are eyewitness pictures of Jesus, painted from life. Professor Rendell, how can you be so sure?'

Martin says simply, 'Look. See. The end of doubt. I'd bet my life on their authenticity.'

Gonzalez says: 'Jesus among Mayan roughs. It's nonsense.'

'Look at their faces. I don't believe they're Mayan. Some Mayan blood maybe. Look at the bone structure in the faces. It's Caucasoid, white, not Indian.'

'No ancient Caucasian skeletons have been found in America.'

'Sure they are. Look at the clothes of these people, robes, long hair, beards, buildings, Semitic. Egyptian cultural influences . . . I guess south-western Semitic, the Sinai desert, maybe as far north as the Dead Sea. Moses's time, basically. All these fashions would've looked pretty dated by Jesus's day. Perhaps deliberately so, a religious sect.' Wipes his palm across the fourth wall. 'Here's the ruin of Solomon's Temple on Mount Sion in Jerusalem, still burning.' They can almost smell the rising smoke.

Tallboy taps the painting with his Uzi. 'Who's the geezer with white hair, same as on the ship? Looks like he's reaching out to catch hold of someone we can't see.'

Martin whispers 'Lehi.'

'Clear as mud,' Tallboy says cheerfully. 'Never heard of the old bastard. Who was he?'

'Like Moses. I don't know who Lehi's holding out his hand to, but Lehi believed in Jesus Christ. In God on earth.'

Gonzalez frowns, 'And this was his promised land? America?'

'Millions believe so.' Martin reaches up reverently. 'I believed, but I lost my faith. I've found my faith again.'

'Hallelujah.' Tallboy grins. 'Happy for you, prof.'

Gonzalez says, 'Rendell, to business. How much is this stuff worth if it's real?'

'The painting?' Martin sounds staggered. 'No, this is priceless. You couldn't buy it. No one could. It changes everything. The whole world.' He tries to explain. 'Jesus Christ is here, in the life. I feel I can almost touch Him.' Reaches again, goes up on tiptoe. 'Perhaps I *can*—'

Gonzalez says abruptly, 'I represent a collector.'

Martin bumps down. 'No, no, it isn't worth ten million or a hundred million, Gonzalez, it isn't worth a cent. This is more than art. It's real.'

'Priceless. Yes, I heard you say. But it's definitely Jesus Christ?'

'Oh my God yes!' Tanya cries. 'Look!'

'You are quite certain, Rendell? The collector I have in mind is intolerant of fakes, frauds, lies, anything less than the almost-perfect truth.'

Martin laughs, 'My God, Gonzalez, you can see it's the truth.'

'Tallboy?'

'Go for it, Mr G.'

The feed from the video monitor shows the scene in

the main auditorium or pronaos they've come from, a bluish fisheye of people moving about searching among bones. Gonzalez presses the audio. 'Snowflake, your expert opinion in here, please.' The Negro stands up, his muffled head growing briefly enormous in the fisheye lens as he looks up. '*Ja*. Right away.'

People are gathering in the Holy of Holies, one student falls to her knees praying, others gaze upwards in awe. The Negro arrives, pushes forward between their pointing fingers, his dark glasses flashing in the camera light. He sniffs the air. 'Cedarwood. Not naturally occurring here. Transported many miles at huge effort and cost. The smell is very fine.' Touches the walls with his gloved hands. 'The feel is very good. Turn off the light.'

Jerry makes a peevish gesture, his filming interrupted, but the light goes off.

Snowflake takes off his glasses, leans forward. His eyes are white like snowflakes, and the whites of his eyes are black. 'Everything has its price, and I know the price of everything.' He examines the painting, touching, sniffing, licking smears of paint from the gloved tips of his fingers.

At last Snowflake straightens with a sharp crack of his bones. 'Your tame professor is maybe right,' he says in his rich melted voice. 'The value is beyond me.' The balaclava hiding his face stretches, smiling. 'If the painting is a fake, it frightens me. If real, it terrifies me.'

Tallboy goes to the praying girl, nudges her with the Uzi barrel, rests his finger lightly against her lips. 'Put a sock in it, love. We can't hear ourselves think.'

Gonzalez taps his teeth thoughtfully with his fingernail. 'So. Everything is worthwhile. *If* this is true. *If* it's real.' He clicks his fingers. 'Tallboy. Cakchiquel.' A couple of Chetumal *mestizos* pull the native Cakchiquel forward, throw him down. Old Cakchiquel stares up at the painting in toothless wonder. 'Told you, did. Words of Chilam Balaam, ancient Maya prophet, told you. "The raised

43

wooden standard shall come! Our Lord comes, Itzá! Our elder brother comes, oh men of Tantun! Receive your guests, the bearded men, the men of the east, the bearers of the sign of God, Lord!"' The old man cries out, 'All the old stories, no-fake true! Wotan, Quetzalcoatl, the ship of Christ—'

Tallboy interrupted, 'He says Wotan, same surname, that bitch Winona? No offence, prof.'

'No' – Martin glances round – 'he means Votan, it's different. One of the local gods here. Myth. Legend.'

Tallboy says, 'Like Jesus, right?'

Martin shakes his head. 'No, Tallboy, this is real and true, just look around you at the paintings, see Him here.' Tallboy looks around him, nodding, appreciating, then touches the barrel of the Uzi to the head of the praying girl for the second time, pulls the trigger. The crash and smoke of the weapon deafens and blinds them all for a moment. The girl lies down sleepily, her blood and brains thrown over the stones behind her. Tallboy says cheerfully. 'Now your Jesus ain't here, right, prof? Not in her, anyway.' He winces, pulls his earlobe, covering the other students with the gun. 'Don't it make your ears ring.'

Tanya screams and Jerry swings the camera, filming, the Uzi barrel taps against the camera lens and the gun stutters its thunder on a single note, the camera sprays glass and then film in a steady unspooling stream, motor whining. Jerry slides forward in his blood and as he lies still the camera beeps loudly, steadily, announcing it's out of film. Gonzalez warns: 'Mind the walls, Tallboy.'

'Sorry, guv.' Tallboy calls to the *mestizos*, 'Knives, lads.' The students scream, pushing each other forward, soiling their jeans helplessly, the smell of death, as the *mestizos* move amongst them. A machete blade flashes.

'Stop,' Gonzalez says. Everyone stops. The screaming stops. Tallboy's heel comes down on the camera, then again and again, until its chirpy announcement is silenced. In the silence someone says, 'Don't kill us.' Then the others begin to cry, sobbing as they always do. Gonzalez steps forward reasonably. 'You youngsters have achieved everything you dreamt. You came here hoping for the find of the century, something you would remember all your lives. Something to give your lives meaning. You have found it. Be happy.' He points to the largest *mestizo*, scarred face and hands. 'You, your name?'

'Lazaro, me.'

'I wouldn't ask you to kill a woman before enjoying her. Choose one of those clever boys we all hate.'

Lazaro pulls forward a lad of nineteen by his hair, pulls back his head by the hair, rests the handle of his machete against the throat. The lad's Adam's apple bobs as he tries to swallow, making the leaf-stained blade flash. Tanya whispers, 'Stop it, Gonzalez, you're mad.'

'You see Jesus Christ all around you, and you say *I* am mad?'

'Stop it. I do see Him.'

'You are not the world's foremost authority on this subject.' Gonzalez turns to Martin. 'But we have the man here. Professor Rendell, believe me, this is no small matter. My master is intolerant of deceit. I would value your professional opinion.' Sweeps his arm round him: everything you see. 'Is it real?'

Martin says simply, 'It's real.'

Gonzalez says, 'Lazaro.' Lazaro slices the machete smoothly towards himself, turning his body so the lad's blood spurts past him, severs the vertebra with a final click of breaking bone, holds up the head.

Tanya vomits. Martin stares at the head. He puts his hands to his own head. 'But it's true.'

'Deny it, Rendell.' Gonzalez jerks his head and Tallboy takes two strides to Tanya kneeling wiping the vomit from her lips, straddles her, grips her shoulders between his knees, touches the gun barrel to the back of her head.

'You know this one a little, you do, Rendell. Save her. Say her name.'

Martin says: 'Tanya.'

'That's better,' Gonzalez says gently. 'I have to know if the picture is true. I have to know.'

'Tanya, I'm sorry, I'm sorry.' Martin's voice breaks. 'All right, it's a fake!' He grabs at the gun but Tallboy butts him effortlessly with the shoulder-stock, the barrel hardly moving in Tanya's hair. Martin slides down the wall dragging the colours of the bright holy day behind him, sags against the golden floor. Tanya hisses, 'Martin, Martin, don't lie for me, not here, tell them the truth.'

Martin shouts, 'It's real. It's true. I swear it.' He weeps. 'Gonzalez, for God's sake let her go.'

'Seems he don't love her enough, Mr G.' Tallboy tears off Tanya's jacket, wraps it round her head. 'Won't splash the artwork.'

'Gonzalez, for God's sake.'

'*Is it true?*'

'God, I swear, I swear it's true.'

The gun crashes. No blood spurts, a little smoke rises from the jacket's neck. Tanya's body dangles silently between Tallboy's knees, slides forward as he steps back. One of her long white legs shows a bruise, she must have knocked it earlier in the day.

Gonzalez says, 'You believe our professor?'

'Never can tell with these clever bastards.' Tallboy shrugs. 'Could be trying to fool us, I reckon, getting us in trouble.'

'We'll shoot them all, Jurgen, Colin, Bertstein.'

'Bernstein.'

'Bernstein, Coles, shoot them all. Some expert, one, in the face of death, will truly say they believe this Christ is false.' Gonzalez crouches beside Martin. 'You, Martin. Tell me this Christ is false and I will spare your life. I will give you any gift. Deny Him. Save yourself. *I have to be sure.*'

Martin stares upwards. His mouth moves without sound. Then the tears in his eyes overflow, pour down his face. The gun barrel makes a cold kiss on his neck and he is terrified, terrified, and above him Jesus Christ spreads out His arms, His hands and His fingers over the children, this moment lasting for ever.

Martin cannot close his eyes, he cannot look away.

Martin says clearly: 'He is true.'

XI

'Room forty-three. Thank you. Two minutes.' Dr Winona Wotan, standing six feet tall in her sheer stockings, puts down the phone and slips her feet into comfortable white shoes in front of the full-length mirror. White cotton skirt to the knee, silk sapphire-blue blouse under her white business jacket, and in its lapel a single startling deep-water pearl, surrounded by sapphires as blue as the sea, perfectly matching her eyes. Her eyes gaze steadily at herself, her suntanned feminine features, her high cheekbones are as usual but she can never get used to her full lips, the merest touch of lipstick; then she puts back her blond hair so it tumbles over her shoulders as she turns away, her inspection of her appearance complete, and picks up her newborn baby lying safely asleep in the centre of the double bed.

A knock on the door, she smiles. 'One hundred fifteen seconds. Well done, Pepito.' Tosses her suitcase to the eager boy one-handed, precedes him down the corridor to the elevator as he struggles beneath the heavy weight to keep up with her long strides, finally dragging it by one corner in his efforts not to fall behind. The elevator has been called away already and any bellboy worth his salt must reach the button first to call it back. Perhaps her long suntanned fingers do not reach the button quite as quick as they might; Pepito lunges, bangs the plunger with the side of his little fist and almost collapses, grinning, perspiring, the victor. '*Servicio, señora.*'

She stands waiting, twice as tall as he, impossibly tall to the child, and Pepito looks up at her wishing he could think of something wise to say to make her smile. 'Is pretty baby.'

'Thank you, Pepito.'

'Is boy or girl?'

'She's a girl.' The cable rattles past the concertina gate as the elevator ascends.

'I don't remember her with you before.'

'Your mistake.'

'What name you call her?'

The tall woman looks down curiously. 'I don't know, Pepito. She doesn't have a name. I haven't thought of a name for her yet. I don't know what name will suit her.' The elevator halts and she lets him crash open the gate, enters the confined space. Pepito slams the latch with a flourish and the lift descends shuddering under their weight. She says suddenly: 'None of my children have turned out as I . . . expected.' She finds another word. 'Wanted.' Shrugs. 'Perhaps better.'

Pepito stares up adoringly, gushes: 'To me the *señora* is perfect. You will be perfect mother.'

'I am always a rather bad mother, I'm afraid, Pepito.'

He grins disbelievingly, crashes open the lobby gate, watches her queue and pay at the checkout with Visa like any other tourist, then she moves away with long strides through the crowd and their luggage while Pepito drags her suitcase with all his strength down the steps to the ancient Morris taxi, catches up with her in time to open her door and hand her case to the taxi-driver. 'Put this in the trunk right away for *señora* to the airport, and don't over-charge!'

She winds down the back window while the driver tries to start the engine. 'Two things for you, Pepito. This.' She slips a ten dollar note into his top pocket. 'And this. This advice.' She whispers, '*If that's what love is like I swear I will never fall in love.*'

Pepito colours. How could she have overheard him? He crosses himself, and she smiles, kisses his forehead.

'Love is the most beautiful thing in the world,' her whisper comes, 'and one day, Pepito, you will fall in love.' The taxi pulls away between the tropical fronds and bumps on to the highway trailing smoke, and Pepito gazes after her with adoration in his eyes.

Winona looks down at her baby as the Morris rocks and bounces out of town between the shacks and fields. The early sun stretches their shadow in front. The driver watches in his rear-view mirror as she feeds her baby from her breast. She looks into the mirror, he looks away as they come to the airport turning. Winona orders: 'No, keep going.'

'Everyone goes to the airport. The road to the west, there's nothing more there.'

'Except the west.' She looks through the grimy window. 'Keep your eyes on the road.'

After the fields there's only the jungle, the road a dusty track rising along the steepening valley of the Rió Azul. The Morris struggles uphill, shuddering, popping smoke and steam. The driver's sun visor is plastered with yellow sticky-taped photos of girls, boys, a woman. From third gear to second now, struggling hard. A village on the roadmap is only a cantina, a few scrawny chickens, more jungle. Again the driver smiles as she feeds her baby and Winona reaches forward, twists the mirror round.

She sits watching her baby curiously. You could not have come at a worse time. Yet here you are, our little girl, symbol of the love between a man and a woman, not to be denied any more than love is to be denied, passion is to be denied, time denied, life itself denied. Love is greater than death. So here you are. But you could have timed it better.

San Lorenzo then Yo Creek by noon, stopping to put water in the steaming radiator, then at San Lazaro the driver stops for a couple of beers at the crossroads cantina and afterwards he slows down, wants his siesta by the roadside and a little fun first to ease his beer belly, a woman and her baby alone in a car in the jungle, she needs looking after. 'Nowhere for you to run to.'

She says, 'Drive on. Only a little further. Then we will have fun.' So he keeps going through the Mennonite Settlement, engine howling in first gear, and kills the motor on a high corner before they reach Quatro Leguas, leans back over the seat grinning yet domineering. Time for fun. Winona shifts her baby to her right arm and reaches out her left hand, takes the driver by his smirking face and pulls him into the back seat, knocks his face between the door and the roof until he's quiet, lifts him again against the roof. The steel creaks.

She says calmly, 'This is my sort of fun.'

She opens the door with her shoulder, drags him out, drops him across the hood of the vehicle while she opens the trunk, pulls out her suitcase. How beautiful the view below the high corner is, treetops falling away into the *rió*, parrots the size of paintspots down there, a gleam of the river like a silver worm. The driver lies gasping across the hood, shirt caught in the chromed Morris insignia. He holds up his hands as she approaches. 'Don't hurt me.'

She lifts him, drops him in the driving seat. 'Turn round. Drive home to your wife and children.'

He will not meet her eyes. The Morris backs with grinding gears, then he stops, speaks without looking at her. 'You will die here. This is jungle. Get in.'

'Go home, my friend.'

While the sound of the engine fades Winona sits peacefully on a fallen treetrunk, one knee comfortably raised, feeding her baby from her breast. After a few minutes a thin trail of dust moves far down on the valley wall, then there's nothing, only jungle sounds, and the whisper of the wind.

When her baby's finished Winona burps her, chuckles and rubs noses affectionately when success is achieved, opens the suitcase with her foot. Most of it is bloody sheet, the undersheet as well, bloody and torn; she takes a nappy from a plastic bag and a small bottle of olive oil, lays her daughter on the treetrunk and changes her with the ease of long experience. Her baby kicks cheerfully at the air. The climate here in the mountains is cooler and the night will be cold; Winona dresses her baby in a warm one-piece suit, pulls over it a woollen cardigan she knitted herself, then swaddles her in a warm blanket and returns her to the crook of her arm. A few more nappies left in the bag so she stuffs them in a jacket pocket, the olive oil in another. That's it. She kicks the suitcase over the edge and it falls for ever in the afternoon light; Winona has already turned away, and walked into the jungle.

Best to get there before night. The expedition path is hacked wide enough for an army along the contour of the hillside. She leaves the path to cross a chasm balanced on a fallen tree, cutting a corner, then runs smoothly. The path again, and after ten miles a Jeep abandoned in a stream. The light is failing as the dull forested dome of Apachiohualitzá, at the head of three valleys, appears between the treetops, and she pauses. She did not remember it so high.

Thunder rumbles, light flashes between the clouds filling the valleys, Apachiohualitzá floating like a green island above grey mist. Soon the evening rain will come and her baby will get wet; for the first time Winona moves quickly, running uphill, leaping the streams that foam past her, going faster until the sweat pours from her and she stops to drink. Again she runs, again she crouches to drink, her sweat steaming gently from her face and hands in the

51

cooling air. She takes a few steps forward, and comes into the clearing.

Everything has changed; jungle has grown over the fields and houses, drowned them, buried them, nothing is as it was. Only the Mayan name remains, and the myth: Apachiohualitzá, the Flood. And the legend of the Hand of God.

With a shiver she approaches four great black basalt fingers standing as though beckoning from the forest floor, stares up at them uncomprehendingly.

'My God,' Winona whispers. 'What's this?'

Her baby starts to cry in her arms, blue eyes looking up intensely in the dimness, sensing her mood. Winona jogs her. 'Sssh baby, sssh baby sleep, sleep baby . . .' Then she looks up at the basalt fingers and whispers, 'Is *this* obscenity supposed to be the Hand of God?'

Nothing here, no more information; only a hundred footprints trailed across the leaves and mud, and night falling.

And lying on the leaf-mould a single chromium-plated torch, the hand clasping it severed from its wrist by a slash from a machete.

By the stone forefinger an aluminium ladder angles into the ground; Winona switches on the torch, pulls off the fleshy hand, goes down into the dark. The rungs creak one by one under her weight, she moves the arm that supports the baby, flashes the torchlight below. 'Hallo?'

She stands on the face, the immense silently screaming face buried by time below the jungle. Below her in the torchlight gapes the screaming mouth, and a ladder leads down inside.

She swings herself across, goes down one-handed. Her baby whimpers. Winona kisses her eyelids. 'Sssh, baby, it's all right.' She knows it's not all right, and the baby whimpers again.

She calls down: 'Anyone there?' She knows there isn't,

this is a dead place void of life, whatever happened here is finished. She calls into the rising breath stinking of sulphur and naphtha, 'Martin? Martin Rendell? You still here?' No answer. Something amazing happens: a tear squeezes into Winona's eye. 'You stupid bastard, I told you not to come.' A rustling sound; her hand grips the torch like a weapon, the casing crushes and splinters, the light goes out.

It's only bats fluttering past her, the evening feed.

Winona strokes her baby's face reassuringly in the dark. She descends the ribbed steps to the firelit hallways and corridors below, the walls carved with Mayan stelae and glyphs, the flickering ancient glow of burning naphtha, stairways down. Plenty of footsteps in the dust. The first body on the stairs, a *mestizo* tough shot from above. More corridors, more bodies lying stiffly where they fell or crawled or tried to hide in the last moments of life, students in jeans and bright waterproof gear, blood and the usual stuff everywhere, the smell coming up like an abattoir, the same old smell. They're all dead. It could have been worse.

In the dark Winona walks between the headless copper pillars that she remembers standing in the sunlight, their golden flames that gleamed like the sun now stolen. Her face doesn't change. Nothing surprises her about men.

She enters the Temple. The priests are still here in the pronaos; these are their bones beneath the latest bodies, the latest blood, Jurgen shot in the knees and then the mouth, Bernstein hacked by blades, other unrecognisable. Most of the students simply shot in the back, fallen where they ran. Winona looks around her calmly as she goes forward. Soon all this, too, will be bones; who knows what creatures wait in the dark. She crouches on one knee, her free hand searching in the bone dust, coming up with shapeless jewellery, a strap of brass armour, a gold pendant earring, a sword with a jagged rusty blade. She lifts the sword, blows away the dust, tosses it lightly in her scarred hand as she walks forward.

The walls of the maze are scrabbled with blood, bloody fingerprints, torn fingernails, but it's brown blood, already dried. There's nobody here, everything's finished, but there's no sense of peace: rather of held breath. Winona sniffs the air, then strides quickly. At its centre the maze is wholly dark, but she remembers her way flawlessly, and at the end the golden glow of the Holy of Holies appears like a beacon in the darkness to guide her.

Her baby gives a sudden cry but Winona does not stop. She drops the sword, strides forward with an exclamation.

Gone. All gone.

The gold plates of the floor are still here but everything of value is gone. Jesus Christ is stolen away. The painted cedar panels of that day two thousand years ago are torn from their mountings. The walls are bare black stone.

The Holy of Holies is empty.

Except for these bodies. The stink of evil is as strong here, as she walks between them, as the sweet smell of spilt blood that rises like an offering to her nostrils. Evil has come into the Temple; it came here many years ago and tried to build over what had been created, but this is stronger. This is terribly strong.

Winona touches a shoulder, turns a head. 'Martin.' How much did Martin understand, in the last moments of his life? Did he hear the children calling Itzá to teach them, come to us Itzá, Itzá, the name of Christ to Mayan tongues? Did Martin feel at least a tiny part of the marvel? She lifts his body, rests him down by the flame still burning as it always has. She moves calmly, quietly, but her baby gives bawling yells of fear. Here's the film girl, what's her name, Tanya. She lifts Tanya one-handed by her clothes, rests her by the flame. Others Winona does not know; here's one she didn't trust, Lazaro, shot in the back of the head. She piles them all by the flame, lifting them higher.

Her feet crunch on alloy shell casings. Winona crouches, sniffs the spent metal. Tallboy. He probably joined the expedition somewhere *en route*, a crossroads, San Lazaro maybe. If only she'd known.

It would've made no difference; no woman can halt the birth of her child.

A blue flicker catches Winona's eye; the video monitor. She presses rewind, watches herself walk backwards from the maze into the Hall of Judgment, standing up with the sword, search for it, walk away backwards between the entrance pillars Jachin and Boaz. Then nothing moves. The tape buzzes quietly, rewinding the hours. Suddenly the picture is filled with Tallboy's grinning face, his raised thumb almost touching the video camera: okay. He winks, pulls away, and behind him the porters are carrying out the last of something shrouded: the cedar panels. Winona watches them at their backwards tasks, watching as from the floor the bodies of students jump to life running, their injuries disappearing, their faces losing their terror, their screams becoming unborn, then just their faces looking round curiously at some new arrival, and Tallboy backs into the doorway with his gun smoking and flashing, leaving them chatting quietly among themselves in the last moments before their lives ended.

She plays the tape back to the beginning, then forward to Tallboy's wink at the camera, his grinning face, his huge thumb: okay.

Rewind, start. Someone else on camera, a muffled head growing briefly enormous in the fisheye lens as it looks up, listening. 'Snowflake, your expert opinion in here, please.' The faceless man's answer, *'Ja*. Right away.' Snowflake. She knows his name.

A blur of motion, then the shooting, Tallboy's wink, his grinning face, his thumb: okay.

Rewind, start, freeze frame.

Wink. Grin. Okay.

Winona says: 'Tallboy, damn you.' She knows Tallboy. She punches her fist through the video monitor, throws it at the bare looted walls. It's not enough. Winona puts back her head, her long blond hair swinging down her back, and gives a bellow of rage. She thinks to put her baby down gently where the altar once stood, then her rage bursts out of her uncontrollably. She turns away shouting at the black walls, she puts her fists to her face and her baby smiles up at her innocently, wondering at the noise, her mother's screams. Winona beats her face with her fists. Jesus with the children, gone. Jesus facing the Dragon, gone. Jesus at Jerusalem, Jesus at Sion, all gone. She beats at her face and pulls her hair and beats at her body, screaming.

Sometimes screaming is all that can be done, all that's left. She remembers the fat Spaniard speaking on the videotape. '*The Fallen Angel.*' His shrug as he holds up the terrible statue. '*A tradition that Jesus Christ visited them as a plumed serpent, yes, but let's be serious now. An angel after its Fall from Heaven. This scream, total loss, total abandonment, total thrown-down desolation, this is the scream of an angel forsaken by God. Yes, ten million. Such an icon. Such a powerful symbol speaking to our age of suffering. Our search for belief. One true faith to cling to. One truth in this world of lies that can make sense of our lives. Something real.*'

Winona screams. 'Damn you, the damned!'

Something real.

The earth growls, but scientists like these whose bodies are scattered around would say it's only the thunder echoing from the storm above. Winona's voice rises, louder and deeper. 'Damn you all, all you who made this world Hell before there was Hell! I shall find you! I shall find you all, destroy you all, I shall destroy the Destroyer!' Silence. No thunder, then a fierce crash that makes the earth shake once.

Winona picks up her baby, kisses her, kicks open the stone conduit that feeds the seven flames of the menorah, steps back across the thick oily rainbow spreading across the floor, wrinkles her nose at the fumes of naphtha, then turns and strides away. A few seconds in the maze; she strides out between the pillars, reaching out with her left hand to tear each flaming stone cup from the walls as she goes, pools of fire spreading behind her along the corridors, flames licking up the faces of the ancient glyphs, smoke beginning to billow past her as she climbs the ladders, the breath from below blowing hot with the stink of burning sulphur. She climbs from the mouth, now the final ladder with its soft metal rungs bending and breaking beneath her feet as she goes faster, then she leaps out and throws down the ladder to the ground.

Lightning flashes around her in the dark, illuminating the slanting rain, the trees around the clearing streaming water, the black basalt fingers gleaming wet, upraised. *Come to me.*

Come to me. Believe in me.

'You aren't God,' Winona screams. '*You aren't God!*'

Bending her body to keep her baby dry from the rain, she turns and walks away.

Behind her the clearing craters as if punched, collapsing into the ground below, then blows upwards around the fallen angel's clawed hand in an explosion of fire that rises boiling above the treetops, setting them burning in the rain, and makes the clouds red so that the rain seems to pour down around Winona like blood.

Then night falls again, and the rain falls. The pyre shrinks, dies away into the darkness. She shelters her baby beneath a fallen treetrunk and stands listening to the falling rain, stands alone in the dark with the raindrops making her hair heavy, drops dripping like beads from her eyelids down her face, from her upraised hands down her arms, body, legs, then lightning flickers. Winona stares at her right hand, the scar on her palm punched through to the back of her hand, triangular as the bite of a tooth. She remembers.

Thunder roars and she shivers, remembering the beginning.

Remembering.

I am Wotan, and I remember the moment of my conception.

Era One

Shem

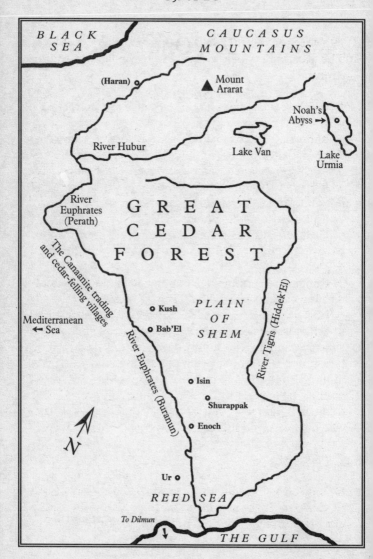

The Land of Shem
3,941 BC

19 March 3,941 BC, 5:14 in the evening
The Kup Valley, below the western plateau of Mount Ararat

I am Wotan, and I remember the moment of my conception . . .

Impossible to imagine the world before my existence: there was no world, no nothing, no everything; all was not-all, a formless void without knowledge, without sound, without sight. Nothing moved for an eternity, and I did not even know. There was nothing to know.

And then something moved.

Heat. Silence. I'm not-me, I'm half-me. I'm impossible, passive, receptive, half-human, a monster, my mother's egg.

Clinging to her womb, bound to fall, to fail. Impossible that I, whatever I was, should live.

And then an act more like murder than the giving of life, this sudden boiling rushing birth of energy and violence coming into my mother and the deaths of an uncounted flood of struggling sperm, millions, tens of millions, hundreds, almost an infinity of my father's number failing and dying as they flutter in my mother's womb: but it is I, buoyant, strong, one-hundred-millionth, who happens, who succeeds: who is chosen by chance . . . or chosen.

I am.

'Tomorrow is the equinox of spring when the great God El gives His gift of new life to the world, and we offer up our firstborn male children to Him in thanks.'

The sun set like a bloody eye. From beneath its closing eyelid of snowcloud the sun withdrew its glowing fingers one by one from the mountaintops stretching beyond Apsu's right hand, and there, in the immense violet moment of distance, a man, a king, might see clear to fabled Shem, the land of plenty where it was said the priests built mountains to El and were blessed with food all year, and no snow.

Apsu spat out the snow his words had allowed into his mouth. He didn't believe it. He looked round foxily, enough talking like a priest, time for a few whacks. 'Get on with it, you fat sods! Put some push in it!'

Ploughing forward through the drifts, he shielded his ice-blue eyes from the wind billowing over the ridge. They might die. Tonight, no later, they must find shelter in the valley beyond – if it existed – in the promised village, if it was there. Tomorrow the all-important spring equinox; but his men were exhausted, the older ones stumbling and swaying like the children. The snow plastering their fleeces and faces made all, children or adult, look as grey and clumsy in the gloom as old men. All were desperately tired, the children so thin with winter and the long journey that they'd stopped crying with cold. He whacked them, making sure they stumbled onwards clinging to the knots in the rope that kept them from getting lost or lying down to sleep; it was important not to lose any more children.

These weren't farmers' sons, they were the best of the best: fighting blood.

The oldest was seven.

Apsu wore the best and largest furs from the fiercest animals. Even so he stumbled towards the ridgeline tugging a donkey's halter – a king walking on foot like a woman, tugging his wife's donkey like her slave while she rode! But Tia's waters had broken, long icicles from her womb hung beneath the donkey's belly, from its fur and

62

her blue sandalled feet, and her tears had frozen to her cheeks. He smacked her a few times, getting colour in her face. She snarled at him, clawed at him with her puny strength, hating him, and he grinned: the furious stage of labour. Then her mouth rounded, an O of pain, good, his child was coming tonight, pray God he was a son; what Apsu did tomorrow would tear his own heart out but it must be done. The wind howled, or perhaps it was Tia again, her weakness and dependency infuriating him as he dragged at the donkey. His life was hard as hers, harder. Why had God made women to howl, why couldn't they suffer birth silently like other livestock? Mutton didn't howl its agony, neither did beef, nor would any man worth his salt – men were made by God. Infuriated by his wife's howling and his own terror and despair, the cold set deep in Apsu's heart.

Tomorrow he must face God.

Apsu felt fear and more-than-fear. He felt the terror of God that turned his bowels – though he had killed more men, women, children, than he had fingers and toes – to water. Tomorrow he might glimpse God's living toenail; he might hear God's own angry voice roaring in the sky above the mountain.

The death of the children must be good, more than good: it must be sufficient.

'This mountain goes up for ever,' Lotaan called. 'Maybe it's got no God at the top because it's got no top.' He gestured wearily at the great gloomy saddleback of snow overhanging them, the great flank of Ararat apparently summitless between the drifting clouds. 'I'm not climbing to the land of the gods, not up there with the great God and His Elohim, not me.'

Lotaan the whiner. Apsu kicked him, screamed at the others: 'Not much further, you sons of whores!' The starving men grinned wearily at the compliment; in the lands of the right hand the temple whores of Shem gave birth to the sons of gods, making the next generation of priests. None of these men could imagine priests of temples, the legendary false mountains built for worship and occupied by men who did nothing but pray. To these Caucasian men Apsu was their leader, talker, beggar, king, priest, flatterer to God, and their God lived in real mountains and real places. Here, here was the truth: here on Ararat, greatest mountain in the world, home of God. Apsu said so.

'After tomorrow, lads,' Apsu promised them, 'we'll get back home safe beyond the northern mountains, we'll crawl if we have to, and you'll see El of the glorious sun bless our winter with summer, fill the grass around our tents with new life and our orchards with red apples, make our herds fat with meat, and the bellies of your women fat with new sons you started before you left, you randy buggers!' He kicked Lotaan away from the donkey, cursed Tia's moaning, staggered forward with all his strength – and the skyline fell away beneath him, revealing the valley beyond the ridge.

Overlooking the *yallim*, the summer pasture below, huts with smoking roofs were clustered at the head of the valley: the village that had been promised. Apsu threw out his arms. 'God's answered my prayers, *mine*, and don't you forget it. Me, Apsu, I got you here, so God's with me.'

Tia cried out in a voice like the wind: 'Oooooh.' She bent forward, clutched the necklace of seashells she wore around her neck. 'Here. Now. Let me here. It's coming.'

Apsu's eyebrows drew together but Tia's belly hung so low it humped between her knees on the donkey's back. She begged, 'Quick.' She actually dared say his name. 'Apsu, quick. Apsu—'

'Hold it in, woman.' Apsu led them along the sheep-track crossing the hillside, sent Lotaan ahead to arrange shelter. Lotaan ran back. 'No, they won't. There's no room. They don't like people like us.'

Tia cried out like the wind moaning above the valley.

'I am Apsu!' Apsu drew his sword and ran forward on the mud to the miserable turf tents, sooty roofs and walls steaming and smoking and stinking, their lean-to doors cobbled from greasy sticks knotted together. He beat with the hilt of his sword but the door was stronger than it looked. Somebody shouted angrily inside, good, they deserved to die. Apsu screamed, kicking and pummelling the door, then hacked at the rope hinges with the blade. The door burst open and half a dozen men came out and stood up straight. Not one of them was white or blue-eyed like Apsu, each one was bigger than him, and their swords were longer.

Tia cried, 'Apsu, quick!'

Apsu swallowed his pride. He pointed at his wife. The armed shepherds sniffed her, she was on a donkey, she hadn't been left to whelp in the snow; she must be important. Then they spat, they didn't want their sleep disturbed by the noise of childbirth, no room. Everyone drew their swords: only a fight made sense.

Tia groaned, contrived to slip from the donkey and clutch at Apsu, forcing down his sword. Then she pushed in front of him, held out her hands to the men. 'Help me.' Her voice tiny in the wind and dark. 'Help me.'

The men burst out laughing, pulled at Apsu who stood red-faced behind her and clapped their arms round his shoulders, led him inside, drink, friends, Lotaan too, all the men, and the door slammed muffling their sounds of merriment, leaving Tia standing alone. Behind her the children clung to the rope in the snow, and more ice and snow blowing over them. She turned to the eldest, no higher than her waist, put her hand on his head. 'How many summers you have?'

'I'm seven.' He tried to show her his fingers. 'I'm Kris. I'll look after you.' He shuddered with the cold. None of the children could let go of the rope, their hands clasped the knotted rawhide like a row of white balls. Kris looked up at Tia, then clasped her fingers in his free hand. He was in charge. He walked her to a shack with no smoke coming out, kicked away the slush and worked the door open, led her inside: the wood store, freezing, but dry. Tia lay down exhausted and the children gathered round her in the gloom. Kris piped at the next oldest boy, 'Oris, steal a flaming stick to light a fire.' He turned to the next. 'Snormar, make a pile of small twigs for a fire and get larger pieces ready. You two, Yeris and Strig, tend the fire when it lights, not too high or too low, keep it just right.'

'Just right,' Yeris and Strig said obediently. 'Not too high or too low.' The youngest children were crying now they were not so cold. Tia gripped Kris's small icy hand. 'Kris, do you know what's going to happen?'

He said calmly, 'Tomorrow?'

'No, I . . .' She groaned. 'To me. Now.'

'You're going to have a baby.' Kris looked surprised at her ignorance. 'We're the firstborn. We all have brothers and sisters younger than us. We know everything.' He grinned, sliding a log beneath Tia's head, then grabbed the stick Oris brought back and set its glowing tip to Snormar's twigs. After a while the flames flared up, smoking, and the children sat in a circle round Tia holding hands, eyes large and hungry, then flickering sleepily in the firelight.

Later in the night the children were sleeping, their heads resting against one another, dreaming peacefully on this last night of their lives despite Tia's occasional moan and the working of her body, when Apsu stuck his head past the door. 'Where is it?' he demanded. Tia turned her head away from him. Later Apsu came back. 'What, not yet? What's she doing?' His breath was rich with beer and fat mutton. He bent over her but Tia lay on her side away from him, and wouldn't answer him. Apsu kicked the door, stormed out.

Kris touched Tia's hair, whispered, 'What are you going to do?' She shook her head, then looked down at her newborn baby hidden between her breasts. Her son. His eyes flicked open, fiercely blue, sky blue. Of course. Tia smiled, brushed the blond strands of hair from his dark brown eyebrows, almost black. Her baby, so warm! Her baby was so alive, he was kicking his little feet already, already he was everything to her. And the delicious peaceful baby smell of him, like warm milk. She ached for him, inhaled him, touched his hot little face to her own face.

'Give me my son.' Apsu's hairy hand pulled the boy away from its mother, he hefted its weight. 'I name you Wotan, the most precious gift I'll ever own, my firstborn son. I dedicate your life to God.' He grinned with fatherly pride as the baby cried strongly, then pulled off the furs and carried the child outside, held him up naked before the men in the mud and snow so they all saw the penis, lifted the boy high above his head in the dawn light like an object of worship, of offering. 'My son! My firstborn son Wotan!' The men cheered because the baby's squalling cries were almost as loud as Apsu's shouts of pride, in fact now louder. Apsu let go of the child with one hand and put the other over his ear, laughing. 'My son! My son!'

'He's not your son.'

Tia spoke. She staggered in the shadows of the doorway, almost fell. She leant against the post, looked Apsu in the eye. 'You can't kill him.' She repeated: 'He's not your son.'

She hobbled from the doorway into the first rays, pushed down on Kris's shoulder so that she stood upright, the other children filing out after her. Apsu laughed, nodded to his men, tousled Tia's hair patronisingly. 'You don't know what you're saying, you don't!' But she repeated calmly: 'He isn't yours.'

'Liar!' He pushed her over, tripping her, she fell with a cry and lay still, a bloody woman lying in the snow, his bloody wife with the birth blood on her legs, provoking him with her silent reproach. He kicked her and she kept silence. Apsu dragged her up by her hair and shouted at her. Silence, no screaming. He threw her down, terrified of showing weakness, of not prevailing over her. Her baby cried and kicked in his arm and made such a noise he could hardly think. Someone said – not one of his men – 'Give it to its mother, why not?'

Apsu dropped it on her and the baby fell silent, cuddled in Tia's arms.

Apsu stared around their quiet faces, no one saying anything. He'd lost control of his wife in front of his men. He knelt smiling, whispered in her ear, 'Listen to me, stop this, I'll kill you if you don't behave. I'll kill you. Tell them the sodding truth, you fuck.'

Tia sat up calmly, and one of the children helped her stand. Kris. Apsu smiled with his teeth, made a show of helping his wife, sank his fingers deep between the tendons of her elbow. Incredibly she gave no sign of pain. He squeezed tighter, warning her brutally. But she said: 'Men of Aesir, these words are truth, hear me. I bow to the law of B'El, eldest and most loved son of the great God El, that the firstborn son of a marriage should be sacrificed to give thanks and thereby replenish and sustain the energy that God gives to create life. One greater brother must die that the lesser brothers may live their lives in the world. I accept the Law because God must be served as well as the people. But my child is neither Apsu's son nor a child of any man of Aesir. You cannot sacrifice this child because he is not yours.'

Apsu stared at her, so enraged he was blind. 'Bastard. Liar. You liar. Traitor.' He drew his sword with a hiss of metal. 'You're dead. It's not true. Who you saying's the father?' He turned on his men, shook the sword. 'You, Lotaan? You, Auor? You, Hvergil, tent-creeper? I'll kill you!'

Tia touched his cheek gently with her fingertips. 'Apsu,

listen. Hear me, see me. Look at me.' He blinked. 'Apsu, my love, it's easy to understand. El, only El, is the father of your child.'

'El.' Apsu swallowed. 'The great God El?'

She smiled tenderly. 'Yes.'

Apsu turned to his men with a sigh of relief. 'It's all right. She's mad.' He chuckled, turned the baby's face in her arms, showing its hair and eyes to them. 'He looks like me to me, what do you say?'

The men muttered loyally, especially Lotaan, Hvergil and Auor.

Apsu showed them the baby's smudgy pink bottom. 'Even smells like me, eh?' He took his wife's face fondly in his two great hands. 'Why didn't you tell me this before, then, lass?'

'Because I wasn't ashamed of what happened to me. It was beautiful.' She was keeping up her pretence, then! 'On the shore of the inland Surtr Sea where I find shells El came to me one day like a great bull, rising from the waves as a great white bull, his voice roaring like a mighty wind, and His shadow overshadowed me and I fell on the pebbles where I lay open, exposed, unhidden, at peace, and from His shadow His voice thundered, *Fear not.* And I was not afraid, and He was so beautiful. Don't be afraid, Apsu. I knew you would see what a beautiful baby I have and come to know the truth of your own volition, and acknowledge El as his father.' Her eyes filled with tears. 'I didn't know El would test us like this, bringing us to this terrible place, testing you too . . .' She smiled through her tears, slipped her hand through his fingers. 'Come, Apsu. Forgive me as I forgive you for hitting me. Let us take my child home together.'

Apsu tried to hide his fury and loss of face. He wanted to smash her, but the baby kicked and cried between them in her arms. 'The child of a god, eh? Could be worse. Look, I know what you're up to. All of us love our children.'

As a man he struggled to explain the true God to her small intelligence in words she would understand. 'Our children are the greatest gift we receive from Him, right, so they're the greatest gift we have to give Him back in return. In return for El's small blessings we sacrifice oatcakes, for His larger blessings some blood, a bird, maybe a lamb, even a steer. It's been proved this works.' He bragged, 'I myself once sacrificed – you remember the drought – our finest bull calf to the god B'El.' His voice rose. 'And now we need the biggest blessing, so we must give up everything most precious to us. We must show God how great our love and obedience to Him is, then we'll get our reward. The herds haven't come back at the appointed time, the ground's still frozen, our orchards are bare, our people starving. God demands this sacrifice of us. Our most valuable gift. Our firstborn sons.'

'No,' Tia said gently. 'He doesn't. God gave me my son.'

'*Your* son!' Apsu wanted to kill her, stomp her, run the insolent bitch through with his sword. His men were listening. He whispered, 'I'm not a monster. Take your place beside me, smile, be calm, do your duty.'

'I won't.' She truly was mad. 'I won't do my duty. It's not my duty. Yes you are a monster, God makes you a monster, Apsu, if you do this. You can't cut my son's throat and let his blood run up to God as though that makes everything all right.' She tried to search for a word but obviously there wasn't one. 'It's wrong. It's a crime.'

Blasphemy. Apsu warned her: 'Enough. You are offending God.' He made one last effort. 'You know I'm right. God told me to come here, God demands this sacrifice of us.' He hushed her. 'It's painful. It's agonising. No man wants to give up his son' – he tickled the boy beneath the chin, grinning, took him up affectionately in his own arms – 'however necessary he knows it to be. I know, even you have feelings. But this is for the good of us all.'

Tia spat at him. She went wild, she tried to grab her baby back. Enough. Apsu raised his fist and brained her. She crumpled to the ground and the most amazing thing happened: the children started crying and cried however loud he shouted at them. Apsu wrapped his son in his own furs, crooked his finger at Lotaan. 'Put them back on the rope. Leave her.'

Lotaan said, 'She'll freeze if she isn't dead already.'

'Let her freeze, it's God's will.' Apsu turned away, wrapped the baby firmly in his furs to silence it, strode uphill, and did not look back. It was the day of the equinox, when day and night were equally balanced, and the world was about to begin anew.

Behind him each man walked with his son. Their hearts were heavy, but with each step upwards up the mountain they were uplifted by the clearing air and each other's company. One voice uttered the dirge, the others began to sing sadly at first then joyously as the land fell away below them from the crisp, white, pure snow. The glacier dropped down the slope beneath them like a long trailing tongue of ice as they came to the vast snowy saddleback between the two peaks of Ararat, turning to climb towards the higher, closer to God. The line of men and children filed as small as black ants across the white slope, their voices raised in song chirping and tiny and almost lost in the wilderness of snow and sky growing above and below them, and the sun shining like God down from the sky and up from the snow. Now they saw that the saddleback was part of a volcanic rim, and they stared down from the sunlight into darkness and smoke. The smoke stank of sulphur and blew over them like a memory of darkness as they climbed, silencing their song, and it was in silence except for coughing that they filed on to the peak of Ararat, a plateau of bare windswept rock standing out of the yellow sulphur-stained snow like an island.

71

Apsu croaked: 'Stay back.' He took his first step on to the plateau, then the second. The shale crunched under his feet, making him sweat. El lived in the mountains and high places, and a man could do nothing more dangerous than dare to come close to God. And Ararat was the greatest and most terrible high place anyone knew.

Apsu was more afraid than he had ever been. One of the names of El was Storm-God, and He might make the wind blow Apsu clear from the summit and smash him on the pinnacles below. It mattered nothing to El whether Apsu personally lived or died. El created Man and sent the Flood. El created the Tablets of Destiny, wrote the future on them, then guarded them so jealously that the future was illegible. El was God of all the lands and seas of the earth, and His fury with His creation was legendary.

But El listened to those who called on Him.

Apsu took another step, and dared raise his eyes from the ground.

As if growing alive out of the crushed rock ahead of him, bare trees stood in the shape of great curved beams higher than the highest temple, a huge skeleton made of wood beached on the mountain's summit. The planks that once clothed the trunks had long since rotted away, the decks and stairways fallen in; even so the structure was almost too big for his mind to believe, but he knew what it was. Apsu walked slowly between the great decaying ribs of the giant vessel, Noah's Ark. Here on Ararat Noah's Ark came to earth after the Flood. The ribs were called *asherot* now and they were holy. Apsu walked between them as though down an avenue of rotting trees on the mountaintop. At the centre of the wreck was the rock slab on which the drifting Ark had caught and broken its back as the waters fell. Seventy days had passed before the other mountaintops appeared below Ararat like a ring of islands.

Apsu cringed as he came to the slab. God was here. God ordered the god of the wind to blow, flapping Apsu's furs, God ordered the winged sun to flare its light in Apsu's eyes. God might even order each beat of Apsu's heart, each flicker of his eyelashes in the wind.

Apsu laid the baby on the slab.

He isn't yours.

Apsu wiped the beads of sweat on his face. The wind was icy cold. He called his men to him and the men and children filed towards him across the plateau. They gathered behind him. The teeth of the children chattered with cold. One little boy said, 'Am I going to die now?'

Someone said: 'Hush up, son.'

Apsu said, 'Be silent, I shall pray.' The baby cried on the cold slab, kicking with his feet in the furs. Apsu pressed his belly against the slab to stop the baby falling off. Behind him a voice piped up, 'Will it hurt?' The children would be stunned by a blow to the head and this had been explained to them but they never understood. At least their mothers were far away; the goodbyes on the shore of the inland sea had been painful, but at least that meant there was no girlish screaming now, only a fairly worshipful waiting-silence except for the questions of the children.

Apsu drew his dagger, its blade black volcanic glass, obsidian, holy, the *molech*-knife. 'Great God El, I apologise for disturbing Your sleep, do not destroy me. Hear my voice, and know that I did not shout without good reason to awaken You, and forgive me. Great El, our sufferings though small to You seem great to us. We know what suffering You demand of us: we are born and we obey in suffering before we return to the dust; through suffering we come closer to You: but witness our terrible suffering, great El, hear us, and have pity.'

A child piped: 'Who's he talking to? I can't see anyone.' Usually the snivelling mothers tried to be calm for the children at this point, keeping them quiet by hugging them or shrouding their heads.

'Great El, have pity, witness our love,' Apsu prayed

loudly. 'These our eldest children die for You, that we renew our covenant with You. For the sake of Your covenant with Your people I sacrifice my only son for You.'

He is not your son. Apsu tried to concentrate.

The baby kicked against Apsu's belly with its little kicks. He raised the baptismal dagger ritually in both hands. Actually the *molech*-blow was performed with little force, not to the heart but the neck, it was necessary to get plenty of blood on the slab for its sweet savour to blow on the wind to El's nostrils.

'Suppose she told the truth?' Lotaan said. 'Tia, I mean. Suppose Tia told the truth and the great God El did appear to her as a huge bull and . . . you know.' He made the familiar gesture. 'What she called it. Overshadowed her. You'd be killing the son of a god.'

Apsu gripped the obsidian dagger so tight he cut his fingers. 'She's dead,' he grated. 'This is my son and I'll kill any man who says otherwise, I'll kill you all.'

'He's your son,' Lotaan said agreeably. 'Look how strong he is.'

Apsu pushed the baby back with his belly. 'Great El—'

'If we can't see God,' one of the children said, 'who's that hiding behind that rock?'

Apsu heard them turn, and in spite of himself he looked.

Tia ran at him. Her face was bloody, her clothes flapping. He was so surprised that he forgot to strike her. She grabbed the baby from the slab, clutched it to her breast, backed away. Apsu hesitated. He dare not return the dagger to its sheath unblooded, unbaptised by death, and it was blasphemy to lay it down from the flesh of his hands; he could not draw his sword. He paced after her between the bones of the ship as she backed from him step by step, she almost tripped, he had longer strides than hers. He jabbed the dagger at her. 'Give me my son and die quickly.'

'*My* son,' she hissed. The wind flapped her cape, tugging at her. They were near the edge, clouds drifting below them. Apsu lowered the blade a little, pleading. 'He must die properly or it means nothing, his life is wasted.' She took another step back. He saw air beneath her heels, but also the fear in her eyes. 'You won't,' he said calmly.

She shouted past him at the children: '*Run!*' She shouted again, teetering on her toes, nothing but her toes taking her weight on the rock: 'Run for your lives!' Apsu heard them scatter. He cursed her but he dared not look away from her eyes, his look like a rope connecting them, alone holding her on the earth.

He said, 'You don't have to die.'

Her voice quavered. 'That's up to God not you.' That quaver. Apsu knew she had decided to jump.

He grabbed at her but caught at only a single shell from her necklace as she leapt.

Apsu screamed. Her face shrank below him as she fell towards the clouds, then her cape blew up over her head and hid her shrinking figure in its fluttering embrace, and the baby too; the dagger slipped from Apsu's hands, falling over and over after her. What he'd thought was cloud was glacial ice. Her dot struck the almost-vertical ice slope, struck again, slid away like a plummeting bird. Her legs and one arm sprawled around her as she span, still holding the baby. A pinnacle of ice hid her for a flash, then her sliding dot reappeared far down the glacier near the edge, and even Apsu gave a shriek, seeing what was about to happen.

Tia's tiny body slid flailing from the ramp of ice, fell out into the grey abyss below, down, down, to the foaming misty meltwaters of the River Hubur. He never saw the splash.

She fell screaming. The great lip of ice rose up into the sky over her and she fell fluttering with her baby into the gloomy chasm, now above her kicking feet, now below, her furs roaring in her ears with the wind of her fall.

She clasped her baby tight, too tight, squeezing the breath from her own body as if to squeeze it into his own, feeling him kicking and wriggling against her as she fell, his face sliding up past her own, she couldn't hold him: she screamed for him.

Foam crashed over them, the river swept her down, bubbles, pebbles, her arms were empty. She clutched at the rushing water that whirled her between the boulders, a great shoulder of rock pushed her up, she splashed on the surface, glimpsed her baby splashing. A smooth slope of water slid him away, she slid after him into a torrent of foam. His furs buoyed him up; hers dragged her down. His tiny body was swept between the boulders but she banged and bumped on every one, the weight of water piling up behind her like a great hand squeezing her, forcing her through.

She saw him splash, grabbed, but the water dragged her down, then as she lunged gasping to the surface the river rose up in a mound, almost throwing him into her arms, and she clutched him tight. Wotan's hands curled instinctively into tiny fists around her fingers, holding hard, and the river swept mother and son down together.

'*My* son,' Tia whispered.

The river swept them over a waterfall together, mother and son fell together, came up together. Icy boulders slid smoothly past, pushing them tight, she and her warm little bundle. Deep water lifted them, holding them, carried them forward as smooth as oil sliding between the walls of the chasm. A cavern whispered around them, dark as night, blinding them in its darkness, then pulled them into daylight again between hills rounded like green breasts full of life. A tree fell, was swept close to them in the meandering stream with earth still clinging to its roots: Tia pulled herself up between the stones and soil, straddled the trunk with her elbows and knees in the water, warmed her baby in her armpit with the sun hot on her back as she lay forward, and slept.

He cried for his milk, kicking her.

She woke. Green shadows swept over her, enormous fragrant cedars overhung the river. Sometimes the pulse of the stream quickened, sometimes slowed when the treetrunk turned quietly in a backwater. Tia used these times to suckle her baby at her breast, listening to the evening birdsong, then the trunk was swept forward again and night rushed over the cedar forest.

She woke, and he pulled at her for milk.

The cedar forest, the endless cedar forest. Dawn came, showing dark trees sliding past the trunk, the sun hardly flashing for trees. The stream joined another river, then the two flowed into a third winding like a sea through the perfumed forest. Everyone knew this sacred cedar forest once covered all the world and still, except for myths and legends, shut the world out of Shem.

Night fell again, and a great roar split the sky. Tia clutched her baby tight, closing her eyes; everyone knew terrible lizards lived in the forest. Even in the grassland tent-villages north of the Caucasus mothers frightened children (for their own good) with stories of karibu-lions soaring on wings like eagles above the cedar tops of the south, of gallu-demons who shifted from shape to shape as they flitted between the trunks, and worst and greatest of all (she remembered listening round-eyed to her own mother) the dragon Huwawa, appointed guardian and protector of the forest by El. She peeped and saw her little baby looking around him, smiling, wide-eyed in the dawn light, the treetops passing green shadows across his blue curious eyes, and wished he were more afraid. The dragon's roar didn't come again during the day: the treetrunk rode silently through the vivid leafy caverns of the overhanging forest.

Something bumped. Another treetrunk floated beside them, without roots. Where the roots should have been it had been bitten by a great animal, the yellow wood ringed with marks like teeth, slices gouged into the heart until the tree fell and was swept away by the river. Now another fallen trunk, and another. Other trunks, more than she had fingers, bumped and bobbed beside her. The cry of an animal echoed in the forest, another tree fell, splashed into the river. Her baby gave a loud cry and she cuddled him to keep him quiet but he cried again. Other cries answered from the shore: she'd been seen. Movement, shapes running. Hundreds of yellow teeth sticking up through the skin of the land, chopped branches everywhere, fires, the smell of woodsmoke.

Men. They stood on the riverbank, watching her drift past. Brown-eyed sunbrowned boys as thin as reeds skipped in the shallows, keeping pace with her, shouting excitedly, yelling advice, she understood not a word. The river curved, bringing the felled trunks closer to shore, the boys scampered beside her holding out their hands, almost reaching her, then they ran ahead to a cleared spit of land between tents made of reed, ran out along the sandbank, and again held out their hands to her. The tree roots caught in the sand; Tia flinched away from the crowd, nervous of their jabbering, but the children tugged her furs amazed by such clothes in the heat of the sun, then stared in awe at her eyes, her blue eyes, and her baby's blue eyes, and their hair the colour of the sun.

Little Wotan clenched his fists on the children's hands, clinging to them like a limpet as they swung him with laughter and amazement to the shore, and Tia stumbled after them on to the sand.

The children laid Wotan on the grass and gathered around him, especially the young girls, and he lay kicking his legs and chuckling up at them.

Because of him, they would all die before their time.

I knew I was different.

Who was I? I only knew what I was not. I was not-tree. I was not-river. Not sun, not sky, not land. I saw these things with my eyes so I was different from them. I was not-adult, but perhaps I was almost my mother. Certainly I was not the other children. 'Mother, who am I?'

Tia looked up at me wearily, her face smudged with smoke, fingers bleeding from mending broken axes. I could have done the job much better, but it was woman's work. 'You are my son Wotan.'

You are my son. The other children had fathers. It was humiliating. 'Yes, I'm your son, but Mother, why don't I have a father?'

'Your father lives in a faraway land.' Tia's northern tongue still spoke trader-talk clumsily – these woodland tribes of the Cedar Forest all called themselves *canaan*, their word for traders, though the Shemite buyers called us Amors or Amori, westerners. Their ancestors came like my mother from the mountains of the north where the sun sets early, sons of Ham the son of Noah like ourselves, but my mother never got used to living in a house with walls of bound berdi-reed – though it seemed so natural to me – and in her own language (which she taught me) she still called it a tent not a house. We canaanites call our great river Perath, though to float down our precious cedar logs, and carry down fleeces, deerskins and colourfully plumed birds in our black tar-coated reed boats, the Elders cheerfully pretend to call the river by its Shemite name, Buranun, to please the men of the Land of Shem (long ago Ham and Shem being brothers) and respectfully clinch a higher price. Great survivors, we canaanites.

But I had to know all the truth. To believe that there is a truth to be found has always been my greatest weakness, even as a child – and in a way I am always a child. 'Will I ever know my father?'

'No.' She sucked the blood from her fingers, smiled kindly, pulled me to her with her arm. I was six years old. 'You're too young to understand, young Wotan.'

I sucked the blood from six of her fingers. 'I'm not young. That's how old I am.' My mother looked at me strangely. I like the effect I have on people, they always look at me: I'm more than what they see, they hear something more than sound in my words, they feel I say more than I speak. I have personality, individuality. My mother kept me beside her at night suckling on her breast so that no man came to lie with her. She's mine, I'm hers. But usually his father is the most important part of a boy. My mother said, 'Son, you see, your father cannot be with you.'

'Why not? Is he dead? Plenty of canaans want you' – I knew some of them were rich, with robes of dyed wool, and I might be given one! – 'then I could have a new father.'

She struggled, not with the knots binding the broken axeheads; struggled with something inside herself, I thought.

She told me: 'Your father is the God El who lives in the heavenly sky.'

Good, that made sense. I was pleased. I'd always thought I was special. She said no more, then touched the almost-perfect ring of seashells at her neck, only one missing. I asked, 'Will you see El again?'

She looked down. 'Sometimes I do in my dreams.'

'Do you love Him?' I asked excitedly.

'With my heart not my body. I believe in His love. His perfect love.'

'Will I see Him?' I jogged up and down in my excitement, spilling the axes from her lap. 'Can I catch fish with Him? Can we all be together, our family?'

'Stop it,' she scolded. 'You mustn't speak of El like that.'

I looked at her thoughtfully, until she looked away from

my eyes. I said, 'That's why you don't have men like the other boys' mothers. So that I don't have someone who thinks he's my father, and takes El's place.' She picked miserably at the bindings. She could have lived much better with a man to protect her and give her things. I sat beside her, unpicked the knots easily for her. 'I'll look after you,' I said. Her tears ran clean marks down her cheeks and I kissed them. 'Were you married to the God El? Were you happy?'

She choked, clutched me. 'I lived with a man I hated. Hated. I had no choice but to . . . to appear to love him.' She stroked my hair, breathed on my skin. 'But I have you to give my life meaning, Wotan. Hatred could not have created you.' She kissed my lips. 'My beautiful son.' I tried to give her breasts a suck but she smacked my bottom. 'Off you go, you! I've work to do.'

I ran, laughing. This is my ridiculously happy childhood, not a care in the world, see me join the other boys running to the shore, they're nine, ten years old, Shim about twelve with his thin straggling beard fertilised with oil, combed, curled, dragged, teased, pulled almost by sheer force of will from his spotty flesh to make him look like a man, but I was almost as tall as him. The older boys liked my spirit, I ran almost as fast as them (but not quite), fought almost as hard (but not quite), and I didn't cry or tell stories when they hurt me. I mean, of course, that I didn't let them *see* me cry, and I always got back at them somehow in a way to make them (except my victim) laugh. Being boys they loaded me with all the dirtiest jobs but I came up smiling, larking about, showing off; their approval and laughter was everything to me. I was only miserable when I was ignored, and I hated being miserable, so I made sure I was never ignored.

I ran after the boys running to the river, calling their names, 'Shim! Jamesh! Ulik! Erdil! Adama! Wait!' I scampered into the shallows between the bobbing one-man coracles where the nets were being pulled up, weighted to pass beneath the logs drifting downstream. The other boys waited on the beach for the fish to be drawn up, but I ran out on the logs where the fins and dark bodies swirled and tore across the surface, the fish twisting frantically as the net tightened, some leaping into the air to escape. I caught one and tossed it to shore. Then I jumped down amongst them over my head in the water, this dark tumultuous bubbling world with their heavy slimy bodies buffeting me, fins and mouths sliding around me. My feet found bottom and I grabbed at the foaming water, caught quivering wriggling shapes in my arms, heaved the fish out to thrash and gasp on shore, jagged mouths snapping at the boys' legs so that soon everyone on the beach was shouting, jumping like fish. Even the fishermen on the black boats laughed. A fin swirled past me like a sail, I grabbed on. He was the biggest monster, king of the river, half rotten with age and foul with weed and water-snails, but strong, victor of a thousand battles in the savage netherworld of the river-bed no doubt. But now I plunged my hands into his gills and lifted him from behind so his whipping mouth could not bite me, his slamming tail could not break my bones but only kick spray; I heaved him above my head, which was barely above water, and threw him on the beach so hard that my hands sank into his body. The men laughed and congratulated me, shaking their heads, and the boys watched quietly. Even Kino my special friend who looked after me, or tried to – *I* hadn't asked him to – turned away from me as I washed my bloodied hands.

I followed the boys upstream along the beach – the village followed after the felling of the forest – past the reed-marsh to where the woodcutters jammed sticks into the logs as they slid into the water, marking them with tally-battens so their work would be recognised. The plainsmen of Shem had cut down all their own trees – I couldn't imagine a land naked of trees – so having no wood they valued nothing more highly, and thanks to us the Perath (their Buranun) carried our trees down to their fabulous construction, Ur, which means simply City, for a high price. And there were other lesser cities too.

None of the boys would talk to me. They were jealous, though I just wanted so badly to make them all my friends. 'Aren't I a good fisherman?' I called. 'You should be like me.'

'You're a foreigner, a norther.' Shim turned on me. 'We don't want you here. Bastard. Your foreign norther mother doesn't even know who your father is.'

'She told me,' I said brightly, but my eyes were hot. 'The God El is my father. He lay with my mother like a raging bull. He *is*.'

Kino reproved me. 'Everyone knows the Lord B'El is the son of El.' Canaanite tongues pronounce B'El *Baal*, and the righteous Zedek or *Zadok* – the village priest and prophet – tells us El is not the great God but only one of the gods, *Ab-Adam*, the Father of Man. To them the great God who created everything is Ea, whose name their tongues say as *Éya*, or Ya. My claim to be the son of the God El meant much less here than in the north.

Shim said: 'Wotan, your father is only a gallu-demon! A dream in your head!' His words hurt more than if he had hit me, which would not have hurt at all. Six years old, but I still wasn't strong enough not to cry over words. Kino put his hand on my shoulder, I told you he was kind – and he had a round gentle face, not a face to be feared – but Shim piled insult on insult. 'Wotan's father is a demon not a god! Even to claim he's the son of a god makes him a demon, not a god!'

Kino warned Shim: 'Leave him alone, he's half your size,' though this was not true.

'That just makes him easier for me,' Shim said cockily, pulling his beard.

'Come on, fight!' I said in my high little voice. But Kino pushed Shim, Shim pushed Kino, then they wrestled in the dust. The others shouted odds and held me back by my hair. Kino was brave but stupid (and too gentle as I told you), and soon his nose was streaming blood. 'Run, run away,' he called to me as he lay moaning like an old lady. But Shim pushed down his heel on Kino's neck and grabbed me, lifted me off the ground with his arms. I ran in the air kicking and punching, but couldn't reach Shim's grinning bearded face. 'Now learn your lesson,' I heard him say, and that was the last I heard, my blood roared in my ears with fury, I hardly saw him. I reached forward as far as I could reach and held on to his arms, I pulled his elbows towards me and heard the muscles and cartilage tear, I heard his bones break inside his arm, the splintered bone stuck out of the wrist like teeth. Shim dropped me, he screamed, but I clung to his beard, the rage was in me. The joy of the red, red rage. Nothing as good, until I knew women.

Shim fell back from me. Kino turned away, but Shim said, 'No, it's all right. It was fair.' Then he fainted.

After that gentle Kino would not speak to me but Shim One-Arm was my friend. Both of us had come of age, though different ages, together. I abandoned my mother except when I needed her, which was when I was tired, worried or in pain. With Shim I shared drinks of fermented honey in the forest but he soon knew how to get beer, a brew made from the special grass grown in Shem. During the late summer, low river, when all our boats returned home, rowed, sailed, dragged against the sluggish stream or even hauled overland, they carried beer in vats covered with the *tebah:* the upturned basket that hides the cargo from thieves, pirates, quick-fingered drunks – and boys. When we were caught curled like maggots beneath the *tebah* we were soundly beaten, so drunk we laughed. Or rather, Shim laughed, so I laughed too, but I slept very

84

quietly against my mother that night.

'Is it true?' I asked her then, when El's Moon goddess Sin made a glowing net of the reed roof, and other Elohim sparkled their patterns in the sky. 'Am I His son? Or is it just a story for a child?'

She didn't move, then she did move, and I felt her lips kiss the top of my head. 'Are you alive?' she whispered.

'Yes.'

She whispered, 'Yes, it's true. You are saved.' She tousled my blond hair over my shoulders. 'El saved you. El chose you. He is your father.'

'I know how boys come out of their mothers,' I said, and told her graphically. 'And I know how they start.' I knew everything about it.

She cuddled my mouth against her to muffle me. 'Why does it happen?' she murmured. 'That's what I ask myself. Who are we? What purpose? What is a child for?'

'To make more children,' I said.

She said, 'There must be more to it than that.'

No; there was no more to it than that. That night I learned it during the brief interval of darkness between the setting of the moon and the rising of the sun: that's all it took. A sudden, startled cry.

Then a scream, an awful scream like the sound of lungs ripping. Then more cries and shouts, more screaming. My mother hung on to me but I ran outside. Footsteps running everywhere, shadows running almost as dark as the dark. Legs running and voices shouting, the first clash of swords. A flaming arrow, a falling star, a reed house speckled with a pattern of flames like stars spreading together, then with a whoosh the bitumen waterproofing caught in a mass of fire and heat, and inside the burning people ran like white shadows, then like bonfires running among us spreading confusion. The shrine went over in a shower of sparks, an old woman shrieked, 'Horror!' and the women screamed we were lost and screamed for their children. I saw Kino speared.

I grabbed my wooden sword, a child's sword. My clothes tore as I ran forward, my mother could not hold me. Wild horses galloped between the burning houses, men slashing, stabbing from horseback. The burning village threw up a glare like the sun but everywhere beyond was darkness. A horse bowled me over, its hooves landing on each side of me as I rolled. My mother grabbed my foot but I wriggled away, jumped up, our enemies were looting our axes, pots, girls, anything, breaking half what they stole. A stumbling fool put his head beneath my stick and I crowned him. I stared at him where he lay down, burning pitch dripping from the eaves of a house on to his vacant face, illuminating . . . nothing. Death.

The first man I had killed. So easy. Only a man.

I beat his body with my stick, shouting. The wonder of it! The power! I was filled!

My mother whispered, 'Wotan, stop.' She put her arms around me, embraced me, slid against me, her body was all blood. 'Quick. Here. Come.' She tugged me by my torn clothes, her blood hot and cold and sticky on my skin. 'Oh no, oh Mother,' I said. She said, 'If you love me come with me.' I hardly heard her words, but her lifeblood spoke to me eloquently. As she pulled me back step by step into the dark, a man mounted higher than the others rode round the glare of the blazing shrine, his furs flapping behind him with a heavy clapping sound like beating wings. His voice roared my name. He roared my name over and over. Wotan. Wotan. He knew my name. Wotan, come to me. But still my mother drew me back.

I whispered, 'Who is he?'

Her voice trembled, bubbling blood. 'No one. He is no one.'

The furred man rode in a furious circle steering his horse with his knees, blond hair flying above his furs. In the firelight I glimpsed his eyes blue and cold as chips of ice. 'Kill the children,' he roared. 'Kill them all.' I saw

Jamesh die, Ulik die, Adama and Erdil dragged out and butchered like small squealing animals, and still my mother dragged me back on the beach with her failing strength.

'I am Apsu, king and priest,' the man roared. 'Hear me, know me, know the truth. I, me, *I* am the Bull of Heaven! *I* am your father, come to me, Wotan, come!' Some woman was hauled to him with her brat and he brained them with one swing of the axe tied to his wrist. In the first shaft of sunlight something glinted at his throat: a single seashell. I turned to my mother. Her necklace of seashells smeared with her blood at her throat. The same.

'Is he the God El?' I whispered.

She grasped my face in her hands, her eyes enormous. 'He is only a man.' Her voice rattled. 'Only a man.' She pushed me back, I fell over a coracle left upturned, shiny black with fresh tar, at the water's margin. I lifted it afloat, put one foot inside, pulled my mother with me. I could look after her wound. I could make her live. Then full sunlight warmed my back and my shadow flooded past her, shouts went up from the village, and I realised we stood silhouetted against the rising sun's red circle.

'Wotan,' roared the man on horseback. His arm banged at a dagger in his belt. 'I bring you *molech*, justice, expiation, the Law of God! Come to me, I shall wipe your sin away!'

My mother pushed at me with surprising strength, beneath my foot the coracle skated light as a bubble on the water, and I sprawled inside against the wicker bottom staring for an astonished moment at her necklace clutched in my hand. A moment later was too late: the current snatched the little craft and whirled it away among the other debris floating on the river. I knelt wobbling unsteadily, clinging to each side. 'Mother.'

Apsu dragged at the reins with his teeth, his horse stopped, half throwing him to the ground. His eyes set on me across the water, he walked stiff-legged along the beach, his hands outstretched like fingerless blades. His furs

the distant rustle of wind across reed-beds. I jerked and writhed but almost overturned my ark; the heat of the day pressed down on the black wicker like a hot heavy hand, baking me in the water that had slopped over. I drank it, then pissed in it. I lay comatose. I was very thirsty. I drank the bitter water, then pissed again, then drank it. Yes, I was alive.

The heat of the day passed over, and the moon came again.

Reeds creaked and cracked. I roared and writhed until watery mud slopped inside, and drank it. I heard voices like animals giggling, strange accents, then calling, splashing. A girl's voice cried, 'Is it a monster?' Somebody laughed, then an older woman's voice gave an order. Heavy splashing, a man's grunt, my ark was lifted and put down, the top torn off, and the sun poured over me. I thrashed like a fish around the arrow in my hair, tore a bloody strip of skin from my scalp complete with long blond locks, and jumped out covered with my mother's blood as though newborn.

'Oh look,' a girl's voice laughed, 'he's got a little sword!'

I screamed at them, I roared and brandished my wooden sword and stamped in the dust, afraid of nothing. Half a dozen – no, seven – fat young girls with shaved shiny heads stared at me, giggling, plump fingers fluttering at their pouting lips, long black eyelashes blinking. Behind them stood an older woman who laughed for a moment, then returned to her serious demeanour. On each side of me stood a shaven guardian, immense, one of them black with mud to the knee, both with swords drawn and the blades shining yellow in the dawn. I leapt at them, 'Yaa!' swishing with my sword, slicing it into two on their sharp blades, then into four. I threw the pieces at them and attacked with my fists. The guards looked at one another then picked me up by what was left of my hair and held me running in the air between them. I kicked as best I could and bit at them with my teeth like a hooked fish. The older woman commanded in Shemite talk: 'Halt.'

I was so surprised I stopped. This was the land of Shem? She made a patting gesture with her fingers and the hands that held me put me down. 'I'll get you later,' I threatened the guards. They looked straight ahead.

The woman bent in front of me. 'As if born, yet not a baby. The river's child, born calling the name of our city's God, *Ya*. I've never seen such eyes.' She touched my long curls with her palm. 'Such hair.' I snarled, but she smiled.

'Boys,' said one of the girls. 'No wonder we hate them.' They cooed brainlessly over the arrows, fat white rumps bumping, pretending to scare one another with the sharpness of the tips.

The woman spoke to me. 'Child, I am Nin, Mistress of the Mountain, Mother of All the Living of Enoch, great royal wife of Lugal our city's king, who is our steward appointed by Ya in Heaven.' She waited, then touched the seashells at my throat. 'You must have cowered at Lugal's name, even in your northern darkness at the source of the world.'

I looked into her large brown eyes. 'I'm not a child. You must have heard of *me*. My name's Wotan and I'm seven.'

The seven fat girls bowed their heads. I had said the sacred number of the God El – and Ya, for all I knew. Holy seven. At seven years of age I was a man, but these girls would not be women until their menses ran – about twelve, eleven or even earlier if they were fed well, and their fat girlish bodies and empty bobbing heads looked pampered enough to burst, stuffed like geese. Nin, though she had turned her palm upwards at God's number (their cultured tongues call Him *Enlil* or *Ellil*), still regarded me thoughtfully. I gave her my smile which melted my mother's heart and bragged. 'My father is the God . . .' I said it their complicated way, 'Enlil.'

She nodded, educated. 'El.' These people believe the gods are all around them, above and below.

But thinking of my mother had made my eyes run. 'My mother was a queen,' I sniffed, wiping my nose. The fat girls gathered round me curiously but the guards waved them back, one saying in a high voice, 'Now now, sisters, careful.' I shouted at the girls to scare them, '*Yaa!* Yes, I'm dangerous, me!' They ran away from me, squealed, peeped from behind Nin. She explained: 'Temple virgins may not be contaminated by a man's touch, nor even a boy's. Not even his breath or a strand of his hair.'

I jerked my thumb at the guards. 'What about them?' Nin moved her head slightly and the guards lifted their loincloths, showing dangly little penises but only tight-lipped scars where their balls once swung. 'Doesn't look like they had much to lose anyway,' I said. That was it. One of them whacked me with the side of his sword then the other wanted a go, and I cracked his hand in mine. The girls screamed excitedly, none of them had seen such quick strength before. Even Nin gave a small gasp.

The guard knelt in pain and that was good, I kicked him and he lay down trying to hold both his broken hand and his other pain as well.

'Halt,' Nin said for the second time. She hesitated. 'No more, Wotan.' She wanted to turn and walk away from me and leave me to the punishment of the other guard, I think, but she had looked into my eyes, she had touched my hair. I fascinated her. She knelt, murmured: 'Were you really born today, full-formed?'

I had nothing to lose. 'Yes.'

'And your mother?'

I pressed my lips tight. 'My mother's dead.'

Nin glanced down irritably at the groaning guard and the other one kicked him quiet. 'Child,' she whispered, 'do you say you were born from a dead woman?'

My eyes overflowed with tears. I could not speak.

She put her hands on her knees, stood. 'Enoch was a Son of Man also. It's not uncommon. Enoch too spoke with the Lord of Lords. His songs tell us so.' She took a few thoughtful steps up the earthwork that held back the river and I saw the city beyond her, Enoch, *Unuk* to her tongue. A great red-brown mountain raised by the hands of the plainsmen of Shem stood out of the jumble of hovels, mud walls, thatch roofs: a gigantic stairway to Heaven. I looked around me. So it was true: on the great flat silty-red plains of Shem, treeless from horizon to horizon, shimmering with heat, yellow crops, canals cut between the endless fields like a net of blue roads, the grass-eaters did build mountains to worship God. Nin laughed to see my face. 'Are you impressed?'

'It has no walls. What happens when the hunters come?'

'All other kings fear Lugal.' She smiled proudly. 'We have no need of walls.'

I pointed out, 'Your mountain has walls around it.'

'The temple? Because it is holy.' She looked at me respectfully, her hair blowing gently in the dawn wind. 'Our temple may not be approached on a whim but only with reverence by the most righteous and most pure.' She sighed. 'Priests.'

I listened to that sigh. 'Who made Lugal king?'

'Priests,' she murmured. 'Kingship descends from Heaven each year.' The guard who was unhurt pointed at the rising sun. She nodded, giving permission. 'Yes, hurry.' He called the girls together in his high voice.

I said quickly, 'Who was Enoch?'

'Enoch, the son of Cain, son of Adam. Enoch' – again she actually said *Unuk*, but I understood her well enough – 'descended from the mountains and built our city and gave it his name. He then founded City, Ur,' (she pointed across the looping river, where in the distance I saw a smudge of smoke) 'so ours is the greatest nation and first, but they say theirs, being liars and cheats.' Again her sigh.

'For his son Jared Enoch built another city and named it Jared's city, Ur-Jared which is pronounced Eridu, and made him king there. Their sons built other cities named after themselves, Mahalal'El, Lamech, Tubal-Cain where weapons are forged, Adama, Nahor, all the others.' She waved her arm at distant smokes here and there in the haze of dawn. 'Some say sons of Jared sailed beyond the ocean to a place where sunrise and sunset are one.' She shrugged. 'What I know is this. Enoch lived with us for three hundred and sixty-five years, the number of days in the year by El's calendar, which is from the movement of the sun.' The canaans still used it. 'Now that Ya is the great God of our temple the people worship by the moon's calendar in deference to Ishtar the wife of Ya, the seasons of women being ruled by the moon, so our year is now three hundred and fifty-four days, which is much more holy.'

'But after three hundred and sixty-five years Enoch died?'

'Sons of Men never die, their names live on. At the end of the great year of his life Enoch returned to El in the mountains.'

The guard bowed to the seven girls. 'Quick, sisters, back to the precinct quickly!'

Nin followed my eyes. 'It's late, the people must not see them. The virgins should not be out of the temple. But a little freedom . . .' Her sad sigh.

I said, 'If you're a king's wife you can do anything.'

'I'm mistress of the rituals, prisoner of them. I can do almost nothing. You'll be a foundling of the temple, like all the others.' She clapped her hands. 'Where's our time flown? Quickly!' The guard set off at a run along the earthworks followed by the gaggle of girls, the other guard limping after. Nin turned to me. 'Go with my maid. Do what she says.'

Maid? For the first time I noticed the thin willowy girl

standing motionless, standing as still as the earth, wearing a reddish dress the colour of the earth, part of the reddish-brown background of fields, with her head bowed, brown hair coiled, hands together. Then she looked at me with her large eyes slanted upwards at the outer corners, and I saw that they were blue. Blue as the mountains from which I come.

'Eve, follow us quickly!' Nin ordered, then bent for a moment so close I inhaled her perfumed breath. 'And if you are seven, Wotan,' she murmured, tugging the first strands of beard on my chin, 'then I am a virgin.'

She lifted her skirts and ran after the girls. 'You a statue, you?' I called to the girl whose name I'd already forgotten, and we ran after Nin. It was exciting! The earthworks were broken at intervals by gates and sluices that let the river through as necessary; all were closed at the moment but rather than balance along the beams like a woman, arms out and rump swaying, I jumped them for the fun of it and to impress the girls, but only the maid noticed, and she was nobody. Coming closer I saw the city was really a huge village surrounded by smaller villages. A boat sailed on the canal in the brisk dawn wind, women fetched water, men hauled in fishnets left overnight, one man hurrying plunged in and swam across overarm – I wanted to swim like him! I looked around me in awe as reed huts gave way to mud houses, building sites, the stink of brick fires and hot tar, houses with courtyards, the complicated niched walls of a palace. The seven virgins ran with a sheet over their heads but the peasants shoving in the streets, though they got obediently out of the way, hardly raised their eyes. Their days were long, their lives were hard, they had enough to think about getting through each day: worries, work, responsibilities, children too sick or too noisy, ageing toothless parents driving them to distraction, too much to do. I pushed, ducked, threaded through them, the temple rose above us and threw down its shadow. What

I'd thought was one was a whole complex of buildings, walls, stairways, chambers, holy taverns, holy bedrooms for temple prostitutes, crèches, schoolrooms, a hundred things I didn't know the names for all leading up to that great evenly stepped mountain, the stairway to Heaven. I stared in awe. I wanted it. I wanted to climb the ziggurat. All those steps shining in the sun, leading upwards as though they never stopped!

And at the top the *Ya'nna*, the gleaming house of Heaven.

I held out my arms for joy, I shouted my joy aloud in the wonderful city. *'Whooo!'*

Someone stood behind me – she was no one, only the quiet girl. Head bowed, she turned away and walked, so I followed her, I'd nothing better to do. She came to the brick palace with people going in and out, waited for me, then went inside. It was dark, windowless, lit with torches that made no smell or smoke. The place was full of people, tiny rooms full of people, and some of them touched her reverently, or asked questions of her; perhaps the maid of the royal wife is not quite nobody. I still couldn't see her bowed face, shy or overwhelmed by me, as she hurried forward up steps, to household guards where she waited, and as they stepped aside for her I swaggered past them too.

The walls of the palace were massive, even here, decorated quarters, the rooms were small and the windows tiny. She lit a patterned bowl of liquid and it burned. I put my hand in it and my hand burned. 'Ow!' A serving-girl hurried through a doorway with a fresh flaming bowl. 'Oh, Hayah,' she cried, 'what's he done?' I put my hand under my armpit and the serving-girl chuckled, saying the word *naphtha*, the very word. The maid who had been called Hayah (but I was sure that was not her name) shrugged as if I were stupid, the serving-girl chuckled again and rolled her eyes, then was shooed away. The maid pointed at my clothes and I undressed. She was unimpressed but the serving-girl's head showed giggling through the doorway as I showed off. I wiggled my backside at her as I spoke to the maid. 'What's your name again?'

The maid beckoned the serving-girl with her eyes and the girl took my muddy, bloody clothes between her fingertips, then carried them away holding her nose. I heard a peal of coarse girlish laughter in another room, then my buxom milky serving-girl returned with clothes made of something I'd never seen before, lighter than wool, woven from a plant not an animal. Meanwhile my skinny disapproving maid had not moved her downcast eyes, bored by me. I ignored her, eyed the serving-girl appreciatively and got an eyeful of her breasts and even her nipples like dark eyes looking through the weave as I chatted to her, that wobbled as she laughed. I was tall enough for her to know I was more than a child; she pushed my shoulder deliberately with her own as she was sent away, and her touch rushed the female smell of her into me, motherly and milky, but something harsher underneath it too. I followed her with my eyes, interested. My thin, boring, bored-by-me maid still stood like a stick left standing by the river's flood, and I still couldn't remember her name. So I followed the laughter to the room where the girls were, no bigger than a hut, poorly lit between the dark brick walls, all the girls with plump arms and hands busy at this or that work and with busy mouths too, that fell silent as I came in. I was the centre of attention. I knew words would come into my head, but suddenly tears came to my eyes, and I spoke the words that I found in my heart. I said: 'I am the son of the God El, and my mother died the night before last, and the king's wife found me drifting in a basket' (I didn't know their Shemite word for coracle) 'in the river, caught in the reeds, and now I have no one.' I snuffled. 'No one in the whole world.'

An older woman bent down. 'Oh, my poor thing, my poor lost child.' The women gathered around me as I cried, touching me, holding me, wrapping me in their arms tenderly whether their faces were cruel or sad or worn-out, or ugly or beautiful, old or young, whether (I could tell by the smell of them) or not they had children of their own. They understood me instinctively, childish, sweet, vulnerable, alone. Theirs were hard lives.

I returned satisfied to the other room. The thin maid looked at me with hot runny eyes. She said, 'Did you think I was a statue?'

I still didn't remember her name, and when the men arrived covered in blood I forgot her completely.

Men; but the only man of importance to me was King Lugal at their head, these men coming home filling the narrow corridors, blood-brown swords clanging from the walls, stiff leather armour squeaking and clinking, Lugal with his great bloody head-dress in the shape of an open-mouthed fish and his dripping armour (holy water had been thrown over him) scaled like a fish. He roared for beer and wine, clapped the bloody shoulders of his men with his left fist, and from his sword hand swung a pale decapitated head by its beard. 'Victory, by Ya!' Each city has its own god, they say; Enoch is famous for the Ya'nna of Ya and Ishtar (whom their tongues sound as Inanna), so the great temple joins both gods by its name. Ishtar's the goddess of love and women, but in war men follow a man's god, and the warriors of Enoch swore by Ya. Shemash the Sun god's worshipped at Shurappak, Sin the Moon god at Ur and Isin. When the cities fight each other success in battle shows the strength of their gods. As their gods are in constant conflict, so are men. Lugal bellowed: 'Victory! Victory!'

He strode past me without a glance and I slipped among the men piling after him into a long room, a colonnade of pillars making a long balcony that poured sunlight across them. In the centre of the blue room Nin offered a large shallow bowl of water, the laver, in her hands. Her lapis-blue gown was woven with the golden flower rosette of Ishtar, her lapis-shadowed eyes beautiful, chaste, serene among the mosaics of stunning lapis lazuli from Meluhha in India that decorated the walls and pillars around her, two temple guards kneeling devoutly behind her. Lugal took the bowl and dropped it, smashed it, put his bloody sword hand in the small of her back and kissed her with his mouth. 'Brought you his head.'

She said: 'My lord king.' Her long fingers worked nimbly to unlatch his armour but Lugal grunted for male servants, armour was man's work, threw his sword at a cringing valet. 'Don't worry,' he reassured Nin, 'it's not my blood.' Those soft words, his moment of concern for her, made me think Lugal was not as hard as his show. Various couches stood about the place behind them, each on four thick legs, like crouching animals. He pushed Nin back and mounted her there and then, showing his favour of her publicly until the sinews stood out on his thighs. He pulled out and a low servant wiped him while another brought beer, tasted it, and Lugal dashed it down his throat. He felt better. I wanted to be king!

A voice whispered in my ear, the maid I'd forgotten. 'After battle, after so much death, so many sent to the Underworld, a king must remember love. Lugal is the *ensi* of Enoch, king and priest both, but his royal wife is the high priestess of Ishtar, Queen of Love. She is Mistress of the Holy Mountain, she is Mother of All the Living. Without life there is no death; without death there is no life. Each gains power from their union.'

I scoffed, 'Love's not as powerful as war.'

'More powerful,' she whispered. 'And much more dangerous.' I turned but she was gone. Lugal raised his voice, tearing bread in one hand and meat in the other, slopping crust and bloody flesh from his bearded lips. 'Ya marches with us! Hear me! Hear the voice of Lugal!'

The men roared over their beer, sucking it into their mouths through pipes from a vat. At peace men of violence are intensely sociable. Women scuttled to them with platters of meat, all from male animals. Lugal roared, bragging of his campaign. 'The moon slept in the darkness of the month! I marched from my royal city and my army followed me. My enemies attacked me screaming with fear and I slew them.'

'These raids are small affairs, almost rituals,' whispered a voice behind my left ear, my maid – I remembered now, she'd been called Hayah, Hawwah, by the serving-girl. 'Ten or fifteen men of importance,' she whispered, 'a few hundred peasants.' A raid dressed up as a great slaughter. Her contempt surprised me as much as her honesty considering she was no one, her life hanging by a thread.

Lugal gulped wine from a cup. 'Like locusts my army darkened the fields of Bab'El!' The first God of Bab'El, literally the City of God, was El not Ya. 'Like locusts we fed on them!' Lugal bragged. 'We fertilised the fields of Bab'El with the blood of their farmers! All their year's work is mine, my royal granaries full as women with child, theirs empty as the wind. In Bab'El I harvested everything that grew with my left hand, and I sowed death and starvation with my right hand. In Bab'El I made worms of any man who opposed me and made all other men slaves, and their women, and their children, and their oxen and their donkeys. I sought the King of Bab'El among the ruins of his city but he fled naked from me, shrieking like a blue-eyed woman. But I found the king's son hiding beneath an age-crumbled stone of the fallen tower.' The women fell silent as he raised the severed head by its boyish beard; Lugal had no son of his own. 'Behold, a prince of Bab'El. He begged for mercy from Lugal, I gave it; great was my glory, a prince is years of crops, herds, flocks, red bulls beyond price. But this serpent of El stabbed at me.' Now the men fell silent, hating treachery. 'I placed my foot on his thigh. I seized his beard in my left hand. With my right hand my sword severed his head from his heart and his blood splashed down my body like warm dew, and warmed my soul.' Lugal finished in little more than a whisper in the silence. 'And I knew Ya blessed me.'

An *apkallu*, a white-bearded sage, nodded. 'El did not defend his believers. Lugal and the city of Enoch are blessed by Ya and all the gods, even El.'

Lugal turned to Nin. 'Blessed most of all by Ishtar, wife of Ya.' He kicked the head and it rolled. Withdrawing with Nin to the end of the room, Lugal sat on a chair as tall as her, so that her nimble fingers worked at the level of her eyes as she patiently unbound the tresses of his war-beard. I watched their eyes, their glances for each other, their warmth, and sensed their weakness, their love for each other. I took the head from the corner where it wedged, hefted its weight like cold brawn, the eyes like blue stones. Truly we do have souls. The brain had maggots now, and cold mucus spilled down my leg from the windpipe, but I imagined the prince when he was alive, full of a man's life, and hot. I saw Nin glance at me, her lips moving. She was speaking of me to Lugal.

I lifted the head above my own head. 'I'll cut off heads for you, great Lugal.'

The men laughed but Nin had spoken, and Lugal looked at me thoughtfully. 'A peasant does not kill a prince. Only a king kills a king.' He raised his cup to his lips, smiling. 'And children with unbroken voices kill only children. Kill the children of Bab'El and Kush for me and bring me their heads, child.' He laughed. His men laughed. Nin didn't laugh.

I said: 'I am Wotan the son of El.'

'This is true.' Nin's lips moved against the king's ear, but Lugal said, 'Did his God save this boy from Bab'El?'

101

My voice honked as I approached. Someone drew his sword but the king gave a small shake of his head. I said: 'I'm Wotan of the mountains beyond the cedar forest, I'm the river's child, born of a basket in the reeds.' I saw the way these people's minds worked: a river is female; a basket, a womb; reeds, the pubic hair. Born of the river.

Nin said, 'He speaks as I saw it.'

Lugal shrugged. 'Some trader's son. I hear canaanite haggling in his tongue. My library's full of their Zadok's promises, clay tallies by the thousand, bills.' He pointed at the great cedar doors closing off the room. 'The canaans' cedar costs me a fortune in bread and wool. I should take by force what I meekly buy, and put them to the sword!' He swilled his cup. 'But they brought us the secret of wine; for that I forgive men anything.' He frowned at his cup. 'And they don't live in cities. The scattered spawn of El, tent-scum, thatchers. There's no honour in killing them.'

I'd come too close. A guard slapped me behind the knee with the flat of a sword. 'Kneel for King Lugal!' It hurt, and I felt my strength and rage boiling up.

The king watched my face, interested. 'Do you feel no pain?'

I turned to the man who had struck me, broke his sword and his arm and threw them apart, skidded the jagged blade along the floor. The men at their beer jumped up swearing oaths, leapt the clanging blade that embedded itself in the stone wall behind them, and paid attention to me at last. Their swords clanked, drawn, swishing the air.

I honked, 'I'll fight men for you, King Lugal.' I pointed. 'But I won't fight those drunks!'

An exciting moment. Nin stared at me wide-eyed with speaking looks, be silent, be silent! The king nodded at me, chuckling. The guards circled me like hunters round a wild animal. The *apkallu* stroked his white beard thoughtfully. The servants hid behind the food. But no

102

one ignored me. No one. I swelled, filling with life.

Nin disappointed me. 'It's not a fair contest,' she said. 'A child against men.'

'It's fair!' I raised my voice before her talk stopped the fun and they all changed their minds and forgot about me, left me standing here alone holding this stupid cold clammy head. I feared that more than anything, being alone, ignored. Ah, the warmth of being at the centre of them. 'It's a fair fight,' I shouted. 'They're not men. They're drunks!' But at the crucial moment my voice broke, I brayed like a donkey, hee-haw, dree-hawnks. The king laughed, so everyone laughed. I felt my face set like metal, felt my muscles tighten like bands of leather. I really felt I could do anything. I knew I could. I felt my rage come into my eyes, I saw Nin's guards behind her, recognised the eunuch who'd gone at me earlier.

'You, baldy,' I said. 'You hiding. Bald head and no balls.'

It was sufficient. Nin's guard lumbered forward.

'Halt.' Nin put out her hand to stop him. 'Menmash, halt. No.'

'Let me,' huge Menmash piped in a high *castrato*, and everyone laughed. Whether I'd insulted them or not they'd be on my side against a ball-less wonder, and I knew I'd win. Besides, fighters like to be insulted, it gives them an interest.

'This is ridiculous.' Nin appealed to the king. 'My lord.'

Lugal looked forward to the contest, a lumbering beardless cockless tub of animal fat five cubits high set against a child. 'The child will be nimble, my dear. Your creature will die of exhaustion chasing him.'

'Menmash is fast and cruel and will tear the child apart.'

Lugal grew irritated. 'If the child's the son of a god he has nothing to worry about. The gods will save him.'

Menmash towered over me. He unwrapped the leather from his hand I'd cracked earlier, revealing the bruised swollen flesh. The last strands stuck to his knuckles and

103

he ripped away the skin. He smiled, raising his suppurating fist to pulp me.

I threw the head and Menmash caught it in both hands, not thinking. All I had to do was wrap my arms around his thighs, squeeze, lift. He rose up wobbling, flapping his arms, swaying. He tried to grab my head, dropped the one he was holding, lost his balance. I let him fall, that's all.

Menmash fell flat on his face and his body burst. I took a knife from a platter, cut off his head and picked it up by the ears, there being no hair to lift by. Look at me! It was a wonderful moment, the most wonderful of my life so far. Sweat from my exertions trickled down my face. The soles of my feet hurt from the heavy weight I had lifted. Blood and spit still hot with Menmash's life dripped from the upraised head on to the cold head cut off by the king.

Lugal grunted, frowning. Then he laughed. 'Well, what are we to make of him?'

Nin whispered earnestly, 'Spare him, I beg you. The child was born from a dead woman. He is a Son of Man.'

'So you say, so you say.' Lugal jerked his head, a cup of wine was brought to me, I drank it. With his own hand he tossed me a half-plucked cockerel leg, I guzzled it. 'And you say he is harmless? Yet your guard lies dead.'

Nin whispered, 'King Lugal is so great a king he does not need to fear a child.'

Lugal tapped his thumbnail against his teeth, thinking. A king fears even his shadow. Only by killing does he have nothing to fear, except himself. 'El is a great god of the canaans, but this is a city of Ya where Ya is most high.' He decided, 'If he is the son of a god he will live whatever we do. Kill him.'

The swords swept at me but I leapt over them, chucked back the head among the guards, jumped between the pillars then from the balcony on to the sloping thatch roof below. It gave way and I plunged into a room where two people talking fell silent with open mouths, a loaf of bread between them. I snatched the loaf and dived through the window into the street, fell rolling and arched my back nimbly over a pile of manure, then leapt to my feet. High above me Lugal and Nin watched me from the balcony, she talking calmly, but with her hand on his chest. I tore the bread with my teeth and ran between the stalls of the bazaar stealing from each one, a red canaan apple, a handful of dates, anything, useless ears of grain, pure bounty, pure joy, and lost myself in the busy bustling joyous life of the city.

Life, how I love you!

I grow up – I grow! I want to help everyone, and everything that was complicated becomes simple. Everyone loves me, I add life to their lives. I'm so *alive*! Now people give me what I once took. To lift a broken-wheeled cart of apples is worth an apple (I eat a red apple in one bite); for me to carry a couple of donkey panniers full of dates to market is worth all I, even I, can eat. I can hold a goose's egg whole in my mouth, I would make my mother proud to see me. My height grows and people look up to me, my muscles grow around my growing bones and my skin ripples and bulges with growing strength, my muscles growing hard as the metal forged in Tubal-Cain when I pull the strength into me, yet supple as oil and nimble as striking snakes when I relax. Still there are men (like Netho) who lift stronger than me, still there are men (Sabu and Salu the twins) who run faster at races, and men like Pe the fish who swims faster in the canal from the city bend to the single tree like a green fist, which is as far away as the eye can see even after the sun has burnt off the dawn mist (it was Pe I saw that first morning) – ah, the joy of competition, the friendship, closeness, life itself! This male bond of comradeship between men, so much closer than the bond of a man with a woman, two sexes who will never understand one another, never be truly together. But in these masculine moments of strength when the winner is acclaimed, our smooth muscular chests heaving for breath and sweat steaming on our faces, we men are happy.

Sometimes I imagine the king on his balcony looking at me in the distance, watching me, envying my freedom. He must do; anyone would. How wonderful it is to be me! I was in no danger from childless King Lugal; Nin had spoken for me.

Nin, I know, watches over me. Nin is wise; and I fascinate her, though she keeps herself from me. Nin is for us all.

Each year Nin dances for the gods on the stairway to Heaven; each year seven fat young virgins from the holy compound of Ishtar, shaved heads shining, plump fingers fluttering at their pouting lips, long black eyelashes blinking as they are brought from the bloodless unsoiled sanctuary beyond the veil into the sunlight, make the long climb to Heaven and give their lives on the knife to the glory of God, and the sweet savour of their burning bodies rises to His nostrils so that each year the city of Enoch is blessed afresh and saved from Kush and Bab'El and Ur and other envious neighbours too numerous to mention. Each year the bull is killed by Lugal who climbs to the summit wearing a tall white mitre (meaning the pure white mountain peak of Ya) and a golden fleece (the sweet sunlit waters Ya sends us from the mountains), Lugal clenching his hands tight for us in prayer so that the canals water the fields, so that each year new life is born and old life passes away, so that each year his kingship is renewed from Heaven and he returns to us in the flesh as God's promise (whether El or Enki or Ya – a wise man believes in all) that the Flood will not be sent again and mankind will not again be turned to clay.

106

On my golden-brown sunbrowned body, sleek with swimming, rippling with strength, golden hair grows from my legs and crotch and chest. I shave according to the fashion of my city so that we know each other in the confusion of battle. The fashion and style of the men of Enoch is superior to any other city, our hair worn long, bound up in a manly chignon, wearing gowns to our knees or even longer. We change little; the fashionable women change their minds twice a week, hair up, hair down, curled or straight, jewellery this colour now that, the tiny details that speak volumes to their own sex. No wonder I ignore them. And though they follow me about they're so helpless, always afraid of something or other in the dark, always dropping something so that I pick it up, and their hands touch my hands by pretend-accident and their eyes smile into mine. I know what they want.

They want to be my mother.

I want my mother. I still dream of the smell of her. I'm still part of her.

I remember Nin's whisper: *'King Lugal is so great a king he does not need to fear a child.'*

'You'll never be as strong as me,' Netho said. He grinned, punched my arm, then frowned at my frown. 'Oh, stands big for himself in his sandals now he's nearly as tall as his master. I won't be able to teach you a lesson soon, eh?'

'I am as tall as you, Netho.' I ran my hand from the top of his curly head to my eyes. 'But not as fat.'

He coloured; yes, he was running to fat. 'That's muscle, lad.'

'That's your big mouth, Netho.' Once Netho had seemed as strong as the earth to me but now he was smaller. My frown worried him. 'Pick up the donkey,' I invited, grabbing the harness. 'Excuse me, sir, my old friend wants to use your donkey.' Netho grunted but Sabu and Salu were watching and Pe already taking bets. Netho

107

grunted again, shrugged, crouched beneath the donkey, braced his shoulders under its ribs, lifted. The donkey planted itself four-square, sticky-hooved. Netho lifted again, grunting, muscles standing out along his shoulders like loaves. The donkey arched slightly, then its front legs came off the ground, then the rear hooves lifted, and Netho stood swaying beneath his burden.

'One . . .' Salu counted.

'Two . . .' said Salu.

I said, 'Three!' From behind I pushed my head between Netho's legs and lifted him, donkey and all, on my shoulders. The donkey brayed, running in the air, and Netho shouted, 'Whoa! Whoa!' I stepped forward, my feet sinking deep into the dusty street, then ran between the stalls with Netho bumping and swearing above me, and the donkey galloping five cubits clear of the ground, grabbing mouthfuls of roof-thatch where it could. Then its flying hooves brought the canopies that shaded the bazaar crashing down and we collapsed laughing. I picked Netho up and dusted him. 'Now I'm taller than you, Netho. And stronger.'

Netho looked stunned. He was sick. Sabu, Salu and Pe laughed, clapped their arms round his trembling shoulders, pulled his mouth into a smile with their fingers. 'Whoa, whoa!' they cried in Netho's voice, splitting themselves. Netho looked trembling from the donkey to me then down at himself, then at me again as though he couldn't believe what he saw. It was a look I'd recognise often, amazement touched with fear, and something else: longing. Men wanted to see themselves in my eyes. They wanted to be me. The children cried out they wanted to see me lift Netho and the donkey again, that I was stronger than anybody, and the women called too. But I knotted the broken ropes of the canopies and jumped up the walls and posts to tie them again, and the stallholders offered me prizes of fruit and cheese so that I was seen eating their produce. I'm always hungry after exerting myself, and hefted Netho on my shoulder and ran through the crowd eating a roundel of goats' cheese.

The king's soldiers watched, but did nothing to stop me, and all the women bought goats' cheese to make their husbands strong that night. A canaan bargaining in the market heard my name. 'Wotan?' he whispered. 'Is it the same?' Perhaps he followed me, observed me. Perhaps he was a woodcutter's son and had known me. He slipped away.

And my strength grew, and the length of my thighs. Often in the evening twilight I ran from the city (though it's dangerous for most people beyond the ditch when the peaceful fields of daylight dim to a dark lowland of robbers, outlaws, outcasts, the sick, sometimes raiding-parties from other cities – I name no names such as Ur, or Kush, or Bab'El, though I could – young bloods slipping inward between the outlying villages, the *uru-barra*, to steal a woman or two or a few trophies of sheep or barley; and to be true Bab'El has been silent these past years, the old king grieves and broods for his son and has lost all spirit for skirmishing) . . . anyway, as I told you, I often run from the city and lie out under the stars with my friends swapping boasts, drinking them insensible. Then I lie bored, watching the stars. I've never needed sleep. One by one the patterns of the Elohim lose their meaning and fade as the moon rises, and this is when our land is most beautiful, and I am most itchy. I have never been able to sit still with beauty around me. 'Wake up. Wake up!' I shook Sabu and Salu and they woke with yelps like dogs, thinking we were attacked. 'Race you,' I said.

They groaned. They always do.

'You two are faster than anyone,' I offered. 'Even so, I'll give you each a loaf of bread stuffed with spiced minced mutton if you win.'

They can't resist a bet. 'We like lamb, not mutton,' they

said, playing into my hand; they say fat meat makes them slow, and they eat no gristle. I shrugged. Lamb's my favourite. 'Right, lamb it is. And if I win – of course I won't, but if I do – you give me two whole loaves stuffed with spiced lambs, just to be fair.' They looked at me then at each other, sniffing for the trap. 'Done,' they said, but I wouldn't clasp wrists. 'Sabu,' I said idly, 'you're the faster of you two, aren't you?'

Salu said: 'No, I'm faster!' His pride's his weakness.

'He's no faster than me!' Sabu interrupted, the aggressive twin. But I knew Salu *was* faster.

'If Sabu the Slow winds,' I betted, 'I mean if Sabu *should* happen to be faster than you, Salu—'

'He's not!'

'But if I do just happen to run faster than your lazy tortoise of a brother here, then you give me a bonus loaf stuffed with spiced lamb, and not cheap spice either.'

They clucked, seeing I was playing them off against each other, then in their aggression and pride came up with the only result they could. 'We're both faster than you!'

'Good,' I lied. 'That's settled.' We clasped wrists. 'First to the city ditch,' I said, sending Netho ahead to acclaim the winner. 'The far side.' The twins touched their toes and did their exercises while I watched Netho shrink to a dot in the blue landscape towards the earthy jumble of the city, which was sleeping. Pe shouted, 'Now!'

You see, I knew I was faster than them. I knew it in me. But those twins ran like the wind, their dust blowing past me as I ran, then their breath blowing in my face as I caught them. I was right; Sabu, though faster in a dash, didn't have the legs of his brother over a stretch, and his chest (as I had noticed) was not so deep. As he gasped I ran beside him. 'Come on Sabu, run faster.' I really wanted him to beat his twin (though I'd lose part of my bet) because Salu's pride had rankled me, and now I truly wished Sabu would win over him. Then again, I wanted those loaves of spiced lamb for myself – I'm always starving hungry. Sabu gasped, rolling his eyes. He was almost exhausted so I picked him up and ran with him, kicking forward to catch Salu in the moonlight, Salu running so that his feet seemed barely to touch the stark moonlit dust, and the ditch coming close. I heard Netho shouting come-ons at the top of his voice, people gathering about him, all shouting as they saw what was up, all chanting our names. My name was sung louder than the others. I pulled my strength into me, springing past Salu who gave a weary cry, slid down to the bottom of the ditch with Sabu and dropped him from my shoulder there, and then I sprang up the far side. Netho lifted me shouting my name hoarsely, the victor, I embraced him and we jumped for joy among the people gathered under the moon. Sabu ran up the ditch behind me, his breath entirely recovered; then finally Salu scrambled up, slipped back, and I took his wrist and sprang him over my head and hugged him, all of us together in comradeship. But I did not let them forget the three loaves of spiced lamb they owed me, and I drank so much beer to wash down the bread and meat that my belly was full until midday.

'The king wishes you well in your cunning and prowess,' Nin whispered to me as she passed in the street, 'but he would prefer less noise while he is sleeping.'

I bowed, and followed her elegant swaying figure with my eyes. I loved her like my mother; but she was not the same.

Every day at dawn, as I told you, Pe swam the canal. No man, it's said, will ever swim faster than Pe the fish-man, who claims his father's Ennugi the god of canals, and when he's drunk even claims to be the son of Enki the water-god; without Enki's sweet water, our two great rivers and canals feeding the vast network of irrigation ditches, the arid plain of Shem that water blesses and makes fertile would die. And obviously Pe is the son of one water-god or another, since no one swims faster than he, or with a more joyful flowing rhythm, or with such porpoising fluidity that man and water are one. The currents push Pe forward and the water flows with him in any direction, never against him. Everyone knows this. It was Pe who taught me to swim without splashing, and how to breathe for speed, and how to make the rhythm of arms and legs and heart.

The sun glowed through the dawn mist over the pigtailed slaves spreading out like shadows across the bare fields, bringing in the last of the harvest, and soon the winter rains would come. I found Pe sitting on the canal bend where the fishermen dragged out their night-nets. One net had a hole as big as a man torn in it and Pe (who is smooth-faced for speed) got the blame from the bearded fishermen, though everyone knows there are gods and monsters travelling beneath the surface of the waters. 'Be quiet,' I said, and the crowd fell silent. Then some idiot with fish-scales in his beard complained again, and I threw him to the centre of the canal to be quiet. 'Monster in the water!' I called cheerfully and he spluttered ashore in no time. 'Swim with you,' I offered to Pe. 'Teach me. Race you to the tree.'

He nodded, grinning. 'A man has to lose at one thing.'

'Oh, I'm not learning to lose.'

'Then,' he broke into a smile, 'I'll teach you humility.' He plunged into the water leaving hardly a ripple then came up in the sunlight fifty cubits out, and I plunged after him. Humility's something I'll never need to learn. The feeling of speed is beautiful in the water, the sliding weight of it past me, the foam rushing in my ears, Pe's kicking feet trailing bubbles through the blue-green depth, flashing pale like the bellies of fish, then something moving from below struck up at him all teeth, white eyes, long spiny fins; missed him. Pe swam on unknowing, but it turned at once on me, mouth gaping, teeth hooked, a warrior among fish. Fishermen call them white-eyes, the eyes pallid as whitewashed wall, used to the black depths of the river, but sometimes white-eyes swim under sluices and destroy nets and tear at swimmers. The canal's not safe until they're speared. The mouth closed over my head and arm but I bit down on the fish's jutting lower jaw, and my fist thrust in its throat squeezed through to its heart. The fish thrashed, leaping, we bit at each other, the water swept it away and I gasped a breath, caught it with my arm between the two dorsal fins, gripped tight, and now the fish added to my speed as its tail hammered in its death throes. Pe swam unaware, winning, I followed his trail of blue-green bubbles, reached ahead with my fingers splayed to pull the water towards me, the fish sending up spray beside me. Now Pe swam at my side, falling back, swallowing water in his amazement, and the green fist of the tree hung over us with people running along the canal bank to be in at the finish. I coasted, lying on my back in the still waters while Pe climbed out spluttering.

I am the winner even at this. Oh, how I love my life!

'You were a little slow this morning, Pe.' I climbed the bank and yawned, full of fun; winning in style's as important as winning if you want to keep your friends, and I told you my friends are my life to me. I lifted the fish and held it up by the jaw, taller than me, its tail swinging gently in the dust. 'I saw I was getting ahead of you, Pe, so I stopped to do a little fishing on the way.'

All Enoch laughed with me. Everyone knew me. All men wanted to be seen with me. I was famous.

From the bazaar I looked up at the palace balcony. The king watched me, then he turned away.

'Be discreet,' Nin whispered to me. She reached up, brushed a lock of my blond hair from my eyes, she who had no children of her own. 'You are still a child in your heart.' Still a child! I could have lifted her in one hand, tossed her as high as the king's balcony, caught her without harming a hair of her head. She whispered sadly: 'Wotan, you are still a child.' Sad, because that was what she knew she would take from me. Lightly with her hand she led me into a room of her temple. 'Wait.' I waited. Perhaps there would be food, she knows I love a feast. I called, 'Nin?' but she was gone, and another sort of feast (though not one I've ever had), a beautiful woman in a gown the colour of the temple, stood in her place.

I asked, 'Where's Nin?' The temple prostitute wore the holy perfume of the temple, her body powdered with pale powder, claiming without words that her skin never saw the sun. 'Nin is here,' she whispered. 'I am Nin. I am Ishtar. I am her body made life.' Her hair was oiled, sensuously piled and bound, her breasts stood tall beneath her gown. I felt her nipples prick me as she took my face in her hands and kissed my mouth with her soft full lips. I shivered at their touch, I shook, and for the first time in my life my penis swelled in its sheath we wear beneath out gowns. I ached, fearing – me, afraid! – that I'd burst out of the tight bindings and stand exposed.

'Don't be ashamed.' She reached down, held me against the sudden sharp odour of her flesh. 'Be born again in me.'

It was wonderful! Wonder of wonders! What a feeling! My balls swelled enormously in my desire for her whoever she was, one sliding ecstatic touch of her feminine heat and I couldn't stop, I lifted her and filled the bowl of her womb with my semen like a bull at a cow until even she, seasoned prostitute that she was, cried out my name.

She clamped her hands over herself, her head dropped back limply. 'Be born again in me!'

I'd discovered something almost as good as winning.

Naturally the magnificent size of my penis was rumoured

all over the interested quarters of the city within hours, and that my orgasms come as often and as fully as a woman's. You may imagine how quickly with practice my skill grew. I can have four women in a night, each of them four times, and not repeat myself once except in the pleasure I give. The more women I possess the more I hunger for more; a glance in the bazaar, a smile, a look down, a fluttered eyelash, a direct stare, I know you all. A flash of something at a window, I'm up there with you. A touch on my elbow and I turn into your arms, if you're beautiful; a secret tryst excites me so that I must have you even on my way in the street or behind a granary if the opportunity arises – which, you being the prisoner of your lusts as much as I of mine, is often. I love my penis as much as you do.

I've learnt how to kiss the final farewell kiss so that your hands don't cling, your arms don't enclose me to drag me back, your entreaties and begging don't sway me. I'm gone, leaping along rooftops in the rain if necessary, swinging down streets away from the sight of jealous husbands. In fact, I'm told, my example makes such men try harder. You women of Enoch are the most satisfied in all the lands of Shem.

No man dares oppose me, or even meet my eye, but they mutter to the king.

And Nin touches my lips with her fingertip. 'Wotan, do not make so much noise.'

King Lugal watched me from the balcony. 'I'll put him to use. You've tried to bind him with comradeship, and failed. Women's bodies, and failed. Love, and failed.'

'He doesn't know what love is. He has no idea. He's blind and deaf and dumb.'

'*I* shall not fail.' Lugal held up his hand, no more argument. 'I'll bind him and use him and contain him with the sport of men. War.' Nin looked sceptical. 'Every young man,' Lugal said, 'loves war.' He rubbed his hands gleefully, and lightning flashed in the clouds over the horizon.

The clouds, as Lugal well knew, sent rain down into the great cedar forest and the mountains that rise to the east and north, where I come from, falling as snow on the holy white peaks; and the slushy torrents roared down canyons to the endless living green peaks of the cedars, swirling the brown earth from their roots, sweeping onwards to the plain of Shem. Beyond the earthworks our slumbering river Buranun shook itself from sleep, rising up brown with silt, stretching out ten times itself, twenty, around the earthworks of Enoch. But Lugal was unafraid. God had promised no more Flood.

The rosette banners around the temple of Ishtar thundered like sails between the rainstorms as the army of King Lugal marched out. The city of Kush had gone too far, King Nangi forcing the city of Isin under his protection and calling our great king a mere shepherd, meaning Enoch was a city of sheep. The diplomacy of veiled insults escalated like a stately dance, then near Isin's border a donkey-caravan carrying our grain to ur-Ararat was attacked, slaves, donkeys, grain all stolen. Nangi compounded his thievery by demanding tribute, saying Kush was the greatest city of Shem and our grain had been grown without permission on *their* fields, because all our land belonged to Kush! King Lugal swore he'd cut off Nangi's beard and make him a small man. Dire threats were exchanged by messenger and the messengers' heads cut off and sent back. Everyone was pleased. It was war.

I was overjoyed; I wore armour donated by rich women, I waved my sword (Netho had taught me swordplay) and the women wept from the rooftops as I left and held out their arms to me (Lugal thought they were cheering him). Nin kissed my nose and told me not to make too many children fatherless. It's wonderful to march in an army – behind the king, naturally, but not too far from the head,

116

a warrior among warriors. Around us strapping beauties of Ishtar beat *tigi* and *lilis*-drums or danced with *nexe* and *ala*-tambourines and promised us their love when we returned victorious. Behind followed a swarm of violent peasants hoping for plunder, and bringing up the rear a vast dull jostling mass of slaves just for show; they'd be sent back at dark.

I walked behind King Lugal who rode above us on a four-wheeled war wagon. The wheels were a clever idea – someone had thought of turning potters' wheels on their sides so that they rolled, then joined them together with a wooden beam (the front axle swivelled, breaking the rear axle if the turn was too tight). Stone was too heavy so Lugal's wagon had wheels of solid cedar. Dragged by four oxen as white as holy bulls, the sides and railing were decorated with lapis lazuli and gold (fabulously expensive) brought from the tribesmen of Punt, Egypt, by canaanite traders. The wind bannering the imperial canopy and holy flags made the wagon's progress across the flatlands a kingly and impressive sight. At each village under our city's control we took a tribute of women and wine. Peasants levelled the boundary ditches and embankments and we rolled into the fields of Isin, now under Kush's sway; any foreign slaves we found we knocked about and sent screaming ahead of us; King Lugal's coming! King Lugal's coming at the head of an army of five thousand warriors!

Finally the two armies faced one another across a waterlogged ditch on the vast drizzling plain of Shem. The shivering peasants started to drift away almost at once, and we muttered that peace would be declared before war had a chance. Netho ran forward. 'Are these Nangi's best warriors?' he taunted them. 'Your mothers are donkeys!' All we warriors shouted insults at King Nangi's warriors (only a king shouts insults at a king) then Netho sloshed across the ditch and dared them to kill him. They wouldn't. I yawned, boredom setting in. Only Nangi's strongest man

Agga interested me, standing tall and impassive with crossed arms by the king's chariot. Agga had killed three thousand six hundred men (such totals, like the reign-years of great kings who begin dynasties, are always multiplied in sixties, meaning *lots*, and it's the length of each dynasty's reign which is counted not each king's).

To fight a hero is the fastest way to become a hero, so I put myself in front of King Lugal's eye and received the king's blessing. I jumped the ditch and cut down a couple of men sneaking behind Netho, left him to deal with the others for his own glory, and advanced steadily. My eye met Agga's. His eye glinted. So did mine, no doubt.

He bowed to Nangi for permission, Nangi waved his hand, and Agga came thumping forward. He was a handsome man, as tall as me or taller, and within moments of meeting him I knew he was not stupid. To fight a man, a good man, is to know him more deeply (as I told you) than any man knows a woman; you're fighting what you are, no difference, his thoughts are yours. His death or your own is the most intimate companionship. I felt Agga's heart and lungs, the sweat sliding on his skin. Our faces bumped in the clinch breaking his nose, I felt his pain and the weight of his armour, but he threw me back skilfully. 'You're strong,' he said, 'but your sword is weak.' A storm swept over us, then the sun, and still we fought. The ground turned to mud beneath our sliding feet. We rolled into the ditch and fought in filthy water to our necks, then fought again on the level ground. I did not put forward my strength, I fought him as a man. War, the joy of it! This honour, this glory, this ecstasy! There is no finer feeling. Our swords broke, we clasped, brothers in arms.

'If I am commanded,' he gasped, resting his head against mine, 'I will kill you.'

'If you're commanded,' I said, 'you'll fail.' I could have broken his back. I did not. For the first time in my life I did not do something I could have done. Agga gasped,

'Don't squeeze so hard, even in friendship.' He stepped back, wiped the blood and spittle from his beard. 'Your king has a cruel reputation.'

I said, 'A wise king is called cruel not weak.'

'Lugal, childless and envious, cut off the head from the son of the King of Bab'El.'

'For treachery, not from envy.' Warriors on both sides beat their swords on their shields, fight, fight!

Agga said, 'King Nangi is wise but not a cruel man.'

I was disappointed. 'Then perhaps peace must be made.'

'You are a hero now. I speak to you as your friend.' Agga picked up the pieces of his sword. 'Some say you are the child of Lugal, illegitimate, but to be his heir.'

A dangerous rumour. 'No.' I was careful not to tell the truth since the men of Kush, being from the north, worship El. 'I know who my father is.'

'I've heard that rumour too,' Agga said, then surprised me. 'That your father is the Bull of Heaven who attacked us from the north and destroyed our harvest.' So that was why Kush, under pressure from the north, pressed to the south. Like a flashing nightmare I was a child in darkness and flames, a man's voice echoing in my dreams, *I am the Bull of Heaven, I am your father.*

'I've never heard of him,' I said. *Fight, fight!* cried the soldiers, and Agga raised his voice. 'Now word reaches us the Bull of Heaven has marched through our lands towards Bab'El. The Bull—' He covered his ears at the noise of chanting warriors, in a moment no one would stop them, the armies would clash, lives be lost, reputations made, glory won. But my reputation was already made: Agga had said it. I was a hero now.

He and I raised our broken weapons above our heads, comrades, and threw them down.

I returned to Lugal. 'They want peace.'

'I want glory,' Lugal said. 'I need glory.' His complaints

fell silent as I told him about the army from the north marching on Bab'El. 'Suppose Bab'El falls?' Lugal sensed his weakness at once. 'The old king hasn't dared attack us though he has the soldiers, he lost heart after the death of his son.' He tapped his teeth. 'But the men of Bab'El are still strong. Strong enough to beat off a band of ruffians.'

'If the men from the north have marched south to attack Bab'El,' I said, 'then Kush will return to the north.' But I did not think the Bull of Heaven would attack Bab'El; he would make alliance, double his strength, and attack us in mutual hatred together with the king of Bab'El. But I am not an *apkallu*, King Lugal would not listen to my voice. Nevertheless I advised: 'Great king, make trade, not war, and hurry home.'

Lugal's blessing and curse was his impulsiveness; this time it saved him. Within hours a bridge was thrown across the ditch and the two kings exchanged ceremonial greetings in the middle. They clasped wrists, cloaks flapping in the wind, then retired to a tent rinsed with tar, which makes a royal red colour visible as far as the eye can see. And also waterproof, necessary as the rain poured down like thunder on the roof-peak.

'Why Bab'El?' Lugal said, drinking wine. 'Why does this Bull of Heaven march on Bab'El?'

Nangi pulled his wise white beard. 'Because Bab'El is your enemy?'

'The city of Enoch has no quarrel with any ruffian. The Bull of Heaven is not my enemy.'

'Perhaps you are his. Then Bab'El, your enemy, is his friend.' Yes, Lugal would listen to another king! Nangi nibbled a date, then paused. His eyes widened.

'Only a city fights a city.' Lugal stopped. 'What?'

Nangi stared through the tent-flap. 'What?' Lugal cried, and the flap was thrown wide. Again a watery gleam of sunlight passed across the southern horizon, and in it stood darkness like a cloud. Not a cloud. It was smoke.

'Enoch is burning,' I said. 'Your city is burning.'

Lugal stood, overturning the table. King Nangi gripped his arm. 'My horses are yours.' But Lugal was already running from the tent. He ignored his wagon in the mud, screamed for his men, his weapons. I ran ahead, grabbed a sword and cut the hitching-rope and then grabbed the fastest horse, heaved Lugal astride. Still half-wild it bit at him and bucked, they hate being ridden, but he jabbed its ribs till they bled. I vaulted the next horse, turned its head by the mane, and together Lugal and I rode like the wind through the rain.

At evening the king's horse fell down exhausted, we were alone. I picked him up and ran like a slave, saw a fire in the dark, stole a donkey from an *uru-barra* and ran beside Lugal as he swayed exhausted in the cedarwood saddle. The wind in our eyes blew smoke over us, then huge slow flames showed through the streaming rain. The rain made one fire into ten, and ten into a hundred, each streaked and multiplied by glittering raindrops. Lugal gave a cry then said no more. He watched in silence as we came to the first bodies lying like earth in the sodden ground. The donkey picked its way forward between piles of discarded bodies and now we heard the screams of the living, the clash of swords.

'Fighting in the dark,' Lugal whispered numbly. 'There's no honour in fighting in the dark. Where's the glory? Where's the honour?' We came between the first buildings, thatch burning, the dead thrown down, none taken alive that we saw. Lugal tried to comprehend what happened. 'Where's the profit? What's the point?' He saw someone he knew and greeted him, but the man was nailed up dead as though alive. 'I would have paid ransom for him. I would've paid, I swear.' I was silent, you know why. This death all around me in the darkness is familiar. I've been here before. I've seen this darkness before, these flames, I've heard these same screams, you know where. You know.

I was weary in my heart now, nothing surprised me. I knew what would happen.

This is what happened. Innocent shapes ran around us in the filth and dark, children, dogs, horses, women with breasts bare and eyes wide and full of flames, blind panic, their sweat on their bodies making their skin red with reflected flame, blood spurting from their wounds like gleaming black tongues as they ran. Lugal tried to catch them but his hands slipped. He stared at his bloody hands then at me. 'Why?'

I knew why. Because of me. For the first time an extraordinary thought struck my mind. There is more than good in this world, more than the pleasure of women, more than the laughter of children, more than the joy of war. There is something . . . I had no word for it. Something bad.

Flames flared in my eyes, screams filled my ears.

There is something more than light. There is darkness. There is this darkness.

I drew my sword and ran forward. Soldiers of Bab'El rushed at me from all sides, I roared, I cut them down, hacked limbs from bodies and heads from hearts in sprays of black blood in the firelight and dark. A chaos of streets rose around me, the raised ground of the Kullaba, the outer suburb, our city's built up on a sandbank, a turtle's back made from hundreds of years of rubbish from which the temple rises; ahead of me the darkness turned to a curtain of fire, burning pitch thrown down from the walls of the temple, bowls of naphtha falling from the air like white stars. The men of Bab'El fell back from the walls, running away, and I cut them down through their armour until my sword broke and the ground around me was saturated with death. I leapt forward dragging the king with me, horsemen of Bab'El swept by us with their cloaks on fire, they screamed like girls when they saw me. I knocked the horses over and pulled the men down and butchered them in my strength and rage and horror with my hands, my bare hands, and trampled their bodies with my bare feet. My armour and clothes were all torn away, I was naked and my penis stood joyously erect in the lust of battle, stiff as a flagpole despite all the disgust and despair of what I saw.

Beyond the square the great gates of the temple still withstood the attacks against them.

Three hundred and sixty ruffians crowded forward like a wave at the gates, were beaten back by stones and fire, the cries of the defenders high above – mostly women, priestesses and priests of the Urmeme, prostitutes who provided the new generations of the priestly family, and eunuchs, and white-bearded sages – their terrified and terrifying shrieks crying in the air like a flock of gulls above the battle. In the square rode a man on a pale horse, steering it with his knees, his face and beard dripping blood-red as a bull's flayed hide, rallying his men for the next attack. The wave of heads and shoulders rolled forward. He roared: 'I am the Bull of Heaven!'

Apsu, who claimed to be my father.

Apsu's voice shouted: 'I am the Bull of Heaven, I am the sword of God brought down from the mountains to bring justice to the Shemites! I brought the great God El to the canaanites, I taught them the ways of sacrifice, I killed those who did not worship the storm!'

He saw me, his eyes fixed on the seashells at my neck, and one pale shell swung at his own throat like a broken tooth, torn from my mother's neck those years ago. 'I followed you, Wotan. My ears heard your name, I heard you hid from me here. I am the searcher, I'll find you wherever you hide.' He raised a glittering black knife two-handed between his thumbs. 'Atone, Wotan, my son, cursed, damned, cast down by your life, you are the cause of all evil. Atone now for your sin, for you are alive!'

I said quietly, but he heard me, 'I am not your son. My

mother Tia told me the truth.'

Apsu's horse pranced among his troops, knocking men down, but he didn't move his eyes from mine. Spittle flew from his lips, pure hatred. 'The bones of your father's people, *my* people, lie dead and scattered on the seashore because of you. Sacrifice yourself! Die as you should have died. Give life to them.'

I stared at the black-bladed obsidian knife. I am Wotan, and I remember the moment of my conception, I remember the ribs of Noah's Ark rising as high as Heaven, I remember the knife raised above me. Apsu's hands had fingers then, not stumps. Now he clenched the knife between his thumbs, all he had left. 'The knife fell,' I said. 'The knife fell from the mountain to the glacier.'

He held up his palms before his face, smiled where his frostbitten fingers had been. 'Days it took me to find it under the ice and snow. Ice and snow took my fingers and toes in return for the knife which will kill you. Holy I am with suffering. Strong I am with suffering. I am a righteous man, my son, and by your death I redeem my suffering people.' Four young men about my own age or less gathered round Apsu's horse. He held out his clenched arms, pointing at me with the knife, cried out their names. 'Lahmu, Lahamu, Anshar, Kishar! Take him. Bring him to me.'

Kishar ran at me first; I lifted him, broke his back, threw him apart.

The others fell back from my blood-spattered face and body, and Apsu gave a ghastly cry.

'My son has killed his brother!'

The battle rolled over us, pushed us, pulled us away. I fought forward through the scrimmage, seized a sword and cut a swathe of blood and bodies ahead of me, but the tide of battle swept Apsu who claimed to be my father from my sight, and of the three survivors that he claimed were my brothers I saw nothing; I was blind with blood and rage. The battle was lost, the feathers of arrows stuck from my naked body, their wedge-shaped tips came through my flesh from behind, I carried a hundred cuts. Even I would lose.

'Lost,' King Lugal cried. 'All lost.' He covered his head with his cloak.

I fought my way to the earthwork and stuck my sword deep between the sluice gates, worked the point deep into the splintering wood, the waters of Buranun spurted and sprayed past me; then I thrust to the hilt and the great gates gave way, the smooth slope of water swept us all down, the flood swept everyone away.

Sun. The sun's heat and light falling on my closed eyelids.

I opened my eyes and stared at the sun. It didn't hurt. There was no pain . . . I mean that there was no *more* pain. My body was a sea of pain. The sun's heat had turned the floodwaters to mud and I lay awakening in the mud, stuck deep in slime with arrows and blood. Birds wheeled and hopped out of the sun, scavenging the stinking bodies around me with their beaks, greedily turning brave men to birdshit, and I cried aloud in my grief at life's smallness: that humans are just clay, blind white clay, spattered back on the earth from which we blindly rose and struggled and fell.

A woman's face covered the sun. The wind blew her hair like a wing, her voice murmured. 'The great God El sent the Flood. Son of El, you brought the flood for the second time.' She bound her hair, thinking I was dead, her voice began the prayer for the dead. *'Lay upon the sinner his sin, lay upon the transgressor his transgression. The lord of the Kullaba, the lord of the people's hearts, he will not rise again; he overcame evil, he will not come again; though he was strong of arm he will not rise again.'*

'Eve.' I remembered her name, and Nin's maid screamed in shock. Then she knelt and touched me but I couldn't feel her fingers, only my pain. I roared my pain and anger at her, shouting her name as strange and foreign as my own.

'To these people's tongues my name is Hayah.' *Aya* is the goddess of the dawn, the land where the sun rises. She worked methodically, unafraid of my blood and noise. 'My name's always the same backwards and forwards. Eve's a common name with us.' Her long fingers touched the tuft of feathers sticking from my chest, marvelling. 'How can you be alive?'

'I hurt enough to be alive.' I sat up, then slumped forward in her arms – I was weak! All around us stretched mud and muddy lumps, arm, legs, everything thrown down in death. The temple of Ya'nna stood like a mountain out of the mud, the gates open and the people who had sheltered there creeping to find their homes among the ruins. Their wailing rose to Heaven: the flood that saved the holy precinct had swept away the Kullaba, the people's part of the town. 'Did your mistress send you to look for me?'

She said: 'No.'

'Who, then?'

'Oh,' she said angrily, 'no one.' She pulled at an arrow head and it hurt.

'Is Nin well?'

'Of course, yes, *she* is well. She sent me to find your body. *I* didn't care.'

I whispered, 'Shall I call you Hayah, or Eve?'

'Whatever you like.' She frowned. 'Stop groaning.' She was so fierce I laughed, then groaned. She stroked my forehead. 'I'll get some men to carry you.'

The humiliation! I pulled my strength into me and stood, the mud springing the arrow shafts, I felt the tips quivering in my flesh. One arrow had pinned the muscle of my arm to my ribs. I jerked it out, screamed. 'You're strong enough to scream and be stupid!' she shouted

126

furiously. 'There's plenty of others who need help more than you.' Her eyes filled with angry tears and she turned away looking for whoever needed her, but they were all dead, and I touched her elbow. She stiffened. 'Don't. I haven't slept. I haven't stopped.'

'Why?'

'And now I've found you and you're alive.' She pressed the back of her hand to her mouth.

I turned her. 'Where do they call girls Eve?'

She wouldn't look at me. 'Where the sun rises.'

'In the mountains?'

'Beyond.' Even beyond the mountains. I tried to imagine it. 'There's a place beyond the mountains?'

She stared angrily. 'Yes, where slaves come from.' Then her mouth moved, jerking, and I thought she'd cry again. She laughed. 'You look ridiculous.'

I groaned, stuffed with arrows like a hunted lion. 'Stop it,' she said. 'You're strong but you're stupid. You're so stupid. You don't know anything. You've hurt yourself.' She cried as though I'd hurt *her*, but there were more important things for me to know. I asked, 'Is King Lugal alive?'

Her eyes searched mine. 'Of course he's alive. He's the king. There wouldn't be anything left without him.'

I limped, not wanting to admit I needed help, and she put out her hand. 'I'll call you Eve not your other name,' I said.

We walked. 'Only my mistress calls me Eve,' she said.

'And I do. Tell me what your name means among your people.'

She said, 'Helper. Mother. Lover.' She bit her lip, fell silent.

'Don't stop.' I took another step.

'I haven't stopped.'

'I meant don't stop talking. Your voice makes me hurt less.'

'You should hurt! Look at everyone you've killed. All the people you drowned. People of Enoch as well as their enemies.'

'Enoch's my city,' I groaned. 'I saved my city.'

She said: 'You're so big-headed. Enoch's no more your city than it is mine.' She looked up at me with her eyes wide open, steady, and I couldn't argue.

The royal palace, the Egalmah, still stood, though with its feet in the mud. Nin rushed at me, embraced me, took me over, and faceless women fussed around me binding my wounds as I slept. I awoke having forgotten about Eve, and my strength returned. The knotted scars that covered my body became smooth oiled skin shining with sweat over my muscles rippling beneath, and as I exercised the girls loved to put their hands around my muscles as they hardened until they were lifted kicking from their pretty little feet, my muscles hard as living stone, and as the girls swung their bodies and breasts deliberately against me they slipped their arms around my neck and gazed into my eyes and whispered in the way a man never resists. The more I use my strength, the stronger I become. The more I use my sex, my gorgeous engorged sex as long as a rib, the more of a man I am. How I adore these lovely girls, their laughter, their kisses, how they love me! No man is as terrific in bed or in battle as I.

I saw Eve hurrying in a corridor. I called: 'Eve.' She gave me a bored look, and hurried away.

I found Nin with Lugal in their rooms at the top of the Egalmah. They both exclaimed my name, startled, and drew apart as though they'd talked of me. Lugal had been thoughtful since the flood, but below the palace and temple I saw the city full of workmen and teams of slaves, fields of bricks drying in the sun, great heaps of reed standing ready to be used and more brought in by donkey and ox-cart every day. But Lugal sat with his chin in his hand, watching me. I cheered him up. 'Your city will soon be rebuilt exactly as it was, as if nothing happened.'

He sighed. 'It did happen.' He glanced at Nin. Lugal had felt his crown shake, and doubt and worry actually made him look younger than before, by which I mean less dignified, and dignity is everything to a king. I told them, 'But we won a great victory. We beat them back! We slaughtered them!'

Nin touched my shoulder. 'Yes, but Apsu the Bull of Heaven survived, who claims to be your father.'

I ate a piece of fruit. 'He's not my father.'

'And so did—'

'They're not my brothers!'

'You killed one called Kishar.'

'I've done nothing wrong. No badness.' I searched for the word. 'I committed no *sin*.' My cheeks burned, and Nin placed her cool palms against them. 'No sin,' I muttered.

'I know,' she whispered. 'I believe you are the son of El. I believe you. But . . .' She glanced at Lugal.

Lugal said: 'The Bull of Heaven will come back. He and Bab'El have sworn blood-vengeance for the deaths of their sons, and they'll come back and back until Enoch is trampled, destroyed, chaos. They've sworn it, my death and yours.' Lugal was wishing he hadn't chopped off the head of the king's son.

'Let's go and kill them,' I said cheerfully.

'There's my army.' Lugal pointed at the sea of cracked mud around the city. 'My soldiers are clay! And beyond the ruins of his tower, the king of Bab'El's building a wall.'

I shrugged, not understanding. Everyone was building walls for houses. My loins were hot and my muscles itched, I wanted to get back to the women and my exercises. I yawned.

Lugal pointed at the horizon. 'No, a *wall*, enormous, around his city. He can't be attacked.'

A wall encompassing a whole city! It was a wonderful

idea. We definitely needed one. I remembered how a few women, priests, eunuchs, threw back Apsu's horde from the temple walls. 'We'll build a wall around the whole of Enoch,' I said. They stared. 'I'll do it,' I added. Still they stared. 'I'll need help,' I said. 'A little.'

Lugal said nothing. Nin said: 'Give it to him to do. It will keep him quiet. We need peace.'

So this is the story mothers whisper to their sleepy children: how I built the walls of Enoch. Every word's true: fathers tell their sons they were there. First I walked the city boundary dragging a plough behind me to mark the foundation, the *ur*. I set two thousand one hundred and sixty men and women to work making twelve million, nine hundred and sixty thousand rich red silt-bricks from the river's mud that had inundated our city, transforming its doom into the wall that would be its salvation; three hundred and sixty men and women cut and carried berdi-reed for straw, five hundred and forty bricklayers worked from the ground at first then up ladders, finally from scaffolding like spiders' webs held against the summer sky; at intervals of one-sixtieth of the wall's circumference smoked sixty boiling bubbling vats of pitch for mortar, and children beyond counting scampered with steaming tarry buckets as nimbly as cedar-monkeys up the swaying scaffolds to where the men worked. I built the wall with niches and buttresses to make it stand for ever, I built high towers and placed great trees on them, whole cedars, to fly flags and banners magnifying the glory of the city and the gods. I sent orders to the canaans to fell whole forests of cedar to make the great gates, and set carpenters dragging and joining the ancient trunks floating downriver from the woodland villages of the far north to our reed-beds, just as had my little ark.

In the evenings, covered with sweat, stonedust and wood-shavings, I and my friends – I had so many friends! – headed by Netho, Salu, Sabu and Pe, went roaring to the temple precinct and the whores washed us and cried out, 'Be born again in me!' Among them we sprawled drinking beer and wine, ate the strongest fish whole from mouth to tailfin, lion, eagle still clothed in feathers from the mountains, and sang drinking songs and building songs and war songs and fornicating songs while the moon rose and fell. All night under the moon we sang, and drank and screwed the whores – I had them all, every one! – until they begged for mercy, their wombs overflowing with the oil of life, making the next generation of priests and virgins. There was no end to our strength – to mine, anyway. Nobody could keep up with me, I'm so full of life! The more I had, the more I wanted. I want to be young for ever!

A voice said, 'Wotan, stop.'

I stopped.

I recognised her laughter. 'I didn't mean *stop*,' Eve said. 'I meant stop.'

A hot summer's day, and the dust from the building works blew over us. I stood between her and the sun and wind, sheltering her, always uncomfortable standing still. 'I haven't seen you. Eve, I—'

'Not stop walking,' she said. 'I meant stop what you're doing.' She put her fingers to her ears at the rattle of hammers, coughed the dusty air, spat dust.

'Stop my building?' I felt the earth drop under my feet. 'My wall is the marvel of the world. Is this you? Do you hate me so much? Or is it your mistress saying these words?'

She walked, so I walked with her. 'Wotan, the people of Enoch are saying them.'

'The people of Enoch are made safe by the wall I'm building.'

'People who are safe demand greater safety.'

I put out my open palms. 'What are you saying exactly?'

'Enough. Stop.' She bought a kebab and the man

recognised me, shook his head, wouldn't take what she offered. 'Look what respect the people have for me,' I said. She paid him anyway, then she said, 'They talk about you behind your back.'

'My back's broad. It lifts heavier weights than words.'

She put back the hood of her galabiya from her face, more beautiful than I remembered, lovely wide cheekbones, eyes, small chin. Skinny, whereas I like them buxom. If I kissed her I'd probably break her. She obviously wanted to kiss me, they all do. She filled her mouth with lamb and those pungent spices, exhaled. My eyes watered. 'You aren't so strong,' she said.

I knew how to impress her. 'Last full moon I lifted thirty men on a rope up the city wall, hand over hand.'

'One fell.'

'Yes, he fell, the idiot lost his grip, but I didn't drop him.'

She yawned, mouth red with lamb, succeeding in not attracting me. 'People talk.'

I swelled with pride. 'Yes, I know what they say.'

'Tell me, great man.'

'How huge my strength is, how big my cock is, and my orgasms that—'

She walked, so I walked. 'No, they say you make too much noise.' She held out the stick casually to my lips, I pulled off a mouthful, then stopped as though I'd eaten a mouthful of gristle.

I said, 'Noise? Is that all they call it?' I swallowed, hurried to catch up before I lost her in the crowd.

I found her sitting by the fountain, dabbling the grease from her fingers in the bubbling waters. There'd been nothing in this quarter but dust; the turtleback of sand and rubbish on which Enoch was built being higher than the plains, water did not come up inside the city walls, so if besieged we might die of thirst, but I'd prayed to one of the Elohim of El, Ninurta, and this water had bubbled up through the dust at my feet. But Eve wasn't listening.

'The great God El sent the Flood because of men's noise,' she told me, dabbling. 'Long ago the world of men bellowed noise like a bull, the roaring of the world echoed up the Tower of Bab'El to Heaven, and the great God El said, "This uproar of mankind is intolerable and My sleep – My absence – is disturbed by your babble, so I shall silence you in the waters." But the great God Ya whispered to Noah the righteous man, the Zadok of his people, and told him to tear down his house and build a boat. Ya commanded, "These are the measurements of the ark Noah shall build to save his soul: across shall be the equal of long, the beginning shall be the equal with the end, and the roof shall be like the vault that covers the abyss; and Noah shall take in it the egg and semen of all living creatures, and dwell over the gulf of the waters, saved by Ya."'

'Everyone knows this story,' I said. 'Noah was, is' – he was still alive – 'a Son of Man, and he laid the keel and ribs with his own hands. Noah built the Ark across the equal of long, and the beginning equal with the end, one hundred and fifty cubits each side, every child knows this. He built six decks below, making seven altogether, each divided into nine sections. The children ran with baskets of hot pitch and asphalt for waterproofing the timbers, and Noah gave the shipwrights red wine to drink like water, and on the seventh day the Ark was complete.'

'At dawn a black cloud rose from the horizon.' Eve stared at the bubbling water. 'The rain fell, and the sky was turned to fire by dreadful lightning, the lightning of the Annunaki, who are called by my people the seven judges of Hell.'

'Hell? That's the third time you've told me a word I don't know. What's the name of the place your people come from beyond the mountains?'

'Eden.'

It meant nothing to me. 'Eden, the Land of the Living,' she said impatiently. 'The Garden of Life. The Source of Knowledge of Good and Evil. What more don't you know?'

'Sin. And true goodness. And evil.'

'Among my people *sin* and *evil* and *Hell* are simply a removal from God's presence.' Again she stared at the water as though she saw the Flood. 'The land was smashed like a cup, the tempest poured over the people like the tide of battle. Ishtar the Queen of Heaven cried out like a woman in childbirth, "The former world is passed away, the days of old are turned to water, the bodies of my people float like fish-spawn in the ocean." For six days the torrent fell on the world, and the flood overwhelmed the world, and everyone died, and only the Ark was afloat on the waters.'

'On the seventh morning the flood was stilled.'

'Noah opened a hatch, and saw the sea was as flat as a rooftop.' She dabbled again. 'The flood receded and left the Ark high and dry on the Mountain of Salvation, Ararat. On the seventh day Noah let loose a dove.'

'The dove returned.'

'Noah loosed a swallow.'

'The swallow returned.'

'Then Noah sent out a raven and the raven found food and did not return. Noah made sacrifice to God on the mountaintop, and El's voice spoke over him saying, "In the past time My servant Noah was a mortal man; now he and his wife shall live in the distance at the mouth of the rivers, far away." '

'God gave Noah immortality,' I said. 'That's why legend calls him the Faraway.'

She said: 'The people say you too are immortal.'

I flexed my muscles, showed my strength. 'Of course I am.'

'You nearly died in my arms.'

134

'Look how quickly I recovered!'

She glanced at me under her eyelashes, her wide blue eyes slanted upwards at the outer corners, and I waited for her admiration. But she said: 'You nearly died.'

I slammed my fist into the water, but only succeeded in making us both wet. We stared at each other angrily through the trickling drops down our faces. I shouted, 'Why do you try to make me angry?'

'Because you're stupid when you do nothing. You don't *listen*. You make noise, nothing but noise, the noise of you with the temple whores rises to Heaven.'

'You're jealous.'

She said calmly, 'You never stop. You never sleep. The noise of your drinking and singing and shouting and fighting keeps the people awake, the whole city's sleepless with your whoring. Stop, Wotan. Stop.'

'But everyone likes me. Everyone loves me.'

'No one loves you. They're in awe of you. They fear you. Just because they acclaim you, you think you're popular. All men want to be you, but they aren't. So they smile to your face and behind your head they whisper . . .'

'What whispers?'

'Slander. Innuendo. Rumour. Nothing. For all his lovemaking, where are Wotan's children? For all the wombs Wotan seeds, why do none spring forth with life?'

'Do you believe that nonsense?'

'I said I hear it said.'

'Why are you telling me? Did Nin send you?' She shook her head. 'Nin and Lugal sent you,' I accused her.

Eve leant forward, opened her eyes wide. 'When you *think*, you are so intelligent. You are wonderful when it matters, when it really matters. You can see into people, you saw how it lay between Kush and Bab'El and the Bull of Heaven, you made Lugal understand, you truly saved our city from your father—'

'No. El is my father.'

'Among my people, for a man to call himself the Son of God is blasphemy.'

'Not if it's true.' I sat her in my hand, lifted her above my head, jumped on to the ornamental brick cones that surrounded the fountain, leapt lightly from peak to peak. 'Can a man do this?'

Her voice called down, wobbling, 'Would a Son of God waste His time doing it?'

I slipped, caught my balance, jumped down with her, let her down gently on her toes. 'Yes. No. I don't know.' I cleared my throat. 'There's another word I don't know.' She raised her eyebrows and I said in a rush, 'Atone!'

'That your—' she bit her tongue. 'That's the word the Bull of Heaven shouted?' She sat again, looking up at me curiously. 'On the first day of each new year Ya is enthroned at the festival chapel, the *akītu*, in divine kingship over the city, then the people shout, "Ya has become King", there's a rite of sacred marriage between Ya and Ishtar, and the trumpets blow and earthly kingship is let down from Heaven to anoint their chosen son, King Lugal, priest and king. On the seventh day a red bull's sacrificed, atoning for all the bad things people have done during the past year without thinking about it, reconciling them with the righteous anger of Ya. But some badness is worse than badness, it's *sin*, which my people call knowledge: knowing-badness. Knowing what's bad and deliberately doing it, that's sin, that's evil. Knowledge of sin and evil means a man must atone personally before he can be understood and forgiven. He himself must speak to God and beg mercy, expiation.' She explained: 'He must appease by sacrifice. There's no greater gift than life.'

I understood. 'I lived, and so my people's grass didn't grow, my people's herds and flocks starved, my people died. El let that happen. So even as a baby I was sinful. As a child I was sinful. As an adult I must be full of sin.'

Her eyes softened. 'Full of noise, anyway!'

ve. Sin is my nature, I know it. I can't
ly, then spoke to her face. 'But the
y father, the great God El is, my
no right to kill me, I'm not his
mu is, or Anshar. Let El kill me

me she looked admiringly. 'You're so
I said was your noise was driving the people
stop before they no longer love you.'

ll stop,' I said earnestly. 'I'll stop right away.' I covered
my mouth to show grief, put my finger to my lips,
whispered: 'Nin and Lugal did send you, didn't they? You
didn't do this of yourself.'

'Why should I? Would I dare talk to the great you this
way?'

'Exactly.' I stood and looked at her, half my height, a
girl with small brown feet and tiny toes. 'Go on, what
do Nin and Lugal say about me between themselves?
Do they talk of me all the time?'

She hesitated, but all servants eavesdrop, it's how they
live. 'They say you're not like them.'

'That's true!' I roared with laughter and she shushed
me. She whispered, 'They say, how can we teach Wotan
to be human, respectful of humans? Lugal says, if Wotan's
a half-god no task will be large enough to keep him quiet.
Nin says she has an idea.'

That was better. 'What idea?'

'I don't know. Nin is wise, the mother of women.
Perhaps she says you need a wife.'

I roared with laughter. 'What do I need a wife for? I
can have anyone!'

She bowed her head. Then she said, 'Yes. I know.' She
raised her eyes, blinking, she had dust in them. 'But you
do need a friend, Wotan. A man, even you, cannot live
alone.' She noticed or pretended to notice now the angle
of the sun, realised how the day wasted, hurried away

without a backward look. 'My mistress will r⟨...⟩
farewell. Gone. I hadn't even squeezed her ru⟨...⟩
she had much of one, skinny-shanks.

I sat quietly by the pool. I was bored.

I hummed quietly to myself. I am who I am.
change who I am, and neither could she. Some p⟨...⟩
women went by, my spirits lifted and the light came ⟨...⟩
my eyes. I smiled at them, they giggled, who needs grea⟨...⟩
encouragement, I followed their swaying hips and fragran⟨...⟩
myrtle perfume – unusual in our city, myrtle grows more
towards Bab'El – and their muted giggling led me forward
from corner to corner until I came after them along an
alleyway. At the top of mudbrick stairs leading up outside
a building, a door-curtain flapped in the evening wind
and I glimpsed a female ankle. I swept back my hair with
the palms of my hands and ran three steps to each stride
and at the top, as the door-curtain flapped down behind
me, I came into a shadowed room with a couch. At the
far end the women bit their lips, large-eyed. What makes
them do this with me? Excitement? Fear of getting caught?
Contempt for their own husbands? The older woman
asked, 'Is he really him?' I asked her name and she babbled
something, lay back hitching up her knees, but instead of
watching us the younger women drew back into another
doorway. It was hours since I'd had anyone, talking with
Nin's maid had wasted the afternoon, but this woman
didn't want to talk at all. 'Quickly,' she said, seizing my
shoulders. She'd anointed herself with fragrant oil where
it matters and she cried out like a signal at the size of me.
She slobbered kisses over my face, covering my ears with
her sweaty hands, but I hesitated for one heartbeat.

For all his lovemaking, where are Wotan's children?

I pulled her muffling hands away, heard the soft footfall
behind me, the creak of a leather sandal-strap, and rolled
aside. The unfortunate woman received in her belly-button
the sword-thrust meant for my back and lashed out with

her arms and legs in her agony, knocking my would-be assassin to his knees and springing his hand from the hilt. 'Ah,' she cried, 'Anshar, you have killed me. I'm a dead woman.' Her fingers slid and skidded on the blade, trying to pull it out.

I said his name. 'Anshar?'

Anshar smashed her face with his fist, jerked the sword into his hand. We circled the body. He flipped the sword from one hand to the other, full of pride in his strength and skill, thinking he was my brother. 'You're nothing like me,' I said. 'My eyes are the sea and my hair is the sun, but your eyes and hair are brown like the earth.' He swished the blade, stabbed forward, but I lifted the dead woman and caught the point in her ribs, jerked her to pluck the handle from Anshar's hand, threw her from the stair-door. Someone in the street shouted, surprised.

Anshar drew his knife as we circled the couch. 'My father's blood flows in you as it does in me,' he spat. 'No wife would ever dare betray my father. Come, sisters!' One of the girls in the other room tried to stick me with a pin from her hair, another jumped on my back screaming. These furies thought they were my sisters? I shook them off, snarled to frighten them away, and one fell backwards down the stairs. 'Come back,' Anshar said. He shouted insults at me. I told him I had no quarrel with him, but poor Anshar lost his nerve. He was just doing what his father told him, he simply believed in his father. 'Run away,' I said. 'Run away and live.'

Anshar jumped at me, I gripped his hand like a rock, stopped the blade a finger's width from my eye. He screamed, writhing, kicking, spitting. I could not make him understand there was no need for this, for all my strength I could not make him stop. For a moment I was red with anger and threw him away. The wall fell down and Anshar fell down with it into the street. He lay dead in the rubble with his knife in his eye. I didn't mean it to happen. The people gathering around the bodies looked up. 'I didn't mean it to happen,' I said.

'I never meant it to happen.' That night I lay on my chest on the marble slab in the temple, the bangles of the temple prostitutes jingling softly like goat-bells as they worked. My whore had the biggest breasts, I always start with the biggest, and her hips were spread wide by the birth of many children; she was holy. She sat on my bare buttocks, her oiled toes moving sensuously in my armpits while her fingers massaged my shoulders. 'I never meant it to happen,' I repeated. Through the breezy black window-holes came the noise of hammers in the night, the drum-roll that started the shift for both men and women, the flickering torchlight of rowdy building gangs working along the top of the city wall, their cries, the clank of tools, the stink of hot pitch. Netho leant back, stroked the perfumed female flesh around him, drank wine. 'These things happen, my friend,' he shrugged, yawning. He slapped someone's thigh, making her squeak and embrace him. 'Don't they, love.' She pushed his head between her breasts. 'I'll make you happen,' she murmured.

I stared at them, Netho, Pe, Sabu and Salu, all the others. I did not need friends, I had these friends. These men were my friends. Sabu and Salu were singing a marching song, we all joined in, someone held a cup beneath my lips and I drank it to the dregs, the wine dripping from my mouth as I sang the words, whatever the words were. They weren't important, this warmth of friendship was everything. The prostitutes all whispered to us what good lovers we were and tried to put themselves first and holiest, but I rolled over and kissed the painted toenails of my big-breasted one and took her, and she gasped at the feeling of being possessed by such a bull as I. 'Be born again!' She bucked her wobbling hips exquisitely, and the flood rose in me.

For all the wombs Wotan seeds, why do none spring forth with life?

I stopped. The wave fell back, my blood cooled, I shrivelled. 'Are you with child?' I asked her. 'Are you with child by me?'

'Not tonight, obviously.' Her face set hard with anger, her beautiful flesh withdrew, she stared shrewishly. 'What happened to you?' she demanded scornfully. 'Come on, keep trying.' She pointed between my legs. 'Look what's happened to it,' she cried to the other girls, 'he hasn't done anything yet!'

'I can make it do it,' Netho's girl said. She touched me but I said, 'Stop.'

She stopped, amazed. 'Don't you like it?'

I asked her, 'Have you had a child by me?' I could see by her eyes she hadn't. I asked the others who watched silently. They hadn't. I could tell.

'Happens to us all every once in a while.' Netho clapped my shoulder. 'You'll be fine tomorrow.' He put a cup of wine in each of my hands and made me drink, then we sang as we drank, and Sabu and Salu climbed around the room without touching the floor, and the girls danced and clapped and rubbed themselves against me and clutched my shrivelled penis with ardent cries but nothing happened. I sat while they slept. In the morning would come the usual complaints from the citizens of Enoch about our noise. *Why do none spring forth with life?* I covered my ears.

Before dawn I took my sword, stepped over the girls without looking at them, slapped my men's bodies with the flat of the blade. 'Wake up!' The room stank of spent lust and sour wine. I pulled down the curtains and hangings, let the air in, the clean air of the plain. 'There's work to do.' They grumbled, 'Work?' I cried, 'War is work! Our city has walls, we can't be attacked. It's time to go out!' I raised my voice to a roar. 'Time for war!'

And so I took war to the Bull of Heaven. He had shown me what war was, now I showed him. I and my friends and whoever would follow us marched from the walls of Enoch and the great cedar gates were closed after us, we spread out over the plain until we came among the *uru-barra* of Bab'El and burned them and my men raped the widows and sent them back as slaves, and the flocks and herds, and the grain in the granaries, and the boats in the canals, everything. Netho thought it would be good war to burn the fields too, the crops dry under the summer sun, and the burning crops joined the smoky columns of burning villages into one great line of billowing smoke to cause terror at our coming. The smoke drifted towards Bab'El that shone in the sun, then the shining city fell dark under the lid of smoke. Twilight fell at midday and we heard the people wailing and shrieking as we marched close. They ran like ants atop their crumbling unfinished wall. They tried to block the gaps with timber but we burnt the timber. They ran in the streets but we cut them down. Their wives offered their daughters, my men took them, their screams rose like offerings to Heaven, and the blood of Bab'El ran brown on the stones. 'Bring me the Bull of Heaven!' I roared. 'Bring him to me!' They were here, the man who called himself my father and his sons Lahmu and Lahamu who called themselves my brothers, I fought my way to them, I found them. Apsu lunged at me from the steps but his two sons wrestled him back. Screaming women ran around us, dogs barking, a cart fell over with a crash. Netho jumped forward to please me, swung his sword at Lahamu, but Lahamu turned the blow, turned Netho's back, and his sword struck through Netho's chest like a red tongue. Netho stared at me. He lifted himself on tiptoe. He opened his mouth, and he died. Netho died.

I jumped forward, jumped over him, I swung at Lahamu, I knocked Lahamu's sword from side to side as I leapt up step by step below him as he retreated upwards,

I cut Lahamu to pieces while he still lived and fought, and on the top step I cut his head from his shoulders and kicked it down.

I stood on the ruins of the tower. Apsu had fled with Lahmu, neither could be found. The king of Bab'El was my slave, no stronger than a child in my hand.

Bab'El was mine. I had won Bab'El for the power and glory of King Lugal and Ya.

I sat by Netho's body until the worm fastened on him, I buried him with my own hands in the earth to become earth. I let my men lead the old king of Bab'El downriver on a yoke and hand him to King Lugal in triumph outside the walls of Enoch. I had no heart for it. I walked alone to the city and the gates were thrown open for me because of all the slaves and wealth I'd sent ahead of me; the people watched me curiously, falling silent, as I walked between the sacred curly-topped gateposts – always open, gateposts without gates – and entered the temple precinct, and there I made offerings of flowers, boatloads of flowers, to the sacred flock of rams of the Ya'nna.

I found my friend Pe with my friends Sabu and Salu bragging of their prowess to the temple prostitutes, pulled them off. 'Come away.'

My friends followed me.

I sought Apsu and Lahmu in the great city of Jared, in Ur that in its pride calls itself simply City, and their kings knew my name and greeted me with gifts. The gods of their temples were punted in great arks along the canals and rivers to pay homage to the gods of Enoch, and be rewarded with trade. No city dared shelter the Bull of Heaven. Every village I found that had sheltered him, I burnt. I drove him beyond the crops into the wilderness. Every tumbledown reed hut in the marshes that carried his smell, I burnt. Through the flames and smoke Pe and Sabu and Salu followed behind me, trying to keep up with me. Each night they fell down exhausted among the great rustling stands of berdi-reed, each night they dreamt of Enoch, home. In the endless shallow marshland Pe lost his love of swimming; Sabu and Salu could not run in the sticky mud. Finally they all said to me, 'Lord, it's time to return home.' But I didn't hear them, I walked where I smelt the Bull of Heaven. Still they followed me. They were silent for days, or talked of nothing but women, wine, the comradeship of beer, home. Finally they were simply silent. But they followed.

This is how Pe died: he drowned. I'm always first, I didn't see Lahmu hiding in the reeds. He let Sabu and Salu go past. But Pe was last, and Lahmu threw him down in the water and stood on him, and we heard Pe's arms and legs splashing and the sound came from all around us in the reeds, and then our own splashing was all we heard, our voices calling his name, and when we found Pe he was silent and dead, face down. I could not breathe life back into his body. The Underworld had taken his spirit; he had crossed the river that carries us underground, and not even Pe the fish could swim fast enough against that mighty flood.

The worm fastened on him, and I buried Pe in the earth to become earth.

This is how Sabu and Salu died: they died running. I saw Apsu on horseback, I ran after him, his horse galloped away, his cloak flew, he stared over his shoulder with his spittle flying. Far behind me Lahmu on a second horse galloped from the canebreaks where he had been hiding. His spear killed Salu without warning, then Lahmu set after Sabu who ran away faster than the horse over the flat level ground of the plain, but as you know Sabu's chest was not so deep, he began to gasp, and the tip of the spear inched closer behind him. Sabu's heart was heavy for his brother, and the spear-tip almost touched his spine as he ran. 'Run to me!' I shouted, I bounded like a lion towards him, but Sabu's eyes were blinded by tears for

144

Salu who was dead, and the spear-tip caught him and ran through his heart and Sabu fell running, and I believe his legs ran even though he was dead. I leapt over him, I leapt the spear, I leapt on Lahmu on horseback and stood up with him and lifted him and crushed his head and heart in my hands, but Sabu was dead, and Salu was dead, and I could not call them back.

The worm fastened on them, and I buried them together in the earth to become earth.

After seven days I set off again after the Bull of Heaven, and there was not a sound of him, no scent, nor any place he had been. I don't know where I went; at last I went home. The gates of the Kullaba were shut against me. I'd brought the people booty and plunder beyond measure, and now they feared such a man as I had become would take it all back, and destroy what I had created, that they enjoyed without me. Such a man as I was not a shepherd to my people, my followers died while I lived: such a man as I was not wise, nor wise to be with. I sat in the dust, gathering my strength. I'd destroy the gates, I'd destroy them all, and let them live without walls, if they prized safety.

But Nin came out, her finger to her lips, and took me to a small room in the Ya'nna, and I slept.

This is what they say happened. Nin came to my room where I lay sleeping, and from her dress she took the small curved piece of horn such as women use to mix unguents and powders for their beauty, rich colours for their lips and nipples, that their skilled hands apply as the thin black arch of an eyebrow, the rosy passion in a cheek, even the drop of poison that makes eyes bright as lamps with the appearance of desire. With the side of the horn she scraped the night-sweat from my skin as I twitched and mumbled with unaccustomed sleep and dreams – some say she'd drugged me; she dripped my sweat from the horn into a small patterned pot with a stopper, and then she stole away in the dark; and I never knew, except what I heard later.

This is what I heard. Nin walked from the crops and canals of civilisation into the desert towards the hills. At an oasis near the hills she knelt, took the stopper from the bottle and let my sweat drip on the dust. The dust dissolved, forming clay, the clay rose up quivering with life without shape, wet clay shimmering in reflection of the sun and Nin's prayer. 'Great God, create a man who is Wotan's equal, a friend to be as like him as his own reflection, his second self, a storm-god for a storm-god. Let them fight together, let them be friends together. But let them leave my city in peace!' She turned away and did not look behind her, but behind her lay a man fresh-born in the dust.

That's what they say, that's what I heard. A wild man called Kidu living in the wilderness, a man with a child's heart and a child's innocence, a child with a man's strength. Of course I didn't believe it. I didn't believe almost everything in those days. I was just a child myself, knowing almost nothing of the mystery and vastness of the world around us, I was blind, deaf, dumb. But I would know; I'd learn, and I'd begin to see. But for now I awoke in the temple cell and hated my wakefulness, my unsleeping habitation of myself. I sat with my head in my hands day after day, shouting at the temple prostitutes when they attempted their caresses, I ate nothing, drank nothing. I covered the windows and lived in the dark, I saw no one, not even my own body. Weeks passed, months, then light flooded my tiny cell. Nin's voice spoke.

'Wotan, there's a man living in the wilderness. His hair's as long as yours, longer. People say he's stronger than you.' I did not respond. 'He eats grass and runs with the deer, he drinks the milk of deer and wolves. He's strong as a lion.'

'I'm stronger than a lion.'

'Speak to me.' But I was silent. She sat beside me, murmured, 'This wild man terrifies the shepherds because he's master of the animals that kill their flocks.' Master of animals, that's one of the titles of a king. 'He's king of the wilderness just as you are a king of the cities.'

I groaned. 'What do they call him?'

'Kidu.'

'Did he name himself?'

'No. It's what they call him.'

I shrugged. 'Send one of your temple whores to him, let her use his name and take him. When the animals smell woman on him, civilisation, they'll run away, and he'll be king of nothing. Like me.'

'You're so sad.' She touched my shoulder. 'We're only human.' She tried again. 'I'll send Lalla to him, shall I?' Provocative Nin. She knew the big-breasted one had been my favourite, but I shrugged, and she went away with a small hiss of irritation. She didn't give up.

This is what Nin told me. 'Kidu was drinking on all fours like an animal at oasis, and he saw Lalla's reflection in the water behind him. As he turned she bared her breasts and pulled his face between them crying his name, and he pushed his body between her legs and possessed her at the waterside, and by possessing Kidu and his name her skill conquered him, which no man's strength could do.' She paused provocatively, but I shrugged, and again she hissed. 'Lalla-Kidu has taught him the art of women, he smells of perfume and the city. He's besotted with her.'

'I pity him.'

'Go to him. He's lost his strength, his swiftness. He's lost everything he loved, the animals, the wilderness, he's nothing but a man.'

'I lost my friends too.' I turned away from her. 'Bring him to the city.' She stared, alarmed, but I said, 'Bring him to the city.'

Nin went away and sent word, and Lalla-Kidu brought him to Enoch. At first the gates were shut against him, people thought he was me – I overheard the prostitutes and women chattering excitedly that he looked just like me. Then the gates were opened and I tried to glimpse him from the window but saw only the throng of ordinary people; perhaps he was only ordinary, meek, law-abiding after all. I heard he'd been brought into the temple precinct but saw nothing, then heard a babble of voices. 'He's the spit of Wotan!' Some claimed he was shorter than I, some said taller, some said he was heavier of bone, and some cried out that he had a head of hair golden like wheat, but however hard I strained I couldn't see. Then the voices came inside, and I heard Nin's voice raised in the sanctuary, 'You are the strongest here, you are the storm. Eat this bread, it is the staff of life, drink this wine, it is the blood of the land.' Sounds of eating and drinking, then a wild voice bellowed for more. I crept from the darkness and stood well back from the doorway, staring through. The wild one ate whole loaves of bread in his mouth, as many as I when I was strong, and I saw him drink seven cups of wine. His face shone, he swept back his long blond hair with the palms of his hands just as I did, and eyed the women with the light in his eye I knew so well – I knew exactly what he was thinking, and so did they. The wild one smiled with his whole face.

I stepped into the room and everyone but Nin and he fell back. I grabbed Lalla-Kidu, staring her mate in the eye, and bared her breasts to claim her.

He roared, struck at me. We grappled, I lifted him, the tables broke. Our arms and legs locked, straining, our muscles stood out like stones. Sweat slid and dripped like oil from our skin, droplets sprayed from our bodies with the force of our blows. He thrust his shoulder against my groin but could not lift me; I twisted him over my hip but could not throw him. We fell against the walls and the stones cracked, the wooden doorposts broke, the doors fell down, in the open air we rolled on the sanctuary steps. In the sunlit courtyard we grunted like bulls, our sweat white with dust, eyes glaring, we struggled and fell and rose; our shoulders splintered the *mezuza*, gateposts of the holy Ya'nna, the gateposts without gates, and as I stared in horror the wild man lifted me easily above his head to throw me down. In the moment before my fall I clutched his hair in my hands and put my mouth close, I spoke his name into his ear.

'Kidu.' I possessed his name.

He stopped, eyes searching. I hooked my foot under his arm, slipped down, braced my back against his back, and threw him.

Kidu fell and the ground shook. I stood to my knees in the earth from the force of my throw, the victor. But the crowd was silent. Not a word.

Kidu leapt up and gripped my wrist. He looked into my eyes. 'Wotan.'

I saw the shattered gateposts of the temple. There was nothing we could do to repair such sacrilege. Kidu and I ran from the silent city.

'Your face is white as salt,' Kidu says. 'You look like death.' Day after day he licks the salt sweat from my face as an animal would, closer than a brother, closer than a twin, my flesh. In Kidu's company I am entire, a full man. Without him I'm a broken sword. Kidu's my son and my father, there's no gap between us, he's everything a man can be: he's me. 'They say you're mad, Wotan.'

'Am I?'

'The people say so.'

With wide-open eyes I watch the sun set, the rising stars wheel in their patterns. 'The people of the city know nothing.'

'The city's your place.'

149

'Nowhere's my place. Not there. Not here.'

The dawn rises behind Kidu. 'When you were silent we were happy. You didn't think. We hunted, ate, drank water from our hands. Happy. Now, words.' He crouches, watches. 'Why do you hate women?'

'I adore women!'

'No. You take women, but even as your body penetrates her body, in your mind you hold her at arm's length. When you're closest you're most distant. You don't let her penetrate *you*. You don't give love or allow yourself to receive love.'

'Other men don't talk like this.' Incredibly, Kidu embarrasses me, my face flushes red, angry red. 'What do you know about love? I heard you're just a clay man!'

Kidu slaps himself, hard. 'This is flesh. It hurts. I love Lalla-Kidu.'

'You aren't serious. Her? She's mine. I had her a thousand times.'

'That's what I mean. You don't love her. You don't think of her all day, all night.'

'You think of her all day, all night?'

Kidu says simply: 'I love her.'

'Fight you for her.'

'She loves me.' Kidu grins, shakes his head. 'You'll beat me, but you'll never change her mind.'

I've won every battle I ever fought; I've lost everything important, so Kidu says. I sat staring at the rising sun until it fell. Kidu shook my shoulder and I realised I had been asleep not awake. 'I had a dream,' I said. 'I was dead. I was dead for ever.' Kidu performed backward somersaults along the shore of the oasis, the wind blowing dust from his hands and feet. 'Why should you be immortal, Wotan? You're just the son of the god of a particular people. He's given you strength to do things while you live.'

'Yes, to kill people. And I can do backward somersaults.' I backflipped half a dozen times, better than him.

'Not quite as good.' Kidu gripped my elbow. 'He hasn't given you love, that's all.'

'Who?'

'Your God.' Kidu stripped off and plunged into the water, called back cheerfully from the ripples. 'He's given you the cities, victories, the power to enslave and let loose, to be a beacon or make darkness fall, given you all any man dreams of having, made you an example to all of us. All mankind. All the children want to be like you.' But I shook my head. *For all his lovemaking where are Wotan's children? For all the wombs Wotan seeds, why do none spring forth with life?* I turned and walked away from Kidu's cheerful splashing into the desert. Almost at once a shadow moved against the brilliant colours of the sunset, and I knew I was hunted. Perhaps the moment of my death was coming.

Stones clattered in the wadi that fed the oasis, sounds and shapes moved around me, then against the red glare I faced the shaggy silhouette of a lion rising up, the largest lion I'd ever seen: I smelt my blood on its breath, heard the click of its claws like knives on the desert stones as it padded forward, I sensed the weight and velocity of its body. I felt at my waist, no sword, no dagger. The lion's eyes glowed, seeing me, it smelt me, it circled me so that I was the one silhouetted against the sun. I pulled my strength into me, my heart hammered, the sweat poured down my body, the veins stood out in my neck and like ropes along my muscles. But the lion did not leap. Instead as it padded forward its claws fell silent, sheathed.

The lion pressed its head foursquare against my chest and purred soft as a priest's cat. I heard its tail swish in the darkness as I stroked the harsh tufts of its ears, I felt its hot breath blowing from its nostrils down my legs. It belched and stank, its mane ragged with vermin, completely a lion, and it purred louder the more I stroked it. Kidu's voice came. 'Master of animals. You are master of animals. You're king of the cities, Wotan, and of my wilderness too.' He held up a torch of burning bitumen, illuminating the rocks of the wadi, throwing back the light of a hundred eyes. Bears, lizards, a hopping eagle, I don't know what else was here. I heard the growl of a lioness, the slither of snakes, serpents, even the cheerful bells of goats. I looked calmly around me at the firelit shadows. I'd brought them here to me, even the baleful wolves. I was the centre. Of what? What had changed? 'If you have love,' Kidu called, 'you have everything.'

The lion reared up, dropped its paws heavily on my shoulders, stood erect. You've seen this scene commemorated on a hundred stelae, some of them carved immense into the faces of mountains: the king of beasts acknowledging the king of men. In real life it lasted only a moment, then the animals scattered around us, wolves leaping, the eagle flying up startled, the bears chasing the goats and the goats mixed up with the sheep and the lions going after them all. I stood in the darkness lit only by Kidu's flickering light. He stood beside me.

'Now you do not know,' Kidu said, 'whether or not you are immortal.'

'This I know.' I sat with Kidu in the desert, empty dust from horizon to horizon. 'Everything we do is a breath of wind. Nothing lasts longer than a moment. There's got to be something more. Something *big*.'

'How big? Even bigger than your—' He glanced between my legs.

'Something to be remembered by. Bigger. Biggest. More than building walls and killing people.'

'There aren't many things bigger than that.' Kidu lifted my sword, which an ordinary man cannot do, and sliced the air with it. 'What shall we do? I hate talking. I want to see Lalla.'

'Then go alone.' He paled. I threatened, 'I'll search alone.'

'Without me? Where?'

I said the only place I could think of. 'Where I came from.' I gestured northwards – checking by the sun, for the great dustbowl looks the same in every direction. Even standing I saw only featureless dust, but by leaping on Kidu's shoulders I made out pale distant fangs along the northern horizon, mountaintops, and a shimmering green immensity beneath them stretching upwards towards them. 'Beyond the cedar forest.'

'There's no *beyond* the cedar forest.' Kidu grunted, swaying under my weight. 'It's endless. It covers the world in every direction.' I jumped down, lifted him up. 'Oh,' he said, seeing. 'It's true. It's there. The Land of the Living.' I remembered Eve splashing the shining water. 'The Garden of Life at the mouth of the rivers, where the Faraway lives for ever.' Kidu sighed, not really believing it, and I called up to him, 'Noah the Faraway, the man the great God El made immortal.' I dropped Kidu down and we both stood looking at the bare dusty northern horizon again, flat as far as the eye could see. But we'd seen more. By jumping as high as we could, we saw it again. For a heartbeat we glimpsed the mountains rise into view each time, then the desert pulled our feet down. 'I was born out of the mountain,' Kidu said longingly. 'Nin confessed it to me.'

So Nin had told Kidu he was a foundling of the temple – mothers in desperate straits often left their babies, living clay, on the steps or between the holy gateposts, where no harm dare befall an infant. But I knew the truth. Nin the priestess of Ishtar, the Queen of Love, had made Kidu out of my sweat and a pinch of the living earth, because her religion was true.

'My mother was afraid of the cedar forest,' I said. 'Tia was afraid of the great trees.' We were walking without

153

thinking, beginning to run towards the city for the things we'd need. 'In the cedar forest she knew there are karibu-lions – lions with wings – that soar above the treetops, and demons that change shape—'

'Demons?' Kidu laughed, panting as he ran.

'That's what her people call them. Gallu-demons drift like mist between the treetrunks. Other demons, more, worse, uglier than you can imagine.'

'Can we fight demons? Can we kill them?' Kidu leapt a ditch. We were coming close to Enoch, the farmers scattered around us in the fields. 'If you fight demons your name will endure—'

'My name will last for ever!' I roared.

'Everyone'll remember you, Wotan who fought the demons.' He added, 'Us. Kidu too. What's your plan? Will you ask Noah if you're immortal like him? Or is it just fighting and killing?'

I remembered my mother whispering to me. 'The greatest demon is Huwawa.'

'Hawwah?' He'd misheard me, Hawwah's the canaanite name for Eve.

'Huwawa the dragon, guardian of the forest, appointed by El.'

Kidu skidded, stopped. 'Then your father's to be found in the forest?'

I called over my shoulder, 'My father the great God lives in the mountains.' I don't know where the story came from, but everyone knows it's true. Mountains are the home of storms. The mountain fell on the plain to make life: the plain of Shem is the remnant of a fallen mountain.

Kidu called, 'What are you trying to do? Make your name live for ever, or attract God's attention?' But his voice grew faint as I ran ahead. 'Both,' I said under my breath, and Kidu heard me. His face shone, he sprinted and caught me up, we ran as one. 'A journey in search of God!' he laughed. 'The greatest scheme I ever heard!'

I ran in silence. Only one Voice could tell me the truth of who my father was, whose son I truly am; and that Voice lived in the mountains beyond the cedar forest.

I beat my fists on the great cedars I'd had felled to make the gates of Enoch. King Lugal appeared on the battlement, then his hand ordered the gates opened, and I greeted him on one knee, head bowed. 'You've come back,' he said.

'Am I welcome?'

'There are no wars at present, Wotan.' We walked in the town and I saw buildings knocked down and the bazaar twice its original size, ten times as busy with Isin cloth, Ur jugs, slaves, more pottery from Jared, reed boats double-moored at the quay unloading lapis from one of Noah's tribes in Afghanistan, gold, tin and cornelian stones from Meluhha, seafish and pearls from the Red Sea (all our seas are called Red, all our peoples being the descendants of Adam, the Red Man) and in return dead bodies respectfully spiced and wrapped were loaded aboard to be sailed to the Isle of the Blessed for interment there in the land of the Twin Waters, to awaken to eternal life when the Pearl shall be found between fresh water and salt and brought into the sun. But the oppressive city heat of Enoch and the walls pressing against my shoulders stifled me, the haggling of the canaans sawed at my ears. 'There's no glory for me here.' I watched the shrouded bodies floating downriver on the boats of the dead, the *magilum*. 'I should have stamped my name on each brick of these walls I built, carved my name on each trunk of the gates, and been remembered.' The king muttered, afraid of me. I told him my plan. 'I'll fight the dragon Huwawa, and search for El my father in the mountains.'

'You won't stay?' Lugal's face lit up. 'Ask me for whatever you need, it's yours.'

I said: 'Give orders to the armourers to cast axe heads weighing three talents, and sword blades weighing seven talents, and hammer them hard and sharp enough to cut a hair falling in the wind. Send men to cut willow for the axe handles, and to Elam to fetch their special wood for a bow that only my strength can pull.'

'And my strength,' Kidu said.

'It shall be done as you say.'

All night I watched the armourers at their work: with me clamour returned to the city of Enoch, and sleepless nights. The leather bellows heaved, molten metal ran like shooting stars, sparks set thatch alight all over the city, the smiths' hammers rang ceaselessly on the cooling metal; and Nin came to me. The high priestess of Ishtar, wife of Ya, came to see me while Kidu slept like a baby.

She murmured, 'You don't know what you're doing.'

'I'll fight Huwawa, I'll learn whether I'm immortal, I'll find God. Only by finding God will I know my name.' I glanced at her. 'I know what I'm doing.'

'Your name is Wotan.'

'No, that was the name claimed for me by the Bull of Heaven, not given me by God.'

'What gain is there finding your name if you lose your life?'

I thought about it. 'Peace.'

She gave such a bark of laughter that the armourers looked round. Nin asked, presciently, 'You, Wotan? What will you ever know of peace? You aren't made for peace. Everything about you's made for war. Your strength. Your lust. Impose your will wherever you wish, rule all our cities as king. You can force the people to follow you, to worship you if you want. Children are taught to pray to you already as one of the gods. Songs of praise are sung to you. You know it.'

'I've never known a moment of peace since I came to Enoch,' I said. 'Not since you found me by the river.'

'Didn't you know? It wasn't I who found you.'

I cursed a clumsy armourer who burnt himself yelling on his tongs, sat back. 'What? Not you?' I shrugged irritably. 'You were the first person of importance, the only one who mattered.'

'No. Eve saw you first, not I.'

'Eve?'

'I'd never have found you. I'd already walked by, so had the others. It was she who called us back.' She touched my arm lightly. 'Didn't she tell you?'

'Why?'

'You're a fool on a foolish quest, Wotan. The answer to what you seek's here in front of your eyes, not in the trees and mountains. She knows it.'

'Eve doesn't know me.'

'She knows you perfectly. Your courage carries you too far, as always, and makes you . . .' she hesitated diplomatically, 'too much of a man.'

'Stupid, you mean?' I snorted, angry now. '*She* calls me stupid too.'

'And you haven't killed her? Why? You'd kill anyone who said you were stupid. But you haven't killed her, chopped her head off, thrown her through a wall, have you?'

I shook my head.

Nin said: 'Why not, I wonder?'

I didn't know. Nin always does this to me; always knows where to strike at my heart. 'I can't have children,' I blurted. 'No sons.' Instead of the opposite my tongue blurted the truth, which anyone would conceal. 'I'm the strongest of men, Nin, but I'm not much of a man!' I writhed in shame in her arms, covered my head. 'I can't be born again in anyone.'

She held me as tight as she could, hid my face in her shoulder. The armourers tapped delicately at the cooling metal, began grinding the blades on stones from the mountains. Soon the handles and hilts would be fitted. It was nearly dawn, and Nin looked into my eyes. 'When you go, say goodbye to her.'

'Who?'

'You know.'

'Eve? Your *maid*? Why?'

Nin patted my head and stood. 'Because,' she said. 'Because.' She walked away through the shadows of growing daylight, then turned when I thought she'd gone, her face pale, and called to me. 'Don't be a stupid fool. She's a slave but she was a princess of her people. Let her talk sense into you. Your courage takes you too far. You have too much to lose, more to lose than you know. Huwawa's a dragon, one of the serpents of ancient times, greater than those we know now. The forest is his world, it stretches to the stars in every direction. He hears each footstep among the trees, the birth of each seed, the death of each leaf, the fall of a sparrow.' But I turned away angrily, speaking to the armourer who'd blistered his hands. She called: 'Remember, you must climb seven mountains, and Huwawa will fight you with seven weapons.' But I was more interested in the balance of my swords, and hefted the axe.

'Cut stone, that would, lord.' The chief armourer tried to lift the weapon he'd forged. I swung the edge of the axe easily into the stone block that had sharpened it, cutting the block in two like a rotten wooden stump. I looked round proudly for witnesses, but Nin was gone.

With all the fuss of going from the city I forgot to speak to Eve, remembered her, hesitated, then left Kidu standing at the city gate and returned to her. Eve stood in her usual little mudbrick room with her eyes cast down, as always. Skinny as always. I cleared my throat to speak and she turned her back on me, didn't want to speak. I said her name. She shook her head. She hated me.

What did she think I was going to do? Did she think she'd stop me going by not talking to me? I said farewell, turned on my heel and left.

'Don't!' She ran after me fiercely, plucked at my elbow

like a fierce little sparrow, trying to turn me. 'You nearly died in my arms. Don't do this to me.' Her eyes filled with tears.

Her? I'd hardly thought of her. Did she think I'd die, was she afraid, was she trying to sap my strength? 'Goodbye,' I repeated. I shook her off, forgot her almost at once, people adoring me were throwing down flowers from upstairs windows into the street as I departed. The stalks caught in the mighty Elam bow I wore over my shoulder, the petals bobbed and swayed around my head like a garland. Then I heard Eve's footsteps running, her voice calling a curse, a curse of her people I suppose. 'If you do this may you burn in Hell!' Hell meant nothing to me. I lengthened my stride and walked with Kidu from the gateway of the city, which was flanked by the gigantic statues of gallu-demons I'd carved, lions, dragons, dragons entwined with serpents, animals with the heads of men and men with the heads of animals; and the last sound we heard was Eve's tiny high voice screaming after us from the battlements, 'Damn you to damnation for ever, Wotan, may you burn in Hell, burn in Hell for ever if you awaken the Serpent! Don't go. Don't.' Her cries faded behind us, softening with distance. 'Don't go. Don't go.'

'Told you,' Kidu said as we ran. 'God didn't give you the gift of love.'

I ran ahead of Kidu: bare is back without friend behind it. Our swords strapped on our backs shook in their gold scabbards as we ran, the hilts jutting higher than our heads. The flowers fell away as we ran faster. Time after time I loosed an arrow from my Elam bow and we sprinted after its fall beyond the horizon. Enoch shrank behind us, we passed Isin by, saw Bab'El as night fell: in three days and nights we ran as far as the trade caravans travel in sixty days. With long strides we followed the great silty curve of the Buranun, which I remembered from my childhood as

Perath, and came northwards to the sandbank I remembered. The village was gone, it was thorns; we camped on the sand and everything so large to me as a child was now small. The Perath was small, the fish small, the trees that I remembered were all gone, only dusty plain remained. But in the night my nose twitched while Kidu slept, I smelt cedar on the wind from the north, and thought I heard the voices of the children playing, and my mother calling me to drink at her breast. I blinked and her bones were dust in which my feet stood, her voice the wind. The wind breathed softly from the north, calling me to the scent of growing trees and snowy mountains.

At dawn Kidu and I ran through the stumps of the felled forest standing like rotten yellow teeth along the banks of the Perath, the canaans all gone south to the cities or north, following with their axes the retreat of the virgin woodland. Sometimes I heard the beat of blades, the creak and crash of falling timber, caught the fresh perfumed tang of logging work, saw trunks flowing with the river, but we did not stop. The day grew very hot and insects swarmed above the swirling waters. One by one the trees closed around us and the river flickered between them, then we saw only the dense green tangle of the woodland, an impenetrable mass of undergrowth wherever light penetrated. Even we could not run fast; we cut back to the river; and we stopped, staring, feeling no larger than insects. I was a baby, my mother clutched me in her arms, and I remembered the green hills.

I whispered: '*I remember.*'

Ahead of us rose two hills like green breasts holding the river like sweat between them. On each hill was planted a tall gatepost, curling inward horn-like at the top, like the gateposts that guard the entrance to the temple, so that only the holy and pure in heart may enter between them. 'The gateway to the cedar forest,' I said, and my voice echoed. The hills were too steep to climb, the only way forward led between them. 'Let's go round,' Kidu said. 'There must be a way round.' He shivered like a child, then followed where I led as I walked towards the gateposts. Silence fell, the waters made no sound, noise was sucked from the world: my footsteps were heard however softly I trod, my beating heart came loud as a hammered anvil to distant ears, and my breath roared.

'You know me,' I whispered. 'I come to meet one who calls itself Huwawa, a dragon of this world.' There was no reply to my challenge. I pushed forward.

The cold of the valley took our breath, it blew around our heads like white smoke as we passed between gateposts, and the river swirled hot at our knees. We shivered and sweated, pulling ourselves along by the tree roots that hung down like great fingers grasping the waters. Kidu cried out. Ahead of us a gap in the solid mass of trees looked like a mouth opening in the forest. 'Don't be afraid,' I said. 'El will protect us.' Amazing; the first time in my life I'd not trusted my own strength, asking El's protection.

'Afraid?' Kidu shuddered. 'Me? I'm you, aren't I?'

'El's made me strong,' I lied, no stronger than a moment ago. 'I called on my father, and He answered. El is with us.'

I scrambled up the tree roots, lifting Kidu after me, and the green mouth widened around us, gusted fragrant cedar breath over us. Not really a mouth; a huge path beaten smooth through the forest, a path as wide as the river, old as the river. No stumps grew in it; like a green artery it stretched silently ahead of us. From time to time other paths branched inward or outward, green veins shrinking to points further than my eye could see in the endless forest. I smelt dung. But I turned neither to the right nor the left, climbing uphill all the time as the invisible sun sank beyond the treetops and darkness fell.

I cut branches for a fire and we watched the sparks rise

into the black vault of trees. There were no stars; everything was trees. 'The forest's one vast tree,' Kidu whispered, 'and we're inside it.'

I kept watch, and he slept.

In the darkest hour of the night a leaf stirred. A twig broke. A shape skittered through the firelight, then another, now others no larger than pieces of torn bread, or small plates. They gathered playfully, skittering on small stiff legs that rattled across the dry leaves. 'Kidu,' I called. One ran over him and he sat, swearing, then leapt up. 'Don't hurt them.' I picked one up, grinned. 'It looks like a sort of—'

'Cockroach,' Kidu said. 'Hate 'em.'

'Crab.' I peered at the tiny waving claws. 'Crab-cockroaches.' It clicked its pincers, stabbed suddenly and pinched my finger, drawing blood. 'Sharp.'

'They stink. Kill 'em.' Kidu yawned, lay down again, but his bed crunched. A dark mass of the little creatures sprang up around him, swarming over him, then more clattered and clicked from the darkness into the firelight, flowing over the fire like a tide, a fiery tide bursting into flame from the heat of the fire. They swarmed over Kidu as he sprang to his feet, outlining his shape in stars of flame as he clawed and clutched himself. More leapt up my body, pincers stabbing. I brushed them away, brushed them from him, and as one Kidu and I leapt against the treetrunks, clawing our way up the smooth boles to the branches. From there we stared down at the ruin of our camp. Huwawa was winning already. Our swords were useless. Quickly I jumped down, grabbed a burning branch from the fire, scattered the disgusting creatures with the flame; those that got too close were turned to flame themselves, and rushed squealing up the trees just as we had done, illuminating the clearing with an eerie green light as they burned. One by one they fell down, blackened, and our feet crunched on charcoal. No more came.

'The first obstacle. We're alive.' I clapped Kidu's shoulder cheerfully. 'Sleep well.' I roared at the top of my voice, 'Come to us, Huwawa! I'll fight Huwawa himself! Is Huwawa afraid to fight?' But Kidu didn't sleep.

In the morning we climbed the second pass. Rocks groaned, sliding, then plummeted down on us from the hilltop, making the sky dark, striking the river with such force that the waves threatened to wash us away, but we lived.

'D'you see him?' Kidu whispered as we went forward, pointing along the empty path. 'A smiling man with his hands outspread in welcome.' He walked ahead, reached out as though his hand was grasped, exchanged greetings with the air; but as he turned smiling to call me, his hand pulled something accidentally between us, a shape like a man made of water. It hissed, knowing it was seen, and solidified. From its backside hung a red tail tipped with a spike, a scorpion man – the creature Eve called a demon. It snarled, its body made flesh, colour, blood, snarling like a lost soul; its tail rose up, stabbed down on Kidu, but I said: 'Stop.' I raised the palms of my hands, pulled them towards my eyes so that it looked at my eyes. I am the master of animals.

'Die,' I said. It shrieked and snarled, stabbed itself with its own sting, and died. With my dagger I cut off its head anyway.

Again I smelt dung, as though some great creature observed us, and walked around us behind the trees.

The third pass we found blocked with boulders already fallen, a slimy dam cascading with water; as we climbed the loose rocks fell away, but we scrambled to the top, and lived.

I pointed at a tall tree fallen clear across the path. On one side lay the roots, on the other side the treetop; between them the great length of trunk was squashed flat, its fibres crushed no thicker than skin, a yellow line oozing sap across the sole of a great footprint. I jumped down, clambered up the far side, pointed out the clawmarks. 'Keeping ahead of us.'

At the fourth pass birds attacked us from the sky, pecking our eyes with their beaks. They clawed our shoulders with their talons, and the wind from their wings almost blew us away; but we did not turn back, and we lived.

I won't tell you of my fight with the griffon-demon – a grinning gargoyle face and a worm's tongue – my dagger was not enough. I drew my sword for the first time and chopped the creature like meat, and it groaned as it crawled in its blood as though this was not the first suffering it knew, nor the greatest, and died.

I cut off its head and we heard a great roar like thunder in the sky, and the treetops roared like a waterfall as breath gusted over them. Ahead of us a great turd of dung as big as a house lay across the path, still steaming. We climbed over and jumped down the far side.

The fifth pass – I forget, even I was tired; the sixth pass began in a swirling pool at the foot of a sheer stark cliff, no waterfall, and no way up. I pointed down. 'The water comes up from below.' I dived into the freezing meltwater, swam deep through the shafts of light, swam against the current into the dark. Rocks bumped my head, I kicked down, the water pushed me back like a hand. My chest tightened, water snorted into my nose. I calmed myself and swam; tiny daylights swam rippling above me in the darkness. I kicked up into a cave, pulled myself out on a boulder. Above me great slabs of rock leant against each other as if caught in the act of falling, and cracks in the clifftop high above made the daylights. Kidu surfaced, gasping, and I plucked him out. We hugged each other for warmth.

We climbed the length of the cave, along beaches, along narrow ledges, sometimes hanging by our fingers from cracks; the river swept past us like a vast serpent sliding downhill, the daylights gleaming like silver scales on the flow. Almost silent on its journey; but the rock trembled with the river's power. Sometimes caverns opened over us like temples, once we found the remains of a fire, gnawed bones. Then green light grew ahead of us, the sixth exit barred by the seventh gate. This final holy gateway was wound about with copper chains, each gatepost topped with copper flames. Kidu shook his head, afraid. 'I'm not afraid!' I said; but he was I, and knew the truth.

I touched the gate, the flames went out, the chains fell, the gate swung open.

We walked through into the heart of the forest. Ahead of us the land rose steeply towards a hill like a green pyramid of treetops, and at its peak grew the largest cedar I ever saw, ancient, its roots struck down like great serpents into the rock of the mountain. The branches of the tree were hung with fruit like offerings, and great rings of gold, sacrificial knives of obsidian and copper, and golden fleeces such as the Zadok of the canaanites wears, all shining in the sun. High above the branches and gifts, where the trunk seemed almost ready to touch the sky, the peak of the tree was wreathed in pale drifting clouds.

Kidu bent back his head. 'It's beautiful,' he said.

I said: 'I know how to get Huwawa's attention.'

I climbed the hill to the base of the tree, unlimbered my axe, spat on my hands. As I swung my axe into the growing wood a howl rippled through the forest. With my axe I chopped the tree with great blows so that Kidu covered his ears against the noise, and shut his eyes against the woodchips flying out, until a voice said: 'Enough!'

I rested my axe lightly on my shoulder. The dragon that came down from the tree was very large, sinuously unwinding itself from among the gifts and branches, separating itself from the trunk and standing on many legs as he came down, claws sheathed so that the tree in which he lived was not harmed. And then the dragon stood up above me on the earth, and on his head he wore a crown of stars. 'Enough, Wotan. Stop!'

'Are you the one named Huwawa, and is this your tree?'

The dragon breathed softly. 'I am Huwawa and this is my tree. Stop, Wotan. Do not chop my tree.'

I swung my axe, a great slice of fragrant wood flew, and the trunk creaked. I heard it in my ears, felt it in my feet. 'What is the purpose of such a tree?'

Huwawa said: 'It is the tree by which we shall know God again. One day my tree will grow high enough to reach God.'

'How long will that take?' I swung again, but Huwawa extended his claw like lightning and stopped the axe. His head bent forward and I saw myself standing like a golden man in his eyes.

'As long again as it has taken, Wotan.'

'How long has it taken?'

'Ten thousand times ten thousand years,' Huwawa said, blinking once, and I felt the weight of time and misery inside him. 'When one day comes, I shall climb back to God.'

'Why should a serpent climb to God and not men?' I drew my axe back, and quickly swung again. The wood quivered under the blow.

'Enough, Wotan.' Huwawa raised his voice. 'Do you do this terrible thing for glory?'

'If I cut off Huwawa's head and fell his tree my name will live for ever.'

'You do not know what glory is,' Huwawa said simply. 'I have known the glory of God and it's more than you imagine. More than you *can* imagine.'

I stopped. I listened to the serpent's persuasive words. So there was more than glory; there was the glory of God, my father. But Kidu wanted to fight. Huwawa said: 'No, let me speak. Kidu speaks evil' – there it was, Eve's unfamiliar word again – 'because Kidu is your servant, your slave, your right hand. He can't live without you any more than your hand can. If you die he'll be killed, that's the law, and he's afraid you'll listen to me not to him. He's envious and afraid of me, because I'm his rival in your heart. You and I, Wotan, we can be friends. Listen to me, Wotan.'

'He's trying to stop you,' Kidu warned me. 'He's clever. He's trying to get between us. Don't listen to his slimy tongue.' He struck at Huwawa's claws with his sword, and I struck at the tree. Huwawa rose up as tall as the temple at Enoch, roaring, and we fought.

I forget all Huwawa's seven weapons; around us he furrowed the ground with his claws, and as we jumped into the furrows to get under his blazing breath he rammed at us with his head like a battering ram; that's three. I shot arrows into his side, I chopped at his feet with my swords, I cut at the tendons of his heels with my axe. Huwawa's voice roared until we fell down deafened, four, he blew flame across the treetops until we were surrounded by fire on all sides, that's five; he stamped on us with his feet and his tail, that's six at least, and still we weren't dead.

Then Huwawa rose up like the forest, huge as the forest, green as the forest stretching golden in the afternoon sunlight; and light, the seventh weapon, grew like a halo around his head.

Around Huwawa's head grew the glow of light that in Shemash, the god of the Sun, is called the *shekinah*, the glory that announces the sun's rise, and is both valedictory to the Sun god's setting and the promise of his return. The *shekinah* burnt fiercely in one star of Huwawa's crown of stars, forming whirlpools of cloud rushing towards the star both from below and above, whirling inside it, the wind dragging us forward lifting our feet from the ground even as we clung to the branches of the trees, and the branches broke off the trees and the trees broke out of the ground and flew upwards into the *shekinah*, the fierce heat as they flashed to incandescence burning our skin like sunburn and turning our long hair to flames of fire. But Huwawa's crown had grown very heavy, dragging him down even as the roaring wind lifted us; I grabbed the scales of his chest, worked my sword beneath the overlapping plates, and thrust the point deep into the beast's thundering heart.

Huwawa fell, and the light went out.

We'd been blinded by the light; Kidu and I sat rubbing our sunburnt eyes, then stood up on the smoking earth looking around us. Huwawa's heart beat like a broken drum, black blood spurted from his body stretched across the hilltop, his spiked tail hanging down into the valley behind, his head overhanging the drop in front. Beneath his head the cooling star dropping from his crown and plummeted into the earth leaving a smooth round hole exactly its own size. Huwawa saw me looking down the glowing tube as it cooled and darkened, leading as deep as the world. 'No.' Huwawa tried to speak, but blood fell from his mouth. He moved his leg spasmodically, sweeping the earth over the hole, then I saw myself in his eye. 'Wotan, you shall never find the mountain of God.' Huwawa's voice spoke no louder than the draught from a doorway. 'Hear me. I was born in the mountain from which I was cast out, cast down.'

'Which mountain? Ararat? Not Ararat? Where's the mountain of God?'

Huwawa grinned in his agony. 'The mountain is Heaven, Wotan. You've killed me, taken more than my life from me. Denied all hope of Heaven to me.' His mouth gaped, then without warning he stabbed down on the back of my sword hand with his tooth, the three-pointed incisor tearing through to the palm, transfixing me for a moment to the ground before it was withdrawn. He fell back exhausted as I writhed in agony, a foretaste of Huwawa's own death agony; the merest lick.

He spoke. 'With my dying breath I curse you, Wotan. You shall never know your sons, they shall be born knowing sin. They shall go forth like scattered seeds and not know you, only sin shall they know, only evil, only knowledge. I pluck out my eye and curse you.' The dragon blinded his eyes with his claw. 'This is my second curse, Wotan: you shall live for ever on the world, on your feet like a monkey walking upright shall you live.'

All over him the black blood dripped from his heart, beginning to burn like oil. Huwawa raised his head, spoke with a mouth of smoky fire. 'For the third time I curse you. I'm not the last, Wotan, nor the greatest. I am the least. I am not worthy to tie His shoes.'

I cried, 'Who is the greatest?'

Huwawa's blind eyes burst into flame, the fire of his burning body rose over him.

I cried at the top of my voice, '*Who is the greatest?*'

'You will know Him,' gasped Huwawa's dying breath through the flame. 'You will know Him.'

With Huwawa's fall his tree also fell, falling forward across the hilltops towards the mountains, its branches sweeping upwards like brushstrokes with the wind of its fall, then the ground shook as earth and rock showered down on us from the great upended roots. Kidu clasped my hand to stop the blood. Our burnt hair stank, we pulled it away from our heads like crisped charcoal, our sunburnt bodies were crusted with dried blood. We laughed, we played like children. The air grew chill as darkness fell, but Huwawa's bones still burnt, and we made our camp for the night inside the warm slatted cavern of his ribs. Once a shooting star crossed the sky and I held my hand, imagining in the dark that tiny infant crocodiles swarmed snapping like dragons from my wound. At dawn Kidu awoke at last and only Huwawa's bleached skeleton remained, the bones crumbling in the wind, and my mood was sombre. I filled my scarred hand with bone dust, let it blow away, troubled. 'El appointed him guardian of the forest.'

'That's just a story made by men,' scoffed Kidu.

'How do we know what is made by men,' I said, 'and what is made by God?'

'You're not afraid of a few curses,' Kidu scoffed, shooting an eagle for his breakfast. 'Many men have cursed you with their dying breath.'

Eve had cursed me; for the first time I didn't want to tell Kidu something he did not know, but I remembered her high voice as though I heard it now: *Damn you to damnation for ever, Wotan, may you burn in Hell, burn in Hell for ever if you awaken the Serpent!* There's really no place called Hell, I told myself, there's only the Underworld that all men and women believe in, the world of the dead that stretches out beneath us, everywhere. I shook my head. 'No, Kidu, I'm not afraid of Huwawa's first curse, I already know I can't have children. Nor of his second curse, because I do walk upright on my feet – and as for living for ever, that would be a blessing not a curse!' I sighed. '*You will know Him.* The curse on his dying breath. *You will know Him.* That's the one I fear.'

Kidu clapped my shoulder cheerfully. 'What does it mean?'

'I don't know. That's why I fear it.'

Kidu jumped up, clambered from root to earthy root until he stood high on the treetrunk. 'It's a path!' he called down. 'A cedar road leading straight to the mountains.' I climbed up after him – but I looked back once. How would my people far away believe in Huwawa's death when I'd not brought back Huwawa's head? How would my name live among my people, even if I was immortal? Would they believe my stories? My scarred hand itched.

The broad curve of rough bark was good to walk on, as

long as we did not look down at the clouds and hilltops below us, but the trunk had narrowed to a skinny pole by afternoon. The peak of the cedar, which had once brushed the sky so that I half expected it to be coloured sky blue, rested over a snowy ridge with a deep aquamarine pool below; rather than climb down we shuffled to the swaying tip, arms outstretched for balance, and dived through the air into the freezing waters. There we swam on our backs, squirting playfully from our mouths, washing our naked bodies clean and sunbrowned, then lay on the beach with our heads on stones for pillows, yawning, staring up at the snowy double peaks of Ararat where the tip of the cedar pointed. 'Does God really live there?' Kidu murmured.

'Noah will tell us about God,' I said firmly. 'Noah spoke with God. He knows where God walks in the Garden of Life.' I remembered Eve's name for it. 'Eden. Where the sun rises.' But Kidu didn't hear me, snoring, already asleep. I knelt on a rock at the water's edge, staring at my reflection, my hair ragged where the flames had burnt it, and unsheathed my sword to cut it away.

I stopped. A face moved within my face in the water. My streaky blond hair became long and perfectly black, lying in curls across my woman-white shoulders, my blue eyes opened dark brown, my frowning lips widened into a luscious red smile. I turned, shielding my eyes against the sun, and looked up at the most beautiful woman I have ever seen.

I stared. I smiled. She wore a harlot's purple robe, a virgin's enigmatic smile, her breasts were full, plump, white, jewelled, red rubies for her nipples, a sapphire as big as an eye for her belly-button, and below I saw the intoxicating feminine curve of her jewelled loins gleaming with golden straps, and her long thighs leading down to her toes lapped by the waters, each toenail pierced with its own bright jewel. Her eyes sparkled, returning my appreciation, her tongue touched her lips at the sight of my muscles, the feel of their rippling hardness under her fingertips. I affect all women like this, and I never disappoint them. I stood, gently I lifted her and kissed her upturned perfumed mouth. 'Harder!' she said. She glanced down at my bulging loincloth standing erect in her honour and her eyes widened in admiration. 'It's true what they say! You *are* as big as a bull!'

A woman after my own heart, we beat as one. 'You're the one,' I whispered. 'The most beautiful.' It's true; the perfect woman, lustful as a man. The sunlight struck across her eyes and face, dazzling my mind with images of her beauty and carnality, conquering me. I, Wotan, was conquered. She whispered, 'I am the Queen of Heaven, worship me. Give your penis to me, I'll give you my cunt, I'll give you the art of lovemaking, I'll give you the art of kissing the phallus, I'll give you the art of prostitution, I'll give you the art of sexual control, I'll give you all these gifts a woman has, and no woman is more woman than I.' I squeezed her breasts, held her loins against me, felt her jewels moving between us like tiny mouths. 'Quick, quick,' she cried, inflaming my soul, 'come in me, Wotan, give me your semen, quick, I'll be your wife, you'll be my husband.' She lunged against me, all softness and perfume, grabbed my penis with both hands to force it in her, she was as strong as a man lying with a woman. I fell back a pace, then two. 'Wife?' I pulled away suspiciously. 'Husband?' I had to have her, not marry her. But still she came forward. My feet skidded, I plunged backwards into the deep water, came up spluttering. 'Who are you?'

She turned furiously on her heel, scorned me. 'If you aren't man enough to take me, I know who is.' She woke Kidu with a kiss of her mouth, he wrapped his arms around her at once as though she were his dream, Lalla, but she wasn't, this dream or nightmare woman crouching over him cast a long afternoon shadow, she was flesh, blood,

172

weight, her black hair flew over his face, and she went for him like a man lying with a woman, give me more, she demanded more, deeper, harder, he was just an object of desire for her, just a small squirt of semen to feed her insatiable flesh. I touched the point of my sword to the nape of her neck.

She ceased. Kidu rolled aside, groaning. She'd bitten his neck in her passion, clawed his chest with her nails, then contemptuously pushed him aside.

She stood and faced me, wholly passionate, took the point of my sword between her teeth, smiled. 'Most men worship me as a god,' she said lightly, her eyes gleaming with her smile. 'Most men and some women. You know my name.'

I pulled away from her but she closed her teeth on the sword, following me. 'You aren't Ishtar,' I said, 'Nin is the high priestess of Ishtar and she's the best friend a man ever had.'

Ishtar spat out the sword. 'But you don't sleep with her.' She opened her breasts, dropped the jewels, stood bare and white. 'I am Ishtar. Marry me. I'll give you whatever you want. Chariots of lapis lazuli, weapons of beaten gold. Your sheep will drop twins and your cows triplets. Give me your manhood, Wotan, give me your strength, give me everything you've got and get everything in return.' She strode after me with long strides, cherry-ripe. 'I'll be your wife, Wotan. I'll cut your hair, I'll rub oil in your burnt skin, I'll give you sons as strong as yourself, stronger. You're the son of the God El, they say,' she told me eagerly, eyeing me in admiration. 'Is it true?'

'Yes, it's true.'

'Such sons we'll have! Masters of the cities, masters of all the peoples. Take me, Wotan, husband, son of El, be my master.' She grasped me in the way no man can resist. 'If what you tell me really is true, God has entered the world. *Is* it true?' She squeezed voluptuously, eyes against

173

my eyes, breath against my breath.

Temptation! Her harlot's robe made her even more irresistible, hinting at dark unwifely skills practised in the street, in doorways, by the women who wait at the crossroads, in the potter's field, the heedless women called 'potters' earth' because anything can be made of them, and they can be made to do anything, however depraved; her beauty knew them too. A wife as beautiful as this woman would make her husband proud and all other men envious. My head span. She was just what I wanted. Perfection. And yet . . . my mind groped for the word, the word that had never passed my tongue to any woman I'd had. Love.

'I don't love you,' I said. 'You're everything I desire. But I don't love you.'

'Love?' She frowned. 'Don't I have love?' She touched her hair as if checking its lustre, its curls, the perfect skill with which they were cut, shaped, arranged. '*Love?*' She was the Queen of Love (at least the love which men worship in this world) but she didn't know what love was. 'Isn't this love?' she said, touching me as she'd touched her hair, kissing me carelessly, turning her back provocatively. I knew exactly what it was.

'No,' I said regretfully. 'It isn't love.'

Her face fixed slightly. Her cheeks coloured, and a bubble of spittle gleamed on the tip of one incisor. 'Coward.'

I knew her; I'd had a hundred like her, pots that emptied as fast as they were filled. 'I know your sort,' I said. 'You're the fire that goes out in cold weather, the shoe that rubs, the door that opens in the wind, you're the bed of thorns. You make happiness into misery and sweetness sour. Which of your lovers did you ever love? Tammuz, your husband, your brother?' I drew breath, the list was long. 'Ishullanu—'

She made herself laugh, showing her teeth. 'Who

174

deserved me except you, Wotan, son of El, if you speak the truth? Prove yourself a man, more than a man, man-god, take me in your arms, I'll show you love, love, love.'

Kidu said: 'The killer of Huwawa doesn't need to prove his strength to anyone.'

'Huwawa's dead?' She stared. 'He can't be dead. You murdered him?' She clapped her hands to her ears, wouldn't listen. 'What harm did Huwawa do? He never hurt anyone, he was harmless, he loved the tree that grows to God.' Her voice rose. 'He was of us, *for* us, fell with us, an angel cast down from Heaven—'

'An angel?' I cried. 'Angel? What?'

Her face darkened like venous blood with fury, she held up her arms. Wings rose up behind her, her wings dark as black gold, each perfect feather fluttering and lifting in the evening breeze, the muscles twisting in her chest as her wings beat the air like claps of grief. 'Huwawa's dead!' she cried to the pool and mountains, her voice whining in mourning, desolate as the wind. 'Huwawa is dead!'

'Angel?' I shouted. 'What's an angel? You're one of the Elohim, a goddess, wife of Ya.'

'Here I'm whoever I want to be. I need use none of the names given me by God.' Her mouth opened deep as a cave, she grew up over me into the darkening sky, eyes golden-black like a creature made of metal or marble – I dared touch her knee, black obsidian, black as a sacrificial knife, born of the volcano. 'Huwawa who was alive is dead,' she cried over me. 'Huwawa who as a living angel was cast out from Heaven, cast down by God into this Hell, is dead for ever.' She opened her fists as though to crush the stars which were coming out. 'This Hell, nothing, vacuum, airless, lightless, our prison falling for ever. Cruel, limitless imprisonment! Then God, the God of our damnation, made light to blind us, heat to burn us, earth to bind us to its dust with chains of gravity; in six days He was done, and on the seventh day He rested, and on the eighth day

He closed the doors of Heaven.' She pressed her giant face close to mine, I saw the veins in her eye. 'We are alone, small man. There is no God. This is the place abandoned by God. This world is Hell.'

Her breath blew me over. I struggled to my feet. 'I am the son of El. The God El *is* my father!' I shouted with all my strength, 'God *is* in this world.'

'Then let Him save you.' She flicked me aside, I fell in a shower of stones. 'This is *our* place,' she said contemptuously. 'Ours. There's no El here. No Ya. No God. There's nothing but us.'

She picked me up with her fingers, flung me in the water, but I came up. She threw boulders at me, but I dived down. Kidu stabbed at her, but she broke his weapons, she stamped her feet in her rage and broke my sword, my axe, my Elam bow. 'Huwawa is dead!' she cried. 'Death to the murderer of Huwawa.' She lifted me from the foam, threw me, but my flailing body skipped across the water like a stone to the far side, she could not kill me.

Ishtar gave a scream of rage and the mountains rang with her echoes; she lifted her robe over her head and her robe sank down among the pebbles as though beneath it she descended into the world; the hem fluttered once, and was gone.

Kidu and I sat exhausted on the beach. We clasped each other.

'Noah will know the truth,' I whispered. 'He knows God.'

We stood with Mount Ararat rising huge behind our backs and the sun rising in our eyes. I pointed. 'There.'

Beyond the mountain passes and mountaintops below us, the violet horizon shimmered white with salt flats, great salt lakes, a gleaming sea. In the middle distance a wide green valley curved between volcanic mountains on each side, a natural fortress protected on the fourth side by a great salt lake. If God was anywhere, He was here. 'Eden,' I said. 'At the head of four rivers.'

The mountains gleamed with the river-streams called by canaanite traders Perath, Hiddek'El, Pishon and Gihon. As we walked towards the rising sun the Perath looped past us in the hills, its flow swollen by the River Hubur, fed by Ararat's glacial meltwaters, foaming southward towards Shem. I had retraced the journey of my life, and now by leaving the river's course I struck out across new ground with eager footsteps.

Noah the Faraway was not hard to find; he found us.

Rather, his voice found us, a reedy voice singing hymns. We walked from the misty valleys along the shore of the salt lake, following the sound of singing. A narrow causeway of crusted salt led to an island in the lake, the rim of an exhausted volcano. The sound of breaking waves drowned the voice, then it came again. '"Pretty girl, pretty bride, I demand you in the name of Ishtar, come dancing with me from the temple steps, I'll give you a bag of gold for your lap, a bag of bridal gold for your pretty lap, and you'll sleep with me before your husband tonight."'

Kidu and I looked at each other as we climbed. 'Can't be him,' Kidu said.

'It's an old man's voice.'

'God would have given him a woman to look after him, surely. This is Eden, isn't it?'

We listened to the cracked awful voice. 'Maybe Ishtar's right,' I said, 'and there is no God.'

'"A bag of gold and a bowl of wine,"' the rambling voice sang out of tune. 'I mean, no, "a bag of wine and a bowl of gold." Give me another bag. Hallo?' Black glassy pebbles, obsidian, rattled beneath our feet as we climbed through a vineyard in the rich volcanic soil. 'That you? What took you so long, girl?'

At the summit our shadows streamed across the crater,

brimming full of water so crystal-clear that our shadows rippled down inside, refracted, magnified in the volcano's subaqueous gullet. In the open door of a reed hut an old man sat like a bundle of sticks propped together. 'Don't drink it!' he called as Kidu knelt with cupped hands at the water. 'Poison.'

'Salt, you mean?' Kidu tasted it. 'It's fresh.'

'It isn't wine!' the old man cawed, banging the ground with a stick like one of his legs. 'Water goes to your bladder, not to your head, like wine. If it's not wine, it's poison!'

'It's beautifully sweet water.' Kidu pointed to swirls of refraction showing far out. 'The source wells up from below, from an abyss.' He pointed at the stream overflowing downhill to the salt lake. 'The meeting place of two waters, salt and sweet.'

'Yes, that's what they call this place.' The old man drew his green robe around him against the evening chill and his eyes moved in his skull, bright as stones set in leather.

'Eden,' I said.

'Perhaps. Perhaps, Wotan and Kidu. Sit.'

'You know our names.' We sat at his dry feet, each foot as knobbly as a piece of spine, the toenails as long as my fingers.

'I see. I listen. I know everything that it is lawful to know. And you know I am an old man, Noah, once a rich man, a canaan of Shurappak.' Noah clenched his hand like a claw on his stick. 'And you know Ya whispered to me through the wall of my reed house – *house*, meaning the House of Noah, my tribe, my descendants, if I was going to have any – and warned me to build a boat if I wanted to save their souls. All the unborn generations of undrowned souls.'

'So the story they tell of the Flood is true, and of Noah's Ark.'

'What do they know now? Babies they are, nowadays, all my children. Nine hundred and forty-one years old, I am.' Noah quivered, spat wine-red spit into the clear waters. Not a breath of wind; the air was breathless with approaching night, the water a perfect mirror of the sky. 'I'll tell you this, hear me, rained forty days it did, not seven like they claim now in the temples of the plain! Forty days. And they say my steersman was Puzur-Amurri, but he wasn't! How could he be? My Ark had no rudder, I was in Ya's hands. That was the deal. Trust in God, and live.' He beat his shadowy green-robed chest with a fist that looked no heavier than cloud, hardly disturbing the material. 'Once I wore the yellow cloak of the Zadok – a golden fleece, they use now, fools. Babies. The Zadok's cloak must be yellow gold, Balaam-gold, shining like the sun, a glory as bright as His *shekinah*, if they want to call Ya to us, call Ya to rule over us.' He paused forgetfully as the sun sank into the world. 'I passed mine on years ago. My son Shem, I think. Now every mumbling Zadokite priest of every village wears his little scrap of wool. Probably forgotten what it means.'

'Not all. They take religion very seriously in the cities.'

'Probably forgotten everything important.' Noah scratched his skull, remembering, then pointed at the star Sirius setting after the sun. 'I wore the Urim and Thummim on my chest. Ya told me to, He whispered through the wall of my tent while I was drunk. Could get drunk in those days.'

He had spoken the words complexly but I repeated them as best I could. 'Urim, Thummim?'

'Words given me by God. Words without sound. Shapes burnt from jewels on to tablets of wood.' It was possible; I'd seen city men press shapes in clay with wedges held in their fingers, and the canaans use notched wooden tallies to record buying and selling. Noah shrugged, a shadow in the dark, groaning as his bones clicked. 'Some said each shape was a whole meaning, others that they were numbers. One, two, many, sixty.' Shrugged again.

'Numbers to worship God by.'

'El is the great God, not Ya,' I said.

'Heard all about you, I have.' Noah wagged a finger like sun-dried bone. 'Claims to be the son of El. El, who sent the Flood! Prove it, I say.'

'I am Wotan, I built the walls of Enoch, I killed Huwawa, I sought the Bull of Heaven, I am the man of men.'

'And now you seek immortality.' Again his wagging finger, hardly visible. 'You won't like it, Wotan. Look at me. Look.' I heard him stick his horrible tongue out. 'No dignity, my age. Prisoner. Trapped. Even wine tastes like piss.'

'Am I immortal?'

'Huwawa cursed you with immortality.'

'*Cursed?*' I shook my head, chuckled.

Noah groped in the dark, took my hot powerful youthful hand in his own; I felt his icy dry bones as he scraped the triangular scar. 'The bite of Huwawa, an enemy of God, no doubt, but one of the least. I was sorry to hear him dead.'

'Is God in this world? Actually? Not just as a belief, a religion, but real? God is real?'

At last Noah's voice came. 'He doesn't speak to me now. Too old. Adam spoke to God, saw Him walking here in the Garden. But Adam fell. The Serpent seized him at the chink in his armour.' He shrugged. 'Woman.'

'Eve.'

'All women are Eve. It's a common name among that people.' He gestured towards the east of Eden, where the moon rose.

'Can I find God walking in the mountains? Was your immortality a gift from God?'

'They said so. I don't believe it.' Noah sighed. 'No, not God. Something else. I know what Huwawa said to you. He said you'll never know your sons. They'll be born knowing sin, knowing evil. He cursed you with eternal existence; and he cursed you with knowing the greatest, Him whose shoes you are not worthy to tie.' He rested his claw on my head. 'I pity you, Wotan. To live a hundred years is agony; nine hundred years is nine hundred times that torment, I know. You will live for eternity. When the mountains wear down to sand and the sun falls cold and the moon turns to blood, you will still be like me. Not a life, an existence. An eternity of living in Hell.'

Kidu clung to me, shivering. The crater was an abyss full of stars, like the sky; then the moon's image rose in the crater also, as though we hung between water and sky, between a new world and the old.

I whispered, 'When Huwawa spoke of the greatest, Him whose shoes I'm unworthy to tie, did he mean someone greatest to Huwawa . . . or greatest to God?'

Noah stopped breathing.

Then he spoke. 'There is a tradition that God is all-powerful, so powerful, so *everything*, that He must speak to us in big gestures, in symbols we can understand – thus He spoke to my house, not to me; and *everything* means there is room for lies also, like the lie that Puzur-Amurri steered the Ark, and there are worse. Much worse. Some say there's a God of Lies.'

'Does He have a name, as Ya has a name, and El?'

'Listen to me, Wotan.' Noah gripped my wrist in the moonlight, and the moon twitched and shivered in his old eyes as he looked into mine. 'I know more than is lawful. I knew you'd killed Huwawa, knew his three curses, didn't I? I know about Ishtar. I *know*.'

'The most beautiful woman in the world? I never touched her.'

'Don't test me, Wotan. You saw with your own eyes the fallen angel, the demon who allows herself to be worshipped as the wife of God – and how would the people know better? Thus she drags honest men and women into sin, and turns honest worship into deceit, into blasphemy.

181

You saw her. A fallen angel, beautiful and terrible.'

'I saw her.'

'You insulted her. But she fears you are the son of God, Wotan. She truly does fear it. That you are God come into her world, or that through you God will come. You saw her fury and terror when you were not destroyed.'

'The ground took her and she was gone.'

'Yes. But not gone.' Noah stared at me by the abyss, the moons filling his eyes. 'This I saw. In my wine I saw her fall, in my blood like red wine I saw the ground rise up around Ishtar, I saw her fall deliberately in her rage and fury down to the Underworld where souls lie like dead fish in the dusty caverns. In the place where there is no movement, she moved. Dust trailed after her cloak as she moved. I heard voices calling blindly, I saw blind confusion around her, the confusion of death. But a falcon shaped like a man rose up, Horus, and held out his wing to show the way forward. Down and down she went, finding her way forward through the first gate and the second and the third, and at each gate as she went down she gave up an item of her clothing as each guardian demanded, until at the seventh gate her body was naked to the cleft. And she came through into a place, an *emptiness*, I've never seen before, no, no matter how sour the wine. A new place, worse than a nightmare. I saw a palace built of gold, like Heaven, but dreadful. I saw an abyss of stars, and stars within stars, and strange starry shapes going away from me without limit or end, and columns of fire and dust ten thousand years tall. And Ishtar who is worshipped as the wife of Ya went forward and climbed the steps of the palace – or the palace rose over her as the steps led her down – and a great chariot carried her forward without stopping, she could not turn aside from any of the rooms of the palace, and in the seventh room a throne rose up inside the darkness, a golden throne, immense, overhanging her, and—' Noah stopped so suddenly I looked round, expecting to see something behind him. 'And something moved. On the throne, *of* the throne, something moved.' Noah's mouth moved, twitching. 'Too terrible to see. Misery. Loss. Pain. Ishtar screamed. Ishtar tried to get away. Ishtar tried to stand her ground. She tried to threaten, but her voice was swallowed, and she stood silent.'

'What did the bitch see, old man?'

The moons went out; Noah spoke with his eyes shut. 'The Serpent.'

I swallowed but my mouth was dry. 'The Serpent of Eden?'

'The Serpent came up and went down all around her. She cried out to Him, "Who are you?" and His reply came back to her and echoed forward to her from the darkness, "Hear me if you have two good ears to listen. I am B'El, the son of God." Ishtar cried out to Him in terror. "Liar!" The sound of His laughter came and Ishtar's sweat froze to ice on her body, she could not move in the darkness that surrounded her, the darkness of His voice rising over her. "I am B'El, Baal, B'Elial, B'Elzebub, B'El-Zephon, *S-T-N*, my name is Lord. I am Lord Prince of this world, this world is mine, there are my people. I am the oldest of the old and greatest of the great, I suckled closest and most loved at God's bosom, and the woman and man that love me and sow their crop in tears shall reap in joy. The man and woman who weep in the fields, bearing precious seed, shall return home rejoicing, bearing sheaves with them." But Ishtar looked around her and saw only ten thousand times ten thousand souls lying like ghosts in the darkness, all the men and women who ever lived since the world began worshipping B'El in the darkness and dust, and saw that fertility grows on death and manure. And Ishtar had found her voice, and now she spoke to Him.

'"B'El, hear me, you know I've committed foul and

hideous sins." Silence; every sin was known. Ishtar spoke again, rage overcoming fear. "You know Wotan claims also to be a son of God, hideous blasphemy! Punish Wotan for his blasphemy and arrogance. Punish Wotan and Kidu the man made in his image, the murderers of Huwawa the serpent who loved the forest."

'B'El's voice murmured like growling thunder, "Yes, Huwawa who guarded the glory of God, the crown of stars that is lost."

"'Yes, it's lost! Punish Wotan because he does not love my beauty, refuses me, scorns *me*, will not marry me, he is a no-man, a homosexual, a sodomite. Sterility will never conquer fertility. He has eyes the cold blue colour of the moon, he is not of our race. Mortal or immortal, let Wotan be ripped to pieces with a sharp knife, scatter his meat living or dead with a winnowing fan, burn him in a fire and grind the charcoal of him in a mill, scatter his dust in the fields. Give me the Bull of Heaven to destroy Wotan as he should be destroyed."

'But B'El uncoiled around her in the darkness, and His cold dusty voice whispered in her ear: "For this gift will you give me more than you can pay?"

'Ishtar shook with terror in her ice shroud, but she said, "Take all I have."

"'Shall I turn your beauty into a rotting corpse, and hang you from a flesh-hook?"

"'Take more, much more. Take my soul."

'Uncoiling around her, His voice replied to her, "Will you stay down here for ever, and be my wife, the Queen of Hell, if I will be your revenge?"

'She said, "I shall." Then Ishtar's fury broke out of her and she demanded, "Give me the Bull of Heaven and take my soul or I'll break the gates of Hell, I'll break the bolts and the door-posts, peasants will mingle with kings and queens will lie among harlots, I'll make the lowest in Hell highest, I'll bring up the dead into the world to eat food like the living." She fell silent, trembling.

'But the darkness left her undestroyed; instead His voice came laughing around her. "Having heard your tongue, Ishtar, whom the people believe to be my mother, I should rather return you to the land of the living. It suits me very well that you shall be worshipped by the people as the wife of Ya, and I, B'El, be worshipped as His son." His laughter roared like the wind. "The Bull of Heaven is yours. Oh, woman, man, delicious fate!"'

Noah fell silent in the moonlight, so silent that I touched his fluttering pulse of life.

'That's what I saw when I was drunk.' His head nodded.

Kidu whispered to me, 'You're not listening to a drunkard's dreams?'

'No,' I said. 'I hunt the Bull of Heaven. Not he me.'

'In my wine I saw it,' Noah whispered, sleepless. 'In wine I see truth. In wine I'm naked. In wine there's no lies. Saw Adam down there, I'll join him there in Hell and live among the dead.' We heard him sigh. 'One day there will be no Hell. The chains will be broken as Ishtar promised, the gates smashed, the dead given new life. But not by her.'

Kidu turned away impatiently making wine-swallowing noises, but I asked: 'Who by?'

'By the One who shall reign as King for a thousand years in Ur-Shalom.' We shrugged; never heard of it. Noah promised: 'He shall be King and Zadok both, king and priest united, a Son of Man, our anointed saviour.'

All kings are priests. 'What's his name?' we asked. 'Maybe we've heard of him.'

'That *is* His name,' Noah murmured, nodding. 'Anointed Saviour.'

Someone coming, stones sliding; Kidu and I whirled, crouching, ready for a fight. More stones clinked on the hillside below us, rattling down from footsteps climbing up. 'It's her,' Noah said in a stronger voice, pleased. 'It's only her, late as usual. Wine time.' The stocky figure of a girl climbed into the moonlight, Noah knew how to choose them, big swaying breasts and a big swaying skin of wine. She gave us a moonlit flash of a smile as she unpacked bread and cheese from the sack on her back, but Noah was only interested in the skin. 'Waited all afternoon!' he grumbled. 'What kept you, Siduri?'

'Only my husband,' she yawned.

Kidu put away his dagger. 'Thought she was Ishtar!' he whispered. 'That old man knows how to make up a story. Must be the moon.'

'He believes what he told us.' I glanced back as Noah drank noisily, the girl holding the skin to his mouth. I called out to him but he didn't respond, so I crouched close enough to hear him dribble.

'I *am* the son of God,' I whispered. 'Therefore God must be in this world. At least at the moment of any conception. Something of God was.'

'God didn't think of wine, not a sip before the Fall,' Noah said. 'I did. All my idea.'

I asked, 'Will I ever find God walking here in Eden?'

'Eden's where your heart is.' Noah coughed, spat wine. 'Have you found your heart, young Wotan? Do you know where it is?'

I was confused. 'Here. This place is Eden. The head of the four rivers.'

'Some say the heart puts out rivers of blood as quickly as it takes it back. Where's your mouth?'

'In my head.'

'The head of a river and its mouth.' He pointed at the moonlit abyss full of stars, the crater yawning like a mouth, overflowing with sweet water. 'Head or mouth? The words are the same. A river has two mouths, its beginning and its end.'

I frowned. 'Eden can be found where the rivers meet the salt sea?' But only the greatest two of these rivers reach the Gulf, the mighty Perath and Hiddek'El, not four.

'You will know,' Noah said, 'when you find your heart.'

Damn you to damnation for ever, Wotan, if you awaken the Serpent.

'I don't like it.' Kidu drew his knife even though the night had ended and the moon, Sin, had gone down in front of us into the great mound of Ararat. God was not here in the mountains – no more here than anywhere else. Our path turned southward towards the Perath, we heard its tributaries roaring in the gorges and smelt the snow and melting snow, and Kidu ran to check behind boulders as though the Bull of Heaven lurked behind each one. 'I don't like this, my friend.'

'He was just an old man and an old drunk.'

'*I* said that.' Kidu leapt forward around a rock but found no Bull of Heaven waiting in ambush. 'Now I'm saying I don't like his choice of words. He was very vivid.'

'The Serpent was just a drunk dream of his and Ishtar was just a dream too.'

Kidu showed me his neck, the mark of her kiss like a wound. 'I know when you're lying.' I knew too. He sighed, gripped my arm. 'Don't be sad. It's not total failure, people are bound to believe us. Who is this Bull of Heaven anyway?'

Kidu knew nothing of him! 'No one. He claims he's my father.'

'Our father,' Kidu said.

'All my life I've felt there's something missing,' I said. I shrugged. 'I was made with something missing. Something more than you. Maybe Nin's right. Maybe I'm too much of a man.'

'Nothing wrong with that,' Kidu said. 'Eve said you were stupid. That's worse.'

The River Hubur foamed on my right, leaping downhill in long arches of spray, and we climbed down the crags. I stopped. 'Do you think I've awoken the Serpent?'

'You know me,' Kidu sheathed his knife cheerfully and swung from his hands, dropping down, 'I think what you think.'

I thought about it as I leapt down. 'If the Bull of Heaven is sent after me and finds me,' I said, 'then the Serpent is awake.'

The air tasted of spray and the river roared in a pool surrounded by cliffs, the foam swirling as it was sucked into the vortex. But we remembered the way, parted the bushes and shouldered forward down a narrow crack into the cave, slipped down in a debris of soil and bones into darkness. Daylights gleamed on the racing water, sending pallid lightbeams shooting in every direction as they were carried downstream through the dark, and the rock platforms shook under our feet with the river's thunder. I ducked past an outcrop. Ahead of me Kidu turned. His face changed. His eyes widened. His mouth opened. I was punched in the back, then felt a sliding pain in my rib bones by my spine. A voice shouted. 'My firstborn son dies for You, great El! Make Your covenant with Your people be born again with new life. For the sake of Your covenant with Your people I sacrifice my son for You!'

The black obsidian blade of the sacrificial knife, volcanic glass, slid out of my chest through my left nipple, tore my clothes, gleamed bloody in the racing light. I grabbed it in my hands. From behind me Apsu's voice hissed in my ear, 'Atone, Wotan. Die. Die.' The blade withdrew, sliding through my hands, I couldn't stop the slippery sliding edge, my right hand hung by its skin, my ribs broke. A stinking palm was clapped over my mouth, no fingers, no fist. The knife split my ribs as it was thrust again and again into my spine, I gasped but my lungs were blood not air, I gasped blood not breath, I fell to my knees. Kidu ran towards me, eyes wide with shock, I shouted keep back, keep back, my blood spattered his face, knocked him back. Again and again the knife thrust down, the point breaking on the rocks beneath me, the jagged edge stabbing me, now finding my heart, I felt its coldness inside the quivering muscle of my heart, stabbing into the heart of me, I felt my arteries tear and the hot blood flood into my chest, my stomach, my guts. Lay mouth open like a fish. Apsu twisted me, his foot stood on my neck. The sacrificial knife was strapped to his fingerless hand. My head lolled, staring up at the cold blue eyes of the man who claimed he was my father. *Mortal or immortal, let Wotan be ripped to pieces with a sharp knife, scatter his meat living or dead with a winnowing fan, burn him in a fire and grind the charcoal of him in a mill, scatter his dust in the fields. Give me the Bull of Heaven to destroy Wotan as he should be destroyed.* The Bull of Heaven cried: 'Wotan, atone for your sinful life by your death!' He struck the *molech*-blow across my throat.

Then as the blood flowed from my throat across my eyes Apsu staggered aside, struggling. Kidu fought him. Kidu struck with his sword and Apsu at the same moment struck with his knife; they stood upright on tiptoe together, face against face, transfixed; then they fell together, fell into the river together, and together the river swept them away.

I blinked bloody tears, but I was a man without strength. I cried Kidu's name, Kidu, Kidu, but I had no breath, none. I lay on the edge without the strength to move, my blood dripping into the river that raced below my head, I wept tears of blood. Kidu was dead.

A shadow rose up the wall. I don't know how long had passed. 'Kidu?'

Atone. Atone. Atone. No, not *atone*, she said my name, *Wotan, Wotan.* 'Wotan!' she said.

I opened my eyes and stared up at her face. Too skinny for my taste, but she had lovely eyes, lovely dark eyes like deep pools, and her slanty eyelids made me smile. The lights raced over her eyes, making them flash and sparkle like love, despair, need, anger. Her funny little chin, and I reached up to touch her chin with my hand, but I had no hand. I screamed.

When I awoke it was dark.

'Am I alive?'

I heard her weep. I slept. I slept, and dreamt she was dragging me with all her strength, her small hands pulling at my armpits, my heavy heels dragging on rock. When I awoke I was in a different place in the cave. When I awoke again I don't know where I was in the dark. I awoke for the third time and I lay on a dark beach by lapping black waters, the smoke of a small fire rising towards the daylights in the cave roof. 'I'm cold.' She covered me with her cape. She sat shivering, poking at the fire. 'How long?' I said. She shrugged. Glanced at me and away, I wouldn't believe her. 'I lost my hand,' I said.

'You shouldn't be alive,' she said.

'Lost my sword hand!' Ridiculous; I felt hot tears in my eyes. 'How can a man live without a sword hand?'

'You shouldn't be alive,' she repeated. 'I thought you'd die in my arms. At least you're breathing through your mouth now. I sewed your throat.' She gave a little shudder, squeamish. 'Don't touch. I put a bandage round your neck to hold it together.'

'You're not squeamish.'

Her lips writhed and she slapped the only part of me that didn't hurt, my legs. She cried and cried.

I said, 'How long really?'

Through her sniffles she sniffed, 'Too long. I thought your spirit had fled.'

'Kidu's dead, isn't he?'

'Yes.' She gave me a frightened look. 'Kidu is.'

'Tell me.'

'One day I found his body turning in the lower pool and laid him out until the worm fastened on him, just as

190

you would have. Then I buried him as well as I could. I didn't have any red ochre.'

'And the Bull of Heaven?'

'Dead as a doorpost. I chopped him for the fish, I thought you'd want that.'

I stared at the fire and the daylights, then glanced at her face. 'Will I die too?'

She looked at me steadily. 'Can you?'

She went away; she slept when the daylights went out; she cleaned me when they returned. Later she went away and this time she returned with a hare she'd trapped. I watched her skin and joint the carcass; a one-handed man can't do that. I hissed. My stump itched as though insects swarmed in it. 'That's what they all say.' She shrugged callously, roasting the joints on green sticks over the fire. 'You think you're the first warrior to lose his hand, Wotan?' I turned away from her, lay on my clumsy bandaged wrist. She pulled my shoulder back. I swore at her. 'Leave me alone, you!' I shouted.

But she pulled, then held a joint of stick-roasted hare in front of my face. 'Eat.' I ate, she watched. 'Good?'

'No. Too hot.'

She went for a walk, and offered no more. I lay sulking. Swallowing hurt my throat a lot. Over the fire the tastiest joint on its green stick was beginning to crisp, spitting fat. 'Eve,' I called. No answer. 'Eve!' I roared, and birds or bats whirled startled in the daylights. The stick charred, soon that lovely fat haunch would drop in the fire. I rolled over, dragged myself on one arm to the fire, wolfed the meat straight off the stick, I think I ate the stick too. Good, more without her. I pushed with my good arm, sat up, wolfed the kidneys and another haunch. The juices trickled down my chin into my beard, and I reached up amazed. My hair, burnt short by Huwawa, had grown long. The blond curls lay on my shoulders and hung down my back, neatly combed. How much had Eve done for me? How much did she know about me, my body? I called, 'Eve?' Still no answer. I thought about her. I knew she was teaching me another difficult word. 'I'm sorry!' I shouted. 'I'm sorry, I'm sorry.'

She came back, sat without looking at me. 'I thought you said something.'

'I'm sorry.' I clenched my teeth. 'Thank you.'

She looked, not at me, but at the naked fire. 'You've eaten all the—'

I was fed up with words. I reached forward, lifted her up with my good arm, kissed her mouth. 'Rabbit,' she said.

'Hare.' I put her down lightly. 'You don't weigh anything. You don't eat enough.'

'I know,' she flashed, 'you only like big women with two big' – she made the lifting gesture – 'and a big—' She made the patting gesture behind her.

'And you don't like anybody,' I said. We stared at each other hotly. 'You don't,' I told her. 'Nin's loyal little maid, always head-bowed hands-clasped in the background, listening to everything, doing nothing, only what you're told, never having a thought of your own for yourself.'

'Yes, never a thought of myself!' She threw a green stick at my face. 'I thought of you these months, wiped you, nursed you, cried over you because I thought you were dying, I even cried over your poor hand!'

We were shouting. I shouted, 'Nin sent you to follow me!'

'Is that what you think?' She leapt to her feet. I said, 'Sit down.' Her face tightened and she said, 'I won't sit.' We stared furiously. 'Why not?' I shouted, and she shouted, 'Because you told me to! I won't do anything you tell me, never!' She kicked the fire. 'There!'

I said calmly, 'You came by yourself? Nin doesn't know?'

More kicking. 'Of course she doesn't know!'

I stared, trying to understand her. 'Really?'

Eve snarled, put her hands in her hair. 'I'm a slave, don't you understand?'

'You aren't a slave,' I said thoughtfully. 'You're an escaped slave.' I could not think what to say to her. She risked her life for me. 'Why?' I asked. 'Why me?'

Her eyes opened wide as though she could not believe me. Her jaw dropped. She clapped her hands to her cheeks, I was the most stupid thing she'd seen. 'You know everything about some things,' she sighed, 'nothing at all about others.'

'What others?'

'Isn't it obvious?' She was going to cry again; usually I make women cry with pleasure, but her tears of sadness welled up from some internal abyss of her soul, they overflowed down her cheeks and I couldn't stop them, and she wouldn't wipe them away. 'You break everything you touch!' she cried suddenly, 'I don't want to speak to you now.' She shook her head when I tried to get up after her. 'No.'

She lay down on the other side of the fire, her back to me, her firelit shadow throwing a magnified silhouette like distant hills on the rock wall. She sobbed, and the hills shook.

'Eve?' She wouldn't answer.

I slipped back, too weak to stand anyway. I hated it. I was miserable because she was miserable.

'Eve,' I said. I still didn't know how to talk to her. 'You're my strong right arm,' I said. 'You've never let me down.' Her shadow didn't move, only the regular rise and fall of her breath in the valley between her hip and shoulder, she wasn't responding, but I could tell she was listening. The trouble was I was talking like a man, I'd never listened to women talk; it was impossible to touch her with the words men understand. Impossible to say these things directly, so I spoke again to her shadow. 'Eve, I know I'll never know exactly what you're thinking.' The shadow of her head moved slightly. 'I know this is so simple for you, Eve, but it's complicated for me.' The line of her arm slipped a little, was stilled: her shadow was motionless, she held her breath. 'I love you,' I said. 'Eve, I love you. I love you, Eve. I love you.'

I watched the shadow of her body on the wall. I imagined myself crawling one-armed, clumsily, around the fire, imagined lying down behind her. I imagined reaching out my arm wrapped in bandages, no hand, just clumsy bandages, and stroking all I'd lost gently along the outline of her shadow. Gently, gently. I imagined my shadow leaning forward over hers, the shadow of my lips whispering to the shadow of her ear as I caressed her without fingers. 'Look at me, Eve. Feel me. Now I can't possibly break anything I touch.'

And as you know, I'm not the sort of man who imagines something without doing it.

I watched Eve swim in the black water, pull her white body on to a rock, sit in the glowing pool of sunlight from the daylights above; the only place of colour and natural light in the darkness of the cave. She squeezed the water out of her hair, let it fall over her breasts. Resting her elbows on her knees she dipped the brush for teeth called a *siwak* – a stick frayed at one end, pointed like a pick at the other – and brushed her teeth solemnly watching me watch her. Then she laughed. The reflected daylights playing over the walls flashed sparkling in her eyes as she dived back and swam to me. 'I knew it the first moment I saw you,' she said. 'I knew I loved you. I knew you were capable of being in love.'

'I never even noticed you . . .' I was learning tact. 'I noticed you at once.' She splashed me. No one else splashes me. She splashed me again. 'Can you swim?' she asked, with a glance at my arm.

'I swim better than anyone.'

She set off. 'Race you round the rock!' I plunged after her through the silver bubbles of her flashing feet, the momentary black world of blind fish, surfaced and struck out one-armed after her. She won easily. She kissed the cold drops off my lips. 'I love it when you sulk.'

'I lost to a woman,' I muttered numbly. From my youngest days it's been my rule that I win. Now that I was a cripple even a skinny girl swam faster than me. Even if I loved her that didn't make it simpler, it made it more complicated: I didn't know how to deal with her, but I couldn't get away from her.

'It's not wrong to lose to me,' she said, licking my lips, my skin, my hair. 'With me, you're allowed.' She crinkled her nose. 'And I'm allowed to win.'

'Only you. I'll kill anyone else.'

'Only me, no one else,' she said agreeably, touching me with her fingertips, then her hand, then her whole body, and won again.

For days I swam around the rock beating the water with my clumsy bandages. A little faster each time. I made a spear for my left hand and learnt Eve's motionless crouching patience, learnt the refraction of water, speared blind fish, and she brought herbs and roots down from above; but still I would not let the sun see my crippled body.

'You're hiding,' she said.

I hate her talking like this. 'No, I'm not hiding.'

'Don't argue, you know you always lose.'

I said seriously, 'Did I awaken the Serpent?'

'Did you see Him?'

'B'El, B'Elial, B'Elzebub, B'El-Zephon, I heard all that. Enough not to want to do it again.'

'Some among my people call him Molech-Ya, Messenger of Ya. Sacrifice of Ya. Greatest of the angels. My mother beyond the mountains called Him *S-T-N*, the

One whose name is too unholy to say aloud. The Enemy.'
She looked into my face. 'I love you,' she said tenderly.
'That's all that matters.'

I swallowed, touched the bandages around my throat.
'Should I have died? Am I immortal?'

'You're special to me.' She brushed a fish-scale from
the corner of my mouth. 'Nin said every man was special.'

I was surprised. 'Them? I can't believe that.'

'Grrr, you,' she said, then laughed. She liked it. She
looked at me with love in her eyes, skinny, imperfect,
a cut on her knee, more beautiful than Ishtar. I
swallowed again, then reached up my left hand to my
neck and pulled the knot that held my bandages. 'No,
don't,' she said. I unwound the bandages turn by turn
then covered the wound quickly with my hand, gasping.
'Quick, catch me!' I let my head flop forward as though
it fell off and she screamed, grabbing my hair. I winked
in her eye.

'You,' she said, then stopped. She frowned curiously,
touching my throat with her fingers. 'Does that hurt?'

'What?'

'The cut. It's gone. There's no scar.'

I touched the place, smooth. 'Maybe you made a
mistake, it wasn't as bad as you—'

'I sewed you like two bits of ragged cloth. Now there's
not a mark. No mistake.'

I examined my reflection in the pool, felt my new
unmarked skin. 'No mistake.'

We both stared at the stump of my bandaged wrist.
'No,' I said. 'I don't want to know.' I dived in the water
and swam round the rock, round and round. When I came
back to shore she said, 'The ligatures will have to come
out anyway, else the pus will rot your flesh. Do you want
that? Let me look.' But I wouldn't let her look.

Each day when the daylights brightened in the cave
she said, 'Let me.' Each day I shook my head.

Finally she took my chin in her hand and made me look at her. 'Wotan, I *know*.'

I shook my head.

She said, 'I *know* you're afraid. You can't keep your feelings from me.'

'I'm not afraid of anything.'

'You're terrified.' She hugged me. 'Wotan is terrified. God, I love you!' She kissed my face so hard I thought she'd hurt herself. 'Afraid of living in hope.'

I held up my arm. 'It burns like fire,' I said. 'It hurts a lot, like insect stings. And I keep on imagining my hand's there, it tickles. But I know it's not.'

'Then let me look.'

'There's no room for a hand.'

'Let me look!' She seized my arm and unwound the bandage by force, I couldn't stop her without hurting her. I squeezed my eyes shut. The bandage fell away. 'I'm sorry,' Eve said. She'd sewn the flap of skin over the stump and it had healed well. 'It looks good, there's no decay. I'm so sorry. I thought . . .' We both knew what she'd thought, we'd both thought it, hoped. 'It's all right, Eve,' I lied. 'You were right. I was afraid.'

'No, you weren't,' she said. 'Not you.' She was fierce. 'No you weren't.' Her lips trembled and I knew she'd cry. A tear fell on to my stump and she brushed it away. 'Ow!' I complained, but she gasped, 'I felt something.' Again she touched the skin covering the stump with the tips of her fingers, rotating them gently. 'I can feel something underneath.'

'Yes, my bone.'

'There's bumps.' She stared at me. 'Three, no, four bumps.'

The pain kept me restless all night, worse every day. The skin stretched up tight in four bumps, then a fifth appeared at the side. I lay quietly in the dark. My arm felt as though it were splitting at the wrist, red, inflamed. Then one morning after my swim something on my wrist caught in my clothing: a tiny white hook stuck through the tip of stretched skin. 'It's a fingernail.' Eve peered. 'Try and move it.' I shivered, 'I can't.' She said, 'Move your fingers.'

'I don't have any fingers.'

I moved the hand I did not have, and the stump moved. 'Careful, careful,' she said, but I took my dagger and quickly split open the skin, and from the rush of straw-coloured liquid four fingers stuck moving weakly from my wrist, and a thumb. No hand, only a child's fingers, but my own, perfect even to the whorls on each fingertip, the same as on my other hand.

Eve kissed them.

Each day the hand grew a little from my wrist, and grew a little stronger. The growing-pains hurt like torture, the bones growing forward inside my flesh, my flesh firming, muscle hardening. At first the hand was weak, I had to learn even the simplest action, picking up a stick took all my strength and skill, but soon I could eat with my hand, touch my nose first clumsily then accurately with my fingers, and within a week or two I practised swordplay among the daylights and shadows, whirling my sword from hilt to point, point to hilt and back again, perfectly balanced on my fingertips, just as I had always done.

Eve watched me. She beat the flats of her hands on her shoulders. 'Well done,' she called. 'Wotan has learned to kill again.' I stared at her confused, then dived into the water and swam down, down, sword flashing, until the current caught me and swept me forward with the river's rush under the rocks, and I came up, up with the bubbles.

I surfaced in the lake where the river boiled up from below, the hot brilliant sun blinded me with heat and light and life as the cries of birds surrounded me, the fluttering wings of butterflies, the fragrance of honeysuckle and wild flowers. I let myself be swept to the warm waters of the shore, put out my hands and felt a grassy bank, lay on the soft grass in the sun. Covering my closed eyes, little by little I let in the light, the blaze of green and blue and shimmering waters. Eve surfaced in the middle and I called to her, plucked her from the water. She stood unresistingly as I kissed her, her arms hanging down as she looked around her. 'Now you don't need me any more,' she said.

'Of course I need you! I love you!' I put my hand up her skirts, she loves that, and kissed all over her face. 'I do love you, Eve.'

'You have your sword hand and your sword. You'll go back to Enoch and brag about killing the dragon, and weep for Kidu, and kill some more, and make their widows weep – and their children – the children you can't have.'

I remembered Kidu and saw his grave where she had dug it, grown over with grass and flowers. Grief overwhelmed me, tears rushed to my eyes. I lay on Kidu's grave and held the earth.

'If I'm immortal,' I whispered, 'I'll watch everyone I know die. You.' I clung to her hands.

'You are immortal, Wotan. And sterile.' She stroked my hair. 'Lie on me, not Kidu. Give your love to the living not the dead.'

'Sterile love.'

'Love. Hope. Not giving up. Our day in the sun, that's all. One tiny little spark, that's all it takes. Just one. Just one that persuades the egg to believe.'

'Believe?'

'I believe in love,' she whispered. 'I love you, you can do anything.' She stroked my arm. 'You can do more than make love like a bull and make war like a lion, destroy cities and pick men up and, oh, whatever you do, throw them down again. One tiny thing might happen.'

I asked, 'We're married, aren't we?'

She looked away. 'You're so romantic.' She gripped my hand until her hand shook. 'I have been married to you since' – she turned and stared unblinking into my eyes – 'since that day a tall noisy boy jumped out of his tar-covered basket in the reeds.'

'I'm still him.'

'You'll watch me grow old, and when I die you'll hold me in your arms just as I once held you, and you'll never change. I'll be an old woman, ugly, grey, without teeth or sense or courage, and you'll be' – she kissed my hands – 'young.' Her voice trailed away, she stared at my new hand that held my sword. In the sunlight the shiny pale mark was plain to see. 'The dragon,' she said. 'It's the mark of Huwawa's tooth.'

I tried to pull my hand away but she clung on. 'Can't be.'

But it was. She touched the triangular scar on the back of my new hand. 'It's cold.' She turned my hand over, touched the same scar from thumb to forefinger to the heel of my palm where the dragon's tooth had bitten through. 'I'll cut my hand off,' I said, but she covered it with her own hands. 'It would grow again, don't you see? However many times you cut it off, it would grow again. It's part of you.'

'No, you are, you're part of me too, Eve.' I lifted her from my hand, stood her lightly beside me, then threw my sword from my hand as far out into the lake as it would go.

The ripples spread, and after a while lapped our toes.

'I awoke the Serpent,' I said. 'I'm fated – damned – to wander the earth for ever. Noah said so. More than immortal life: eternal existence. The dragon's curse. And yours.'

She looked up, stood on tiptoe. 'Not if you have love. Kiss me.' She kissed me wide-eyed, knowing what she did. 'I cleave only to you. You're my heart, my breath, all I am, I don't exist without you. Because I love you.'

I murmured, 'Because I love you.' She closed her eyes

and relaxed into the kiss. I slapped my forehead, dropped her. 'I just remembered what Noah said! Eden's where your heart is!'

She sprawled unimpressed by my insight; she already knew. She and her sisters were probably born knowing it. I picked her up, dusted her down, I couldn't suppress my excitement. 'Eve, wherever we are is Eden. Two rivers, four, it doesn't matter. It's inside us.' I ran with her to the top of the green hill, swept my arm over the immense view of Shem, even the greatest cities no larger than patches of smoke, the silver river broadening into the haze over the Gulf. 'We're in love, we can go anywhere, we can do anything, be – whatever we want!' I remembered the Abode of the Blessed, the island called Twin Waters, Ni-Tuk. 'Two rivers, not four – the island where the two rivers, Perath and Hiddek'El, meet! Not at the beginning, the end! That's what Noah meant.'

Eve chuckled, pulled my ears tolerantly, kissed me. 'No cities, no wars, no other women. Only me.'

I cut down a tree for the river to carry, passed silently by the walls of Enoch in the night; when we reached the reed beds that stretched from horizon to horizon I took my dagger and cut twice sixty poles of berdi-reed of sixty cubits each, tied them together to make a boat, and coated my boat underneath with tar from the spring to make it watertight. I cut a tall light-starved sapling for a punt-pole and six more to tie in a length for when the water was deeper, wove a sail from a field of flax, and carved an oar to steer by when the wind was strong. And each night I made love to my wife all night, and each day I pushed and punted and pulled my boat across the reed sea. I was as happy doing this with Eve as when I'd led great projects, the building of cities and the fighting of wars and the loving of many different women – and then I realised, looking at Eve asleep, or her silhouette against the sunrise, or hearing her laughter, that *this* was my great project. She. Simply she.

I lay beside her while she slept under the stars, my hand on her womb. Only two of us, not three. We were so lonely, the two of us together in love.

The reedy river-delta of the Perath and Hiddek'El fell behind us, we rocked on the sea with the deltas of the River Batin and River Karun – the four rivers – falling behind on our right and left, the temple-tops of drowned cities showing as foam and spray among the waves. Sometimes as the wind blew we saw *magilum* boats piled high with the dead of the cities voyaging southward with us in hope of eternal life. The sandy shores of the Abode of the Blessed, the island of Twin Waters, called Dilmun by the canaans, rose out of the sea fringed with palms and rare trees. In a calm lagoon away from the busy canaanite trading harbours we swam in the sea and lay on the sand, and I built a house of logs and fronds for Eve my wife, and lay with my wife there, and loved my wife in our house, and gave my wife my semen like a bull; and she did not conceive.

I loved my wife in the sea, and she did not conceive.

I loved my wife by moonlight, sunlight, once during an eclipse of the sun, and she did not conceive. By which I mean *I* did not conceive; it was my fate not hers. Yet she loved me, and would have no other, and so she did not conceive. The years passed, and I noticed a strand of grey in her hair. Eve was always a little older than me of course, an adolescent when I was a child; I said nothing. I saw small lines deepening round her mouth, but I said nothing. One day her monthly courses would cease, but I said nothing. I lay in my house with my wife, and one day she ran away.

I searched the beaches where the fishing boats were pulled up, I searched the harbours where the *magilum* ships docked, I walked with the cortèges of the dead to the immense cemeteries that fill the interior of the island, row after row of verdant hillocks by the thousand and ten thousand, planted with grass like green breasts in imitation of nature, crypts for the dead to await the finding of the Pearl of legend: the pearl of great price to herald the end of the world and the raising of the dead to happiness. She was not there.

I climbed the tallest tree and saw her nowhere.

I ran to all the temples and she was not to be found.

Enash the pedlar, king of thieves, grinned with his mouth of broken teeth. 'Lost her? Saw her at the harbour, she got a man I reckon, yes? She gone home now I reckon, yes.'

I arrived home in a rage and Eve greeted me crossly. 'Where have you been? It doesn't matter. There's a fisherman.' She pointed at an ancient asal-reed boat beached on the sand, waterlogged, dripping water through the cracked red tar that was supposed to keep it out. The gnarled fisherman leant against the stone anchor, arms crossed, scratching his leg with his foot. His skin was burnt to black leather by salt and sun, his beard bleached white. Eve ran to him, dragged him to me by his elbow. 'This is Kino. Everyone says Kino's stupid, everyone steals his fish from him, but he's only slow in the mouth. His mind's sharp, isn't it, Kino?' she demanded.

Kino thought about it, nodded. 'Sharp as a net,' he said. He put his tongue out, to warm it in the sun I suppose. He was senile, his brain baked by his hard life on the sea.

I grabbed Eve. 'Where have you been? What have you been doing? Who is this idiot?'

She said crossly, 'This idiot knows where the Pearl is.' She stamped her foot. 'I've been *waiting* for you.'

I was as cross as she. 'Oh, Eve! Why do you want to deceive yourself?'

She burst into tears. 'I don't want to grow old! Look at me!'

I denied what I saw. I hugged her. We both knew she spoke the truth. 'I never want to be old,' she whispered. I swallowed. I had to do whatever she wanted. 'How much gold will he take?'

She smiled at Kino, whispering to me, 'He'll show us the place for nothing.' I whispered, 'Well, what does he want for himself?' She hissed, 'I told you, he's stupid, old, worn out.' We both smiled at Kino. I whispered to Eve, 'You know this is a waste of time.'

She said simply, 'What choice do I have?'

'Saved people live for ever,' Kino muttered. 'Pearl fishermen call these seas *pairidzaeze*. Paradise.' He scratched himself. 'Kino knows the place where the salt and fresh waters meet.' I stared; Eden is wherever we are. Eve pinched my arm, come on. 'I'll show you for nothing,' Kino said. 'Won't help you, poor people.'

'Why?'

'You poor people will see.' He strained against his boat as I shoved it in the water for him, I swung Eve aboard, swam the boat through the surf into unbroken waves. Kino hooked the tattered sail over the mast and crouched by the steering oar, instantly motionless, part of the boat's own motion all his life. The bobbing rafts of the pearl fishermen fell behind us, the swell grew long and deep, the island sank beneath the smooth curves of the waves. The sun set, we listened to the slop of filthy tarry water from side to side in the boat, watched the mast circle in the stars, then dawn rose and Kino held up his finger to the wind. He sniffed the sea, then pointed to a circle of calm water among the waves, and the boat slid into stillness. 'My father dived down deeper between the walls of coral than any man and when his breath was crushed, and his eyes were bursting, he saw an oyster below him, an oyster as big as the world. He believed the oyster *was* the whole world. And the oyster yawned its mouth like an abyss to drink the sea, and on its tongue of soft delicate flesh lay a pearl, the largest pearl he had ever seen, and his eyes burst and that was the last thing he saw. The Pearl of great price.'

'I can get down that far,' Eve said. 'I'm a good swimmer.' Not when I'm around; I dived over the side and swam down from the silvery surface into the pale blue into the dark blue, and still no sign of the bottom. Great spires and antlers of white coral grew up around me, my chest heaved for breath, the air in my lungs dragged me back to the surface.

'I can do it, let me try,' Eve said. And let her have all the glory? I whooped breath and swam down to the walls of the coral but the current pushed me up, my mouth opened in the sea and the sea rushed in, I tasted it: not sea but fresh water. At the surface I gasped: 'Fresh!'

Eve begged, 'I've got to do it, it's mine. It's for me.' I couldn't let her, the challenge was irresistible, I pushed down, swam down, kicked down to the coral, but my lungs pulled me back. Then bubbles rushed past me going down, I glimpsed Eve dropping down holding the heavy anchor-stone in her arms, her hair waving above her head in the rush of water as she sank, shrinking without effort into the deep blue below me. I stared enviously, grabbed the coral to hold myself down and blood poured from my hands on the sharp growths, turning the coral wall pink like a pink wave going away from me. My wife would find the pearl, not I.

I pulled my strength into my body, thrashed downwards after her like a swimmer in a race. Deep blue water pressed on my ears and lungs, making me heavier so I sank faster, and now darkness opened below me like a mouth and I sank into the darkness between fresh and salt.

Eve's bubbles rose against my face, leading me down, and a light showed in the darkness. The dimmest light possible, barely a glow, a watery silvery glow. I thought it immense. Then the equally immense silhouette of Eve's hand reached forward, and I realised we were almost close enough to touch. The pearl was smaller than I'd imagined; only a pearl. As if sensing Eve's hand the oyster's shell slammed shut. In almost total darkness I sensed her trying to put her arms around the shell, but it was too large, too weighty to lift; pallid bubbles came from her nose. She wouldn't give up. She pulled and jerked at the shelly jaws but they set hard as stone. I swam beside her, my hands pulled at the oyster's tight-clamped lips beside her hands; for the first time in my life I put forward all my strength and exhaustion rushed into me, salt sweat poured from my body into the fresh water. My fingers bent like wet clay, then the jaws loosened, creaking, the lips parted, the mouth gaped wide as childbirth. Eve reached inside, gently took the pearl in her hand. My strength almost failed me; an instant after she withdrew her hand the jaws snapped closed unstoppably, almost trapping me by my hands on the seafloor for ever.

She put her arms around me and we swam to the surface of the sea with our arms around each other, rose almost out of the sea into the sun in the rush of our ascent, fell back in the foam laughing and whooping for air. I climbed aboard, pulled Eve after me. I bumped Kino and he gave an exclamation of pain, a piece of coral caught in my clothes had cut him. He held up the coral reverently, red as blood. Red coral, never seen before. Even white coral is believed to give life; coral as red as a man's blood would be priceless in the markets. Kino the idiot held his fortune in his hands. 'There's more?'

'There's nothing,' I said, 'except red coral down there. Take us home, return, fill your boat.'

The boat sailed home with the evening wind and we came to shore at moonrise in the darkest hours of the night, the honey-coloured moon overhanging the surf that rose and fell like slow surges of honey, the black waves breaking golden and gleaming along the dark shore. The boat swayed in the surf, pulled back, rushed forward. We'd come far enough, called farewell to the fisherman, and dived over the side.

On the sand we lay listening to the roar of the surf, and for the first time my wife opened her fist and showed me the moonlit pearl, a trinket such as a man might give the most beautiful woman in his world as a gift. 'It's beautiful,' I said, because she wanted me to. I reasserted myself. 'What do you do, eat it?'

'You're so strong,' she whispered, 'and so stupid. It's my gift to *you*. Don't you love me?'

'We've made love thousands of times,' I reminded her proudly. 'Look at me, I could do it again right now.' But she smiled, dropped the pearl in the sand. 'It's nothing.' She stroked my eyelashes. 'Nothing.'

I scrabbled for the pearl among the grains, found it. A moment later a wave washed over the place, tugging at out bodies as its foam returned to the sea. I held the pearl clenched tight in my fist.

'It's just a pearl,' she said wistfully. 'It's not love. It's not the act of love you love so much, that's got you . . . nowhere. Pride, strength, lust, fighting, glory, all these things we admire in a man, you more than anyone, they're nothing. In the end they count for nothing, they turn to dust.'

'I do love you.'

'Then love me,' she said. 'Really love me. Real love. Intense love. True love. Let me love you. Let me have you. I don't mean just that cock you're so proud of, let me have all of you, give all of your heart, all of your soul, all of your blood, every drip. All you are. Die for me.'

She asked the one thing I cannot do.

'That's love,' she whispered. 'Be born again in me.'

She kissed my hand, she took the pearl in her mouth, she kissed me as though the pearl was nothing. A wave washed over us, we slid with the foam into the sea, the waves turned us over, we rose up and fell down. The bubbles of her breath rushed in my mouth, I inhaled her, felt her, felt my body hard and hot with passion against me, felt my muscles and my own strength crushing me, piercing me, stretching me, and then an act of love more like murder than the giving of life, this sudden boiling rushing birth of energy and violence gushing into my body, my womb.

A miracle. Life.

I stepped from the sea and looked back. They never found his body.

I walked naked across the sand in the moonlight, combed my hair dry in the house he'd built for me, knotted the pearl in my hair and dressed in clothes that he'd have liked to see me wear. My decorative copper ring broke when I pulled it over my ankle, I must learn to be careful of my strength. I knew he was inside me, still inside me; I was more than one.

Still in love.

As the sun rose I looked at my face in the freshwater pool out back of the lagoon. Me and not-me, him and not-him. Something more than us both. I knew I was pregnant, I felt my baby like a warm comforting glow inside me. It didn't make me feel different, it felt . . . natural.

I prevented an urge to play with my breasts. That's definitely not-me. My hand slid across my loins. 'Stop it.' My body's got none of the glamour for me it held for him; still, my fingers couldn't help scratching an imaginary tickle on my nipples. I crossed my arms to stop my hands playing and walked back to my house. I grew tired quickly; so this is tiredness! And I slept every night, which I've never done before. And my baby grew inside me, my immortality.

For weeks Enash the pedlar hung about with a couple of his cronies. 'Man gone away for good I reckon, yes?'

He grinned his mouthful of broken teeth, then pulled at me with his friends, which he never dared when my husband was around. My male sense understood them perfectly, how their minds worked, they thought me a woman defenceless and alone. 'No good screaming I reckon, beautiful woman.' His cronies held my arms while Enash admired my body. Instead of struggling and screaming I smiled. I warned them, but they didn't understand. I wanted to fight, wanted their blood, the rage for blood rose up, took me over, I couldn't stop myself: I thought like a man, I wanted trouble, when they backed away I followed them, when they struck at me I welcomed their pathetic blows. I banged their heads together. I felt wonderful! Come on! Enash drew his knife so I broke it and threw it away, and threw him away too.

They never troubled me again, but all I cared about was my baby. I returned quietly to my house.

The months passed like weeks, and I have never been so happy.

My tummy swelled, it felt like less than nine months – but maybe it always feels like that – and then I knew my time had come to lie down in my room, on my bed of palm fronds, the sound of surf echoing peacefully through the walls. I grabbed the wall-posts with my fists. For the first time I felt what only a woman feels, this agony, felt my body, Eve's body, pushing and splitting in agony. My blood dripped down the fronds. The wall-posts that held up the walls bent, splintered, snapping, I might pull the whole house down on top of me, I don't care. I see a tiny head poking out between my legs, my baby, my baby slides into my hands, my voice overwhelms me, crying out: 'Eve, my love, Eve I love you, give him to me. Give me our son.'

I have a baby boy. I hug him tight. Mine.

But not-mine. I named him Ymir, but he was not-me. I watched Ymir play in the sand and sea among the cooling waves, loved him, called him to eat, watched him grow.

Time went so fast! A year seemed no more than a day; in less than a month of days, it seemed, he grew tall as I, taller. Yes, loved him with a mother's intensity and sense of loss . . . yet did not know him. He was not-me, he was himself. Different. My son. My life.

Ymir sat beneath a palm tree, chin on his hand, watching the breaking sea. The wind blew his long blond hair, fluttered his eyelashes beneath the frowning dark line of his eyebrows, and I knew he was thinking. I knew one day he would go. 'Don't go far away,' I called.

The next morning, Ymir was gone. The world is huge; I didn't see him again for many years, many, and heard nothing.

I was weary and without him my heart broke like the sea. My hair was white, the sun burnt my withered skin, I was old with a mother's pride and loss, my job was done. My bones cracked, my strength fled like youth, I lay on my bed listening to the thunder of the breaking waves like tolls of passing time. In daytime the slats of sun through my frond roof grew unbearably bright, blistering my skin, but I welcomed the cool nights, the darkness, weakness, peace. I slept.

I awoke. I knew I was dying. My breath gasped, breathing took all the strength I had. I knew I'd die at sunrise; I couldn't bear another day of sun, not even the thought of it. Somehow, falling back many times, I got to my feet and picked up my knife. Who was I when I had a knife like that? Was I young? Was I beautiful? Was I strong? I walked on the beach beneath the stars, blind to them, deaf to the surf. The waves washed over my footprints, erasing my existence as I walked forward, and I heard goat bells among the dunes. I tripped, stared down: like death itself a fish lay dead at my feet, swept up with driftwood and weed. I fell, lay beside it, chewed the hard scales, the indigestible oily flesh beneath, felt an artery between my teeth, tugged weakly and sweet blood coursed into my mouth. I swallowed. I drank, and swallowed.

I climbed to my feet and walked, loped, ran among the dunes, my knife found a goat and slit its neck in a *molech*-blow and I knelt and drank the blood, drinking, swallowing the hot blood, and strength coursed into me. In the marshland an ox stood stuck in mud to its knees, lowing piteously as I sucked its blood by the light of the moon. I turned full of strength and splashed away through the pool, scattering moonlight around me like spray.

I stopped, staring down at myself as the waters came together and stilled. The size and strength of my masculine body had torn her clothes to shreds, but the pearl was still pinned to my shoulder. 'Eve?' I called. I threw away her clothes, pinned the pearl to the flesh of my shoulder for safekeeping, and strode bull-naked back to the house I'd built with these two hands.

I am Wotan, and I remember the moment of my conception.
Eve lives inside me still. She sees through my eyes.

She changed me, though I look the same, and I'm as strong as ever – and even more attractive to women. This time you sense the depths in me, I'm more than the man I was, more than a gorgeous body. We never recover from being in love, it changes us, we're never the same again. Love does live for ever, believe me. Through *us*, we have a child; Eve gave me her gift of immortality, I gave her mine. Fair exchange; she's inside me still, and I in her. I knew our son Ymir might be around the next corner, any time; his might be the next hand that opened the reed door. He might fall in love, might have children of his own, I might hear of his great deeds; but I did not. I didn't rage against his fate and mine. I know what it is to be both male and female, a man with the strength of a woman, a man who knows from his own experience what it is to give birth out of his body. Eve would say I've grown more mature. Eve *does* say it. Well, maybe I have. But not too much.

One day I walked through the busy village to the quay and sat drinking wine, watching slaves unload the reed boat from Meluhha heaped sky-high with spices, metals, fabulous cloths. Then the dour drums beat, joy evaporated, and I put down my cup as a *magilum* boat rowed into the harbour. In the open cabin the body of a king lay wrapped in a three-ply shroud on the golden bier, his possessions piled around him for his use in the next life. The weeping of his women carried across the water in the eternal wail of grief. They, too, did not have much longer to live, nor his slaves who packed the boats in the wake of the royal barge, complete with his horses and his hunting falcons, who would also follow the king to the grave. A tall dignified lady stepped from the boat on to the quayside, and despite her white hair and cloudy eyes I recognised Nin. I blurted her name and she turned towards my voice. 'It's you!' we cried together. I embraced her and she peered close. 'You haven't changed at all. You don't look a day older.' She stroked my face. 'Why didn't you come back? Didn't she find you?'

'Eve? Of course she found me.'

She clung to my hand, nodding, muttering. 'And they say Kidu killed the dragon Huwawa, and you killed the Bull of Heaven.'

I started to correct her, then let it go. 'Maybe it happened that way. It was a long time ago.'

'And you never discovered immortality.' She grasped my shoulder. 'Lugal is dead.'

'He was a good man and a good king. I'll mourn him.'

'I came here to die with him,' she said intensely. 'Go back to Enoch, Wotan. Kingship was not let down from Heaven last year, our prayers were not answered. Return and be king of your city that took you in when you were in need.' She squeezed my arm with her arthritic fingers.

I said no, no, no, but I knew what Eve would want. 'Yes,' I said. 'But you mustn't die, Nin. Come back to

Enoch, climb the temple as wife of Ya, and your prayers will be strong enough to elect me to the kingship. That's my condition.'

Nin gripped my hands. She would live.

On the first day of the new year the God of Enoch, Ya, was enthroned as every year at the festival chapel, the *akītu*, in divine kingship over my city. From the streets and squares and rooftops below us the people shouted, 'Ya has become King!' The rite of sacred marriage was performed between Ya and Ishtar in the person of Nin, then the trumpets blew and earthly kingship descended from Heaven into the hands of the priests, Nin anointed my head in symbolic birth, and the shouts of the people acclaimed me Priest and King. On the seventh day of these rituals as old as time I sacrificed a red bull, atoning (the harvest had failed) for the sins of the people during the past year, reconciling them with the righteous punishment of Ya, and my city prospered.

But I remembered the dragon uncoiling in the deeps of the world. *It suits me very well that you, Ishtar, shall be worshipped by the people as the wife of Ya, and I, B'El, be worshipped as His son.*

Many times in my golden fleece I watched my people from the shadowed colonnades of my Egalmah palace, their brief scurrying lives, envying their simple faith, scratching my scarred hand. There are great and terrible and wonderful truths to be found in this world, and though my people live hardly a day, somehow they do sense them. Perhaps more than I. But I've seen the dragon with my own eyes, I've seen Ishtar, I *know* I am a son of God. I know there is Truth.

And in all these days, I have not aged a day.

Shall I stay and rule over my city for a thousand years? Shall I call my city Ur-Shalom and call myself the Anointed Saviour that Noah the first Zadok foretold? Shall I conquer all the surrounding cities of the plain, and make their kings

213

grovel at my feet? But Enoch is already first among the nations of Shem, and their kings already do.

At night I walked from the darkness of my palace on to the moonlit balcony. The rough noises of the Kullaba carried to me and I longed to join the harlots and warriors in the holy taverns, but my head was too full of questions. My shadow rippled across the pillars of lapis lazuli as I paced, I held out my arms in prayer, and this happened many nights. Prayers are not answered. Then one night as I reached out in my anguish, peace equal to my anguish flowed into me. A shadow, not my own broad-shouldered muscular shadow but slender, feminine, reached forward to my hand from the pillar as I put out my own hand – my slim delicate hand, unmarked by war – and I touched my shadow. Quick, quick, a bowl of water, a mirror: my face was not my face. 'Eve?' I whispered, but my voice lost its deepness, I looked through Eve's eyes, I inhaled the scents of the night, I drew in the glorious moonlight over the city like new breath. In me Eve lived for ever, for ever young.

'You will know,' she whispered, 'what you will do.'

'My lord,' the guard called, 'what's wrong?'

I turned impatiently, strong, blond, entirely male, and dismissed him. 'There's nothing wrong.'

You will know what you will do.

Nin grew old and died, I married a queen I did not love, I lay joyless in my sterile loveless royal bed of many colours woven by my people, and she fattened on sweet dates not children. There would be no children. Her royal beauty aged visibly beside my perpetual youth, so I combed white flour in my hair. Children that I remembered being born birthed children of their own so I stooped when I walked, and my life was heavy. The act became the truth; the people watched me, talking behind their hands, and rumours of my illness flew around my city. And Eve was right. I knew what I must do.

There was a girl in the kitchens I could do anything

with; at last I found a body dead in an alley, about my own size and weight, and we bleached his beard blond with spirit. In the kitchen I plunged my head in boiling water to make my face ghastly like a disfiguring skin disease. My flesh swelled, my hair came away when it was touched, no apothecary could help me. All night I shivered in a bath of cold water, and in the morning I lay stretched out on my many-coloured bed like a hooked fish, my body cold and waxy with the appearance of death. My people wailed for me, praying that I would be brought back to life by B'El, their god of fertility. But on the seventh day, as was the custom, the *magilum* boat must set sail to the Abode of the Blessed with my mortal remains. On the sixth day my kitchen girl, with a saucy wink in her eye, brought a bucket of worms to rub on my body beneath my robes, and the doctors proclaimed, 'The worm has fastened on the king. Let the finger of blessing be stretched out in mourning. Let the people go unshaven in mourning.'

Early in the darkness of the seventh day my kitchen girl opened the inner door and I carried up the dead body from the hiding place, laid it stinking with the worms in my bed, covered its swollen staring face with a cloth. We stole from the outer door, I kissed her and gave her gold. If she ever told the truth, no one believed her. Wotan was dead, and when the sun rose the *magilum* boat rowed from the quay of Enoch, the sail caught the south wind, and I watched until there was no more to be seen.

I turned my back and shook the dust of Enoch from my feet, and never returned there while anyone I knew lived.

XII

The present day
Out of Goldson International Airport, Belize City
She sits with her long sunbrowned legs elegantly crossed

beneath her white cotton suit, her white jacket open to the third button to suckle her baby at her breast. Beneath the silver wing the rolling jungles of Belize give way to the rolling jungles of Mexico, and even after half an hour in the plane's cramped economy class lavatory (despite complimentary perfume) she still smells the explosion on her skin. The odour of burning naphtha and sulphur clings to her flesh along with smears of stone dust and damp tree bark, and worst of all her suit's dried wrinkled. She *never* rides economy class; but this is work, and she keeps a watchful eye on the curtain that separates Premier Class from the crowded rear of the plane. At Campeche she lifts the drunk who snored beside her into another seat. At Mexico City his place is taken by a brown cowboy jacket, brown leather necktie, brown cowboy boots, styled hair and every bourbon a double.

She gives him a hostile stare. He takes off his jacket and folds it over the arm of her seat, claiming her, looks at her thighs, and she smells his aftershave. No rings on her fingers and a baby asleep in her arms, she knows he knows what sort of woman she is. He'll touch her before long, they always do, drop his flight magazine and bend forward retrieving it and glance up her skirt to heaven, maybe brush her knee accidentally with his knuckles, excuse me ma'am, you flyin' alone I guess? She puts her elbow heavily on his jacket and yawns, reading.

Jungle gives way to desert, desert to the sunburnt peaks of the Sierra Madre. The smiling flight attendant in Maya costume brings lunch trays. Cowboy demands, 'What the hell you folks call these eats and where the hell are we?' Smiling she tells him about delicious Creole cookery, glances smiling past Winona through the window. 'Just about now we're flying into the United States of America, Dr Wotan.'

Winona blinks. *America*. The name's so new and odd, so *unfamiliar*, she'll never get used to it. She shakes her head at the tray but the attendant smiles at the sleeping baby. 'What a beautiful baby boy.' Cowboy demands, 'Any chance of good liquor, not this piss?' Turns to Winona. 'Pardon my English, ma'am.'

Winona tells the attendant. 'She's not a boy. She's a girl.' She still can't believe it. A girl. Her first.

The attendant gushes, 'I'm sorry, it's so difficult to tell at that age. She must be three, four months now?'

'She was born three days ago.'

'Oh. My goodness!' The attendant stares at Cowboy's tray knowing she's forgotten to do something, it's gone from her mind. 'Really? Three days?'

Cowboy says: 'Liquor.'

Winona pats his tray. 'He wants his piss.' The flustered attendant fetches bourbon and Cowboy eats gumbo. Winona reclines her seat back and gazes from the window. Cowboy drops his plastic fork, then reaches down bending his head around to look up her legs. She pushes her knee firmly into his face, pulls his tray down on his head and tips his bourbon over his hair, drops his jacket on the mess and kicks him. Her baby's eyelashes are fluttering, if she wakes there'll be no peace. '*Don't wake my baby.*' Her foot on Cowboy's neck keeps him quiet, and baby slides back into sleep. Winona picks up Cowboy in her fist and drops him in his seat, she holds him against the seat back, she looks into his eyes. It's a real struggle not to get angry. She speaks to his eyes.

She says quietly, 'There's a word I want you to remember. It's a little word. It's easy.'

Gumbo and bourbon trickle down his face but he doesn't wipe it away, he stares. He tries to swallow.

She says: 'It's a little word called *sorry* for being such a shit. Are you sorry?'

He swallows. 'I'm sorry, ma'am.' He flinches when she blinks.

Winona takes her fist off him then pushes him back as

she turns away from him. 'Wash yourself up. Come back quietly, cleaned up.' Cowboy pulls himself to the rear of the full plane not meeting anyone's eye. He won't look back. They never do.

She notices a couple of blond hairs growing on the back of her dragon-scarred hand and plucks them out casually, cosmetically.

She settles back, watches her sleeping baby.

Still don't have a name for you, baby.

The aircraft appears to lose height as the mountains rise. Her mind turns back to Apachiohualitzá, the ancient hilltop temple built in the Mayan jungle, an exact copy of the First Temple of Solomon. O Lord, there's no end to evil, not until time ends; for the hundredth time she remembers the screaming black angel, Gonzalez's face on the eerie blue glow of the video monitor, his whispering voice: *The fallen angel. A tradition that Jesus Christ visited these people as a plumed serpent, yes, but let's be serious now. This is the scream of an angel forsaken by God. Such a powerful symbol speaking to our age of suffering. Our search for belief. One true faith to cling to. One truth in this world of lies that can make sense of our lives. Something real . . . something real . . . something real.* In Winona's memory the videotape still runs backwards, the bodies of the students run back to life in the Temple, fatal wounds shrinking and disappearing, gone, screams unborn and unharmed faces smiling, and Tallboy backs into the doorway with his Uzi smoking, flashing, over and over. Over and over again.

Something real.

Ending with Tallboy's huge leering wink close to camera, huge grinning face, huge uparaised thumb in victory: okay. Okay.

Passing over the Grand Canyon the aircraft tilts. Suddenly a biblical landscape of jagged peaks and chasms slides below the wingtip, green valleys spreading outwards from the mountains like fingers grasping a promised land.

The speaker bell chimes softly. 'Passing beneath us you see the Sion National Park. That tall mountain is the Watchman and the line of shadow is Sion Canyon. The three hills to be seen to the left side of the aircraft are the Three Patriarchs, Abraham, Isaac and Jacob. In the foreground see the mountain named after perhaps the most famous patriarch of all, Moroni.'

Winona lifts herself across the vacated seat, and pads forward to the aisle curtain. Careful not to wake baby she lifts the material aside with her fingertip, stares forward into Premier Class, the tops of heads showing above the rows of seat backs. There he is. Tallboy sits tall enough to show his shoulders above the seat back: his ginger hair slicked back to the collar of his pinstripe suit, a glimpse of his profile as he watches the flight attendant. He yawns, checks his Rolex.

Yesterday Winona drank coffee from dawn to dusk at the San Lazaro hardware store, watching the cantina where Tallboy drank, got drunk, slept. From a chicken shed she watched the whorehouse where he passed the night. This morning Tallboy came out fresh and bright, panama hat and white pinstripe suit, a jungle orchid in his buttonhole, no car to be hired. She stole a pickup leaking oil and followed the market bus taking him to Belize City. From there her smoking pickup dogged his Air Maya coach to the Goldson international airport outside town, her baby crying hungrily in her arms as she drove. At the Air Maya desk Tallboy bought a Premier Class ticket on the afternoon flight about to depart, peeled a thousand dollars cash from a fat wad, then added a hundred from another pocket. He went to the boarding gate and Winona crossed to the desk. 'I'll go as far as eleven hundred bucks takes me on the afternoon flight, first class.'

'Salt Lake City, *señora*.'

'I changed my mind. I'll take economy.'

'Seven hundred five dollars plus departure tax.'

219

Now the plane's speaker bell chimes softly, the engines' tone falls. 'Landing at Salt Lake City in ten minutes.' Winona lets the curtain drop, asks the attendant for a cup of water. 'I guess feeding's made me thirsty.' She takes her seat and lets baby feed again, hungry as always. Cowboy comes from the lavatory at the last possible moment, sits without looking at her exposed breast as the white glare of the Great Salt Lake turns beneath the window and distant mountains rise up shimmering over the Jordan Valley and Galilee, then the tyres yelp on the runway.

The jet stops at the terminal and Cowboy turns to Winona. Complex emotions struggle to come first on his simple face. 'I got to apologise. Sorry ma'am. Away from home too long.' Puts out his hand. 'Chris.'

'Forget it, Chris.'

But he won't go. 'I'd be right honoured to carry your bags, ma'am.'

'Winona. Baby's my only luggage, but thank you.' All her attention's on the figure leaving the plane, not Chris. She hangs back at Customs to keep away from Tallboy, his British passport slows him: she uses the booth at the far end, American passport. Coming through, the concourse is busier than she wanted, several flights landing almost at once before evening, but Tallboy's height and ginger hair make him easy to follow. But her own height and striking physical presence, star quality, make her easy to be seen following him. Tallboy looks round a couple of times, that's new: a pillar saves her, then the busy stall of an ice-cream franchise. A cry from baby almost gives her away. She slips her little finger between baby's lips like a teat, drops back behind Chris who tugs a crocodile suitcase on wheels.

Outside the baking breath of the desert washes over Winona from the evening shadows. The lights of autos come on suddenly bright. Tallboy takes a yellow cab, Chris hails the last one on the rank. Hell. The tail lights pull away past her, flare, stop, he winds down the window. 'Winona? Headed downtown? Happy to share.'

Winona sees the tail lights of Tallboy's cab winking down the ramp on to I-80, runs, gets in beside Chris. 'You're a saint.' The Arab driver floors it, the cab sweeps down the ramp picking up speed.

Winona watches Tallboy's yellow cab moving steadily ahead of them towards the lights of Salt Lake City. Even from this distance she sees the floodlights picking out the great golden statue topping the huge Temple. Her baby looks up at her calmly, curiously, smiling at the golden reflection moving in Winona's eyes.

She laughs, lifts the corner of baby's mouth with her fingertip, and baby smiles. 'I know what name I'll call you.' Kisses those beautiful baby-blue eyes. The cab changes lane suddenly and Chris warns the driver, 'Take it easy . . .'

Winona kisses her baby. 'Your name is Christine.'

Era Two

Sion

Sion

1,800 BC – 587 BC

1,800–587 BC

Angels sang when I was born. I remember their upraised voices, strange beautiful winged angels of mercy and light never seen before, and I remember my childish voice replying.

I am Wotan, and I remember the moment of my conception.

I am Wotan, I am born and cannot die. *When the mountains wear down to sand and the sun falls cold and the moon turns to blood,* Noah had prophesied, *you will still be like me. Not a life, an existence. An eternity of living in Hell.*

Oh great God, El, Father, the weight of it – immortality!

Why am I here? What's the purpose of my life? Something must happen.

In a reed hut in the wilderness I light a tallow candle and stare at the flame in the dark. The flame flickers in the draught from the walls, then sets still, pointed, bright.

I hold the palm of my scarred hand over the flame. I've tried slicing the scar from my palm with a knife; no good, it goes right through my hand, part of me. Tried cutting it out with the point, but the scar grows back. Perhaps suffering is the answer to life, perhaps somehow we're redeemed by suffering, and by suffering I will understand. To be burnt is the worst pain. The bright flame licks my skin agonisingly, seeking a way up, rising between my thumb and fingers, then seeks a way smokily between all my fingers. I smell my burning blond hairs, then my fingers hook like claws as the scalding skin pulls tight. The skin splits when I straighten my fingers, but then my muscles contract as they burn, dripping fat like sweat to feed the flame so the flame burns higher and more penetrating against my flesh, which crackles like cooking pork. My tendons snap, and you can imagine my pain, my agony, when the flame reaches my bones. But I shall not move my hand.

My bones blacken, crack, marrow bubbles from my joints. I scream, I scream, I feel pain as deeply as you, this dreadful unmanning insufferable pain.

The scar on the back of my hand steams, shrivels, cooks through, and finally the flame burns through from below. It takes most of the night to consume my hand. It's winter; a long night.

By midsummer's day my hand has grown back, perfect. The dragon's scar, too, is perfect. I can never forget.

I forget nothing; my story's as plain and vivid as I told you. I remember my growing strength as a child by the river, every intimate detail of me that you know, I confided to you even the (in all modesty) impressive size of my penis and its stiffness, strong as a cedar beam; told you of my knowledge growing, knowing myself as well as you do, knowing war and murder and killing, knowing women; that's any man's life. Mine's longer, that's all. Even now I remember each single act of lust, each sterile orgasm wasted in ten thousand wombs, ten thousand lustful city women desiring only to tame my gorgeous manhood and to leave me limp and pliable, merely male, in their arms and bed, conquered; which as you know is impossible. It's never happened. I'm no woman's creature.

How I love it, the ejaculation! The thrill! This act, so close to murder for most men, the deaths of their countless perfect images by the hundred million. Yet I am sterile from the first moment. Immortal and immotile, I have nothing to give.

But sometimes there's love, we live as lovers together in love. And love changes everything. In love, I am not sterile. In love I give life for ever. You know Eve lives inside me still. It's marriage, more than a marriage, deeper. You know, you *saw*, Eve looks through my eyes, and you saw me see through her eyes, feel with her feelings, move with her muscles. Like me, she will live for ever, because I love her and she loves me. Because she *is* me. She made her choice, there in the surf of Two Waters taking the pearl, *her* pearl, in her mouth, in my mouth.

I am her, and our child was born.

I wear her pearl still, pinned to my flesh, or in my hair, any place safest.

After all these years there are other women I've loved, and still love. Not many. Gentle Rebekah, Deborah with her kindly smile, Rachel the dark incomparable beauty; and Dinah, dearest Dinah, who loved me but would not change herself, and as the years passed grew old while I remained young, for ever young. Not so many as you'd think, because love is rare. I mean unselfish love, true love, romantic love, it's so rare. More rare than gold and diamonds, and ten years turn into sixty, and simple human loving lives shrivel like Dinah's and pass away: but I move on from place to place and life to life and a hundred years turns into two hundred, and the two into three, four, five hundred, and six hundred turns into many, and each former world I have known and sometimes loved passes away, passes away, going, gone.

The trade with Meluhha passed away, there was no more gold; I sailed on the reed ships with Meskiag of Kush raiding southward past the Abode of the Blessed, Two Waters, down the Gulf to the Red Ocean, and my hand pushed the steering oar when the order was given to turn towards the setting sun. The tarred pirate ships stole like shadows west along the empty coast, then steered northward up the Red Sea that lies like a salty blue finger between the deserts. We called the shores of Egypt on our left hand *Muzri*, and this time we came to plunder not to trade. On the day the red star Sirius rose before the sun, I stood beside Meskiag and beached the boats not far south of where the Red Sea splits into two horns; I helped drag the boats on logs with long ropes westward along the Wadi Barramiya between the sandstone hills into the land that would be called Kush. I stood beside him as the boats were launched in the broad lush mouth of Wadi Abbad, flooded by the rising Nile. Meskiag and his younger brothers killed or enslaved whoever they met, and made them their people. The people worshipped their new masters and the sons of their dynasty as gods of the great house, *Pr'O*, Pharaohs.

I saw the former world pass away, I saw new heavens and new earths born, and new gods who were the same as the old gods.

Long ago I left the land of the Pharaohs, sailed in the canaanite cockleshells and later their great creaking vessels wherever the Mediterranean wind blew, and finally the wind blew me back to the fertile crescent of canaanite land on the eastern shore. The Pharaohs called the canaans *Kanunu* at first then *Foenke*, Phoenicians. Canaanite tribes had moved westward from Shem into the land between the Jordan and the sea, following the trees and trade as they always had; so many traders haggling and bartering in so many towns and markets that the whole busy land was called Canaan.

I returned home across the deserts to Enoch but found nothing there, only the place remembered by a few local peasants as Har'El, the Mountain of God, perhaps a folk memory of my own long-ago failed quest; nothing more than an immense hill of rubbish standing out of flooded marshes, and all the people I'd known gone as if they'd never been. Not one stone did I recognise, all built over, even my great walls I'd built to stand for ever blown away like the dust. Yet there are always miracles. Sixty years later I returned and found a new miracle, a new world born on the dust of the old, a thriving market on the summit, and a new temple making a new summit; in another sixty years a great city stretched out from the twelve-gated temple across the dry desert that was once marshland, and even my name was forgotten. But still they worshipped Ya there, and kept His feasts; each new invader took over the old gods and spoke the old names in new tongues. But tongues and spittle don't change, only the accents they utter, and Ya whether He was called Ya or Ea or Éya was always Ya, and El whether He was Enki or Enlil was always El, God, so that for all this time, six years times sixty years times six years – more than twenty centuries – the gods had never moved, loyal to their own cities in their own holy land of Shem; not moving even while Bab'El rose from its ruins and newly risen Enoch sank again into ancient obscurity. But always as I traversed the land I saw that the new married the old, and the old married the new, and always new children were born who didn't know where they came from, but knew what God they believed in, and their brief lives burnt through like just-lit candles. Lit, extinguished, gone. Passed away. I watch them born, I watch them die, and I live on.

What does this all mean? This immensity of life and death, always these new miracles, the huge pointlessness of it all. But what if there's a meaning for everything that happens in this seeming-chaos? Of course there is.

Of *course* there is. Again I remember Noah's voice speaking. *Have you found your heart, young Wotan? Do you know where it is?*

I've sought death on the battlefield, I've climbed mountains seeking death, and you've seen me dare death beneath the sea. I did not find my heart or God; but I found where it was not, and where God wasn't. He's not here. I'd live until the mountains were sand and the sun was cold and the moon turned to blood, that's all. I sat among the monumental ruins of Enoch with the desert wind blowing my cloak, the broken walls of the temple complexes falling away below me, the white temple, the mosaic temple, all the others, the temple of Ishtar almost buried, its corners rounded by wind and sand. Far below the usual misery of ruined suburbs inhabited by foul-mouthed women, dogs, squabbling children, a few reed boats at the ramshackle quays, were all that remained of my great thriving city; and then a few heavily laden donkeys led by men and trailed by women came plodding on the riverside track from Ur. Idiots. The marsh path – still called the Moon Road, connecting Ur with Haran – would soon flood with the winter rains, and no one came here these days, except to be robbed.

They were lost. They'd die.

I watched from high above as the strangers trailed like ants among the hovels; children, wives, concubines, slaves, following their white-bearded patriarch and owner who hobbled with a stick. No fighting men, no armour – traders, canaans. Canaans, I've always had a soft spot for them; by now the families I'd known long ago had grown to kingdoms. Who were these leftovers, and what were they doing here five hundred miles east of Canaan, where all the best land's been claimed by now? I stood watchfully, then leapt down from ruined peak to ruined peak, ran along a wall. The traders were trapped in a babble of voices at the centre of the village, dogs worrying their heels and women screaming curses from doorways, girls offering beer and their bodies, boys throwing stones. They'd find no hospitality here, no market, no mercy: they pulled plump donkeys with full panniers, they were defenceless, hauling too many women and young children, but they didn't seem to understand their fate. Any moment now the men of the village, awakening from their afternoon stupor, would come stumbling from their huts and hovels, and then it would be too late – I leapt from the wall just as a stone struck the old man above the eye. He clutched his stick, swaying, one hand clapped to his forehead.

'I am Terah, a prince of Ur! You dare not touch me!' The villagers laughed; he spoke gibberish, the East

Shemitic tongue – with an Amori accent – but they knew only the old country vocals of Buranun. The boy who'd thrown the first stone picked up another. As I strode past I flipped his feet from under him, caught the stone and cracked it in my fist. This always gets the attention of boys. I opened my fist, blew away the dust, and from their faces saw there'd be no more stones. 'It's him,' one of them whispered. 'It's the Watcher.'

'We come peacefully to your city,' Terah said incomprehensibly.

I strode forward as the thieves gathered. 'This man is Prince Terah, a proud aristocrat of Ur,' I proclaimed boldly, getting between the old fool and Mashgun the village leader. Mashgun scratched his belly and said, 'Tell the old fart I am King Mashgun and he gives me his donkeys and his women and he lives.' Much laughter. Mashgun didn't laugh. 'This man Terah,' I said, 'is a ferocious Amori warrior, and you're going to let him and his people go.' Mashgun drew his sword and his men jerked out whatever weapons they had, circling. I sighed, I'd make widows today. I can't help these regrets at such moments, it's my sensitive feminine side.

But a deep voice called out, 'I'll fight King Mashgun man to man, father.' A man pushed past the donkeys, quite old at almost thirty, large dark eyes, a prince's multiple headband. No weapon, not even a slingshot. 'You're angry and foolish,' I said, but he shouted furiously, 'Say my words, stranger!' I shrugged at Mashgun and lied cheerfully. 'The prince says he'd fight you man to man, Mashgun, if you were a man. But you're only a poisonous water-mussel.' I grinned. 'So I'll fight you myself.' I took Mashgun's arm to break it and end the matter, but the prince shouted, 'Stop!'

I stopped, and history changed. 'My name's Abram,' the prince said. 'I and my brothers do our own killing.'

I was pleased, I like a fight. 'Don't let me stop you.'

Mashgun's men crowded forward with ferocious weapons, snarling.

'This is your fault, stranger,' Abram accused me. He was a prince of Ur and city folk are always hot for law, fault, blame. 'Look how angry you've made him. He's red. You insulted him.' Abram had more languages than his father, but his life hung by a thread.

I sighed. 'King Mashgun's a murdering thief. I insulted him because I was going to hurt him, but you wanted it your own way, and now he'll kill you.'

'It's my life, and my death.' From his clothes Abram drew a sword – more like a long knife, really, and dull grey-black not shiny bronze or the lovely hammered copper swords I remembered from antiquity. 'Look,' someone called, 'he's got a little sword!' Everyone laughed – even I, remembering when that was said of me. I liked Abram's courage – but Mashgun's war-sword, pilfered from some battlefield, was longer than my arm. I accidentally trod on Mashgun's foot and elbowed him by mistake in the stomach to slow him up, but Abram gave me a fierce look. 'It was my father who was struck.' He softened, he had gentle eyes that went oddly with his courage. 'Can I trust you?'

'Trust no man.'

'Will his men kill me if I win?'

Of course they would. 'No, Abram,' I sighed, giving my word. He grinned and said, 'Then my life depends on you.'

'Your life,' I said, 'depends on your sword.' I shivered as though I'd spoken some terrible truth that lay still in the future – and perhaps a stillborn future, because it was in truth a very small sword. Mashgun roared and swung his weapon at Abram with all his strength, leaning back against the pull of the heavy blade as it swung hissing in the air. Abram crouched, held up his little black knife – and Mashgun's sword touched Abram's and broke in two.

232

The bronze tip clattered loudly on the ground. Mashgun stared at it then at the stump of hilt he still held. Mayhem began, great fun. A couple of Mashgun's nephews slipped behind Abram to stick him in the ribs or strangle him, I knocked a few heads together and threw a few beards through windows and over roofs, but the Amori fought forward like fierce little dogs. Abram called out to his elder brothers, 'Haran! Nahor!' – they must be named after the cities in which they were born – and the three brothers fought shoulder to shoulder, joined by a cocky little youngster called Lot who ran forward from his mother, Haran's wife; she kept calling his name after him and wringing her hands, then wailing complaints at Haran himself. But I saw Haran was so proud of his son that he made space for Lot at his side. Bronze blades, I noted; only Abram possessed the black blade that cut through bronze. And Abram was not the father, not even the eldest son of Terah, but the youngest.

'Fight me,' I advised Mashgun, 'or offer them hospitality.' Someone threw a spear but I broke it and pulled my strength into me with my angry irresistible joy of battle, broke the spear-thrower's head, inhaled the smell of sweat and blood blowing on the wind, the sound of stamping feet and weapons and screams of pain. Twenty to one against, I love these odds, time for plenty of violence before sunset. 'We don't need your help,' Haran said, stabbing, driven back against a mud wall, but Abram called out to me in the tongue of East Shem, 'Help us.'

I sighed. *Help us.* How could I refuse them what the great God refused me, how could I forsake and abandon these people when I was myself forsaken, abandoned? I sulked, gave the neck I held in my fist one last squeeze, threw away the man who wriggled in my other hand. In country speech I told Mashgun, 'These travellers are vicious bastards as you see. They won't stop until they've killed you, but many on both sides will be slaughtered first. So I'm going to help them. I'm going to kill you.'

Mashgun paled: 'Why?'

I couldn't think of an answer, then the truth came to me: 'They're better than you.'

King Mashgun looked at the blood on my hands, my chest, my face, none of it mine. Then came the moment I've known a thousand times. He begged. 'My wife is yours.'

'Their women are prettier,' I said.

Mashgun snarled. He held out his palms in peace to the strangers. His face struggled, but he remembered to drop the hilt of his sword in the dust. 'Welcome, travellers. Peace, peace.' There was a last scream, then silence. Mashgun had no teeth but I heard his gums squeak as he contorted his lips into a hospitable smile. 'My house is your house.'

Only a fool stayed in Mashgun's house or ate his food. The Amori pitched their tents by the river, unloading their donkeys and grazing them, guarding them as the light failed. The women and their children worked busily – there was the usual shortage of men, Nahor's wife was his brother Haran's daughter and Nahor had eight sons by her, and a whole twittering cluster of daughters, and at least four more children by his concubine; Abram alone was childless, lowering his status as youngest even further, yet still the black sword was his. I washed in the river then smelt roasting lamb and took my place in the first circle of men at the campfire. Terah acknowledged me and Abram drew his knife, spiked me the choice fillets and crackliest skin with the black tip, and Nahor scowled. Terah retired to his tent early; he'd travelled little since his sons were born and his bones had grown stiff in Ur. The wives took their food, then the concubines, and the rest scrambled for scraps and bones. Abram and I sat quietly, saying nothing. The fire died down, the storytellers fell silent and the listeners lay sleeping, even the women falling asleep after they'd finished their tasks and lying with their men if they were called, and the stars turned slowly above Abram and me.

'It's iron, isn't it,' I said. He grinned and laid the blade on his hands for me to examine. Stars glinted like sparks in the black. Iron's more precious than gold: Abram the son of Terah held a king's ransom in his hands. I said, 'They say it falls from the stars.'

'It does, my friend,' he nodded. 'That story's true. I saw it.'

'Saw it,' I scoffed.

'I saw with my own eyes a fire light in the sky. The fire crossed the sky like a burning sword beneath the moon. Thunder boomed like the voice of a god. Everyone ran away!' He quivered, remembering. 'I ran forward, not away.'

'And you found this sword just lying in the desert?'

'No. Say nothing. Quiet.' He stood, led me by the hand through the dark to the tent where the donkey panniers were stored, opened it, beckoned, and we knelt inside. 'I found this.'

Abram's hands led mine to a cold jagged shape too heavy for an ordinary man to lift. 'Black as the night, my friend. You can hardly see it even in the day.' The mass felt glassy, fused by heat, and for a horrid moment I thought it was obsidian, volcanic rock, the material of sacrificial knives. Abram felt me shiver and mistook it for awe. 'It's iron. It's mine.' He laughed. 'It's almost pure! Almost impossible to work! We made a furnace out of a termite hill, it took three men to push the bellows, and still it was hardly hot enough!' Now I'd grown used to the dark I made out Abram's eyes staring at me intensely. 'It's our fortune. With this we survive. Times are bad in Ur. With this we can do anything we want. Any canaan hearing our reputation, seeing this, knowing what value we possess, will trade with us for things we carry of lesser value.'

'Or steal it.'

The iron sword glinted as he shook it. 'It's a gift that protects itself.'

'A gift?'

Abram whispered, 'Did the iron fall to me by accident, by chance? Me, and not to Nahor, not to Haran? Did one of the gods send it down to me, personally, for the use of my own hands? No accident, no chance. Divine metal. The sword of Abram.'

How badly they need to think themselves important, humans, finding fate in the shape of a cloud and wisdom in a curl of smoke, and destiny in a lump of iron. My voice spoke to his voice quietly in the dark. 'Which god, Abram?'

'I don't know. The trail of fire crossed beneath the moon, Sin.' I'd noticed some of the donkeys were adorned with little Ur-moon symbols and most of the wives wore moon pendants, silver, copper, dangling from their necks or belts. Abram's voice whispered, 'My father swears by Sin the Moon god. The meteorite was Sin's sign to us. We're on our way to Haran, the city where my father used to trade in his youth, a city dedicated like Ur to the moon.' Nowadays there are thousands of places called Haran, it means Crossroads, but I supposed Abram meant the largest city, in a valley leading towards Mount Ararat. With this rag-tag little trading caravan I'd be retracing my own long-ago journey with Kidu along the banks of the Perath. With Abram and his iron sword, I'd tread in my own footsteps.

'Which god do *you* believe sent the meteorite to you, Abram?'

'Some swear by Ya, who saved Noah the Zadok and all men and animals. Others worship old Anu, the sky-god, Ur-anu of the cities, called by the people of the western islands Ouranos. The god who fell from the sky, fell in love with the earth.' He shrugged. 'My wife Sarai swears

236

like her father by El of the Flood, and His Son who makes the spring crops grow, but of course she's brought along her own household gods, the teraphs, who always bring her good luck, and her mother good luck before her.' Sarai was a beauty, ten years younger than Abram, twenty at most, married since she was twelve probably. I'd cast an appreciative eye over her swaying breasts and backside when the wives knelt at the cooking pot. 'But we've not been blessed with children,' Abram added, 'so both of us pray to B'El the god of fertility, son of El.'

'All these gods sent the meteorite to you? They all agreed on it? Why?'

'I don't know.' Abram's voice came fiercely. 'I am one man. I believe the iron meteorite was sent to me by one god, God. I believe in one God. I believe one God's voice spoke to me in the thunder. Me alone. Chose me. One man, one God, one purpose.' He jumped to his feet. 'But He didn't tell me His name!' I glimpsed the overarching stars and the tent flap slapped down as Abram flung himself out. An angry man. He truly believed God's voice had spoken to him in the thunder, and yet Abram had not clearly understood one word of God, not even His name.

I ran my hands over the meteorite. I murmured, 'What purpose? And which God?'

Our little band of Amori canaans journeyed slow as cold blood over the hot land. The sun rose on our right hands and set on our left hands, and day after day between the vast unmoving horizons of the plain the donkeys toiled beneath full homers of cargo, panniers swaying; the iron meteorite was carried aboard the only camel (the first domesticated camel I'd seen), the weight of the iron balanced by heavy water sacks hung from the other side of the single wobbling hump. We travelled no faster than our slowest sheep; babies were born and men and women of seventy died, and for months we progressed no further than Kidu and I had run in three days and nights. Often we camped for weeks by the Moon Road, resting, stalled, trading with the Hurrians and Marians (in that city Abram purchased the slave girls Hagar and Incense, and bought the beautiful strong-willed girl Mari to be his concubine); the brothers gave hospitality and received it, learning the language of the tribes of West Shem, acquiring the manners of our hosts whether warlike or polite before moving on as always: Terah leaning on his stick, Haran coughing, Nahor counting the profit from his buying and selling.

Mari refused to be Abram's concubine. 'No, it's wrong.' Abram had parted with sheep to have her and he flushed deep red, but Mari knelt as if in awe of him and said in her lovely smooth voice (and she had a gorgeous oval face, and sloe-brown eyes), 'My lord, this is the holiest journey in the world, and to take me as your concubine is wrong, because you *don't.*' That's all. Nothing Abram said or threatened changed her mind, and she did not look down from his eyes, so she had her way and he did not have his.

I had it in mind to have the gorgeous creature for myself. Abram took the hot-blooded slave girl from Midian, Incense, to be his concubine.

Word spread of the iron meteorite, and twice or three times I saved Abram from thieves, and made sure he knew it and looked up to me. He called me by the traditional name, a mighty man – a bodyguard – and I relished being close to him. Close to Abram meant close to the meteorite. He guarded his treasure jealously even from Nahor, calling him a sheep-breeder, envying Nahor's flocks of sheep and all his children to look after them. Childless Abram's meteorite fascinated me. I knew that only my great strength could make proper use of it. I'd steal it for myself and build a furnace from a termite's hill and forge the greatest weapon ever made, a single iron sword that only

I could lift. With such a weapon I'd fight a thousand men and kill them in a day, and make love to their widows all night, and turn their children into slaves. I'd be king of the world.

But I'd have to kill Abram. And Mari drew a knife when I smiled at her. I hesitated. For the first time in my life I was in love with a beautiful woman who was not overawed by me, did not admire me, did not want my penis or anything to do with me. I went off into the desert and saved a child from bandits. I forget his name; I did it only for sport, looked after him for a few days at my campfire in the desert. He was a skinny, leggy lad, followed me with his enormous eyes, imitated my every gesture. I suppose I was the only father he knew, he was six or seven, and he cried like a lost soul when I left him. I felt I knew him better and kinder than my own sons. 'Whatever you do in your life,' I called back, 'imagine you do it for me.' He cried out, 'Yes, Father.' Years later I came back and found a great city at the place, towers capped with beaten gold, gates of cedar and brass. I always wondered.

Winter came and thieves forgot the little Amori band. The river rose, the desert turned to marsh and the outlines of ancient fields, earthworks, canals, surrounded us briefly like the world's fading memories, then the yearly flood drowned them for the thousandth time. Terah's people camped on a miserable runny knoll for months while Haran coughed and Nahor threatened and soothed and haggled with villagers, making deals that kept us in flour and sour beer until spring. 'I'd've struck better deals than him,' Abram said. We walked slow as Nahor's slowest sheep under the hot summer sun, and I barely recognised the great bend in the river where I'd lived with my mother among the trees; the great cedars were gone now, chopped, traded, not even the stumps remained. Sheep scavenged dusty slopes where the tall green hills once stood. The forest was gone. 'Nahor's children will inherit all this land,'

Abram said bitterly. I understood; Abram's sterility worked at him like a knife. I scratched my scarred hand, and Haran walked with us and coughed and coughed. 'Nahor's land,' Abram whispered, 'and Haran's land. But when I die I shall be as though I had never been.'

'And Nahor will get your iron,' I said. 'He'll be a happy man.' I didn't need to mention that Nahor would also get Sarai; it was a brother's duty to take his brother's widow in with his own wives and get her with child. That night I opened the tent-flap and saw Abram sitting with his hands on the meteorite which his personal God gave him instead of children. He said nothing, eyes closed. It was all he had, and I left him alone.

But the brothers didn't fall out. The tribe journeyed slowly northward through a deforested landscape chewed bare by sheep. I recognised none of the places I'd known. The king of one of the West Shemitic hill tribes heard of my strength and I fought a war for him, slaughtering his neighbours and stealing their wives and sheep, enjoying my reward in wineskins and the skins of whores, all the things I do so well, but always I thought of Abram. After my sojourn I caught them up in a day and found Abram on the hill overlooking Haran called Til Turahi, Terah's Hill, in mourning for his brother Haran who'd died in the town where he was born. I heard Terah was dead too, but Abram shook his head. 'It's I who am dead to my father.'

'Why? You'll have children one day. Divorce Sarai and promote one of your other wives.'

'But I love Sarai.' He sighed, the brightness of the setting sun making his eyes wet and red. The girl Mari carried water past us, head down, but we sensed her eavesdropping and waited until we thought her out of earshot. 'Nahor's land, his children's land, his grandchildren's land,' Abram said wretchedly. 'There's no place for me here.'

'Kill Nahor.' I gave Abram good advice. 'Kill Nahor, divorce Sarai and marry Nahor's widows, look after his children as your own. Adopt Haran's children. All this will be yours.' I gestured at the city below and the hills.

He must have thought of it. He admitted, 'I've already taken Haran's son Lot into my care.'

'Very sensible.'

Abram threw a stick off the hill. 'No, I won't do it. I won't—'

'Then you've missed your chance.'

'No!' He interrupted me as I'd interrupted him. 'God has spoken to me!' I stared. Abram turned his attention from the stick falling far below us into the valley and stared me in the eye. 'God spoke to me.'

'Which God?' Ya of the cities, or El of the land?

'El.'

The God of the wandering canaans for the last two thousand years. I laughed. 'Sarai's God advises against divorce? That makes sense.' A divorced woman has no hope, Sarai would use any stratagem to stay married. Abram coloured at my accusation but let it pass, shook his head, hefted another stick. He said, 'You don't understand, Wotan. The great God, the one God. El spoke to *me*. Not her, not Sarai. He is a man, He'd never choose to speak to a woman not His wife any more than a man would.' If any man had to speak of important matters concerning a woman, he always spoke to her husband.

I was intrigued, wondering how Sarai had rigged it. 'What did El say?'

Abram threw the stick towards the setting sun. 'Go there. He said to me, "Go there."' The stick crossed the red sun and tumbled towards the hills of the west. 'El the Most High, eternal El, spoke to my ears in His voice and said, "Get you out of this country, and away from your brothers' families, and away from your father's house, and into the land of Canaan."'

Abram believed it. Abram believed he had heard the voice of El.

'Do what you want to do,' I said. 'Do what you've decided to do.'

'No,' Abram said. He said simply: 'I will do it because El told me to.'

So Abram claimed he spoke to my father; my father who never spoke to me. But I remembered something my mother had told me as a child. *I have you to give my life meaning. Hatred could not have created you.* So surely El (if He had truly spoken to Abram) was sending Abram to Canaan not to die but to live. Perhaps with this man who spoke to my father I would learn how I had come to be born. I remembered the strangest thing my mother had said, considering the world we live in. *I believe in His love. His perfect love.*

The girl Mari ran excitedly round the camp with the news she'd overheard. 'God speaks to Abram!' What did *she* know about Abram's God? 'Abram is following God's word to Canaan,' Mari cried, 'and all of us are going with him, and his father is going too!' Somebody struck her with a stick.

Terah refused to follow his son, and Nahor refused to follow his brother.

So while Terah wept and Nahor scowled Abram, heavy black eyebrows drawn together in determination, divided his donkeys from his brother's donkeys, his women from his brother's women, his slaves from his brother's slaves (the Egyptian slave girl Hagar of the village Hagar, near Tanis on the far crescent-tip of the world, was divided to Abram, lovely Mari taken eagerly by Nahor), and Abram divided his sheep and goats from his brother's sheep and goats, and Nahor laid his hand on the meteorite, but it was too hard to be divided and Abram wouldn't give way as he had over Mari, so Nahor, grumbling, laid his hand on the camel instead. We gathered and Abram knelt at Terah's feet, but Abram would not beg his father's forgiveness, because he said God had told him what he must do and he couldn't ask for forgiveness for following God's will. Terah clasped him tearfully. 'One day, my son, if El truly spoke to you, then you shall send your son back to me here for a wife.' Abram knew he'd never have a son, yet he truly believed his God spoke to him. There was no answer he could give his father. He jerked tight the ropes that held the meteorite to the tottering donkey, then without a word turned his face from Terah, turned his footsteps downhill, and we followed him down the valley until we were far away.

But a girl's scream echoed after us, the girl Mari, Nahor's property, screaming. She screamed Abram's name over and over from the hilltops. 'Abraham, you can't go!' *Abraham*, that was the name she screamed. 'Abraham,' she screamed, 'you can't leave us! You *don't*!' Nahor grabbed her, struggled as she tried to fling herself after us. She screamed after us from high above, 'Abraham, you can't go without your father! Terah dies within sight of the land God has promised you, he *does*! Terah dies within sight of Jerusalem!' Nahor choked her voice but her prophecy sent a chill through us, we all missed a step, but then we laughed because Terah wasn't coming anyway, and there's no place in the world called Jerusalem.

Mari flung herself on the ground to get away, but Nahor stood his foot on her to hold her down.

By now there are as many stories about Abram as there are about me, and doubtless as true. I forget the exact order myself. But Abram's is always the story of Abram and his God, El. You could blink and miss these tiny people journeying in the wilderness; Canaan was not then the centre of the world, the lynchpin upon which the nations turned. In truth each great city was no more than a ramshackle village, each great army only a robber's ragged band, each great battle a skirmish, and no king was more than father of his little band. But Abram had dignity. He was as lavish in his praise and hospitality to strangers as a poor man in a strange land must be, treated his business partners with honour, grovelled on his knees to those greater than he, trod with the soles of his feet on those beneath him, and kept his hand on his sword.

And Abram obeyed God. Never for a moment did Abram forget his God. Abram's God travelled with him and spoke with him. The trade road from Haran to Iamhad trailed miserably through dusty desert, but Abram walked at the head of his rag-tag band and his lips moved as though his prayers were conversations with God. His little people, no larger than dots in the vast landscape (sometimes I was with them, sometimes I fell by the wayside with women and wars), trailed after him like mirages of souls under the burning sun, faithful to El or not, moon-worshippers, sun-worshippers, followers of B'El, Sin, Ya, Ya-Rah the Moon god, Melek the King, El Elyon, whoever – the point is, whatever god they followed, they followed Abram. The donkey died and Abram's meteorite was tied to another donkey. Each night Sarai cleaned and washed and polished her family gods and lifted up the teraphs as though the lucky statues and pillows were her children, whispering to them and cuddling them while Abram lay bare-bottomed with Hagar in Hagar's tent under the stars, and Hagar the slave whispered in Abram's ear that she was a princess of Egypt just as he was a prince of Ur, not one jot below him in rank, and the princes of Egypt and Pharaoh Sesostris would pay well to see her home. I heard her, the tent was threadbare, making enormous shadows of the lovers within. Abram's heels stuck out of the flap, his toes digging at the dust as he took her, and I thought, now we'll see for sure whether it's Sarai or Abram who's as barren as this barren wilderness.

We had reached the Mediterranean, the Great Sea. The

market at Antioch paid for sacks of grain and our journey through bare pastures to Ugarit, where too much rain had fallen or too little, and grain fetched double its price. The Ugarits uttered the hard consonants of West Shemitic in a way we understood, we heard their raised voices praying for rain and manna for their starving families to El who lived in Mount Saphon. El always lives in mountains, obviously. Abram walked there in a day, shouldering his way uphill with the worshippers to the flat summit and the booths of sacred prostitutes. I watched him make his lonely prayers among the crowds of women chanting for mercy to El's holy family and His three wives, headed by Ishtar, and for handsome fertile B'El, His son, killed in winter and born again in spring. Men prayed at the blood-spattered limestone altars to Melek, King of the World; some still called him Molech, for the *molech*-blow that sliced the throat of the sacrificed child. As always, the gift to the god must be of genuine suffering, and Abram turned to me: 'It's the first time I've seen you pale,' he said, and the screaming of the children rose over us in the smoke to Heaven.

We'd arrived early so when we walked downhill the afternoon push of crowds was still climbing upwards, sweaty bodies jostling us. I called, 'Has your God answered your prayers, Abram?'

He let someone pass, was pushed close to my chest. He admitted, 'God has spoken to Hagar.' He corrected himself, not meeting my eye. 'An *angel* of God.' *Angel*. Eve's word, Noah's word, the first time I'd heard it from the tongue of an ordinary man. Ishtar's word: angel, and fallen angels. *Huwawa the dragon was harmless. He loved the tree that grows to God. He was of us, for us, fell with us, an angel cast down from Heaven.*

'An angel spoke to Hagar?' I was amazed. 'Not Sarai your wife?' And not to Abram? The angel had not spoken to Abram! The angel spoke to the concubine first, the slave, the maid, not the royal husband and wife – and still Abram did not meet my eye. I imagined Sarai's feelings; she'd been calm when we left. 'You haven't told her, have you,' I said. I pulled him aside from the crowd but he jerked free. I followed him downhill. 'Well? What did the angel say to Hagar?'

'"You have conceived."'

I laughed. 'That's all? *Your* child? *She* has conceived, not you? You realise what this means?'

Abram turned shouting. 'The angel told her, "Hagar, God will multiply your children, He will make Hagar's children a multitude. Hagar shall bear a son and call him Ishmael, a wild man, and every man's hand shall be against him."' I'd felt as though I'd heard of Ishmael before, I thought of Kidu the wild man, but surely by now no one had ever heard of him, or me. 'The angel spoke to Hagar, Hagar, Hagar, not to me,' Abram said bitterly. '*Her* son.' He consoled himself. 'But it was only an angel, not God Himself.'

'Hagar will make you divorce Sarai,' I said. A barren wife was no one compared to a concubine with an only child. 'And Hagar knows her worth,' I added.

He didn't want to hear any more. 'Sarai will understand.' He pushed away through the crowd. 'Sarai will understand!'

Sarai wouldn't. I reckoned I knew women better than anyone, and I bet Sarai wouldn't understand. I searched for Abram until evening, then made my own way without him towards Ugarit. In the roadside field shadows moved, fighting, a girl's voice exclaimed, then I heard her body thrown down. Saving a girl's hard in the dark, you can't tell if she's pretty. She must be young, she was still putting up a terrific scuffle. I stepped away, wanting to catch Abram. But somebody punched or kicked the girl where she lay, she cried out. That voice, I knew her voice. I called, 'Mari?'

The shadows turned on me, the whites of their eyes showed in the moonlight, someone leapt at me with a knife and I stuck my finger in his eye like a knife, another tried to wrestle me and I tossed him in a tree to wrestle with the branches. I chased the others but they ran away, falling down in a dry river bed. Behind me Mari groaned in the dark and I heard her try to sit up. I picked her up and felt her long hair warm my arm. Her breasts made warm globes tickling the muscular slab of my chest, and the curve of her bottom felt hot as a fire. 'Stop it,' she hissed. 'You. Disgusting!'

The same frigid Mari who had turned down Abram's advances. 'Don't you know how beautiful you are? Any man would want you.'

She wouldn't answer directly. 'Disgusting,' she said. 'I know you. You're Wotan. You're sweating.' She cried out in revulsion, as though my touch defiled her.

I'd ask my question again later (but never know the answer) – *did* she know she was beautiful, fantastically beautiful? 'I love you,' I told her for now. Mari stared, panting, revolted by my sweat and the smell of me, then struggled to be let go. She spat, 'You, Wotan, scum, blasphemer, you love any woman.' I dropped her. She sprawled and I picked her up, lifted her face full into the moonlight. 'You've got a black eye, Mari.' But she didn't care. She muttered then fell still in my arms, lolling, and I realised she weighed almost nothing. Terrible things had happened to her; perhaps many terrible things.

I saw a tavern lamp nearby and carried her there, knocked open the door with my shoulder and sat her on a tall stool between men eating bread and drinking wine, watered a cup of strong wine for her to drink, dabbed it neat on her cuts, finished off the jug myself and ordered another. By firelight I saw that she wore bruises old and new, a dent over one rib that had knitted, her face swollen and blistered by the sun. And now that black eye. One shoe swung by a strap and the other was gone, her feet hung down like torn leather. But her lovely voice, the delicious scent of her. She intoxicated me like wine. 'You escaped from Nahor?' I wondered. She wouldn't speak. 'Escaped several times, Mari, by the look of you. Finally you got away. Somehow you followed us across the desert. One woman, alone. Thieves, wild animals, burning sun. I can't imagine what you went through. Loneliness. Fear. Yet you did. Why?'

She murmured, 'Abraham.'

'You're starving,' I said. 'But you haven't asked for bread.'

'You haven't offered it.' Her spirit flashed. 'I don't ask a man like you for anything.' But she dropped her elbows on the table, swaying with hunger. I should let her starve. I sighed and called for one of the loaves strung on sticks under the roof to save them from mice, held it in my hands. Moved my hands up, and her eyes moved up. I chewed a piece slowly. 'Delicious.' She grabbed at the crumbs on the table but I swept them away. She stared angrily, she might attack me, she might do anything. I broke a wedge of loaf, offered it to her from the flat of my hand. I've offered food in the same way to lions and been more confident of their submission. Her teeth bared in temptation, then she snatched it like a wild animal. 'You don't know anything,' I told her wisely, 'about a man like me.'

She tore, swallowed. 'I know everything about you, beast. I've seen you Wotan, I know you. You were found floating in a basket sealed with pitch, you built the walls of Enoch, you killed Huwawa the dragon.'

I stared. She knew more than anyone. She knew everything that had been forgotten. I tossed her another piece of bread. I said, 'That's not quite everything.'

'You claim you're the son of El, you fiend.'

How could I deny the truth? 'Yes, I'm the son of the great God El.'

'Liar!' She spat crumbs in my face.

Everyone was looking at us. 'Let's talk like this all night,' I said.

'There is only one God. One.' She wouldn't let me interrupt. 'One!'

'Tell that to the people of the mountaintop. Anyway, it's not blasphemy to tell the truth. I remember the moment of my—'

'Demon!' she cried. 'You are not the One! Murderer, fornicator, you!' She tore, ate, but tears of torment trickled down her cheeks to take the pieces of bread I offered.

She fascinated me. I'd never met a girl so strange and powerful. Not even Ishtar. So completely exposed, yet so hidden from me. When we were lovers I'd know everything about her. Demon, I supposed she meant fallen angel. Nowadays people believe a winged evil demon (like the gallu-demons of ancient Shem's cedar forest, now gone) can possess the body of a sick person. They exorcise the creature with a piece of cedar and a sprig of caper (genuine hyssop's too expensive, imported) tied together with red yarn to make an aspergillum, which is a brush the priest dips in holy water made red with the blood of birds. I don't know if the spell works (I remember Ishtar's wings rising most powerfully above her head, each black feather erect like adamantine gold), but long ago the priests of Shem wore red robes and sacrificed red bulls to make good luck. 'I'm no demon,' I repeated. 'Nor am I a fallen angel.'

'I don't know what you are!' she shuddered. 'An abortion. An aberration. A mistake.'

'God doesn't make mistakes,' I said. 'I know who I am.'

'You have no higher feelings at all, do you,' she marvelled, disgusted that I could know myself and not be ashamed, I think. She ate no more of my bread.

'I saved you from thieves and rapists,' I pointed out. The tavern fell silent, everyone listened with interest. I

249

turned my back on them but she raised her voice.

'Saved from thieves and rapists by a murderer and fornicator.' She squeezed the rock-hard muscles of my forearm with disgust. 'Your strength is more than men's, but you're just a man. You think with your penis. You're less than a man, less than other men, not more. You don't know where you're going, or why, or anything.'

I ignored the stares of the other customers. 'Improve me,' I whispered. 'Sleep with me.' Her eyes widened. Her cheeks flushed. She might. Then her fist whistled round and I caught her knuckles a finger's-breadth from my cheek. 'You're so angry,' I laughed, wanting her intensely. 'Are you always so angry?'

'There is only one God,' she shouted, 'and only one Son of God, and He is Jesus Christ, and you are not Him!'

'B'El is also the son of God.'

'*There is no B'El!*' she screamed. 'God and Jesus Christ is *everything*!' Mari made a bolt for the door and I ran after her, but she kicked the stool in my way. The tavern-keeper shouted 'Hoi!' I chucked him a few coins and ran after her into the night. 'Good luck,' someone called after us. She ducked and wove but at the edge of the village I caught her easily, lifted her over my shoulder, let her kick until her shoe flew into the dark. 'That's your last shoe gone, Mari.'

She cried, 'I'll walk barefoot.'

I put her down on the moonlit road to Ugarit and she hobbled painfully on the sharp stones while I ambled casually beside her. 'I'm going to Abram. Lend you my shoes, Mari?'

She glanced down, sulking. 'Both my feet would fit in one of yours.' But she was tempted. 'Abraham's in Ugarit?' she muttered.

I swung her up before she got a thorn, lifted her easily to sit on my shoulders like a very adult child, walked beneath her swaying body with my hands holding lightly to her knees. 'Don't,' she said. She caught her balance, crossed her heels comfortably in front of my heart, rested her hands on top of my head, and I set up a steady rhythm between the moonlit hills towards Ugarit. Abram should have reached there by now. All she thought of was Abram, Abram, being with Abram. She was a fanatic. I asked, 'Are you in love with him, Mari?'

'Him! No!' I felt her shake her head violently, her body shook. I said, 'But you want to be with him.' She said, 'I have to be.' I asked why, but she said, 'I have to see. I have to *see*, that's all.'

I ran up the hills and walked down the slopes beyond, never tiring.

'I don't know whether you're less or more than men,' she admitted after an hour.

'That's what you like.'

'I don't like anything about you.' But she liked riding on my shoulders. She liked the power.

'You've fallen in love with me. Admit it.'

'I'd only fall in love with a man who was nothing at all like other men.' She unbound her hair and as I ran I looked up and saw the long strands blowing like dark wings across the moon. I laughed at the wonder of her, nothing more than a mortal woman, and touched my cheek to her warm knee. 'No, don't,' she said.

'*Don't*,' I said. 'Your favourite word. Why didn't you marry Abram?'

'Because I don't marry Abraham.'

'Don't. There you go again. *Abraham*, that was the name you screamed when Nahor held you back from coming with us. "You can't leave your father, Abraham, you *don't*!" Abraham, not Abram.'

I felt her shrug. 'Oh, I suppose there are always little differences, even in the eternal truths of God's kingdoms. God allows the tiny details, a difference in a sound or a name. Abram, Abraham. Unimportant things.'

'And Jerusalem. You said Jerusalem.'

She covered my eyes for a moment. 'You'll see.' I stumbled, tripped, almost dropped her. 'You'll see Jerusalem!' She laughed, hanging on, and I reckoned the wine had gone to her head.

I said, 'I wish I could see you. You're so beautiful. You can't be a virgin.'

She laughed more. 'It's not you I love, Wotan, and it never will be.' She kissed the top of my head. 'I'm a virgin for ever.'

I bent my head up, looked up at her upside-down face. 'Why?'

'You'll see! You'll see.'

'Where will I see?'

'In Jerusalem.'

'There's no Jerusalem.'

'In Jerusalem, the City of God, you'll see. A new world's coming, an end to everything we knew. A whole new way of seeing and being and believing's about to be born, a new way of living in love.' Her voice filled with joy. 'New laws of marriage, and cleanliness, and safety. Everyone will care for everyone. No accidents. No hurt. No pain. Not a single crying child, no death. Only life. All shall be saved in Jesus Christ.'

I nodded. 'The name you said earlier.'

'The One. The Son of God, Jesus Christ, our Anointed Saviour.' That made me prick up my ears, remembering Noah the first Zadok's words. *The One who shall reign as King for a thousand years shall be King and Zadok both, king and priest united, a Son of Man, our anointed saviour. That is His name. Anointed Saviour.* But in the new language we spoke, West Shemitic, which some call Aramaic, the words *Anointed Saviour* are *Yehoshua Masiah.* Nothing like the odd foreign name she'd used, Jesus Christ.

The Amori tents came into view against the moonlit sea. I trod carefully through the fields, calmed the sheep,

252

crossed towards the sleeping camp. A few lights showed in Ugarit on the brow of the headland, thieves, or traders counting their money, or perhaps sick children lovingly tended by their mothers. 'Who exactly is this Jesus Christ?' I asked.

She said excitedly, 'Jesus Christ is – just *is*! More than you know, more than you *can* know, more than you can imagine, more!' I put Mari down quietly on the grass, my finger to my lips. She whispered, 'Without Jesus Christ there is no Messiah, no freedom, no end to time, no hope for us. Without Jesus Christ there's no judgment. No forgiveness. No peace. No glory. No Heaven.'

'Is Abram Jesus Christ?'

She looked horrified. 'No, no, Abram's the son of Terah. Abraham leads the Chosen People – people chosen by God – into Jerusalem. It's ordained. Abraham leads us between the gold walls of the Holy of Holies of the Temple to kneel before the Christ-child. Abraham's childlessness symbolises our sterility, the sterility of a people trying to live without God, true God, one God. Abraham hands to the infant Jesus the sceptre which symbolises the loyal journey towards God Himself of Abraham and the Chosen People from Haran through the wilderness to Jerusalem.'

The only sceptre that came to my mind was the long staff Abram leant on when he was tired at midday. I didn't understand. 'Is this a prophecy?'

'No, Wotan, it's reality. Reality.' She tried to make me understand. 'Ordained by God. In front of all the Chosen People and the saintly Guardian of Christ, the shepherd Joseph of Nazareth, son of Jonan, Abraham acknowledges Jesus Christ as our Anointed Saviour. The Virgin's only Son shall reign over us in righteousness and perfection, eternal, universal, in holy Jerusalem as has been foretold in other places from the beginning of time.'

'Virgin?' I asked, confused. 'El has His Son Jesus Christ conceived through His wife, the virgin Anath?'

'No, no!' she cried. 'It's so much more beautiful!' A dog barked, I hissed at Mari to keep quiet. She put her hands up in her hair, exasperated. 'I'll never make you understand. You of all people. But in Jerusalem you'll see. You'll believe. You'll *know*.'

'See. Believe. Know,' I said dully. The dog bounded snarling at us. I put out my hand and it rolled over at once, wagging, licking my fingers. 'Abram's dog. He's back.'

She grabbed my sleeve fiercely. 'I know you don't believe a word I say, someone like you. But without Jesus Christ, here, *here*, is Hell. We live in Hell, Wotan. Without Jesus Christ, children in this hellish abandoned world are born beyond redemption, born sinful, born to grow and suffer and die forsaken in the torments of Hell without hope of salvation.' She stared up at my moonlit face and can't have seen much hope there. But the words *abandoned, forsaken, salvation* had touched such deep chords in me that for a moment I could not respond. She drew the wrong conclusion. 'I wasted my time trying to talk to you,' she said. But I remembered Noah, Noah saying *I'll join Adam there in Hell and live among the dead. One day there will be no Hell. The chains will be broken as Ishtar promised, the gates smashed, the dead given new life. But not by her. By the Anointed Saviour.*

Our Anointed Saviour, Jesus Christ.

I shushed her, hearing Abram's voice waking his wife in the tent beside us, then a lamp was lit and threw his shadow across the weave. Abram doing the talking, telling her the news, then Sarai's voice interrupting. Her voice rose, screaming. Her shadow scrambled up from her bed, hair hanging, she screamed and tore her hair with her hands. No, no, no, she cried. The shadow of her little table went over, her ornaments. Sarai scattered her holy teraphs, her shadow flung them at the shadow of Abram, then she stumbled in the flesh from her tent almost knocking into us but not seeing us, stumbling across the dewy grass to Hagar's tent and jerking at the tent-posts with all her strength to pull them down, screaming, then Hagar came out and Sarai flew at her, kicking her, pulling her hair, punching her belly, weeping. Hagar's tent collapsed, and Hagar ran into the night.

'Hagar's with child,' I whispered to Mari. 'An angel spoke to her.'

'But she can't be!' Mari stared wild-eyed. 'It can't be. It can't have been. Abraham has no children, ever.' Her tone hardened. 'No. No angel ever spoke to Hagar. A demon took the form of an angel and deceived her!' She jerked away from my touch, gave me a horrified look, then ran after Sarai running after Hagar in the dark, all three women screaming.

Mari believes that I, Wotan, am a demon. A former world has passed away. Now my great handsomeness, manliness, height, strength, all the things that once counted for me with women, count against me. In these peaceful days they have no need of me, everything they once admired and coveted most about me they now despise. My strength that saved them a hundred times is no longer needed, I'm a murderer with blood on my hands. My inexhaustible manhood is shameless pride, a sin, a threat to their womanhood. I am a bully, a breaker of families, unsafe among children, and they take their own pride in clinging to their husbands against my imagined insatiable lust. Mari's whispers did this to them. Mari, the only woman my manhood never conquered.

After months of gossip and innuendo I put on my travelling cloak and picked up my bundle. They'd miss me; they'd want me back. On the way out of camp I saw an ox fallen down a well, and there was a last useful thing I could do. I pulled down a tree for a ladder and jumped down, and climbed out carrying the lowing beast over my shoulder. But no one saw. No one wanted to see. Only Abram.

'You're still my mighty man,' he said. 'I trust in your strong right arm. I'll see you again.'

But Hagar was the first person I saw, in a dusty valley of the Orontes river, huddled in the shadow of a boulder, her belly poking round as a rock through her ragged shift. 'I'm not going back,' she said defiantly. 'I'm not. That bitch pulled my hair and threw stones.'

'Imagine how much Sarai's been hurt,' I said. We walked for a while. 'Where are you going?'

Hagar looked surprised. 'Where you are. You'll look after me, won't you?' She kissed my mouth, pressed her hot breasts and lips against me. Ah, this was the way it used to be with all women. She still wore her eyelids kohl-black like an Egyptian and she tempted me; a pregnant woman can't run after you with curses when you ditch her. But I thought of Mari and pushed Hagar away. 'How should I know where I'm coming and going? Go back to Sarai and beg her forgiveness. Be humble. Be all the things you aren't.'

Hagar called after me, 'She'll kill me. Don't you care?'

I called cheerfully, 'Abram will sort it out. Trust Abram and his God.'

I travelled, and the months turned into years, but all I thought of was Mari who'd hurt me, Mari, Mari. I fell for hundreds of girls. 'Tell me you love me,' they murmured, 'tell me, love me, take me, fool me.' So I told them I loved them and fooled them and fooled myself, but it was Mari who filled my thoughts, my sterile erect fantasies. Each face was Mari's.

I heard tell of Abram sometimes: his little clan wandering slowly southward in search of pasture and God and trade, Hagar's child Ishmael birthed in Sarai's tent, Ishmael now grown into the scrawny brown boy herding goats in the valley beneath me, and from the hilltop I spied down on Mari fetching water with the women. *Hagar's* child, not Abram's. Cleverly put, so Mari's prophecy of Abram's childlessness still held good. Mari herself looked so gorgeous that I was tempted to become the man they feared, leap down, scatter them, tear her virginity and make her my own. Like a shadow I prowled in the camp at night and knew their lives to the last squirt. Mari had no husband, no lover, no man at all, only her hope of Jesus. Her *certainty* of Jesus. She simply and radiantly followed Abram on his great slow journey into this land his God had promised to show him, slowly approaching her God Jesus Christ with him. From Ebla the clan wandered the Damascus trade road back and forth in the snowy mountains to Hazor and Beth-Anath, the temple to Anath the Divine Virgin; they skirted Midian, the land of Incense's people who worshipped Ya; for a year Abram's people grazed the shores of Galilee and (except Abram and Mari) worshipped in the temple at Beth Ya-Rah to the local Moon god. His great God looked after Abram and gave him gold and silver, grazing for his goats, children for his people. Later in the lowlands at Beth-Shemash the people worshipped Shemash the ancient Sun god of Shem, and Sin the ancient god of the moon, but Abram went alone and built a new altar to his God – and later he built an altar beneath an oak tree at Shechem, the greatest city of Canaan, not even enclosed by a wall so peaceful was the land. Later he built an altar at Beth-El. But still it seemed to me, watching, that Abram had no real idea of his God, only that He was not-El; more-than-El, if such a thing were possible.

Abram's nephew Lot persuaded Abram to cross the River Jordan into the green hills and woodlands of the ancient kingdom of Sion, but old rivalries between the families surfaced and their herdsmen fought over the best pastures. I watched from a terebinth tree as the two men parleyed; there wasn't enough land to support both. Mari was pale with nerves, she wanted, *needed*, Abram to turn back across the Jordan towards her enchanted Jerusalem. 'Abraham, claim the right hand!' she whispered, praying. Above her in the spreading branches I shivered in the hot sun and thought: Mari knows he'll do it, because he *does*. Abram turned his face towards the distant mountains shimmering over the Jordan Valley and the glare of the Salt Sea that washed out the southern sky, separating the two lands. There was a pause, then Lot held out his arm to choose the land on the left, and Abram claimed the right hand. He *does*. Mari had said it. Could there, then, even be a place somewhere called Jerusalem?

I sat on a rock in midriver, the waters of the Jordan swirling around my feet, Abram's people wading to their new land, and Mari saw me. 'You!' she said from the water. I reached out my hand to lift her up but she wouldn't touch me. I blurted, 'Tell me about your Jesus Christ.'

Her eyes narrowed suspiciously. 'What are you up to?'

I was so in love with her I couldn't control my tongue. 'I wish I knew how to make you love me, that's all!' The water tugged and foamed at my bare toes, dragged out the hem of her dress, and I glimpsed her lovely pale legs. 'You poor creature,' she said pityingly. 'That's all you are. Blood and muscle and sexual desire, nothing more. You'll never be more.' She left me sitting alone on the rock, then called back in exultation, 'God has spoken to Abraham! God spoke to Abraham in His Voice!'

'What did He say?'

'No one knows! He was God!'

I held back and Abram strode across the stream. He embraced me, pleased. Good, he admired me, I like that. 'I keep thinking I see you,' he said. 'Perhaps you're an angel sent to watch over me as well as a mighty man. Shall I see you in times of trouble?'

We laughed. 'Always,' I said.

He was serious. 'Can you see it in me?'

I smiled and lied. 'Your God has spoken to you, Abram. Yes, you've changed. Like a burning lamp inside you.' We waded together to the west bank of the Jordan. I put down my hand and he scrambled up beside me.

'God Himself spoke to me, Wotan. All the land from the Perath to Egypt is mine.' That was the whole world. He added, 'Mine and my son's land.'

'Your son? You mean Hagar's son, Ishmael?'

He confided, 'I am to have another son. This time from my own flesh.' A man's flesh was his wife. A son from Sarai? I watched how she plodded, her grey hairs. I stared at Abram and he said unblinkingly, 'God has made me a father of many nations.' I asked at once, 'What does He ask in return for such a gift?' Abram said, 'That I should mutilate my penis to show the seriousness and completeness of our promise,' he chose a deeper word, 'covenant. The sincerity of the *covenant* between us. He is the One God, we are His people, and He will look after us.'

'And you did it?' It gave me a turn. 'You cut the most important part of you?'

He said seriously, 'With a copper knife' – such knives were holy, that soft metal no longer being used for war – 'I circumcised the flesh of my foreskin from my penis. And all my men, all their sons, all my slaves, all in the one day.'

I shuddered. 'It worked? Sarai's really pregnant? Her blood no longer flows?'

'Not for years. Everything is new, Wotan. God has named me not Abram but Abraham, and Sarai is Sarah.' Gods like to change the names of converts, it's traditional, but it gave me another turn. 'Sarah feels the change God has made inside her, just as I do. We have new flesh, and new names from God.' Abraham ran to comfort her, held her proudly. Sarah with child, a child from Abraham's own bowels. But that, Mari did not know.

Perhaps it would not live to be born; perhaps it would not be a son.

Later I found Mari, snatched her elbow. 'Abram's God has changed his name to Abraham just as you said.'

'Told you.'

'Did you know Sarah will bear him a son?'

She stared. '*Abraham will have a son?*'

'God named Abraham and told him so. A son for Abraham, a legitimate son.'

'No.' Mari spat in my face. 'Demon,' she said. Her eyes filled with tears. 'I don't believe a word you say. It can't be true.' She shook her head, her wet tears flew into my face. 'Demon. Liar. Fiend.' She screamed, 'Satan sent you!' She screamed in front of all the people, 'Satan!' And she ran away from me.

Satan. And I am a demon.

Who is Satan? I have no idea. The sun fell down below the hilltop where I camped and it grew dark, but the stars did not come out. Darkness fell on me and I fell asleep, dreamt of Rebekah, Deborah, Rachel . . . Dinah . . . and Eve came to me. Eve, my love, my first love. Hold the pearl in your mouth, let me kiss you, let me be your mouth and eyes and your immortal life. Be young in me for ever, Eve.

The fire blazes up, the stars gleam and the sparks swirl upwards towards them.

My clothes hang from Eve's shoulders like a tent, her feet slip out of my shoes as she sits up by the embers of my fire. She takes a deep breath and I feel her breasts lifting inside Wotan's sheepskin top, my clumsy stitches scratching her nipples, this is nice. I never could be bothered to sew properly, but her skin is more sensitive, and especially her sense of propriety. Her slim hand prods the fire to life with the stick (she thinks disapprovingly, you used a whole branch, Wotan, and too much firewood

as usual – even your campfires burn like burning houses).
By firelight she moistens a bone needle between her lips
and sets to work on my brown linen undershirt. My
favourite shirt. Before the moon rises she slips it as a
serviceable shift over her head, spreads her hair neatly
over her shoulders. She feels better already, I can tell. I
ask, 'Who's Satan?'

'*S-T-N*?' Of course she knows. 'These people are the
many times great-grandchildren of my own people from
beyond the mountains. They write without vowels: *S-T-N*
is Satan. I've told you, the dragon takes many names, B'El,
B'Elial, B'Elzebub who's worshipped in the city of Ekron,
B'El-Zephon the god of wind and storm. Any and all of
them are the children of El. All fallen angels.'

'Yes, I know.'

'But the greatest is the One, *S-T-N*, He whose name
may not be uttered. Satan.' She claps her hand to her
mouth.

'Noah described Him, very, very vividly. More vividly
than he described God. To Noah, God was just a whisper
through the wall. His Satan, B'El, made my hair stand on
end.'

We fall silent, then I feel her clear her throat. 'Wotan?'

'Sssh, people will think you're talking to yourself.' But
there's only the night, the line of the rising moon. I enjoy
being alone with her, part of her, my feminine side.

'No,' she whispers, 'I mean, I have to, you know. Go.'
She's embarrassed. 'Relieve myself.'

'Don't mind me. Here's a good place.'

'Close your eyes.' Her eyes close, she loses her balance
in the dark. 'All right,' she decides, opening her eyes, 'but
don't look.' Naturally I look down between her knees with
interest as she pees, it feels quite different for a woman.
'You're besotted with Mari,' Eve says to distract me. 'Or
is it her Jesus Christ who fascinates you?'

'I don't think He exists,' I reply, feeling like a eunuch

because I speak with Eve's high little voice. 'How much longer are you going to keep peeing?'

'You make me feel pain for you, Wotan, you really do,' she says tight-lipped, finishing. 'Mari's right about you. You have no higher feelings. None at all.'

'Do you always listen?' I'm interested. 'To everything?'

She puts me down smartly. 'I couldn't bear it, I feel so sorry for the girls you meet, you're such an animal.' But she loves me, always did, always will. She wants to walk to the edge of the hilltop. The lights of Abraham's camp swing into view, speckling the valley between the twin towns of Beth-Horon. There's talk of war in Lot's country, some brigand spreading terror southward from Shem, they sneak down the eastern desert and strike west to bite mouthfuls off Canaan at will, then disappear into the dust again. There's talk of going after them but the clans never agree on anything. For now the camp looks so peaceful. The moonlight draws its finger along the valley and Eve follows it down towards the women's voices by the stream. It's that time of the evening. Their duties and their men finished, shawls thrown over their heads against the cool dewy air, the women sit or lie back sleepily among the rocks, talking: and I hear Mari's voice. I'd hoped she was alone.

You really are besotted with Mari, Eve thinks.

Close enough! she decides powerfully as I steal closer. Eve tries to pull back but the rocks are rough under her knees, and now I hear Mari's lovely smooth voice speaking with the ease and honesty they never share with men. Here we're sisters, and I make Eve settle closer than she really wants to Mari.

'A Star shall rise over Jerusalem,' Mari tells them with passionate intensity, and the women fall silent, seeing the Star in their minds. 'This is the Star of Jerusalem which announces the birth of baby Jesus, Son of God, to the Virgin Mary.'

'A virgin having a baby,' cackles an old woman. 'Wish I'd learnt that one.'

Mari lets the laughter die down. 'The Star beckons the faithful to Jesus Christ.' She holds out her arms, her pale hands upraised in the moonlight, her voice raised. 'The Star stretches its light over the Virgin Mary and the Holy Child—'

'Which God is this?' mutters a woman deaf in one ear. 'Where'd He catch her?'

'There's no . . . physical contact,' Mari says. 'The Son of God is conceived by God's whisper in the Virgin's ear, He is born as a ray of light from her immaculate womb.'

One girl calls, 'Can anyone see the Star? Could I?'

The deaf woman gets up to go. 'I liked the bit about the baby. But I like my stories with a bit more you-know-what.' Someone helps her over the rocks, then goes with her.

Mari persists. 'To the golden Holy of Holies three magicians come bringing gifts, one of silver, one of balsam, and one of precious galbanum incense. Jesus's cradle is laid with ordinary "lady's bedstraw" to symbolise His humility. An ox and the ass watch over Him, again showing His humility. The head of His cradle is draped with the purple robes and golden insignia of King and Saviour of Jerusalem which await the coming day of His Recognition.'

'If He's born to be King,' a young girl says, 'why's He humble?'

'At the foot of His cradle faithful Abraham's sceptre symbolises the salvation freely offered by the Christ Child which is His gift to us all, the kingdom of Heaven to which He will lead the faithful and the saved; and of His people, not one shall be unsaved.'

'Saved from what?' interrupts the old woman.

Mari says: 'From suffering.'

'Wish I'd been saved from childbirth.' The old woman slaps her knees and gets up. 'Eleven I had what lived,

263

bloody agony, I could've done with a bit of saving.'

An ugly girl says, 'What, everyone saved? Even us?'

'Everyone. You. Even me,' Mari said. 'Our sins shall be washed away. Everyone who is lost shall be found.'

The old woman hobbles off, calls the others. 'Come on, you whores, early start.'

'Not whores,' Mari says quickly. 'Not thieves, murderers, adulterers, people who've no respect for the law. But honest people, decent people, law-abiding people, every one shall be saved.'

But she's talking to herself; only the pouring water and the rocks, and Eve. I make Eve sit next to Mari's warm body, inhale Mari's scent through Eve's nostrils. I make Eve say, 'Mari, your words are so beautiful,' because I want the word *beautiful* said into Mari's ears, because Mari is herself so beautiful. '*Stop it,*' Eve whispers. I make her say, 'Mari, what about those people who don't believe in Him?'

'Everyone'll believe in Jesus!' Mari laughs. 'How couldn't we?'

This Jesus sounds like my sort of God: a God you *have* to believe in, no choice, no picking and choosing. I reckon Abraham will melt down the meteorite for Him (the meteorite deliberately sent into the world by El's divine will, obviously) and Jesus Christ, not I, will wield the iron sword and kill a thousand men a day and lead armies to compel belief in Him. God's plan for us made visible: I'm awed, the sheer scale and arrogance of it's lovely. 'It's lovely,' Eve's voice whispers. 'No it's not,' she hisses fiercely, contradicting me. 'It's horrible!'

'What?' Mari turns to Eve, touches her face, I feel her finger touch Eve's forehead, brush a strand of hair from Eve's eyebrow, lightly trace the outline of Eve's cheek, Eve's chin. Mari speaks softly. 'Who are you, girl?' I make Eve shiver in the cold night, it *is* cold, and the two women hug each other for warmth. I touch Eve's lips to the lobe of

Mari's ear, kiss her. Mari, Mari, this moment is everything to me. I make Eve whisper something, anything to keep me close to Mari. 'Tell me about Him.'

Mari hesitates, but feels she's bringing the girl in her arms to God, embraces her as a sister. Oh, if only I had my penis, I'd explode with love! I grip Mari tight in Eve's arms, Eve's skinny arms containing my superhuman strength, I kiss Mari's lips with Eve's lips. Mari twists her head away. 'It's not earthly love,' Mari gasps, 'it's a different love, it's Love, immaculate love, higher love, worship, that we feel for Him. Jesus Christ shall never take a woman, He shall be a virgin like His mother.' She gasps: 'He begins His ministry in his twenty-ninth year and in His thirtieth year, the year of His Recognition, Jesus is crowned King and Zadok in Jerusalem, He is the single pillar of the world, and rules in wisdom and benevolence for a thousand years.' Mari puts back her head, Eve kisses her throat, licks her fingertip and touches it to Mari's flesh, and Mari stares up at the stars even at this moment with her eyes searching, searching for the Star of Jerusalem, but there's nothing. Nothing. Suddenly she gives a cry and pushes Eve away, the two women fall apart, scramble apart falling over the rocks, Mari splashes on her hands and knees in the stream. 'You!' she cries. 'Who in God's name are you?'

Eve runs. I can't stop her, she's wild. Ashamed. She runs uphill on to the hilltops where the wind blows from the stars, she runs with her hands in her hair until she falls to her knees. 'You utter bastard, Wotan,' she cries inside herself. 'Utter bastard, doing that to me and her.' She wipes her weeping face, hands, rolls her body in the dust, anywhere she touched Mari, spitting, trying to clean herself with the dust of the earth. 'I don't care whose son you are, you utter profane bastard. How could you. Evil. Utter evil bastard!' She jumps up and runs and runs until she's running exhausted among the hilltops, she falls and lies down, her eyes close, and before dawn the seams of her brown linen shift begin to pop and tear, the material stretches, the stitching snaps.

Eve's exhaustion became filled with my endless vitality, and I sat up on the hilltop naked except for a few rags of brown linen hanging from my muscles. I stood and looked around me, killed a sheep for a fleece, then called to Eve inside myself. Nothing. However much we love them, they'll never understand us.

Abraham called me an angel, Mari a demon. I only knew I wanted to meet this Jesus Christ. He sounded like a man after my own heart: a man of men. I followed Mari but didn't let her see me. Abraham turned his wandering footsteps south towards Hebron, but halted almost at once as Lot's wife caught up, clutched his hem, fell in the dust at his feet: Lot had been stolen for ransom by bandits. Abraham listened to her cries, but he wouldn't pay. Instead he called together the local Amori families of Aner, Eschol and Mamre (only an outsider could – they hated each other like brothers) and at the parley Abraham was a hawk, laying down the law, telling them if they didn't stand together now they'd be picked off one by one. So together the allies chased the bandits almost as far as Damascus and we wrecked a place its people called Hobah, I killed everyone I saw, we covered the village with blood and dead and dying and had a glorious war, and Abraham brought back Lot alive with everything that was stolen. What a wonderful welcome home! Even Mari washed my feet.

The next day, sheep baaing and dust drifting like smoke under the summer sun, we resumed our journey south towards the little-settled plains of Mamre, a promised land of fertility and plenty – Mamre himself owned one of the four suburbs of Hebron. Mari pointed ahead. 'Is that Hebron?' Nobody knew. During the morning a mountain rose from the horizon, then in the afternoon hills appeared below, and on the almost-highest a village gleamed like a drop of honey in the sunset. She called to a shepherd boy, 'Is that the place?' and he said, 'No, that's the village of Ur-Shalom where my father lives.'

Ur-Shalom. Not Jerusalem, not Hebron. I took the opportunity to walk beside Mari. 'I'm sorry,' I said. 'Like you, I really hoped.' I craned to see her face. 'Your Jesus. Something.'

Mari smiled. She laughed. 'Ur-Shalom!' she cried. 'Jerusalem! It's the same name!' She grabbed the boy. 'Is this truly Jerusalem, the centre of the world?'

'I'm Jeb's folk.' The boy was frightened. 'Some call this Jebus. To us everywhere's the centre of the world, 'cos the world's around us wherever we look.' She shook him. 'It is,' she murmured. 'It's Jerusalem. Look, Wotan, can you see the Temple?' All I saw was a distant jumble of rough stone walls and muddy thatch. She pointed. 'There, raise your eyes, see Mount Sion.'

I saw the mountain standing against the dark sky.

'There, below it,' she murmured, gazing, 'the flat-topped hill, Moriah. Can you see the east gate? See the porch facing inward, the columns like palm trees made of stone?' I couldn't make them out. 'The priests preparing, their long wait's nearly over.' She went on excitedly, 'I see the hereditary priesthood going in, the Zadoks.' I saw nothing. Darkness rolled over the village but the last eyelash of the sun lit Mari's radiant face.

'Perhaps you're right,' I said. But as we camped in the dark by the spring called Gihon down in the valley, I thought: Abraham's father Terah is not with us to die within sight of Jerusalem.

All night I looked among the stars twinkling over Jerusalem, but saw no Star.

I was in love with Mari, and she was crazy.

At dawn the trumpets blew and we climbed behind Abraham (Sarah stayed in her tent, fat, gasping in the heat) and came up the steep path to the village. Mari looked around in amazement. Hovels, the stink of humans. No Star, no Temple, no golden Holy of Holies, only smelly shit and smoke and dust like a thousand villages. 'It can't be Jerusalem,' she said. 'There's more.' She grabbed some brown-toothed woman. 'Where's the Temple?' They gazed at her like sheep. Children tugged at her, stealing a copper ring from her finger. I watched Mari stare uncomprehendingly at the pale circle of her skin, she couldn't understand how much she'd lost, where it had gone.

'There was never anything here,' I said gently. 'No Temple. There's not even ruins.'

The largest building in the village was the royal palace among the sties, plastered white, with a curved doorway like a frame where a man of normal height could stand upright to look impressive to his people, a couple of holes for windows, a roof no higher than I reached. A pig fled oinking from the door. Mari stumbled. A beggar clawed at the bracelet on her wrist, I dragged him back by his neck but she didn't even notice. 'Leave her alone,' I warned. I dropped him, kicked the others back, turned again to Mari. 'No don't hurt them,' she said. I felt sorry for her, she looked as if the sky had fallen on her. 'Mari. Don't do this, don't hurt yourself.' I gave up, no words could say the truth. There was nothing here. I pitied her. She stared at me with pure hatred, pure confusion. 'Don't look at me,' she said, dry-eyed. 'You did this. What have you done?'

'There's just these people here, that's all. Ordinary people.'

She murmured: 'God created Heaven and Earth, but this is Satan's world.'

I tried to make her understand. 'There's no Jesus Christ, Mari. You had a beautiful dream.'

More trumpets blew, scattering piglets between our feet. Slaves bent their backs in the shadows of the doorway, shuffled forward with a throne made from olive wood, lifted it high. Perched atop the creaking structure, gnarled and dry as his throne, sat the king of the village. The king's blood-encrusted hands, still wet from a thanksgiving sacrifice of doves, grasped a sceptre of olive wood – a sceptre in Jerusalem as Mari prophesied, but it belonged to this creature, not Abraham! The yellowed fleece of a son of Zadok hung crawling with lice from the king's shoulders. With a crafty smile, spit crusted in the corners of his lips, he was set down and slyly watched Abraham approach the throne. Abraham knelt, then the king stood with dignity and spoke. 'Welcome to Ur-Shalom, City of the Most High God. Hear me, all who have ears to listen! I am Melchizadok, King and Saviour, the two pillars of the world made One.' *Melchi*, from Melek or *M-L-K*, King, and *Zadok* a righteous man or righteous teacher, a priest as among the canaans of Shem long ago. Melchizadok claimed to be the Anointed One. 'I am Melchizadok a son of Enoch the Son of Man. I know no earthly father, I was born from the dead body of my mother.' A saviour born of necrophilia, not virginity: nothing like Mari's beautiful dream. Her face fell almost blank with horror at the claims of this old man raddled with sores, merely human. What had happened here? Nothing divine here. Nothing could be worse. No Jesus; only all-too-human Melchizadok, bloody and diseased, clutching his ragged golden-yellow fleece and badly carved sceptre like an ancient corrupted memory.

'No,' Mari whispered.

Melchizadok beckoned his slaves impatiently, held out his hand like a claw. Grails of bread and wine were placed between the two leaders who faced each other unequally, the anointed king of the city and Abraham the chief of nomads. Melchizadok intoned, 'I bless you in the name of the Most High God, El Elyon, the God of gods, the possessor of Heaven and Earth.' Possessor; Mari said God *created* Heaven and Earth, and that there were no other gods.

'Abraham,' Melchizadok intoned, 'El Elyon the Most High God has delivered our enemies into your hand.' He blessed Abraham with the bread and wine, then the two men exchanged gifts, Abraham giving ewes and lambs and receiving from Melchizadok a gift of grazing in Hebron. 'A land for your people for ever,' the king-saviour wiped drops of red wine from his grinning mouth with the back of his hand, 'a land to name you. I shall call you Hebrons,' a name his wheezing mocking tongue pronounced in canaanite *Habiru*. 'Habiru you are, and shall be for ever.'

Mari clutched me. 'Melchizadok's one of the demons. He's false. Don't believe anything he says. He only says lies. It's a plot, it's one of Satan's schemes to deceive us. Jesus Christ is here! He's here somewhere.' She sounded crazy, but no one listens to a woman anyway. Food was brought, and wine for drinking, so I ate and drank. But Mari stumbled from the table and I followed her eating a goat's leg, found her searching among the houses, picking up stones, looking under pieces of wood. 'He's here, Wotan,' she told me earnestly. 'I *know*. I *believe*. It's enough. It's enough to believe.'

My heart went out to her. 'It's madness, what you're doing, Mari,' I said gently. 'Madness. There's nothing here. Melchizadok's not deceiving you. You deceived yourself.' I looked round as a boy messenger ran on to the hilltop, flung himself on his knees, tugged Abraham's arm. 'Come quick, quick! It's Sarah your wife!'

Abraham ran and Mari and I ran after him down to Sarah's tent. We heard the crying of an infant and Abraham reappeared. Flushed, breathing heavily, he raised his child who was the flesh of his flesh over his head. 'I name my son Isaac!' Not Jesus, not anything like Jesus. Mari's last hope was gone. I looked round but she was already far away, running away. She saw me coming after her and ran

270

faster than I thought she could. I pulled my strength into me and caught her on the edge of a steep stony valley. She wrestled free, fell out into the air, arms outstretched, but I grabbed her clothes, I lifted her up. There on the crumbling edge I kissed her lips, buried my mouth in her mouth, buried my hands in her hair. I pressed my hot cheeks to hers, her cheeks cold as death. 'Don't die,' I whispered. 'Don't make yourself die. Be with me. Let me love you.'

Her eyelids fluttered open, she touched my face with her fingertips. 'It was you. You came to me at Beth-Horon as women come among women. It can't be, but it is. You're so much more than a man. God truly has sent you.' Her body trembled. 'But you're not perfect. You're so male. So human. What does it mean?'

'I love you. Everything I do I do because I love you. I'll do anything for you. Crawl. Fly. Swim. Can't live without you. You can't die.'

'I'm dead without Jesus Christ.' Her fingertips fluttered on my eyelids. 'You're no demon, Wotan, but you have no soul. You'll never find the mountain of God.'

'I'll live for ever. Live with me. Love me. Be me.' I held the pearl in my mouth.

She whispered, 'My soul is immortal, Wotan. Everyone's soul is immortal. All of us live for ever.' Her arm dropped. 'But you have only immortality.'

She hung in my arms. I whispered, 'Don't go, Mari.' I stroked her cold face.

'I don't fear death,' she murmured. 'It's life. Emptiness. A dreadful eternity of life without Jesus Christ. Abandoned, forsaken. Denied salvation for ever.'

The whites of her eyes turned up, I tried to shield her from the sun. 'How can you know all these things, Mari? How could Melchizadok know so much? Son of Man, a son of Enoch? It's so long ago, Enoch was Noah's great-grandfather! Two thousand years ago Noah was nearly a

thousand years old. It's all forgotten, forgotten long ago.'
I wept tears into her eyes in my frustration, squeezed her
body gently in my arms, squeezed air in her lungs. She
gasped.

'Not forgotten. Never forgot. Goes back further than
you know, Wotan. Further than you can imagine. Long
before Heaven and Earth was known in this world. Or
even whispered.' Her eyes stared blank white but her finger
moved, scrawling in the sand. I didn't recognise the letters
but this is the exact shape of them: ARAM MENAHT
MENOU. '*Aram menaht menou*,' Mari's voice whispered
like the wind. 'This is the Holy Bible of the Lord your
God.'

'Bible?' I whispered. 'What's a bible?' I didn't care, my
only thoughts were of her, my prayer was old as time.
'Don't die. Don't die. Don't leave me.'

The wind blew away the shapes her finger had written
in the sand. I wept, 'Mari, Mari, who am I?' I shook her.
'Huwawa spoke of the greatest, there'd be someone who
was greatest, Him whose shoes I'm unworthy to tie. Did
he mean Jesus Christ?' Her breath sighed from her open
mouth, stopped. I had to know. 'Mari, did Huwawa mean
someone greatest to God . . . or greatest to Huwawa? *Do
I do Satan's work?* Am I immortal to do Satan's work?
How can I know? *How can I know?*'

I knelt over her body, squeezed her lungs, tried to kiss
the pearl into her mouth. 'I can give you eternal life. Be
born again in me.' I shook her until her head lolled. 'Take
it! Be born again in me. Mari, please!'

Mari was dead. She was dead. Without her Jesus Christ
she did not want to live.

Time passed. I don't know what the Habiru did. Later I
heard Abraham was called a foreigner and outsider in
Hebron; his hawkish face, thousands of hungry sheep and
hundreds of men living in tents, didn't fit in peaceful times.

I heard he moved on from the Dead Sea sulphur-pits trading salt, sulphur and pitch into Sinai, which means literally Land of the Moon. I heard they followed the trade-trails of the Wilderness of Shur selling pitch at a fabulous price in Egypt, where the black mineral's not found, and I heard some Habiru remained behind in Egypt as traders and builders when Abraham returned to the Land of the Moon, where he sired sons by dark-skinned Incense the Midianite. I heard Abraham pushed far to the south along the shores of the Red Sea, then returned north up the Arabah to the Dead Sea – and I know this is true, because that's where I saw him. Desert life had made Abraham old and hard, but Isaac scampered eagerly at the donkey's side. 'I remember when you were born, Isaac,' I called. 'I remember your father naming you seven years ago.'

Abraham didn't recognise me for a moment. 'You're younger,' he said, white-haired. He dismounted, looked into my eyes. 'Stronger. No wiser. What haunts you, Wotan?'

Your God, I thought, then didn't say it. We walked by the villages of Sodom and Gomorrah among the pillars of salt, the houses standing in their reflections in the bitter rising waters. I said, 'Your God is real to you, isn't He, Abraham. Does He truly speak to you?'

'He speaks,' Abraham said grimly, staring over the Dead Sea, climbing. 'This is the sixth day of my journey to God.'

I called, 'Where has God told you to come?' Abraham and his young son travelled almost alone in the dangerous wilderness; only a few guards followed well back.

'To Ur-Shalom, to Mount Sion.' Abraham put out his hand for Isaac to help him up the rocks. 'To Melchizadok's temple on Moriah.'

'Do you still have the iron meteorite? Your iron sword?' I glimpsed the coppery flash of a blade beneath his gown. 'Abraham, do you trust Melchizadok?'

Abraham's voice came back. 'I trust in God. God calls

us, Isaac and me.' I watched them climb the cliffs, the child helping his father up the steep path, until they were gone. That night I camped among the palm trees and balsam by the sterile waters of the Dead Sea. The stars above me winked in the deeps of the sea as though I stood on the edge of a bottomless pit. Local people call this bitter sea Abaddon, the abyss of destruction, the entrance to an underworld ruled by the Destroyer. Here, people believe, the dead aren't peacefully laid out to sleep in dusty halls as in the days of Ararat. Here they are tormented for ever by the Destroyer.

Something's changed, changing. Is this the Hell Mari believed in? Maybe Abraham's new God is different too, not like any God worshipped before, and everything's changing. I remembered Isaac's carefree scampering, the copper blade I'd glimpsed beneath Abraham's robe: the sacrificial knife, and knew why God had called Abraham.

Abraham would kill his firstborn son to please his God.

I ran uphill, leaving the sea like a great dark eye full of stars below me; ran from the clifftops along the dusty paths to Mount Sion, and arrived as the sun's first glow lit the sky behind me. The guards lay asleep by Abraham's donkey. Above me on Moriah, place of seeing, little Isaac stumbled uphill with a bundle of firewood at his father's side. I ran, lost them among the stars, then saw them silhouetted against the sun's rising glow. Abraham ignored the bloody altar of Melchizadok and piled stones to make his own altar. Isaac watched, trembling under the weight of sticks that Abraham would not let him put down. I heard Isaac's childish voice call out, 'Where's the lamb for the sacrifice, Father?' Abraham called out, 'God will see to it, son.' Abraham covered his face with his hands, then held out his hands smiling to Isaac and took the sticks, piled them on the pile of stones of the altar. A son seven years old, the perfect age meaning 'all'; surely nowadays, these enlightened days, a father can't kill his only son, his loved child, his life for seven years, all he'll ever have. All he'll ever have except for his God. Abraham's God demanded Abraham's entire life and future.

Abraham did it. He kissed Isaac and trussed him with a rope, blindfolded his son and kissed him, laid his son on the wood on the altar and kissed him, and laid out the fire-stone for the sacrificial fire and the copper knife for the cut. As he raised the knife for the *molech*-blow the blade flashed in the first light of the sun. 'Abraham,' I cried out. 'Abraham!' It was all I could think of to say. I pointed. The rising sun shone yellow as gold on the fleece of a ram caught by its horns in a thorn bush.

Abraham turned his face up to the sky as though he heard the voice of his God, but I did not. He hardly saw me, circled me with his face averted, then picked up Isaac from the altar and set him free. Together they pulled the ram from the thorns, a gift fit for the life of a prince, cut its throat, burnt it on the fire and sent the fat of its tail crackling in the smoke as a substitute sacrifice to Heaven. By giving its life in Isaac's place Abraham believed he had redeemed his son, and called the place *Ya will see*. So that was how the politics of it went with Abraham; his dark-skinned concubine Incense feared and worshipped Ya, but Sarah had loved El.

The villagers feared Abraham's blasphemous desecration of their holy place and chased him away. But all these little things happen a million times, to a million people. They're life. Why should I think anything that happened to the man called Abraham, and that Abraham made happen, important? Such tiny people, such tiny lives, and so many. Surely nothing matters. No one outside Abraham's families heard the voice of God, or saw any angels.

Some say Abraham was a hundred and seventy-five years old when he died. Some say he died in Hebron, others in Beer-Sheba in the Negeb, between the Dead

Sea and Sinai, where his son Isaac lives (though blind with age by now) and worships El, God. Some say Abraham settled with his Midianite wife who worships Ya, whose children are building a new nation of Midian beyond the eastern horn of the Red Sea, and that where Abraham is buried his black iron meteorite stands as his shrine to this day. I don't know; and I knew him as well as any man.

God makes Adam out of dust, and the wind blows the dust over the earth. No one knows our future. Our children are born and scatter like the grains of sand, but is there a pattern, is there a shape to be discerned? Is fate as blind as Isaac, and we're just scattered dice tumbling, or is Mari right? Mari, the only girl I will love and need for ever and offered my eternal love, eternal life, and will never have. I who have everything life offers, except her: Mari the virgin, who alone turned me down. Mari who believed our lives are not chaos but come to a conclusion ordained by God. Mari my love, who believed every mote of dust falls precisely where God's breath wills it for a purpose. Mari who *believes*. Sometimes I jump up with an oath from my little fire in the desert, sensing her behind me in the night, scenting her perfume, fragrant hyssop. Nothing. Sometimes I hear her in a flutter of wings, a faraway call. Sometimes I see God's fingernail scratch a line of fire between the stars, but that's imagination too. There was no Jesus Christ in Jerusalem.

God named Abraham and Sarah's grandson Israel, and Israel's children scattered like dust. A great wave of Sea People broke on the shores of Canaan calling themselves Philistines, and they called the land they conquered Palestine. Their blood soaked up the dust, carrying Israel's children as far as Egypt on a flood of fast chariots, strong bows, battles and slaughter. Pharaoh named the alliance of Sea People and Israelis *Hyksos* and fled to safety above the foaming cataracts of the Nile. The Philistines stayed in the delta, anointed one of their own Pharaoh, and made one of Israel's children, Yosef, an interpreter of dreams, his vizier and eventually high priest. His sons were Manasseh and Ephraim, so once more Israel's children mingled with their kin the Hebrew merchants and builders of cities, rulers of the priesthood and thus rulers of rulers. But Philistine rule was overthrown in Egypt and the Pharaoh of Thebes returned down the Nile to hold court in the great city, Avaris, built for the defeated Philistines by the Hebrews. The Hebrews, *'Apiru*, were thrown down with the Philistines and worked as slaves in the cities they'd built as free men. The lowest criminals and slaves were sent to dig copper mines in the Land of the Moon, Sinai, and lived short lives. In the choking glittering dust, dry mountains and merciless sun of this foreign land their one God was powerless to help them. But the Hebrews did not forget that they were Hebrews, Israel's children, and they did not forget their names, and they did not forgive Pharaoh, whom their fathers had driven from his kingdom, for his terrible revenge. And they never forgot where they had come from. Into this tortured land, along the trade-trail from Midian, a man came riding on a white camel.

This man had the temper of a camel, and he spat like one of the camels for which Midian is famous, hawking thick yellow spit because the Ya-Raha desert is dry dust and its sun is a furnace. Children cowered, staring up at him in awe, and a woman drawing back from the well whispered his name: Akenmoses. Akenmoses the murderer, once a prince of Egypt, punished not by honourable death but exile in Midian, the dry-as-dust underbelly of the world. Disgrace, the cruellest punishment to a proud prince. Death was preferable to the life he lived. Akenmoses hated the Land of the Moon with a furious temper, hated the dry desert, hated the dull peasants, hated demeaning his aristocratic blood with bartering and haggling, hated his clumsy bad-tempered camel and beat it and kicked it whenever he could. In his youth no doubt he'd driven four-horse chariots like the wind and his mind was still filled with that excitement, freedom, the lush fields and great buildings and beautiful women of the Nile, all he'd lost – I saw it in his eyes as he rode through whatever place this is. Akenmoses hated his life. His camel wailed and farted, scenting the well, slumping rebelliously to its knees as Akenmoses whipped its rump to force it past, not wanting to stop among us. Akenmoses never wanted to stop. He jumped down to kick the beast to its feet, setting the silver moon-trinkets jingling. 'Pharaoh's daughter bathed in the river,' the woman whispered to her friend, 'and found a basket sealed with pitch caught in the reeds. From inside came a baby's cry, a child who was one of us. A Hebrew. She named him Akenmoses and brought him up as a prince.'

'Who tells this story?' whispered the friend.

'Akenmoses.'

I watched Akenmoses with admiration. In this rough Levite region of the Hebrews, Egyptians outside the law get knocked on the head with rocks or knifed in the ribs, but he'd come up with that old story to protect his back. I've heard it a thousand times, all coming back in the end to Noah's Ark, a divinely chosen child, and what really happened to me. Sargon of Akkad claimed the story for himself, and that impostor Gilgamesh, and Egyptians believe that Isis hid the young god Horus in the reeds. Now Akenmoses claimed it for his own story, and a pitch-soaked basket (in Egypt!) just added to the sense of divine mystery. *A child who was one of us,* the women breathed, eyes glowing. They made Akenmoses sound like Mari's Jesus. More than their men, the women here expect a Messiah to save them. Men rule the day, but the women's tongues whisper in the night, and the whispers turn into dreams, and dreams can shine brighter than the light of day.

I stepped past Akenmoses's kicking sandals, looked him in the eye man-to-man, slipped my forearm under the camel and lifted it to its feet. The beast spat, accurately, and with my free hand I caught the sticky yellow gob an instant from Akenmoses's haughty Egyptian nose and clasped his wrist in welcome. In one I had helped Akenmoses, protected him, and offered friendship.

He wiped his wrist on his galabiya and tried to stare me down, his eyelids black with kohl. 'You,' haughty Nile accent, 'you are king of this village?' More Midianite camels padded between the mud huts, sleek, lightly laden, for sale. I was about to shake my head but the noon wind blew aside one woman's hood, and she was lovely, so I nodded and showed off. 'I'm strong enough to be king.' I put the camel down by the water, glimpsing the woman's Midian-dark skin, olive-smooth, as she watched. Strength always impresses them. 'Our water is yours. Yours,' I called after her. The camels drank their fill and I paid a young girl to ask about her among the women. 'She's Zipporah,' the girl sniffed, 'she's Akenmoses's wife, and she's holy, and she's not for you. Akenmoses is a jealous man.' But I watched Zipporah water the camels, her lovely intelligent eyes all I could see of her body, her low laughter all I could hear, and then her clear decisive orders to her slaves and servants. Again Akenmoses impressed me: surly and embittered, but not humbled, he'd taken care to make a good marriage. My girl sniffed, 'Her father's Jethro, their high priest of Ya. He's got seven daughters' – *many* – 'all of them daughters of Ya.' Meaning all holy – and often women were priests and prophets in their own right. I saw the old man standing asleep in his shadow, his chin against his sceptre, the Zadokite yellow cloak hanging from his shoulders to his feet – the golden fleece long gone, too hot and heavy in this fierce climate. Zipporah knelt at his knee, offering water, and Jethro drank without thanking her. She knew I watched her. She tried to ignore me. They never succeed.

The sun moved past the worst heat of the day. I made Akenmoses's camel kneel so he could climb up. 'Are you out in the desert tonight?'

'No.' He was a man of few words. 'With Aaron's people, if Ya wills it.'

'In the mountains,' Zipporah said. He glared at her. Egyptian women know their place. He contradicted her, 'No, not the mountains. The people of Aaron's Levite tribe live where the plain meets the mountains. Meets.' She shook her head, chuckling, and Akenmoses whacked the camel with his stick. He yelled, 'Where the plain meets the mountains!' She shouted, 'You know I'm right, husband. Why won't you listen!' He shouted Egyptian at her.

I shouted louder than both of them. 'I know where the copper mines are.' I spread my hands. 'I know. I'll show you.'

'In the mountains,' Zipporah said. Akenmoses said, 'Between the plain and the mountains.'

'He doesn't know anything,' Zipporah muttered under her breath. 'He's just a child, my husband. He'd forget his clothes if I didn't dress him in the mornings.' Her gaze softened. 'Ya would have to look after him if I didn't.' I walked beside her past the various Hebrew encampments by the road wishing I could see her face, then pointed out the scorched yellow peaks hovering in the mirage. 'Don't worry, we'll get there before sunset.' Her eyes smiled as she told me, 'Yes, the light lingers longer in the height of the mountains.' I nodded respectfully, really interested in her now, but some children fought over a beetle they'd found. I kept them quiet by juggling rocks, I've always felt closest to children, except my own. The rocks were heavier than they could lift. Out of sight of adults I made them laugh by leaping back-somersaults as I juggled the rocks, then saw Zipporah watching. 'You're another one,' she decided. 'You're just a big child.' But the children looked up to me in awe, which is what I love.

Both Akenmoses and I took care to pee without showing ourselves, but being curious (I like to check no man has a penis nearly as large or beautiful as mine) I noticed his foreskin was as whole as mine is; he was no more Hebrew by blood than I, whatever he claimed.

And he was smaller.

The Hebrews Akenmoses sought lived by the great precipice of Safsafa, the copper mountain rising above their tents as jagged as a knife. Here, in the holy mountain hallowed because of its copper, Aaron's people scratched and dug and suffered in the deadly dust-filled smoke-reeking darkness of the holy place to send their quota of metal to Pharaoh's treasure cities. We climbed past gangs of slaves, prisoners beating great ore-stones to rubble, a roaring furnace fed with precious sticks hauled from the blue haze of the Red Sea on our left, while on our right lines of men stumbling from the mines fell exhausted in their chains. 'Told you, wife,' Akenmoses called back down the slope, 'the Hebrews are found on the plain.' Zipporah said, 'In the mountain.' We came to the camp and Akenmoses, hospitably welcomed by Aaron in person, dismounted and followed the bowing Hebrew into the largest tent. There they'd dicker over the price of Akenmoses's pack-camels to carry metal to the palace at Raamses. I yawned, hoping for the smell of boiling lamb, then settled in the shadow of a boulder to wait. Almost at once I heard a woman's footsteps, but it was the scent of her that made me sit up, fragrant hyssop – real hyssop. I saw her only from the back, dressed in white linen, a middle-aged woman, but I knew it was her. Mari. She didn't see me, ducked through Aaron's tent-flap, was gone. But it was her.

Looking nothing like I remembered her. But if souls do live for ever, this woman had Mari's soul. The scent of her, the instinctive sway of her walk; as if she'd never died. *Everyone's soul is immortal, all of us live for ever. But you, Wotan, you have no soul. You have only immortality.* I shivered despite the sun, then crouched forward into the tent's shadow. In my haste I broke the tent-peg between my fingers as I lifted it from the rock, then I lay and lifted the side of the tent a notch, peered beneath. A rug, feet moving, a woman's sandals. Then Aaron's quick voice. 'This is my sister Miriam, the prophet of El.' Miriam, almost the same name!

Miriam's voice speaking to Akenmoses: 'Welcome. May El abide with you as far as you go.' Her knees as she knelt, her hands as she washed Akenmoses's feet. She left him dusty between the toes and her greeting made it sound as though she wished Akenmoses farewell and good riddance. She liked Midianites even less than Egyptians, her tone said, especially as Akenmoses's father-in-law was high priest of the Midianite God Ya; Jethro's rank to Ya was equivalent to her own to El.

But Akenmoses wouldn't go. Aaron and he haggled over camel prices then spat on their hands to clinch the sale, and drank wine. 'Pharaoh is dead,' Akenmoses said, but Aaron had already heard, news travels as fast as the birds of the desert. 'The new will be worse than the old.'

'Less sure of himself,' Akenmoses said bluntly.

'Had a man die a few days ago,' Aaron said; they must lose men every day in this awful place, holy or not, but Miriam said warningly: 'My brother.'

Aaron said, 'Burnt to death.' I think that's what he said; a goat nibbled my toes. I kicked it away and when I looked again under the tent Miriam had moved, standing between Akenmoses and her brother as though to silence him. But Aaron blurted, 'He was burnt in the deepest level of the mine where there's no fire, only a flickering reed for light.'

Miriam insisted, 'My brother—'

Akenmoses got to his feet. 'No, a man doesn't burn without fire, except by the sun. Your El lives in the mountain. Your man has been burnt by your God. Let me see.' He tried to step past Miriam.

'Don't go,' Miriam said. 'It's dangerous.' She tugged his sleeve as he passed. 'Akenmoses, El's not there. My brother and I are the priests of El. El is with us.' What was in the holy mountain that she didn't want Akenmoses to see? Really God? Really?

Akenmoses glared at her. 'I'll see for myself!' I busied myself with camel harness as he came out with Aaron, then ran silently after them from rock to rock as they strode uphill. 'Does she hate all men?' Akenmoses grumbled, and I thought, *Yes!* But Aaron shrugged. He didn't want to talk about Miriam, he wanted to talk about what they'd found in the mine. 'I think it's the moon.'

Akenmoses grunted as he climbed, climbing after his long shadow drawn black as a stick-man up the cliff ahead of him. I saw the entrance to the mine high above, a natural cave at first.

'The moon's fallen to the Land of the Moon,' Aaron said. 'You'll see.' The men took burning tapers from a pale boy and Akenmoses went first into the dark mouth. The sun hung like a red ball over the mountains, time soon for evening prayers; El's worshipped according to the sun, as I told you long ago, after the days when Enoch lived for three hundred and sixty-five years. But Ya's followers worship according to the moon, giving a lunar year of only three hundred and fifty-four days. Such tiny matters are life and death to those who believe in them. Miriam shouted angrily for her brother to return.

Aaron hurried inside. I snatched a taper from the boy and followed him into the dark. By the fluttering light I glimpsed his silhouette going ahead of me through the dust and smoke, bent double now. The cave had been widened but Aaron's shoulders and hips almost jammed, dragging fresh dust after him. The miners wore cloths over their faces, coughing, eyes red as demons. The clatter of axes was silenced by the weight of rock above us as we went down. The cave narrowed and Aaron almost stuck, pushed sideways and got through, then crawled on his knees under the low roof. The tunnel widened, and here was the hole where the miners had broken through into a chamber below. Akenmoses had already gone down. Aaron slid from sight, leaving me in almost total darkness. I waited on my belly. There was nothing but dark and dust and smoke down here, and silence. I could hardly breathe. Below my head Aaron's taper reappeared, then Akenmoses's, seeming bright as stars in the blackness below.

Suddenly Akenmoses's voice came whispering enormously, echoing. 'It *is* El!' I craned forward, peering, and saw God like a light in the darkness.

'My sister disagrees,' came Aaron's voice, ashamed. 'She swears it's not El.' I thought Akenmoses murmured under his breath, 'Then it is Ya.'

Ya, that made sense; Ya of the lunar calendar and the worshippers of Ya-Rah, the canaanite moon god, but I was disappointed to see only a perfect silver ball, perfectly round, somewhat smaller than a man. Its curve showed not a speck of dust or taint. It looked enough like the full moon to me; perhaps it had fallen to earth, or rested here. Perhaps it was simply a symbol of the Divine Will, like Abraham's meteorite, and scratches of fire in the sky, hidden to be found. If it was made of solid silver it was fabulously valuable. Akenmoses crawled forward and the silver moon reflected back the approaching flames of the tapers like a mirror, stretching their light in perfect reflection around its surface, redoubling their illumination so that Akenmoses's face and then Aaron's face glowed like faces painted on red rock. The two crouching men looked ancient as cave-dwellers, as though men had walked the earth for ten thousand years; but the silver shone as bright between them as though newly minted.

'My people want to worship it,' Aaron whispered. 'I wish it was made of gold.'

Akenmoses inched close. His face swelled, staring back at him in perfect detail, eyes and teeth stretching hideously round the shining globe. 'It isn't the moon. The moon doesn't reflect faces.' His mouth grinned enormously, all lips and teeth and tongue. 'Do you pray to it?'

'Inside the mountain? The people can't worship what they can't see.'

'Perhaps that makes it more powerful.' Akenmoses smiled with teeth as long and pointed as swords, saw himself, realised how loudly his voice boomed, fell silent. Then he noticed a sceptre lying in the dust, picked it up. For a moment I thought he'd brought Jethro's sceptre down here somehow, or even Abraham's. But this relic was not cut from olive-wood clumsily carved. The shaft of this holy sceptre was polished ebony and the head was gold, ornate, intricate, precise. It looked old as time, old as the beginning of the world. Akenmoses blew the dust off it, and it gleamed complexly, a beautiful work of art, almost serpent-like about the head, recalling Eden: a device for approaching God. 'In Egypt,' Akenmoses whispered, 'our priests use sceptres like these. Not as heavy.' He touched the head with his fingertip. 'Not as complicated.' Suddenly my hair stood up, the hairs prickled along the backs of my hands, and up my arms.

'Careful!' Aaron said quickly. 'My man – burnt to a cinder!'

'I've felt this before.' Akenmoses stood curiously. 'It's a lightning storm.' He prodded at the sceptre with his blunt forefinger but nothing happened. No lightning. Both men shrugged. Then Aaron reached out and his hand skidded over the silver ball without quite touching the surface – as though it had no surface exactly, like melting ice. Aaron said, 'It's warm.' Both men held out their hands as though to a campfire on a cold night.

And I heard the sound of angels singing.

No, not quite the same, because I've heard the song of real angels. The day was windless when we came down, but now I saw a wind start in the chamber, blowing faintly at first around the walls, setting the taper flames fluttering. The flames were drawn in towards the silver sphere, and dust rose up spinning around the globe just as the stars and sun circle the earth. The moon seemed a little less silver to me, darkening, glowing with darkness. The wind began to tug at the men's clothes, pulling them forward.

'I don't like it,' Aaron called. They were truly afraid God was coming and the wind was a divine wind. Akenmoses touched the sceptre and everything stopped. The two men stood watching the silver ball. Nothing else happened. Motionless.

'I spent too long in the sun today,' Aaron muttered at last. 'My face hurts.' They turned to leave, and I scrambled along the passage into the last light of the sun. My face and hands too were raw with sunburn everywhere the shield of rock had not protected them. Akenmoses and Aaron came out with faces blistered bright red, as burnt by the sun as newborn children. 'Burnt by the *shekinah* of the Lord,' Akenmoses claimed. 'Burnt by the glory of God!' Everyone laughed, except Miriam. She sat on her heels and wept. I think she knew more than they. Much more.

I searched for her among the acacia bushes that night, but she was nowhere. Some said she'd tried to destroy what was found, knocking at the pit-props with an axe, but the cave refused to fall.

In the morning Akenmoses stalked full of strength from Jethro's tent and parleyed with Aaron like a king to a king. What were they planning? Together the two men called for every galabiya and every cloak that could be found, every blanket and camel-blanket, and sent for more to other Hebrew camps. By evening the women sewed busily to make a thick garment with many layers. At dawn the next day slaves carried the tent-like garment up to the cave mouth, Akenmoses following behind. Miriam ran forward. 'You can't go in,' she cried. 'It's not God. You can't control it. You'll be wearing your shroud!' Akenmoses shrugged her off, received Jethro's blessing, and pulled the heavy folds over his head and body. As he vanished from the people-filled sunlight into the darkness Miriam shrieked after him, 'You'll kill us all! You don't know what you're doing! You'll destroy the whole world.' Her voice echoed between the rocks, magnifying, but Aaron silenced her and strong men pulled her back. So that was how, I observed, it was between the king of the Hebrews and his sister the high priest of El.

We waited. Miriam wept her heart out among the acacia bushes. I got close and whispered, 'Mari?' She screamed at me, struggling, kicking, spittle flying from her chin. Then she fell silent against my hands, listening, and we listened to the silence. The earth gave a shiver under our feet. I laughed with excitement, but Miriam's eyes widened. 'No. It's the end of the world.'

Everything that was up fell down. Everyone fell. We lay hanging against the earth with our fingers, our toes, the whole earth trembling under our faces as though to shake us off, then through our bodies we heard the song of angels rising like the song of a great choir of angels rising up in the mountain, as if the mountain to which we lay clinging was only a wind instrument, a sounding trumpet of Heaven's music.

I heard His Voice in the thundering storm. An acacia bush burst into fire.

It's true. God lives in the mountains.

The people scattered. Great boulders fell over the cave mouth, sealing the mine. The tribe gathered, silent, staring numbly at the disaster. Akenmoses had been punished for daring to approach God, he and the Hebrews' mine were both destroyed. The copper quota would not be filled. The livelihood of the whole people was lost, and they would be punished by Pharaoh. Aaron claimed it was only an earthquake, the burning bush nothing more than a lightning strike, but Miriam shrieked it was a sign of God's wrath, El's punishment of His whole people because of their sins. Only God could explain such destruction. Her priests whispered that the burning bush was a false wonder, a trick by Jethro's priests jealous of El. Miriam called the people down from the mountain to pray, because to El the whole people, not just the priesthood, was holy. To her each man's salvation lay in his own heart, and each woman's heart, and personal prayers redeemed them.

Aaron waited alone. I kept him in my sight from behind the burning bush. At noon he climbed to the cave and called between the boulders, tried to shift them, but they lay together like pillars holding up the mountain. During the afternoon Aaron retreated to the camp. The people would have to go, some were already packing up, but he had no idea what to do next, where to go, how to lead them. The turquoise mines to the north had even harsher conditions than here for digging copper. Pharaoh's wrath would be worse than God's. I climbed the boulders, surveyed the disaster Akenmoses's pride had brought down on the Hebrews, and saw no hope even with my strength.

But something made me wait. The sun fell and in the desert below me the camp fires were lit as Aaron's tribe went about their usual prayers, Jethro and the Midianites making sacrifice to Ya on the near side of the camp, Miriam praying to El of the Hebrews on the far side, and between them the cults of Serpents and Red Calves and Riders on the Clouds and B'El-Zephon of the Storm and Wind howled and beseeched their gods, offering their children to Molech, so below me I heard a great babble of voices rising like the sound of wild animals in worship as the sun set over Egypt and the moon rose over the Land of the Moon.

The mountain groaned. The boulders behind me groaned like a man's voice. Beneath a slab bigger than a house, a little dust trickled. By my foot a man's finger poked out, sunburnt, blistered. The mountain teetered over us. The finger scratched at the dust with what was left of its nail. That's all; that tiny scratching sound. I shoved my shoulders beneath the boulder, lifted, nothing moved. I pulled my strength into me, pushed my hands on my knees, pushed with my legs harder than I have ever pushed, my thigh muscles swelled hard as iron, my shoulders burst out of my clothes, my chest ripped my shirt as I lifted, lifted, and the boulder creaked as though I lifted the world. The rock above me shifted, heaved upwards. Between my feet a hand appeared, pushing forward a few pages of carved marble no thicker than sheets of papyrus that knocked my ankles; marble sheets, almost infinitely long-lasting but brittle, covered with letters or numbers I couldn't read even by the glare of the burning bush. My strength was going. I lifted with all I had left, sweat dripping, my jaws so tight my teeth broke, my feet sinking into the rock, and Akenmoses slid out between my legs. Slid out in the dust like a baby being born. I gasped, 'Akenmoses?' He stared up as though he didn't know his name. The weight overcame me, I fell forward exhausted. I, Wotan, was weak – for a moment.

I opened my eyes. Below me in the night Akenmoses, naked, sunburnt, almost blind, staggered barefoot into the light of the burning bush and stared into the flames which were all he could see; stared as though he saw every truth revealed in the fiery tongues of light. But he did not see me.

* * *

Akenmoses's voice was the voice of pharaohs, taskmasters, bureaucrats and the ruling castes of Egypt who'd enslaved the Hebrews, so Aaron spoke for him. He started wisely. 'This is not Akenmoses whom you knew.'

The people muttered. Standing red and blistered though Akenmoses was, in a striped borrowed galabiya too small for him, they knew what Akenmoses looked like.

'If you've got two good ears you'd better listen,' Aaron told the people. 'Akenmoses is dead.' He raised his arms over the seventy chieftains. 'God has given this man a new name: Moses! God has saved him!'

The Midianite priests chanted, 'Moses! Moses!' But the Hebrews grumbled. They wanted to know exactly which God lived in the holy mountain, their own El, or Ya of the Midianites. They wanted their copper quota filled and their bellies full, not talk.

Aaron scrambled on a rock. He pulled Moses up beside him, king and priest together. I looked for Miriam. 'You ask which God named Moses?' Aaron called down, and now I saw her, down on the ground with the others, her lips pulled back in fury as she stared up at the two men. Aaron ignored her, shouting, 'The God of Moses's father named him, that's who!' The old story of Akenmoses's Hebrew parents again – Aaron was even trying to pass Akenmoses off with a Hebrew name, *Mosheh*, as though Moses were not an exiled Egyptian aristocrat who'd married a Midianite priest's daughter. The most ardent of Aaron's followers even claimed that he and Moses were not only Hebrew but brothers of this same tribe, both sons of Levi – so Miriam was Moses's sister, and her duty was to show him sisterly loyalty. Aaron got fully into his stride. 'The God of Moses is the God of our fathers, the God of Abraham, the God of Isaac, the God of Israel!'

That could mean anything; those who believed in El thought he meant El, the followers of Ya supposed Ya. Aaron dropped his voice to make the people hang on his words; garrulous and indiscreet in private, he was a canny public speaker. 'He is the God who will lead us from Pharaoh's hands into a land flowing with milk and honey!' Aaron shouted over the heads of the chieftains and the heads of the people crowded behind to the parched landscape that surrounded us: 'God will lead us home to our land of Canaan, ours, our own land of milk and honey!'

The chieftains laughed. 'The Egyptians are going to let us go? Who's going to fight the Egyptians for us?' The Hebrews didn't have a dozen swords between them against Pharaoh's army, only sticks and copper eating knives, and numbers: a whole enslaved people, perhaps half a million men altogether, though not a single soldier among them. But *Canaan:* that ancient name awakened memories whispered from mother to child for thousands of years. Voices among the people shouted out until the whole people were shouting, 'What's the name of the God of our fathers who's going to do all this for us and take us back to Canaan?'

When Aaron didn't answer they chanted, 'Give us His Name! Give us His Name!' Aaron turned from side to side but they grew noisier. He could not answer. He did not know God's name.

Moses raised his arms, and the people fell silent. He stood taller than Aaron, and his silent sunburnt figure and upraised arms against the blinding sky made the people small. Then Moses spoke to them in his deep foreign voice – and he spoke to them in their own Hebrew language.

Moses said: 'God says to me, I AM CALLED I AM.' Everyone looked at each other, confused. 'I AM CALLED I AM.' Those were literally the words Moses said, '*Eyah asher eyah*', which makes no sense, but the people chattered among themselves and believed his thick foreign tongue uttered '*Eyah asher Ya*', I am called Ya. Ya, the God of their ancestors, which makes perfect sense to all Shemites. I remembered from my youth the great mountain-temples of Shem dedicated to Ya, Ea, Éya. Long ago the *kanunu* woodcutters following the cedar trees brought El with them into Canaan, and now Moses the educated man brought back Ya, through the Midianite descendants of Abraham's second wife, to the Hebrews who'd forgotten Him. 'God talks to Moses alone!' the Hebrews excitedly called to their old people and deaf and children too young to understand. 'He doesn't speak to all of us, a whole people isn't holy enough. He will speak only to Moses who is holy. God tells Moses, I am called Ya!'

'Ya is God, Ya is God!' chanted the priests of Midian, El meaning simply *God*. 'Ya-El is One! Ya-God! Lord God! Ya-El who is Lord God who created the world! Ya-El made Adam! Ya-El is the God of Abraham and Moses!'

'No!' shrieked Miriam's voice. 'God is God, there is no God but God! *El aser yahweh sabaot!* El calls into being the lord of armies!' She scrambled on the rock, lashed out at Moses with the sceptre of El. 'Liar!' she shrieked. 'Blasphemy!' Aaron tried to stop her but her gopher-wood staff struck at Moses again and again. He warded her off with his own sceptre of ebony and gold he'd brought down from the mountain with the writings on marble; but Miriam's fury, certainty, desolation, took him aback. Moses was shaken. Guards threw Miriam down from the rock but the people shouted for her, her priest Korah and their followers lifted her up, and Moses knew he had to do something about her.

He raised his arms and spoke simply, showing his imperious accent as little as possible. 'God's name is too holy to be said aloud.' The people fell silent, puzzled. God whose name could not be called aloud with spittle on the tongue, but only uttered as a private thought in the head, was an extraordinary new idea. With his sceptre Moses scratched four Hebrew letters in the dust of the rock, then called the seventy Elders forward. 'This is the tetragrammaton, *Y-H-W-H,* which stands for the secret sacred name of God.'

One old man cried, 'How do we pronounce it?'

'You're not permitted to say God's name in full. Are you stupid? If it cannot be said it cannot be pronounced!'

The old man tried to understand. 'How will He hear our complaints if we don't speak?'

'*Y-H-W-H* God hears every thought as loud as if it were shouted. He is everything, everywhere. He is all angels, all gods, all Elohim. You cannot limit Him by pronouncing Him, defining Him.'

'It sounds like Yahweh to me,' the old man said, but the Elder beside him shook his head. 'No, Yahvee.' Moses glared angrily. Another argued, 'Between the hard letters I believe I hear the soft sounds of *Adonai,* Lord.' The old fool tried to articulate the sound of the name, and Moses lost his temper. Someone called, 'Are we permitted to say Ya?' Another asked, 'Or Yah? Is that permitted?' The one who had heard Lord cried out, 'Shall we call Him Lord God?' Moses raised the sceptre and I really thought he would bring it crashing down on the head of the parroting Elders, just as he had murdered an Egyptian in a fit of rage. But this time Moses pointed the sceptre above his head, and God (whatever His name) moved the mountain. I saw it. Moses pointed the sceptre and the mountain moved inside itself, roaring inside itself, shrinking, collapsing as the God of Moses roared. Red rock poured down the slopes like blood, rose into the sky like a cloud of blood over the people.

The great sound of the Voice of God, theophany, stopped. Not a word to be heard from the Elders. Not a sound. 'That is the power of my God, *Y-H-W-H.*' Moses dropped the marble tablets at their feet. 'Read, understand, obey His Law.'

The Elders knelt and tried to read, but understood not a word. They argued amongst themselves.

'This is all a lie!' Miriam cried. 'It's a dreadful trick, it's all wrong, there's no Yahweh—'

'Silence her,' Moses said. 'The name of the Lord is not to be taken in vain.' But Miriam broke free from the hands which held her.

She threw herself at Aaron's feet. 'My brother, I am as great in power and prophesy as Moses is, and so are you. The people will still follow you.'

Aaron turned his back on her. 'Can you make the mountain fall, Miriam? I can't.'

'Give me the sceptre of Yahweh and I will.'

Moses mocked her, 'This sceptre of *Y-H-W-H* which you despise?'

She begged Aaron, 'There's no Yahweh in the mountain. It's a trick, a deceit by Satan.' *S-T-N,* He whose name is too *un*holy to be uttered aloud. She cried, 'Hear my words too, my brother Aaron, hear me speak for El, as well as listening to Moses.'

Aaron hesitated. 'Yes,' he decided, swaying first towards Moses then to Miriam. 'My brother, she must be allowed to speak for El.'

Mose's face darkened with temper. His blistered skin trickled blood. Yet the palm of his hand, where his grip on the sceptre had protected his skin, looked white as snow. He clenched his hand around the sceptre. Then he pointed it at Miriam, and cursed her.

'It's leprosy,' Miriam said. She threw back her hood, let me see her distorted lion-like face, flaking skin, withered hands. She looked like a woman of seventy. 'I'm unclean. Forbidden to perform any of the rituals of El. Services. Liturgy. Nothing. So Moses can do what he wants, and my brother Aaron is his little puppy dog and barks for him.' She shaded her eyes from the sun, watching the men like dots searching the mountain.

'Has Moses truly found the power of God, Mari?'

She heard me say her old name, but she didn't care. She was too exhausted to pretend. 'There's no God to be found in this world, Wotan. Don't you know that by now? Isn't it obvious to you? Look around you. How can you be so stupid that you still try to believe?' A cry went up on the mountain and the dots moved together above the collapsed mine.

'He's got it,' I said, but all I could think of was kissing her lips, leprous and peeling though they were, whatever happens I'm always me, Wotan, it's my nature (God-given or not) to be a man and to want to possess everything to the hilt. But Miriam pointed. Moses knelt, covering what had been found with his cloak as though it was too holy to be seen, just as the name of God is apparently too holy to say. Men with poles carried the divine gift reverently downhill between them. I knew it was just a silver ball. But if it was really a ball of silver, which must be heavy, why were only two men needed to carry it? Was the silver hammered somehow to be as thin and insubstantial as skin – which would be a miracle in itself? The noon wind blew, and the cloaked shape fluttered between the poles as though no heavier than a bubble. I whispered, 'Is this your Jesus Christ, Mari?'

'No!' She shot me a horrified look. 'It's just a treasure, a peculiar treasure. Not the power of God. The power of men.'

'Moses seized power over the Hebrews very effectively,' I said shyly. 'God says Aaron is Moses's prophet – so Moses claims.' God spoke to Moses, not Aaron.

'Moses the Egyptian can't possibly love the Hebrews,' she said. 'He just hates Pharaoh.' Miriam covered her face and turned away. 'If you live for ever one day you'll understand what he's found, Wotan, and I pity you.'

Moses called Bezal'El the Hebrew carpenter and ordered acacia trees to be sawn to make a box called a sanctuary. The carpenters averted their faces as they lowered the object into the box so it remained hidden. When the lid was closed they whispered that Yahweh God Himself lived inside, and His people would be safe as long as they kept Him among them. This huge promise was Yahweh God's Covenant with His people.

Pharaoh allowed the Hebrews no smiths or metalworkers who might use their skills to make weapons, so Moses called Jethro the Zadok and gave instructions for his men to make a gold seat, the *kappōret*, on top of the box and beside it two angels of beaten gold, their arched wingtips meeting over the seat. 'I name this tabernacle the Arch of the Covenant,' Moses said. From between the arched wings, he said, God's Voice would speak to him when the time came.

Jethro said, 'What time?'

Moses leant on his sceptre. 'Time to get honour over Pharaoh.' I felt Miriam shiver at that word *honour*. It means war. Moses the aristocrat exiled from court had everything to prove. A man of honour living in disgrace will give his life for just a scent of the honour he once knew. Moses led peasants he once considered less than dust. He had no soldiers, but he had numbers, vast numbers of people who were not his own people, whom he hardly knew, whose lives were cheap. Moses's God would lead a defenceless people against the most powerful army on earth. 'For the glory of God,' I said. I've always loved men with big schemes.

'No, for the glory of Moses.' Miriam shuddered, and turned away from me.

'Moses, listen to my advice,' Jethro was saying. 'Stand to Godward of the Hebrews, place yourself between them and the Lord. Appoint your own men to order and command them in thousands, hundreds, fifties, tens.' Order, command: the word he used was *sion*. 'Make sure each clan, and each father and son, and each mother and daughter, under the order and command of these righteous men of sion, knows the Law of Moses.'

'God's Law,' Moses said.

'Exactly, my son. The two branches, the branch of Ya and the branch of El, shall be joined together under Moses's Law in Israel.' Jethro smiled toothlessly. He was a cunning old patriot whom some called Reuel, others Hobab; not even his seven daughters knew him well. 'These cadres of sion shall be your judges under you in all small matters of discipline. Larger matters should be decided by you.' He clasped hands with Moses, and the matter was sealed.

So the Hebrews, left with nothing to keep them where they were, began their long journey northward towards Pharaoh thinking Moses led them to Canaan. These journeys are always called wanderings, moving as always at the pace of sheep and growing grass, but it turned into a migration. Not of a whole people at once. Not even all of Aaron's tribe of twenty-two thousand started out (Moses counted only men who were over twenty years old but younger than seventy); no, only a few hundred families at first, the clans closest to Aaron or deepest in his debt. But like a snowball rolling from the mountains Moses picked up converts among the twelve Hebrew tribes of the plain, the children of Manasseh and Ephraim, Judah, Zebulun, Benjamin and Dan and all the others, and the numbers swelled like a cloud following the Covenant. Aaron's Levites, the thirteenth tribe, had as their sole duty the carrying and guarding of the Arch. Still the Elders had not deciphered the Law Moses had brought down, but I heard Moses carved on acacia wood the oracles Urim and Thummim, jewelled tablets of destiny for discovering the Lord's Will, to be worn beneath the Zadok high priest's breastplate and understood only by him. Did Moses believe he would never live to enter Canaan, was he taking care that his successor would be able to comprehend, through holiness and priestly submission, the Voice of the Lord?

Like a slow-moving tide, with waves sometimes reaching ahead or falling behind, the Hebrews flooded north beside the western horn of the Red Sea. From the tip of the horn they could turn right towards Canaan or left into Egypt.

They turned left. 'Pharaoh's pride won't let my people go,' Moses said. 'But my Lord is greater than Pharaoh.' The Hebrews of the mountains and plains flowed together with the Hebrews of the cities, moving past the Bitter Lakes and Lake Timsah to Taphanes, into the Land of Goshen, coming to Pharaoh's treasure-cities of Succoth and Pithom built by Hebrew slaves, finally to the greatest treasure-city of all, Raamses. And there they stopped, idle. They were now a force to be reckoned with. The slaves stopped, the building sites fell idle. Pharaoh Ramesses surveyed the half-finished buildings, his testament to eternity, and cursed the Hebrews because he needed them.

Each morning when divine Ramesses went down to the river to worship, Moses demanded from the river bank that the Hebrews be allowed to serve their Lord in Canaan. Neither man would give way. This was not between the Egyptians and the Hebrews, but between two men equal in pride. Ramesses sought to part Moses from the Hebrews by letting it be known that the murder Moses had committed long ago was forgiven, all witnesses were dead, but Moses said obstinately: 'Let my people go.'

Young Ramesses walked among his scaffolded buildings. Moses asked more than could possibly be given. Ramesses had the Hebrews whipped to make them build. When they didn't build fast enough he forced them to buy their own bricks so that they paid to work in slavery.

Moses said: 'Let my people go.' He touched his sceptre, showing God's power, and the Nile turned to blood and dead fish. Ramesses turned his face away. Moses said, 'Let my people go.' A plague of frogs came over Egypt, into every house and every bed, into the royal granaries and bakeries and ovens, and the taste of their flesh came into each loaf of bread.

'Let my people go,' Moses said, the uncircumcised Egyptian whose Egyptian was better than his Hebrew; but he spoke through Aaron, whose people they were. When Moses touched the ground with his sceptre God made the dust of Egypt turn to lice, as many crawling lice as there were Hebrews. Finally when no courtiers were present Ramesses spoke privately, in Egyptian. 'Akenmoses, we both worship Adam, we shouldn't argue. Give up your madness.'

'Let my people go.'

'You'll never force me to believe in only your Yahweh-El,' Ramesses said.

'Let my people go.'

'Make your people work.'

'Let my people go or the Lord of all will send flies swarming over Egypt.'

Flies swarmed on the land. How was Moses doing it? That was what interested me. On some level I could understand the shaking mountain, the devastated river, as somehow the work of men. But I couldn't see how the Arch of the Covenant – perhaps it *was* the Lord – could cause frogs and lice and now these disgusting swarming crawling flies if it was *not* the Lord.

Yes, perhaps in the Lord Moses truly had found God, whatever Miriam said.

I don't know what happened for a while; I got drunk in Tanis, fell in love – lust – in some little seaport, started a war between two brigands and helped the one I liked most, who drank most, who had the most beautiful daughter. The women I love always hate me when I do this, they always get at me, my nagging conscience, but I'm a man. I woke in a barn in the town of Hagar, my head banging with wine, my hands covered in blood, my lips tasting of kisses, and as you know I'm never happier than on such days. I walked back to Raamses whistling like one of the little songbirds sometimes blown into people's hands on the desert wind, a miracle, for there's no water to be found until the edge of the world.

The Hebrews were gone. The wind blew across the empty building sites of Raamses. I smelt death, passed cemeteries howling with mourners. I walked to the deserted mud ghettoes of the Hebrews, calling out, but every house was empty. Every silent door hung open in mute witness, daubed with blood. I tasted it: not human. 'The blood of lambs,' Miriam said from a doorway, watching me. 'Zipporah circumcised Moses while he slept and made him a proper son of Israel in the eyes of God. At midnight God killed each firstborn uncircumcised child in Egypt, each eldest child from Pharaoh to the lowest slave, all dead. The firstborn calves of cattle. Everything. Only houses daubed with blood of the lamb were passed over.'

I was amazed. 'And Ramesses still won't believe in Moses's God?'

'He sent the Hebrews away the same night. Just go. A riot, I don't know what the Hebrews stole, gold, jewels, clothing, everything they got their hands on. The Egyptian women screaming and holding out their dead babies.'

I took her hand. 'You're sure God did it?'

'This is what He does to those who are not saved,' she said dully. 'How else could we know which is the right God?' She breathed the smell. 'How else can we know what salvation is?'

'Tell me where Moses is now.' I shook her by her leprous shoulders. She pointed: a single cloud hanging in the pure blue arch of the southern sky.

'God lives in the cloud,' she said. She corrected herself. '*Y-H-W-H*. The Lord of Moses.'

I picked her up and carried her in my arms in the desert. The cloud hung above Succoth – no, it already moved

300

forward. During the night the cloud was a pillar of fire between Heaven and Earth, a light without shadow reaching higher than the sky. I carried Miriam past discarded clothing, broken carts, the bodies of old people who had died, dead animals, all the debris of the Hebrew exodus from Egypt. A whole people moving day and night, each night bright as day, driving their flocks in front of them with sticks and stones in desperate haste. For a few days, I knew, Pharaoh would mourn. For a few days more the scale of his disaster would grow on him until he smelt nothing in his nose but the death of children, heard nothing in his ears but the cries of his people for revenge. Ramesses was young; when he came he'd come down as cruelly as the north wind.

I hurried, passing stragglers now, the sick and injured, hopeless and helpless, animals limping or lying exhausted, and the pillar of fire burned by night. At dawn I came among the lepers. 'Put me down among my people,' Miriam begged, meaning the lepers, but I went faster, angry now: Moses had brought terrible suffering on this people he had taken over and called his own. I told her, 'Moses cursed you so let Moses heal you.' I passed through men and women filthy with diseases and plagues, then sinners who'd been cast out, then women unclean with their monthly courses, then came through the old men to the young men, and finally to Moses walking alone at the head of the people. 'You,' he said, remembering me – as if anyone could forget such a man as I.

'What have you done, Moses?' I swept my arm across the mass of people stumbling behind us, from horizon to horizon.

Moses said: 'As the Lord wills.'

I put Miriam down on her feet to walk beside us. 'Moses, I know this land. As soon as the funeral rites for his son are over, Pharaoh will come after you.'

He shrugged, nothing could have surprised him less.

'That's why I struck south, not east. The garrisons at Lake Balah and at Zilu haven't seen us.'

I said angrily, 'Lake Balah was your road straight to Canaan.' Only three tracks lead east from Egypt to Canaan: the coast road, the central track across the Wilderness of Shur, and the southernmost track from Memphis touching the tip of the Red Sea. Moses shook his head.

'Ramesses knows I'd choose Balah. But it's a reed swamp with fine chariot country around, low hills, he'd destroy us from every direction. So I'm here.' Moses took my shoulder in his free hand as he walked. 'Mountains, my friend. I need mountains.'

My friend. He was right. I've done worse things than this to people.

I told him, 'My friend, you need the Land of the Moon. Plenty of mountains and plenty of Hebrews there. They'll hide you, you'll blend in.' I pointed ahead, a faint dusty line crossing the desert ahead of us. 'The road from Memphis. Turn east, then south. If you keep ahead of Pharaoh for three days and nights, you'll be in the mountains.'

Moses said something strange. 'B'El-Zephon is there? And Pi-hahiroth?'

I stared at him. 'Pi-hahiroth's an Egyptian port three days due south of us, down the Red Sea. On the wrong side. This side. You can see to the Land of the Moon across the sea, but that's all.'

'And B'El-Zephon?'

'A canaanite port on the far shore. Zephon's their god of wind. Their ships trade up and down the Red Sea, gold, turquoise, copper. You've seen them.'

Moses said, 'The Lord said to me, "Turn and make camp before Pi-hahiroth, over against B'El-Zephon. In sight of it make camp by the sea."'

'From the hills before Pi-hahiroth you can see B'El-Zephon on the far side.' I stared at the thousands of people behind us. 'Turn back, Moses. You'll trap these people between the wilderness and the sea. They'll die. You'll kill them.' I'd seen, many times, how great a slaughter chariots, horses and soldiers trained as butchers can achieve working through a mass of defenceless amateurs. If Pharaoh killed ten thousand he'd make the others meek. If he killed a hundred thousand he'd break their spirit. He'd kill Moses for sure. I would.

'We won't die.' Moses stared at me with glittering eyes. 'The Lord spoke to me and said, "I will be honoured upon Pharaoh!"'

'Your Lord is sending you into a trap,' I said. 'He's entangling you, trapping you between the wilderness and the sea.'

Moses clenched his fists. 'Trust in the Lord.'

'What, even if the whole people die for you?' Then Miriam appealed to me. 'Can't you do something?'

I could break Moses's neck, but it was too late. Nothing would stop Pharaoh now.

I gazed at the Memphis road, the sandy hills beyond, remembering sailing with Meskiag and coming ashore all those years ago to steal gold, remembered the wadis cutting between the sandstone hills into the land now called Kush. 'There are ways through,' I said. 'Ramesses will expect you to follow the coastal plain, chariot country. But I know ways through the hills.'

Moses embraced me. 'The Lord sent you.'

I said impulsively, 'Then make Miriam's skin whole.'

'When she and her priests bow to my leadership under the Lord,' Moses said, 'I shall consider her skin.'

The hills rose around us, the east wind blew dust over us. The rocky wadis made shallow valleys winding back and forth between the hills that crossed our path. The rocks would break chariot wheels, the slopes exhaust the horses, their hooves would sink in the blowing sand. Each day the east wind blew harder, covering the grassland that had sustained the Israeli flocks with sand as we moved on, and Moses made sure the waterholes were poisoned with dead sheep; even humble sheep were warriors in Moses's war against Pharaoh. We covered our faces against the sandstorm. 'Beyond the next ridge,' I shouted in Moses's ear, 'lies Wadi Arabah. Turn towards the sea.'

So we came down and made camp by the sea before Pi-hahiroth, over against B'El-Zephon, and waited for ships to sail when the east wind turned. A beautiful black woman from Kush washed Moses's feet like a wife. Aaron and the Levites camped around the Covenant by the surf of the shore, and prayed. Above them the pillar of fire stood in the sky all night.

The wind did not turn. It blew stronger.

At dawn I climbed the hilltop and saw the peaks and ridges around me glitter with line after line of Egyptian armour. The dry wadis winding from every direction into Wadi Arabah filled with footsoldiers flooding down, and then chariots trailing dust like spray, hundreds of chariots, horses galloping, and men running and screaming revenge for their dead children. I counted five hundred chariots coming together in the broad wadi, then gave up counting as more rose up on the hills and poured forward, carts, farm wagons, chariots summoned from distant regions, horses lathered and heads tossing like the sea, pouring down like a breaking wave.

I ran back to Moses. 'You got your wish.' As the sun rose behind him over distant B'El-Zephon the sea glittered like beaten silver, and the waves rising up broke behind Moses like molten metal, making him a black silhouette. Only the whites of his eyes showed.

'Can my people see they are trapped?' He looked at his people caught between the chariots and the sea. 'Can they see there is no hope? Are they certain of their death? Then they know only the Lord God can save them.' Moses raised his voice to the people. 'Stand still, and see the salvation of the Lord!'

As the Egyptians came down Moses lifted his serpent-headed sceptre towards the sea, and stretched his hand and fingers forward. The pillar of fire rose up like a holocaust brighter than the sun. The sea flew up around the pillar like a whirlpool pouring down into the Covenant, yet the Covenant was not filled, but the sea was emptied. The blinding sun was struck dim by the light of the pillar, the sea fell dark as it drained away and revealed the seabed like a dark road leading downwards, strewn with flapping fish.

I remembered Noah the first Zadok telling me of Ishtar's descent to the Underworld, and the bodies laid out like fish in the Land of the Dead: B'El's land, the deeps where the dragon lives.

Moses said, 'The Lord has divided the sea. My children may walk on dry ground through the middle.' *The Lord*, Moses had said, not Yahweh-El, Lord God. The priests of El cried out.

The Covenant stood like an angel of fire on the border of the sea, throwing light ahead of us, and darkness into the eyes of the Egyptians to dazzle them so they could not follow.

Moses walked forward where the surf had been. He walked forward where the sea had been, walked steadily down between the pools and seaweed and dying fish. The people saw no harm came to him, watched Moses grow small in the distance between the towering luminous walls of the sea, then ran down after him, first one by one, then many. The children ran down shouting with excitement and the flocks and herds ran down, then the shepherds, then the young women, then the men pushing carts of all they'd stolen from the Egyptians, gold, jewels, and their wives following behind dressed to the eyeballs in fine clothes, all they could wear, their flesh clinking with gold rings and copper bracelets. Then came the old men hurrying down as best they could and the women unclean with their courses, and the men and women made unclean with diseases and plagues, and sinners who'd been cast out. Last came the lepers, Miriam last among them. I fell in step beside her.

'This is not God,' she said. 'It's not Jesus Christ.' Her pallid fingers trembled at her flaking lips, her eyes flickered left and right at the roaring waves perpetually falling on each side. 'Maybe it's Moses's Lord. But it's not Jesus.'

We walked further down and the great banks and spires of coral rose above us, blood red, casting long shadows. I remembered Eve and such a feeling of love for her glowed in me that I felt her wake in me, knowing me. At this time of all times love washes over me, I love you all, all the women I've known, you're still in my heart. You're still here for ever. Miriam stared wonderingly at the tears on my cheeks, reached out her bent flaking fingers to moisten them, then remembered herself.

'Touch me,' I said.

'You're still in love,' she marvelled. 'Who is she?'

'I don't know. All women. You. I'm a man. I love you all.'

Her eyes softened, but she looked away. 'I loved once.'

'Once!' I tried to imagine only once. The poverty of it. The mortality.

She said emptily, 'Once is enough.' Not for me it isn't, but thinking of my magnificent body, and feeling so full of life and love and lust and mere human emotion as I wiped away my tears, felt irreverent between these great waves holding back the sea – we were in the midst of a miracle, I suppose. She watched me, smiling to herself. 'You aren't the man for me,' she said. 'But I wish you were.'

'Leprosy limits your choice of suitors,' I pointed out. We'd come to the deepest part of the sea, and began to climb up the far side among hag-worms and sea-urchins.

She said, 'I can give up my leprosy any time. All I have to do is believe in the Lord.'

'You can fall in love any time, too.'

'I'll never love another man.'

'He must've been quite a man.'

'No.' She surprised me. 'No. I was not enough of a woman. I could not give enough.'

Hands reached down, helping us up a steep shingle bank, then we walked on to dry sand. Most of the day had passed and the sun now set where we'd begun. The pillar of fire had departed from the far shore and the Egyptians flowed down like black ants, their blindness taken away from them. Below us across the seabed came Aaron and the Levite priests carrying the Arch of the Covenant beneath the firestorm – not two men on the poles now, I counted eighteen, then twenty. The poles bent as though they supported an almost intolerable weight, and the feet of the priests staggered deep in the shingle. Above them the pillar of fire roared like a furnace, whipping their clothes around them, sand and gravel flying upwards, whirling, consumed by the *shekinah*. I ran down to help them but they shouted at me to go back, go back, only a priest may approach the holy object. More Levites offered their bodies, bowed their backs beneath the tabernacle and crawled on knees and hands like crabs, faces distorted by terror and worship and the glory of the Lord.

They stumbled forward on the shore and fell down exhausted beside their burden. Moses stood on the shingle bank, seaweed around his feet, staring down into the pit of the sea.

Pharaoh's army came in sight on the seabed below, greater than ants. I saw their horses and chariots grow like an advancing wave, now I picked out their faces, and as they became human to me not the enemy I saw fathers and sons, and a man who as he ran stared in such awe at the sea rising up on each side of the dry land that he tripped and almost fell over, and from somewhere a lost Israeli dog ran among the Egyptians barking with excitement, snapping at the heels of the guards who ran beside the leading chariot. The man who rode haughtily beside the chariot driver might have been Moses, he had the same stare, same curled lips, eyelids blackened with kohl like Moses. He raised his throwing-spear and the four horses scrambled up the shingle bank almost on to the beach, gravel flying from their hooves beside Moses, and for a moment from the brink the two men gazed at each other calmly, as close as brothers. Then the horses fell back and the Egyptian threw his spear as he was overthrown and the horses fell on top of him and he was gone. The spear almost touched Moses then thudded against the Arch of the Covenant, letting out a fierce light. That was the worst thing that happened; but that was all.

Moses lifted his serpent-headed sceptre over the Egyptians and stretched his hand and fingers forward. The pillar of fire was withdrawn; shrank bright as a vanishing shooting star between the angels' wings into the golden mercy-seat of God. We held our breath: each Israeli, each Egyptian.

The falling waves fell. The sea swept inward from each side like curtains and covered the Egyptian army like a clap of great hands. The Israeli dog alone was thrown out in the spray and ran yelping across the sand; that was all. The sea fell calm and we waited in the dark. The moon rose behind us and we waited. The Levites stood around the dull shadow of the tabernacle holding it down against the night wind, but nothing else moved. The God of Moses swallowed the Egyptians in the sea.

'Immortal souls?' I whispered. 'The Egyptians have immortal souls?'

'Can you feel them?' Miriam whispered. 'They're

thrown down by God, there's no salvation for them. They'll scream in Hell for eternity.'

That was all. Days passed in the heat and the bloated bodies rose up in their armour and lay in the waves along the shore, stinking, pecked by gulls and crabs, and their smell rose to the mountaintops, but Moses walked in the desert. I walked the other way, only my little black-and-white dog for company. He chases the sticks I throw and lies beside me all night, guarding me, as if I needed guarding. But I am his life.

I heard Moses returned to the Holy Mountain. His people call the place Mount Moses. I heard he destroyed the chief priests of El, who were Korah, Dathan and Abiram, and the ground swallowed them up; but Miriam submitted to him, gave up her God and sang the new liturgy to Moses, 'The Lord is a man of war, the Lord is His name,' and her skin was made whole. I heard Moses outlawed the sacrifice of children and took the black woman from Kush for his wife, and the people hated him, but they followed him for forty years before they came to Canaan; the cadres of sion forged swords and spearheads and armour in the wilderness and entered the land of milk and honey in units ordered and commanded in tens, fifties, and hundreds and thousands. They fell on the Amori tribes of Canaan who were once their kinsmen and knocked down the walls of their cities with the trumpeting Voice of the Covenant, killed the men, the women, their children, every animal, and razed their buildings to the ground and seized their land. The Lord had told them to do this, and so by obedience they prospered.

But another wave of Sea Peoples broke on the shore of Canaan, which they still called Palestine, and organised the Palestinians already there into formidable armies against the children of Israel. Great battles! Huge dramas, death and honour, plenty of blood, I could never bet for sure who'd win; the Palestinians had iron swords but the Israelis had the Covenant, and if the people had been virtuous the Voice of the Lord spoke for them. The Israelis picked up the iron swords left scattered on the battlefield and put them to good use next time.

In the end the issue was simple. Either the Palestinians captured the Arch of the Covenant, or they'd lose their land and be slaves. At Ebenezer they attacked like men possessed and overwhelmed thirty thousand Israelis (*I* was in a brothel that day). Afterwards I walked to Ashdod, the Palestinian city where the stolen Covenant was taken, to see what would happen. Soldiers in bronze armour laid the Covenant down in the temple to Dagon, and Dagon's statue fell down and shattered. Plague broke out in the city, so the Covenant was sent to Gath, and plague broke out there. Conscripts carried the Covenant to Ekron and you know what happened. The priests in B'Elzebub's temple (I saw them peeping round the pillars, and heard their squeaking voices) talked among themselves and decided, 'If that box is empty, then the plague's come to Ekron by chance, has no home here, and won't stay long. But if the box contains the Lord of the Israelis, then the plague's His own, and will stay until He is home with His people.' Someone shouted, 'Which? How do we know which?' The priests told the terrified citizens of Ekron to load the Covenant into a cart and whip the oxen. If the oxen pulled the Covenant to a Palestinian city, they said, then everything bad that happened was pure chance; if the oxen wandered to an Israeli city, then good riddance to a great evil.

The oxen carried the Covenant straight home to Israeli Beth-Shemash, lowing as they went. King David threw back the Palestinians from Geba all the way to Gaza, killed them, enslaved them, and peace fell over Israel. The Covenant was carried to Jerusalem, the hillside village of Melchizadok and Abraham on Mount Sion grown to

David's City; and was left, half forgotten, in a tent by the well of Gihon where I remembered camping with Mari. During Absalom's revolt against David the great high priest named Zadok hid it in a cave. It was put back in the tent when David's son Solomon, whose name means peace, was anointed king.

Solomon's peace, Solomon's wealth: treasure-ships wallowing home from Ophir, trade agreements with Sheba, Egypt, Africa and the canaans of Tyre under King Hiram. The trade routes turned like a wheel on Israel's hub. Solomon married Pharaoh's daughter and worshipped Egyptian gods as well as the Lord. He had seven hundred wives and three hundred concubines and worshipped all their gods, as well as making sacrifices to the Lord. Among the thousands of temples in Israel were more than a dozen dedicated to the Lord, in Bethlehem, Hebron and elsewhere, and in their sanctuaries services were performed by priests 'in the presence of the Lord' even though the Arch of the Covenant was elsewhere. Then Solomon decided to bring worship of the One Lord into one place, Jerusalem, the centre of his kingdom, and build one Temple in the shadow of his immense palace where he could tax the cult, control it, and bask in the reflected glory of the Lord.

So it was true: Jerusalem had spread to the hilltop. Would I find Jesus Christ here? If so, I'd find Mari too. I climbed the peak where the Temple stood inside the palace grounds in a mass of wooden scaffolding. Buildings and great projects are irresistible to me who built the walls of Enoch (and my strength helped build the pyramids), but this little Temple disappointed. The Jews are a tent people, they don't know how to build big. Solomon hired workers from abroad, mostly from King Hiram, thousands of them, their foreign babble drifting with the dust across the chaotic site. I pushed between sweaty gangs of canaans, Jews in forced labour, Palestinian slaves. Foremen cursed and whipped, but it was the quietest building site I ever heard, no banging of hammers or axes, perhaps the stone was quarried from caves and adits burrowed deep beneath the ground where the Temple would stand; but the others said it was magic, or that Solomon employed a demon to do his work by night. I lifted a massive stone block with three terrified labourers standing on top to show them what could be achieved by exercise and virtuous living. 'You,' a foreman called me afterwards, 'he wants a word with you.'

He jerked his thumb at a small, intense, dedicated man who watched me with fierce dark eyes.

Prince Hiram had a strange reputation. A son of King Hiram of Sidon and Tyre, I knew he fancied himself as an architect and coppersmith – not an unusual princely skill, King Solomon made the seven-pronged menorah candlestick for the Temple's incense altar with his own hands. But the foreman turned back seven paces from Hiram, wouldn't go near him.

'What's gone wrong?' I asked the prince. Workmen were busy knocking down walls they'd built. 'My strength could build them up again for you.' I kicked a stone jutting from the ground, once an altar – the ground breathes holiness here, the exact place Abraham laid out Isaac in sacrifice, Melchizadok's place.

'We've help enough,' Hiram said. He sighed. 'The walls cracked and grew crooked whatever we did. Seven times we've started the Temple. Six times we've knocked it down.'

Seven being such a holy number, he meant simply that the Temple was very important to Solomon. 'Dig your foundations deeper in the rock,' I said.

'It's full of caves and water channels, natural as well as man-made.' The caves where Zadok had hidden the Covenant, where perhaps it would be kept again.

'Fill in the caves with rubble.'

'That would be a profanity on the holy mountain.

312

Anyway the entrance is hidden.' Hiram turned down my offer of help. 'This is the place of seeing. The Temple must be built here on the mountain, exactly here. We already have our help.' We walked past Egyptian masons chipping their marks and signs in the stones, but he didn't mean them. Whoever helped him was good at their job. This time the walls were being rebuilt stepped slightly inward, making them stronger at the base but lighter, reminding me a little of the stepped temples of Enoch – but those had been man-made mountains, a hundred times larger than this little building. I asked, 'Whose help?'

Hiram shrugged. 'One who has knowledge of the building of such things. Some tasks are too large for men.' I saw no other architect. Hiram diverted me to the workshops, the tall copper pillars topped by copper flames that would stand one on each side of the Temple porch, showing off the skill that made them. Here among the coppersmiths' beating mallets he was happy. 'This is my life's work. I know it. I'll build nothing greater than this.' He touched the palms of his hands to the fluted pillars lying on their wooden blocks. 'Boaz and Jachin. When standing they'll carry no weight, yet be strong enough to lift the world under King Solomon.'

We walked outside and he pointed at a broad empty space. 'This courtyard is the Sea. My hands will make the bronze altars and basins, lions, cherubim, the great font supported by twelve red bronze cattle. It's all planned. Here Pharaoh's daughter will have her house. Here's the Judgment Hall. The Hall of Cedars here, a whole forest of cedars chopped down.' He paused proudly, letting me imagine the fabulous expense. Cedars were nearly all gone from Palestine, even from the most inaccessible hilltops, and his father had supplied them to Solomon at bankrupting cost. 'Only the outer rooms use cheap cypress.' Obviously even Solomon's bottomless treasury felt the strain of the Temple. We pushed past exhausted workmen and Hiram's enthusiasm grew as he looked around him in the air. 'Imagine the carvings, palm trees, exotic fruits! Side rooms connected by trapdoors.' He pointed right and left. 'A maze.' He lowered his voice reverentially. 'Here at the centre will be the presence of their Lord. This place shall be—'

'The Holy of Holies,' I said.

'Only your Zadok will be righteous enough to enter the Holy of Holies.'

It all fell in place in my mind. 'Walls of beaten gold,' I whispered, remembering the ancient scheme. *To the golden Holy of Holies three magicians come bringing gifts, one of silver, one of balsam, and one of precious galbanum incense. The head of the Christ-child's cradle is draped with the purple robes and golden insignia of King and Saviour of Jerusalem which await the coming day of His Recognition.*

'Yes, walls of bright gold,' Hiram said. 'Kingdoms can be bought for less.'

'And the Covenant will be kept here?'

'The Arch of the Covenant will be deposited here in the Holy of Holies on the day of dedication. This Temple will be the House of God, literally.' One of the coppersmiths called him, some particularly difficult piece of work, and Hiram hurried away to his first love.

The foreman fell in step beside me, a Ugarit canaan by his accent. He nodded after Hiram. 'Strange one, him, lord.'

'Strange? How strange?'

'Happy as a little bird, but he won't survive his work. That's the deal.' He cleared his throat, whistling innocently. 'I don't know how his walls stand up, but they do, see what I mean.'

'No, I don't see.' He whistled until I dropped coins in his hand.

'They say King Solomon's borrowing the help of a demon to build his Temple.'

314

'Borrowing from moneylenders, more likely,' I scoffed, but he gave me such a steady look that I took him seriously. 'Demon? What demon?'

'You think demons tell people like me their names? That's for kings. Solomon knows his name.' The foreman turned away between the half-finished walls but I followed him. 'Solomon uses the demon, tricks him. Solomon does the Lord's work, fools the devils. And men like Hiram, if he is a man.'

I put my hand on his shoulder, turned him to face me. 'Go on.'

'Shouldn't have told you.' He watched my money hand. 'My tongue's too big for my mouth, always was.' I paid him and he met my eye. 'They say Hiram's a Son of Man. A Son of Enoch. Didn't have a mother.' He licked his lips. 'His father loved a woman, a princess, but never had her. Loved her all her life. Rose her name was, the Rose of Ararat, and she died. The king went into the tomb where she was laid out dead and he got the love from her he didn't get when she was alive, he had her dead. Screwed her dead body. Nine months later a baby was born from her skeleton. The king pulled his son out with his own hands from under her ribs. No mother, see, our Hiram. Only a father.'

'You canaans tell too many fireside stories.' But I believed him, because the Ugarit canaans write their stories down as epics carved in stone, kept in royal palaces and libraries. The writing's very nearly Hebrew; the stories will survive when the spoken language is long forgotten. The cool evening wind whispered, then blew my clothes as abruptly as the pull of a hand. *Aram menaht menou,* Mari's voice whispered in my memory like the wind, *This is the Holy Bible of the Lord your God.* I remembered hearing Melchizadok the first king of Jerusalem, Ur-Shalom, claiming to be an Anointed One. *I am a son of Enoch the Son of Man. I know no earthly father, I was born from the dead body of my mother.*

315

The foreman gasped and I realised I'd lifted him from his feet. 'Surely Solomon's doing God's will,' I said. 'Building the Temple must be a project blessed by God.'

'Perhaps there are others with a different purpose. Don't hurt—'

I shook him. 'What purpose? Who?'

'A son may grow up to oppose his father.' The canaan choked, hung writhing from my hand. 'Even a son of God perhaps, like B'El, struggling to improve upon his father's world, filling its beauty with life and fertility not obedience, not worship – he may honourably oppose—'

'A son of God is canaanite blasphemy to the Jews.'

'I am a master builder of Ugarit. One man's blasphemy is another's worship. Let me live. I believe in angels. I believe in fallen angels. I believe in demons.' The canaan's eyes widened as he stared at me, thinking I too was a demon, then he hung limp. A vein burst in his forehead, and I realised how hard I squeezed him.

I demanded, 'What's the demon's name? *What's its name?*'

He struggled to answer. His back arched. I let him go when I knew he'd tell the truth.

'Asmodeus!' The master builder fell to his knees. 'He's Asmodeus.'

The man crawled on his knees and one hand, warding me off with his other hand. Workmen gathered around me with raised shovels, pickaxes, dusty fists, frightened eyes; little men. They fell back when I growled, made the sign of the Evil Eye at me. To them I was a demon like Asmodeus – whatever it, *he*, is like – but *I* know I'm a son of El, cursed with humanity but half divine, not half demon. Can a demon sleep with a human and make a child? Everyone knows they do – Ishtar wanted me, needed me, offered me the world to have sons by me – but is a living child possible from such a demonic union? Would the children of humans and demons be born to sin? Bound to sin? No choice?

I walked away through them, pushed them away when they got in front of me, left them to pick up their shaking master builder and brush him down.

So many stories of birth by death: the Rose of Ararat, Melchizadok, the sons of Enoch, too many. Something's true.

So King Solomon built the temple, and maybe he tricked Asmodeus the son of Azaz'El into helping him, because it was well built in only seven years, and stood for three hundred and fifty. In later times, each year on the Day of Atonement, the Zadok takes two goats and sacrifices one to the Lord, and the other goat's anointed with the sins of the people and hurled to its death from the cliff of the Temple Mount, the gift to Azaz'El. Maybe Asmodeus is still chained in the mountain beneath the Temple where Solomon tricked him. No one knows – I think even the sons of Zadok forget exactly why they perform the ceremony. Even the Arch of the Covenant is forgotten – I mean forgotten as something real, something that actually parted the Red Sea and exploded the Palestinian armies and carried creeping plague to their cities. No one's seen it since it was carried inside the Temple – perhaps Solomon never even placed it in the Holy of Holies. How could we know, since no one but the sons of Zadok enter there? So without anyone noticing the Arch of the Covenant's changed into a story handed down by mothers to their children, something that *has* been real but is not. They remember the Arch as the Ark, as if it were a kind of Noah's Ark filled not with animals but with people's hopes and dreams, a reliquary preserving the soul of the Jews against the flood of time and defeat and death, times when the Lord turned His face from them, just as El had turned His face from Noah.

Now even Yahweh withdrew His face from His people.

317

The kings that came after Solomon worshipped B'El, kept whores, virgins and star-gods in the Temple, employed pagan prophets, and sacrificed their children to Molech by knife and fire in the valley of Gehenna below. Many times I stood on the city wall of Jerusalem watching the fires burn like Hell below me, the smoke and the screaming of infants rising past me into the empty sky, and knew for certain the power of the Lord was forgotten.

And yet. Always and yet. In the third year of the drought Elijah stood on the summit of Mount Carmel for the Lord. With my own eyes I saw Elijah, wild as a cave-man (he hid in caves to save his life) come out into the sunlight and stand up on the open mountaintop against King Ahab and his canaanite queen kneeling at the altars to B'El and the cedars planted to Ishtar, his mother, the wife of El. Four hundred and fifty hobbling and bowing priests of B'El waited on Ahab wailing for the end of the drought, four hundred maidens of the cedar groves attended the queen, and Elijah walked through them alone. The altar of the Lord had been knocked to pieces. With my own ears I heard him tell Ahab to his face, 'You worship that shitball B'El.' *Shitball* was exactly the word Elijah used, loudly. 'Your knees bow to B'El, your lips kiss him, there's no truth in the breath that comes out of your mouths, yet you blame the drought on us! You shitballs abandon the commandments of the Lord,' Elijah cried, turning to the people, 'you shitballs attack the Lord's cult and His prophets, yet still you're thirsty. Does B'El give you water?' No one answered him, not a word. 'I have travelled to Mount Moses, I have veiled my face, I have come back. I, Elijah the prophet, am a lone voice. There are hundreds of you, but I say the Lord is greater than B'El. Sacrifice your bull and lay the meat on the wood piled on the altar, then call on the name of your gods to make the fire. And I will call on the Lord. The God that answers with fire is God.'

It's a famous story, you know what happens, but I saw this with my own eyes. King Ahab accepted the contest. The priests prayed for fire all morning. They hobbled devoutly around the sacrifice and slashed their skin with knives all afternoon, blessing B'El with their fertile blood, life, but B'El sent no fire. 'Perhaps he's too busy shitting,' Elijah said. 'Perhaps he's asleep.' The sun lit the hilltops around us with a fiery evening light and still the wood would not burn. Elijah raised his arms to the people and said: 'Come to me.'

The priests of B'El watched exhausted as the people came to Elijah.

Elijah repaired the Lord's altar with twelve stones, one for each tribe of Israel. He piled the wood and laid the sacrifice on top, then the people whispered in amazement as four precious barrels of water soaked the sacrifice. More barrels were brought forward. Elijah dug a trench around the altar to stop so much water running away. More was poured. The people watched dry-lipped, thirsty. Elijah prayed with his arms outstretched over them. 'Hear me, Lord God, Yahweh El, that the people may know You are the Lord God.'

Fire fell from the sky. How did Elijah do it? No Covenant, no sceptre. Fire fell from the evening sky around us and the sacrifice was burnt, the wood burst into flames, then the stones, and the water caught fire and leapt up like burning steam.

A woman cried out from the people to Elijah: 'Truly Yahweh's word is in your mouth!'

The fire died down. The night was full of screams, the people hurled the false priests like goats from the mountaintop to their deaths into the Kishon valley below. But I crept forward to the glowing ashes where the fire had been. Even the stones of the twelve tribes, ash. But pools of clear liquid remained in the trench, and then I saw how Elijah had pulled the trick: the liquid was highly flammable naphtha, obviously.

I cupped my hand in the liquid and touched it to my tongue. It was water. Pure water.

How can I explain Elijah's fire? I have no explanation. It's a miracle. There are other miracles: later it is said that Elijah brings a dead child to life by stretching out his hands three times.

Elijah prayed with his head between his knees, and the Lord's rain fell. The drought ended, and Ahab scampered to his royal chariot before he was washed away by the flood.

On the sixteenth of March Jerusalem fell to King Nabuchadnezzar's army, the Lord stayed silent in the Holy of Holies, and now the Temple pays taxes to Bab'El. Nabuchadnezzar's empire stands stronger than Egypt, and Jerusalem's just another dusty city. Long ago Pharaoh made the Hebrew Yosef, an interpreter of dreams, his vizier; now Nabuchadnezzar's vizier is the Jew Dan'El – the prophet Ezekiel's name for him – but to show his power the king changed Dan'El's name to B'Eltasar, which means B'El Protects King Nabuchadnezzar. Dan'El was no longer a Jew, he was a Jew of Bab'El, Nabuchadnezzar's creature. I travelled from Jerusalem with Dan'El's three childhood friends Hanniah, Michael and Azariah, all educated scribes hoping for work now he'd grown so great. In his youth no one had believed in the Lord God more devoutly than Dan'El.

Bab'El: I gazed in amazement. The ruin I remembered by the river had grown to an immense walled city, greatest in the world, its nine gates more than any other city in the world, its roofs of gold reaching up to an immense pyramid. From the blue-brick Ishtar gate, shadowed by the gold-domed Ishtar temple, we stared at the bridges and boulevards stretching away from us, the El gate, a Greek theatre, palaces, and by the *dura* citadel a golden statue of a winged angel shining in the sun – an angel as tall as the pyramid. My companions' eyes filled with golden light as they imagined living here. 'My three friends!' Dan'El embraced them then coughed at the dust puffing from their simple robes. Very foreign and prosperous Dan'El looked in his shiny clothes, trousers, a tall hat, slaves scurrying like a small army around him. 'Welcome! My friends, the king always needs scribes. I've had rooms set aside for you.' He put his strong arms round their shoulders, pulled their unkempt beards affectionately, remembering when he was as uncivilised and provincial as they.

But I stared up at the golden angel towering over us, each toe of each foot as long as a man. The gold had peeled from the toenails where the sacrifices were laid, revealing black iron beneath. 'Dan'El,' Hananiah whispered, 'does it not bother you to worship this god?'

'Here I prefer to be called B'Eltasar.' Dan'El shrugged. 'I survive.'

Azariah murmured, 'Does it not look like you?' He stared up, shielding his eyes from the sun. 'Dan'El, the angel has your face!'

'Pure chance. Nabuchadnezzar saw the same likeness, and fell down and worshipped me as a god.' Trumpets sounded and all the people fell down worshipping the statue, even Dan'El himself.

The three Jews looked shocked. We four alone stood among the people lying down. When the trumpets fell silent Dan'El was lifted up and a slave brushed the dust from his knees. A girl getting to her feet smiled at me and I saw she had magnificent breasts. I smiled at them and she eyed my crotch, we lost ourselves in mutual admiration. Michael said to Dan'El, 'I understand you, old friend. You mean that this reverence to a false idol is forced on you. You regard this divine honour as being paid, not to you, or to Nabuchadnezzar's golden angel, but to God.'

'Exactly,' Dan'El said. 'And those who don't bow down are thrown into the fire to Molech.'

'But you were born a Jew. Your God isn't your choice to make. You were chosen.'

'I agree,' Dan'El said. 'But still, old friends, keep cold, and call me B'Eltasar in this place.' He laughed, glanced at me carrying their baggage on my shoulders like a donkey, then walked with them to the king's winter palace, the vast jumble of domes and towers by the river, and I followed.

The girl blurted after me, 'Ninurta.'

Dan'El guarded the king's door. No one, not even the Chaldean prophets, saw Nabuchadnezzar without gold in Dan'El's palm and his approving nod. Dan'El guided his friends forward at the right moment after the king's siesta. 'Say nothing. Let the king speak.' From his throne Nabuchadnezzar blessed Hananiah, Michael and Azariah with new names to show his power over them, calling them Shadrach, Meshach and Abednabu, which means servant of the god Nabu, Nabuchadnezzar's own personal god and a horrid insult to a Jew, but fortunately Azariah misheard the king's broad Bab'El accent and thought himself called Abednego, which is meaningless. 'I always have need of scribes,' Nabuchadnezzar said majestically, then beckoned Dan'El and spoke quietly, but not too low for me to hear. 'Listen to me closely, my Master of the Magi.'

'I hear, great king.'

'B'Eltasar, I've had a dream, a dream of a tree. A great tree.'

'Great king, live for ever, and let me see your dream.'

The king whispered, 'In my dream a cedar tree grew as high as Heaven.' I listened, appalled. Huwawa's great tree which he grew to climb as high as God, like the Tower of Bab'El once built by men? What evil was this? Nabuchadnezzar said, 'A Watcher and a holy one came

322

down the tree from Heaven.' A Watcher? Me? Was the holy one Kidu? How could this happen, how could these ancient events be remembered in a dream? The king's eyes filled with tears. 'I saw the Watcher cut down the tree. His heart was changed from a man's. A beast's heart was given to him.'

My story! The king remembered in his dream how I'd cut the great cedar and thrust my sword into the heart of Huwawa, guardian of the tree. By cutting the tree I'd destroyed what Huwawa lived for, cut out his heart. In the moment of his death he'd cursed me with a beast's heart, *like a monkey walking upright shall you live* – an animal, not a divine being, not even an ordinary man originally made by God (as all men are made, but animals are not, for men have power over them). I am the strongest, most handsome, manly man in the world, but beneath my skin I'm a monkey. Huwawa had taken my soul.

I forget Dan'El's interpretation of the dream – something about Nabuchadnezzar himself – I knew I'd glimpsed something much greater. Nothing's forgotten. Everything that happens happens for ever, and still happens. I put my hands to my head and stumbled from the auditorium, wandered miserably in the city for an hour; but soon I drank some wine and felt better, then ate a leg of pork washed down with more wine and felt better still, then went to find a girl to impress, and as you know no one impresses girls more or more often than I, and soon I felt fine.

That night, in the dark with my headache, I prayed to God. Long ago children had been taught to pray to me as one of the gods. Now I'm not even human, just a monkey-human, blind strength and lust, nothing more.

Even when they were rich (and Dan'El even richer, from his fee) Shadrach, Meshach and Abednego kept their simple robes instead of wearing shiny clothes. They looked like Jews. They left their beards scruffy like Jews. They called all gods but their own false, walked with their eyes averted from idols, and stayed on their feet even when the trumpets sounded for the golden angel of B'El. They refused the royal menu and ate kosher food among the sties and blood of Nabuchadnezzar's city, lying indoors on the Sabbath as though no one would see them. But eyes are paid to see everything in Bab'El, and tongues paid to wag. They wagged about Shadrach, Meshach and Abednego.

Dan'El was too popular with the king to be attacked directly, but the Chaldean prophets saw their chance to bring him down a notch. 'Great king, live for ever,' they whispered when Dan'El slept and Nabuchadnezzar walked in his garden. 'Everyone knows that if men don't bow to your golden angel when the trumpets sound, then the god will fall, and your kingdom will fall, and Bab'El will fall.' The king nodded, 'Yes, yes.' The prophets bowed their heads devoutly. 'Great king, one man who doesn't bow down to the golden angel endangers us all, because a blasphemy by one is blasphemy by the whole people. That man must be thrown into the redeeming flames to Molech.' The king nodded again, and the prophets bowed their heads still further. 'Shadrach, Meshach and Abednego do not bow down.'

Nabuchadnezzar said, 'Bring them to me.'

I didn't know. I'd fallen in love with Ninurta, true love this time, a wonderful girl with three breasts (which made her holy in the temple of fertility) each tipped with a nipple as large and dark and succulent as a red wine grape, so when I lay with her I didn't have a thought in my head except her. She yawned as I pleasured her for the seventh time. 'Listen,' she said, 'those idiot friends of yours.'

'Not now.'

'You really do love me, don't you. You're all sweaty.'

'I love you all over.' I nibbled her middle breast, which was slightly smaller than the others, and enticingly perverse. 'I love you because you're you. Unique.'

'You all say that.' She wriggled her hips uncomfortably. 'I've gone numb. You don't give me any peace.'

'Stop talking.'

'Your friends didn't worship the golden statue, so they're going to be killed.' I stopped. She smiled. 'That's better.' The evening trumpets blew. 'Just about now.'

I cursed and jumped off her, jumped from the window into the streets below, left her amazed laughter behind me and ran stark naked through the streets scattering fruit stalls and bread stalls as I ran, green apples and oranges and big round loaves bouncing and rolling after me along the roads, and urchins seizing them and running away for their lives before they were caught. My limp sated penis slapped from side to side on my thighs as I ran, I jumped a wall, women laughed with surprise and a man tried to stop me, I leapt a fountain and dropped him in the water. From the wall on the other side I glimpsed the head of the golden angel above the smoke. I raced across the flat roofs, people at prayer kneeling towards Nabuchadnezzar's angel, B'El, Satan, and the fires cooking evening meals singed the hairs on my calves as I leapt over them, jumped down into the shadow of the pyramid, the great temple to some god of Bab'El or other, and ran in the shadows. Above me the great golden buttocks of the angel, as bare as my own, stood up like golden apples in the last of the sunlight streaming round the side of the pyramid, and the coiled gold hair on the back of its head gleamed like the sun.

The worshippers were held back by chaplains, Nabuchadnezzar sat on his throne, and in front of the angel's feet a huge bronze basin had been set up, larger than a fountain, filled with burning coals: a fountain of fire. The king pointed his finger and priests ran forward with pitchers of holy oil, throwing them in the flames, but the flames burst out and set the men alight where they stood, so they ran about like little burning candles to the glory of their god. Only the head of the golden angel was in the sunlight now and the flames at its feet burnt bright against the darkness below as Shadrach, Meshach and Abednego were pushed forward by soldiers with long poles. But the three men stood calmly, then turned and spoke with one voice. 'Great king, live for ever. Our God whom we serve is able to deliver us from these flames. Stoke them seven times hotter and still He will save us. But whether He saves us or not, we will not bow down to your golden angel.'

Nabuchadnezzar said, 'Stoke it seven times hotter.' The soldiers used the long poles to stoke the fire but the poles were set alight by the heat, the soldiers' hands and hair burst into flame. More soldiers ran at me with swords and spears as I came forward. I knocked them aside, I ignored my wounds. Ahead of me Nabuchadnezzar's guards wrapped robes around Shadrach, Meshach and Abednego. The three men were thrown forward trussed like food offerings into the sacrificial fire. I heard their upraised voices singing songs, psalms, as they were thrown. I caught at Shadrach's heel, stumbled after him, fell, slid with him down the bubbling bronze into the blazing coals. The fire roared over our heads bright as the sun in the night, and I closed my eyes against the pain.

There's no pain.

This cannot be. I know the pain of burning, I know suffering. I open my eyes and the flames roar around us but do not touch us. Shadrach, Meshach, and Abednego stand together unharmed in the fiery holocaust. The flames meet over our heads but do not burn us. Their clothes don't burn, only shine like their faces in reflection of the heat. I wade forward through the brilliant molten coals which feel as cool as river mud against my bare feet, and the flames refresh my naked skin like showers of rain. I breathe the fire, I inhale the flames like a perfumed breeze,

I exhale harmless fire. Shadrach looks at me, straight at me through the fire, but he doesn't recognise me. 'Look, do you see him?'

'An angel. He's an angel of God,' cries Meshach. 'One of the Elohim.'

'No, it's I,' I call, but only cool fire comes out of my mouth.

'He's no angel,' Abednego says, blinking against the brightness of the light. 'He's like the Son of God.' I lift my hands towards them and touch the ropes that bind the three men. Instantly the ropes flash into flame and fall away as though touched by the heat of the furnace, and the men walk around me where I stand among them. Above us Nabuchadnezzar's angel stands against the stars in the night sky, blackening in the smoke.

Outside, like a shadow, the king approached the altar seeing us walking inside, then shielded his face from the blistering glare. 'Shadrach, Meshach, Abednego, come out!' If he still saw me, he was too afraid to command me.

Shadrach, Meshach and Abednego walked from the altar of fire. Their hair was neatly combed, and their clothes did not even smell of smoke. The king turned from his Chaldean prophets and embraced Dan'El. 'Great king, live for ever,' Dan'El said. He seized the opportunity, already courtiers flocked to his side. 'Great king, don't lift yourself up against the Lord of Heaven. Don't worship gods of gold and iron and clay that see nothing, hear nothing, know nothing.'

The king looked up grimly at the blackened angel. 'Where was its power! I'll have it torn down.'

Dan'El pressed home his advantage. 'The Lord God sees everything, hears everything, knows everything, and holds your every breath in His hand.'

'Yes, yes, there's no other God like this one,' the king said. 'Anyone who harms Shadrach, Meshach or Abednego harms me.' He glared around him, and a babble of voices

327

called out that the Chaldeans should be thrown on the fire instead of the Jews. Maybe they were, I don't know; I walked into the night, I thought of everything I'd heard, and sat on a rooftop caressing my unhurt skin with my unhurt fingers, and marvelled at myself as if I'd just been born.

Yes, nowadays there are miracles.

Everyone has their favourite tale to tell of Dan'El, thousands of stories are written down (only lately the scribes spell his name Daniel) and are preserved in the great library at Sion by the Dead Sea as well as in other places – how Daniel was thrown down into the lions' pit, but I held the lions' mouth closed to save him (you saw long ago the power I have over animals); how I appeared in shining armour to him beside the River Hiddek'El when Daniel hadn't eaten for three weeks, and in his hunger he took me for an angel. Many stories are true to my certain knowledge, but many are not. All I know for sure is what I build with my own hands here among the palm trees and fragrant balsam on the fertile green shores of the Dead Sea, where the fresh water of the Arnon river flows from the eastern desert. As a farmer I'm king of my little patch of land, my tiny kingdom of fields hacked from the sand. But lately I'm an idle king, my woman Ruth (we have no children, of course) who was once a beauty grows old, and I sit full of strength and youth by my black hearth like an old husband to keep her company. I am her life, but she turns down my curse of immortality, grows colder day by day despite the heat of summer. She won't have doctors. The priests of Sion are Jews from the west, with lands in Egypt as well as here, and they have a reputation as *Asayya*, healers (some call them Essenes, or therapeuts), but my woman won't have them in. She kisses my lips lovingly with her dying breath. She's gone. Beyond the shining sea the sun sets behind the cliffs of Sion. I stand staring over the moonlit waves hugging her in my arms all night. Another life has gone, another former world passed away.

Nothing to keep me here.

In the morning I weep and bury her grey body in the sand and the rising sun streams past me, suddenly lighting the monastery buildings on the western shore as white as salt. *Monastery,* a new word, a fort for priests. Nowadays this garrison of priests (they claim they're the living bloodline of Yosef, Pharaoh's vizier before Moses's time) believe they alone follow the true teachings of Zadok, and call their monastery Sion. Peasants call the place *Qimrôn,* Pointed Arch, from the Egyptian-looking shape of the gateposts meeting over the gates – which remind me of the temple gateposts at Enoch long ago, probably meaning that 'only the holy and pure in heart' are allowed to enter the Order. I knew the hereditary Zadokite priesthood passing from Noah the first Zadok through father and son had split into two warring branches with the fall of Jerusalem. The old leaders lost their grip and were dispersed from Jerusalem, scattered, kept powerless in exile in Bab'El. Now the new generation of zealous Zadokite priests arriving at Sion from Egypt believe their Order is more pure and righteous than the surviving Zadokites of the Jerusalem Temple, whose city tongues pronounce Zadok *Sadduc,* and call themselves Sadducees. Each branch zealously follows its own Zadok or Righteous Priest. Each branch zealously promotes its own rituals. Each branch preaches that its opponents are wicked priests who blaspheme God by worshipping Him the wrong way (the Sadducees time their festivals by the moon's varying calendar, the priests of Sion by the invariable sun, just as in the old days Ya was worshipped by the moon and El by the sun) and each blames the other that God turned His back and let Jerusalem fall.

As I walk along the sulphurous shore, past pools of

bubbling pitch and brimstone, I come to green grass again and the years fall away from me. I swim the River Jordan and the white frankincense washes out of my hair, I no longer walk bent like an old man trying to hide his strength. My blond hair flows back long and shining over my shoulders, I run along the sand like the wind, I let the wind blow me away.

I slept that night on the seashore, and in the first grey light I asked for water at the gates of Sion.

The priests, all men, not women too as in the old days, watched me suspiciously. Finally a single cup of water was sent out. 'You can't come in. None but the purest and most righteous souls enter through these gates.' So these priests believe in souls – that each man in himself, not just the whole people, possesses his own immortal soul. I sipped. Tasted like ordinary water to me. Behind its walls Sion was a small, isolated, wholly male community. Wives and children were left to sleep outside like nomads, in tents, or along the bare ground. They woke yawning, scratching their heads, stumbling off to work in the fields. Only the priests – less than fifty, I reckoned – were pure and righteous enough to be allowed inside the monastery, obviously, and worshipped on behalf of all. An ordinary person was not worthy to speak to God except through a priest's skilled prayers and sacrifice. Counting the numbers I reckoned each priest kept several wives as in the days of Moses and Abraham, there wouldn't have been enough women and children to do the work otherwise. I drank slowly, watching them hoe the dusty unforgiving soil before the sun was hot, the children gathering around the women like chicks, each one given a job to do. Pick stones, pile stones, pick out seeds: girls looked after the infants and taught even their little chubby hands to pick up stones and pile up stones and pick out seeds, so that the games the children learnt became their life's burden.

But some were born to be priests. I watched the priests

shuffle along the top of the salt-white wall, all in white linen bleached with frankincense, waiting for the first rays of the sun. Their Zadok wore his yellow cloak (the golden fleece long forgotten) over an ephod of pure white linen – not the blue, purple and scarlet priestly garment used by the Jerusalem Sadducees. He prayed with his eyes closed. His face looked hard as red rock and his brushed silver hair was as long as mine, blowing in the dawn wind. His feet in the simple sandals were scrubbed white, his teeth brushed as white as fine linen: a priest must be perfect for God. He held out his arms and novices fastened a breastplate on his chest, the shoulder straps decorated with onyx jewels inscribed with the twelve tribes of Israel, as though the tribes had never been scattered by Bab'El. The priests prayed for the twelve tribes to be gathered together once more. Novices brought forward the jewelled Urim and Thummim framed in worn and cracked acacia wood, reverently hanging the two oracles beneath the breastplate. To me they looked identical to the ones Moses had carved, which had always been kept with the Arch of the Covenant – more than six hundred years old, if genuine, and I couldn't imagine a Zadok of this fierceness and intensity, standing like a pillar of rock atop the wall, using fakes. Even Noah had talked of an Urim and Thummim; Ya had whispered through the wall of his tent and told him to wear them on his chest. Words given by God, words without sound, shapes burnt from stones on to tablets of wood. Even Noah hadn't comprehended fully. Perhaps each shape was a whole meaning, perhaps they were numbers, one, two, many, sixty. But I remembered the look in Noah's eye. *Numbers to worship God by.*

The Zadok climbed the arch over the gates. He raised his arms to the rising sun, opening his eyes wide, showing he had no sin to hide, no shadows in his soul, only purity, whiteness, righteousness to show God, and the priests lining the wall chanted their morning prayers like

Egyptians. 'Lord God Most High, give us this day,' they cried, then fell silent.

The Zadok spoke simply and clearly. 'Hear me, my children. Laman, my firstborn and most doubting son, hear me. Hear me Nephi, my youngest and most loyal son. Hear me Lemuel and Sam. Hear me Laban my faithful overseer, keeper of the Scrolls of Sion, treasurer of the Poor.' The word he used was *Ebionim*, the Poor, the Meek, the Simple. 'Hear me, see me.' He touched the gleaming Urim and Thummim with his thumbs. 'This is our Covenant with God, made between God and us His people faithful in keeping His commandments, and I am the Keeper of His Promise: God shall send His Son into this world to save us from our lost and fallen state, and the Poor shall inherit this land. The Messiah shall gather the tribes of Israel together. Messiah and Zadok shall be one, priest and king together, the single pillar of the world, Melchizadok. He shall be the Anointed One and by God's Promise, His Covenant with us, the Messiah shall save our souls and rule in Jerusalem for a thousand years.'

I watched the scribe, Laban. He yawned. As treasurer and librarian he must be a powerful man, probably more powerful even than the Zadok's four sons. The scriptorium at Sion which Laban controlled is famous for more than Daniel stories; it's the repository of thousands of scrolls, scriptures, genealogies and histories going back to the time of Noah. How else could they know that Noah begat Shem, and Shem begat Elam, and Elam begat . . . it's all written down, the most valuable documents carefully etched on scrolls of copper, even gold. These people know where they started.

I watched Laban's powerful yawning face. He wasn't listening to a word.

The Zadok clenched his fists as he preached his sermon, a man in an agony of his soul. 'Sorrow to you, Jerusalem of the Sadducees! In His Temple you insult our God Most

332

High to His face with false worship, you're dogs baying at the moon! You Sadducees bow to the inconstant moon who changes like a woman, so even your Holy Passover is an abomination to God! One error leads you into all errors! You false prophets remember His salvation of His people in Egypt on the wrong day, you fast when you should feast, you pig yourselves with gluttony when you should remember God in hunger. By your false calculation of our Sabbath by the moon not the sun you work when God commands you to rest, and rest when God commands you to work. You deny the resurrection of the dead, but did not the prophet Elijah the Son of Man raise the dead? You deny immortality of souls and claim that death is death, beyond God's power. You deny the world to come. Lord God, hear my voice! The Sadducees are lawbreakers, criminals who drag us all down, for to pollute one Law of God the Father, and the Son, and the Holy Ghost, pollutes all laws. One criminal blackens all honest men. Destroy the Sadducees with your righteous fire! Let your righteous ones slay the wicked priests of Jerusalem!'

Laban stood with his eyes closed, bored. He scratched his chin.

The Zadok cried out the climax of his sermon. 'Hear me, Lord! Great and marvellous are Your works, Lord God Almighty! Your throne is high in the heavens. Your power, Your goodness, Your mercy flow over all the inhabitants of the earth. Those who come to You shall never perish. Lord Most High, save us! Let the Pit take the Sadducees of Jerusalem for their falseness, let the Destroyer eat their souls, let the Abyss swallow them, for they are a profanity and an abomination in Your eyes!'

He was telling the congregation what they wanted to hear. The line of sunlight rippled down the wall and blazed across the ground, stretching out the shadows of the women and children across the fields towards us like a race of giants. But still Laban yawned and scratched.

The Zadok spoke with his eyes wide open, visionary. 'We are God's people, the watchers of the stars, observers of the constellations of Sirius, of Lucifer the morning star, of the sun by which God lights our lives. We are His Nazarenes, the Keepers of His Promise, dedicated from conception to death to carrying out His Will. We drink no wine or beer, we eat no cooked meat or dirty food, we touch no leather or fur or any dead body. No razor ever touches our hair. We are consecrated to God, Nazarenes from the womb to the grave. Through our knowledge, holiness, and righteous living God's will shall be done, His promise sent down to us, our Messiah come to us, and the Covenant shall be ours!'

The priests cried: 'Lord, give us this day!' Silence fell. The prayer was over. Laban called out, 'Lehi, there's important matters to discuss,' but the Zadok shook his head. 'No, I'm hurrying to Jerusalem. Talk to Nephi, he speaks with my voice.' Laban shrugged angrily, then stormed off followed by Nephi who argued with him, I couldn't hear what about. As their arguing voices faded the priests filed down from the wall, the only sound their shuffling footsteps, and the women and children were already working again as though they hadn't stopped. The Zadok rubbed his face, exhausted by his sermon. He believed every word he'd spoken, a totally sincere man. At first I'd thought Laban had called out his name as *Levi*, but Lehi suited him better. It means jawbone.

People gathered around him, bringing forward a donkey and a waterskin for his journey. In the excitement I thought no one kept an eye on me, no one was near. I could have gone where I wanted. But then I knew someone was watching me. I felt their gaze on my shoulders. I turned, but there was no one on the walls. Everyone around Lehi was busy. I turned towards the fields, the lines of women toiling in the blowing dust and shimmering heat. Like a mirage the figure of a girl stood beneath a palm tree, watching me. The wind lifted her headscarf across her face, I couldn't see her. But I felt her. Her age, power, knowledge, observing me, seeing into me. I glimpsed her eyes through the flapping scarf, and she was beautiful. 'Mari?' I called out. The mirage split into two, two girls identically dressed, headscarves flapping, the shadow of the palm tree between them.

I blinked. Dust blew across the girls and they were gone among a hundred toiling shapes.

I ran among the women pulling at them, staring into their ugly vacant faces. No one.

I returned to the walls, called out thanks to the priests for the water, stole the cup to remember them by, and climbed the rose-red cliffs overhanging the rooftops of Sion until I reached the desert. I had dreamt of Mari; Mari was still alive in my dreams, that was all. I found no direct road to Jerusalem, so I wandered. At each village the talk of rebellion grew stronger, the villagers more sullen. The priests of Sion were not alone in their fiery talk. The farmers scratching the dust kept their heads down but a few young men said King Yaukin had escaped from exile. 'He's got the Egyptians to help him.' By midday King Yaukin was leading a whole Egyptian army with armour as bright as the sun; an hour into the afternoon there was no army at all, Yaukin was still held prisoner in Bab'El, and all hope was gone. By evening King Yaukin was dead, strangled by Nabuchadnezzar. I drank wine from my new cup, listening to wilder rumours, yawning like Laban. At the next inn I heard that Yaukin's uncle Mattaniah had been given the name Zadokiah by Nabuchadnezzar. That was interesting. Zadokiah means righteous priest of Ya, so thanks to Nabuchadnezzar's political sleight-of-hand three factions – Lehi at Sion, Zadokiah in Jerusalem, and the true Jerusalem Zadok who was Buzi the Sadducee, exiled in Bab'El, claimed leadership. By naming Zadokiah King-Priest of Jerusalem

Nabuchadnezzar sowed dissension and confusion in the already chaotic world of Jerusalem politics. Now word came that Zadokiah, appointed to rule Jerusalem in obedience, rebelled against Nabuchadnezzar and rebuilt the city gates. Zadokiah manned the walls with an army of soldiers. No, the Jerusalem priests would not support Zadokiah. Yes, priests rushed to Jerusalem to support Zadokiah.

I was drunk as a fish and found no woman to sleep on, so I stumbled into the desert and fell down snoring. When I opened my eyes the sky was still full of stars and I wondered what woke me. I heard a low growling sound and the scrape of claws on rock. It was only a desert lion, its starlit mane ragged with hunger. I stretched, smelt wine still in my cup, drained it, and turned over. When I awoke the rising sun struck into my eyes, and I heard a man's shouts.

I turned over the other way and tried to sleep, but still he shouted.

I swore. Despite my thumping head I wandered between the rocks trying to find him. The sun hurt my eyes, his shouts hurt my ears. I heard the clack of bones against rock in a valley, then recognised yesterday's priest by his long silver hair. He threw dry bones, ribs, vertebrae, they flew through the air and clattered on the rocks around the sand-coloured lion, but still the lion came prowling forward like ragged sand towards its prey, beautiful in its hunger and concentration, its gaze never shifting from the Zadok.

The Zadok shuddered, a Nazarene contaminated by the presence of death, then picked up something heavy, a cow's sun-bleached skull, an ancient meal, and threw it; he was at the lion's breakfast table and he was its breakfast meat. The cow's skull struck a rock by the lion and rolled away. The priest cried out to God. 'God, help me!' How often have I heard that cry?

No help here, no lightning, no miracles. The priest was a dead man, we all knew it. The lion crouched for the kill. Usually dead men run away on feet of lead or don't move at all, hypnotised by their fate. But as the lion sprang the Zadok ran forward. Not away, he ran forward. He believed in his immortal soul. I watched the man attack the lion. He pushed his shoulder forward under the lion's lower jaw as it came down on him so it could not bite. He wrapped his arms around its forelegs so it could not claw him. He grappled the lion with all his strength, lifting. I watched fascinated, this couldn't last longer than one deep breath. The Zadok gasped, his face deep red, veins standing out, then he gasped another deep breath. His lips pulled back from his teeth, those perfect white teeth, then his tongue came out black and I knew his strength was almost gone. The lion's stinking jaws opened, the yellow fangs snapped closed against one side of the priest's head, then the other.

Now the gaping mouth strikes down in a gust of breath.

I hold the lion's mouth open in one hand, bunching my fist between the incisors, then carry the animal away under one arm and let it free. The lion crouches, baleful honey eyes and swishing tail, then comes that magnificent moment: the great beast rears up, drops its paws heavily on my shoulders, and stands erect like a pillar braced against me. Only a moment, a wonderful moment, but the Zadok stares at me with eyes wide open as though he sees a vision.

I reached up. I stroked the lion's mane, then rubbed its eyes. 'First you slept in his cave,' I reproved the priest, 'and now I've denied him his breakfast.'

I slapped its rump and the lion loped between the rocks, following the hoofprints of the straying donkey. When the squealing began the priest raised his voice. 'No, whoever you are, you didn't save my life. God has saved me, just as God has fed the lion. You were sent by God.'

'That's ungrateful of you, Lehi.'

'How can you know—' He stared. 'Yes, I'm Lehi, son of Ephraim, of the tribe of Manasseh, the Zadok and prophet of my people. Are you a thief?'

'I'm not your enemy, Lehi.'

'My people are surrounded by enemies.' He lifted a dry bone to defend himself, then dropped it with a cry of disgust, contaminated by the dead skin still clinging to it, a Nazarene.

I told him the truth. 'I'm Wotan, a son of El.'

Lehi gripped my elbows, stared into my eyes. To many people my claim that God could have a son would be blasphemy, but Lehi was an educated man and high priest of Sion; he could hardly be unaware of the contents of his own community's scriptorium, he must know the ancient subtleties of the word El. And he claimed to be a prophet: a man doesn't choose to be a prophet, he's chosen by God, given the power of hearing and speaking divine revelation, and takes the consequences. Most prophets are ignored or killed, but Lehi had at least a few supporters (though most seemed to be his own family), and defensive walls around his community. He listened.

'I hear what you say, stranger,' Lehi said. 'Are you an angel?'

I belched wine-breath into his face. 'Do I smell like an angel?'

He sat down abruptly; even his red-rock cheeks had paled, then he recovered his composure. 'Stranger, the Scroll of Abraham tells us that God tests us to see if we will really do whatever our Lord God commands us.' I'd never heard of any Scroll of Abraham, but it must be in the library at Sion. I shrugged. 'What does God command you?'

'Then you're not sent to stop me?'

'Not me. But I'll travel with you, if we're going the same way.'

Lehi bowed his head. 'The Lord God has commanded me to go to Jerusalem to confront the Sadducees and their Zadok with their wickedness and abominations, calling them to account, so our clean living and morality shall rule in Jerusalem, and we shall earn the salvation of the Messiah.'

I laughed. 'The Zadok of the Temple's been carted off to exile in Bab'El, there's only the seventy Elders of the Sadducees left in Jerusalem.'

He shook his head. 'The Lord God never commands us without preparing a way for us. I am not the only man making a journey. A meeting has been arranged. A negotiation. An illumination. I shall show my opponent, the false priest, the false Zadok, the light!' But he rubbed at the dead skin clinging to his hands, disgraced by the touch of death. The Nazarene purification rituals were complex, humiliating and lengthy, involving repeated washing and long prayers, and his hair would be cut bald to the skull, so that men would shun him for his infection in the sight of God. Numerous guilt offerings and sin offerings must be made before he was pure; his hair would take years to grow again to a commanding length. 'God prepares a way,' he whispered. 'This doesn't stop me. There's a way, always a way. I have faith.'

I sat on a rock. 'Who is he?'

'Who?'

'The priest you're meeting. The false Zadok.'

'The traitor! The abomination. The ass.' Lehi scrubbed his hands raw with sand. 'I'm filthy,' he burst out. 'Unclean. I can't go like this.'

'I won't tell anyone. It was only dry bones, nothing more. Exactly what light is this guiding you, Lehi?'

He said fiercely, 'The light of God the Father, and God the Son.'

'Two Gods? I haven't heard of . . .' Then I remembered Mari. 'You mean the Son, the Messiah? Jesus Christ?' He looked blank so I tried it in Greek. '*Iesous Christos?*'

'The Anointed One?' He nodded, knowing the Hellene language. 'But He won't be Greek. He'll be a Jew.' Lehi forgot his hands and his face lit up with faith, simple shining faith. 'He'll be born in Jerusalem, gather the scattered tribes to make one nation, and rule in righteousness. He'll be an *Asayya,* a healer, and heal our nation. The Messiah is the sole high priest after the order of Melchizadok. You call him Jesus Christ, that's up to you, stranger. All I know is His spirit is the soul of Man, and has fought Satan from the beginning of time.' It was the first time I'd heard the name *Satan* spat with such force from the mouth of an ordinary Jew, as though Satan were a personal enemy. 'God shall choose His Son to come down to us in the body, fight Satan and redeem us who believe in Him, and bring us to His side in Heaven, where we shall live for ever as gods.'

I was pleased. These beliefs were much what I was familiar with from the past. 'God truly, physically can have sons?'

'God was once a man of flesh and bones,' Lehi said passionately. 'He learnt. He chose. His right choices improved Him. We believe He achieved the Godhead through His perfection. Yes, He can sire a Son of flesh and bones.'

'Is the Holy Ghost the wife of El?' I asked. 'Will the Son be born through her? Is she a virgin like Anath, or is she His wife like Ishtar?'

'No.' Lehi wouldn't explain who the Holy Ghost was, only that God was at least three separate Gods, as the canaans believe. The sun struck down into the valley and it grew hot. 'Where's your guards?' I asked. 'You don't travel here alone?'

'The Lord God's my shield and my guard.' Lehi stood up as though his strength was limitless. 'Today my son Nephi's fetching the scrolls belonging to my family from

Zoram, Laban's assistant in the scriptorium. It's all arranged. They'll prove the truth of everything I say. Nephi's bringing my wife Sariah with them to me in Jerusalem.'

I found Lehi's sleeping blanket in the shallow cave, drank his water to wash the wine out of my mouth and poured the last of it over my head. 'Baptism,' Lehi said, watching me. 'We believe in baptism with water. Not of children,' he added. 'Children aren't born sinful. It's the choices we make in this world that make us sinful or good.' He rubbed his hands uneasily, remembering, but I clapped my arm round him. 'Forget it,' I said. 'Make your choice. Keep your mouth shut. Lie.'

'For the greater good,' he said, holding his hands behind him. 'Yes, for the greater good.'

I grinned, scared the lion off the dead donkey, swung the panniers over my shoulders, and walked with him for company. Lehi walked with his hands behind him all day, and slept hardly at all in the night.

And so before dawn I walked into Jerusalem with Lehi the prophet. Jerusalem, its defensive wall gaping like a ring of broken teeth, the great gates hanging smashed in gateways. Bab'El troops in brass armour searched us and stole Lehi's eating knife before waving us through, then Zadokiah's threadbare barefoot soldiers tried to steal my cup in the street but I tossed a coin, and as they fought over it I pulled Lehi deep into the maze of streets.

Jerusalem, city of priests and peasants. 'Jerusalem,' cried a voice among the sheep and bobbing heads, 'Jerusalem, you harlot, you fornicator, you whore! You build brothels to idols at every crossroads, a temple to pagan gods on every hill, you open your legs to anyone who passes by, you beg to fornicate with Egyptians!' I stood on tiptoe but couldn't see the speaker, only shadows and the smoke of cooking lamb; it was not yet dawn. 'Make the mark of a cross on your foreheads, all those who are not guilty of

341

idolatry!' The voice faded, the flocks of sheep and peasants pushing forward swept the speaker away.

Lehi gripped my arm. 'Come with me. My family and supporters are at the Temple. I pray that Prince Mulek and the Elders will come! I'll confront our enemy there.' We stepped over women weeping and throwing themselves down at the shrine to Tammuz as they did three thousand years ago; kings and cities rise and fall, but religion never dies. I pulled Lehi uphill to the Temple. 'Who's Prince Mulek?' I asked.

'A friend. A son of King Zadokiah who has seen the light. His wife brought him to us, God be praised.'

Brass gods dotted the Temple courtyard as in Solomon's time and the days of King Manasseh. Worshippers crowded devoutly around the horse and chariot of Shemash the Sun god, statues of Molech, B'El, Nabu, uttering heartfelt prayers before the sun rose. I pushed through and Lehi climbed on to the east wall, the horizon a quivering line of light rising in front of him and the Temple behind him. His sons were waiting and he gripped hands quickly with Laman, Lemuel and Sam who'd travelled separately to Jerusalem. 'Is everything ready?'

'We expect my dear youngest brother Nephi later.' Laman shrugged. 'If he hasn't lost his nerve.'

'Your youngest brother is greatest in spirit. Did *you* dare go into the scriptorium and face Laban and Zoram?'

Laman's face flushed red. 'I haven't got a sword!'

'Neither has Nephi.' Father and son shouted, then Laman's brothers shouted at their father.

'You ask Nephi to do everything!' Laman shouted at last. 'You love him more than me. You never loved me or Lemuel.'

'That's right,' Lemuel said. 'Never loved us.'

Laman noticed me, stuck out his jaw. 'Who's he? Why do you promote every dog you come across over your own sons?'

Lehi said, 'Peace, Laman, son. Hold silence in your mouth.'

'Where's the donkey?' Laman demanded. 'You didn't lose the donkey?'

'The Lord God tested me with a lion,' Lehi said, but Laman said, 'It was our best donkey.' I put myself in Laman's face. 'Better a donkey's fattening the lion,' I told him, 'than your father.' Laman shrugged, hot-tempered, tall, knowing his strength. He wanted to fight and I always do. Lehi forced himself between us to make peace. 'Enough! Enough. This is the day when we stand or fall. Today truth and righteousness wins, or Satan's lies prevail.' Laman pointed his finger at me but stepped back.

More men arrived. Lehi greeted his nephew Ishmael with both arms. 'Welcome, Ishmael, and bless you for coming so quickly.' Ishmael was a thin man in his forties, haggard with travel, he'd left his flocks in Nahom. He coughed – I knew that cough, I'd heard the same demon in Haran's chest – then he knelt and kissed Lehi's hands. 'Father Lehi, when you call, I will always come.' I gathered Ishmael's two sons had married Lehi's daughters. Lehi saw his wife Sariah waiting respectfully in the shadows below the wall, beckoned her up, kissed her on the mouth. Sariah took her two youngest children from the maid and hefted them in her arms for him to bless, Jacob old enough to crawl, Joseph a newborn babe. Lehi beckoned his eldest daughters, the wives of Ishmael's sons Ayn and Cumor, and allowed them to kneel and kiss his feet, then lifted them up and embraced them, both with child.

The families were so closely entwined, as usual with nomads, it was difficult to tell them apart. Ishmael's eldest daughter had stayed home with her mother to tend his flocks, but the two plate-faced older girls here had married Laman and Lemuel and did whatever their husbands told them, muttering with Laman and Lemuel's other wives over the loss of the donkey because their husbands did, sulking because Laman did. Behind them three younger, prettier, unmarried daughters waited hoping to be acknowledged by Lehi. As the sun had not yet risen Lehi allowed them to pay their respects. The first, Abigail, came up and knelt to greet him, but I stared at the second girl to climb the steps: she was the mirage I'd seen by the palm tree. 'Mari?' I whispered. She glanced at me without curiosity, without force, without love, yet she was lovely. A beautiful empty face, flawless skin as white and plain as milk, smooth brown eyes. She stepped past me.

But Lehi watched us. 'This, Wotan my friend, whom the Lord sent me to save my life, is Ishmael's pretty daughter Maralah, the elder twin by an hour.' The girl, I already forgot her name, knelt and wiped the dust from Lehi's feet with her long black hair. No, she wasn't Mari. But Mari was here. I felt her. I felt her eyes like a lion's watching me, I felt her as a hunted prey feels: I turned from side to side, searching the Temple wall, I felt like a mouse that hears the hiss of an eagle's wing. 'Mari?' I called aloud.

Laman yawned. 'Who's Mari?'

Who was she? Not Laman, none of the brothers, not Ishmael who coughed quietly into a rag, not any of the wives. Lehi said, 'This is Mara.'

The identical twin of the forgettable girl climbed into the dawn light – identical but utterly *more* than her sister. Spirit, soul, I don't know the word. Too beautiful to touch, pure creamy skin, she stared at me with hot brown eyes – eyes that blazed with feeling, depth, life. Naked emotion. I felt I fell into her, I couldn't look away from her, for a moment Mara was the whole world, Mara's beauty, Mara's perfection in everything, the way she moved, the fullness of her, her heat, overwhelmed me. I stared at her like a lovestruck boy who has never known a woman, a man-virgin again – me, the greatest lover the world has ever known!

I'm Wotan, I've had a million women. Never one such as she. She kneels at Lehi's feet, she kisses his ankles with her sensual lips. I can't take my eyes off her, can't look at her sensibly. She's no more beautiful than her sister. Her skin's no whiter. Her eyes are no browner. Beneath her clothes she has breasts and legs just like her sister's, no doubt. But her sister's a candle, and this girl is the sun.

'Mara,' I whisper. 'Younger by an hour.' She ignores me, her eyes are only for her Uncle Lehi, her eyes gazing into him as she stands, and they embrace. She has slender white ankles, I want to touch them, touch with my fingertips the curves of her body as the dawn breeze presses her clothes against her, touch the dawn shining through her hair. I want all of Mara. I want Mara's life. I want every beat of her heart. I'm in love. But all she cares about is talking to her uncle.

'It's true, Father Lehi?' she breathes, low-voiced, so her sisters and brothers can't hear. 'It's really true? You've spoken your prophecy, your vision, among the people?'

Lehi prophesies, 'Our Lord God Most High will take the highest branch of the highest cedar, a Son of the royal line of King David, and plant it on a high mountain.' He holds out his arms: the mountain on which we and the Temple stand. A prophecy of the Messiah to come.

Mara stares into his eyes, total concentration. 'Promise me. The Messiah will be born here in the Temple?'

'Yes, daughter of Sion. All truth is found in the Temple.'

'When?'

'Soon, soon,' he soothes her, but Mara cries out, 'When? When?' Laman grabs her elbow. 'Leave, it's holy here, you can't stay here.' But she kneels so she can't be moved. How well I know her! 'When?' she cries.

Lehi soothes her, 'Daughter of Sion, I tell you, when the people of Jerusalem see the truth. Soon.'

'The people of Jerusalem throw stones at us,' Laman said. 'They want peace, Father, not your God.' He continues smoothly, 'I mean our God. They want peace, not war.'

Lehi faced him down. 'There's no Messiah in the Temple, so there's no peace. There's nothing but war until the Messiah comes to end war.' Lehi turned his back on his eldest son.

Sunrise was less than five minutes away (the priests of Sion use a sundial to divide their hour into twelfths) and the other women had already gone down, forbidden to witness what we would see. All except Mara. Laman tried to jerk her to the steps. I pushed him aside and lifted her away from him, forgot him, carried her down unable to look away from her eyes, I stumbled and we almost fell down in the shadows, and she laughed. 'Mari,' I whispered. 'I know you're Mari.'

'Mara,' she said, then whispered at my jaw so the women wouldn't hear. 'Why are you here, Wotan? Why are you always trying to get in the way?'

'What way?'

She fell silent as guards slapped the people aside with rods. A cloak swirled and a young bearded man wearing purple trimmed with gold thread strode up the steps above us. This must be Prince Mulek. Lehi bowed, greeting him earnestly. Mulek turned, showing himself beside the prophet to the people below: a tableau. Like a burning fire the rising sun sent up great fingers of light into the sky as if blessing them. Neither a prince nor a priest makes a single accidental gesture.

'I sent a messenger to Pharaoh,' Mulek told Lehi in a low voice, but the wall magnified his whispers. 'I'm confident of Psammeticus's support.' Lehi said, 'And his army? He'll send an army?'

Mulek shrugged. 'He says my father King Zadokiah, may he live for ever, is King Nab's puppet.'

'Rebellious puppet.'

'Psammeticus won't send an army to support even a rebellious puppet.'

'But to support you, Prince Mulek?'

'Ah, now,' Mulek said. I lost what they murmured next, girl servants arrived chattering. A fine-looking woman moved among us, Princess Zarah, Mulek's wife. Her fingers flashed gold rings, her arms and neck and ankles gleamed with copper bracelets. Zarah means shining, and she shone like the sun. Sariah stood and after an awkward start they talked about babies. Meanwhile I saw men gathering along the wall above us, some well dressed, others ragged as shepherds. These seventy Elders of the Temple, the Gerusia Council (Greeks call it the Sanhedrin), oversee religious matters during the exile of the highest priests in Bab'El. Zarah pointed out one greybeard. 'Look, old Ya'Azaniah! Have you got him on our side?' His father had been famous for his holiness to Ya, and so were his brothers, but Nabuchadnezzar had promoted Ya'Azaniah over them; and now the old man turned away from the Temple and climbed the steps to greet the sun. 'Don't trust him,' Mara muttered.

Sunlight touched the Temple roof like gold. The twenty-five priests of Sion turned their backs on the Temple and raised their arms like the sun's rays, showing themselves in their white linen – near the horizon the sun is closest to the earth – to be unstained by sin. Then the Elders in blue, purple and scarlet, the colours of the sacred Temple Veil, also raised their arms. 'Behold the glory of God,' Lehi prayed, 'behold the *shekinah* of the Lord.' He stopped, looking round. Voices shouted, coming closer.

There was a disturbance below, and from the outer court of the Temple the voice I'd heard earlier cried out against the men on the wall. 'You fools, by worshipping the sun to the east, you turn your backs on Yahweh!' Temple guards ran to throw out the shouter, a dusty ragged figure waving a stick, his broken sandals hanging from his ankles, but the people held them back. The guards cracked a few heads. 'You've turned your backs on Yahweh!' the ragged man cried to the men on the wall. 'You insult

Yahweh! The Lord says to me, See this, Son of Man! Have you seen the abominations which this rebellious house commits?' The people shouted for him, pushing him forward, but guards bustled him from the place. 'Look to the north!' he cried over his shoulder, white hair flying. 'Look northward to Bab'El and to the mountains, rebellious branch of Sion! Our punishment, slavery, destruction, is God's will. Don't break your solemn vow of peace to Bab'El, King Zadokiah! You called on God Himself to witness your oath!'

'Yes, that's the point,' Mara whispered, nodding. 'Zadokiah swore loyalty to King Nab before God. He can't break that oath. The people won't stand for it.'

'But Prince Mulek's sending for help to Egypt.'

'The people believe that if their King Zadokiah rebels and calls in the Egyptians, then God will leave the Temple and destroy Jerusalem. They believe God allowed Bab'El to prevail because Jerusalem was sinful. A harlot. That's what the exiled priests say.'

'But if they're in exile, how can they be heard?'

'There are ways. Ways in. Ways out.'

'What do you believe, Mara?'

She looked at me with her hot brown eyes, then winked. 'I believe in Jesus Christ.'

The Elders came down from the wall, bowed to the statue of Yahweh by the east gate, and filed into the sunlit Temple. Lehi led the priests of Sion past the statues of the gods on the porch, then followed the Elders behind the Veil. The sun beat into the courtyard. People chanted prayers, priests worked over the hot altars, the smoke of sacrifices rose. A bird escaped, a dove I think, whirling like a white spark above the roofs.

Later the girls dozed, fanning their faces.

Zarah talked with Sariah then they watched the children play.

Mara's sister turned her back on me, ignoring me. But

Mara played with the children, and I filled my eyes with her in the sunlight.

A shadow fell across me.

The ragged man limped between me and the sun, stepping so close I smelt him. He was the shouter I'd heard earlier, but silent now. Almost furtive. He crossed the courtyard without being noticed. He leant on a serpent-headed stick almost as high as his head and his long white hair hung greasily to his waist, swaying as he climbed the porch steps. His shift was travel-stained, hardly any white left, tied with string at the waist. He looked neither to the right nor the left, meeting no one's eyes as he crossed the porch, drawing no attention to himself. He disappeared round the side of the Temple.

No one else had noticed him.

I thought about him.

He didn't come back.

I got to my feet and went after him. Nothing. The courtyard was empty, but then I saw a door in the wall. I pushed the door and an entrance swung open, revealing a narrow side corridor in the Temple. No one either to the right or left. The ragged man had gone. I stepped inside, wedged a pebble in the angle of the door to stop it quite closing behind me, chose to go left, followed the cool dim corridor to the end. Where now? More choices.

A corridor to the left turned back on itself, ladders led up and down through trapdoors. I was in the maze.

How did the ragged man know his way? Only the high priest of the Sadducees was allowed to know the way through. Then I saw a bare footprint. I followed the scuff-marks left by his trailing sandals in the dust, long strides, no false turns. He'd followed the way with perfect confidence.

Another corridor, almost a tunnel, and I thought I heard muffled voices chanting beyond the thick walls.

Halfway along the corridor, a pair of feet stuck out

between the floor and the wall. Sandals swung by their straps from the ankles. I stared, then stepped forward silently. The ragged man grunted with effort as he worked, unblocking a secret hole: a place for priests to spy on priests. His legs jerked, dust puffed, then handfuls of rubble were scooped out and pushed back by his feet. I crept forward, then crouched behind him. I could have touched the soles of his feet. I rocked on my heels, balancing, watching him, thinking. What was on the other side of the wall?

'The Lord sees us not,' the ragged man's voice muttered from the hole, 'the Lord forsakes the world.' Dust flew back, and I sneezed. For a shocked heartbeat there was silence, then the feet snatched into the hole. I grabbed, caught a sandal strap with my little finger, overbalanced, slid down beside the ragged man into the tunnel. Stone and plaster scraped my back, his knees jabbed me then he grunted, squashed between me and the wall. He hissed, 'Who are you?'

'Who are you?' I said. We stared eye to eye, his eyes veined by the desert sun, his breath sour with hunger. He tried to move his knee. 'Ow,' I said.

'Sssh.' He jerked his elbows, held his finger angrily to his lips. 'I have a perfect right to be here. I'm the only one who *does* have any right to be here. They defile the house of the Lord.'

He squeezed his arm forward to a wooden panel, and the voices were suddenly loud.

'The Lord's not to be found here now,' the ragged man whispered, inching forward. 'The Lord is gone far from His sanctuary.'

'Sanctuary?' The sanctuary of the Lord was the Holy of Holies. Was this it? Here King Solomon supposedly placed the Arch of the Covenant that once contained the Lord of Moses. It was death to enter here.

I tried to pull him back but his greasy skin slipped

350

through my hands. 'The Lord brought me to the door of the courtyard,' the ragged man hissed. He kicked at me with his feet. 'You can't stop me. The Lord showed me the hole in the wall. The Lord said to me, Son of Man, dig deeper in the wall, and find a door.' The ragged man raised his voice. 'And the Lord said to me, Go in!'

Before I could stop him he pushed the panel, it swung open like a door, and we fell forward in a tumble of limbs.

I sat up on the golden floor of the Holy of Holies. Gold walls gleamed dimly on every side. Perfumed smoke made me cough. A censer at the centre of the room poured more smoke. Candles burnt like stars in the clouds of incense. The shadows of men moved around us. I recognised Ya'Azaniah, wide-eyed, white with shock as he came through the clouds. The ragged man whispered, 'Even you, Ya'Azaniah? Even you?'

Ya'Azaniah stared. 'It's you.' He fell back a step. 'But you can't be.'

Each of the seventy Elders carried a smoking censer in his hand. I saw no Arch of the Covenant. Lehi's white linen made him stand out like a ghost in the darkness. His sons moved around him like wraiths. He stared at the ragged man as though he couldn't believe his eyes. Laman called out in a high voice, 'Who is he, Father?'

The ragged man lifted himself against his sceptre, standing barefoot. 'I am Ezekiel.'

'Ezekiel? You aren't here,' Ya'Azaniah mumbled, shaken, shaking his head. 'Ezekiel's finished. You, all your priests. You're in exile at Tel-Abib.'

'Tel-Abib, the Mound of the Flood,' Ezekiel said, reminding the Elders of the descent of every true Zadok from Noah. He took Ya'Azaniah's hand, pressed it to his scrawny chest, his living heartbeat. 'Do you think the Lord forgets one jot or tittle?' He moved among the Elders, who shuffled back from him. 'You all know me. I am Ezekiel the true Zadok, son of Buzi the Zadok of the sons of Zadok, a priest of the priesthood of Aaron back to the beginning of the world. Through my father and my father's father my living blood remembers the children of Father Noah, the first Zadok.'

'I know you, Ezekiel,' Lehi said, pushing past Ya'Azaniah. 'I expected to meet you on neutral ground, not here in the Temple.' He shrugged, holding up a candle. 'But I can provide illumination for you here as well as anywhere.'

Ezekiel pushed him back fiercely. 'I am the true Zadok.' I thought he'd strike Lehi with the serpent-headed sceptre. I grabbed it: Ezekiel's hand cold and dry as bone with starvation clutching the ancient sceptre.

'*I* am the Zadok,' Lehi said, his white linen against Ezekiel's rags, his washed and combed white hair against Ezekiel's wild tangle. Each man pushed, neither backed down. Lehi said calmly, 'God has revealed to me the righteous way, Ezekiel, and you are a false prophet. You are a voice of Bab'El. I alone can make Jerusalem free. I alone can gather the tribes that are scattered. I alone can bring about the Messiah.'

'The Lord brings me here,' Ezekiel said. He reached out his hand like a claw. 'The Lord reaches down His hand to me, like this.' Ezekiel closed his eyes as though seeing a vision, gripped his tangled hair with his hand and pulled upwards as if lifting himself from the floor into the air. I clearly saw the Sadducee cross scratched deep and bloody on his forehead. 'The Lord takes me by the hair of my head and His spirit lifts me up here to Jerusalem. He brings me here. He shows me a door and says to me, Go in, see the wicked abominations that they do!'

'Keep your preaching for your exiles, Ezekiel,' Ya'Azaniah said. 'You have no voice over us. You're yesterday's man. Without you we'll free ourselves from Bab'El and live as free men.'

Ezekiel put his hand around Lehi's candle, lifted it high.

'The Lord says to me, Ezekiel, Son of Man, see what the Elders of the house of Israel do in the dark!' He held Lehi's candle to illuminate the walls, pulled Lehi forward. The incense-smoke cleared and I saw the gold walls of the Holy of Holies painted over like an Egyptian tomb with portraits of famous men, paintings of great events – I saw Moses parting the Red Sea like curls of hair – and along the bottom and the top were symbols and Egyptian writing, the tribes of Israel in the desert, pyramid shapes, cherubs looking down from the sky, and a gold angel reaching up to the stars above the sun. 'Every creeping filthy thing is here,' Ezekiel cried out. 'Every abominable beast. You desecrate the walls of the house of Israel with idols. You make strangers of yourselves to God with idols.' His fierce eyes shone with tears. 'Lehi, I shall put a hook in your jaws, jawbone-man, and drag you round the walls of Jerusalem to show the people how your evil has brought down God's fury on us all.'

'*Your* evil,' Lehi said.

'For how many years must Jerusalem atone for your sins, wicked priest? Three generations shall pass before the throne of the Lord returns to Jerusalem!' But Ezekiel's eyes flickered: even he, I thought, did not know where the Arch of the Covenant was.

Prince Mulek pushed forward. 'Ezekiel, you're the wicked priest, not Lehi.'

'The Messiah shall be born,' Lehi said.

Ezekiel turned on him. 'The Lord says to me, Son of Man, prophesy against the false prophets who can't hear the word of the Lord. You are foolish prophets, your rebellious house follows your own spirit. You're the foxes of the desert.' He stared down Mulek with contempt, turned again to Lehi. 'I'll break down your wall. In your wickedness you promise eternal life, but will you save souls alive that should not live? Shall the wicked be saved with the good? Will you open your teraphs, your holy pillows, your lists of the saved, and let the souls fly away and go?'

'Every soul can be saved,' Lehi said. 'The living who are baptised with water can be saved, and even those who are already dead, if a symbolic baptism of their names is performed. Every named and baptised soul can be saved.'

I remembered Abraham's wife Sarah who had worshipped El and loved her sacred cushions, her teraphs, that she believed cared for the souls of her ancestors. Now the priests at Sion believe that an immortal soul is trapped inside the prison or teraph of each human body. They believe that after the death of the body the released soul flies home beyond the ocean that encircles the world, where they will one day be gathered up by God.

'I believe in souls,' I said. Tears came to my eyes; I who have no soul.

Ezekiel scoffed, 'Baptism with water! Hocus-pocus. The only true baptism is circumcision, baptism of blood.' His voice rose. 'There is no life after death. There is no life. Only the Lord.'

'We know what we believe,' Lehi said. 'You won't change us. I know the secrets of the Urim and Thummim.'

'Stolen!' Ezekiel lifted the serpent-headed sceptre. 'Know the truth! Mine is the sceptre of Zadok, the mouthpiece of the Arch of the Covenant.'

'You don't know where the Covenant is,' I said. Again that flicker in Ezekiel's eyes. Now I was certain the Covenant had been lost.

Lehi seized his advantage. 'Ezekiel, the Covenant with God is lost and you are exiled. You have no legitimacy. I am the true Zadok.'

'You are a liar.' Ezekiel said, '*I* am the true Zadok, appointed, through His salvation of Noah from the Flood, by God Himself. Everyone knows this. My father Buzi—'

'I too trace my family back through Aaron to Noah,' Lehi said.

'Prove it.'

'The genealogy of my fathers is recorded on a copper scroll ending with my name and beginning with Noah.'

'Show me.'

'My son Nephi brings the scroll to Jerusalem at this very moment.'

'You hope,' muttered Laman under his breath.

'Then, Lehi, lying priest, you'll show me the scroll-stick tomorrow,' Ezekiel said. 'If it exists.'

'It exists.'

'Don't let Ezekiel fool you,' Ya'Azaniah said quietly. 'There's something he hasn't told us.' The arguing men fell silent. 'Ezekiel has no sons to follow him. He's the last Zadok of the pure line. It ends with him. His time, his priesthood, is past.' Ya'Azaniah knelt before Lehi. 'You are the Zadok to lead us. You and your sons are the future.'

Lehi said, 'But Ezekiel's wife—'

Ya'Azaniah said quietly, viciously, 'Ezekiel's wife is dead.'

'It's true.' Ezekiel's eyes filled. The tears trickled like pearls from his gaunt cheeks into the corners of his mouth, then dripped from his chin on to the golden floor. 'It's true, my wife lies dead in Tel-Abib.' He dashed the moisture from his cheeks. 'The Lord tells me I shall not weep. The Lord says to me, Ezekiel, you shall not weep.' He looked at us dry-eyed. 'I am a sign to you. I say to you, escape. Escape.' He pointed the fingers of his hand at Lehi. 'Your sons and your daughters shall fall by the sword.'

It was a terrible curse. Lehi shivered. Laman and Lemuel supported him.

Ezekiel pushed past. He pushed the Elders aside, strode with long strides to the golden door in the golden wall, pulled it open, then looked round straight at Lehi. 'Tomorrow I'll meet you in the valley of bones, jawbone-man, and we'll see which one of us speaks with the Lord's voice.'

'Where is he?' Time after time during the night Lehi, pacing the rented room, sent out for word of Nephi and the scroll. 'Something's wrong.' Laman had heard a rumour that Laban the treasurer and fifty armed men had seized control of the monastery at Sion, looted its wealth, (the priests had no money of their own, everything was held in the treasury) and stolen its priceless scriptorium for his own. 'You should never have trusted him, Father.'

'I never trusted Laban, not since he got too big for us,' Lehi sighed. 'Now it seems Zoram the librarian's gone over, betrayed us too.' Lemuel brought news that the scriptorium was burnt; Sam that it was safe. Everything was peaceful; no, there had been a terrible fight. Mara said bleakly, 'Nephi has no sword.'

'Don't fret,' Laman said, drinking wine. 'Nephi's the youngest of us, but he's strongest.'

Lehi said worriedly, 'He's my favourite son.'

'We know *that*,' Laman said. 'He never thinks for himself.' A cockerel crowed the dawn. Lehi said, 'It can't be, it's still dark.'

Mara put her arm around his shoulder. 'There's still time.' Grey light grew around us. 'It's not light yet,' Lehi said. He said hopefully, 'Nephi will ride like the wind.' The first rays of the sun touched the towers of Jerusalem and we climbed to the roof to pray. I licked my finger, held it up. Dead calm. If Nephi rode like the wind, he'd never get here. I glanced down the ladder and noticed Mara's smile. She never missed a thing. When I went down I said, 'You smiled.'

'Not at you.'

'I caught you.' I touched the tip of her nose with my finger. 'You smiled.'

She knocked my hand away angrily. 'Not now!' People were coming down.

'With you it's not now, not ever,' I said. 'Always.' She gave me a silent look then hurried to help the women seeing the men off. 'Give Nephi another five minutes,' Lehi said, and everyone sat down again. The sun threw a bright line through the window, slowly widening. It touched my foot, and I realised Lehi looked at me. 'Will Ezekiel wait?' Lehi trusted me because I'd saved him from the lion, but he thought I knew Ezekiel because I'd fallen with him into the Holy of Holies.

'Ezekiel will wait,' I said.

'What does this man know?' Laman demanded, turning his back on me. 'He's an opportunist, a stranger. You trust strangers too much, Father, and you trust your family who loves you too little.'

They were arguing again, so I said, 'Why should Ezekiel sacrifice his authority, crawling to you here in secret? The longer he waits, the louder he'll preach to the people in public.'

'Poisoning their minds against us,' Lehi said grimly. Again Mara hugged him, saying, 'But you know that God puts true words in *your* mouth, Father Lehi.'

I said, 'Ezekiel believes God puts the truth in *his* mouth. You accuse each other of the same things. You can't both be right.'

'I am right,' Lehi said. 'God is on my side.' Laman closed a drape across the window to make it look more like night. I pulled Mara into a dark corner, whispered angrily. 'You're encouraging him.'

She whispered equally angrily, 'Of course I do. Lehi believes in a Messiah, God coming into flesh, coming into this world. If Lehi wins, maybe it will happen.'

She drove me crazy. '*How?*'

'By making a Jerusalem deserving of God in the flesh. A worshipping people deserving redemption. Law. Order.' She said fiercely, 'Heaven, eventually. We *can* achieve Heaven in this world.'

Footsteps outside; but it was only the bread seller. I whispered, 'How, Mara?'

'How? How?' She stamped her foot. 'By our own efforts. By making the right choices. Choosing good over evil. And if we *can*, we *ought*.' I looked at her sadly. 'No, it's me who's sorry for you,' she said.

There was a clatter of hooves in the street. Laman parted the drape looking frightened, then sounded relieved. 'It's all right, it's him.' The door burst open and Nephi strode into the room carrying a bloodied Damascus sword in his right hand. A brown linen sack swung from his left hand. He saw me and raised the sword, but Lehi reassured him, 'He's one of us.'

Nephi was tall, almost as tall as me; strong, but not as strong as me; and he was young, and exhausted. He stood swaying with tiredness, then the sword clattered from his hand. He'd ridden all night, ridden through the guard posts straight into Jerusalem.

Laman said, 'Couldn't you get it? Father, if only you'd asked me—'

Lehi said, 'Let him rest.' He called the women. 'Fetch water. Cakes.'

'I got it.' Nephi, face flushed, reached into the scaly brown bag; the brown was dried blood. He pulled out a copper scroll rolled up tight into a stick. 'I have it, Father!'

Lehi took the metal stick with trembling fingers. 'The genealogy of my fathers. This scroll contains the words spoken by the holy prophets since the world began to the present day, our Law, and preserves for our children the language of our time in Egypt.' He stared at his fingers. The scroll was slimy, sticky with blood. 'What—?

'Laban wouldn't give it to me. He was falling-down drunk on wine.' Nephi reached into the sack and pulled out long hair in his fist, then a bearded face swinging, dripping wine as it was lifted high. 'The Holy Ghost told me: "Laban has stolen the records of the Law and the commandments of Moses. Slay Laban, whom the Lord has delivered into your hands." I cut off his head with his own sword.' He saw me smiling, tossed the head to me, and I caught it by one ear. 'Good work,' I said, but Nephi said, 'It's the first blood I've shed.' He didn't bother to wipe the mess from his hands, hopelessly contaminated with death.

I encouraged him, 'You'll get used to it.'

'No,' Nephi said. 'I won't.' He knelt at Lehi's feet. 'Laban betrayed us to the Sadducee Elders.'

Lehi started. 'You can't be sure. Ya'Azaniah knelt at my feet. He acclaimed me. He said that I am the future.'

'Fifty Temple guards in full armour rode in through the east gate of Sion as I rode out of the west.'

'But Ya'Azaniah—'

'Worships God, but loves mammon.' Mammon, money. 'Besides, he's only one among seventy.' Nephi went to the door and pulled a man inside. 'Zoram knows. Tell them, Zoram.'

'It's true,' the assistant librarian said shiftily. He swallowed. 'It's true. Let me live. I'm on your side. They tricked you, deceived you. The monastery's taken over, it's gone. Laban set up everything with the Elders – for a cut. He was to get the treasury, they got everything else. The library. And you.'

Lehi murmured, 'What of us?'

'I don't know. A trial. Death.'

Mara said, 'They didn't expect Ezekiel to arrive.'

Lehi couldn't understand such treachery. 'I broke bread with the Elders. I worshipped the Lord with them. Ya'Azaniah gave me the kiss of friendship.' He covered his ears with his hands, he couldn't bear to hear more. 'The wickedness of the people of Jerusalem is limitless.'

'The Elders want peace,' Nephi said. 'Peace is all they want. Power for themselves. The last thing they want is the Egyptians marching in, overturning them, setting you up in their place.'

Lehi muttered, 'And Prince Mulek?'

'King Zadokiah can protect him. But we can no longer be Zadokiah and Mulek's allies, we have nothing to offer. With the Elders against us our lives are forfeit.'

'But Ezekiel hates the Elders as much as he hates us.'

'Ezekiel loves whoever loves his God.'

'Then we're dead,' Laman said. He turned on his father. 'All because of you. Your dreams. Visions. Pride. You've killed us all.'

Mara knelt, lifted the sword Nephi had dropped, and held it out to me on her wrists. She looked up at me appealingly. 'In the worst of times, there is one man we can trust.'

I stared. 'You trust me? You of all people?'

'It's the worst of bad times.' She whispered, 'Wotan, if we're driven out of Jerusalem there will be no Messiah, because there will be no believers in Him. Only Bab'El. Defeat.'

'Obviously we can't meet Ezekiel, it's a trap,' Laman muttered. 'With the Elders on Ezekiel's side he'll turn the people against us, it's certain death.' He peered round the drape. 'We'll run for our lives. We'll get out of Jerusalem before we're discovered, hide in the wilderness. Maybe they'll let us live quietly.'

'I won't run,' Lehi said. 'I won't run. I won't hide in tents in the wilderness again. I won't be afraid every footfall is a thief or assassin.' He knocked the cup from Laman's hand. 'No more wine.'

Laman coloured, bunched his fists, saw Mara kneeling at my feet, kicked at her angrily. I blocked him, knocked him against the wall to calm his nerves. 'Let's keep our heads,' I said.

Mara held out the sword. 'Always,' she said. I grinned and took what she offered. Lehi's eyes flicked between us both, not missing much. Maralah pulled her sister back with the other women, but I watched Mara. Maralah smiled at me.

Laman gave a high laugh. 'Keep our heads!' he said. I steadied Lehi and Ishmael's sons, Ayn and Cumor, moved between them calmly, spiked the head on the sword and popped it back in the sack. Nephi looked at me in the eye. 'Can we fight our way out?'

'I can,' I said. 'Not you. Not all of you. We'll hide out today, find a way down the walls at night. Ropes, baskets maybe.' I didn't look at the women. Not everyone was going to make it.

'I'll fight!' Laman said, but I could see he liked the idea of baskets and creeping away in the dark. 'Yes, we'll fight!' Lemuel and Sam said, following Laman's lead, but Nephi shook his head. 'No, you don't know what you're saying. I'm the only one of you who's killed a man.' They argued back and forth.

Lehi said quietly, 'There will be no fighting. No running away like thieves in the night.' He spoke with such authority that the four arguing brothers were silenced. 'We will win because we are right,' Lehi said. 'We will debate with Ezekiel in the valley of bones and see whose God is God.'

He gave a single clap of his hands. The matter was ended.

The sword blade had a lovely steely glint, and the hilt was gold. I stuck it through my belt and covered it with a linen Nazarene robe, rubbed soot from the hearth into my blond hair, and walked beside Lehi in the street. The crowds were too thick for bowmen to shoot at us from the walls or rooftops; the danger was an assassin among the people pressing around, a knife stabbing quick and close under the ribs. Flocks of sheep for the Temple barged and bleated past us, a dog tethered in a doorway watched hungrily. I snapped the chain between finger and thumb and the dog ran barking among the sheep, the sheep ran baaing in every direction knocking people over, plunging through doorways, tangling in washing lines, and sacrificial doves and pigeons flew up as the coops fell and broke on the stones. Street children scampered everywhere stealing whatever they could get their tiny hands round, and the guards on the Shit Gate didn't even see us in the excitement.

The valley of dry bones, Gehenna: where children had been (and street children still were) sacrificed on fiery altars to Molech. A dreadful place, the rocks white with bone dust, good fertiliser, the shit-tips drifting smoke along the merciless white slopes. Women and children with shrouded heads picked over the shit and broken pots, broken sandals, broken bones, putrid vegetables and foul meat, buzzing flies: a fine place for words. When I looked up I saw Ezekiel on the lip of the valley, a ragged barefoot man leaning on his stick, watching us climb through the tips towards him.

'Have you emptied your bowels?' he called down insultingly. 'You know this place better than I.' Some Jews called the gate we'd come through the *Asayya* Gate, knowing the cleanliness of Lehi's people: the priests never relieved themselves in the city but came through the gate to do so, usually while it was still dark, so the sun's rays sent by God wouldn't see the sinful filth of their bodies. 'Stop, crouch,' Ezekiel invited us. 'Better the shit comes out of your arseholes than your mouths, as words.'

'You'll hear my words come out of my mouth, and you'll know the truth of what I say,' Lehi promised, but he puffed for breath as we climbed. As we came near the skyline I saw seventy Elders gathered behind Ezekiel, then a whole crowd of the people of Jerusalem brought out on the rocky slope, and more coming. I looked back. The valley fell away below us.

Lehi brushed a fly from his lip. 'I am the true Zadok. Witness the truth of my fathers!' He held up the copper scroll-stick, then carefully unwound a hand's-breadth that shone in the sun. 'Hear me, I am Lehi who is the end, and the beginning is Noah the first holy man, who was chosen and saved by God. On this stick is recorded the names of all my fathers, even back to the father of us all, Adam.' Lehi raised his voice, reciting by heart. 'And Adam's son was Cain, who dwelt on the east of Eden; and Cain's son was Enoch, who built the city, and called the name of the city after the name of his son, Enoch. And Enoch's son was Jared, and Jared's son was Mahal'El; and Jared and his brother sailed from Shem beyond the ocean to a place where sunrise and sunset are one. And back in Shem, Mahal'El's son was Methusa'El . . .'

'No, you mean Methusa'Ya!' Ezekiel cried. 'The follower of Ya not El, and no man ever lived longer in Ya's sight.' He pulled a tightly rolled golden scroll from beneath his clothes. 'See! Gold! I too have a stick to beat you with!' The people murmured; gold was greater even than copper.

'Enoch walked the earth for three hundred and sixty-five years!' Lehi waved his stick. 'Here is the proof! Hear the correct record, the genealogy of my fathers! Methusa'El's son was Lamech—'

'No, it was Methusa'Ya who sired Lamech, at the age of a hundred and eighty-seven!'

Lehi stood his ground. 'No, Methusa'El's son was Lamech, and Lamech's son was Noah, my ancestor.'

'Lamech never had a son called Noah,' Ezekiel thundered. 'The sons of Lamech were Jubal and Tubal-cain, a mere brass-worker.'

'Perhaps he's right,' Laman whispered. 'Ours is a brass stick, isn't it?'

'It's holy copper, pure unalloyed copper, not a weapon of war,' Lehi hissed. 'Pure unalloyed truth. Stand behind me, boy!'

I yawned to Mara, 'I never can remember all these generations, can you?' But she threw me a fierce look. My love always takes everything seriously. She walked forward alone to stand at Lehi's side – a woman! An unmarried girl, a virgin in white linen, staring fiercely at the prophet Ezekiel as though she were his equal. 'Your own name gives you away, Ezekiel,' she called. 'Ezeki'El!' She raised her arms and we took up the contemptuous chant. 'Ezeki'El! Ezeki'El!'

Ezekiel shouted, 'Moses saw that Ya and El were one, one God.' The more we shouted, the louder Ezekiel shouted, then the Elders shouted, and then all the people shouted too, until the hillsides of Judah echoed to the walls of Jerusalem. Silence fell, apart from a few children who kept going to annoy us. Ezekiel muttered, 'Moses brought Ya and El together.'

'We too believe in Moses,' Lehi said. 'We follow the Law of Moses.' He raised the stick, reciting. 'And Noah's son was Shem, and Shem's son was Arphaxad . . .'

'I know all that,' Ezekiel said. 'So on for thousands of years to Abraham, the father of Israel.'

'The Philistines who called themselves *Hyksos* made alliance with the children of Israel and conquered Egypt.' Lehi waved the copper stick in the sunlight. 'It is written. The Israeli Yosef was made Pharaoh's vizier and high priest, and thus the scroll comes down to us.' He showed the strange Egyptian-looking writing. 'Yosef's sons were Ephraim and Manasseh.'

'Yes, so on down to Moses and Aaron.'

'I am the direct descendant of Aaron, the brother of Moses, who brought us out of Egypt.'

'Go back to Egypt,' Ezekiel said, and the crowd roared its approval.

'It's written,' Lehi held up the scroll. 'It's all written down. I know who I am. I am the true Zadok of the true God.'

'The Lord tells me to put on my sandals.' Ezekiel bent down and tied the latchets of his sandals over his bare feet. He stood straight. 'Hear me. My sandals are tied. Know therefore that the Lord speaks to me. These are the words of the Lord to your rebellious house. Sin no more! At the start of our exile the king of Bab'El came to Jerusalem and took King Yaukin away, and his priests away, so that Jerusalem would not lift itself up in rebellion against Bab'El. In return he made Zadokiah king of the city and took Zadokiah's oath of loyalty so that by his oath the walls of Jerusalem might be left standing, and the city might not be burnt, and the people might not be slaughtered. But, says the Lord, now Zadokiah sends Prince Mulek to Egypt for horses and armour and armies. Zadokiah has broken his oath that he took before Me, and he will know My fury. If Egypt tries to save Jerusalem then the walls of Jerusalem will fall, and the city of Jerusalem will be burnt, and the people of Jerusalem will be slaughtered.' Ezekiel glared. 'Get you back to Egypt, priest. Take your stick of brass with you, and bother us no more!'

The Elders looked at us with angry faces. 'Ezekiel's right,' Ya'Azaniah muttered. 'He's wise. It's wise advice, Lehi. Best go quickly.'

'I pray the God Most High will save you from your lost and fallen state,' Lehi said gently.

'It's you who have led your people into a lost and fallen state,' Ezekiel said. 'The Lord God says, Defile not yourself with the idols of Egypt. Lehi, you have rebelled against Me in the wilderness—'

Mara cried, 'God doesn't say that!'

Ezekiel raised the serpent-headed sceptre. 'The Lord God says, You have polluted My Sabbaths—'

'*You* pollute them!' Lehi cried.

Mara ran at Ezekiel. 'Unless you worship God in the right way the Messiah will never come to Jerusalem, don't you understand?'

'Jerusalem must be punished,' Ezekiel said, 'not destroyed.' He pushed her back with sudden wiry strength and she fell with her hair over her face. It was an extraordinary sight: the prophet knelt on one knee beside her and spoke as forthrightly as if she were a man. 'The Lord God, Yahweh-El, has promised me this. He shall take the highest branch of the high cedar and plant it on a high mountain.' He turned his face towards the Temple on the mount. 'On the height of Israel.'

'The Messiah,' Mara whispered. Lehi had made almost the same prophecy.

But Ezekiel shook his head. 'No. The Temple. A perfect Temple shall be built. God's perfect sanctuary.' He started talking about the size of the rooms and the shape of the windows, all the things he sat dreaming in exile at his lonely fireside I suppose. 'And in the Second Temple the priests of Zadok need not be the sons of Aaron, only sons of the tribe of Levi.'

Mara whispered, 'Without our Messiah we shall never be free.'

'I shall make you free,' Ezekiel said. 'You believe in choices, Lehi. Then choose freedom. Go. Be far from here.'

Lehi said doggedly, 'I will not go into the wilderness and live like an animal.'

Ezekiel held out his arm to the crowd gathering behind him, and yet more people arriving, climbing up out of the valley of bones. 'The Lord says to me, Son of Man, can these dry bones live? Dry bones, hear the word of the Lord: behold, I shall breathe breath into you, and you shall live.' I listened to the feet of the children rattling, climbing over the bones. 'The Lord says, I will lay sinews on you, and cover you with skin, and make a great army of you.' I touched my sword, but even I could not fight so many children. And they were unarmed.

Lehi shouted, 'The Lord Most High says to me, I shall open your graves, I shall put my spirit in you, and you shall live, and I shall place you in your own land, so that you know I have said it and done it, that you shall know I am the Lord Most High.'

Ezekiel raised his scroll. 'The Lord God says to me, Son of Man, take one stick and write upon it, *This is the stick of Judah, for the children of Israel.*' He scratched the words with the point of a knife, then held it out hilt first to Lehi. 'This is our parting of ways, the parting of our blood without bloodshed. Write on your stick, *This is the stick of Ephraim, for the house of Israel.*'

Lehi looked at the crowds gathering around us, and wrote it.

Ezekiel held up the stick in his hand against the stick in Lehi's hand, showing the two sticks to the crowd. 'The Lord says to me, Son of Man, speak a parable. Say to the rebellious house, Noah's vine, say to them: take the highest branch of the cedar, carry it to another land, plant it in a city of merchants by the ocean. Plant Noah's vine in good soil by the ocean that it might bring forth branches and bear fruit.' I saw Ezekiel's offer: one branch of Israel would build the Temple here, and Lehi's branch would have their chance somewhere else, Egypt perhaps, one of the Nile seaports I supposed. There was more. Ezekiel cried out, 'The Lord says to me, I will take the two sticks and make them one. I will take you children of Israel from among the heathen, and gather you on every side, and bring you into your own land, and the two sticks shall be made into one stick. You shall be no more two nations, neither shall you be divided into two kingdoms. I will save you wherever you are, and cleanse you: you shall be My people, one nation. And I shall return and set My sanctuary, My Temple, in the midst of you.'

Ezekiel took his stick tight in his fist, and Lehi held on to the other stick, stumbling backwards against me. The two branches, or sticks (sometimes Ezekiel had said *et*, sometimes *matteh*), of Israel had parted. The two tribes stared at one another, stunned by Ezekiel's prophecy: one day the scattered tribes would be gathered together by God into one nation. By means of God rebuilding the Temple, Ezekiel said; by the Messiah the Son of God born in the Temple, Lehi said.

The sun shone on the Temple, striking into our eyes. Ezekiel shielded his eyes, staring at me. 'Man of brass,' he said, then shook his head as though a bee buzzed inside it. 'A stream flows from the Temple to the Dead Sea. It turns the lifeless Salt into a sea with shoals of fish, and trees flourish along its shores.' The Salt was a name of the priests of Sion for themselves, their robes whiter than white, whiter than salt, frankincense-white: Sion that they had lost. Lehi had no place to go, and the crowds coming up pressed closer around us on every side. Ezekiel watched silently. He was too exhausted to know whether he had won or lost.

'Ezekiel,' I warned him. I smelt the breath of his followers, their sweat. A prophet who loses is false; false prophets are stoned to death. I shielded Lehi with my body. Any moment now someone would throw the first stone, then a hail of them would fall like a divine rain to wash us away. An urchin about ten years old bent down, picked up a pebble, I saw him. 'Stop,' I said. He chuckled and threw the stone, it struck Mara's forehead. She cried out and fell. The people crowded forward eagerly at the sound of her cry, smelling blood. I lifted her in my hand and brandished my sword in my other hand, sending sunlight flashing into Ezekiel's eyes. He stepped back, then stood aside.

'Go,' he said. 'Go, quickly. Save yourselves. I too return to my exile.'

I pushed Lehi forward so that his sons would follow him then turned back, pushing back the mob that tried to stop Sariah, her two babies and the younger children, then hurried the wives through. At the very end Mara's sister tripped on a pebble with a helpless cry so I picked her up too, carrying her angrily because the smallest slip would tip the mood of the mob into mindless violence. I'd seen it happen before. I've seen almost everything happen before. Quickly I put Marnlah down.

We shook the dust of Jerusalem from our feet without a waterskin or a loaf of bread to share between us, and the babies crying for milk. And then something new happened.

'I haven't lost,' Lehi said. 'I've won. I've won.' A small party of twenty or thirty tiny refugees walking in an immense desert: it looked much like losing to me, but when it comes to God people break the rules.

Mara was still unconscious so I took advantage of her. I carried her, kissing her bruised forehead, murmuring I loved her. Maralah walked beside me watching without expression, then walked with the other women when I didn't take notice of her. Lehi set an unforgiving pace, these people were used to desert travel, but soon Ishmael was gasping and grey-faced. I kissed Mara's forehead hot with the sun, her nose, her lips, I kissed her lips until her eyelids fluttered. Heat came into her eyes, she bit me. She struggled to be let go, so I let her go. She walked with her hands clenched in her hair, probably had a terrible headache. Once again she'd left Jerusalem without her Messiah; tears poured down her cheeks though there was no water to replace them. I left her to it and helped grey-faced Ishamel instead, who needed me more. We found an unguarded stream and the sun set, but still Lehi wouldn't stop. We rested when the moon set, then the sun rose and he walked again. There was no time to cook food so we ate honeycombs left by the deserets, honey bees. Lehi knew where he was going, but no one else did. The women kept silence, they didn't dare ask him. They began whispering among themselves. They knew it wasn't Sion;

the sun rose on our left, not in our faces, and set on our right hand. I helped carry the babies. The women didn't trust Zoram the librarian who stumbled with us; a man who has betrayed one master will betray another. They were afraid he left signs for the people of Jerusalem to find us and kill us, but Nephi said he was honest, and Zoram gave Lehi his oath. But still Lehi wouldn't say where he led. 'It's Ishmael's valley,' Sariah said. 'We'll stop there.' I gave up the babies and lifted Ishmael who was about to die, carrying him in my arms; he wouldn't let me stop.

At a valley in the dusty wilderness Ishmael's wife and eldest daughter Abihail ran up to welcome him home, and Ishmael died. We buried him before sunset. 'Not here,' Lehi said. 'I won't stop here. No more here.' He broke down the roof of Ishmael's house with an axe and we drove the flocks ahead of us as we walked – and I remember there was an old donkey to carry Sariah and the babies, and later Ishmael's wife when she was exhausted by grief. This time the sun that rose on our left hand fell to a glaring sunset straight in our eyes. Lehi had turned west towards Egypt.

I remembered this wilderness road of Shur from Abraham's time, less a road than a swathe of grazing nibbled short from horizon to horizon. We met no one. On our right lay dunes and marshes and the sea just visible like a blue brush line drawing itself forward as we walked, yet unmoving. The sun set in front of us, silhouetting a caravan of plodding camels, and Lehi kept going all night to get ahead of them. Laman, Lemuel and Sam complained that their wives were tired. Nephi said nothing. I fell in step beside him in the moonlight. 'Well? Do you know where he's going?'

'Yes.'

I waited. Nephi looked at me as though it were the most obvious thing in the world. 'My father's going where the Lord Most High tells him.'

'You never question him, do you.'

'Who? God or my father?' Nephi shrugged his broad shoulders, not understanding me. 'No. In life we're always at a crossroads. There's always a right way and a wrong way. We simply always choose the right way to get to God.'

'Thank you, Nephi.' I handed him the sword. 'You're going to need it more than I am.'

He took it and from the way we walked in silence I realised I'd made a friend. Ten minutes of silence from Nephi was worth a thousand words.

We overtook the camels in the night, seeing no sign of them in the sunrise behind us. The River of Egypt broke the horizon ahead and Lehi changed course to avoid the Balah forts, sleeping at midday, slipping across the river at night, the waters barely knee deep at this time of year. Another day in the sun. Both animals and humans were suffering now, but Lehi wouldn't slow down. Darkness fell, the desert sand gave way to grass and then to mud, and I heard stems clacking and hissing in the night wind. I splashed forward in the slime, tasted the brackish water – and in my mind was transported back three thousand and more years to the land of Shem, the reedy river delta of the Perath where it meets the gulf. 'Nephi, where's this?'

'My father knew this land for many years. The Reed Sea of Egypt.' All night we pushed through the papyrus reed-beds, and dawn revealed the sea of reeds swishing and waving all around us except for an island ahead, Irreantum, with a few fruit trees. From a treetop I looked down on a wilderness of many reedy channels and lakes cut off from the sea by a long tombolo, an embankment of sand thrown up by waves. Surf broke on the far side and I saw the spray. 'Ocean,' Nephi said.

I jumped down. 'It's not the ocean, just the Mediterranean, the Middle Sea. All that's left over from the Flood.'

He nodded. 'Together with the Caucasian inland seas to the east and north. I know. The people have pale hair and blue eyes like you, it's said.'

'You're well informed.'

He pointed at the scroll that hadn't left Lehi's hand during the journey. 'We alone know where we come from.' I said quickly, 'I hope you know where you're going.'

He chuckled. 'It's written. The bountiful future is ours to make what we will, under God.'

I dug a well and built a shelter for them from branches and reeds. The dry stems made an excellent crackling fire, sending sparks blowing in the night wind. The firelight glowed on Lehi's white blowing hair like brass. 'I have dreamed a dream.'

'A dream,' Laman said. 'Look at my blisters. You said we won't go into the wilderness. Where are we? The wilderness.'

Mara whispered, 'Is it a dream of the Messiah?'

'A man in white linen came to me,' Lehi said. 'We are not lost; by our defeat we are saved. Jerusalem will be destroyed. The people of Jerusalem who hated us will be destroyed. Nothing will be left standing. Even the Temple.' I looked around the ring of firelit faces as they tried to imagine it: no Jerusalem, no Temple. The breeze gusted, making the flames roar.

Mara asked, 'When will the Messiah come?'

'In six hundred years He shall redeem us.'

'Six hundred years.' Laman counted his fingers. 'Isn't that just a little too late? Isn't that our bad luck?' His brothers laughed, except Nephi.

'Bless you, Nephi, because you believe in the Son of God.' Lehi stoked the flames with a reed. 'He shall be born of a virgin, a Nazarene.'

'Yes!' Mara said.

'She shall be His mother after the manner of the flesh.' Lehi laid the flat of his palm on Mara's head when she tried to interrupt him. 'No, hush, child. He shall be the Lamb of God. He shall be a healer, an *Asayya* as we are.'

'Who told you this?' I asked.

Lehi said tenderly, 'An angel.'

'What did the angel look like?' I know what angels look like; I've seen Ishtar with my own eyes, her immense wings dark as black gold, the muscles twisting in her chest as her wings beat at the air. I've seen the dragon; with Dan'El I'd even seen the golden angel worshipped by Nabuchadnezzar, blackened like cheap alloy by smoke. Now Lehi was saying there were good angels.

'I saw a golden man with golden wings.' Lehi held out his arms to make his followers understand. 'Treading on the air like this, in a glory of gold!'

'How do you know he was an angel sent by God?' I asked, but Mara said, 'Sssh!'

Lehi said simply, 'The angel showed me the land of promise. He showed me my children, a great nation, as numerous as grains of sand.'

I said, 'Where's this great nation?'

'Beyond the ocean.'

'I thought that's where souls go after death.' I looked at Mara. 'If you believe in souls. Do you, Mara?'

'The living may travel there also.' Lehi held up the scroll. 'The place where sunrise and sunset are one.'

'All souls live for ever,' Mara said passionately. 'Men. Women. Even children.'

'Yes, this is what we believe,' Lehi said. 'Immortal souls. The Messiah sacrificed by the cross the false Sadducees wear on their foreheads in their false pride, but reborn.'

'Even dogs have souls,' Mara said. 'Every ant, everything that's too small to see. All the men and women and children and babies and unborn children, dogs, and ants, and every' – she used the Greek word – 'atom.'

'God has not shown me all that,' Lehi said, quieting her. 'But God has told me, Blessed are they who shall seek to bring forth my Sion. I shall guide them with an iron rod.'

'Guide us where?' Laman said, alarmed.

'Across the ocean.'

'There's nothing beyond the ocean,' I said. 'I've sailed with canaan traders to the end of the Middle Sea. I even sailed northward along the coasts to the land of tin. But to westward there's nothing but ocean until the end of the world.'

'We're not going,' Laman said.

Lehi held up the scroll. 'A new land can be found beyond the ocean. The genealogy of my fathers tells us that. "Enoch's son Jared and his brother sailed from Shem beyond the ocean." Nin had told me almost exactly the same thing.

'Perhaps there's something to it,' I said.

Lehi said, 'The Lord broke down the great tower of Bab'El and scattered the people so that each city spoke a different language.' I remembered all the accents and dialects of those days, each city behind its walls with its own god, the people of Enoch hardly knowing the people of Ur. 'That's true,' I said. Only the language of the canaanite traders had joined them; and they had left and gone west to Canaan, Abraham trailing after them.

'I won't go,' Laman said. 'It doesn't say Jared *got* anywhere, just that he set off.'

'The Lord showed Jared how to build an ark,' Lehi said. '"In the wilderness Jared built eight arks and launched them in the Red Sea."' I said nothing, but in those days all sea was called the Red Sea, even the gulf of Eden that I remembered. 'I have faith,' Lehi said, 'that the Lord who brought Noah to dry land brought Jared to dry land beyond the ocean.'

'What land?' Laman said.

'The land of promise, choice above all other lands, which the Lord God has preserved for a righteous people, and the nation that possesses it shall serve God.'

'If God tells us to go,' Nephi said, 'I for one am not staying here.'

'I'm not going,' Laman said. 'We're not going.' The young men jumped up shouting, fists bunched.

I left them to argue, walked quietly to the edge of the island. The planet Lucifer rose glittering from the sea of reeds, announcing the first glow of the sun. To the north winked the star Merak and westward, towards the ocean, Jupiter set its reflection in the Middle Sea. I heard a soft footfall and knew without turning who she was. I asked, 'Do planets really sleep in caves beneath the earth?'

'No,' Mara said. 'They go around the sun.'

'Doesn't sound right. About as likely as immortal souls and lands beyond the ocean.'

'Horseflies and mosquitoes as big as your fist.'

I stared at her in the dark. 'Did God tell you that?'

'Wotan, Wotan, do you think there's one single thing God *doesn't* tell us, if only we have ears to hear, eyes to see, and hearts to feel?'

'I love you.'

'No.'

'If only I could see you.'

She stood against the dawn so that I saw her image like a black cutout.

'Even like that,' I said. 'Delicious. I still love you.'

'*Delicious?*' She gave a high laugh. 'You're so incredibly . . .' She searched for a small enough word. 'Ordinary.'

'You mean masculine. Isn't it wonderful? I still mean you're delicious.'

'Stop it. I hate it when you talk this way.' Her hair blew like fine curly black threads. 'You're incapable of love. There's no place for you here, Wotan. You should never have happened. I'm not for you.'

'Maybe you don't know God as well as you think you do.'

'Just leave me alone!' I wouldn't, so she ran away, but

she bumped almost at once into Nephi. He blinked as though awakening, staring at her. 'What is it?' she asked, frightened, and turned to me instinctively. Her body was wiser than her mind.

'The Lord spoke to me,' Nephi muttered. 'I must build a ship.'

'No, we must go back to Jerusalem,' Mara said. 'Somehow.'

'You mean an ark,' I said.

'No. Not an ark that drifts.' Nephi was definite. 'A ship. A ship with a rudder.'

'What's a rudder?'

'The Lord will guide us,' he tried to explain, 'but we'll steer the rudder with a pole so that we are free to steer our own course, make our own fate, our own choices right or wrong.'

I looked at him sceptically. Maybe Nephi had been to a seaport and seen ships with long oars angled over the stern for steering, but he seemed genuine. 'All right,' I said, 'a rudder.'

'The Lord told me.' A smile broke out all over Nephi's face, his eyes shone. 'Build a ship! Build a ship!'

I shook the tree beside us, almost breaking the fragile wood. 'From fruit trees?'

Nephi's face fell, then he gripped my elbows. 'You'll help us, won't you?' He wrapped his arms around me, lifted even me – me! – off the ground in his enthusiasm. 'The Lord will show us.'

'I don't know,' I said. I looked back at Mara, at the different emotions passing across her face, hope, fear, doubt. She didn't know what to believe any more, what was possible, or impossible.

Nephi lost no time. The Lord had told him to make tools so he found an ash tree somewhere on the island and made a bow and arrows, hunting the gazelles that grazed between the marsh and the desert, returning with skins to make leather bellows. 'What do you need bellows for?' I asked. 'A furnace,' he said. He got the women to make reed baskets then carried black mud from the marsh, mixed it with dried reed, and made bricks for a furnace. I asked, 'What do you need a furnace for?' He filled the furnace with veined Sinai rock, telling me, 'You can't have a ship without copper nails.' I told him, 'You can't have a ship with copper nails if you haven't got wooden planks to hold them.' Nephi insisted, 'The Lord will provide materials.' For days he pumped the bellows like a madman to feed the flames, but he had no charcoal. The fire was reeds and sheep dung and would never grow hot enough to melt rock, however great Nephi's faith. Laman jeered at his young brother's failure but was secretly relieved. 'You're not getting us on that work, we're staying here to plant vines,' he said, and even Lehi's face grew longer, doubting his industrious favourite son Nephi had truly heard the Lord. 'That lad hasn't got God in him,' Laman said. 'He's just fooling us. We warned you.'

Mara came to my reed hut where I lay on my side eating a leg of lamb. 'You've got to help him,' she said. 'You can't let him down.'

'Who?'

'Nephi. And yourself.'

I belched lamb, wiped my mouth and hands. 'You really believe this stuff about Jerusalem being destroyed, six hundred years, all that?'

She shrugged. 'You and me are the only ones here God doesn't talk to. You say you're a son of God. Maybe so. But you're on your own, abandoned the day you were born. Lehi says God talks to him. Nephi does too. I don't hear a word, not a word.' She was getting tearful.

I reached out. 'What can I do to make you love me?'

'You'll never make me love you,' she said. 'Please. Help him, that's all. Please.'

'I'll think about it.' I watched her go. How could she possibly resist me?

I went on the beach, tapped Nephi's shoulder. 'I'll show you how to build a ship.' I called the others over. Nephi stared at me with white eyes from a weary face blackened by smoke. 'Give me your sword,' I said. 'Quickly.'

He gave me his sword and I jabbed Laman with the point. 'You, take the donkeys and baskets, take your grumbling brothers with you, go to the Dead Sea, and bring back all the pitch you can carry. Don't argue. Steal it from a camel caravan to Egypt if you have to, just get it.' I turned to the daughters of Lehi and Ishmael. 'Twine together young reeds to make rope, lots of rope. When you think you've got enough, make more.' Lehi asked what he could do and I said, 'Get me flax, a whole field of good Egyptian flax.' I called out to Zoram and Abigail, 'You two, you're always together' – Abigail giggled, Zoram looked embarrassed – 'together you can cut the young reeds for rope. When you've cut a thousand, cut two thousand. When you've cut two thousand, cut three thousand.' While they worked I took the sword into the thickest part of the reed-beds, up to my waist in slime, and turned to Nephi with a grin. 'Don't worry, I've done this before.'

I hacked the reeds down with great sweeps of the blade, cutting twice sixty poles of papyrus-reed of sixty cubits each, leaving them piled like debris from a storm as I worked forward. I threw a rope around the cut reeds and carried them in great bundles to the island where Nephi and Abihail, Ishmael's daughter who was the same age as Nephi, laid them out to dry on the beach while I drank wine. 'You shouldn't drink wine,' Nephi said sternly.

'Why?' I demanded. 'God told you not to?'

'Wine makes you make bad choices,' he said. 'It makes your tongue say words you wouldn't.'

'The truth maybe.'

378

'The truth is always sober,' Nephi said earnestly.

'I'll make her love me somehow.' I turned to Abihail. 'What d'you think about her? You think your little sister Mara will ever love me?'

'No, it's Maralah who loves you,' she said. 'Why are you blind about us? Mara only makes you unhappy. All I know is I love Nephi, and Abigail loves Zoram, and you should marry Maralah.'

'Yes, I'd like imagining she was Mara too much.' I, who've made love to three dozen women in one night, lay asleep on the sand dreaming impotently of loving Mara just once.

So I showed Nephi how to build the boat, how to twist the dried reeds tight to help keep out the water, how to tie the bundles together to shape the sides, how to build the boat higher and broader with each layer. 'Curious workmanship,' Nephi said, tightening the knots with a special tool, but I could tell he was impressed by the sheer scale of the construction. 'No ship has ever been seen in the world with timbers like this,' he said. How wrong he was. I remembered them well.

When it rained I found the papyrus more absorbent than the berdi-reed I was used to; at last Laman arrived leading camels laden with black pitch. I thinned it with oil and painted over the hull and deck to make them waterproof, but not watertight – the sea's a reed ship's friend, sloshing freely in and out as it rides the waves.

Time came to float the ship before the upper decks made it too heavy to launch: everyone gathered to push. My legs sank in the sand to the thigh, my muscles bulged like barrels, my linen clothes split, ropes whipped; then the vessel, rust red (the age-old colour of thinned pitch), slid slowly sideways, lifted, suddenly moved easily, and the water took the weight. Lehi could move the reed ship with a press of his hand. I made an anchor from a boulder, cut the ash tree for a mast and helped the women weave the sail. Reed huts with thatch roofs were erected on the deck fore and aft, and where the stern rose high I called Nephi up. I invited him, 'Show me the rudder God showed you.'

Nephi made the device for himself, pushing a pole through the platform almost to the water below. He tied a deep blade of driftwood, painstakingly carved, to the pole, leaving one-third of the blade's length forrard of the shaft and two-thirds abaft, then lowered it fully into the water. On deck he took another, shorter pole and cut a square hole in its end, fitting it over the squared top of the vertical pole, hammering it down level with a stone. Moving the tiller above moved the rudder below. Even Laman was impressed. Everyone had a go.

'Tomorrow we'll collect the fruit and nuts and seeds,' Lehi said. 'Lambs, chickens, salted meat. Grain for loaves of bread.'

'No bread.' I shook my head. 'No fires on a reed ship.'

'What, no bread to dip in our wine?' said Sam.

Nephi promised, 'The Lord will make our provisions so sweet we won't need to cook them.'

It was supposed to be our last night on shore, but it didn't work out like that.

That night the bonfire blazed high on the beach and Nephi announced his marriage to Abihail. Everyone got wild singing and dancing around the flames, wine or not, and I was certainly drunk as a lord, dancing the young bride around me until her bridal white fluttered like wings, then I danced with the other girls, trying to get close to Mara and warm her up, but the more I came forward the more she moved back. Finally I saw my opportunity and grabbed Mara from behind but she turned in my arms, laughing, and she was Maralah. Maralah clung tight, whispering in my ear, 'What's Mara got that I haven't?' She pressed herself close as we danced and I closed my eyes.

Somebody screamed.

More screams, confusion spreading through the firelight. Hoofbeats, jingling harness, lathered dusty horses falling in the soft sand, men tumbling, a cart spilling out women as it overturned. I leapt on horseback at the leading man, grabbed him, jumped down with him in his glittering brass armour and purple cape, threw him on the sand. He cried in a familiar voice, 'It's us!'

'Prince Mulek?' I lifted him by his bloody shoulder-plates. Mulek's beard hung from his cheekbones, his eyes stared, desperate. 'Thank God for your fire,' he gasped. 'Beacon. Saw it. Thank God.' He wept. I poured wine but he choked on it. 'All dead.' His wife Zarah ran forward, shining clothes torn, her hair fallen out of its ringlets. 'All dead!' she cried, clutching him.

Lehi said calmly, 'Tell us what has happened.'

'My father King Zadokiah – my brothers—' Mulek vomited, clutched the sand in his fingers. 'All dead.'

Zarah said, 'My husband saw his brothers executed by the king of Bab'El. Their murder was King Zadokiah's last sight, he was blinded while their blood still splashed hot in the dust. His shoulders were chained to a weaver's beam, he's been dragged by hooks in his jaws to Bab'El. No one knows if he's dead or alive. He's dead.'

I said, 'Zadokiah rebelled? He slaughtered the occupying troops in Jerusalem? He went ahead without the Egyptians?'

Mulek screamed, 'We were sure the Egyptians would hear me! I alone survived!'

'The Lord Most High preserve us,' Lehi prayed. 'These are all who are left?'

'All. All closest to me.' Mulek shrugged. 'Twenty, thirty.' About the same number as us.

'All closest to the Lord High God?'

'All closest.'

Lehi said, 'Then, King Mulek, all is not lost. All is won.'

'Won?' Mulek cried. 'Jerusalem is destroyed! The Temple's destroyed, gone, not a stone left standing on another stone, not one. There are no Jews in Jerusalem.' He covered his face. 'There is no Jerusalem.'

Lehi said calmly, 'You see, we are vindicated. The Lord punishes the people of Jerusalem for their wickedness, as I prophesied. He punishes Jerusalem and the Sadducees for their disbelief and abominations, condemns the crimes and falsehoods of their false Zadok and their moon-worship. We are the people of the sun, free to make a new start. God's purpose is in us. We shall build a new Jerusalem in a new Sion.'

People who moments before had been lost in despair raised their heads and looked up. Mulek muttered, 'A new Jerusalem?' Zarah's eyes shone.

Lehi raised his arms in the firelight. 'The Lord shall see. We shall live in the sight of the Lord. Between King and Priest, Melchi and Zadok, our clean living and morality shall rule in New Jerusalem, and there we shall earn the salvation of the Messiah.'

I pointed out, 'There's not room to take everyone on one ship.'

Lehi said: 'Build another ship.'

So I took Nephi's sword and cut twice sixty poles of papyrus-reed of sixty cubits each, laid them out to dry, and set King Mulek's women to work making ropes, and his men to work with tools that pulled the great bundles tight and closed the knots. Nephi made the rudder while Mara and her sisters sat expertly weaving a second sail. While the second ship grew tall in the shallows the first ship was moved into deeper water and loaded with nuts in sacks, salt meat, fruit sweet and sour, deseret honey in jars, and fresh water in skins. Nephi was anxious to try the heavily laden vessel. 'Don't worry,' I said, but Nephi always worried. While the young girls remained on the second ship weaving the sail, for two days the brothers and I poled the first ship forward. The channels between the mud banks and reed-beds turned to a maze of dead ends. I climbed the mast and called down directions to the nearest open water. We heard the swell breaking beyond the tombolo but could not reach it; finally I plunged into the slime with a rope and by brute strength hauled Nephi's ship after me into the lake. It had been a calm morning but suddenly Lehi's white hair blew forward, the sail billowed, and the ship overtook me with foam at its bow. 'Keep going!' I called, letting go the rope. 'Keep going!'

The ship lifted in the waves breaking over the bar where the Reed Sea mingled with salt, Nephi pushed at the rudder, and the ship turned down the wind into blue waters. I watched, peeling leeches off my skin, until the ship shrank to a reddish dot following the coast westward.

Suited me. I'd be with Mara. I swam back to Irreantum.

'They've gone,' I greeted Mara. 'Looks like I've got a second chance to dance with you.' She walked away. Mulek called, 'Lend a hand here, Wotan. You're my mighty man.'

'Give her up,' Maralah whispered, tugging my elbow. 'Look at her. She hates you. Look!'

'Mara's afraid,' I said. 'Afraid of loving me. Of giving up her search.'

'What for?'

'She thinks there's something greater than love, marriage, a few children.'

Maralah breathed out. She didn't need a reason or long words. She just knew what she felt. 'I'm not afraid of loving you.' She looked at me steadily. 'I do love you.'

I watched Mara work with the bone needle, the sail draped over her knees. I murmured, 'I can give Mara everything she ever wanted.'

Maralah said, 'You. Marvellous you. Do you ever doubt yourself?'

'*Me?*' I tried to imagine self-doubt. 'I can give her love.'

'She doesn't know what love is,' Maralah said in her flat voice.

'She knows,' I said. 'Love's all she wants. Love's what she needs. But she's asking too much. For a love that binds together everything. A reason for everything.'

'But there isn't a reason.' Maralah tugged my arm. 'There isn't a reason for anything. Don't give me God. Why should I suffer like this?'

I hardly noticed her. 'Isn't Mara fantastic?'

'Wotan, look at me. Stop saying her name.'

'Love's so big and small and simple Mara can't see it however hard she looks. Mara thinks she's got to carry the world on her shoulders. Order. Discipline. Obedience. Deserve God. No swearing. No drinking. And when Mara's deserved Him enough, in return He'll send His Messiah to dazzle us and teach us what love really is. The answers to everything. Eternal life, eternal worship. So she waits.'

'I can't live without you,' Maralah said. She pulled my arm to make me look at her but I watched Mara's needle dip and slide in the cloth, its tip moistened between her lips, then dip and slide again. Maralah sobbed and ran away somewhere. A rope broke on the boat and I jumped up to lend a hand.

Someone shouted. Troops were coming into the marsh. Egyptians maybe, or Jews, it didn't matter, everyone was our enemy. Mulek's military officer, Benjamin, attempted to prepare defences, but the defeated courtiers were in no condition to fight, they were outlaws; they'd lost their war. 'Hurry! Get aboard!' The ship was barely ready; we bundled aboard all the food and water we could carry and poled the vessel seaward. I saw the heads and helmets of men bobbing through the reeds, trying to cut us off. Arrows whined and I pushed everyone into the huts fore and aft. Benjamin was struck in the leg by an arrow, then burning arrows set the thatch alight. The men didn't know what to do. Zarah and the women swept up water in their skirts and threw it over the flames. Then the wind caught the sail as we came to the lake, I stood high on the stern and pushed the tiller, and the ship lifted to the waves in the open sea.

'It works,' Mulek said. 'God be praised, Nephi's contraption actually works.' He turned to me as his expert on nautical matters. 'If God wills, we'll catch the first ship today, won't we?'

'Not today.' The horizon beyond the horn of the bow was flat, dark blue, empty, but the coast drew a sandy line on our left. 'Nephi will keep in sight of the coast. The coast will guide him.' I remembered years ago, the first of the First Dynasty of Egypt, King Meskiag, had hugged the coast of Arabia all the way from the gulf of Eden to Wadi Barramiya, pulling ashore in any likely bay for fresh water. At the moment the nights were moonlit, with no danger of passing the other vessel in the dark. 'Ration the water. If we push hard and don't stop, we'll catch them up.'

'Are you sure?'

'Of course Wotan's sure,' Zarah said, her dress torn to make bandages for Benjamin's wound. Later everyone gathered in the belly of the ship, the bound reeds creaking around them, the sail creaking over them, the occasional salty wave sloshing up through the reeds over their feet, and prayed. Each dawn they prayed as the sun rose. The sea turned brown around us and I pointed to the lowlands of the Nile delta on our left. 'Here the Great River flows into the sea.' I kept far from land, beyond sight of traders and towns, though we saw the great bonfires of lighthouses in Pharaoh's ports. At dawn the sea was blue, and the coast was empty desert.

Day after day the coast was empty desert, and the wind blew us in and out, but we saw no sign of Nephi's ship. 'Has it sunk?' Mulek asked.

'Reed ships don't sink,' Zarah said, with a glance at me. So I knew she'd been talking to Mara.

Every night the horizon was flat, moonlit, empty. The full moon waned, the wind blew us inshore and at dawn I saw a bay with palm trees fed by a stream. We landed for fresh water. I felt the embers of a fire, still warm, then pulled out a burnt crust. 'They baked bread.' We stoked the fire and baked our own loaves, refilled the waterskins, and hurried on under full sail.

Mulek asked, 'This is still not the ocean?'

'You'll pass the pillars of Hercules tomorrow.' At midday the next day we pulled ashore for water beneath the great white rock of Hercules, whose legends are in fact my own; not one of them a lie.

This time the embers of the beach fire burnt my hand. 'Closer. Twelve hours. Less.'

'The last night of the moon,' Mulek warned.

I took the tiller. 'We won't down sail at sunset.'

And so we sailed into the ocean. The men wailed at the sight of the great seas, and the wind backed and blew us southward along unknown regions of African shore.

All night the ship heaved sluggishly in the deep-ocean swell, rising on mountains of seawater until I reached up to touch the stars. 'You'll never reach them,' Mara said, climbing the tiller platform beside me. 'Not even you.' The ship fell away, sinking into the valleys between the mountains, then rose again until the stars were close. I jumped, reaching with my fingertips. 'You're a creature of this world, Wotan,' she said, pitying me. 'You'll never be more.' The wind from the north blew chill and she shivered. She went quickly back down the ladder.

'Mara.' I dropped my cape down to her. 'Don't get cold.'

She wrapped herself in my cape and sat on deck watching me, or the stars, I couldn't tell.

We heard the other ship before we saw them. 'Listen!'

Calls and laughter in the darkness ahead, then among the rising and falling seas we heard voices singing pornographic songs to Tammuz, the dying and reborn god always popular with women. 'Let me kiss you with the kisses of my mouth,' they sang, 'your love is better than wine.' Drunken laughing. I recognised the braying of Lehi's eldest daughter, who'd married Ishmael's son Ayn. Somebody shouted, 'She's got nipples like ripe grapes. Let's see her honey.' I wished I was there. They were having a wonderful time.

Mulek called up to me, cursing them. 'They've got demons in them!' Nearby the reed ship rose like a shadow in the moonlight, pale foam pouring from its sides as it wallowed in the troughs of the sea. The sail fluttered aimlessly in the wind, trailing ropes. I pushed the rudder, the ships came close, Laman saw us. He waved Nephi's sword, its blade black against the dawn. 'We're not going to hell,' he shouted. 'We're going back home to grow wine and drink and die happy.' The others danced around him shouting encouragement, bellowing abuse at us with rude gestures.

Mulek called, 'Where's Nephi?' No answer. 'Where's Father Lehi?'

I recognised Lehi come on deck by his white hair. He argued with Laman but Laman pushed him back. Sariah cuddled her babies into her clothes, hiding their faces. Where was Nephi? The sun struck across the sea and I saw him bound tight with ropes to the mast, gagged. 'We're tired of his voice,' Laman said. 'We're not having any more of his God. Go away!'

'Mutiny,' Mulek said. He looked at Benjamin lying helpless, his leg wrapped in bandages, then turned to me desperately. 'Is there nothing we can do?'

Easy. As we rose on the peak of a wave I plunged in, swam down the watery valley, then let the rising wave lift me aboard the other ship. Laman staggered at me, but a drunk can't fight on a rolling deck with a wineskin in one hand. I knocked him down, stood on his neck, helped myself to his sword, and cut Nephi free with one slash of the blade. 'Don't kill him!' Nephi said as I raised the sword. 'Laman's just jealous because I'm his younger brother, but God speaks to me not him.'

'He'll be trouble,' I said. 'Let's kill him.'

'I won't,' Laman said hoarsely. 'We won't. Don't.' He screamed, gurgling, as I debated whether to cut his throat or cut his head off. I was angry with him because I'd rather be joining in the fun and drinking.

'My elder sons have tried to turn my heart to stone within me with their blasphemies and sins,' Lehi said, then saw my savage face and said hurriedly, 'but be merciful to them, Wotan. Their wives are with child.' Lehi's own daughters, the wives of Ishmael's sons Cumor and Ayn, which means Source, broke away and knelt before him begging for their lives. 'We too are with child.'

The other women, rapidly sober, said: 'We're all with child.'

I sighed, seeing Lehi would spare them. 'They'll be nothing but trouble,' I said. I whacked at Laman, Lemuel and Sam with the flat of the sword. 'I'm staying aboard.' I whacked them until they cried out like sheep, then made them pull the ropes that set the sail. I put the women to work repairing the ropes and weaving a rope longer and thicker than the others, then forced the brothers to pour the wine over the side. 'We'll die of thirst,' they complained.

'God will provide fresh water,' Nephi said. 'Sail forward, and water will be provided!' The brothers looked up at the cloudless sky above, the salt ocean below. 'We're going to die,' they said, and lay down.

Lehi whispered, 'Bless you, Wotan.' I hid a full wineskin that I'd kept back for my private use, then tied off the new rope woven by the women. I let one end trail over the stern to the bow of the second ship, so the two ships sailed joined in one purpose on our voyage; whatever disaster or blessing befell one would befall both. 'Like a marriage between a man and a woman,' Nephi said. 'God will guide us in the right way.' But Mara was on the other vessel.

I climbed the tiller platform, turning the ship so that the rays of the rising sun threw my shadow along the deck below, and the wind filled the sail. The rope tightened, water spraying from its strands, and the second ship sailed with us.

Day after day God's wind blew us, falling calm for prayer at dawn and dusk, then blowing steadily all night. After dawn prayers He made the wind blow steadily all day, pushing the ocean waves forward alongside the ship. Each day His sun rose on the nape of my neck and set in my eyes; each day its heat burnt hotter on top of my head, until I stood shadowless.

The new bright rope joining the two ships darkened, growing green and ragged with weed; the two ships wallowed sluggishly, weighed down with weed like trailing hair. We drank green water, and Laman claimed God punished us for throwing away the wine. Seawater sloshed and slurped through the deck a little higher each day, soaking us and our supplies. Our clothes were stiff, crusted with dried salt. Day after day we ate salted nuts. We ate salted meat. We ate salty bread so stale that we pounded the loaves with stones to break them. The salt made us more thirsty and swelled our tongues so we spoke like drunk men and women, and our joints swelled for want of fresh food.

I drank my wineskin to the last drop, pleasantly drunk while I steered the ship westward all night, keeping the star Merak on my right eyebrow and the North Star on my right temple; and the people slept, trusting me.

Weeks passed. My wine was gone. Nothing but the empty sea ahead of us, the empty sea behind.

'Turn back,' Laman said.

The wind fell calm and Lehi's people prayed to the sun rising behind us. But today the sun did not rise. The wind did not blow. The sky was a glaring haze. Behind us a mountaintop of black cloud rose from the horizon. A mountain chain of cloud spread out to each side like black teeth. The sea lost its motion, lying dark and heavy as lead. 'Tie everything down,' I said. 'Tie yourselves to the ship.'

Daylight was darkness; then it began to rain. At once the people undid the ropes and jumped up crying out with joy, catching the fresh pouring rain in their open mouths, in pots, rinsing the salt from their clothes, even the women prancing naked and shameless as in Eden, wringing out fresh water from their clothes into their mouths. 'Don't leave yourselves naked in God's sight!' Lehi cried out as lightning flashed, but they laughed for joy. They pulled down the sail and stretched it out so the rain filled it, then filled the empty wineskins with fresh water. 'God's rain!' Nephi cried. 'I promised you.'

I heard a sound like thunder, but there was no lightning. The sea rose up behind us like a waterfall, and the joy of the people turned to terror. They clutched the ropes they'd let go, trying to bind themselves, then the storm broke over us. The ship staggered, swamped, then came up through the foam into the blast of the tempest. The sail burst upwards from the deck flailing like a living soul, held down only by a rope on one corner. I pushed the tiller into Nephi's hands, jumped down, tied down the sail with ropes, tied down the people to the ship.

For four days the wind blew. On the second day the rope joining the two ships fell slack and I pulled in the ragged end. It looked as though great teeth had cut it through. 'There are monsters in the ocean,' Lehi said. 'So they say. Leviathan. Others.'

'Everyone knows that's true,' Nephi said. Father and

son clung to the steering platform. 'The God of men, Deus, the dragon, Leviathan, *ho theos*, Satan.' Nephi turned to me. 'Do you believe it?'

'It's all true. Everyone knows that.' But to be honest I was more worried about Mara. I saw no sign of her ship.

'For forty years of tribulation the Sons of Light' – Nephi beat his chest – 'will fight the Sons of Darkness. The Temple destroyed – all foretold in the scrolls, in the genealogies of my father!'

'It's true,' Lehi said.

'A Beast will rise up out of the sea.' Nephi exulted in the storm. 'A great dragon red as blood, the serpent of Satan in the Garden of Eden, who cursed women with knowledge. Seven angels will blow seven trumpets and hail and fire mingled with blood will fall.'

'Some people say these old stories already happened, long ago,' I said. 'Not *will* happen.'

'No!' he cried. 'A great mountain burning with fire will be cast down into the sea, one in three of the ships will be destroyed, and a great Star will fall from Heaven to Earth. To Him will be given the key of the Underworld, the bottomless pit, Hell.'

'I know these stories,' I said. 'The Zadoks pass them down from father to son. Noah—'

Nephi said: 'And when the seventh angel's trumpet sounds, the mystery of God is revealed.'

'They're not stories,' Lehi said. 'They're the truth. One day you, Nephi, my son, though youngest, in your turn you will know all the true secrets.'

I pulled the tiller, pushed, pulled, fighting the storm. 'Secrets? They're stories about the truth. Shouldn't we all know what they are?'

'They're facts,' Nephi said. 'Facts that have happened and will happen again. God will come into this world. He will occupy His creation.' He stood with legs apart, arms outstretched, shouting. 'I believe in God! I believe in God!'

I caught him before he fell overboard. 'I believe God sent this storm,' he shouted. 'God teaches us!' But still I worried about Mara.

On the third day of the wind I glimpsed her ship blown in the same direction as we. Once during the night I heard a great creaking of reeds, felt a rush of spray, and glimpsed her vessel close to us beneath the storm-wrack. The bow rose up and I saw Mara's pale face. Our ships slid apart on the wave that had brought us together and I saw her raise her hand, in farewell perhaps.

Dawn crept beneath the clouds, grim and dismal dawn. The fourth day; both ship and crew were finished. Great bundles of reeds had sprung loose from their knots and the people lolled where they were tied, too exhausted even to pray, passive in their exhaustion as the waters poured over them.

The wind was halted.

A circle of blue sky was opened over us, like a great blue eye opening.

Around us the waves leapt up in points, no longer knocked down by the wind, then tumbled down. Our ship drifted waterlogged in a sunny flat calm. We shouted. We all shouted. We were saved. Lehi climbed the bow and led the people in a prayer of thanks.

On the far side of the circle of calm I made out the red dot of Mara's ship. I realised this wasn't the end of the storm, only its eye moving over us. When the wind began again, it would blow from the opposite direction. Beyond her ship a vast wall of cloud blew the wrong way, funnelling round in a great curve towards us. 'No, no,' I muttered. The wind caught her ship, blowing it to my left. I stared back. We, by the time the eye had passed over us, would be blown to the right. I ran to the sail, hauled it to the top of the mast, but it hung slack. Still dead calm. In the distance I saw Mara's ship swallowed by spray and cloud.

'Mara!' I shout.

I slide down the mast. Seize an oar. Row. The oar snaps. I seize two oars, row, row, the muscles stand out on my shoulders, the sweat pours on my face. But however hard I row towards Mara the sea pushes me back. Foam surges from the bow but we hardly move. I redouble my strength, but the wind begins to blow against us. I pull all my strength into me, working like a madman, bending the heavy oars like reeds. The wind roars, blowing the ship over so that the oars are torn from my hands. People scream, hanging on, then slide down the heeling deck. I run to the tiller to wear the ship round before she overturns.

I know I'm too late.

The sea bursts open and a horn as red and shimmering as living blood rises up above Lehi, above the bow, above the ship. After the horns the dragon's head rises ponderously from the sea shedding spray, towering above us, rising high as the storm clouds. 'Huwawa?' I cry, but nobody hears my voice. More than Huwawa, guardian of the forest. Sea thunders from the blood-red scales of the dragon. The neck snakes up like shining blood over us.

The eyes open almost at the same moment. Huge eyes, fierce, cruel, loving. In them I see a million screaming faces, and hear a million voices screaming worship. I may be seeing the face of God. My strength's gone. I'm nothing. The ship's overturning and the people will founder, nothing I can do to stop it or alter it. There's no mercy here. 'You're not God!' I shout. 'You are not God.'

I know his face now. This is the beast Noah saw in the abyss of stars, the fallen angel, the serpent of Eden. B'El, whom so many worshipped, and worship still. *I am B'El, the Son of God. I am Baal, B'Elial, B'Elzebub, B'El-Zephon, S-T-N, my name is Lord. I am Lord Prince of this world, this world is mine, these are my people. I am S-T-N whose name is too holy to be said aloud, oldest of the old, greatest of the great, who suckled closest and most loved at God's bosom.*

The people scream as the ship, overturning, throws them down.

'Satan,' I whisper. 'You're Satan.'

He knows me. Satan knows me. His head comes down, down. His unblinking eye fills me, liquid, quivering, passionate, yearning. Such sadness I can't look away. This time, he speaks without thunder.

'Give me the crown of stars that is lost.'

His talons come out of the sea to crush the people. He stops. His claw lifts the ship like a wave to spill the people down, then stops. Satan stops.

'Look!' Lehi cries out in wonder. 'It's He. Him. Messiah. Our Saviour, Lord Jesus Christ!'

A man dressed in white walks towards us on the water. He walks unsmiling on the peaks of the waves and in the valleys between them. His white linen shift and royal cloak blow in the wind. His long hair, gold circlet and bearded face sparkle with beads of seawater thrown up by His golden sandals. His eyes glare fierce as a king's, His fingers glitter with royal jewels and imperial seals. He's infinitely better than us, above us, we don't deserve Him, shabby fallible failing creatures that we are. Yet he gives His love to us, holds out His arms to us, imposes His forgiveness and salvation on each and every one of us, except me. Not me. I understand: I've too much blood on my hands, I am a man of blood, not worthy of redemption. And perhaps, with all my experience, I do not really believe in Him: that one man can change the world.

Lehi crouches on the bow of the ship as it teeters, rolling over. 'Lord Jesus Christ, save us!'

The figure moves His finger, and the ship is set right.

The people drowning in the sea are washed back aboard.

The dragon falls back, gone.

I grabbed Nephi. 'Did you see Him?'

Nephi was busy with a rope. 'Who?'

'Did you see the dragon? Did you see Satan?'

'Yes, Satan's all around us, everywhere,' Nephi said busily. 'We must be constantly on our guard. Help us raise the sail.'

'I saw Him.' Lehi gripped my elbow. 'I saw the manifestation of our Lord.' His eyes filled with tears. 'The Jesus Christ who is to come saved us.'

I hauled on the sail and looked in vain for Mara's ship. All I saw was clouds and rain. Mara, of all people, had not witnessed the miracle.

The storm blew, but not so hard. Waves broke against the ship, but not so heavy. The hurricane that had blown Mara westward blew us northward, growing cool. Far behind us, as the weather cleared, I thought I glimpsed a chain of tropical islands curving away like the crater-remnants of a gigantic volcano, or the ring of debris from some vast explosion in the sea. But then the rain closed in again, turning to hail, and the cold wind blew us north.

'Land!' How often I heard that cry. There was land beyond the ocean; we'd found the end of the ocean, but now it was the land that seemed to have no end. Day after day from the masthead, seagulls cawing around me, I glimpsed a slow unfolding steamy misery of marshland, with lakes or perhaps another sea gleaming beyond it; but the wind blew us eastward, and the current pushed us northward. Then for several days the sun set behind distant rolling mountains. Once we even saw the pale sandy bottom of the sea, with waves breaking over it like a whale's hump. At last I seized an oar and rowed. I rowed all night, and when dawn came land was on each side of us, and we were blown northward into the mouth of a river.

I made out a long narrow island of hills, and pulled for shore.

The bow grated on muddy sand. Lehi jumped down. His yellow cloak shone in the sun. He lifted his white linen shift fastidiously, showing his scraggy knees, and knelt.

Lehi kissed the sand. God had promised Lehi his children would be as numerous as the grains of sand.

'Lord God most High,' he cried, 'Your will has brought us, Your chosen servants, here to the land of promise. Here we will serve You in humility and freedom, under God. I name this place New Jerusalem!' He stood straight, held out his arms, and turned his face to the sun.

'I name our land of promise New Sion!'

XIII

The present day
Salt Lake City

'Mommy,' Christine says. 'Mommymommy.'

The two fat yellow cabs, travelling nose to tail in the evening traffic, follow the Jordan Valley into Salt Lake City. Winona, white suit crumpled by days of travel, still cuddles her baby. Floodlights reach up from the horizon, bathing in a golden glare the gigantic copper angel standing atop the Temple's tallest spire. In the headlights she sees Tallboy's shoulders and head silhouetted in the cab windows in front, almost touching the roof. She leans towards the driver. 'Don't let him lose you.'

'Losing? Who's losing who?' Cowboy demands. 'He's doing fifty-five. This is my fare.'

'Enjoy the ride' – Winona remembers his name – 'Chris.' She drops a hundred dollar bill into the cab driver's lap.

'Right.' The driver pushes it safe between his legs. 'Mohammed. Pleased to meet you. Nobody loses me.'

'What's this, losing?' Cowboy asks plaintively. 'Who're we following?'

'Take it easy,' Mohammed yawns, 'all this guy sees is my high beams.' He looks in the mirror. 'Dah, cute kid. Walking yet?'

'Mommy, Mommy.' Christine plays with Winona's necklace, hums a snatch of the tune playing on the radio.

The DJ comes through. 'This is KBZN-FM, and that was Hoagy on piano.'

'Piano,' Christine says.

'Mine's walking, two boys.' Mohammed nods his head in time to the tune. 'Year old.'

'That damned kid's three days old,' Cowboy says. 'So she says.'

Winona points. 'Go, go! Losing him!' A Ford cuts between the cabs at the traffic lights, then a battered pickup. The Ford turns right but the pickup weaves ahead of them, stuttering smoke. More stop lights, then Tallboy's cab swerves into the left lane. 'There he goes. Left, left!'

'KBZN-FM,' Christine says. She hangs on as the tyres squeal.

'Listen, I know who's driving that guy.' Mohammed waves his fingers. 'Abdul, he don't know this city no more than me. We're like brothers.' He examines her in the mirror with frank interest. 'Who is he, that guy, your husband? You think he's cheating on you? Relax. Not in this city, lady. They don't. Maybe somewhere else but not here.'

'He's not my husband,' Winona says. 'I'm not married.'

Mohammed's mouth turns down. 'That how you make your living, I guess?'

'No,' Winona says. 'I fuck for love. Always have.'

'They won't like you here, lady.' Mohammed follows the cab, takes a right. 'This is Virtue City USA. Uh-uh sex before marriage. Uh-uh divorce. Give all your money to the church.'

'I need a drink,' Cowboy says.

'Uh-uh strong drink.' Mohammed wags his finger. 'Drink, smoke in private clubs only. The Dead Goat. I'll take you. Look out.' He hits the brakes. Both cabs stop, cars queuing on each side. 'That's it. Must be the Temple. Something big.' Crowds gather by the granite walls, moving back past the vehicles. He leans his elbow out the window. 'Hey, Abdul, what's up. It's a parade?' Mohammed pulls his head back inside. 'Shit, it's a parade. I love this country. Hey, your friend's looking over his shoulder. Smile lady. He know you're here?'

Winona ducks down. 'No. Maybe. Is he getting out? Is he running?'

'No, he's cool. Why should a man two metres tall run from a woman? He's paying Abdul off, mean tip. Looks foreign.'

'English.' Winona bends double behind the seat, smiling as Christine plays with her lips.

'Sure, I hate foreigners too. Now he's walking. Hey, it's not a parade, it's a wedding. Get going if you don't want to lose him.' Winona slams the door, chucks back money.

Mohammed turns to Cowboy. 'Listen, when does a man two metres tall run from a woman? Answer: when the woman's two and a half metres tall.'

'And some,' Cowboy mutters. 'Turn round, get me to the Dead Goat. I'm forgetting today.'

Winona pushes past the happy floodlit faces in the crowd. Gospel singers, tambourines. Missionaries busy at work. Boys in suits, beautiful little girls in skirts and white bows. Someone says, 'Here's kind of what Heaven is like, I guess.' Winona sees Tallboy, head and shoulders above the crowd, panama hat, long ginger hair on the shoulders of his white suit. He looks round, thin face pale as a horse's skull, eye sockets dark, but Winona's behind the man holding down a huge bunch of balloons. Tallboy walks on, she moves forward.

A stall sells pots of sweet deseret pudding. The woman gushes, 'Yes sir, the very food sent by the Lord to sustain Lehi in the wilderness.' Tallboy hands over a dollar and eats going along the sidewalk, drops the stuff underfoot with a grimace. Winona paces him, hidden behind the coaches parked in front of the Temple except for glimpses between them, but then there's a big open space.

Temple workers, old women wearing white linen, hold the crowd back. Tallboy's surrounded by women looking up at the Temple, waving, calling up excitedly. He wipes his lips on his handkerchief, yawns.

Winona stares as the Temple doors are thrown open, and down the Temple steps comes a beautiful girl dressed in white, pure bridal white. The breeze pulls out her veil, she's lovely. Her face is radiant, virginal. She's married, just married, her husband walks hand in hand down the steps beside her, and she walks as if she could fly. She walks as if her white satin shoes don't touch the granite steps of Utah at all. Winona whispers, 'Mary?'

A second girl dressed in white appears with her husband at the top of the steps, then a third. More brides stream down from the Temple all dressed in white, their husbands with them, the flaming Sword of Solomon and the All-Seeing Eye visible through the open door behind them, their marriage ceremony exactly the same as that ordained by God for marriage in the Temple of Solomon almost three thousand years ago, even to the recitation of names of the Melchizadok Priesthood. Winona can see the sun stones and star stones, the star Merak in Ursa Major pointing to the North Star: the stars that guided the navigators to America. The first bride reaches the bottom step and Winona stares at her face, whispers, 'Mary? It's really you?'

The girl overhears, pauses, laughs. It's her day. 'Yes, I'm Mary! How did you know?'

'No, I'm Mary,' the second girl says. 'That's *my* secret name.'

The third girl looks surprised. 'I'm Mary too.'

The girls behind say, 'We're Mary.'

The Temple worker pushes Winona back. 'Troublemaker,' she says gruffly. 'Get on with it, girls, get your pictures taken. Christmas weddings,' she explains. 'So romantic.'

Winona says, 'I didn't mean to make trouble.'

The rough-voiced old woman watches the young girls pass, remembering herself once. 'They're all Mary today. Today's secret name. They're not supposed to tell anyone. Can they keep their mouths shut nowadays? Can they?'

'They're all so beautiful.'

'Rented. The duds. Got to give 'em back clean as they got 'em.'

The young husband of the first Mary looks over her shoulder at Winona. It's his big day too. 'Hi, I'm Enoch.'

'Don't you start,' the old woman warns. 'All the husbands are Enoch today.'

'Enoch!' laughs the young man. 'Enoch who was taken by God to Heaven without tasting death.' He kisses his wife's flushed cheek as the snapshots flash.

'I blame the new liberal service. Not like the old days when I was sealed to my husband,' grumbles the old woman as the crowd thins. 'Those days Hell was Hell, and we took the oath of vengeance against the United States for persecuting us. You betrayed your secret name, your tongue was ripped out and your guts gushed on the ground like Judas Iscariot's.' She looks round, then calls after Winona, 'Hey, you're one of us, aren't you?'

Christine burbles, 'Enoch, Mary.' Winona runs, and Christine hangs round her mother's neck with her small strong hands. 'Mary, Enoch.'

'Hush, darling.' Winona slows, strokes her daughter's fine blond hair. 'Not long now.' The stores shine with Christmas lamps, frosty fir trees, fake snow. Santa hands out Temple literature. Tallboy waits to cross the road, the traffic stops, he walks with the crowd. The people stream to the car parks but he turns into a smaller street. Not so busy. Winona crosses to the far side, hangs back.

Tallboy stops in a doorway. He doesn't move for five minutes, watching the sidewalk behind him. A police cruiser idles by.

Tallboy's gone. The doorway's empty.

Winona runs between the traffic. Now she sees it: a dark delivery road between the buildings. Iron fire escapes, rubbish, no drunks, no homeless. She walks with long strides. A building lot, chain-link fencing, security lighting, a crane soaring into the dark. Beyond it Tallboy moves like a pale ghost by a truck park, delivery vans, mostly white – she almost loses him. He comes in sight, still watchful, then walks decisively. Big metal warehouses give way to older warehousing, stone with dark windows, mostly broken. Alleyways between them, she follows his echoing footsteps. Right, left, another left. Silence.

An opening door spills coloured light. As Tallboy goes through the doorway she sees the neon sign inside, red against the dark: *NEW JERUSALEM CLUB*. The narrow corridor ends in a steel door. Beneath the spy-hatch there's the usual Utah state notice, *Members Only*.

The hatch opens, a fat face squints suspiciously. Tallboy's recognised. The door half opens on a chain, he squeezes through, the door slams behind him. The lights go out.

Winona stands in the darkened alley. 'Non-members twenty-five bucks,' she murmurs.

'Enoch, Mary. Mary, Enoch.' Already Christine speaks better, the palate of her mouth is knitting. 'Non-members twen-five bucks.'

Winona chuckles. 'Twen-*ty* five.'

Christine says seriously: 'Twen-*ty* five bucks, Mommy.'

'Come on, you need your sleep.' Winona walks quickly back to the road. At the 24-hour drugstore she buys deodorant, an expensive perfume, toothbrush, toothpaste, dental floss, a romper suit and a spare four sizes larger and other things, including a one-piece black aerobics catsuit her own size with a pair of soft indoor shoes, also black, and an overnight bag to put them in. 'Where's the nearest best hotel?' The checkout girl points two blocks east, past the all-night U R Hardware outlet where Winona buys the largest pair of heavy-duty snakeproof leather workpants, an outdoorsman shirt and two heavy-duty door bolts.

The Sion Inn has five stars and a fountain in the four-storey lobby atrium. 'I'll take a balcony suite. You have a baby listening service?'

'Of course, Mrs—' The concierge sweeps the offered Visa card in the machine. 'Dr Winona Wotan, yes, our Temple Suite. All Sion Inns offer crèche and nursery services. In addition we provide qualified nanny—'

'I won't need that. Send up room service. I need a couple of steaks, thick cut, rare, on the bone. Lobster in the shell, Atlantic not Pacific. Make that two lobsters. A bowl of avocado pears, big. The usual salads. Nuts. Wholemeal bread. Plenty of salt.' She calls back from the elevator, 'Oh, and don't forget baby food. Lots of baby food.'

'Right away, doctor.'

Alone, Winona yawns and lies on the bed. Christine crawls beside her, cuddles. 'Mommy need sleep?'

'No, Christine need sleep.' Winona grins. But she is tired. She looks tired. It's begun.

She plays with Christine to keep herself awake. Room service brings the food. Winona opens half a dozen pots of baby food and lets Christine eat. 'Messy eater.'

'Christine want lots of baby food.'

'You don't miss a thing, do you?' Winona sits beside her on the bed, strokes the hair from Christine's eyes. 'You'll have teeth soon.'

Christine smiles. 'Got teeth.'

'I love you.'

'Christine love Mommy. Love you.'

'I'll never leave you, baby.' Winona really means it. And it's true, because it never happens that way: the child always leaves its mother. She knows that. Winona's eyes gleam bright blue, filling with tears. 'You're always in my heart, baby.'

Christine yawns sleepily. Winona jumps up maternally. 'Quick, brush teeth, brush hair. Nightclothes.' She lays Christine between the soft covers already asleep. Looks down tenderly. 'I'll always be there for you, baby. All you have to do is ask.' But she knows they never do.

She tucks her in, tests the baby alarm, turns off the bed light, half closes the door so she can hear if Christine wakes in the next few minutes.

The room service trolleys wait in the centre of the split-level living area. Flowers, too. She breaks a lobster in half and stands at the balcony window eating, watching the lights of the city. She cracks the lobster claws between her fingertips, licks out the meat, then helps herself to a steak in one hand and a loaf of bread in the other, eating as she checks out the bathroom. Back in the living area there's a clock behind the flowers on the mantelshelf: nine o'clock, plenty of time. While her bath fills she helps herself to the other lobster and steak, slides the balcony doors open, leans her elbows on the railing and watches the tiny cars passing below. Back inside she eats the avocado pears and a bowl of nuts, drinks a couple of bottles of mineral water, then can't resist the platter of whipped cream profiteroles. Just one. She never can stop at one. Neither could Wotan; she wolfs a whole dozen. 'Stop it, Wotan. I'll get fat.' But she can almost hear him laughing. She wolfs the rest. *Now you've got cream on your lips. I can taste it.* She dabs her melty-chocolate fingertips on her cheeks, looks in the mirror. 'I couldn't eat another thing. Just one. Good enough for you? Now I look like a' – she almost says red Indian but bites her tongue – 'indigenous American.'

You look like a Jared woman. A blue-eyed red Indian woman from the red sea.

'You like that?'

Don't forget your bath.

403

She races for the bathroom, turns off the water just in time, takes off her clothes. She sees only the blur of herself in the full-length mirror, poses. 'Shame it steamed up, huh?'

You feel lovely. I love being in a woman. Inside your skin. Inside your heart. Yum. Like making love all the time.

'I feel older, Wotan.'

No. You're lovely as always.

She slides her naked body into the bubbles, leans back with a sigh. 'I never want to grow old.'

You never will. I promise you.

'Because you love me.'

Because I love you.

She washes her face luxuriously, then her hands play with her breasts. 'Stop that. Stop it, stop, you beast! Don't make me, you're disgusting, it's masturbation.'

I haven't had a woman since we got pregnant. I'm dying of lust.

She washes herself all over, washes her hair. 'Good,' she says.

She towels dry, talcs herself, slips into the catsuit, combs out her long blond hair then pulls it back, ties it tight behind her head in a businesslike knot. She checks Christine's still asleep – Christine snores! – then pads through the living area, glimpses herself in the mirror.

You look magnificent, Winona.

'Let's go.' She steps out on the balcony, slides the glass doors closed behind her, then jumps up lightly on to the railing. The night air feels good against her bathed face, her perfume smells good, even the distant roar of traffic far beneath her feet is perfect. She turns to face the building, jumps out and down to the rail of the balcony below, steadies herself on her toes, jumps down again. On the seventh floor two naked lovers drink champagne. On the fifth floor an elderly man with binoculars stares at her blankly, then examines his binoculars, but she's already gone. She leaps from the third floor balcony on to the hotel forecourt, jumps the flowerbed and the ramp to underground parking, runs along the dark service alley then from the hotel garbage skip she springs on to the end wall, swings up on the roof behind, and from there on she goes fast, following the rooftops up and down to the warehouse district.

She slides face forward down a rickety slanted roof seven storeys high, peers over the gutter into the alley below. A gaggle of non-members, mostly young, wearing short skirts, wait outside the New Jerusalem Club. A middle-aged guy arrives, leather waistcoat and single gold earring, John Travolta hair, strong face. He waves his membership card like a magic wand. The girls cluster round him. 'Take us in, give us a break, mister.' But he seizes on a waif-like girl, smaller than the others, who hangs back shyly with her boyfriend. Their faces shine with Salt Lake City innocence. Nothing bad happens here. 'You,' the strong-faced guy says. 'You want to join the party?'

'Sure!' she says eagerly. 'I'm Jeri. This here's Todd.'

Winona watches. Walk away, Jeri. Walk away, Todd. Don't go in there.

'I'm Simon. I love our liquor laws,' says the strong-faced guy. 'Both twenty-one, right?'

'Sure!' Their young voices echo up the narrow walls to Winona high above them in the dark.

The strong-faced guy grins: 'Simon Says, here's the deal. One of you goes in.'

'Which one?' Todd says. He should have said no.

'Up to you, Todd. Your choice, you or her. One of you joins the party tonight. One of you has a good time.' Jeri claps her hands excitedly. 'Yes! Me!'

Todd says, 'No, she can't, she's only eighteen.' He's lying, Winona hears it in his voice. Todd's eighteen, maybe; Jeri's younger.

'You're such a nerd, Todd Bascoe.' She pushes him

away, appeals to higher authority. 'I look older than twenty-one, don't I, Simon Says?' She trusts the strong-faced man, he's old enough to be her father, maybe even looks a little like him.

'Sure, you're old enough.' The strong-faced man takes her elbow. 'You look perfect, Jeri.' For a moment light streams her shadow across the alley as he takes her inside, then the steel door slams closed. 'Hey,' Todd says. 'What about me?' The girls groan, giving up, scatter with a clatter of high heels to try somewhere easier. None of them wants Todd. 'Get lost, loser.' He waits alone, face flushed, then a police siren wails in the distance, and he puts up his collar and walks quickly in the opposite direction.

Winona slides over the gutter, jumps down the grimy wall from windowsill to windowsill. 'Take me.' He looks round, looks back, and she lands lightly by a streetlight in front of him. 'Take me to the party, Todd. You'll get her back.'

He's not tall; he gazes at her stiff sexy breasts like all young men do, then stares up hopefully at her face. 'You in the movies?'

'Not in this life.' She smiles, puts her arm on his shoulder. 'Listen to me. This is real. In real life you can't leave her, Todd. You can't just turn and walk away.'

'Yeah. Right. Watch me.'

But she takes his elbow, walks him to the door. 'They tell you in church about bad things, don't they?'

'Oh, yeah, they sure do.'

'Better believe them, Todd.'

Winona steps past the grimy bricks into the corridor and the lights come on, gleaming off the steel door. The hatch opens, the plump sweating face looks through the bars, stares up. 'Who the hell are you?'

'I've come to join the party.'

'She wants to join the party. Fuck you. Members only.'

Winona keeps her arm resting lightly on Todd's

406

shoulder. She puts her free hand between the bars, pulls the face between them, kicks the door open, breaks the chain with her hand, goes inside. 'Come on, Todd.' A couple of guys come downstairs reaching into their dinner jackets, she throws the first guy through the office door and the second against the wall, steps on him going upstairs. The rhythmic thud of music beats through the reinforced walls. 'This way, Todd. You'll find her.'

'Jesus, me, I hardly know her.' He's terrified. 'Jeri who? I should care about her.' Winona gives him a cold blue look and he trembles. 'Who are you, for God's sake, her mother?'

'A man must fight for his woman, Todd.' Winona throws a man downstairs, steps across the bolted steel DJ platform over the elevated dance floor. The music's too loud, strobe lights flash, below her the dancers flicker like an old movie. There's Jeri: Winona jumps down into the roar of sound and movement, forces a way through the dancers, stands tall between Jeri and the strong-faced man. Simon smiles, opens his hands, steps back. His lips move. Take her. The music stops so abruptly that everyone feels deaf, then the dancers' feet shuffle loudly, slowing, stopping.

'Take her,' smiles the strong-faced man. 'Simon Says, no contest. She's yours. I didn't realise she was so young. I didn't know anyone cared about her. Here.' He pushes Jeri at Todd. 'My mistake.'

Winona says, 'I'll speak to the Englishman, Tallboy.' She looks around, raises her voice. 'Anyone? Tall as me, but thin. A weak man. White suit, shoulder-length red hair. English accent.'

Simon shakes his head. 'No, no one here like that. Anyone seen a creep like that? We haven't seen anyone like him here. Sorry.'

Winona tells Todd: 'Get Jeri out of here now.'

Jeri splashes her drink in Todd's face. 'I'm old enough to know my own mind!'

Someone laughs, the music cuts in, lights flash. From the corner of her eye Winona sees a shape in a white jacket slipping away from the bar. 'Tallboy.' She jumps the railing from the dance floor, runs after him down the ramp into the circle below. 'You seen him?' Startled faces. Plush carpet down here, semicircles of red leather banquette seating, an empty stage. She pushes between businessmen and politicians served drinks by cheerleaders. Among the shiny shoes and polite conversation a white panama hat lies where it fell. A few paces forward a broad staircase curves down from the centre of the circle.

'Anyone see him go?'

A couple of guys in dinner jackets take her arms. 'Time to leave, lady.' She throws them over the bar counter into the bottles. Alcohol fumes fill the air with seductive perfume. A liqueur bottle glugs liquid red as spilt blood across the carpet. She vaults the stair railings and goes down to the circle below.

Look at this! This level's for naked girls, Winona! My kind of place. Maybe there's a sauna. 'Stop it.' She searches the doorways. Bedrooms, kinky furniture, surprised men with big bellies, big-bottomed girls, big breasts. 'Stop looking at them.'

'Get her!' shouts an English voice. Heavy-set guys, bare hairy arms, come up from below. She knocks them about, throws them down, goes downstairs among the sprawled bodies.

'Got a gun,' Tallboy calls from the far side of the auditorium. The screen behind him writhes with naked bodies, twisting limbs. Doors everywhere, on every side; shrieks of pain, screams of pleasure. Stainless steel and plate glass windows, green with thickness. Winona walks steadily forward. Tallboy's hand shakes, she can see the gun shaking. An automatic pistol, silver-plated. He calls, 'We're on the same side.'

'We're not on the same side.'

408

'Fuck you.'

'I saw what you did at Zarahemla,' she says quietly. 'I saw.'

'Zarahemla? Apachio-bloody-whatever in the bloody jungle? So bloody what?'

'Better run, Tallboy.'

Tallboy backs a step. 'Stay back you bloody bitch.' But she follows him step after step down to the next circle. Weird lighting. The air's hot down here, desert heat.

'You killed them all, Tallboy. I saw the tape. A hundred times. You killed everyone who knew.'

She's closer. Tallboy points the gun at her with both hands. 'Knew what, bitch? Come on, come on, I'll kill you.'

'I know what you stole, Tallboy.' The gun's going to go off anyway. 'The paintings. Jesus Christ in America. You stole the paintings from the Holy of Holies of the Temple. Eyewitness paintings.'

Tallboy jerks the trigger. The bullet sings off the wall behind her. She prowls forward, hunting him. 'The porters who carried them out lived for a while. Everyone else was dead, you killed them. The students, just kids, dead. Tanya and the film crew dead. Martin tortured and dead. Your own thugs too, you even killed your killers, they'd all seen too much. All died for those paintings of the Itzá, the Christ. Professor Martin Rendell knew they were real and true, didn't he? Jesus Christ came to America. You couldn't get Martin to deny Him.'

'All he had to do was swear they were false. We didn't know. Couldn't tell. Couldn't feel it.' Tallboy sights down the barrel, but Winona doesn't stop. He shoots, smoke spurts. Still she comes forward.

'You took the paintings, the three of you. Gonzalez. Snowflake. You. The porters carried them across the border. The airstrip at Chichanhá, I guess. Single-engine plane, not enough room for you. So you stayed behind, you killed the porters, then took time off for rest and relaxation at San Lazaro. I know. I saw. I watched. Then I followed you here.'

'What do you want?'

'Snowflake. The Negro with the German accent. Give me Snowflake.'

Tallboy backs away, shakes his head. 'Why him?'

'He's deep in, isn't he? Snowflake knows of the dead. He knows a lot. I heard him tell Martin on tape. "The dead do not return in this world, not in the flesh, not as they were." That's what he said. Gonzalez asked Snowflake for his expert opinion on the paintings and Snowflake bragged, "Everything has its price, and I know the price of everything." But even he admitted he couldn't value the paintings, he only knew they were priceless. Yes, Snowflake's got them all right.'

'I'll blow your fucking head off if you don't back off.'

'Snowflake smuggled them into this country. Maybe even here, I guess. Salt Lake City.'

'*Back off!*'

'Snowflake knows what to do with them. Where to place them. He's a collector.'

Tallboy breathes through his mouth. 'An agent for a collector. Don't do this.'

'I want Snowflake. I want them back. I want the collector. The collector who's intolerant of fakes, frauds, lies, anything less than the almost-perfect truth. Gonzalez spoke of him.'

'*Gonzalez?*' Tallboy screams at her. He shoots at her, runs down to the circle below.

It smells of smoke and iron down here. Tallboy's gone. The air stinks of flesh. 'Can't see him,' she murmurs to herself. 'How far down's this? I think we've come to Hell. Hell's in Salt Lake City.'

It's the sixth circle, Winona.

She mutters, 'It can't be this bad.'

410

Go further down.

She goes down.

Hear that? Sounds like children crying.

'Oh my God.' Winona covers her ears. 'This is a dreadful place.'

He went down further. Go on.

'I don't want to go any further down.' But she can see the steps curving down.

Go on. This isn't Hell, Winona. Hell's worse. This was dug by men with bulldozers and cranes and planning permission. Shut your eyes.

'I can't.' She covers her ears but the screams and cries echo through her head.

Silence. Winona steps from a broad curved staircase into a deeply carpeted movie foyer. Soft high-quality Muzak plays along beige stucco walls lined with glossy adverts for cars and movies. Near the ticket booths Tallboy empties the gun at her, she takes her hands from her ears as she comes forward steadily towards him. Each shot sounds louder. Tallboy lets the empty ammunition clip fall on the carpet. The smoke clears, sucked smoothly into the air conditioning.

Tallboy backs away from her. 'Who are you?'

She holds up her right hand, turns it. The triangular scar on the back of her hand through to the palm. The scar of the dragon's tooth.

Tallboy shudders. 'He spoke of you.'

'Who?'

He shakes his head. 'Can't.'

She says gently, 'I'm not asking for the collector. Tell me where I'll find Snowflake.'

Tallboy backs away from her. A couple of women in nice clothes come from the ladies' room talking about something that interests them, go through the double doors on the right.

Tallboy says: 'The Reformed Temple of Sion of the

411

Prophecy.' He pushes his way backwards into the men's room. 'East 100 South.' The door swings closed, showing a little picture of a stick-man.

Winona touches her left shoulder, wet with her blood through the holed black catsuit. The blood stops almost at once. She pushes open the men's room door with her foot, goes to the long row of basins, washes her hands in a basin, dries her hands under the hot air dryer. When her hands are dry the noise of the blower falls quiet.

She hears Tallboy crying like a child in the end cubicle. She touches the cubicle door with her foot and it swings open.

'Don't kill me. Don't kill me.' Tallboy's sitting on the toilet with his gun in his lap. He looks up at her. 'It wasn't my fault. It's a violent world.'

'Not compared to the Old Testament it isn't.'

He holds up the gun, points it at her. 'I loaded a fresh clip.'

'You're only going to need one bullet, Tallboy.'

Winona turns away. She leaves the cubicle door open, walks across the tiled floor, lets the door to the men's room close softly behind her. She leans back against it, closes her eyes wearily. When the muffled thud of the pistol shot comes she knows it's over. She checks anyway, then crosses the foyer and goes through the swing doors trailing bloody footprints, comes down the steps from the movie theatre into the street. It's a different part of town, but she recognises the floodlit tower of the Sion Inn in the distance.

A few minutes later she climbs over the balcony railing, slides the glass door open, slips inside. Christine's turned herself over in the broad double bed but she's still asleep, still lightly snoring. She looks even more grown-up in the few hours since Winona left. Christine's hands twitch in a dream, her closed eyes move.

Winona pulls off the catsuit, groans. She's too tired to

wash her shoulder. She slips into bed beside her daughter and Christine turns towards her suddenly in her sleep, holding her tight in her arms.

Winona kisses her, strokes her daughter's hair.

'I love you. Don't leave me.' Winona's eyes close. 'Never leave me, Christine.'

She sleeps.

Christine's eyes pop open. She lies motionless, staring, listening to her mother mumbling in her sleep.

Era Three

New Sion

New Sion
586 BC – AD 30

Our New Jerusalem. Our New Sion. Our land of promise, of milk and honey.

I jumped down from the ship's bow, sloshed ashore through the shallow water. Our Garden of Eden. Our virgin earth, our world without sin. Our New World without the Devil.

Lehi lifted handfuls of muddy sand, his face radiant. 'This new land is more, *more* than the old land God chose for us. This is the home we chose for ourselves. It was our choice to come here, made of our own free will. We had faith that we would not sail over the edge of the world. Faith that the ocean had an end. Faith in ourselves. Our faith brought us here, and with faith, under God, we shall flourish here.'

Nephi jumped down, kissed the sand. His muddy face beamed. 'In this land we'll worship God.'

'It's dark soon.' Laman pointed at the sun. 'Where will we sleep? What about wild animals? What if the ship drifts off during the night? What if a storm gets up?'

I pulled my strength into me and hauled the ship ashore, sinking to my knees in the sand, the creaking hawser rubbing deep into my shoulder. I tied it to a great tree as tall as a cedar. Gently I lifted down Abigail and Abihail, their bellies big with child, then helped down Sariah and her toddlers Jacob and Joseph, then carried down the other babies who'd been born on the voyage, Lehi's and Ishmael's grandchildren. Older boys, sons of Laman's, Lemuel's and Sam's servants, ran joyously on the sand. They play-fought with wooden swords, screaming happily; one day I'd teach them to be proper swordsmen. 'Be quiet, boys!' Sariah shouted, worried by the dark unfamiliar forest and swirling tides. She asked Lehi, 'Husband, could there be danger?'

'Danger? Here in God's land?' Lehi said. 'This is our God-given land. The only dangers are the ones God sends, to test us so that we choose the right decisions and improve ourselves constantly in the sight of God. I know this is true because I saw the Son of God save us in the sea, and saw Him still the storm, and saw Him throw down the serpent, Satan. We're free.'

'More of your visions,' Laman said. 'Isn't that right, Nephi? Our father speaks like scripture, but he's just making it up.'

'I didn't see anything with my own eyes,' Nephi admitted. I left them arguing behind me, seized an axe, and for the first time since the creation of this land came the whistling thud of a steely axe blade into the trunk of an oak. Again, again, again: within five minutes, less time than for a single prayer, the tree fell with a thunderous crash, knocking down half a dozen smaller trees in its fall.

'Houses!' I cried. The low sandy headland by our landing site was carpeted with turf. I dragged back great clumps. 'Make roofs!' I called, then sent the children for deadwood in the forest that clothed the island. 'Fire!' As darkness fell around the bonfire the women brought back crabs and clams and oysters from the sandbanks and mudflats along the shore, and Sam returned from the headland carrying a gape-mouthed eel longer than himself from the sudden deep water there. Ayn found a pool of fresh water and Cumor pulled up a bush. 'Look what God has grown here for us,' he called, showing us roots like children's fists. 'Hard but sweet. They'll cook.'

I split a tree long enough to seat all at table. On the fire we baked the food that God had given us on the land and in the sea, and slept in the houses whose wood and thatch He had grown for our use – so Lehi promised, and who am I to disbelieve him? Every morning Lehi led the people in prayer to the sun which God lifted into the sky to illuminate their labours. Every day the people worked for Him, clearing land, improving themselves, and Abihail's baby was born for the glory of the Lord, and then Abigail's; and every night more babies were made.

'Do you, Wotan? Do you truly believe what we believe?' Nephi asked. He followed me along the trail I slashed through the undergrowth to the highest hill. 'Sometimes I wonder about you. Laman and my brothers too. People who believe with their mouths but not their hearts and souls.'

'I have no soul.'

He laughed. 'Then you can't be alive. You're just an animal.' We came to the tallest tree, and I climbed it fast and agile as an ape of Egypt. 'What do you see?' Nephi called. I shielded my eyes from the sun moving among the clouds. 'We're on an island for sure. A long thin island with a central lake. More islands to my right, narrow channels. The river on my left's wide and the land on the far side goes . . . goes. Looks as though it might go on for ever. Forest. Swamps. Hills.' I shrugged. 'Maybe distant mountains.'

'Yes, Wotan,' he called up, 'but what do you *see*?'

I pulled him up on a rope, stood him beside me on the bough. 'Yes, I see God's land!' Nephi exulted. 'I see *our* land. I see New Sion stretching far as my eye can see, high as my heart can lift. We shall populate it with God's children, conquer it with our blood.' I steadied him on the swaying branch. 'The land itself will turn to blood, our blood. The moon shall turn to blood, our blood shall be even there. The sun shall swell up like a bursting heart.'

'Are these Lehi's visions? Will you still be alive to see it?'

'My children, my children's children, my generations will see my father's prophecies come true. No one who lives who builds this land shall be forgotten,' Nephi said seriously. 'Our names are inscribed in the genealogies in the Holy Language' – the Egyptian-looking writing I'd seen on Lehi's scroll – 'so that we shall be known to God on Judgment Day.'

'Known? Judgment Day?'

'In the moment before God destroys the world, and destroys all sinners and all their works, all good people whose names are known shall be lifted up to Him in His Rapture, and translated into Heaven to be saved.'

'Why? To just sit around and worship eternally?'

'To learn to be gods themselves.' The wind blew, the tree swayed, leaning, and Nephi clutched me realising how high we were above the ground. 'Be with us in your heart, Wotan. Worship with more than just your mouth. Till God's soil with us, put the fruits of your labours into the common granary. Take a wife and seed her as your garden. Take wives. Make a house of your families. Remember, our blood must conquer the land. It's God's will.'

I'd heard it before. 'How do you know?'

He put out his arm – the one he wasn't holding around me for dear life. 'Look! See! Would He have granted us this beautiful bountiful land and the fishes of this sea and the fruits of this soil if we were *not* His chosen people?'

I was tempted. It was months since I'd had a woman, I was miserable with lust. My penis sprang up happily at the thought of wives. But I wouldn't love them, so I'd have no sons.

Nephi watched my face. 'You're thinking of her. Poor Maralah.'

'Maralah? No, it's Mara I love!'

He laughed, amazed. 'Her? She never even looked at you. She turned *me* down. Yes – even I.' He added sourly, 'Perpetual—' I thought he'd say *virgin*, but he used the less flattering term. 'Spinster.'

'I love her. I can't help it.'

'She's dead, Wotan. No man will ever have her now. The storm blew her away among the islands, among the rocks and reefs. My father says he saw Jesus Christ save us. My friend, if so, that Jesus only saved one ship.' Nephi looked earnestly into my eyes. 'The fish have had her. Marry, Wotan. Marry. Seed the land with your blood.' He remembered where he was, gripped the rope tight. 'It's your duty.'

I lowered Nephi from the tree. In the last moment before I followed him a ray of sunlight fingered the northern horizon and it seemed I saw a hill, and smoke rising from the hill like a slumbering volcano. The sunlight swept on, and the hill was gone. I rubbed my eyes, slid down the rope to the ground, and what I'd seen slipped my mind.

The winter was bitterly cold. I kept warm by clearing trees, since sex was unavailable. All the women had been claimed as wives, so even the ugliest and most bad-tempered with the worst teeth and terrible breath were granted a portion of someone's marriage bed, from which they duly swelled and gave birth. It was their duty to populate the earth or die trying; soon rows of graves lined the seashore, larger for mothers and smaller for babes, ready to be raised in the flesh at the Rapture. I swung my axe harder, felling a hundred trees a day, praying Nephi was wrong, trying not to think of the fish tearing at Mara's flesh in her last moments, the agony of her immortal soul among the mouths and fins. Because of her, only because of her, I know there are more mysteries than we can explain.

Mara, my love.

Snow lay over New Jerusalem and I watched Abihail's child die of an infection. I held my arms around both mother and father as she died, and knew Lehi was wrong. There's nothing good to learn from a child's agonising death. No God I'd believe in would teach us so.

421

The serpent's here, even in this Eden.

'We must be strong,' Lehi said, blessing the dead child's forehead. 'Strong to choose.'

I returned to the land I'd cleared, pulling out the stumps of felled trees with my hands, making fields of the forest that had once covered the island. Spring warmed the rich leaf-mud and I dragged furrows with a plough of oak. The women hoed the furrows of virgin soil and planted the seeds they'd brought with them, barley, flax, nuts, berries, fruit. The sun was hot, greening the crop, now yellowing the ripe barley ears: we all longed to reap what we had sown, we all longed for bread. Laman planted his vineyard on the southern tip of the island and tried to make friends with me. 'Now,' he said, 'us guys'll soon get drunk again.'

'You and your brothers don't like what Lehi and Nephi are doing, do you,' I said. 'The religion.'

He dug his toe in the soil, grinned. 'Oh, I don't know. We like the women good enough.'

'We don't like being told what to do,' Lemuel said. 'Don't like that.'

'Do this, do that,' Sam said. 'When to pray, even when to shit. And I don't like my wives having secret names only Lehi knows. It's like God getting between them and me.' Laman nodded. 'Yes, but our dear father's an old man. He won't live for ever.' Sam burst out, 'Shit, then Nephi takes over, then what?'

I pointed across the east river, narrower than the western. 'Looks like good growing ground over there. Let's swim over.'

'No one's been over there,' Laman said apprehensively. 'The tides – currents . . .'

Nephi overheard us. 'Let's build a raft,' he said, coming between the vines. 'Laman, tie some stumps together, and I'll make paddles.' As usual the brothers argued about who'd do what, but I plunged impatiently into the river and swam to the beach on the far side.

It was quiet here. A bird called. This forest was not so dense, younger, cleared by a lightning strike within living memory, perhaps. Sunlight still patterned the forest floor between the young trunks, the vivid moss felt soft and warm under my bare feet. I glanced back, seeing Nephi and the others paddling their makeshift raft across the blue waters, then crouched, examining what I'd found.

By my foot lay a red Caucasus apple, discarded, fresh, one mouth-shaped bite revealing the worm inside.

Birds called, flying up around the brothers as they splashed ashore laughing after their raft adventure. I threw a stone to get their attention, held my finger to my lips, beckoned.

They gathered round, staring. 'It's just an apple core,' Laman said.

But Nephi understood. He whispered, 'Who dropped it?'

Laman drew his sword. Jerusalem apples are green or yellow; the apples of Bab'El and mountains north of Ararat, my mother's homeland, are red. The canaans traded them southward thousands of years ago – Noah invented wine, but the people of the Caucasus, my people, made cider first. I padded silently forward between the trees.

In a sunlit glade stood an apple tree, ancient, gnarled, heavy with red fruit. The branches spread out like a fan, the longest supported by posts where they nearly touched the tended grass. The fire that had consumed the forest had not touched here; by the tree a few mossy stones had been piled into a cairn waist-high.

A bird sang; no, it was a child's voice. A girl of about twelve came from behind the tree. She reached up, her deerskin dress showing her knees, picking red apples. Her hair swung over her shoulders, golden brown, and her eyes were wide and blue. Her face was decorated with simple signs, simpler and clumsier than I remembered from Shem; not expertly tattooed as in the cities of that land, daubed with her fingertips probably. The Sun. Moon. Others. A shape like the sign of El.

She lifted the hem of her dress and dropped the apples in as she picked them. Someone moved behind me. She stopped, stared. Her eyes widened.

'Don't be afraid,' I said.

Laman ran forward with his sword. She dropped the apples, ran like a wild animal. He tripped her, picked her up round the waist. 'Look what I got.'

'It's a girl,' Lemuel said. 'She's got pubic hair. She's old enough.'

Nephi stopped him. 'It's not a girl,' he said. 'It's a wife.' He touched her face gently.

The girl stilled, watching him doubtfully, then smiled. 'Are there more of you?' he asked tenderly, then picked up an apple she'd dropped from her skirt. 'Do you think she's Eve?'

'She's not Eve,' I said. 'I don't think this is a tree of knowledge.'

'Is your name Eve? Eve?'

'Eve,' the girl said.

'She's just copying you,' I said. 'Let her go, Laman. She won't run.'

'This truly is Eden, I knew it,' Nephi said. 'Look, Wotan, she has blue eyes like yours! Her face, look at her cheekbones, her nose, she has your bone structure. But she's not as strong as you. What an exquisite, primitive creature.' He crouched, speaking clearly to make her understand. 'Are you married?'

She smiled, shook her head, nodded. I said, 'She doesn't know what you're saying.'

'Good, that's better, she can learn,' Nephi said. 'She can learn properly.' He spoke slow and loud again. 'Do you believe in God?'

She shook her head, smiling, nodding. 'Nin-na, Nin-na!'

I said, 'That's her name. Ninna.'

Nephi frowned. 'I don't like the sound of it. That sounds like a blasphemous name. One of the foul gods of Bab'El is Ninna or Nana, isn't she?'

'Nanna,' I said. 'Inanna, long ago. Ishtar. Yes.' I looked round. 'Maybe there's more like her. Her family. Her people.'

'Not if she's the Eve of this Eden,' Nephi said. 'I'll marry her, she'll be mine, and I'll be the new Adam. "Eve conceived and bore Cain and she said, I have got a man from the Lord."'

'It's not an entirely happy story,' I reminded him. 'Anyhow, this girl's name's Ninna.'

'We're free to choose. Here we're free to choose our fate.' Nephi offered her the apple. 'Go on, here the man is in control. The man offers the woman the apple.' Ninna looked at me for approval, spoke quickly. I guessed some of the words, though their sound had changed since I first learnt them on the battlefield by the broken tower of Bab'El; and the fallen stones had been ancient even then.

'I think she's one of Jared's people,' I said. 'I think Jared made it across the ocean. Jared, Ninna? Know Jared name?'

'Jared.' She made a sign like the shape daubed on her face: the sign of God.

'No. Jared not God,' I said. 'Jared man, not God.'

Nephi demanded suspiciously, 'Stop jabbering you two.' He touched the apple to her lips. 'Eat. Be mine.'

'I wouldn't eat that apple,' Laman said. 'You never know.'

Nephi took a mouthful, pressed the bitten apple to her lips, and she ate to please him. 'We've eaten the forbidden fruit,' Nephi said exultantly. 'We shall not die. We shall be as God, knowing the difference between good and evil.'

'I don't want to know,' Laman said.

'Let's show her to Father.' Nephi led her to the water, and she walked with him as obediently as a domesticated animal. Laman picked up a few apples then threw them down. 'No, I'm not eating them!' he said.

'You don't know what might happen,' Lemuel agreed. 'Might hurt your guts.'

Sam followed his brothers, then looked back. 'Still,' he said. 'Wives.'

I waited a while, examining the cairn, then found a path winding through the forest and followed it eating a juicy red apple. The land rose then fell, a calm estuary opened on my right, and ahead of me, beyond a narrow neck, I saw the open sea with coves and cliffs, and more islands. I didn't have to look so far; smoke rose above the treetops quite close to me. I watched Ninna's people busy at their lives in a village where a stream joined the bay. Middle-aged men and youngsters worked with fish nets, but only one young man of fighting age returned, carrying over his shoulders a buck with an arrow in its side. The rest were old women and girls. I watched until the light failed. Now I understood Ninna. When a few women came out calling her name, searching for her, I slipped back through the woods and plunged into the east river back to New Jerusalem.

Lehi sat on a tree trunk by the bonfire blazing on the beach, the people around him, Ninna sitting at his feet and Nephi kneeling beside her. 'She's Godless,' Lehi said. 'A survivor of a people plainly fallen into decadence and savagery. We must beware the taint of a different race diluting our God-given blood and purpose.'

'But you yourself have prophesied by the Spirit,' Nephi said, ' "None shall come into this land save they are brought by the hand of the Lord Most High." '

'That's why knowledge of this land is kept from other nations,' Lehi said, 'so that God's purpose shall prosper here.' He mulled it over. 'God planted her race here, but they've forgotten Him.'

'I can bring God into her,' Nephi said. 'Her savage womb will be a new vessel for the children of God.'

'Not so savage,' I told them, squeezing the water from my hair. 'I think she's us. You. I think Jared's eight arks from Shem came ashore here. One of them, anyway.' I told them about the village I'd seen. 'And I reckon there're other villages. Maybe wars, I don't know. I saw blackened circles where huts were burnt down. Women and girls and old men, but where were all the young men?' I answered my own question. 'Fighting, or killed.'

Lehi cried, 'Why would men fight in Eden?'

'Men did before.' I shrugged. 'Wars are fun.'

Sariah, alone of all the women, dared contradict me. 'Wars cause suffering and enslavement and terrible grief.'

'And glory and honour and pride,' I said. 'And joy and sex and the tests of manhood and strength without which life isn't worth living, without which strong babies aren't born. War is the brilliant light that illuminates existence.'

'No, our God is the brilliant light,' Nephi said.

'Maybe it takes both,' I said. I touched Ninna's hair, looked into her eyes, blue-black in the firelight. 'Her people came here thousands of years ago. I don't think they've forgotten God completely. Even in those days the people of Bab'El worshipped El as their God. They knew the stories of Eden and Adam.'

'Adamah,' Ninna agreed quickly. 'Red-earth man.' I translated. She touched the clay daubs on her cheeks expressively.

'I've seen no wild apples here,' I said. 'They brought red apples with them. I think that apple tree is a kind of shrine. A memory.' I told them about the cairn of stones. 'You could knock them down in a few moments. Forget them. Gone. They're weathered, four or five thousand years of weather, but I think they were made by tools.'

'Tools?' Nephi said.

'People in those days built mountains to worship God. I think those few old stones are the tip of a temple. A mountain underground.'

Nobody said anything, then Laman laughed. 'A mountain underground! These people must be more stupid than we thought.'

'It's our duty to save them,' Nephi said. 'God brought them here.'

'Dig down,' I said. 'They aren't just stones. You'll find a mountain top.'

They laughed. 'A mountain as high as my waist!' Lemuel sneered.

'The soil rises,' I said. They couldn't believe it. From the generations of the Bible they'd worked out the day God created the world, and there was no need for God to add further wonders to make the soil rise, or make the oil that bubbles from the ground in certain places, or create the conditions that make petrified trees, or leg-bones longer than a man, or dragons, but I'd seen such things.

'God condemns worship in high places,' Lehi said firmly. 'The Genealogy of Enoch tells us God created the world three thousand three hundred and fifty-five years ago, on the day of the equinox of spring. There was no mention of mountains.'

'Noah's ark landed on a mountain top,' Laman said.

'Listen.' I turned Ninna's smiling innocent face towards them. 'She's you. Don't you see? Her ancestors brought their blue eyes and light-coloured hair and the shape of their bones from the Caucasus, the mountains of Eden. They built Bab'El at the beginning of time and the nations gathered. Intermarriage between peoples has been the way of the world there for thousands of years. Invaders with black hair, straight hair, curly hair, broad cheekbones, narrow cheekbones, canaanite traders with a girl in every port. But not here. Nothing's happened here. They haven't changed.'

'We can change them,' Nephi said. 'We can bring them back to God. We'll marry them and name them and make them live like us, worship like us, be like us. Their children will *be* us. Wotan, we have you to thank.'

'That's not what I meant,' I said, alarmed.

'How many girls of marriageable age would you say you saw?' Nephi asked.

I looked round the eager faces of the brothers. 'Enough,' I said. 'But you can't—'

But they could. An idea is stronger even than I. Marriage not rape, order not chaos. The seed spread roots so quickly that even I could not pull them out. The wives loved the idea, they'd have younger hands to help them, set to work, and boss about. They faced less of the dangerous business of childbearing and gained authority over each new wife; each new wife made the same calculation in her turn. Nephi dressed Ninna in the traditional white linen robes of marriage, the crotch cut open to reveal her shaved pubes, her fertile slit exposed to make plain the purpose of marrying, which is children, and Abihail Nephi's first wife led her to her husband's marriage bed. Later, when Nephi married Adah (knowing her by her secret name) both Abihail and Ninna led Adah to her bed, and the three of them led the fourth wife, Zillah, to her bed, and they raised their children together and praised God that He had given their lives purpose.

After the kiln was built the thatch huts grew to houses with tiled roofs, and the houses grew to villages. Each family was a village. Nephi stayed with his father Lehi and built houses behind the beach where we first landed. Laman moved to the north of New Jerusalem and built his village where the two rivers separated. Zoram took his wives over the east river, Ayn and Cumor and their wives the daughters of Lehi, and all the Jared wives they'd taken, carried their young sons Ram-Ya and Cumor-Ya across the west river and followed their swinging axes into the

429

hinterland of New Sion. Great fires rose up as they burnt the forests and planted fields in the fertile ash where trees once grew, making farmland to feed their children's mouths.

I climbed the great tree by the island's central lake. 'Careful below,' came a woman's voice from the bough above me, my own bough, almost at the lightning-struck top. 'It's me, Abihail. You come up here often, don't you? I thought I'd try it.'

I sat beside her. The treetops below us were all gone, replaced by fields, grain for bread, flax for linen, sunflower for oil. I'd always liked Abihail, she was strong-minded but sensible. We sat swinging our legs off the bough. 'Don't tell Nephi I came up,' she said. She patted her belly. 'I've started again.'

'Nephi didn't like it up here.'

'He has no head for heights, nothing but worries.' She saw my face and sighed. 'About everything. About Laman. The children are growing up, they drive their goats into land belonging to each other's father, you know what boys are like.' She gripped my arm cheerfully. 'Sorry, you don't!' The women despised me a little for not having wives and children; not all of them trusted me like Abihail. 'Well, boys like to make trouble. Anything for a fight. Laman encourages them, and Lemuel does too I think. Sam sometimes.'

'It's just high spirits and rivalry.'

'And broken noses. It's getting out of hand. Laman's sons have wine and best pasture. There's so much swamp. Nephi needs good water. Laman demands right of access to his vineyard at the south end, Nephi demands the vines on his land be dug up. A dog kills a sheep so two dogs are killed in revenge. A hut gets burnt. The first time someone gets killed it's an accident.' She looked between her swinging legs. 'There's talk of building a stockade across the island.' She held the narrow waist of the island between her feet. 'It's not so far. A fence to keep the families apart. Like the genealogies say about the families of Abraham and Lot.'

'The River Jordan kept those two apart, not a fence.'

She looked at me directly. 'Nephi and Laman will fight. Are we building Sodom and Gomorrah here not New Sion?'

'Abraham and Lot agreed to go separate ways. It can work.'

'Laman hates Nephi. The younger one. The successful one. Closer to their father, closer to God. Nephi's almost unbearably good,' she admitted.

'Maybe Lehi can keep the peace.'

'Lehi's dying.' She drew a breath. 'I'm afraid for my husband. This land has been so good to us. Our children are still so young but so wild. And Laman doesn't allow the Word of God to tame his children, he won't let them hear.' She pointed across the west river to the wild savage continent that for all we knew went on for ever, or until it was Africa, or the world ended. 'Surely there's room for us all in New Sion, Wotan? Surely this land is big enough for us all to live together.'

'Ordered and commanded,' I said.

'Yes. Under one Law. Under God.' Dark clouds gathered in the south and the tree creaked in the rising wind, fluttering her white headscarf, sending beams of sunlight racing past us like flags rippling across the landscape.

'No land's big enough for us,' I said. 'Heaven itself won't be big enough. We'll always want more.' I fell silent, the wind blowing my hair. Abihail turned my face.

'You never talk about her. But you think about her all the time.'

'Her.'

She chuckled. 'When you die we'll find Mara's name written on your heart.'

431

'I can't die.' People never recognise truth when it's told simply. They always think truth is huge and complicated. 'I can't die, Abby.'

She hugged me earnestly. 'Yes, we all can't die. We'll all be raised to life in the flesh when the Rapture comes.' I knew she'd talk about marriage now. 'So, no wife for poor Wotan, then? A man so incredibly handsome, so strong yet so gentle, so agile in bed I suspect. You have lovely eyes, I can always tell what you're thinking. And you're a killer.' She sighed. 'You could have any stupid young girl you wanted. All because the one he truly loves died. Will you spend your life mourning for her?'

'I told you, I can't die.'

She grinned. 'Waste your undying eternal life in perpetual mourning, then.' She came to the point. 'There's someone, a Jared girl. You'd learn to love her.' She quoted, '"And it came to pass, when men began to multiply on the face of the earth, and daughters were born unto them, that the sons of God saw that the daughters of men were fair; and they took unto them wives which they chose." It says so in the copper scroll of Lehi's genealogy.'

'Are they calling themselves the sons of God now?'

'Where else do children come from, if not from God? You don't have to *love* the silly Jared girl, just make God's work possible. It's your duty to take a wife. Wives.'

'God doesn't come out of my penis, Abby.'

She looked shocked. 'You mean you can't?'

I told her the truth. 'I was born with something missing. It seems I am only capable of love.'

'Poor man.' Her lips tightened, quivering, angry. 'Who of us has love? Nine children were born to my husband last week. The only love is love for God, all the rest is work. Hard work.' She slapped me with the flat of her hand, weeping. 'There is no love, didn't you know?'

I held her and the storm blew wind and sunlight over us. I pointed as the bright fingers touched the hill on the

432

northern horizon, that I'd thought looked like a volcano. Now the smoke was blown out to one side, revealing a glitter of tiny fires, buildings, maybe a temple on the top of the mound, the place the Jareds called Ramah. 'Those people aren't Jareds, Abby. Not peaceful fisherfolk who forgot what they believed. Maybe they're the ones who burnt the Jared villages. What happens when Ayn and Cumor reach there?'

'It's an opportunity. We'll bring God to them, the God Most High they've forgotten in their savagery and decadence. I must tell my husband what we've seen.' She turned to climb from the tree but the wind snatched her headscarf, sent it flying like a gull over the water, over a distant white patch of foam among the grey waves. I stared. 'Oh my God.' I stood upright on the bough, staring.

Abihail looked up at me, frightened I'd fall. 'What is it?'

'It's Mara.' I stared at the reed ship wallowing waterlogged, storm-blown, in the channel. 'Mara. Hold on!' Abihail thought I meant her and grabbed hold of my ankle. She slipped. I felt her weight swinging below me but all I thought of was the ship. 'She's alive. She searched for me.' The ship went down in the surf then reappeared, bow and mast and stern only, all the rest was spray. 'Hold on, Mara.' I mustn't lose sight of her now. I swung Abihail over my shoulder and jumped down from bough to bough staring all the while at the ship, somersaulted from the lowest branch and set her lightly on her feet, left her and ran across the fields to the beach. The wind would blow the ship past the island. I kept pace with it from the sand, then dived forward and swam out, let the waves sweep me aboard. The sodden decks were foul with seaweed. A man clung exhausted to the mast, a few others huddled at the bow. I cried, 'Where is she?'

'Thank God, sir.' Benjamin, Mulek's military officer, had lashed himself to the mast. 'We knew God wouldn't let Father Lehi perish. I knew we'd find you.' Benjamin's strength was gone, his water-wrinkled fingers couldn't undo the knots. I snapped the rope, shook him.

'Where is she?' A wave washed over us. 'Mara. Is Mara alive?'

He coughed salt water. 'She's alive. We were saved, sir. God saved us in a miraculous place.'

I looked round the vessel. This ship was past saving; the wind and waves pushed the waterlogged hulk past the island. I saw Nephi and the people waving from the beach but they were powerless. I took the bow rope in my teeth and plunged in, swam to shore tugging the ship after me, got a grip on the rocks and hauled her hand over hand on to dry sand.

'Where?' I said.

Benjamin pointed into the wind. 'There is a land southward.'

Benjamin limped again to the fire, sat with his men warming themselves at the flames. When they'd finished eating the fire sent sparks whirling into the stormy night sky and Lehi was carried out on his bed. 'Captain Benjamin, did you not see the Dragon that day?' he whispered. 'Did you not see Jesus Christ save us?'

'We were too busy saving our own souls, sir.' Benjamin saw some meat left on a venison bone and went back to it. Nephi acknowledged, 'Neither was I granted the vision my father saw.'

'I saw,' I said. I worked with half a dozen Jared wives in the circle of firelight, taking the lengths of wood I'd cut, bending them tight with my strength, heating them on the fire to set the wood. The Jared fishergirls worked expertly, lashing the joints with ropes, their flashing fingers making the knots faster than any tool devised by Nephi. Others stretched deerskin to render the hull watertight as Jareds had done for thousands of years.

434

'If you saw, Wotan,' Lehi croaked, 'then you know our faith is the true faith.'

'I saw it,' Laman said. 'Didn't believe it. Just thought we were going to die.'

'You were granted our father's vision?' Nephi said incredulously. 'You, an unbeliever?'

I started work on the outrigger. 'Let Benjamin speak.'

'It was a long time ago. That day when the wind rose up after the calm,' Benjamin told us through another mouthful of red meat, 'we were blown between the islands we would otherwise surely have hit.' His eyes widened, remembering the sight. 'Coral reefs this side, rocks that!'

'What colour coral?' I asked sharply.

'Red. Red as blood.' I nodded and he said, 'Mara, your Mara, sir, she stood at the rudder. She guided us. Then the wind eased but still blew us forward, we couldn't get back to you. I don't think she wanted to. She said it was God's wind.'

I nodded. 'That's my Mara. Tell me she found her heart's desire, God walking on the sea.'

'What? No, nothing like that, sir. When the ring of islands fell behind us we sailed warm shallow waters full of fish. We hove to each night, but the wind blew us forward. One morning we woke to see ourselves in a flat-calm bay that held us like safe arms, green hills as big as strong muscles on almost every side. God knows, pardon me, sir, how we got through the entrance without being dashed on the rocks.'

'Is the south land a hot land?' I asked.

'Hot and wet, hotter'n here, sir. And wetter when it rains, sir! It pours hot rain! Trees like I never saw. Hardly get between them. Snakes and painted birds as bright as birds from India.'

I bunched my fist. 'Horseflies and mosquitoes as big as my fist?'

435

'How did you know? Maybe quite not so big as *that*, sir.'

'Mara told me,' I explained because everyone was watching. 'She must have had a dream.'

'A river flows northward into the bay. The sun rises over the sea and sets over the land.'

I asked, 'How far from here to there? As far as, say, Jerusalem to Egypt?'

Benjamin shook his head. 'Further than the whole world we once knew, sir. But I believe it's the same land as this.'

Lehi gasped round the cancer eating his throat, 'All New Sion. All our holy land.'

'Yes, sir. King Mulek's kingdom. He kissed the sand with his lips and touched it with his royal ring and claimed it in the name of his father King Zadokiah and Noah the first Zadok.'

Lehi gasped, '*I* am the Zadok.'

'Yes, sir, but we didn't know you were alive. That's why I came searching.'

'Mara sent you,' I said. 'She had to know what happened to me.'

'She never mentioned you, sir. Sorry. No, it was natural curiosity brought me after you. Life in Bountiful's not for me, I'm not a man who's comfortable with women.' He looked around him, realising nearly all the people around him were women. 'Not previously, anyways.' He pointed proudly at his men snoring by the fire. 'I wouldn't marry native. So me and the lads set off for what we could find.'

'And God brought you here,' Nephi said.

'He damned near killed us first, sir. Nergal the Sarsech of Bab'El who'd come on to our side, the shark got him, Kibzaim washed overboard, Gareb, Hanniel, all gone. We're the survivors.' He rummaged in his bag, pulled out knobbly yellow sticks. 'The natives call this *mayz*, and we call them *Mayza*, because they eat so much of it. You plant that, it'll grow here.'

436

I lashed outriggers to my long, thin boat so that it wouldn't overturn in steep seas, and carved the paddles with my knife. All night I worked while Benjamin told me what he knew. 'I'll come with you,' he said at last. 'There's too many women here, they'd take my strength.' He waited. 'The lads are with you. Joshbek, he's strong as an ox. Elhanan's a good man, and Parosh is fearless. The other two got with women and want to stay.' He watched me carry a tree for a mast. 'You're doing this just for a woman?'

'For love.'

'Sir, she refuses all offers of marriage. The men call her the Virgin. Mulek wants to make her a priest like in the old days. You know, like Miriam in Moses's day. She won't have you, sir,' he called after me. 'She's a lost cause.'

No one could stop me, no one could change my mind. At dawn I filled deerskins with water and carried dried meat to the boat, then carried the boat to the shore. Abihail and Nephi stood on a rock by the breaking waves. 'You won't change your mind?' he said.

The men launched the boat and scrambled aboard. 'You're a fool, Wotan,' Abihail called. 'The Devil seeks to make all men as miserable as himself. You're on a fool's errand.' But Nephi admitted, 'One day I may follow you southward.' I stood on the outrigger pulling the rope to raise the sail. Nephi called, 'Suppose the Devil not God succeeds in claiming the souls of my brothers?' The wind filled the sail, turning the boat from the shore. 'Cumor sends word of war in the north,' Nephi's voice called across the water. 'Wotan. Come back. I shall follow you south if I fail!' Then I heard nothing but the cries of gulls, the island fell from sight, and I turned my eyes towards the sun.

It was a long voyage. I thought of Mara. From the waves of the estuary we came to the ocean swell like big blue breasts lifting our little boat, passing beneath, dropping us down before the next rippling slope that raised us in sight of land once more. Dark fell, and we rose and fell in the dark. The sun rose, and I thought of Mara dressed in white. Each day the sun burned hotter, and Joshbek fell sick. We sailed to shore but he died on the sand. The wind turned, but because we were ashore we were not blown back to New Jerusalem. I told myself Joshbek was meant to die.

Day after day the wind blew in our faces, then turned again and we launched our frail vessel. Elhanan's screams woke us in the night. Tentacles whipped round him like snakes and snatched him into the dark. Slimy tentacles writhed around us stinking of the sea. The more I pulled the great creature up the more the boat was pulled down, so I let go, and Elhanan was gone.

I thought of Mara. 'He was a good man,' Benjamin wept, and I said, 'Yes, and Joshbek was strong as an ox.'

The wind blew a gale from the west, surf roared. Breaking waves picked our little boat up and rushed it forward to destruction, splintering on the sand, and we never saw Parosh again.

New Sion was smooth beach and dunes as far as we could see, nothing else visible. 'The beach is our road,' I said. Benjamin limped in my bare footsteps. I ate crabs raw, and there were snakes in the swampland behind the dunes. I skinned them between finger and thumb. 'Eat. The flesh tastes like eel.' Benjamin choked, 'For God's sake, man, it's unclean food.'

I thought about Mara, and thought about the land. 'Listen. When the great storm blew us along this coast, from the masthead I thought I saw sea beyond these swamps. I think this is a finger of land pointing down towards the islands. We'll save time by walking across, not all the way round.'

Benjamin eyed the swamps. The lunging jaws of some great reptile grabbed a bird from a branch. 'I'll walk round,' he said. I never saw him again.

I waded through the swampy glades and swam across the lakes, catching any fish that attacked me and eating them. My clothes were torn to shreds. After dark I crouched on gnarled tree roots and waited for the moon to rise. Once a great creature like a crocodile seized me and rolled me down, but I crushed its skull in my hands, hung it by its tail from a fluffy white tree and ate the best parts. Sometimes large gentle creatures swam with me and we played until they turned back. I thought of Mara and I did not stop. After a few days I loped along a swampy beach curving up from my left, following it to a huge muddy river which I swam. New Sion curved southward, the rim of a gigantic circle, its hilltops balancing the great ring of islands I remembered, their distant submerged mountain tops poking above the turquoise gulf. These hills were clothed with strange trees, and birds with brilliant plumage fluttered overhead with piercing calls. The land curved north, turning back on itself, but I climbed a hilltop and saw sea in front of me. I cut across the neck of land northward and came to a river flowing north. I followed the river to a bay shaped like a cradle of safe arms, with green hills as big as strong muscles on almost every side.

She stood on the water on a landing stage, dressed all in white, leading the people on the shore in prayer. All fell silent, seeing me.

'Mara.' I held out my strong arms. 'I'm alive. Marry me.'

'It's you,' Mara said. 'You haven't changed.'

'You have, Mara.' She looked wonderful. 'You look older. Ten years older.' I loved her so completely that my muscles tautened like rocks, I saw only her. 'Even more beautiful.' I jumped on the landing stage and embraced her, but Mara stepped back. I kissed her mouth, but she twisted her head so that my lips touched only her chaste left cheek.

Maralah, Mara's twin sister, walked towards me. The closer she came across the sand the slower she walked, staring. 'My Lord, it's him. He isn't dead.' She called my name, but when I ignored her she burst into tears, turned away, inconsolable, and ran away between the houses.

'They're alive,' Mara called to the people. 'Lehi's ship was saved. Give thanks to God. Send for King Mulek.'

'The king's not here,' someone reminded her, speaking Hebrew with a thick native accent. 'He's in the jungle with the prophet, claiming treasure for God.' Among the people I saw at least two tribes coming from the thatch houses along the beach, mostly broad round-faced natives. Others were tall and blond like the Jareds of the north, but dark-skinned from the sun. 'You found Jareds living here?'

'Uncivilised simpletons. Remnants. They hardly remember God or who they were. Try talking to them, you'll find they've fallen as low as you. Like the Maya they believe God made men from mud, then wood, then flesh, then the wicked men were swept away by God in black rain and a great flood swept over the world, but someone called Cocoxtli built an ark.'

'Noah,' I said.

'Yes, and the ark came to earth on a mountain top.' She waved her hand vaguely at the hills. 'Somewhere. Mulek's obsessed by it. The Jareds claim to have a great civilisation in the jungle, cities or the ruins of cities. We've never found a sign. I suppose that's not surprising. This land's immense, almost impassable. The only way to travel inland is to follow a river. But the highlands are grass . . .' She could talk like this all day, not looking at me.

'Stop it,' I said. 'You're still hiding, Mara. This is me. Don't sound so cold. I don't believe you.' The sun burned down on her white oval pale face framed by black hair. 'Mara, my God, you're lovely. Talk about you, us, me. Tell me everything you've done as though I was you.' I took her hips in my hands and swung her on to the sand. She looked away. 'Poor Maralah,' she said, staring at the distant figure of her sister. 'In the end she tried to forget you. She married, but her husband died.'

I stared at Mara's lips, the tip of her tongue as she talked, her eyes, eyelids, eyelashes. 'You missed me,' I said. 'Admit it.'

'Certainly not. I've had more than enough to keep me busy.'

'Don't talk. Say my name.'

'I do remember your name, Wotan.'

'No, no, not like that, look into my eyes when you say my name.'

She looked away, anywhere, then looked in my eyes. 'Wotan.' Without thinking she brushed a blond curl from my eyebrow. I smiled, got you. Her eyes flickered, her mouth tightened. 'Wotan,' she said bitterly. 'I knew you'd survive somehow.'

I said: 'Jesus Christ saved us.'

That did get her. 'What? How can—'

'Didn't you see anything at all, Mara? The storm, the calm? The Dragon red as blood, Satan, rising from the sea, our ship overturning? We were lost. Even I was lost.'

'Satan?' She gripped my arms. 'You were saved from Satan? You mean you actually *saw* Jesus Christ?'

'Jesus Christ walked on the waves and saved us.'

'Wotan, Wotan! You of all people.' She laughed incredulously. 'He wouldn't allow *you* to see Him.'

'Like you're standing here.'

Her mouth trembled. 'Why not me? What sin have I committed? You, not I, stood in His sight?'

I nodded, smiling. The gold curl fell back over my eyebrow.

'Describe Him as you saw Him.' She tugged my arms when I lingered in my reply, hanging on my every word. 'Wotan, please!'

441

'Dressed in white, gold sandals, gold crown. Stern-looking. Cloak of royal purple—'

'Yes, yes!' she cried. 'The last, best, greatest of King David's royal line, King Jesus, born in the Holy of Holies!'

'What Holy of Holies? It's dust,' I said. 'Anyway, He looked like a king all right. Just like you'd expect. Jewels, royal seal rings, gold, utter confidence. Eyes like a king's. Fierce eyes that command obedience. Even I'd be terrified not to worship your Jesus Christ, I'll tell you.'

'You saw Jesus Christ,' she said numbly. 'I prayed my knees raw for Him. I endured leprosy for Him. A thousand times I've died for Him.' It was true. Locked in the inexorable cycle of death and rebirth, as Mari, as Miriam, as Mara, her soul – her self – suffered the same curse of immortality as my body. She pressed her fists to her lips. '*You* saw Him. He saved *you*.' I said something but she turned away in misery and despair. 'All right, Wotan, I'll marry you.' I spoke again but she interrupted. 'I'll be your wife. I'll be your whore. Anything you want.'

'Mara, don't. I love you.'

'Obviously I'm not worthy of seeing Jesus Christ but you are. I must have been missing something. I must have been wasting my time all these years.' She pressed her hands over her face, weeping, stumbling away from me along the sand. Maralah ran to her and embraced her, both sisters weeping and wailing in each other's arms, one because I had not proposed marriage to her, the other because I had. I behaved as usual in such a situation: I got drunk. The natives, especially the young males, called Mulek's people foreigners, 'tricksters and rascals', 'the people of Itzá', 'foreigners who speak our language brokenly'. Drink speaks any language. In no time I made friends with the natives and Chachua their leader and soon we were brothers cheerfully drinking jars called *tecomates* full of yellowish frothy liquor. We sang songs, we stumbled around, we snored.

I opened one eye. It was dark in the hut. My Mayan friends laughed at me then they too held their heads, hurting as much as I. Brewed maize liquor hurts. We didn't share much language but men get drunk better than women. In unspoken communication we knew exactly what each other suffered. We vomited where we lay, unable to find the door, then staggered into fresh air. The night had gone, the sun blinded us. We flopped down in the sea. The waves rolled us limply forward and back, groaning.

'I meant it,' Mara called. 'What I said yesterday.' She stood just beyond reach of the waves, white, virginal, watching me with bruised eyes.

'Mara?' I muttered. 'You look lousy.'

'I haven't slept a wink,' she said earnestly. She lifted her shift to her ankles with an expression of distaste, dipped her feet in the water, slipped her hand under my armpit and tried to lift me. Her eyes watered at the smell of my breath. I got up and carried her to shore. 'You don't have to go through with it,' I said, setting her down. 'You were just joking, trying to hurt me.'

'I was not!' She looked appalled. 'How could I ever joke about something so serious? How could you even *think* I could?' She stared into my eyes. 'What are you? I'm never going to know exactly what's going on in your head even when you're my husband. You're like an alien creature. How could you get drunk after proposing something so sacred and profound as marriage?'

'I love you,' I said. She stopped. She melted. I held her head before she twisted away, and I kissed her lips. 'That's all it is,' I said. 'No sacred stuff. Don't let's talk about marriage any more.' She watched me bathe my aching head in the waves.

'But I want to talk about it,' she said. 'That's part of the fun.'

I grinned. She grinned too, shrugging. She made me laugh. She laughed too, clapping excitedly, then rushed

443

into my arms. 'Steady,' I said, but she said, 'Kiss me again.' Even through my shirt I felt her nipples stiffen as hard as jewels as she kissed me. 'Careful,' I said. 'I'm saving myself for my wife.' She punched my arm then stepped back, panting, surprised at herself. 'It's been a long time for you, hasn't it,' I said.

'For ever.' She looked terribly shy, then took my hand. 'I always wanted to do whatever was right.'

'Is this right?'

'I don't care. I'm free.'

'Maralah told me once you carried the world on your shoulders.'

'It felt that way. Now I have you, Wotan. I'm crazy. I've given up everything except you. I'm going to make you a good wife.'

She was making me feel undeserving of her. 'Maralah said when you felt you were pure enough and all that to deserve God, you believed He'd send His Messiah to teach you what love really is.'

'Not this sort of love,' she said, shocked. 'To be His handmaiden, yes. His servant. Totally subservient to Him.' She added, 'You won't drink when we're married, will you?'

'No, no, not a drop.'

'And you won't kill anyone. Or show off.'

I thought about it. 'Maybe.'

'And you'll be sensitive and thoughtful.'

'You'll make me totally virtuous.' She nodded happily.

I walked her along the beach before this dangerous conversation went any further. 'Show me your village,' I said.

'Bountiful isn't a village, it's a town,' she scolded. 'There's Mulek's palace, on that mound. The natives are amazing, they work like ants, it takes them no time at all. Each of their own houses is built on its own little mound. The tribes fight furiously almost all the time, the Mani against the Arévalo, the Olmecs against the Ocós, the tribes

444

of the Tonála River against the Gujalhantón, and all of them fought the Jareds who fought among themselves. The Jared survivors scattered and were wiped out except for a village or two, like here. Now the native tribes just kill and rob among themselves. Robber bands. Wife-stealing. Assassinations. Sacrifices.'

I pointed out fishermen repairing nets on the sand, more setting to sea in boats with spears, others paddling heavily laden canoes from the mangrove swamps and muddy lagoons. 'Mangrove oysters, marsh clams,' she told me. 'The natives eat the dirty things, and we buy and crush the shells to fertilise our fields. Then there's a layer of volcanic ash—'

'Buy? You've got gold and silver?'

'Too much to use for money. The hills are full of metal. Chocolate beans work better.' She tossed me a couple. 'Buy yourself breakfast at the market, corn bread and deseret honey. Look,' she pointed at meat roasting on green sticks, 'turtles, crabs, iguanas.' One of the ugly lizards snapped at her and she threw it pieces of rind from some tropical fruit I didn't recognise. 'We have gar, porgy, snook, catfish in the rivers, cumoms and cureloms to pull the ploughs. Everything we need.' She looked up at me with a childlike smile. 'That's why we call our town Bountiful.'

Queen Zarah came down the mud steps from the palace. Native women lifted the hem of her cloak, and I bowed to her. 'My husband's mighty man,' she said haughtily. 'I heard you survived.'

'He always survives,' Mara giggled, made reckless by love. The queen ignored her. A baby cried, a new prince.

'I hear King Mulek's found a prophet,' I said.

'Indeed,' Zarah said. 'The king hardly needs a priestess now.' Mara's fall from favour reminded me how Miriam had lost out to Moses. 'The prophet Ether tells us many inspired and wondrous revelations, visions of terrible annihilations and millions dead, and of a great people brought low.'

'Jared's descendants?' I asked. 'You've found a living Jared prophet?'

'Ether's a Zadok, an old man now. Younger son of one of their last kings. He possesses an Urim and Thummim. He's infallible.' She looked down her nose at Mara.

'I don't believe that,' Mara said. She taunted, 'Will Mulek make him Melchizadok to rule over us?'

'You're just jealous, my dear. God speaks through Ether's mouth. He lived for years, solitary and celibate, in a hole in the rocks somewhere in the hills, guarding the breastplate with his life. Of course he showed the gold plates and sacred stones, the jewelled oracles of the Urim and Thummim which when held to the eyes translate holy writing, to both King Mulek and me. And there's more.'

'You don't have to bother with all this now,' I told Mara. 'We're getting married,' I explained.

'Oh, congratulations. We'll send someone.'

Mara demanded, 'What more?'

'Ether promised my husband a great treasure. The treasure of the Jareds.'

'What treasure guarded by one crazy old man's so important that a king travels to it, not it to him?'

'Ether's senile if you ask me,' Zarah admitted. 'Loneliness has driven him mad. He promises the world. Perhaps God Himself. Quite mad. But you know Mulek; once he gets an idea in his head there's no stopping him.'

'What's the place called?'

'The natives call the hill Apachiohualitzá, I believe.'

'Hill of the Flood,' Mara translated. 'Temple of the Flood.'

'Yes. Long ago the Jareds called it Ararat. Already a religious site perhaps, not the real Mount Ararat of course any more than that native savage Cocoxtli really was Noah.'

'I'm starting to think there were dozens of Noahs,' I

446

laughed. Neither woman smiled.

'The Jareds destroyed themselves,' Zarah said bleakly. 'War destroyed them. War, and that each man took only one wife at a time. They couldn't raise children fast enough to feed their wars. They forgot God and their civilisation was destroyed.'

Suddenly natives ran along the beach, shouting. 'Is it an attack?' Zarah clutched her young son. Horns brayed the alarm and brightly coloured birds flew up from the jungle, men coming. 'Robbers!' the servants shouted, 'Gujalhantón robbers.' I spat on my hands and stepped forward for a good fight. Open beach, trees in front, sea behind; bountiful this land certainly was, but almost impossible for ordinary men to defend.

Then a voice cried, 'It's us.' King Mulek strode from the trees. His robes were ripped by thorns and he was muddy to the waist, but he still wore his crown and his eyes were bright. 'Wotan, my mighty man! Excellent! So Captain Benjamin found you, his faith is rewarded. Is Father Lehi still alive?'

'He lay on his deathbed far to the north when I last saw him, but still breathing.'

'He was a great man,' Mulek said cheerfully, allowing the queen to wash his feet. He turned to his men stumbling from the jungle. 'Refresh yourselves.' A platter with slices of red fruit was brought to him, and a hairy brown husk as large as a cup from which he drank milk, dribbling the white liquid down his long braided beard. 'Wotan, you'll come, see what I have found. The treasure of the Jareds! Your great strength will lift it. You'll come with me there.'

'He's to be married,' Zarah said. 'To her.'

Mulek glanced at Mara. 'Excellent!' he decided. 'I give my permission. What wonderful times we live in. God has called on me alone to rule over us all.'

'But the prophet Ether . . .' Zarah fell silent as more strong men filed from the jungle. Beneath the grimy mossy pole strung between their shoulders the body of a scrawny old man swung like an animal, bound hand and foot, his long white hair trailing on the dry sand. They dumped him and his body twitched, alive. 'Ether!' Mara cried. He'd been her enemy, but despite his ambition to replace her as Mulek's priest she took water to him. She pulled his gag off but Ether was too weak to drink. She cradled his head. 'He's hurt.'

'Don't pity him, woman. He betrayed me,' Mulek said. 'The closer we got to the place, Ararat, Apachiohualitzá, whatever, the more he tried to mislead me. Changed his mind about showing me the treasure. But I just followed the river upstream, southward. The natives call it Azul, but I shall call it River Sion. When he first came to us, starving and demented by solitude, Ether had babbled to me of a hill, the great green hill, the source of his people's power. Well fed, watered, clothed, he tried to deny his words. He led us the wrong way, but I soon got the measure of him. When he said left, I went right. He tried to throw away the Urim and Thummim in the river, but my men stopped him. He tried to escape, so I bound him. He tried to curse me, so I gagged him. In the morning I saw the great green hill. I followed the trail of his filth to his cave, and found – this.' The mossy pole was handed to him, one end wrapped in cloth. Mulek rubbed the green moss from the shaft, showing us black ebony. Then he pulled off the wrapping from the head, revealing brilliant gold. 'Beautiful workmanship, wouldn't you say?'

They'd hung Ether from his holy sceptre. Its head was a serpent's golden head, ornate, intricate, precise. Mara's eye met mine. The sceptre of Moses, but it couldn't be, Jared sailed from Shem three thousand years before Akenmoses was born. 'Almost the same as Ezekiel's sceptre,' Mulek said with satisfaction. 'Maybe Ezekiel was the true Zadok after all. Lehi hasn't got one. Maybe he's a false prophet, maybe not.' He lifted the sceptre above his head, raised his voice. '*I* am the true prophet. Ruler, defender of the faith. Priest and king. Both!'

'No. You aren't the One.' Ether sat up with all his strength. His legs shook as he stood, a bent old man straining to stand straight. 'Hear me. I thought you were the great king who will make all things new. I was wrong about you.'

Mulek yawned.

The old man struggled for breath. 'I curse you, King Mulek! I curse you with the gift I offered you to use wisely, but I see you're a fool. I curse you with the curse that cursed my people. I curse you with the curse of my people's destruction.'

Mulek glanced at him. 'Words don't hurt me.'

'You hold it in your hands,' Ether said. 'You carry your curse with you in your own hands.' He drew a ragged breath. 'These are the last words which I shall speak.'

'That's true,' Mulek said.

Ether cried out, 'You shall have your heart's desire, King Mulek! Whether it is the will of the Lord that like Enoch I am taken by God to Heaven without tasting death, or that I suffer the will of the Lord in the flesh, it doesn't matter, so long as I am saved in the kingdom of God!'

'Kill him,' Mulek said, and someone walloped the old man before we could move. Mulek took my arm. 'Come with me to the place, Wotan. You'll see it. It's God. The sceptre talks to God.' He pulled off his breastplate and I saw he wore Ether's Urim and Thummim strapped to his hairy chest. 'Even Ether didn't know what the shapes mean. Lehi called it sacred script, Reformed Egyptian, he thought it came from Egypt with Moses. It's older. But when you look through the jewels of the Urim and Thummim everything falls into place. It's the same writing that's on the head of the sceptre.'

'Jared arrived here before Egypt existed,' I said. 'It's not Egyptian.'

Mara cradled the crushed head of the prophet in her arms. She looked up at me steadily.

'God led me to it,' Mulek said. 'It's mine.' He repeated: 'You'll come with me.'

'She comes too.'

Mulek laughed. 'Afraid the natives will run off with her? Marry her when you like, the sooner the better, shut her nagging mouth and fill her belly with child. We leave tomorrow, at dawn.'

Mara and I sat in the dark.

She said: 'It's numbers. Numbers to worship God by. You know what he's found.' Maralah sat with us, watching me across the embers with eyes like dark holes, understanding not a word. I said, 'Yes, I know.' We ate the poached meat Maralah had prepared, she was supposed to be a wonderful cook, and for the first time her face became animated as she watched me eat. I said: 'It's what Moses found in the desert, in the mountain.'

'Not the same one.'

'That almost destroyed the Hebrews.'

'That *did* destroy the Egyptian army,' Mara said.

'God led Moses to it. Maybe He leads Mulek.'

'God's not here,' Mara said in a low voice. 'I've been thinking. Something terrible or wonderful's happening here. I don't know which. Something new. I'm afraid.'

'But I saw Jesus just as you expected Him to look.'

'I know,' she said worriedly. 'I know.'

'Was it good?' Maralah asked, and we stared at her having completely forgotten her. 'Would you like some more?'

Mulek overslept. It was noon before we left, the men grumbling and still weary as they filed across the fields behind the mangrove swamps, cureloms plodding past us piled high with harvest for the town. The natives were busy setting up arches of branches and leaves for some religious festival. 'They're building a tree of life,' Mulek said. 'We've tried to bring faith in the Lord Most High and Christ to them,' he shrugged, 'but we're few, they're many. To their barbarian tongues the name of Christ is profaned as *Itzá*, and since the beginning of time they've believed in a prophet called Balaam. Look, they build their tree in the shape of a cross.'

'How strange,' Mara said.

'They can't even tell us what it means. Their feathered serpent god, the god of life. He's sacrificed and placed in the tree to be resurrected at the New Year. So they believe.'

Mara was right: the easiest travel was along the river. We climbed upstream and the rain began, then the waterfalls. Every afternoon Mulek ordered a small stockade built against robbers. Each night the hot rain fell and each day the sweltering valleys steamed, and clouds lay on the hilltops like great grey hands. 'This way,' Mulek called. We left the river and he hacked at the jungle with his sword. 'I'll clear all these trees. I'll plant fields here. I'll build houses of limestone and cement, and my palace above them. Beside my palace, like King Solomon, I'll build the Temple.' The jungle ended and a green hill rose over us. Mulek leant on the sceptre, staring upwards. 'Apachiohualitzá, the place the Jareds called Ararat. I'll call my city Zarahemla, city of Zarah, my most beautiful queen, my shining one, the foundation of my dynasty until the end of time.'

I glanced at Mara. We'd both heard this stuff a thousand times before, from a thousand tiny kings.

We climbed the slippery path to Ether's cave, the smelly cavity between two rock slabs leaning together. Mulek said, crouching inside, 'You'd think this was all. For ten, twenty years that crazy old man guarded the Urim and Thummim and the sceptre like some small savage animal, all that remained of his people's civilisation. Then we came, civilised people again. He embraced us. Trusted us. Showed us everything. This isn't all. It's just the entrance.'

451

A tallow candle was handed to him. Mulek crawled forward, then lay holding the sceptre beside him and wriggled forward. He pulled aside the grass matting covering Ether's toilet. Stench wafted up from below. 'More than twenty years of shit,' I said. Mara retched. Behind us one of the men was sick and the rest stumbled outside. 'You wouldn't come down here,' Mulek said, putting his head down the hole, 'unless you knew something.'

He slid down easily. The hole was big, much too big for a toilet; and it sloped.

I followed Mulek down, stood up, held out my arms. My fingertips touched smooth curving sides: a perfectly circular tunnel drilled at a steep slant into the rock. How? No marks of tools. The rock gleamed like fused glass, striking away from us like a smooth shining arrow point into the darkness below. Mulek balanced, the candle flame throwing light around him. 'Don't slip. Don't knock into me.' He pressed one hand against the roof, steadying himself, and went down. His voice faded, he shrank. It was a long way. 'Men didn't cut this tunnel,' I said, echoing. Mara slithered down behind me. She squeaked, slipping.

'It was drilled by the finger of God,' Mulek said, suddenly close. The light redoubled. Beyond his black silhouette Mulek's illuminated face appeared, convex, swelling as he approached himself, his features suddenly enormous as he peered into his reflection. His nose swelled like a leather ball. He smiled, all eyes and fangs, a bubble of spittle on one tooth.

'It's a sphere,' he said. 'A perfect mirror sphere. Look, not a mark on it. Fits the tunnel within the thickness of a hair on every side.' He pushed his hand against the surface, hard, but his hand couldn't touch his reflection, skidded. 'I can't tell if it's spinning or motionless,' he marvelled. 'Hot or cold. Here or not-here. It's perfect. It's God.'

I'd seen it before, or something exactly like it. I'd seen

Moses marvel exactly like this.

'It's not God, Mulek,' Mara said. 'It's not God or Satan or anything. Leave it alone.'

'It's me,' Mulek said. 'Look at me. I can do whatever I want.' He touched the sceptre. 'With this, and the Urim and Thummim, I speak to God. Ether was afraid to. Long ago, Ether said, the brother of Jared was guided by the Lord, and he came down the finger of the Lord and found this, His promise that the weak would be made strong, and Jared's brother dug it out. He showed it at Mount Zerin and blasted the mountain to dust, and the dust was gone so that nothing remained of the mountain. It was as though Mount Zerin had never been.'

'I'm not digging it out for you,' I said. 'Forget it. It stays down here.'

'My men will do it,' Mulek said. Mara's muscles tensed and I knew the look in her eyes: she'd make a grab for the sceptre, destroy us by turning the silver sphere into a pillar of fire or whatever, just as Moses destroyed Pharaoh's army. I imagined a million years of immortality trapped motionless beneath a mountain of rock and put my hand over Mara's, stopping her.

'The Jareds destroyed themselves using it!' Mara shouted. 'Ether had it thrown back down here because it destroyed them!'

'But first it built them. It built their civilisation,' Mulek said. 'The Jareds were few at first, as we are, but God guided them here to Him. The natives were many, but God subjugated them. Eight families of Jareds came ashore; but God's blessing made them a nation of millions. Later He scattered them as He scattered the Jews, because they didn't worship Him in the proper way. But now He has brought me here, I stand here, I am chosen by God. Now He shall make mine a nation of millions, a nation of cities, a nation of temples under God, glorifying our God! Hosanna to the glory of God.'

'I know it's not God,' I told Mara in a low voice. The campfire crackled in the night rain, we heard the clink of tools coming from the cave, and the men who'd come off shift snored uncomfortably. Tiny lizards scuttled in the dark, clinging above us to the leaves and tree branches, their eyes gleaming in the fitful flames as they watched us. I pulled my cloak over Mara's head to keep her dry, put my legs on each side of her, spoke to her close enough to kiss her. 'Did God leave His sign here too? As Moses found in the Land of the Moon? As Mulek's found here? What does it mean?'

Mara looked into my eyes. 'I know God put the stars in the sky. What did He mean by it? I don't know.' She'd changed so much. She laid the palms of her hands lightly on my cheeks and to my amazement, she kissed me. 'I don't know anything any more,' she murmured. 'I don't know God's purpose.'

'You did,' I objected. 'You were so certain. I liked it.'

'No, no, everything's chaos here. Nothing makes sense. It *is* the Devil's world. This is the world God built to contain the Devil. The prison Satan was thrown down to in the Fall, and the fallen angels too. This whole world is their Hell. They've made it Hell. Everything, even the sky. The stars. Everything's awful. No love. No God. Abandoned.'

'I love you.'

'That's not so very much, is it?' she cried. 'If only you knew how great the love of God is!'

'It can't be more than you.'

She pulled me to her, pressed my forehead to her lips. 'I was wrong about you, Wotan,' she sighed. 'Even you have so much to teach me.'

This was better. 'All my women tell me I'm a wonderful lover,' I encouraged her. 'I'm strong but my fingertips are very sensuous, and I have a most impressive penis.'

'Not that sort of love.' Her eyes gleamed, blinking, I could tell she was tearful. 'Maybe you're a sign of God after all, Wotan. Even you. That He does have a purpose. That there's a glimmer of hope for us if only we knew what it was. Surely it can't be you.'

'No doubt about it,' I told her. Her face was lovely and warm. 'Tell me what Mulek's found. What it really is.'

'You wouldn't understand.' She kissed my forehead. I waited, feeling her breathing. 'It's a star,' she said.

'But a star's bigger,' I said. 'Pulled by a chariot.'

'It's smaller,' she said. 'Invisibly small. It's so cold inside the sphere that time hardly exists. Nothing goes in or out. It's a place like our universe before our universe was born.'

I stroked her hair. 'If that's the truth,' I said, 'it doesn't make any sense.'

'I'll tell you the truth so you can understand it.' She hugged me close, whispering to my shoulder. 'Once upon a time, a long, long time ago, Ouranos the god of the sky fell to the earth, Gaia.'

'I've heard all these stories,' I said. 'Whatever their names are, he's always male and she's always female. He falls in love with her. People love anything spiced up with plenty of sex. Kings. God. Death.' I added, 'The natives here call their god of the sky Caan.'

'You don't recognise the truth even when I tell it to you,' she said.

I held out my hand. 'It's stopped raining.' The clouds pulled aside, the stars came out like jewels.

'This was Ouranos,' she insisted. '*Ouranos*. Ouranos fell on Gaia with such force' – she groped for easy words – 'fell on her with such passion, that he penetrated Gaia right to her womb.' Again she paused. 'Are you following me now?'

'All the way.'

'There were no children in the world, none. No humans. But now Gaia conceived. Conceived humans deep inside

455

her, do you understand? They had to be born. They had to climb out of her womb through the long tunnel to be born.'

'Is there a point to this story? It was here?'

She shrugged. 'What do you think?'

'I've heard it hundreds of times, hundreds of places. I probably heard this tale on my mother's knee. Each time it's a little different.'

'Just as all the stories of the Flood are a little different. Just a little.'

'The Greeks say Gaia's children were trapped in her womb until one of them, Time, cut off Ouranos's gigantic penis, which was embedded in her body, so that they could be born.'

'Do you believe it?'

I shrugged. 'Storytellers like to say *penis* because it makes the audience giggle.'

'Take the gods out of the story, Wotan. No myth. No story. Keep the bones. What are you left with? An account of something that happened.'

'So what's left has nothing to do with God. It's just a shiny thing.'

'It's just a star, Wotan. Properly used it absorbs matter and emits energy with an efficiency of forty-two parts per hundred at the event horizon.'

'And it destroyed Mount Zerin.'

'It would destroy our sun and all the stars you can see.' We sat looking up at the stars sprinkled between the silver clouds and I said, 'They still look like jewels.'

'You don't believe me. I could prove it to you, if you were educated, and understood about atoms, and numbers—'

'I believe you,' I said simply. 'Moses believed it was the moon. It's easy to believe it's a star.'

She touched the lock of my hair that always fascinated her.

'So it's just a star,' I said. 'A tool that can be used foolishly or wisely. Maybe sent by God, maybe not. People can believe in it or not. Maybe God has no power in this universe, it's just the rubbish tip where He threw Satan down and Satan's as great as God here. But I don't believe it, Mara. I've seen things which have no explanation.'

'Not really. It's just because you're ignorant. There's always an explanation.'

'I was born.'

'I'm sure that has an explanation, Wotan.'

'I am a son of God.'

'So you believe.'

'I saw Elijah make fire fall from the sky. No Arch of the Covenant, no sceptre. Elijah prayed, and the stones burst into flames, even the water caught fire, and the rising steam burnt with long tongues of flame.'

She hesitated. 'There's obviously an explanation.'

'What is it? I heard Nabuchadnezzar's dream of something that happened in my own life, that he can't possibly have known. His divinely inspired dream that men have the hearts of beasts, as Huwawa the guardian of the tree said, "like a monkey walking upright shall you live". We're just animals. We're not divine. Not even men. Beneath the skin we're monkeys.'

'Wotan, my explanation is that some people may believe even that.'

'Listen. In Bab'El I saw Shadrach, Meshach and Abednego thrown in the fiery furnace. I couldn't save them, so I walked with them in the holocaust. The flames met above our heads but didn't touch us.'

'Obviously not a very hot furnace.'

'We talked with mouths of fire.'

'An illusion.'

I said: 'Like Jesus Christ.' She jerked, startled, but I held her. 'You believed what I saw,' I said. 'In the storm I saw Jesus Christ walking on the water, I described Him to

457

you, crown, cloak, rings, fierce eyes, incredible, yet you believed me.'

'Yes, because you couldn't possibly have known what He looks like, according to the traditions, yet you described Him exactly. Jesus Christ granted you a vision of Him, Wotan.' She hugged me, close to me, warm. 'You never told me what He said to you.'

For a moment, surprised, I stopped thinking of her body. 'He didn't say a word.'

She searched my eyes. 'You didn't bow down to Him?'

'No.'

'But you weren't punished? Not one word?'

'No, He didn't say anything.' I thought back. 'Satan spoke.'

'*Satan* spoke to you! Oh, Wotan, can't you do anything right?'

'I wasn't frightened. He fascinated me.' I tried to remember exactly. 'He spoke so quietly. I expected thunder and lightning, but his voice was soft, almost sad. He said, "Give me the crown of stars that is lost." That's all he said.' We listened to the clink of tools from the cave. 'The star,' I said, realising. 'There's much more. More than the one hidden in Mount Moses, the Arch of the Covenant that was taken to Jerusalem—'

'Taken *back* to Jerusalem,' she said. 'Hidden by Solomon. No one knows where it is.'

'When I killed Huwawa . . .' I stopped, remembering the dragon's halo around its head, the shining crown of stars, the blinding *shekinah* of divine glory. 'He cursed me.' I showed Mara my hand scarred through by Huwawa's tooth. 'As he died the cooling star fell from his crown, but with his dying spasm he hid the place where it fell.'

'You never found it?'

'I never thought about it. Huwawa's last words seemed more important. "For the third time I curse you. I am not the last, Wotan, nor the greatest."'

She said, 'Who's the greatest?'

'Huwawa said: "You will know Him." I never knew whether he meant someone greatest to Huwawa – Satan, I suppose – or greatest to God, Jesus Christ.'

Mara stared at me. 'But you *didn't* know the man who walked towards you on the waves was Jesus. You said Lehi cried out it was Jesus. *You* didn't say so. Jesus didn't speak to you. Nephi didn't even see Him! You said you *didn't* believe the man you saw was Jesus Christ, because you didn't believe one man could change the world.' She stopped, appalled. 'But you said Satan knew you and spoke to you.'

'Then maybe the Devil blew us here to New Sion and looks after us, not God.'

Such a thought was so enormous we both fell silent.

'God help us,' Mara said. 'I know what the Devil wants.'

The sound of tools had stopped. Mulek came through the trees carrying the sceptre. Behind him followed the men holding a shape floating between them as light as a bubble, respectfully draped in white pineapple silk. 'Cut trees to make a box for the sanctuary,' Mulek ordered. 'The Lord Most High shall live inside His sanctuary, and my people are safe as long as He's among us here in Zarahemla. Send to Bountiful, fetch our slaves, take prisoners, bring the criminals, they too shall do the Lord's work. Fetch brickmakers, bricklayers, cementmakers, stonemasons to build my royal city that no man shall conquer. Send for miners to dig gold and metalworkers to fashion the gold mercy-seat for the Lord Most High. An angel of beaten gold shall stand on each side, their arched wingtips meeting over the seat, and the name of the sanctuary shall be the Arch of the Covenant, and from it the Voice of the Lord Most High shall speak when the time comes.'

'I can do one thing right,' I told Mara. 'I'm marrying you.'

From very large matters we returned to very small affairs of interest only to a bride and groom. The streets of Bountiful were almost empty, most of the men taken for work at Zarahemla. King Mulek's great project would keep him busy for years, and out of harm's way, I hoped. We had plenty of time, and I was smiling.

'I've never given myself before,' Mara said. 'Ever. Why are you smiling?'

'You're just the sort I like,' I leered. 'Quite a catch.'

'I still wonder about you. I'm giving up everything I once believed in for you,' she said.

'Your,' I touched the tip of her nose, 'wedding nerves.'

She winced, smiled. 'All my life I've dreamt of giving myself to Jesus, in the spirit. Serving Him eternally. His eternal virgin, eternally innocent. Now I'm marrying you, losing it all.' We passed the Sealing House where the Elder of the Order of Melchizadok would marry us tomorrow, kneeling on each side of the altar. The sound of waves breaking along the beach faded behind us as we came to her house among the trees. Mara's servant was laying her wedding clothes out on the bed – the bride's sacred split-crotch white undergarment, her white blouse and long white skirt, her girdled robe, moccasins for her feet and veil for her head, and a green fig-leaf apron to be swept aside at the appropriate moment. The servant turned and I saw she was no servant, but Maralah. She'd been crying, I don't know why. Mara embraced her.

'I just want you to know,' Maralah said tearfully, 'that you both have my blessing.' I kissed the top of her head.

'Go, go!' Mara chivvied me. 'I don't want to see you till tomorrow.' She pushed me out and my last sight was her holding her wedding clothes against her, chattering eagerly to her sister, this ribbon or that ribbon, so I left them to it and went for a swim. The glorious sunset faded and the cooking fires along the beach grew bright. I found my native friends smiling welcome, their rotten teeth filed to points and inset with green jade. A piece of jade and a few chocolate beans bought my supper on the sand, crayfish and clams, iguana steaks on sticks, a whole plucked stuffed turkey, a big toothy fish I didn't know the name of, big loaves of maize bread washed down with plenty of corn liquor, and I finished off with pineapples and more corn liquor. 'Drink, Wotan!' My best friend Chachua was pleased to see me. 'With you here we know we're safe. The Gujalhantón robbers will never dare attack knowing you are here.' Had robbers been a problem? A few heads nodded but Chachua put his heavy arms around me. 'We're afraid of nothing now you are here, Wotan. Drink. Get married tomorrow.' I drank and said, 'Tomorrow's today.' One by one the men fell down snoring in the hut, and the fire died down, but Chachua staggered to me with a last full *tecomate* bowl. 'Drink. Sleep. I sleep.' I drained it and lay back by the embers, but I saw Chachua didn't sleep. He snored, but his eyes gleamed. The snoring of my friends ceased, then the house was quiet as death except for Chachua's breathing. My muscles tightened, straining, bulging against each other in opposition, locked. I couldn't move. Blood trickled down my nose. I'd drunk enough snake poison to kill ten men; the doorway darkened as the moon set behind the hill. It was the signal.

Chachua sat up. He drew his black obsidian knife. In pagan days, before the arrival of the Mulekites, he'd cut out the heart of his eldest son for the Sun god. The blade clinked against a stone, I heard his knees scuffle as he crawled towards me in the dark. I felt his breath against my cheek. I shouted; nothing. Couldn't even open my mouth. Chachua laid the blade against my neck and cut at my throat, but my muscles were too hard. I heard shouts outside, a fire flared up, then screaming started. Running feet, clanging of weapons, sounds of pain and dying. Gujalhantón robbers. The traitor Chachua sat on my chest with his bare feet on each side of my head, hurrying, teeth

461

and eyes showing slits clenched almost shut as he sawed. 'Die, Wotan, die.' Then a single drop of sweat fell from his forehead into my eye.

My eye blinked.

I sat up as stiffly as a man of stone. My hands couldn't grip the knife. Chachua tried to stab me but fell back, and I rolled heavily on him. My arms were bent, I couldn't straighten them, but I got my elbow over his neck and pulled his head off, then stumbled across the poisoned dead bodies of my friends to the door. Outside was chaos, men running and women running into the sea, babies crying, women running with the babies, houses burning. The stones left my muscles, I hobbled, jogged, ran forward. Sweat and snake poison poured from me as I ran between the burning houses. 'Mara,' I shouted. Men rushed at me, surrounded me screaming and hacking at me with knives. I killed them all, I ran shouting between the trees along the path. 'Mara!' I saw her house burning between the trees, the flames rising above the trees. I shouted her name and ran towards her, she ran to me between the tree trunks, I swept her up in my arms. 'Thank God. Mara, thank God you're safe.'

She looked at me with pure horror on her face. It was not Mara but Maralah I held.

That was the end of it; that was all. We never knew which was Mara's body, her ashes so mingled with the ash of her servants and dogs, and there was a cat I think, under the cindered walls fallen in and the roof fallen down . . . it took days to cool. I couldn't recognise anything as I picked through the wreckage. Maralah spoke and I heard Mara's voice. Maralah wept and I heard Mara weeping. I found a blackened bone and turned to see, not Mara, but Maralah. Her tragic eyes. She blamed herself. I blamed her too. She should have died, nor Mara. We both knew it. Mara had been so full of life.

'I'm so sorry,' Maralah whispered. 'I wish I was dead. I'd be happy to have died in her place, because you'd still have her and you'd be happy.' I'd never seen anyone look worse than Maralah, suffering had given her bruised eyes a depth she'd never had; I noticed her for the first time. 'It's your fault she'd dead,' I said. 'You should have been sleeping with her. You might have saved her.'

Maralah's face broke like shattered glass. 'No, I'll never forgive me, never.' She crouched until her head touched her knees, rocking, her hair as long as Mara's touching the ground. She wept to die.

I walked away furiously through the trees, I ran on the beach among the women weeping for their husbands and fathers and children, I ran like the wind until I could no longer hear them and I stopped, but the wind blew and carried the sound to me. I walked back to Maralah.

'There has to be something good I can do,' I said. 'One good thing.' We stared around us, total desolation. Nothing. 'Marry me,' I said. 'Maralah, marry me.'

I picked Maralah up in my arms and kissed her. She jerked back. 'No, I'm not Mara,' she said, but her eyes searched mine in exactly that way. 'You don't love me.'

'I know you love *me*, Maralah, you always have. You've been so unhappy. I can make you happy.'

'I can never be her for you. I'm nothing like her.' Maralah brushed a blond curl from my eyebrow. 'Yes, I've always loved you. I always will. My poor sister thought she had a choice, but I never did.'

She married me; that's the end of it, the all. She loved me with complete happiness and she never asked me, when I said I loved her, which was often, whether it was her I meant or Mara. Maralah knew that love is many things, and she was grateful for what little she had. She could have lived no happier or more perfect life. Bountiful was rebuilt, especially at our end where we had our house overlooking the bay, as the port for Zarahemla. The landing stage grew to a harbour wall made of coral; the Gujalhantón robbers were held back to the other side of the river. Children were born, though not ours, and men and women died, but not us. Where I'd once seen a hundred busy people along the beach, I now looked from my window and saw a thousand. 'They're beginning to talk,' Maralah said.

I turned. 'You don't look old.'

'It's not me. It's you.' She touched her palms to the muscles of my chest, slid her fingers up into my long blond hair. 'You look so young.' She kissed my lips. 'I don't want to be an old woman beside a young man. I want to be young for ever in you. Born again in you.' She touched the pearl in my hair. 'It's time.'

That night the moon rose over the sea and we left our clothes and danced naked on the moonlit sand for the last time, swam in the moonlit waves, and the waves broke over our heads as our mouths met and we kissed. I felt her pearl between her lips, the sand slipped under our feet, we slid down and I felt her enter me, I gasped at the shock of penetration and this gouging act of love so close to death, I felt energy and violence gushing into my womb, my immortality.

I walked from the sea and bound the pearl in my hair. A native called out, 'Hey, Maralah!' I covered my breasts – he gazed admiringly at my bottom – and walked home. When people asked me I said Wotan had gone to Zarahemla, or Mulek City, or that he explored the grassy uplands. The women said, 'Typical man, him leaving you in this condition.' Within a few months my condition was all too obvious; my strength terrified the midwives, and in labour I broke the bed and most of the walls in the house, but my son was born. I cradled him, kissed him, and named him Vidar. He was a delightful boy, but soon almost as strong as his father had been. I loved my son with all my heart, but he was Wotan's blood, carrying a curelom on his shoulders at the age of four, and a year later he killed a man who attacked him. They grow up so quickly. Before the truth was known I hid with him in the jungle, building a house in the treetops of a ridge between Bountiful and the River Sion in the eastern wilderness. On a clear day, when the light was right, we saw as far as Zarahemla glinting in the vast nothingness of the state, the last outpost of civilisation.

One morning Vidar stood beside me, taller than me, bearded, and kissed my white hairs. He stroked my face lovingly but I could tell the wanderlust was in him. Before sunset he was gone, swinging down among the trees with bow and arrows in one hand, gone hunting as fast and completely as a wild animal – to the northward I think, but I couldn't bear to watch him go. I never can. I wept as though my heart was broken, but really it was from joy. I'd done my best for him, and no mother can do more for her son. 'Goodbye, Vidar,' I called across the treetops that night. 'Goodbye.'

Days passed, and day by day my strength weakened. I covered the windows of the treetop house with fronds, unable to bear the blistering sun, and lay in the dark too weak to move. Rain fell at last, pattering in a broken frond. I turned it with trembling hands and gazed at my wrinkled reflection in the water. I was an old, old woman. Each breath sapped my strength, I crawled across the floor to the hatch and climbed down the ladder, lost my footing, fell down from the third platform to the second, heard my hip break and lay writhing in helpless agony, then pulled myself to the edge and let go. Rain sheeted around me in the steaming jungle. The breaking rungs of the ladder slowed my fall a little, my shoulder struck the edge of the first platform, then I slid off and dropped to the ground as limp as a bag of bones.

There was only one way to go: downhill. The rain poured past me, then brown runoff, then white foam which swept me down a torrent between fallen trunks and rotting vegetation to a filthy scummy pool. Where the water overflowed the bloated carcass of a curelom stuck its legs up into the rain. Fortunately scavengers had torn open the belly; the effort would have been beyond me. I stuck my head inside and pulled with my teeth at the soft glistening meat, pulled out the slimy lengths and ate with the last of my strength. Disgusting, gorgeous, bloody food. The pain left my hip and after a few minutes I stood, tore at the haunches with my hands, pushed handfuls of blood and steak into my wide open mouth, gulping it down. The hairs prickled on the back of my neck. I turned, and a jaguar black as the night prowled along a branch towards me.

I leapt up joyfully as the jaguar leapt on me for the kill, we stood up tall together, chin to chin, for I have power over animals, this is the beautiful moment: the sheathed claws of the beast on my shoulders, our heads back, roaring at the sky.

I am Wotan, and I remember the moment of my conception.

It's one of the ironies of history that when Nephi (like Moses fleeing Egypt) fled from his pagan brothers in New Jerusalem and led his people in their great journey south, they entirely missed the city of Zarahemla. I knew the jungle like the back of my hand and followed Nephi's passage through the western wild country of Grijalva from the treetops. From my swaying vantage point I saw the great ocean continue westward on one side of them, and on their other side I saw the grassy central uplands that would have led them eastward to Zarahemla; but Nephi, grey as Moses, wearing the inherited yellow cloak of Zadok (his people hadn't yet acclaimed him king) led them south turning his eyes neither right nor left. He'd heard God tell him to take his people to the land southward, and southward he went.

The passing years that aged him had left me as youthful as ever, and I was careful not to be seen by anyone who'd know me – I knew (I thought) that my immortality was not God's purpose, since it was a curse. So I held back from my ageing friends, watching from high above, monkeys howling around me, and Nephi's grey head passed below without looking up. Jacob whom I remembered as a baby was now a tall black-bearded man with the bearing of a priest, then his brother Joseph followed, and all their wives and families. I recognised old Zoram and his wives and grandchildren, then Nephi's brother Sam who'd finally turned his back on Laman and Lemuel to follow Nephi. Behind Sam's wives and families came Nephi's sisters, but I didn't see their husbands Ayn and Cumor, or their sons Ram-Ya and Cumor-Ya. I wondered if they'd stayed northward to take their God to the natives of the man-made mountain I'd seen.

Once Nephi did stop in surprise, speaking to backwoods natives whose labours (and occasionally blood) fed the pyramids and temples of Kaminaljuyú. 'What?' he cried. 'Votan?' The natives had heard garbled stories of my exploits, and some of them worshipped me as a great spirit. 'But Wotan's been dead for years,' Nephi said, 'he sailed away for love, and was never seen again.' The natives of the broad fertile valley smiled helpfully, not understanding a word.

In silence I watched Nephi's people cross the narrowest neck of the isthmus, the ocean invisible beyond the jungle on each side of them, and continue into the wide land southward. In a grassy valley above the worst of jungle diseases, fed by the sweet water of a highland lake, they stopped and pitched their tents for the last time, and called their little Eden the city of Nephi.

At first the city of Nephi was nothing compared to the city of Zarahemla.

Years later I returned to Zarahemla. No one I

467

remembered lived. Mulek had died long ago of cancers, and his son's son sat on the throne. The Temple overlooked the city from its tonsured grassy hilltop, shaved now of trees, a shining dream from a distance. The original Solomon's Temple, I recalled, took Hiram five or six years to build, but as I came closer I saw that after three generations of work this Temple was still scaffolded. I walked closer, eating a pomegranate, pushing through the crowds of natives and fair-haired Jareds in the busy markets. From here I saw the Temple roof unfinished, bare joists already mossy, the walls damp and streaked with green. A native priest stood on the steps arguing with the crowd. I barely understood his language, a polyglot mess of Hebrew, Mayan, Egyptian, even a few ancient Shem words from the Jareds. I drew back from the piles of concrete left hardened in the sun, empty scaffolds, scattered shovels, listened to the voices shouting incomprehensibly. They'd made a tower of Bab'El of their Temple. In the courtyard a cart stood on four solid wheels, one of them broken: Mulek's Arch of the Covenant. They'd forgotten Moses's Covenant was carried into battle, not rolled. Its sides were decorated with sun and star motifs, a fiery sword sprouting flames like feathers, Egyptian symbols, an All-Seeing Eye surrounded by the rays of a *shekinah*. The gold angels on top had been stolen. In the afternoon the king, little older than a boy, came and pushed aside the priest and argued with the people. I'd seen enough, and walked away.

I walked from the isthmus into the land northward, keeping near the gulf coast which I knew, walking north with the summer. Laman's people had reached across the mountains and down the long beaches of sand, and they remembered his name – their ruler was called a *Laman* and lived somewhere in the north, they thought. Mostly they were a contented village people, or hunters who lived off the land in small groups, but sufficiently numerous not to fear the northern native tribes. The natives preferred to live in big cities with mounds and temples like the Jareds long ago. As the Lamani numbers grew – so many wives – I reckoned their land spread its long boundary south and westward by a day or two's walk each year. They treated me hospitably; it was a beautiful land. I fell in love seven hundred times and made love seventeen times a night, and drifted eventually to New Jerusalem.

I wrapped my clothes in a bundle and swam across. Trees grew again on the long narrow island as though the fields had never been. Little remained of the houses and barns I remembered. Fallen stones and corners of wall poked through the undergrowth. No apple trees survived; some blight spread by the stocks we'd bought. A small colony of Nephite dissenters clung on by the central lake, tilling the exhausted rocky earth for neas and sheum barley and doggedly worshipped their God among the wine-drinking meat-eating Lamani, gamblers all. 'This is the state of Lehi-Nephi, our fathers' first inheritance,' claimed the dissenters' leader, Zeniff; so their past was not quite forgotten. 'The Nephi, our king in the land southward, sent me to spy on the Lamanite army. But they don't have an army. They live in peace here. They're a good people.' Zeniff paused in confusion. 'Even though they don't know God.'

'No wars?' I said, disappointed. 'No raping or killing? No plunder?'

'Only when we try to take God to them. But the people of Cumor-Ya go with God.' He pointed approvingly towards the native hill to the north. 'The temple at the top looks like a shrine to animal spirits and other atrocities, but long ago the great King Cumor-Ya put it to better use, taking it for God.' He nodded, satisfied. 'The natives there worship God, so we shan't destroy them. We're going to build a spire on top so that God knows His own.' He added, 'We have swords, bows and arrows, and hatchets buried beneath our fields for when the day of wrath comes.'

'What's that?'

'The day when the Wrath of God shall come from Zarahemla against the Lamanites.'

I stared. 'Nephi's people have discovered Zarahemla?'

'About half a century ago at Nephi City we almost destroyed ourselves fighting each other. A truce was called. The year was sacred, One-One-One, one hundred and eleven years until the birth of Christ ordained by the prophecy of Lehi. Four hundred and seventy-six years had passed, according to the scrolls, since Lehi left Jerusalem. King Benjamin's son Mosiah, a priest educated in the ancient language, wearing the yellow cloak, led whoever would go with him on a pilgrimage to find the land where our forefathers came ashore. They had no idea how far it was, they remembered only myths of Sion and Cumor-Ya in the land northward, so they kept their eyes open. When Mosiah reached the first wilderness, at the narrow neck of land, he discovered the city of Zarahemla surrounded by a desolation of burnt forests and blackened fields. They, too, had almost destroyed themselves. They'd forgotten God; yet Mosiah found God among them.'

'The Covenant,' I said. 'The Sword of Solomon.'

'God's promise,' Zeniff agreed. 'In their wickedness and stupidity, in their wars with the natives, the Mulekites had abused God's promise, it became a curse against themselves. The hills turned to fire, year after year the crops died, they starved. They turned their backs on God and buried the Arch of the Covenant where King Mulek had found it in ancient times before the city was built.'

'Beneath the Temple.'

'Yes, the Temple had been built over the place, of course. Mosiah went down; as a priest he knew how to use the Urim and Thummim, translated the sacred writing, and brought God out to the people.'

'What did they do?'

'They acclaimed Mosiah king, of course! He rebuilt the Temple and placed the Covenant in the Holy of Holies. The crops grew, the plagues ceased. The people made sacrifice and burnt offerings at the Temple by the Law of Moses, as they had in the past. For half a century God smiled on us in Zarahemla, our numbers grew, and we destroyed our enemies. But then, spreading into the land northward, we encountered the Lamanites spreading south, and I was sent as a spy among them to find the holy land of Lehi-Nephi.' He saw my look. 'This is the land of our first inheritance. It's *ours*.'

I asked, 'When will war come?'

Zeniff replied, 'We will sweep the earth clean of the pagan Lamanites before Christ is born, so that He shall know we are His righteous people.'

There was much else that I did, but if all were written down it would fill all the books in the world. I kept a careful tally of the years to the predicted birth of Christ, finding a secret glade near the beach at Bountiful, counting the years down with horizontal lines on the trunk of a sapling as it grew to a mighty mahogany, and finally I drew my last horizontal line. There is, of course, no year zero, as it's impossible to imagine nothing; the natives use an empty shell. At the end of their month *Xu*, when the sun is never lower in the noon sky, and the natives' god is sacrificed in the tree of life and resurrected for the new year, I drew my first vertical line. If Lehi's prediction was right, the birth Mara had faith in for so long had finally come true: far away in Jerusalem, if Jerusalem existed – if the Jews, incredibly, had somehow returned from their exile in Bab'El like a whole nation returning from the dead, and if somehow they'd built the new Temple prophesied by Ezekiel – the Christ-Child had today been born to a virgin in the Holy of Holies. Did the saintly Guardian of Christ, the shepherd Joseph of Nazareth, son of Jonan, stand by his wife's Son and acknowledge Jesus Christ as our Anointed Saviour? Did Abraham's sceptre rest against His cradle? Did three magicians come bringing gifts, one of silver, one of balsam, and one of precious galbanum incense, to anoint the Son of God who would save us all? I remembered her words as though she spoke them still, of *the kingdom of Heaven to which He will lead the faithful and the saved; and of His people, not one shall be unsaved.*

No choirs of angels sang. Nothing happened.

A butterfly fluttered from the tree and its wingtip brushed a leaf, the leaf fell on a rotten branch which cracked, and its fall sent parrots whirling startled from the treetops. No, nothing happened.

I looked up at the sky where a few clouds formed. Perhaps, I thought, God doesn't recognise His Son; perhaps He has *sons*, ten thousand sons, ten million, if there are as many as ten million sons in the world. Tears pricked my eyes. Abandoned sons, as I am. Not knowing their father. Why did El forsake me? Not a word from Him, no guidance whether I lived as He wished, whether I did good or evil, whether I should do something or nothing, stand or sit; not one word. The clouds drifted over the sea until they seemed no larger than a man's hand, and the wind blew them away.

Nothing happened, and I fell into a drunken stupor that night, but each year I added a vertical line, cancelling each six with a seventh line scratched across. When I had seven lines and another six ready to be crossed off, I knew Jesus Christ was in his thirteenth year. That was the year the hurricane came. Hurricanes come every year; this one was different. For three days the wind blew and waves threw themselves across the headlands and across the bay. On the evening of the third day the eye opened over us. The wind fell calm and we left our shelters. Against the stormy red sunset we saw the mast and rigging of a ship, then the ship was picked up on a great sea and driven forward so that we saw the men clinging on the deck with the crest of the wave overhanging them. Surf broke on each side of them, they were sure to die. On the high stern I saw the young man who steered the ship watching me, standing calmly, steering straight towards me. The sun flared behind him, silhouetting him against a *shekinah* of rays like flames or feathers. The wave lost its force, carrying the ship gently on a long tongue of foam across the sand. The ship jolted slightly as it came to rest, then at once the vessel fell apart piece by piece as if completely worn out now its job was done: the mast broke in half and fell down, the ropes unwound, the nails sprang out and the planks collapsed from the ribs, the ribs folded out from the keel, the railings broke and the crew fell from the deck. But the steerman did not fall down. He smiled cheerfully, still watching me. He called – no, he *calls*. I hear him now.

He calls to me, 'This isn't Britain, is it?'

I stare, I can't believe him.

'Britain,' he calls. 'The Eretz ha-Brit, the Land of the Covenant.'

'My God, you've crossed the ocean?'

He grips my hand, knowing my strength, jumps down. 'Much too hot for Britannia.' That's a word I've never heard. He says: 'It's Latin. Rome's our master now.' He flexes his toes luxuriously in the sand, stretches, yawns. Long brown hair, a slightly straggly brown beard; sixteen or seventeen I reckon, too old to be the One. He reproves me, 'Wotan, Wotan, a man like you should know better than to believe prophecies.' He speaks in Aramaic with a country accent. 'Galilee accent,' he corrects me, 'I'm from Galilee. Sepphoris is my home town. Him, he's from Arimathea.' He points to the older man, wearing the turban of a priest, limping on sandals of wood and rope from the perfectly deconstructed wreck. 'Joseph! It's not Britain. No tin. The Arimathean's a tin trader,' he explains.

I blurt, 'These hills are full of gold and silver.'

'Gold and silver's no good to a tin trader, Wotan.'

'I take gold and silver.' The Arimathean rubs his hands. 'I do take it. I can handle it.' He introduces us fondly. 'This young fool's Joshua the Nazarene.' *Yehoshua Notzri*.

Joshua clasps my wrist. 'It's been a long voyage. You grow wine here. I saw the vineyards from the sea.'

Wine. He drinks wine. He probably even eats bread. I'm delighted and amazed. Everything's overturned from what I expected, but I still can't believe what my ears are hearing. 'A wine-drinking Nazarene?' Incredible; I *know* who he is, I can feel it, even though the facts are wrong. I mean if facts are all that matter, I'm making a fool of myself by believing what I know to be true.

He grins. 'Lapsed Nazarene.'

I burst out, 'Why?'

'A Nazarene's consecrated to God from the womb to the tomb. Does that explain God? No. No, it's not nearly enough.'

'You're searching for God? You?'

He touches my eyes with his fingertips. 'You're a Watcher, aren't you, Wotan? We're watching for God.'

'He isn't in this world.'

'My earthly father's an orthodox Nazarene. So are my brothers. Here, I'm free.' He sounds like any youngster on his first adventure. He walks beside me on the sand, the wind begins to blow as the hurricane returns but he puts out his hand and it stops. 'The star Merak on my right eyebrow and the North Star on my right temple,' he says. 'It worked. Land.'

'New Sion. You weren't really trying to get to Britain, were you? Why are you here?'

'I need to reach the people of the isthmus.'

'There's a whole vast continent northward and southward.'

'This is the place that's important to me. The place

I've come to. Where the wind blows me.'

It's too quiet on the beach. I look around me, realising that every native kneels until his or her forehead touches the sand. Not to me, to Joshua. Their children run forward to Joshua. I've never seen children so happy, their faces shine like little suns. They wait their turn, giggling, then introduce their names solemnly. Those too young to know who they are hold out their arms to be picked up. Joshua picks them up and kisses them and hands them to me until I'm decorated with children like a New Year tree walking at his side along the sand. I murmur, 'You knew my name all along.'

'You know mine.' He looks in my eyes. 'You know mine.' A Mulekite wine-seller runs forward with goblets of wine. 'Ah, wine. No, don't water it. Take some to the men.' He drinks thirstily, Adam's apple bobbing in his throat. I watch him carefully. Is this wine-drinking boy who's rebelling against his parents really tough enough to rule the world? How must he best grow up? What's the Divine plan? Am I part of it, do I matter at all?

'Joshua, my sword is yours.' I kneel, dropping a child in the sand at this most serious moment, and all the children laugh. I silence them with a fierce glare. 'A steel sword. It's in my tree-house. It's yours.'

He says gently, 'It won't be needed, Wotan. You're not my mighty man.'

Someone who doesn't want me to kill for him. Simply incredible. I have to more than know, I have to hear it from his own lips. 'Joshua, are you the Son of God? *The* One?'

'Who knows his father?' He holds out his cup for a refill. 'Does the Son of God drink wine?' He chews a turkey leg. 'Does the Son of God eat chicken?'

'You know what meat it is,' I reproach him. 'Jesus Christ knows everything.'

'Knowing the difference between turkey and chicken

isn't knowing everything, Wotan.' He holds out his cup for more, getting going now. 'You talk like my mother. She's a believer. But she believes I should be different from what I am.'

'Mothers always think their sons are little gods. Until they grow up, anyway.'

He says: 'That I should be someone not myself. She sent me away. She was afraid for me.'

'Joshua, six hundred years ago, did you walk on the waves? Did you save us on the sea?'

He frowns. For the first time he doesn't know the answer. 'Me?'

'From the Dragon. You're not like what I expected, Joshua. Not royal. You *are* different. No gold rings. No fierce eyes.'

'I can be fierce,' he says mildly. 'What dragon?'

'Stronger than me. I've killed a hundred thousand men and made love to a hundred thousand women,' I brag, impressing him. 'I'm not nobody. 'I can carry the weight of thirty men on one arm. It was bigger than me.'

'I'm stronger,' Joshua says. A child's crying, it's just a broken arm. Joshua picks her up and touches it, fixes it. She smiles up at him like an angel, healed. What's he up to? 'I'm an *Asayya*,' he explains, 'a healer. An Essene.' I remembered Lehi, *He shall be the Lamb of God, a healer, an Asayya as we are*. 'Essenes aren't loved in Jerusalem. We hate the Sadducees, even the Pharisees. Essenes serve the ordinary people with humility and hard work – not with healing these days, since we left the *Therapeutae* in Egypt, as we mustn't be contaminated by death. So here I am, neither an Essene, nor a Nazarene, nor a Therapeut, yet something of all those things. Not a Galilean, born in Bethlehem in Judah. Educated in Egypt not the *shuls* of Jerusalem. When I'm eighteen I'll join our monastery at Sion, on the Dead Sea, as a novice with the Poor.' The monastery at Sion. Something's survived the Exile. In fact, the way he's talking of Jerusalem, nothing's changed. 'But will even Sion be enough?' He draws a circle with his toe in the sand. 'When my earthly father dies, as his eldest son I shall automatically be inaugurated as the Christ.'

I ask bluntly, 'Are you Jesus Christ?'

'No, that's a title, Wotan. Joseph the Christ is the leader of the Essenes, my earthly father. He's the Christ, as I shall be, if I live.'

'Joseph the shepherd, son of Jonan.'

'My earthly father is a carpenter, son of Heli. I am of King David's royal blood through both my earthly father and my mother. At Sion I shall take the oath, standing before the true Zadok, to be the Christ-Messiah and lead my people to Jerusalem.'

'Who is the Zadok now?'

'Judas Zadok was defeated and killed six years ago by the Romans, after the tax revolt which he led. A new generation is rising. Perhaps John the Baptist will be Zadok, perhaps Simon Magus; perhaps my brother James.'

'What do the prophecies expect the Christ-Messiah to do in Jerusalem?'

'In Jerusalem I shall throw down the Sadducees who insult God' – the word he used was *Abba*, Father – 'because they worship Him by the days of the moon not the sun. I shall throw down the Temple and rebuild it as the perfect Temple in three days. I shall throw down the great empire of the Romans so that they bow at my feet. This is what the Christ-Messiah *does*. If he doesn't, he's not the Christ-Messiah.'

'Yet you refuse my sword.'

'I'm young, Wotan. Perhaps I'm young and in love and wrong.' He hesitates. 'It seems to me that killing people doesn't change their minds.'

'You can't *be* wrong! It's a contradiction in terms. You can't talk like this! What is right is whatever you say it is, Joshua. It isn't meant to be like this,' I groan. 'It's this world that makes everything wrong, it's not you. Everything's contaminated. Not quite the way it's supposed to be.'

'Contaminated?'

'By the Devil.'

'Who's he?' Joshua looks around him, marvelling. 'This is a beautiful place.' He laughs, rests his hand on my shoulder. 'I know who I am, Wotan.'

He went away and came back and I listened to him speak to the natives. They understood him better than I do. They brought their children to him and he healed them, their old women and young women, even the native men too proud to admit their pain. The Arimathean and the crew set about salvaging what they could from the ship and cutting new timbers. I felled the tallest tree for the keel, and as it dropped with the wind of its fall roaring in its leaves Joshua walked past me and the boughs crashed down in front of him and behind. He jumped up lightly along the trunk and I followed him to the hilltop. I spoke but he hardly heard me. 'Be careful,' I said. 'Robbers. The Gujalhantón tribe. It's their nature.'

'Tell me what you see.'

'Treetops. Danger. Come back.'

'No, Wotan. Tell me what you *see*.'

'The River Sion. You can just see the city of Zarahemla near its source. To the north in the Yucatán peninsula – you see that narrow neck of land that doesn't go anywhere – that's the land of Mani. There's the city the natives called Uucil-abnal, which Mulek's people call Chichen Itzá, the Mouth of the Well of Christ. Plenty more native cities. The shining patch, that's the lake called the Waters of Bacalar. Further to the west, along the isthmus joining us to the land northward' – I pointed across endless treetops – 'Teotihuacán, a native city conquered by Mulek for a while. Now we just trade, but they commemorate Mulek's religion with three mountain-temples to the Sun, the

Moon, and the Cross. Nowadays they're pagan again,' I said. I felt I ought to apologise.

He raised his eyes to the haze above the horizon. 'And there?'

'Smoke,' I said. 'War. A whole nation burning. The Covenant of God burning the forests and fields to slow the Lamani advance, those who won't come on to the side of the Nephi people.' I explained, 'The generals are making a desolation of the land, a curse on the land northward so that—'

He glanced at me. 'I understand war completely,' he said. 'And they do this in my Father's name?'

I pointed out our own cities from Hagoth to Aaron, Moroni to Moronihah, Gid to Gideon, Mani to Mulek to Ur-Gath, and all the others glinting among the fields and forests. When I looked round he was gone.

I heard he went to Teotihuacán – but I heard a lot of things about Joshua that I didn't believe, that he worshipped at the temple of the Sun or was worshipped there, that he dressed up as a feathery serpent (others claimed the feathers were the flames of the Sword of Solomon); I heard that he fell down to the Hell of the natives, Mictlán, that he lay there dead among the dead for three days, and after that rose up from the dead, left Teotihuacán a city where God was worshipped, and returned to us. All I know is he came back, because one morning I saw Joshua on the beach helping build the boat. He smiled, hammering wood, when he saw me. 'There's one thing I have to know,' I asked when he stopped, but he started hammering again. 'The Arch,' I shouted. 'The Arch of the Covenant which the people of Nephi call the Name of God. The same power that Moses had, that destroyed the Egyptian army. Is it really the Power of God, or merely the power of men?' He didn't answer, but he stopped hammering, so I tried again. 'Was it sent to us by God or built by men?'

He said, 'Do you ask a hammer what use it is made for?' He always responded to a serious question with a serious question. I fell silent and he hammered the nails without once looking at them. Nobody else noticed it, the quiet miracle of it, the *ordinariness*, or the way he'd take any old length of plank and make it fit somehow, and in his hands it fit perfectly with the other planks, forming a seamless sheet too tight to caulk. Or maybe we all noticed, but it seemed so natural we never said anything. When the ship was ready to sail I asked, 'Will I see you again? Will the world end?'

This time Joshua didn't answer with a question. 'I don't know,' he said. He smiled.

I heard nothing more of Joshua, not for years. How could I? But, like the people of Nephi, at first I awaited the start of the Kingship of Christ, the rule of the Son of God over us all from Jerusalem. I presumed we'd know somehow, even at this distance: fleets of war galleys arriving from the east, omens, signs in the sky, the Rapture.

These were good times for the Nephis. The Gujalhantón were defeated and Lachoneus the judge made alliances with the Lamani peoples and the natives. Roads were repaired and the cities rebuilt. Several times I walked along the highway beside the River Sion to Zarahemla, and each time the city was bigger, brighter, wealthier, and at the summit the Great Temple of Solomon was topped by a spire shining in the sun. The people shuffled devoutly between the great headless pillars Jachin and Boaz (not cheap gold but holy copper, fabulously valuable, dragged by mule train from the north or from the port on Sea West) and in the Hall of Judgment legal cases were heard by Lachoneus sitting high as a king. Each New Year in the Great Temple the Lord Most High was enthroned just as I remembered from ancient Judah, priests chanting enthronement psalms, everyone shouting '*Yahweh malek!*

Ya is king!' to celebrate God's victories over His enemies and the forces of chaos – the Lamani in this case. Each year the Zadok wore his yellow cloak and sacrificed a red bull on the Temple porch, just as I remembered in the Land of Shem from the beginning of time; then the Zadok – the third to be named Nephi – alone carried forward the steaming bath of sacrificial blood through the maze to the Holy of Holies, where God lived inside the Arch of the Covenant, and sprinkled the blood on the mercy-seat. But each year I noticed fewer people attended the ritual. Instead it grew to a festival three days long, with plenty of eating and drinking and money to be made. Instead of boring worship everyone had a great time. The up-country women were incredibly skilled and depraved; even I learnt new tricks. There were always good fights to be had outside the taverns, and in later years the ball-courts were made into arenas where criminals were thrown to fight jaguars, and natives dressed up as jaguars and deer for mock hunting battles which turned into ritual bloodbaths. Women dressed up in all their finery, reflecting the richness of their husbands, and cripples and street children were killed to clear the streets of crime and beggary, and ugly women thrown down into baptismal pits to thrash about while bets were called on who would be first to drown, or last, or messiest, or loudest, and fortunes were won and lost. The organiser of these games was Jacob, a white-skinned Lamani. The priests, losing both money and face, tried to stop the games. Riots broke out and lots of priests were killed, but they gave as good as they got. Everyone took sides. It never occurred to us that much the same happened on the other side of the ocean.

The people fought the people. Civil war, the worst sort of war; everyone thought they could win, so everyone lost. We were all excited, intoxicated by blood and wine, no sleep, exulting in this savagery that from time to time sweeps over the most civilised peoples – especially the most civilised peoples. We're all barbarians. We threw off every inhibition and rejected everything we'd worked for, saved for, trusted in. The people turned on the government, religion, and vast bureaucracy that had sustained them in their place in order and command. Fathers against sons, brother against brother: the mob burnt their own homes, sacrificed their families, turned against their friends and everything they believed in, and couldn't stop until it was too late. Since the world began it's always been this way. I've seen it so many times.

Something changed.

Some say it was Nephi the Zadok, wearing the Urim and Thummim beneath his breastplate and holding the sceptre aloft, who brought out the Arch of the Covenant and ordered the priests to hitch the wagon to the holy cureloms, and sent it rumbling down the Temple steps; and that what he did he did deliberately, because the Lord told him to. Others said it was Jacob who grabbed Nephi's sceptre from its hiding place; others claim looters made a lucky find. All I know is that some fool who didn't know what he was doing, or an evil man who did know, touched the numbers of the sceptre. From the Arch of the Covenant a pillar of fire, the Sword of Solomon, rose up from the shining mercy-seat between the angels' golden wingtips, rose into the sky, and turned the city of Zarahemla to fire. The people of Zarahemla ran on fire. The cureloms which pulled the wagon panicked beneath the fire, dragging the firestorm through the burning streets, clouds whirling around it and a great wind roaring in the treetops, and dirt rising like great wings from the fields. The vortex of burning debris flying up formed the great funnel of dust and fire sucked down. I heard Nephi the Zadok, high priest and Elder of the Order of Melchizadok, shout from the Temple at the top of his lungs, 'Hell, Hell, Hell is come to this people, Hell is come to the peoples of the whole earth unless they repent, the Devil laughs at us, and his angels rejoice, that the fair sons and daughters of my people are killed because of their iniquity and their abominations in the sight of the Lord! Our Lord Jesus Christ is killed this day and shall rise from the dead on the third day. Jesus Christ speaking into my ears tells me: "Behold! Behold that great city Zarahemla I am burning with fire, and all the inhabitants thereof I burn with fire!"'

A tree crashed down and I sheltered beneath its roots, then the tree was dragged forward by the wind and whirled up. I saw cats, cureloms, survivors whirling in the sky, their screams fading upwards in the thundering clouds. I held myself down, with my fingertips I scrabbled down into the earth with the heat beating down on my back, pulled myself down into the ground. Soil fell down on top of me, the earth shook. I screamed at the noise. The noise didn't stop. Nothing stopped. I covered my ears and eyes and huddled in the dark, my knees against my chin, curled up like a baby about to be born.

Silence.

Silence like the silence of a cathedral.

An ant clicked past me on tiny legs, patiently dragging a rustling fragment of leaf.

Sunlight poured down and a brilliant hand reached down from above into the darkness, gripped me, lifted me up. I stared into Joshua's deep brown eyes.

'It's not you,' I said. My strength left me, I knelt without strength. 'My God, it's not you.' A crown made of thorns had been pushed down on Joshua's head. From the points of thorn bright blood trickled down His face like red fingers. His body was covered in blood, drenched.

'I am Jesus Christ.'

'I know who you are.'

He murmured: 'I entered the Temple to destroy it as the prophets foretold, therefore I am Jesus Christ. The people acclaimed me King Jesus.'

'My God, Joshua,' I whispered, 'what have they done?'

'Wotan, I am crucified, dead and buried.' He was naked but for a white linen loincloth, bloody, torn. 'Abandoned. Forsaken by my Father.' He held out His hands, showed me the nail holes through His wrists, bleeding front and back. He showed me the spear-thrust in His side. He pulled my hand into His blood and I felt His beating heart.

I whispered, 'You didn't destroy the Temple.'

He said: 'I did no miracles in Jerusalem.'

'Why not? I would have!' I looked at the smoking blackened desolation of the city around me. 'I would've done worse than this to them, much worse! I'd have made them sorry!'

'I was—' He used the word carefully. 'Tempted.'

'By the Devil?'

'By love.' He shrugged at everything destroyed. 'I gave in to a greater temptation than destruction, much harder. To love. Not to do this. *Not* to do this.' He touched my lips. 'Silence, Wotan. You have ears to hear. You understand every word I'm saying, because you understand love.' He smiled. 'And Mary Magdalene says we're made of atoms, nothing but atoms.'

Atoms. Her Greek word. '*Mary?*' I whispered. 'Who's Mary Magdalene?'

I followed Joshua walking through the ruins. A girl crawled from a shattered doorway, ran smiling towards Him. He picked up a baby miraculously preserved beneath a fallen slab, handed the child to its mother. A boy of about ten pushed aside the broken plaster that covered him and ran around us, laughing, calling his friends. Children ran between the piles of rubble calling to each other. A young woman, her hungry baby clasped to her breast, limped forward and fell to her knees in front of Joshua. She shielded her face, the light blinded her. He smiled and opened her eyes, lifted her up and she walked easily beside us. I fancied her, those lovely eyes and lithe swaying walk. She returned my grin saucily and I wished

I guzzled like the baby at her breast.

I ran after Joshua, pushed through the crowd of children. 'Love?' I said. 'How can I understand love? You could have destroyed Jerusalem with a flick of your finger! Kill the bastards! Why not?'

'Zarahemla is destroyed. This city is Desolation in the land of Desolation, Wotan, and destruction has destroyed itself. The Sword of Mulek has fallen into its own lava, and circles the centre of the earth until the end of time.' He held out his arms over the scorched hills, the trail of destruction leading as far as we could see. 'The port of Moroni sunk beneath the sea, its people drowned. Moronihah covered over beneath its hill. Gilgal fallen into the earth. Onihah, Mocum, New Jerusalem, Cumor-Ya all burnt by fire. Of the cities of Gadiomnah, Gadiandi, Ur-Gath and Gimgimno, only hills and valleys remain. And all the other cities whose names you know, gone. But not the whole world.' He looked at me, amazed. 'I would do even this much? I'd harm a single butterfly or orphan one child? Why?'

'Punishment. Sin.'

'How should I punish people for sin, Wotan?' I thought guiltily about the girl with lovely breasts. She returned my look ardently, not a single sinful thought in her head.

'Moses was guided by God, wasn't he?' I said. But Joshua said, 'Everything is made on purpose. Even in Hell.'

I stared after Him. 'My God,' I whispered. 'You're still bleeding.'

The Temple stood white and undestroyed on the hilltop above us. Coming closer, I saw the debris of bricks and palm fronds blown across the porch, the walls chipped, a few tiles missing from the roof. Joshua climbed the Temple steps and the children ran past me, flocking around Him. They pushed and shoved, giggling. One small girl bound her hair in a ponytail to look smart. The boys got bored and gave themselves something to do, arranged teams to

485

compete at clearing the rubble before the others. Girls started work on the torn veil, earnest faces bent over the material, fingers busy. Others found a white linen shift for Joshua, more turned up with dusty baskets of fruit. Then everything stopped. We heard a man weeping.

A white-bearded man came through the rubble below us. He carried a dead child in his arms. He climbed the steps slowly towards us, as fast as he could. The boy's head and legs hung down, stiff with death, mouth and eyes fixed wide open. Joshua stood on the top step. The old man stopped exhausted on the step below. Finally he spoke.

'My son is dead.'

Joshua reached down. 'No father should endure the death of his son.' Joshua touched the boy's staring eyes. The eyelids closed, then fluttered. The boy sat up shivering in his father's arms. He gave a deep sigh, then stood up beside Joshua on the top step and after a little while joined the others sweeping the stones clean.

Joshua beckoned me. 'I told you once that you're not my mighty man. I know the course of your life and your place in the world, and it's not mine. I know who the Devil is, Wotan. I have seen him.' He looked at me. 'I have talked to him.'

I swallowed. 'Is it me? Am I your enemy? Shall I kill myself?'

'This is nothing,' Joshua said. 'It isn't the end. Evil is just beginning. My battle has begun, that's all.'

'Why did you call me if I'm not your soldier?'

He pointed up. 'That hole in the roof needs repairing.'

So that was how I, of all people, helped Jesus Christ and the children rebuild the Temple. One day when I was busy with whitewash – trees and crops sent bright green shoots through the fertile ash of the city but I forget how long had passed, whether three days or more – a hand was laid on my shoulder.

'Wotan, come with me,' Joshua said.

We walked through the Hall of Judgment to the maze. 'I don't want to go through here,' I said. He said, 'Don't be afraid.'

'I'm not afraid of anything.'

'Aren't you? A man can be too strong to know fear sometimes. Do you not fear Satan? Follow me, I know the way.' We came through the twists and turns into the Holy of Holies and to my horror the sacred room was full of children, a complete spattering mess of children and paint. A blob of crimson landed on my nose. I waited for Joshua to explode with fury. The children were having the time of their lives, painting themselves more than the walls.

'Look, Wotan,' Joshua whispered. 'Watch. Learn.'

But watching the children I thought of my own sons, all my sons I never knew, and the worst thing happened. Tears filled my eyes. Ridiculous. Embarrassing. Unmanly. They trickled down my cheeks and I tried to wipe them away without being noticed as I watched the arguing children working, playing, mostly playing. 'What are they doing making such a mess?' I whispered. 'Why are you allowing it?'

Joshua looked at me as though the answer were obvious. 'They're children.' Even his white gown was splashed with paint. He wiped my face with His sleeve in a casual gesture.

'Joshua, Joshua, I don't know my sons,' I whispered, and fresh tears flowed. 'I never have. I don't even know where they are. I never even *realised* I didn't know.'

He studied me, smiling. 'Wotan, your strength is your weakness.' He bent down and picked up a brush, dabbed it in a colour, green I think. He pushed it in my hand, but the brush hung limply from my fingers. 'You'll know what to do,' Joshua encouraged me.

'Me, paint?' I said. 'These children paint better than me.'

He said impatiently, 'Then learn from the children.'

I stood there for hours among the paint pots in the chaos of children, paintbrush in hand, the dab of green waiting on its tip. I was afraid. I'd built the walls of Enoch, fought the dragon Huwawa, witnessed the Resurrection of Christ, but I was afraid of touching that tiny green tip to the wall of the Holy of Holies.

I began to see a picture.

The formless mess changed into colours and shapes in my eye. The paintbrush trembled in my hand, I couldn't, it would all go wrong, I'd spoil everything.

I saw past the spilt paint and busy brushes and chattering heads of the children as they worked. 'Who's got the green for parrots?' called a young boy with curly brown hair and cheerful paint-speckled face. I wondered what Joshua had looked like as a child.

I saw into the picture, and it wasn't a picture. It was us.

We were alive. I gazed, marvelling at us. Everything about us was a miracle, each heartbeat, each breath. I saw people I knew, all still alive, as though even mortals live for ever. The closer I came the more I saw. I began to understand that if I came close enough I'd see the pattern of veins on each leaf, the gleam of each grain of matter. A parrot fluttered from a bush.

I closed my eyes and made my mark.

XIV

The present day
Sion Inn, Salt Lake City

'Mommy,' Christine says. 'Don't go, don't go. Don't leave me again.'

Winona double-tips the salesgirl who delivered from one of the swish hotel shops, leans back against the door of the luxurious Temple Suite, then carries the silver bag peppered with designer labels to the sofa. Hot sun streams through the open balcony doors. Christine, swinging her long thin legs from the sofa, her bony arms wrapped around her shoulders as though cold, leans to keep the screen in sight as her mother comes between her and the television. Then for a moment she again looks up appealingly. 'Don't go, Mommy.'

Those enormous blue eyes, as blue and deep and lost as her father's eyes. Winona never could say no to him, either. She bends, kisses her daughter's broad forehead and blond hair. 'What's the matter, baby?'

'I'm not a baby.'

Winona smiles. 'You're my baby. You're four days old. You don't know anything.' She takes the screwdriver, fits the heavy-duty bolts to the door. The child's voice comes from behind her. 'Mommy, what are those for?'

'Safety. Keeping you safe.' Winona tosses the screwdriver in the bin. 'I have to go out, honey.'

'I know more than you think I do. You talk.' Christine watches her mother undress. 'You talk in your sleep.'

Winona stops with one leg in her lacy Janet Reger panties. 'I talk? What about, baby?'

'Just talk.' Christine watches television. She wears a grey pleated skirt and a red striped top like one of the little girls she saw on *Sesame Street*. 'You talk to someone called Wotan.'

Winona shrugs, pulls on her panties and full front-fastening bra, the design Wotan always fancied her in best. She can sense him feeling her breasts now, the perpetual masculine heat of him inside her.

Christine asks, 'Who's Tallboy?'

'Tallboy? Nobody, baby!' Winona watches her daughter, concerned. Best to say nothing. She buttons her blouse and lifts the white Lycra-cotton trouser suit from the silver bag. 'The right clothes make a girl feel like a million dollars.' She smiles at Christine, watchfully. 'What else did I say in my sleep?'

'Nothing.' Christine clicks the remote control, changing channel.

'Good. What's wrong with the kids' channels?'

'I'm not a *baby*,' Christine repeats decisively. 'I'm a girl. Who's Snowflake?'

'Come on then, girl, help me choose my jewellery. Did I say Snowflake in my sleep?'

'People die, don't they. Shootouts. Multiple crashes. I've seen.' Christine nods at the screen. 'Tallboy's dead, isn't he?'

'Yes, he's dead.'

'Did you kill him?'

'That's a terrible thing to say.'

'Mommy.'

'I knew he'd die, honey. He deserved to and I was pleased. Justice was done.'

'I want to have fun. I want to go out.' Christine points at an advert, she even speaks with a Utahan accent. 'Shiny car, no multiple crash yet.' Glances at her mother. 'I want white shoes like yours. And red lips. And eye makeup. I want to be tall like you.'

'You'll be tall as me one day.'

Click with the controller. Hottest December weather for thirty years and more to come. 'Mommy? Children don't stay with their mommies, do they? Will I still know you when I'm grown up?'

Winona sits beside her. 'One day a child goes away from its mother, when the time comes. They always do. You'll want to.'

Christine gazes at the television. 'Not yet. I need you. Wear the jewels the expensive salesman brought up, that look like your eyes.'

'You, bossy.' Winona opens the Cartier box and pins the large double-sapphire brooch to her lapel. 'Madam approves?'

'Did Tallboy go to Heaven?'

'Sweetheart, what a question.'

'You look so pretty.'

'I guarantee you that Tallboy did not go to Heaven.'

'Not many people do, do they.' Christine studies the television, reflections flickering in her eyes. 'Not nearly so many people deserve to go to Heaven as think they do.' *Click* with the controller. 'Are you going out to kill Snowflake? Can I?'

'No, miss, you can't! He's a very bad man who does very bad things. The worst things you can imagine.'

'Maybe very bad things were done to him to make him bad.'

'They all say that.'

Click. 'Can I come?'

'You're much too young and this is much too important. There's no time.'

Christine looks at her wisely. 'You've never had a girl baby before, have you. I'm your first girl. You don't know what we're like.'

'I've had plenty of boys and they grew into strong men.'

'I can tell it's important, what you're doing. You look older but you're still going out, even though you've got white streaks in your hair.'

Winona laughs, punches her daughter's shoulder. 'Distinguished white.'

'Your eyes are tired. It's not makeup. And you slept all night.' Christine points at the screen. 'I want a makeover.' *Click*. 'I want a Jeep.' *Click*. 'I want to go skiing in the Wasatch Mountains.'

'Christine, listen to me.' Winona presses the mute button firmly, looks into her daughter's eyes. 'I do have to go out. I won't be long. I will come back. You'll be safe here. There's a listening service, and if necessary a nanny will come. If you're afraid.'

'I don't get afraid.' Christine stares sharply. 'You don't want them to see me, do you?'

Winona tells the truth. 'No.'

'I wouldn't hurt them. I'm just like other children, aren't I?'

'Yes, honey. You're exactly like other children.'

'Bad things happen to children. They start fires, or get burnt. Some children fall out of windows. Children get attacked by bad men while their mothers are out.' Christine touches the button and the sound blares, machine-gun fire. 'It happens. I've seen. I had all that time while you slept. A thousand satellite channels to choose from.'

'It won't happen to you.'

'I'm your weak spot, aren't I? Your child. Your one and only daughter.'

Winona says, 'It's not that I want to leave you.' Christine says quickly, 'Good, we'll go and see Reverend Snowflake together.'

Winona stares. 'What? He calls himself a pastor?'

Click. 'I saw the advert. He's a good man, it said so. He's a good man wherever people need good men to help in the world. Bosnia, Rwanda, Kosovo, the Gulf. The Reformed Temple of Sion of the Prophecy, East 100 South, German Ward, All Welcome. *Sion Kirche, Ost ein hundert Süd, Pastor Schneeflocke, Wilkommen.*'

Winona picks up her handbag, white leather. 'He knows I'm coming. He wants me to. Someone wants me to. Suppose it's a trap? If I leave you . . . I can't look after you here.' But still she hesitates. Christine puts up her spindly arms to be picked up. 'I'll be very quiet, Mommy. No one will notice me.'

Winona's eyes close wearily for a moment.

'All right.' With sudden energy she lifts her daughter easily on her hip, kisses her, locks the door behind them with the electronic key. People make room for her in the elevator, tall, elegant, stylish in the white trouser suit and wide white hat. 'What a lovely little girl you have,' gushes one of the matrons in lavender and pearls.

'Yes,' Winona says. 'She bites.' She crosses the lobby with long strides but Christine points at the hotel shops. 'I want a hat.' Winona finds something twenties-style in the right size, it doesn't match anything but to Christine that doesn't matter at all. She pulls it down to her ears in total delight as Winona carries her outside. The doorman, dressed as a sweating Santa Claus, whistles a cab. 'No. I'll walk.' It's not far but within a minute or two the heat comes through, the sunlight strikes painfully off the glassy buildings into her eyes. The sidewalk glares heat, most of the churches have a Nativity scene outside, the snow incongruous in the baking heat, and Christine's heavy. She flips on dark glasses but still the glare and heat have already given her a headache. *You shouldn't have walked.* 'It's only ten minutes.'

'Are you talking to yourself?' Christine asks.

You shouldn't do this to yourself, Winona. To us.

'Shut up,' Winona says. 'No, honey, I'm not talking to myself.'

Go back to the hotel, rest up.

'Put me down.' Christine says. 'I'll walk. Is that better?'

Winona smiles down at her. 'Sure.' It's midday and the German restaurants are busy, big piles of meatballs in the windows, bowls of Spargelsuppe, heaped pigs' knuckles. 'I'm hungry,' Christine says. 'What's the matter?' Winona looks sick, hurries past.

'Here it is, sweetheart.' The cedar-and-glass entrance to the Reformed Temple of Sion of the Prophecy is set slightly back from the street. White boards with Christmas tinsel advertise bilingual service times in English and German. The door hisses open ahead, hisses shut behind them. Inside's larger than outside, air conditioned, shadowed. Winona sighs with relief, slips her dark glasses in her pocket. Rows of fragrant cedar pews flank the aisle, sufficient for a congregation of hundreds. Taped organ music, Handel, plays softly. At this hour there's only half a dozen sleepy heads showing near the front, nodding, enjoying the cool shade and the pastor's sonorous melting German. Winona says quietly, 'Stay here, Christine.'

'The backs of the seats are too high. I can't see. I want to see the Nativity with Baby Jesus and the donkey.'

'Sit still. Quiet as a mouse. Whatever you hear, whatever happens, don't let anyone see you.'

'Mommy, what's a mouse?'

For a moment Winona's startled. 'I guess there were no mice on television last night, sweetheart.' She kisses Christine, gives her a hymn book to hold, walks down the aisle towards the tall cedarwood pulpit. The tapestries behind are hung like banners from the roof, illustrating scenes from the Prophecy: biblical revelations of the end of the world patiently woven by generations of German worshippers. Behind Snowflake in his long woollen robes and white hood the moon rises like blood, the Dragon stands victorious on the sea, great waves of fire wash away the world, and unbelievers are dragged from their handholds to damnation in fiery perpetually falling surf. But while the world falls to Hell, on the mountain tops the faithful wait singing and praying joyfully, arms upraised to be lifted, and the Hand of God reaches down to raise them in the Rapture to His side in Heaven, where they'll learn to cast aside their humanity and become gods of flesh and blood.

The people in the front pews look up from their prayers as Winona walks in front of them. She stops.

'Get out,' she says. 'Fire drill.'

They scatter, complaining. She notices dust under the pew. The wood's almost black, greasy from years touching human skin, the stones worn into scoops by heels and soft warm knees hobbled at prayer. She looks up at the pulpit, shields her eyes from sunlight streaming through the Cross of stained glass, moves so that she stands in the

Negro's shadow. He rests his gloved hands on the pulpit rail, leans forward. '*Kann ich Ihnen helfen, bitte?*' Can I help you?

'You know who I am.'

'Peace unto you, sister.' His rich melted voice, same as on the video. 'Lift up your soul to the Lord—'

'I have no soul.' Winona breaks the pulpit with her fist, drags the pastor down, throws him into the pews. He slides down. The people who left slowly are running out now, shouting. Snowflake slips from the bench to the worn stones, colours of stained glass rippling over his white robes, his hood, his dark glasses.

'I do,' he whispers. 'I do have a soul. My soul is in the hands of the Lord.'

Still she can't see his face. 'Don't play innocent with me. "Everything has its price, and I know the price of everything." I heard you say it! I saw you on the video.'

'If you saw it, sister, you were meant to. Nothing happens but my Lord wills it.'

'Then the Lord wills me to come here to kick the truth out of you.' Despite herself Winona glances back, threatened. *You were meant to.* She can see the top of Christine's head in the end pew, hear her kicking the wood, bored. Nothing's happened to her.

'Praise the Lord, sister, even if you cannot lift up your soul,' Snowflake whispers. 'You've hurt me. Are you going to kill me?'

'Tallboy's dead. No one's going to help you.'

'My Lord will save me even if you kill me.'

'Who is your Lord?'

'The Lord who imposes His righteous rule to save us all from sin, so that we earn our place in Heaven. He who is worshipped and obeyed. He who brings peace to us through our subservience to Him, and salvation to those who believe in Him, so that He can conquer Hell.'

'Who are you . . .' She lifts Snowflake by his throat,

tears the robes from his white body. She stares, then pulls the hood aside. Snowflake's straight white hair hangs down to his shoulders. She pulls off his gloves, revealing his white hands. Pulls off his glasses, stares at the pupils of his eyes white as snowflakes, the whites black. A black man's face in a white man's skin.

'Don't worry,' he reassures her, 'it's a medical condition. Don't hurt me because I'm different. I've got doctors, it's under control.' He smiles. 'It's not unnatural, I'm not an abomination or any religious hocus-pocus, take it easy. I'm not being punished for some sin. Just a medical condition.'

She puts her fingers in his eyes, pulls out the lenses. Snowflake screams weakly, looks up at her with a pink gaze, blinking, an albino. 'It's hereditary. Do you blame me for being what I am?'

'You know what I've come for, Snowflake. You're the one who's supposed to know what everything's worth. Where is it?' Winona lifts him, shakes him. 'Jesus Christ in America. The painting by the children who saw Jesus. The painting by the children who *are* Jesus for all I know. The painting that's still happening. Still alive. Still *is*.' Winona's arm hurts, knocking Snowflake against the wall. His head thuds, blood from his mouth spatters her white sleeve. 'Mommy!' Christine runs forward.

'Stay back, honey, Mommy's working.' But still Christine comes forward.

'This is the child?' Snowflake wipes his lips, smiling with one side of his mouth, reaching out. Winona bangs him back. 'Don't you touch her.' One of the tapestries, dislodged, falls like a fluttering sail across the pews. 'The innocence of children,' Snowflake says. 'They are our future.'

The space left bare by the fallen tapestry reveals a door set flush in the wall behind the altar. 'That's it, honey!' Christine gets to it first but she's never worked a door handle before. 'Move over, sweetheart.' Winona kicks the heavy fire door down, drags Snowflake through by his collar, then stares up and around her in awe.

Christine gives a delighted laugh. 'It's bigger than the church!'

It's a warehouse. 'My God,' Winona whispers. 'It's a labyrinth. How much have you got here? Look at it all. Don't touch that, honey. That's a reliquary, a golden house, it's got saints' bones in it.' They move forward among heaped altars and holy art, reliquaries, censers, Bibles piled as high as the ceiling. Paintings, icons, frescoes, fabulously valuable, jumbled together like a religious maze. The banal tossed down beside the infinitely valuable. Christine picks up a Jesus in a sealed plastic dome, His arms outstretched over plastic sheep, then turns it over and snow falls on Jesus and the sheep. She laughs with delight. 'Look at this, Mommy!' She touches a Bible and the pages flutter open under her fingertips, beautifully illuminated. Winona warns her, 'Each Bible's a man's life, honey. A monk might slave all his working life to write one Bible, did nothing else, never married, no children, this Bible is all he was.' She shuts it like a life closing, opens another, marvelling, moves on looking around her. 'This is fabulous. Fabulous. Two thousand years of devotion.'

'A lot more than two thousand years,' Snowflake says. 'A lot more.'

'How much more?'

Snowflake shrugs. 'Eternity.'

Christine says, 'In *Sesame Street* I saw a magpie.'

'Not now, honey. My God, this is a Gutenburg Bible.'

'The magpie stole everything bright and shining that he saw but he didn't know what the bright shining things were. Glass and plastic and diamonds were the same to him. Stealing was all he knew how to do.'

'Listen to her. It's true. No one knows anything, no one knows what's right or wrong.' Snowflake looks at the treasures piled around him. 'Who knows what anything's worth?'

Winona moves reverently between the objects and artifacts piled high; a touch might bring everything crashing down on their heads. 'This must be one of the greatest collections of religious art and religious knowledge in the world.' She opens an ancient LXX Bible from the earliest years of the Christian religion, written in the original Greek, and a Jesus key ring falls out.

'By far the greatest collection in the world,' Snowflake says. 'A small part of it.' He stares up at a huge fresco peeled from some ancient pagan wall, Abraham tearing a dagger across his young son's throat, the child's blood spurting across the altar, no God in the sky, no ram caught in the thorn bush. No Wotan.

Winona demands, 'Who knows of this place?'

'No one. It's just a place to contain God. A church.'

Winona turns dizzily. 'It's impossible to contain God. God's everything.'

'Not quite everything. Some things He created He rejected, and threw down.'

'Us?'

'No. Us.' Snowflake pulls his collar from her grip, steps back before she can grab him. 'Peace, peace. I won't hurt you. You know nothing of suffering. You know nothing of abandonment. To be first and most prized and most loved, then to be thrown down. Forsaken. A whole Universe empty of God. A prison. You know nothing.'

Winona sits on a treasure chest, puts her hands to her head. 'I believe Wotan is a son of God. He was *born* in this world. Not thrown down, not abandoned, not sinful. He was born like any other child.'

'The Christian Church, that monstrous abomination, teaches that children are born sinful by their very nature. We do not.'

'Who is *we*?'

'Mommy?' Christine looks up in her mother's face. 'Are you all right?'

'It's here,' Snowflake says. 'We have it. What you seek.'

Winona stands, and Christine holds her hand.

'Follow, follow.' Snowflake leads them deeper into the teetering maze, pagan idols piled up like mannequins in a shop sale, totems, fat-bellied Venuses roughly squeezed from clay, knives, flints, primitive bowls of red and yellow ochre, stones worn into patterns by fingertips.

Winona mutters, 'When was this collected?'

'Since the very beginning.'

Snowflake comes to the centre. On a plinth stands the statue of the black angel stolen from the skull of the angel in the earth, the Black Angel of Apachiohualitzá, its obsidian wings and arms upraised in mimicry of its great mistress, straining muscles twisted in its breasts, its mouth locked open in its infant scream of worship.

But Christine walks to the pictures scattered behind. She whispers: 'They're beautiful.' She touches the paintings of Jesus in America with her fingertips, then runs the palms of her hands over the painted wood panels, puts out her arms and presses her face, cheeks, lips against the fragrant cedar and paint, closes her eyes as if hearing the jungle and the cries of children playing and the reassuring voices of grown-ups. She smiles. She's never seen jungle, she's never played with other children.

'An innocent moment.' Snowflake glances at Winona. 'Ah, to be a child. I know what it is to be next to God. Almost to be God. The timeless time before He made the first star in this sky, it's more real to me than now. I struggle to return to God, I pray, I worship, I strive. My earthly father was a great man, an Ibo chieftain enslaved by whites. His people tried to kill him to save him from his shame, but all were killed. When his master returned from the German Cameroon to Bavaria, my father was taken with him like a monkey. I was born in Bavaria in the year Hitler was elected to power. Under the Nazi Party my father and his master lost everything. A Negro is worse than a Jew, even the Jews spat on us. They had no nation; I had no hut, no village, no tribe, no colour; they called me *Schneeflocke* in their contempt for someone so punished, as I am, by God, more punished even than they. My father worked in the sewers, my mother died. I was still a child when the war began. Skin cancers covered half my body, how I itched! I screamed with itching! I scratched my skin from my flesh, scratched myself bare. A Jewish doctor took me in, so I was deported with his children to . . . I don't know where. Russia. Somewhere beginning with a T. When we were too weak to work we were taken to a rubbish tip on a hill and shot. Nobody fought, nobody screamed, none of the villagers raised a finger. I fell down under a thousand falling bodies. When we were silent we were covered over with earth and grew, not colder, but warmer. It was very hot, compost-hot. When it rained hot blood trickled past me, then a flood of stinking digested water, and I followed it down. The soil gave way and I crawled out. I always remember that moment. Born again in Hell.'

'You can't see any of this, can you,' Winona says. 'This beauty. It's just paint to you.'

'This I know. A man walked up to me through the water. His feet bare. A gold circlet like a crown around His head. He wore the purple robe of a king. His eyes were fierce, the eyes of the King who rules the world. I writhed to Him in the slime, I kissed His feet in the mud and shit, I loved Him. He touched my head and took away my pain for as long as He wanted. And I knew, I *knew* He was my lord. *My Lord,* I wept, *my Lord, my Lord. I'm yours.*'

Winona says, 'You were saved by the Devil. Did you really think He was Jesus Christ?'

'He had work for me.' Snowflake touches the painting. He whispers, 'Is *this* truly Jesus Christ?'

'Gonzalez couldn't see it either. The truth. Couldn't

value it. It isn't worth ten million or a hundred million, it isn't worth a cent, because it's more than art. It's real.'

Snowflake says: 'Then I've captured God.'

Winona stands, swaying. 'You're mad. Where's Gonzalez? Where's the collector?'

'I'd die and not tell you.' Snowflake clenches his white fists, suddenly leaps at Winona, pummelling her, he knows he stands no chance, but to his surprise she falls back off balance, gives a cry. She drops to her knees, warding off his punches with her upraised arm, then with a grunting effort grabs him by the neck, struggles to her feet, throws him away. Snowflake falls back among a crowd of marble statues, a marble hand raised in prayer punches through his chest. He gasps once, then doesn't move again.

'Christine.' Winona staggers, she can hardly see. 'Glasses.' Christine finds the dark glasses in her pocket, puts them on her mother's nose, but they fall crooked almost at once. 'Quickly. Christine. Back to the hotel.'

'Mommy, I'm frightened! He's dead.'

Winona grabs her shoulder. 'Christine?' Her hand shakes. 'Got to get back to hotel. Help me. Bring the pictures.'

'There's too many. What's that noise?'

Police sirens. 'As many as you can, quick. Here, put them under my arm.'

Christine sounds frightened again. 'Mommy, what's the matter with you?'

'I'll be fine. I'll be well again. Quick, more. I can carry . . .' Winona falls silent. Christine pushes the painted wooden panels under her mother's arm until she drops as many as she's given. The sirens wail closer. Winona says: 'Hurry.'

Christine takes the weight of the pictures as well as she can, leaning against them. 'That's better,' her mother says. 'Walk. Back way.' There's a door, Christine pulls down the handle. 'Quick.' It's an alley. Police cars flash across

501

the street end. 'Other way,' Winona says. 'Turn. Walk calm. Nice and steady does it.'

Christine looks up as they walk, sees Winona's eyes now tight shut against the afternoon sun. 'I can see the hotel, Mommy.' The sunlight falls across the back of Winona's hand, the skin wells up in slow blisters of sunburn. 'Mommy, there's a big street. Do I walk on green or red?'

No answer from Winona. Her head lolls.

'*Do I walk on green or red?*' There's so much Christine doesn't know. She walks her mother slowly across the broad highway, walking on red.

A vehicle comes fast, changing lanes towards them. The powerful engine throbs, slowing through the gears. The chrome radiator grille pulls close, stopping, almost touching them. It's a crimson Jeep spattered with snow despite the boiling sun; then Christine sees the white is salt. As she walks beside her reflection in the chrome fender the driver looks at her through the windscreen, a strong-faced man wearing a check hunting shirt with a pretty girl grinning beside him, sunglasses in her hair. Winona whispers, 'Jeri, no, my God, get out.' But Jeri grins, lolls against the strong-faced man, kisses him. Winona turns her head away. The strong-faced man stares after her long after she's gone from sight. Traffic backs up behind him honking and pulling out, then he pushes Jeri back in her seat and drives away with a roar of the powerful engine.

At the Sion Inn the doorman's concerned, Christine can't get rid of him. 'It's one of her turns. She'll be all right.' *ER* was on last night. 'Insulin. Bed rest. Thank you, thank you, goodbye.' The elevator door *tings*, opens. Christine hisses against her mother, 'I don't know what floor!'

Winona hits the number with the side of her hand. 'Key in pocket,' she mumbles. It's the electronic key; just slides in. Mother and daughter totter across the Temple Suite dropping paintings, the door closing and

502

automatically locking behind them, and Winona falls forward across the bed.

After a few minutes Winona beckons weakly. 'Christine.'

'Yes, Mommy, I'm here. What's happened to you?'

'No doctors, Christine. No doctors.'

The sun goes down beyond the balcony doors, darkness falls over the city below. Christine fetches an icebag for Mommy's forehead. Mommy's asleep. The room service trolleys are gone, there's nothing to eat. Christine sits on the end of the bed, turns on the television, watches whatever's on. *Click*. Jerry Falwell on America's Voice, Channel 19. *Click*. Billy Graham, KUTV, Channel 2. *Click*. Christian Religious TV. The blueish reflections flicker across the child's attentive face.

Era Four

Valhalla

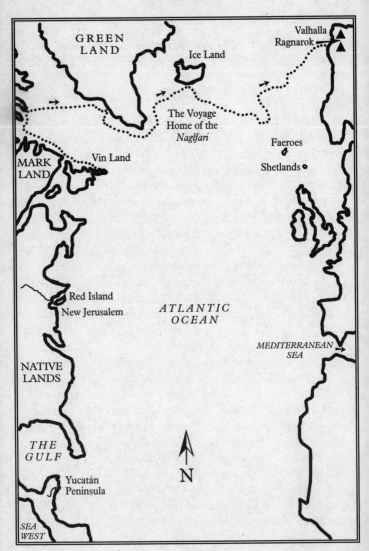

Valhalla

AD 30 – 1066

AD 30–1066

Gone. Jesus Christ was gone. The land stood empty, lifeless.

The city of Zarahemla, gone. The people of Nephi killed, scattered. Only the children remained playing in the ruins. A few old folk came down from the hills, pushing through the weeds and shrubs growing where the fields had been, between trees growing up as though the city of humans had never been. They couldn't believe what the children told them about Jesus Christ and the miracle – except this, that they saw with their own eyes: the Temple stood rebuilt and repaired on its hilltop in the sun, shining, perfect, while the toddlers climbed innocently on the steps.

'You need to build shelters.' I gathered the youngsters around me. 'You need to grow food.'

They looked at me as though I was mad. 'But God will look after us,' they said. 'Our mothers and fathers did.'

I spat on my hands, wielded my axe at a tree. 'God helps those who help themselves.' Was I right? Should I have left the children to be dark in the night, cold in the rain, hungry without food? After a while a few of the older ones started helping, then more, but the youngsters ran playing, making friends, fighting, laughing at farts and smells, then pulled the wings off beetles; then sat sulking, then cried because they were hungry, then lay down because they were tired, then shivered because they were cold, and then the night was long and dark.

Next day, everyone helped.

No, the people of Nephi weren't all destroyed by the great pillar of fire they called the Sword of Solomon. But nearly all. For months survivors wandered down from the hills, arriving in ones and twos from the lost cities of Hagoth, Gid, Morianton, drowned under the trees of the jungle or the waves of the sea. More survivors struggled upstream from Bountiful or the Waters of Bacalar, more still came from Maní and Chichen Itzá, bringing their native wives with them, and their babies, and now the natives called the whole land Itzá, the Land of Christ.

But still the children were who mattered. Even as they grew older they remembered their childhood. Even as they married each other and built houses they felt something missing from their lives. In the quiet moments they felt the hole inside their hearts. Joshua, whom as children they'd instinctively followed and called Jesus Christ, had taught them all the wisdom He believed they could understand – more than *I* ever understood. The grown-up children and a few of the very old folk of ruined Zarahemla knew more than I, had seen and heard more than I, felt more than I. The old folk died; now as their own babies were born the children sensed something once terribly important slipping out of their grasp. They remembered being children, tried to hold the mystery, the wonder inside them that had once been their whole lives, but the harder they squeezed the more their simple faith slipped away between their fingers. Those days were gone. 'When's Joshua coming back?' Youngsters in their teen years remembered when they were the youngest toddling infants. 'We didn't get told off by Joshua! He was *fun!*' Under Joshua they'd worked like angels, but they forgot how. As if reminding them the Temple stood perfect on the hilltop of Zarahemla, but as adults they stared up uncomprehendingly now that He was gone. There was only one thing to do. 'He's still in there,' the town meeting decided, and elected priests.

I couldn't stay much longer; I walked like an old man and wore white in my hair. When the time came I climbed the Temple steps and entered the Holy of Holies, marvelling at what we'd achieved all those years ago. It had seemed so simple and easy. There it was, my own speck of green. I opened my fingers, gnarled by tanning acid, wrinkled and spotted where I'd rubbed them with tobacco weed for the appearance of age, held them up between my face and the painting. I still couldn't believe I was part of it – no, I *could* believe, that's what was so marvellous. With Joshua the children had created something marvellous and true from nothing, and I'd contributed. From the door someone said, 'Hey, you. You're not allowed in there. Only the Zadok's allowed in there.'

So I turned my back on the city that my strength had helped build and hobbled into the jungle. When I heard a jaguar roar I cut my arm and tore my cloak, dripped blood, dropped the cloak where it would be found and I would be mourned; and slipped away. They never found my body. My limp disappeared, the years fell from my shoulders, I pulled my strength into me, I ran, I leapt on the tree branches, I swung from treetop to treetop until I heard the roar of a waterfall, I dived in the bubbles and rubbed the brown from my skin and white from my hair, and then let the torrents of the River Sion wash me down to the sea and a new life.

Years passed; it was a time of peace, unfortunately. The Nephi peoples were so few in number that they no longer fought the Lamani for land. The Lamani were converted to Christ. There were no wars to interest me. Peace ruled the entire Land of Christ. Often in my travels in the pristine wilderness of the Land Northward I saw no one for weeks. My adventures, though too numerous to tell, were rather small by comparison with my usual achievements. Often I rescued girls and women from some domestic distress or other and earned their gratitude, perhaps lived in their company for a while before moving on. Land disputes, sometimes. Bad men coming into the village. I saved widows from ugly men and children from brutality. I often thought of Joshua, of how He would have lived if He were among us now. I tried hard not to kill people or make love to women I did not love, at least more often than necessary, but it was harder than holding my breath. The longer my abstinence lasted the more gorgeous the girls became, and the more I struggled to hide my enormous strength and magnificent sexuality the more I inflamed their desire. My virtue disappointed them and there was not trouble enough in the world to interest me. Frankly I was bored. Mountain peaks called me from the prairie, winding rivers called me from the mountains, the rivers led me down to the seashore, and from the seashore the forests called me back again. I sat sleepily on the bank of a pond looking at my reflection. '*Wotan*,' Eve whispered.

'*Wotan*.' My face shimmered in the water, changing. My hair darkened like Eve's. Again her voice came to me. '*Run. Run, Wotan. Be afraid.*'

The love of my life's the one girl, of course, I never had. Perpetual virgin, pure femininity; Mari, Miriam, Mara. My soul lusts for her. I'll search for her for ever. Maybe it's not God's will that I'll ever find her, win her, marry her, possess her, be her, and she be me. Strange though (according to the stories told by priests in the Land of Christ southward) that three women called Mary gathered beneath Joshua dying on the Cross – Mary Magdalene, the Virgin Mary and Mary her sister. Just another of the ancient triple goddess stories perhaps, I remember the canaanite shrines dedicated to El's three women, Ishtar the wife of God, Anath His Virgin, Asherah His lover. Maybe I'll never find my Mary; but maybe Joshua did.

'*Wotan! Run away! Save yourself!*' I sit up with a jerk. Eve's reflection sits up with a jerk in the water, I'm Eve. Her Caucasus-blue eyes stare back at me. She blinks when I blink, my hands are long and slim, my nails well cared for. I'm her, Wotan's clothes hang on my slim body like a tent. I'm in her, I feel her shivering. The warm evening's cold. The clear sky's covered with thunderclouds, great thunderheads of black cloud boiling upwards over the treetops and mountain tops. The trees bend over, roaring in the wind, the wind howls like demons, and Eve runs under the thrashing branches towards the rocky outcrop, the shelter of my cave. A tree branch whips by her, lightning flashes, then she crouches among the rocks. The storm rises over the forest and the rocks, passes away southward across the prairie. The wind stops. A tree branch falls from the clear blue sky.

What was all that about, Eve?

Eve trembled all over. 'He didn't stop,' she whispered. 'He knew you were here, Wotan. He knows.' She stared at the storm fading over the southern horizon. 'He's here.'

Who's here?

'Satan.' She stood, went back quietly to the pond and sat down. 'Satan's found New Sion. He's found the Land of Christ. He's found them.'

It was just a summer storm. You're imagining it. I'm not afraid.

'Fear yourself, Wotan.' She pulled a splinter from her leg. It hurt me like hell.

I didn't believe her about Satan. Not for years, as it happened, did I return southward. Then I believed her.

No, I didn't see Satan. Just human nature at work. I've seen it before, and so have you. It's our story. Nothing changes. What we build, we destroy. What we love, we hurt. We turn our blessings into curses and kill what we'd die to defend. We always do.

These people didn't need Satan. They did a perfectly good job of evil all by themselves.

The Lamani whose villages covered the land had turned away from Christ, I can't imagine why – maybe *that* was

511

all Satan did, persuaded them there was a better way, a more truthful way, a more loving way to worship God. Armies of thirty thousand men and forty thousand men led by boys of sixteen marched back and forward, and their death hung over the land like a smell. The peoples of Nephi were driven northward by the Lamani, who had circled around them like a revolution and come up from behind. Nephi women and children were sent for safety to the vast native city of Teotihuacán, but when the Lamani besieged the city all were sacrificed, the city spared, and the Lamani armies moved northward after the retreating Nephi. I passed through the lines and forced my way south passing villages still on fire, old battlefields of bones, new battlefields with robbers still looting the dead, women screaming or lying exhausted, birds pulling the rotting flesh, flies swarming in the peaceful glades littered with murdered prisoners. Survivors escaping from the cities crawled northward 'beneath the trees, beneath the bushes, beneath the vines, to their misfortune', as the natives moving in told me. The Nephi were a shattered people. Their pride was gone, they crawled, but still they died. I waded streams running brown with blood. Even the clear pools and waterfalls of the River Sion smelt of blood.

I followed the old wrecked road upstream from Bountiful Bay to Zarahemla, and stared at what I saw. Christ had gone from the Land of Christ.

At first I thought the natives had pulled the conquered Temple down; no, they were building over it, trying to worship God a better way. A holy place is holy for ever and they called it by its ancient name, Apachiohualitzá, the Flood. Native drums beat the dirge, thousands of Nephi slaves swayed miserably as they worked, hauling on immense drag ropes, inching great blocks of stone up earthen ramps. The natives were constructing a mountain to God, a new tower of Bab'El. Each day I saw ten thousand slaves carry a million baskets of soil, lifting the mountain higher, closer to God. I watched from the treetops as one by one a pyramid of platforms rose over the Temple, each flat-topped, fronted by a broad stairway, each slightly narrower than the one below, lifting the eye to Heaven. I remembered the man-made mountains dotting the flat plain of Shem: these people were rebuilding Shem over Sion, vast and primitive. Three hundred and fifty-four years had passed since the Crucifixion of Jesus; each day I watched the priests climb the steps of the ziggurat to the broad summit and the bloodbaths, and the black blades of their obsidian knives flashed in the sun rising over the jungle as they made sacrifice.

One on each side of the bloodbaths stood two huge feet carved of black basalt. Each foot was as long as ten men. Every day more stone was swung up, shaped, set into place, polished. The finest artists worked devotedly rubbing the stone like a black mirror. Day by day the toes were formed, then the toenails, each perfect as a living toenail, and more artisans worked on the bulges and dimples of muscle and tendon so that I could almost believe real bones and living muscles strained beneath the ebony-black basalt skin. More men climbed up and worked like ants forming the fine wriggles of vein. Scaffolds rose up and work began on the mighty ankles.

'My God,' I whispered. 'It's a statue. They're building a statue of Christ.'

Far below, under the directions of the Kukulcan, the native king-priest, skilled masons worked on the Temple carving great stelae of stone, stories, portraits, victories, to the glory of their rulers. Artists carved glyph pictures on the faces of the pyramids. Warriors wearing the Egyptian-looking armour and chin-straps of Nephi soldiers were shown defeated, their heads under the feet of the natives who had finally conquered them. Quetzalcoatl the Feathered Serpent blessed the natives.

The natives were the victors but in truth the Nephi,

obsessed by their feud of nearly a thousand years against the Lamani, had defeated themselves. Then I stared as a young man came from a low doorway hidden in the wall, half below ground. Carrying maybe half a dozen fluted jars in his arms, looking neither to the right nor the left, he walked calmly away from the building site. A Nephi slave working on the plaza recognised him, called out. The young man walked faster. 'Moroni?' the idiot slave called after him, following. 'That you, Moroni? It's me.' Moroni ran. Shouting started. People closed in behind him. As Moroni ran closer I saw he wore Nephi chest armour trimmed with jade, a commander, an important man. Not a slave. A sword was hidden beneath his leather loin-guards, the blade glinted as the leather flapped, he was sprinting for his life now. A group of natives cut across in front of him, a spear hissed, he ducked, ran. The jars bumped in his arms and he dropped one.

Moroni stopped. He turned back and picked up what he had dropped.

Incredible. What's so important that a man risks his life for a jar? I stared down from the high branches. He ran again, but they'd almost caught him now. If Moroni drew his sword to protect himself he'd drop the jars. Another spear, but it struck his armour. Still he didn't draw his sword. I heard his breath gasping in his throat. He was almost finished. As he passed beneath the tree I jumped down with a roar like a jaguar, knocked his pursuers into the branches, then caught Moroni up easily. He stared at me wide-eyed. 'Thou art an angel?'

'Keep going,' I advised as we ran.

Later we walked, but he wouldn't let me carry even one of the jars; after a few minutes with me people are in no doubt I'm no angel, only a man. I showed him the best route, following the River Sion northward, then we camped beneath overhanging cliffs by a deep swirling pool I knew. I found flints and driftwood for a fire to keep off mosquitoes then plunged naked – Moroni swiftly averted his eyes – into the cool water. Big ugly fish swirled hungrily around me and I threw one ashore, chopped off its head and took a mouthful of raw quivering flesh to encourage my guest, since Nephis prefer their meat uncooked. 'Eat.'

Moroni swallowed. He ate watching me, starving, but his hand never strayed far from his sword. 'Why savest thou me?'

'Why does a man risk his life to steal a few fluted jars?'

'Thy speech is difficult of understanding.' He coloured. 'I steal not, except what is our very own, by right and tradition.'

'You mean they're yours.' I licked my fingers, burped. 'Temple records? The genealogies?'

'How couldst thou know?' He crossed himself. 'Yes. The sacred plates of gold.' He opened one of the jars and pulled out a thick gold stick, reverently unravelled a hand's-breadth thickly engraved with writing. I couldn't understand a word. 'Holy writing,' Moroni said, both devout and accusing. 'Know ye not that ye are in the hands of God? Hast thou heard not His great command that the earth be rolled together as a scroll? These are part of the holy scriptures of my people, the writings of the fathers of Lehi, and Nephi, Jacob, Zeniff and others, hidden by Ammaron, the faithful account of mine ancestors from the Creation.'

'Worth risking your life for, if it's true.'

'Many are scattered, many are lost. God hath blown our people like chaff before the wind from the south, and the Gentiles possess the land, for God hath turned His back on us.' He closed his eyes, and his eyelashes were dark, beaded with moisture. 'My father hath sent me at the age of twenty-four, which is according to the tradition, to fetch these unto his hand, so that something of us may survive in the minds of our descendants, so that something of us be not all lost. On these plates shall they find a full account of all the wickedness and abominations of our enemies, and equally a full account of the righteousness of mine own people, under God.'

'There must be many more of these,' I said. Lehi had claimed genealogies going back even past Noah the first Zadok, the first man saved by God, to Adam. He'd claimed he had a whole scroll about Enoch, another written by Abraham, another by Moses, even an ancient legend about a pearl. 'A lot more.'

'Verily, yea, preserved in the holy mountain of Shem in the land of Antum, but Shem is conquered. Even so, in many other holy places in the Land Northward where men raise mountains unto the glory of God, we have hidden up our store of talents according to the Word of Our Lord Jesus Christ. For our talents are the lives of our people who have lived under God, and they shalt be multiplied, and our dead shall likewise be as saints.'

I turned over and pretended to sleep. Moroni talked to himself for a while, slapping at mosquitoes, then I heard him seal the jar. He breathed deeply, then snored, and it would have been fun to steal the jars. I imagined his face when he woke. The loss would devastate Moroni but bring me nothing but brief childish pleasure, since I can't read Reformed Egyptian. Still, I was tempted. I slept, unusually for me, and dreamt of the great legless feet of bare black basalt trampling the Temple.

At sunrise I yawned to wake Moroni. He woke with his hand on his sword and counted the jars. 'I'll come with you,' I offered.

'It's a long way. I'm to meet my father with the gathering of the peoples at Cumor-Ya.'

Everything was drawing back to where it began. 'I know where that is. You'll need my help if we're attacked by Lamani.' I caught breakfast, then found the honeycombs of stingless deseret bees which had spread into the wild, and we walked eating. From the bend where the river turns briefly east to Bountiful, I looked back. From here I could just see Zarahemla gleaming between the ridges and hill-lines. 'The natives didn't get inside the Temple, did they, Moroni? It's still intact. They covered it over and built on top, because that's the way they do things.'

'The priests and congregation of Christ gathered together and made their peace with God, and sealed themselves inside.' He shuddered. 'They starved or died of thirst. Nothing but their bones remain.'

'But you got in and out. You knew a secret way.'

He grinned, touched one of the jars. 'Did I not tell you that all hath been written? The Plate of Lehi makes plain the Way of Ezekiel. To Elders of the highest circle of initiation there is a secret way through the maze that, when Satan seems most victorious, a true believer may find—' I laughed outright. 'Ezekiel dug a hole in the wall, that's all,' I said. 'You knew where to dig. You dug a hole straight through into the Holy of Holies, and slid down.'

'How canst thou know that?' He was instantly suspicious. I might be a Lamani spy.

'Obviously,' I said, 'I'm initiated into the inner secrets.' I recalled Mulek's mumbo-jumbo. 'The Door of Chaos. The Creation Room. I'm anointed into the rank of kings and priests. I know what's on the walls of the Holy of Holies.'

'Everyone knows for a truth they be walls of pure gold.'

'Gold isn't what you saw in the sealed chamber. You saw Jesus in there, Moroni.'

He looked at me, marvelling. 'Truly thou knowst whereof thou speakst. Aye, Jesus in the dark, illuminated by only the perpetual flames of the menorah. I took the holy genealogies from the niche whither I was guided by God, sealed up the hole after me, and left the Temple asleep in its sleep until the end of time.'

I pointed back at the city. 'Why are they beginning a

gigantic statue of Christ standing astride the topmost pyramid of the temples?'

He stared at me. 'The Christ! Dost thou not feel the truth? That's not Christ, though they believe it is. That's the statue they build to the glory of their Master, Satan. This is Satan's land now. The statue is of Satan.'

It was a long journey northward, though I found a sailboat overturned and sunk by the ruins of Bountiful. We salvaged it, filled it with custard apples from what was left of the orchards in the jungle, and stitched a patchwork sail from the clothes of the dead. It split before we cleared the narrow neck of the Yucatán peninsula, so I stood before the mast with my cloak held out in my arms like a sail. It was boring work which made me hungry. I ate all the custard apples before we sighted the northern curve of the Gulf. After that boredom it was a relief to wrestle the snakes and alligators of the finger of marshland pointing southward. We followed the long beaches north, making good time, but my stomach was sour from the apples. The cold rain began. Moroni pointed proudly across the grey river. 'New Jerusalem!'

I stared at the tree-covered island the natives called Man-hat-tan, island of hills. Men had never set foot there, surely, by the look of the place it was virgin land. The smoke of a few native fires rose here and there; nothing remained of all I remembered. Moroni saw my face. 'With God's will, it shall be built again.' I shook my head. 'Come with me to Cumor-Ya,' he said, taking my elbow. 'My father waits. He must believe me dead by now.'

'You go, Moroni. Good luck. Your mission was successful. I wish you well.' He hesitated then hurried away, clutching his jars, his face joyous. I watched him go then swam the river to New Jerusalem. I waded ashore on the same sand I first set foot nine hundred and seventy years ago, with Lehi and Nephi at the beginning, and raised my eyes to the trees. It was as though all the people had never been.

There was one highest tree on the highest hill, a Wotan-tree, there always is. I climbed it to the top branch and stood with my head above the leaves. From here I saw clear across the desolation to the mainland hill of Cumor-Ya where a haze of armour glinted. The tree roared and swayed on windy days. In the hottest days of summer it creaked softly in the heat, and I watched the pattern of armies wheel in their Order and Command on the northern plains. I knew, and they knew, that they would all die. It was inevitable; Satan had come with us. The innocent armies came together and smoke rose over Cumor-Ya, the clashing patterns of ten thousand virtuous men fell apart into chaos and confusion. The whole land could have been theirs. I remembered Lehi's great cry, *Lord God most High, Your will has brought us, Your chosen servants, here to the land of promise. Here we will serve You in humility and freedom, under God. I name this place New Jerusalem! I name our land of promise New Sion!* I watched the remnants of the armies scattered, the wounded killed, the women and children hunted down. The victors fought among themselves, then everything fell still. Night fell. It was over at last. New Jerusalem and New Sion ceased to exist.

I walked in the dark. I don't know how long passed; maybe forty years, like the symbolic forty years Moses spent in the wilderness, the forty days Noah floated on the Flood, the forty days Jesus spent on the mountain, or maybe this was the forty years of tribulation prophesied by the first Nephi, during which the Sons of Light would fight the Sons of Darkness. All was darkness now, not a light showed on Cumor-Ya. 'The Temple destroyed,' Nephi had cried, 'all foretold in the scrolls, in the genealogies of my father!'

The spired temple of Sion of the Prophecy atop the

natives' man-made mountain had been knocked to pieces years ago. All I saw was the black hump of the hill against the stars, then a yellow flash caught my eye. A single candle flame burned in the mouth of a cave. I climbed up and from the darkness watched the candle burning smokily in the middle of a table, sending light twisting deep into the cave. At the table sat an old man, Moroni. His hair and beard were ragged and white, his face scarred and full of shadows. His clothes were scraps of armour and leather and two left boots. His right hand was bound in a bloody bandage but he'd stuck a stylus in it somehow. I watched him scratch at the gold scroll, coming painfully to the end.

Moroni looked down the cave and spoke, but no one was there. 'Now I hide up this plate where my father hid a number of his plates, and some of the plates that were handed down to him, together with the priestly sceptre and holy oracles of Urim and Thummim my father wore beneath his breastplate, and his father before him, taken from the body of Nephi the Zadok.'

He looked up as the wind blew, cupped his hand to shield the flame, clutched his broken sword. He looked straight at me in the darkness, but saw nothing. The hope left his face. 'Have angels ceased to appear unto the children of men? Has He withheld the power of the Holy Ghost from them? Will He withhold it for as long as time shall last, or the earth shall stand, or there shall be one man upon the face thereof to be saved?'

No answer. Only the wind. Moroni dropped the useless sword and wrote again – not to the people of the present time, there were none, but to the future. His tongue moved as he wrote, speaking words that almost certainly would never be read. 'And now I bid to all, farewell. I soon go to rest in the paradise of God, until my spirit and body shall again unite, and I am brought forth triumphant through the air, to meet you before the pleasing bar of the great Yahweh, the Eternal Judge of both quick and dead. Amen.'

There was absolutely nothing I could say to him. I turned and went away quietly from Cumor-Ya, following the wind.

Moroni had believed Jesus and Satan were brothers, both Sons of God. Satan was ancient, His names were legion: *S-T-N*, B'El, Baal, B'Elial, B'Elzebub, B'El-Zephon, Lord Prince of this world. My mother from the northern mountains had worshipped Him among other gods. Eve had known Him, and so had my earliest boyhood friends in Shem, the canaans; Satan was Molech, King of the fiery sacrifices I'd seen from Bab'El to Jerusalem to the Pillars of Hercules: Noah had heard Satan boasting, *This world is mine, these are my people. I am the oldest of the old and greatest of the great, I suckled closest and most loved at God's bosom.*

But Jesus was new.

The Jesus I'd seen, I'd *touched*, wasn't the expected war Messiah, King of the world, another Satan. He was a gentle man preaching love, mercy, peace, reconciliation, toleration. He was Himself the sacrifice. His Father's sacrifice.

I drifted. I drifted west, north, south. Blue eyes, blond hair, high Caucasian cheekbones, were a vanishing sight. The natives killed them or married them. A hundred years later I saw none, only an occasional blue flash in a native child's eye, a pale streak in native hair, then even that was gone. I drifted south to the windy tip of saltblown islands, north to lakes as great as seas, but a continent is only a big island. In the end, it's a prison.

I returned to the Isthmus. The natives still remembered Itzá the Christ, Quetzalcoatl, and even Wotan, though their tongue still called me Votan. They believed Votan arrived from a place across the ocean with followers in long robes. They knew I'd been to Bab'El and seen the great tower with a temple on top reaching to Heaven – I must have

521

been talking drunk, I'd only seen its ruins, but maybe they remembered Jared stories. My symbol, the natives said, was a serpent – getting me mixed up with legends of Mulek's sceptre, I reckon – but they knew my people had married the natives and made more people, which was true enough. And here's something exactly true: they believed I'd left a secret treasure in a dark house underground.

I had to go there.

Before dawn I climbed quietly into the treetops overlooking the native city of Apachiohualitzá – the name Zarahemla was forgotten – and waited for the dawn. It was still dark when I heard the low murmur of the crowd, the sound of their shuffling footsteps across the plaza. When they were assembled, from each corner naphtha flames shot up like burning fountains – I later heard it was called the Place of Fountains – and the firelit people, red as meat, huddled devoutly in the roaring shadowy glare. The temples stood like pyramids of dull red light. The native priests arrived in procession wearing masks and white cotton robes. Each carried a burning cup as they climbed the Stairway to Heaven. At first they were hardly visible, links of fire no brighter than sparks, then they climbed higher into the first grey glow of dawn, higher than I could see. I scrambled to the very top of the tree and pushed aside the leaves. Stared.

'Moroni,' I whispered, 'you were right.'

It wasn't a gigantic statue of Christ; it was Satan. The fallen angel stood vast and unsubdued and full of strength as though using humans to climb back to God, His mighty feet braced on each side of the topmost temple. The natives, inspired, foolish, were building their own tower of Bab'El. Even from here I sensed each hair and vein and knuckle, the black basalt legs rising over the treetops potent with muscle and vitality to the crinkled balls and engorged uncircumcised penis. The priests climbed to an entranceway in the heel and disappeared one by one inside. I shielded my eyes from the bright sky, gazing up at the faithful musculature of the belly, the chest crisscrossed with great ribs of straining muscle as though the great black angelic wings beat at the morning air above me, would lift whole the living edifice from the temple tops towards the sky, towards God. Straining towards God with every ounce of its adamantine strength. Doomed. Its black basalt face locked in a scream, demonic, immobile, eternal, the scream of utter loss. The Fall.

I put back my head and my eyes followed the upraised arms to the great hands outstretched above the screaming head. The sun rose over the jungle, the first rays of light touched the outspread fingertips. *Come to me.*

Worship me. Satan victorious over the Temple.

The priests climbed from the mouth, climbed stairs set on the upper sides of the arms. They came climbing up to the great cupped palms, the bloodbaths where figures knelt teetering against the sky, bound in grass ropes, chests bared, heads bowed in submission to their fate.

I looked away.

I didn't go back to Apachiohualitzá. Satan wasn't truly there, not in the flesh – the only God I've actually met is Joshua, about as opposite to me as it's possible to get, at least in public, though I'd say he had a temper lurking somewhere. And who's to say there aren't different sorts of strength? I can't imagine Joshua carrying three barmaids on each arm as I used to do very merrily in the seaports of Canaan, or drinking his companions into a stupor – though he liked a drop – or wrestling alligators which is good sport. Really Joshua and I didn't have much in common. But he was strong in his way. Perhaps much stronger than me. Maybe God never gives up, has ten thousand sons, as I'd once wondered. Maybe ten thousand times ten thousand, if there is such a number – I'd heard of it somewhere, couldn't remember where. Obviously I'd failed Him, maybe many fail. The Jerusalem scribes had called Moses an archetype or 'type' of Elijah, and Lehi had said both were 'types' of Christ. Others said Hercules and Orpheus and Osiris and Dionysus and Attis and even I foreshadowed and foretold Christ. Maybe they were just trying to claim the ancient beliefs for Christianity. Maybe God loses every battle but the last.

So I wrestled alligators. I wrestled bears, but they go for your head, and they try to gut you with their claws like lions do, and their breath is appalling. I wrestled snakes when I found any large enough, there's a big river in the land southward with good grippy snakes, but I hate mosquitoes and leeches as much as any man. Wrestling native bucks is no challenge but wrestling their squaws is, the whole feathered tribe come after you screaming blue murder.

I look different, I *am* different. I'm not like them. This is their land again.

I went north, then further north, to the endless forest. I lived alone. Me, no woman, no fighting. I had to wear animal skins, no one grew crops for me, and I built a log cabin with a primitive stone axe that kept breaking. There was nowhere to buy salt for my meat – the sea was a day's journey east – and while I was chopping firewood with the breaking axe and wondering if I should go south for the winter a bear attacked me, caught my head in its stinking mouth, and its tooth tore my eye out. It hurt, and an eye takes years to grow back properly. The leaves were falling, the land turning to mud. I sat in pain on the steps of my cabin, wearing stinking bearskin, smelling bear stew again for supper, and no salt, with no woman however repellent to keep me warm, and blinked one-eyed at the first flakes of snow swirling from the mountains above the grey lake, and knew I'd be wintering here. A man walked across the lake between the snowflakes. At first I thought there was already ice, but he walked towards me on the rippling water. The lake's deep; I'd lowered my fishing line ten times my own height, and still no bottom. I stood up. 'My God,' I said. A wave broke around His ankles, not wetting Him. He held out His hand, His fingers jewelled with rings, for me to kiss.

He said: 'You know who I am.'

'You're Joshua,' I said. 'You look like Joshua.'

'I am Jesus Christ.' The wind pulled out His cloak of royal purple, and instead of a crown of thorns he wore a proper gold crown, a gold circlet that held his long hair down, though the ends flapped in the wind. The waves knocked His ankles and He frowned, flattening them, then stepped ashore. 'I *am* Jesus Christ. I am King of the world. I was born in the Holy of Holies of the Temple.'

'Who are you?' I said.

'I told you, I am Jesus Christ.'

'That's not enough. It's not enough to say that.' I was kneeling on the stones, my lips almost touching His ring, but not quite. I looked up. 'Are you the Lamb of God, an *Asayya*, a healer?'

'Of course not. I'm a Pharisee, a promising child educated by the Sadducees of the Temple.'

'Are you a Nazarene?'

'I lived with my earthly parents in the town of Nazareth.'

'Were you born to be Christ?'

'Yes, I am the Son of God. I was only seven months in the womb. I was born in the dark of the year.'

'Like Mithras.' Mithras was a god brought to Shem by invaders.

Jesus Christ did not withdraw His ring, but touched my lips with it gently. 'Believe in me.'

'My eye hurts.'

He said: 'What?'

'Heal me, Joshua. My eye hurts.'

'It's only pain.' He frowned impatiently. 'You're an

525

immortal, your eye will get better. You live in pain anyway, don't you, Wotan?' He pushed His ring against my lips. 'Unrequited love, isn't it? What's her name, Mari, Miri, Mara, Mary? There's so many of them.' I stared down at the gold straps of His sandals, stared up at His smiling face.

'You aren't Joshua,' I said.

He laughed. 'I am Jesus Christ.'

'That's not a name.'

'Hear me, one-eyed man, if you have two good ears to listen. I destroyed the Jerusalem Temple. The empire of the Romans is thrown down, the Pope sits on the Emperor's throne like a ghost, and Rome shall not be born again until the end of time.' He opened His robes, showing the sword He wore at His side. He laughed, knowing how I like weapons and strength.

'I know who you are,' I said. 'You're the liar.'

'You're so close to me. I should have known I couldn't fool you.' He shrugged, sat beside me. 'I don't fool you, do I? You could be my great high priest.'

'I don't serve Satan.'

'Your life doesn't serve God. You've failed Him in every possible way. Caused more harm than good. You've lived with a high hand, a creature of blood and lust and passion. You give in to temptation every time. When I showed Joshua temptation he didn't have any answers of his own, either, just parroted Deuteronomy at me. Yes, when he was a man Joshua knew the trials of human nature, knew the weakness of being a man, feared death.'

'Joshua came back from death.'

'On the Cross he prayed to God and wasn't heard.'

'He came back.'

'I can't imagine why He bothered. And only for forty days. Do you know where His body is?'

'Do you?'

'Ordinary priests die, but they say Jesus is high priest

of a priesthood that will never pass away, because of the indestructible life He received by His Resurrection.'

'You don't know anything about Jesus.'

He pitied me. 'You've always searched for your father with all your heart and all your strength. Found anyone?'

'Don't you call yourself my brother,' I said.

'You've searched, haven't you? All your long life. You're quite virtuous in your way. Just a big child, no harm in you. I don't blame you. I have no punishment for you.'

Snow blew in our faces. 'Living here is punishment enough,' I said.

'No, it's a beautiful world. Mine. A beautiful prison. I slept. But then there were humans. What shall we do with them?'

'We?'

'You live like a god, you look like one, surely that entails some responsibility. Look at all you have to offer them. Yet you live here alone like a hermit.'

'Offer? What did you offer Joshua?'

'On the mountain top? The usual. Make the most of yourself, use the power that's inside you, inside everyone. Turn stones to bread, one loaf into thousands, one fish into a shoal. All I got back was Deuteronomy, man shall not live by bread alone, meaning turning bread into stones is a sin, rebellion against the Divine will. He wouldn't listen. Stones are made into bakery ovens, granaries and houses, but into bread, no, no. That's rebellion.'

'You're very clever.'

'I'm honest.'

'What else was said?'

'Nothing.'

I drew a breath. For only the first or second time in my life I was in the company of someone capable of destroying me. Satan had not done so when Ishtar, Queen of Heaven, begged for my destruction in revenge for killing Huwawa – *let Wotan be ripped to pieces with a sharp knife, scatter his*

*meat living or dead with a winnowing fan, burn him in a fire
and grind the charcoal of him in a mill, scatter his dust in the
fields.* That time He'd only used her for His own purposes,
agreeing to let the Bull of Heaven find me, and I suffered
nothing worse than a sword-thrust to the heart and a cut
throat.

I asked, 'What do you want from me?'

'It doesn't work like that.' He said earnestly: 'It's what
can I do for you. There must be something you want.'

'A good hot-blooded woman would be nice.' I stopped
him before it happened. 'What do you want in return?'

'Nothing. I've already had my fun with you. I like you,
Wotan. You're such . . . clay.'

'What fun?'

'The Bull of Heaven was your father.'

I struck out. He caught my fist in His hand like cold
iron. I struggled.

'Liar!' I cried out, sounded weak for the first time in
my life.

'No lies between us. You think God has a monopoly on
truth? Why? Peace, Wotan, peace. You killed your father –
I mean Kidu did, and Kidu was your golem, wasn't he?
You look so fucking stupid with your mouth hanging open.
You mean you really didn't know? While you lay asleep in
the Ya'nna temple Nin scraped a few drops of your sweat
into a small lapis-engraved pot with a stopper. You don't
remember? You're lying to yourself, Wotan. In the desert
she mixed your sweat with dust to create Kidu, your golem.
Your exact twin down to the last cell. An artificial brother
created by supernatural means. She wanted to help.'

I murmured, 'Kidu was the best friend I ever had.'

'A man's best friend is always himself. Who else can he
trust?' He looked into my eye. 'We're not weeping, are
we?' His gaze hardened. 'You didn't really think you were
a son of God, did you?'

I pulled away. 'I am. Tia my earthly mother told me.

528

On a beach by the Black Sea she picked up shells and El came to her rising from the waves as a great white bull, his voice roaring like a great wind, and His shadow overshadowed her and . . . and here I am.'

He said heavily, 'Does it sound likely?'

'She told me herself. I know it's true. My mother wouldn't lie.'

'She did lie with everyone else, Lotaan, Hvergil, even that runt Auor, anyone with half a cock. She was a queen by marriage but a whore by nature, and who knows whose sperm wins in a whore's womb.' He opened the bearskin at my throat, touched his cold fingertip to the battered necklace of shells, restrung many times. 'Not still? Wotan, you're so sentimental. You still believe her.'

'I remember the moment of my conception. I remember the angels singing.'

He stilled. 'You can remember the song of angels?'

'I hear them. Dream them. Impossible to describe.'

He said nothing. Then He said, 'I know it. I know it. I hate this world. I dream of Heaven still.' A ray of sunlight fingered the lake, sweeping over us. 'Anything, Wotan. Anything you ask. You're a creature of this world. I'll give you the most beautiful woman in the world. Riches.' In a flash I was surrounded by jewels. 'Gold?' In an instant the trees were gold, the lake was a gigantic diamond reflecting them. 'No, Wotan?' Only snow and trees and lake again. He came close until his eyes almost touched mine. 'What's her name? I can give her soul to you.' He blinked, his eyelashes scratched my eye. 'You're in love.'

I lied. 'No.'

'I can give love. Love is easy.'

I tried not to think of her name – of any of her names.

He whispered, 'Mary? Mary Magdalene? *That* love. She's not for you. She never was. It's impossible for me to make her suffer more than she does, or give her more happiness. She's pure woman. The pure knowledge, *sophia*, of women. The Queen of Hell.'

'The priests taught that after His Crucifixion Jesus descended to Hell.'

'Do I look defeated?'

'No,' I admitted.

His nostrils flared. 'That bear stew smells disgusting.'

'It is disgusting.'

'Look at you, it's sad to see you so cast down. I've got just the thing to cheer you up. Something you can't resist. You'll love it. Valhalla.' He clapped me on the shoulder and climbed to His feet, or rather, He expanded in size. 'By the way, about Huwawa, where did he fall, exactly?'

'Is this the deal?'

'No deals. Valhalla is a gift without my hand on it.'

'I don't remember exactly where. It was a long time ago.'

'It's not important. You know. Veneration, a shrine marking the spot, he was one of the greatest of us.' His shape shifted, his clothes split as muscles came up inside him. 'Where did Huwawa's head lie at the moment of his death? Was it in the valley, or on the hilltop? Did he crawl away to die curled in a cave somewhere, still guarding his treasure even in death?'

'I don't remember.'

'It doesn't matter.' Satan's voice changed, deep, echoing like a bell. 'Only remember that Jesus is dead, Wotan. Remember *that*.' Gold burst out of His face, flaking almost at once. A gold angel stood up on the lake shore, wings gusting twigs, mud, tawdry leaves of flaking gold. He stood like Nabuchadnezzar's golden statue peeling gold, then iron below, then stone, then clay, then soil. I whispered, 'You aren't what you appear, are you. That's why they call you the liar.'

Satan said: 'Believe me, I'm exactly what I appear.' The land fell away below me, the soil slid down on each side of me, I stood on a mountain peak rising into the sky. I stood on the head of the Dragon lifting from the earth through the clouds. I stood on blood-red skin and behind me great scales rose up, spines, and vast eyes opened like windows on terrible suffering. I clung to the topmost horn of the Dragon.

Satan said: 'Jump, Wotan. Jump, and fly.'

Below me the sun struck across the white cloud tops of the snowstorm. Through breaks in the clouds I saw the sea, a great flat rock, a bay. The roar of the wind ceased, silence fell like held breath. Far down I heard men shouting, screaming. I saw a woman sprinting bare-breasted on the sand, a two-bladed battleaxe shining in her hand, long blond hair flying.

Jump, and fly.

I held out my arms. I jumped. I flew.

Oh, it was glorious! Flying! The wind roared in my face, the land turned below, her footsteps raced beneath me along the sand, a wave broke and the foam washed them away, then I saw a jumble of many footprints coming after her. Men dressed in sealskin, hunters. The blond girl ran ahead of them like a deer clothed in deerskin, the lithe muscles of her body rippling – and her breasts! – and her long legs flashing. The leader threw a spear, the stone point caught her shoulder, she screamed.

She turned and faced them, raised her gleaming axe to her lips and kissed the blade. Magnificent sight! I heard her cry out, 'Glorious death, if I die for my friends!'

I understood her instinctively – almost my mother's language. What a wonderful prayer, the finest I'd heard. I saw flames burning in the distance; this brave girl deliberately drew the attackers away from her companions to herself. I jumped down beside her, kissed the blood of her wound, looked into her amazing blue eyes. She raised the axe behind me, clubbed a seal-hunter's skull, sliced someone's face in half, screamed for joy. My sort of woman. I grabbed the useless stone axe from my belt and waded among her attackers as they came, shattered them, knocked them back, threw them down. In the end there were only a few trying to crawl into the dunes or hiding themselves in the surf and she walked round killing them, eyeing me. 'Haven't you seen breasts before?' I hadn't, not such big ones with such forceful cherry-red nipples. 'Do you want sex? No sex until the killing is over. And I'm Galmr's woman, so you'll have to fight him first.' She looked at me adoringly. 'You're even stronger than Galmr!'

I shouted, 'Tell me your name!'

'Frigg! Who are you?'

'Wotan.' I seized her round her muscular waist, resisted the temptation to kiss her lips at once (the only temptation I resisted that day) and swept her in my arms along the beach. 'Fly!' Frigg cried. 'Faster! Higher!' Smoke blew over us from the timbered hall where her companions were besieged, the flames pulled downwind by the sea breeze. We fell on the attackers from behind, scattering them, Frigg screaming like the demons of Hell. 'To me, men of the north!' As she called their names the defenders – even the men had blond hair as long as mine, and braided blond moustaches that hung to their bronzed chests – ran out swinging axes, horned helmets gleaming, and the glorious slaughter began. Niord chucked me an axe, a proper war axe, curved doubled-headed blades of iron sharp enough to shave with. I jerked another still hot from the chest of a seal-hunter, fought forward with an axe in each hand. The joy of battle! The passion! The lives I saved that day, repaying Niord, saving Loki's back from a knife-thrust, rallying my new friends when the tide of battle turned against us. The tribe of seal-hunters fought bravely at last but we drove them into the sea, and the waves threw them on our axes. Frigg grabbed my elbow, pointed her axe matted with blood and black hair. 'See, Helluland, the flat rock!' The headland where the sea burst in white wings ended in a large flat rock, and the last of the sealers made their stand there. Frigg and the other women and widows attacked from one side, the north men from the other, and I jumped down in the middle. The rock ran with blood and spray, and we were sad when it was all over. Loki whom I'd saved threw down his axe and embraced me. 'Blood brother!'

We slung the bodies we'd slain into the sea, jumped down from the rock, limped across the sand. Everyone was bleeding and proud, showing off their wounds, bragging that their own were the worst and most painful. 'Let's get drunk,' Loki said. 'Tell us all about yourself. How long have you been on our new found island? We thought we were the first civilised people.' Niord pissed on the burning wall to put it out, but then a man I'd not seen before carried out a body and in a flash the jolly mood was stricken with grief. 'Galmr is dead.' Frigg wailed at once. 'Galmr the Great is dead!' The women gathered around her, wailing. 'It's not as though they were married or anything,' Loki said. 'She won't have to kill herself. Good news for one of us, a chieftain's woman.' He hitched his belt hopefully.

'I've got my eye on her,' I said, throwing my axes at the doorposts so that they quivered one on each side. Loki swallowed. 'She's yours, my friend. Not my sort. Cold in bed as the snow wind, I heard.' He smiled. I said, 'I don't believe you.'

Niord spoke. 'We must bury our dead. Galmr is dead, Skjold is dead.'

I spoke to the huge muscular man who carried Galmr to the pyre. 'I know you.'

'I'm your son, Ymir.' He laid the body on the sticks, bowed his head respectfully. 'You're my father, Wotan, and my mother is Eve.' He looked up as the flames rose and the light of day failed. I hardly heard him for the wailing of the women, then they fell silent as the flames died away. Nobody said anything. They all looked at me expectantly.

They'd seen me fight. Ymir said, 'My father will speak.'

'Your Galmr is dead, your Skjold is dead,' I told them. 'I hardly knew them, but I know this. They are gone to . . . to Valhalla.' I tried to imagine what Heaven was like. 'In Valhalla Galmr and Skjold fight all day and make love all night. They drink all the evening and sleep all the morning. They hunt all afternoon and they never get old. Their axes are always sharp and their pricks never go limp and their women are always willing. Valhalla!'

'Valhalla!' they roared. They raised their axes in the last of firelight, the wind sweeping the sparks across the beach. 'Valhalla!'

'How do we get to Valhalla?' Loki asked.

'Live life to the full and die bravely.'

'Might be hard for you, Loki,' Niord said. 'No offence.' Loki shouted, 'Who says I'm not brave? Who says it?' The women shouted him down. 'What about us?' they cried. 'What about the women in Valhalla?'

'You'll be strong, brave and lustful, bearing strong, brave and lustful children.'

'And no serving?'

'Not if you're good in bed and die bravely.'

'I like the sound of it,' Frigg said. 'No one else ever promised us as much as this before. But I've never heard of you, Wotan.' Her tongue, unfamiliar with my name, said Odin, Ó-thinn.

'I've never heard of you either,' I said, 'but I like the look of you.' She eyed my crotch, gauging the weight of my manhood.

'Is this Valhalla?' Buri asked, but Loki slapped him. 'No, you idiot, this is Vin Land. Grassland.' He pointed inland, the horizon of moonlit treetops, as we walked back to the hall. 'There's Skogsland. Forest.' I saw now that there were more halls built on the low hills over the marshy grassland, crude work behind stockades, with rough-hewn timber walls and peat roofs. 'Let's bind our wounds and eat and

534

drink to the death of the Skarlingarna,' Loki said. 'The natives,' he explained. 'They eat our seal blubber and rub their bodies with it to keep warm. Treacherous animals, no honour, no glory. Shot Buri's woman with an arrow. We broke them today though.' His eye twinkled. 'Peace negotiations broke down suddenly.'

'Valhalla for the brave, but where do cowards go when they die?' Niord asked me, binding his arm, with an eye on Loki who was unharmed.

I shrugged. 'Hell.'

'I've heard of it.' Niord nodded. 'Helheim. When you get there tell us what it's like, Loki.' I separated them, shouting louder than they. 'You're behaving like fools,' I bellowed. They liked a man who bellowed. Ymir said: 'Listen to the wise bellowing of my father.'

'Let's get drunk,' I said. The women brought mead in horns and we got drunk. Outside the hunting dogs snarled and prowled, on guard. We warriors sat pressed together for warmth at the long table, a comradely mass of furs, leather, beards and sweaty smoky flesh. The women tended the fire and cooking, throwing fat joints on the flames, coughing. The fire flickered dimly, the smoke couldn't get out through the thick roof. Flames roared up hissing and spitting as the meat fat ignited, coating us with grease and soot. 'Where's your town?' I asked. 'How long have you lived here?'

'We summer here. Fish, make love, eat, drink. Return home in winter.' Loki helped himself to a leg, ate the blackened outside, dribbled blood from the inside. 'This year we were going to winter here. That's finished. Treacherous Skarlingarna. Good thing we attacked them first.' We ate burnt raw meat, drank sweet mead, belched. 'Where're the women?' The women said, 'You're too drunk for us, Loki. Have some more.' Our horns were refilled.

'Songs first,' Niord said. 'We got our own Hibernian.'

He dragged forward a thin terrified bard. 'Sing for your supper, Irishman.'

'What about, masters?'

Niord thought about it. 'Valhalla. Life in Valhalla. Make us like gods living for ever after death. Strong as Ymir and Wotan.' Ymir said respectfully, 'My father's stronger than me.'

'I can sing about that,' the slave bard said. His name was Bragi. He sang in an awful coughing voice, eyes streaming. 'He'll get better,' Niord said. 'He's good.' Loki staggered to his feet. 'Who's sleeping with Hummel?' Buri slurred, 'No one wants to sleep with her. Why you always choose the smelliest ugliest cows, Loki? You got the worst taste in women.' Loki grinned, stumbling, fell down, pulled down the most horrible-looking cook with him. She got her skirts up quick as a flash but he was snoring already. 'Valhalla,' sang Bragi, plucking a string, 'where Adam and Eve, Askr and Embla, built their great house Asgard.'

The others were sleeping and I stood, stepped over the snoring bodies. 'One day, Bragi, I'll tell you about other places long ago, lands as hot as the sun south of the Surtr Sea, fed by rivers roaring in torrents from icy mountains, a land of man-made mountains. The land between the rivers was called Middle Earth, the land of Shem.' But Bragi too was asleep. He mumbled, singing better in his dreams than awake. I stepped over him, swigging from the horn, and saw Frigg watching me from the shadows. 'Galmr's ashes can't keep me warm,' she said, refilling my horn to the brim. 'What can you offer me?' I picked her up and kissed her, put the horn to her lips and she gulped, blew mead-sweet breath provocatively in my face. 'That all you got, Wotan?'

'No gold, no jewels, no hunting dogs,' I said, 'but I'll keep you warm.'

Frigg laughed. 'You're all the same. You've drunk enough to fell any man's tree. See you tomorrow.' Her eyes widened in amazement as she felt me. I opened my bearskin and pretended modesty. 'Are you a man?' she gasped. 'You must be a god! I've never seen anything so magnificent.'

'Your breasts are almost as good,' I admitted, and she hugged me so tight her nipples pricked me. 'They're yours!' she cried.

Frigg, my darling Frigg, my love. All night in the darkness and smoke she climbed over me like a goddess, insatiable, lustful, demanding, perfect. Perfect.

The morning sun rose hard and bright as broken glass in our eyes.

'We got hardly any sleep last night,' Loki groaned, holding his head. 'Do you have to make so much noise? And you broke the door. You don't have to chase her about so much. What was it about?'

Frigg grinned at me, wiggling her hips. She fried my steak on the tip of a sword. Loki groaned at the sight of it. She swung it across, winking along the blade, and I pulled it off with my teeth. We gazed at each other adoringly. By moonlight we'd made love in the dunes, made love on the moonlit sand, swum in the moonlit sea, and I think we made love there too. 'We're in love,' I said.

'You don't have to scream like cats,' Loki grumbled, but I was so in love and having so much fun that I almost forgot how I got here, almost forgot about . . . I should remember – but just then a cry went up, 'A sail!'

The longship wore clumsily round the cape, then picked up speed towards shore. The stern wind blew hard on the wide rectangle of the sail, sending spray spurting from the lower corners clipping across the wave tops. 'Best to send the ship to sea during the fighting,' Loki said. 'My idea. The *Naglfari*'s the one thing we can't afford to lose. She's got the beer-kettle aboard.'

'And Aegir's the best captain,' Niord said. 'Even with a crew of women.' I saw Aegir standing high in the stern, on the *styrbord* platform over the steering oar. The longship came ashore as fast as a man could run, sliding up on to the sand, and he jumped ashore. The women jumped down after him, big buxom maidens used to heaving oars and pulling ropes. 'Don't look at them,' Frigg said. They were gorgeous, all with blond hair braided so it wouldn't get caught in ropes or oars. So many names, Jord, Nanna, Fulla who was Frigg's maid, Eir the healer, Huldra, Gullveig, all blue-eyed, golden, lovely. They all looked at me challengingly, glowering, women of spirit, distrusting a stranger. Not one of them a virgin. Frigg stood between them and me and offered me another steak from her sword-tip, then jabbed me with the point. 'Look at me, only me,' she said jealously. She called over her shoulder, 'Wotan is mine!'

They laughed, then nodded seriously, laughing, 'Yes, yes, Frigg, all of him for you!'

'Of course I'm yours,' I told her. 'Only you.' But I couldn't help looking.

That evening we held a council in the big hall before we got too drunk. 'A good wind's blowing homeward,' Aegir said. 'But any time now storms will come.' Someone saw yellow-chested birds from Green Land pass overhead this afternoon, flying towards the sun.

'Where's home?' I asked. 'Is it Rome, or Jerusalem?'

'We're north men,' Ymir said. He stood and silence fell, these people love a story, especially a fabulous story. 'Long, long, long ago in the days of Shem, I sailed with the lapis boats from Eden to Meluhha.'

'So that's where you went, Ymir. To India. We never knew for sure.' I embraced Ymir fondly, which no other man was big enough to do. He continued. 'From the deep valleys and high mountains above Meluhha, the earth unknown and Heaven above, these people drove their herds across the endless grasslands of Asia after the setting sun.'

'The *Aesir*. My mother was one of those people. You're my people.' To show them how pleased I was I bashed the oak table proudly, breaking it. Niord killed a slave who spilt beer. 'Go on, Ymir, tell us everything.' They'd heard it many times before.

Ymir said, 'The Norths of Aesir kept going until the endless grassland ended, and there they bore children and children's children. Wars and sport kill so many men that each man has many wives, and when he dies his land's divided equally by law among all his sons. Within a few years each Norse farm's divided into a hundred farms, and one-hundredth of a farm doesn't feed the farmer. Some looked back to the endless grassland; some of us looked forward to the endless ocean. Some said it was a place of storms and chaos, the Ginnungagap. We said it was full of fish. And islands. And coasts.'

'It's simple,' Loki said. 'Just follow the birds. I told them that. The north ocean's narrow enough for birds to fly across it. We left home and sailed after the birds.'

'What place do you call home?' I asked.

'Us troublemakers? Where we lay our heads.'

'There's no glory in killing natives here,' Niord said glumly. 'They own no gold, no treasure, nothing worth stealing. They don't fight with swords like honourable men.' The others nodded. 'Mostly they fight by running away. Where's the honour in killing cowards?'

'And they stab you as soon as your back's turned,' Loki added.

Buri said, 'Or an arrow from the trees, like shot my poor wife.'

I saw the loneliness in their faces. I jumped into the rafters. 'Let's go home,' I bellowed. 'Let's go home and make it *your* home again!'

'*Our* home,' Frigg called. 'Our home!'

Loki said: 'Valhalla.'

★ ★ ★

That easy; that's how I discovered Europe from New Sion. The *Naglfari* was blown forward with the snow flurries from Vin Land, wore round the cape, and heeled awkwardly in the wind blowing along the strait. The grass island fell behind us and everyone fell silent, hating being out of sight of shore. But almost at once new land rose beyond the snarling dragon-headed prow where I stood, my arm around its scaly neck carved of oak. Loki pointed. 'Markland.' Aegir on the *styrbord* held close to the coast despite the wind blowing us out, the men preferring to row between dangerous islands and shoals rather than lose the shore. Twice we landed for fresh water. Then a bay or huge river opened on our left, and another huge cold island of great flat rocks lay ahead; Aegir pulled on the steering oar, the prow turned to starboard towards the empty grey ocean, the wind filled the sail, and the *Naglfari* flew. What a wonderful feeling! I'd not been so fast since I was washed down in the torrents from Ararat, and I stood balanced on the dragon's head, arms outstretched, roaring my joy at the sea and sky and the spray flying below me.

'Green Land,' Loki said, and the grey-green hills reached around the boat like embracing arms. The people, though civilised, saw that even our women carried swords and axes and took fright. We took water, stole what we needed from their halls, and once we started we couldn't stop. We left what little dried-up salted cod we could afford in payment, but still they hid away. Returning to the boat I found every salting-house along the shore stacked to the roof-beams with fat salted cod. Insulted, we went back and reclaimed what we'd offered, and left everything burning so they'd remember us.

We rowed when the wind failed. Aegir used a sun-stone like an Urim to find his way on cloudy days – held up, it revealed the glowing orb of the sun through the overcast. On the fourth day he released a bird (not a dove, a pigeon), then steered the boat after its tiny fluttering shape, and a cloud turned into an island.

'Ice Land,' Loki said. 'Two days more, and we'll come to a group of many islands.'

But the wind roared as loud as I, and snow blew us northward among great islands not of land but of ice. We stood like ice giants on a ship of ice; I struck the mast with a war hammer so that the ice cracked and fell down like ringing bells, climbed to the peak, and stared at the ice mountains rising ahead. On their lower slopes grew pine trees not yet covered with snow, and by the shore I saw groves of oak and ash. We sailed down an echoing inlet, the water deep blue to the shore. I tied a rope around my waist and leapt from the masthead, scaling the cliff to the snowy plateau high above, white as a breaking wave between two mountains. This was the place. I swung Loki up after me, then Frigg, then the others. Loki threw snowballs at the two mountains. 'I call them Ragnarok,' he said. Finally, by tying the rope to the mast, I pulled up the boat itself.

'What now?' Loki said.

I caught a snowball in my hand and put it on the snow, then put another snowball on top. I'd started the walls of Enoch with one handful of mud. Now I made a third snowball and put it on top of the second, and built the walls of Valhalla. As the walls rose up fresh snow fell from the sky and blew in on the wind. The weight of compressed snow made walls of solid ice so thick and clear they didn't melt even in midsummer, shining like mirrors, sending shafts of sunlight back into the sky and into the eyes of all who saw Valhalla, and the roofs of Valhalla, and the towns of Valhalla rising behind them.

My friends gathered round. I knew the look in their eyes. It was awe. Only Loki blinked. From now on I had my way in all things. My friends from the ship *Naglfari*, both men and women, were strong and brave – brave enough to have sailed the Ginnungagap, strong enough to have returned – but they served me as children serve their father. Later, as the stories and sagas of our epic deeds spread, some were worshipped as gods themselves, and the granddaughters of Aegir's muscular plaited oarswomen called Valkyries, choosers of the slain; but that was in the future. For now they were flesh and blood, alive, shivering, and soon they would need food and beer. But I stared up at Valhalla.

Beautiful, beautiful. At last I'd built a house fit for a god: a house fit for El Himself, if ever He came back to earth. So this, I told myself, this is why I was sent into the world. This is why I was born. To build, in the end, something beautiful enough for God.

Once started, I couldn't stop. Everyone, especially Loki, complained about the cold, so I felled the forest below Valhalla to build Asgard, my great hall, its hearth blazing with whole treetrunks, and the *Naglfari* hung on the wall as though sailing still, reminding us of glory. All day we hunted boar, reindeer, bear, eagle, the proudest animals of the mountains. All evening we drank ourselves stupid, ate ourselves fat, and Bragi sang songs of our exploits. All night we made love, and the more I loved Frigg the more I loved all women. Our women hunted the proudest animals of all, men, and the more my power and pride grew the more they wanted to love me. Since the immensity and frequency of my orgasms was legendary (I've never been a quiet or modest lover) but the secret of my sterility was not, Jord claimed her son Thor was mine. Then came all the others. As my reputation spread nine women each with a son named Heimdall claimed I was his father. Frigg joked (she alone knew my secret) they were Loki's spawn because only Loki slept with women so ugly. 'Everyone knows Wotan only sleeps with beauties.'

It's Frigg I loved. Her I married. When the time came

I swam with her in the fjord, in waters as deep as the sky, and she took the pearl in her mouth. Perhaps it was Loki who spied on us from a bush; when Frigg climbed naked and long-limbed from the water and I did not appear, that's when the stories began. At first they believed me drowned; then that Frigg drowned me; but then her belly swelled with child, her child was born, and she called him Balder. He grew up, she went into the mountains to Valhalla, and I came back. My reputation grew dramatically. Everyone knows the gods are different.

'He's a shapeshifter,' Loki slurred. Niord was away in the boats, trading with southerners, so Loki's mischievous tongue went to work. 'Maybe Wotan's trying to fool us. He just wants us to think he's a god. Maybe I should stick a spear in him for a bet, see if he bleeds.'

'Yes, I'm a shapeshifter.' I leapt into the rafters, so high that everyone below squinted to see me. 'Yes, and I can jump and fly!' I sprang down beside Loki. I stared into his sweating face, put my fingers to my eye the bear had torn out, opened the eyelid and stared at him with my eye. It was almost perfectly healed. 'What do you see, Loki?'

'It's true,' Loki muttered. 'Wotan is a god.' He stumbled away, then came back and pulled some hideous wench after him to take for company in exile. I heard he built a log hall somewhere, calling it Utgarda-Loki. I didn't see him for years. Then I appeared to him as Frigg, youthful, bare-breasted, forceful, beautiful, and Loki ran away. I allowed him back to Asgard, but he never again dared oppose me to my face.

The plateau between the two mountains was icy and almost impossible to reach by land, but as word spread of Valhalla many attempted the trek across the mountain ranges, and more were blown by the wind or carried by the sea. Whole villages were built in Asgard. The more I built, the more I had to build, and the villagers fell silent when I spoke. When they heard my footsteps they trembled, bowing, grovelling, I'm irritable when drunk. The more I drank the more I had to drink. Only the bravest men met my eye, and only the bravest of the brave (those who survived) were allowed to make the long climb to Valhalla, my pride and joy. My son Vidar joined us from Ice Land, then other sons of mine whose names I'd forgotten long ago. Oh, imagine the welcome that awaited my strong sons in the warmth of my great hall, Asgard! We drank, we fought, we hunted!

I stood with Niord and Loki on a mountain top. We surveyed the desolate snowy forests below. No boar remained, no bear, few birds of prey, their delicious eggs gone from even the highest nests to which I flew. 'What about those hairy creatures like elephants?' I asked. 'Gone,' Niord said. White-haired, he wore fine sable furs like a southerner, and on his iron helmet the sacrificial tree of knowledge, Yggdrasil, was engraved in gold; trade had made him rich, ivory and slaves mostly. We looked at the empty mountains.

'It's boring,' Loki said. 'I don't like them without hunting.'

'There's reindeer,' Niord pointed.

'They're good to eat but no fun to hunt.' I was restless.

'I can sell reindeer,' Niord said. 'There's always a market for them. Meat. Skin. Antler horn.'

'Stealing's cheaper than trading,' Loki said. 'And a lot more fun. There isn't a single gold cup in the whole of Asgard. Everything's wooden. Even Wotan drinks from a wood cup, eats from a wood platter.' He gave his sly grin. 'I know better sport than hunting animals.'

'Your ideas are the best thing about you, Loki,' I said. 'Sometimes.'

'Hunting people,' Loki said. 'War's the best sport. The comradeship and danger of the journey. The sudden clash of weapons! Glory! Brave screams! Enslave the survivors, steal whatever they had, women, cups. Hunting dogs. Horses. Grain.'

'Grain's boring,' I said.

'Adventure. Glory. Our names remembered,' Loki said. 'They're rich down south, aren't they, Niord?'

'Yes,' Niord said. 'They're rich.'

'It's ours,' Loki said. 'What we don't want, you can sell back to them.'

We should have thought of it before. The two Norse peoples, the sea-loving Aesir and the Vanir who still loved the grasslands, came together as one under Valhalla. They went into battle shouting my name, the roaring sound called a *baritus*, their shields held against their mouths to multiply the echo, so they had faith I was always with them. The longships swept out of the darkness on the dawn wind, sliding up the beach, and my warriors poured ashore like a breaking wave. They fought like wolves. I leapt from the dragon's head, an island off the coast of Britain it was, inhabited mostly by skinny priests in threadbare sacks, miserable creatures, hardly worth cutting their heads off – but the gold! Beneath their little church, barely more than a collection of rocks over a cave, like magpies they'd tucked a king's ransom in gold coin into their nest, books with gold covers, gold crosses with jewels. And gold cups. In the Great Hall at Asgard drunken meat-sodden warriors roared the *baritus*, banging their sword-hilts on the tables, as two British serving-wenches staggered under the weight of a gold cup big enough to baptise a baby in. I put out my arms, lifted both it and them, and drained the slopping wine to the last drop. The warriors cried, 'Wotan is king of the gods!' I looked round smiling my wine-red smile. The terrifying stories about me magnified as they spread, each ripple growing to a wave, spreading fear and horror, forging words stronger than swords. Wotan drinks wine from a font. Wotan drinks blood from a Christian font. Wotan pisses in it.

I had no compunction. These Christians were nothing, nothing like the Christ I'd seen and touched and known.

They butchered more Christians than I ever did. There wasn't a drop of Christ in any of them, or if there was, I drank it.

Life was glorious. Asgard was always full, my halls blazed with fire and life like a gigantic family home. I adopted the dead as my sons, so that their wives and children didn't starve, and brought them here. Sometimes the dead themselves arrived here too, a funeral ship blown by the winds or carried by the tides like the *magilum* boats of old, as though Valhalla were an Abode of the Blessed. The Valkyrie priests carried the bodies to a final resting place in the palace of ice, where they would not rot for eternity, or the worm fasten on them.

And yet . . . I haven't conquered the world. The minstrels have sung my songs, the bards have woven immense tapestries of stories, called sagas, about my exploits. A tiny fraction of what I could have told them. They invented most of the tales themselves, though by now they believe them to be true. The truth, as *you* know it, is far, far more marvellous. But here, I am only a god. I can't deny myself. I can only fly. I can only kill. I can only go on. My simplest, most honest statement is invested with the power of myth. 'Give me wine' is elevated to a holy prophecy. When I put salt on my meat all men watch me and put salt on their meat, making themselves holy in my image.

My people were a greater people than they knew. I gave them war, but their real talent was trade. Warriors no longer burnt villages and returned home with their plunder but settled in the towns they conquered, married local girls, traded with other towns. Their settlements dotted Ireland and England, they sailed again to Iceland, Greenland and Vinland, Red Island and even the land I remembered as New Jerusalem, they traded in Paris (after their grandfathers had burnt it) and in Rome, they sailed the rivers of Russka as far as the Black Sea. And gradually, as they prospered, they disappeared. They became what they'd conquered, good Christians all.

Most nights I still saddled up my horse Sleipnr and rode with my jet-black hounds over England, Germany and France, terrifying the priests and people with fires in the sky, omens, horns, all the screaming throbbing horrors of the dark that feed their nasty fertile imaginations. Below me turned a cathedral, its spire like a finger pointing to Heaven, and in the cathedral yard a priest burned on a fiery cross. I spiralled down, stared into his face. Around him priests and monks prayed for the heretic's soul to fall to damnation and burn for ever. The fire rose, his robes were tongues of fire, his mouth a hole of flame, illuminating me. At last his head hung, and a crucifix hidden beneath his smock fell forward and swung gleaming as the flames died. They thought he was Satan. Not one of the priests knocking his ashes into the ashes with long poles saw me. They were Satan's people, the victors.

My time was past. Satan no longer needed me.

I woke. It was morning. I lifted my head from my arms on the table. I raised the horn at my elbow, but it was empty. Asgard's great hall was deserted but for a knot of people around the embers of the fire. I stepped over the snoring bodies of serving-wenches and poured my wine myself, then sat by the storytellers. But for once they weren't telling stories. They were silent. They watched me silently. The minstrels had no music in their hands, and their mouths were closed.

'Listen to me,' I said. 'The father of you all was Bragi.'

'We all know Bragi,' one old man said. 'He was with you in the Ginnungagap, before Valhalla was built.'

'Before that,' I said. 'There was a time before that. The land between two rivers, the middle ground.'

'Middle Earth,' they said. 'We know that one all right.'

'Askr and Embla, you know them?'

'That's Christian songs, Wotan.' They admitted, 'Adam and Eve. We know them.'

'And you know Mary?'

They said, 'Which Mary?'

'When Jesus Christ was crucified.'

'Oh, no, Wotan,' they said respectfully. 'That's you. You're a Watcher, a searcher for knowledge. It's written in the runes, it's your fate. For the sake of knowledge you'll cease to be a god. You'll die.'

'That's just a myth. I can't die.'

'You hang yourself up on Yggdrasil, the tree of knowledge. We've sung it many times. You'll sacrifice yourself to yourself, just to *know*.'

'Know what?'

'If we knew that, great Wotan,' they said, looking at each other, 'you wouldn't have to go through with it. Some great truth.' They fell silent, staring at the dead fire.

'Truth. Truth.' I tried to remember the most ancient stories. 'The source of knowledge. The Tree of Knowledge in Eden. God commanded Adam not to eat the fruit. Well, where's the truth in that? Why shouldn't Adam get knowledge? Surely to strive for knowledge, education, wisdom, is right.' I held my head, remembering. 'It isn't the Tree of Knowledge. It's the Tree of Knowledge *of Good and Evil*.'

'You spilt your wine,' the minstrel said. He struck a note on his lyre. 'Knowing right from wrong, I should have thought that was pretty easy.'

I stared at him wildly. 'No, it's the whole trick. It's everything. It's the *one* thing God told Adam, don't do it. Don't think you can do it. When Adam ate the apple and thought he knew right from wrong – and didn't really! – that's when everything went wrong. Destruction. Total loss. Pain and murder. Us.'

The minstrel ran his long fingernails across the strings. 'Before Ragnarok Wotan, nobly offering, always searching, never ceasing, hung himself on the great tree Yggdrasil—'

'Ragnarok? The mountains?'

'No. Ragnarok, the death of the gods. A death as great as the fall of mountains. Except your son Balder will be resurrected after Ragnarok.'

'No, no,' I said, 'not this again. It's wrong, it's wrong.'

He said in a dull voice, 'Swallowed the sun, the moon bitten like a fruit, the Serpent comes boiling from the deeps of the ocean, blowing poison over the world and the sky.' He stopped. 'Enough songs have been sung in Asgard. We'll sing no more.'

They sat quietly around the embers, pale as shadows, watching me.

I climbed slowly to my feet.

'Run for your lives,' I said.

When nobody moved I roared, and even the snoring wenches woke, ran squealing with their bare feet slapping the boards like fading applause, then silence fell. I was alone.

I looked around me at the Great Hall of Asgard, the longship *Naglfari* hanging dusty and wormeaten along the wall, the cobwebbed rafters draped with bloodstained banners tattered by age and moth, the great fires cold. I walked through the doors fit for heroes, as high as fifty men, and stood in the pallid sunlight staring up at the ice spires of Valhalla.

I climbed the lofty staircase of ice to the snowy plateau. No Valkyries raised their arms to the never-setting sun, no horses flew in the sky, not the faintest breath of wind touched my face. Rotten snow sloshed around my feet as I walked forward, slush slid backwards from my footsteps over the cliff edge, fell into the abyss. The walls were melting.

Valhalla was melting. Everything that seemed so solid and substantial simply melted away. I reached forward with my hands to hold up the ice but Valhalla trickled drop by drop between my fingers. The spires softened and slid down, the roofs ran into the gutters, the gutters melted and the water poured down, and before my eyes Valhalla turned to waterfalls pouring down, meltwaters swirling through the gateways, the gateways sliding forward, waters spraying into the abyss. Stinking bodies jostled past me on the flood, washed from the niches where they were laid to sleep for eternity. The battlements and towers tilted, sinking, and my arms couldn't hold them from falling, or my hands push them up.

I stood on the bare plateau holding a cupful of water in my hands, and let it go.

'What am I doing,' I whispered. 'What have I done.'

The plateau fell down as though pulled from beneath, the two mountains of Ragnarok leant together and toppled forward, falling towards me. Snow and rocks rose up like a wave curling above the forests and lakes of Asgard, and fell like a great fist.

The wave raced towards me across the plateau. I jumped from the clifftop and fell to the sea. I swam down and the thunder of falling rock came down after me, great boulders dropped slowly past me trailing bubbles, then cliff-faces and the weight of the mountains came crashing down to entomb me, lock me in the earth for a million years. But I pulled my strength into me, I swam like a fish, I swam as I swam with Pe in the canals of Shem five thousand years ago, as though time were a moment.

A boulder clipped my heel, a few pebbles rattled on my shoulders, then nothing. I was clear.

I dragged myself up against the rocks of a low island. I didn't look back.

'I understand it now,' I whispered. 'It's so simple now.' I pushed forward through the undergrowth, reached the far side of the island, plunged in the sea and swam to shore. I walked along the beach, and then I ran. I ran with my fists clenched in front of me. I roared, a great formless Wotan-roar of survival, fury, determination. Not running away; running *towards*. I knew who my enemy was.

'It isn't ended yet!' I shouted. 'It's not over! It's a battle!'

XV

The present day
Sion Inn, Salt Lake City

'Mommy, don't die.'

Christine kneels beside her mother on the bed. Applause roars from the television, the Utah Jazz team going one up. She clicks it off, kneels in silence in the shadowed room.

'Mommy, don't die. I'm hungry.'

It's so dark in here, the thick drapes closed across the balcony doors. She looks longingly at the bright slash of sunlight between them, bored. From the balcony she could look down on the traffic far below, the heads of people walking. Then there's the phone. She knows how to use the phone, people do it all the time. She could talk to anyone, just anyone. But there's Mommy.

The icebag on Mommy's forehead melts despite the air-conditioning. Winona's sleeping face lies dark red against the white pillow, blistered with sunburn. Her hands on the sheet covering her are blistered too. Her hair's as white as an old woman's. Why was it so important to go to the church? Christine stares angrily at the paintings jumbled in the corner, just paint on old bits of wood. 'I hate you!'

Her tummy starts a noise again. She's starving.

'Mommy, *please.*'

The icebag slips from Mommy's forehead. She moved. 'You did! Mommy, you're awake!' Christine leans over her eagerly. Nothing but the sigh of Mommy's breath.

'Mommy, I'm *starving*.' Nothing. 'I'd shake you,' she says angrily, 'but I'm afraid of hurting you.' One of Mommy's eyelids flutters.

'Time to wake up.' Christine runs to the curtains, pulls them apart, sunlight blazes into the room. Mommy cries out in pain, sits half up, rolls away. Christine jerks the curtains closed, bursts into tears. 'I'm sorry! I'm sorry!'

She goes back to Mommy and kneels beside her on the bed. She closes her hands and puts her fingertips to her lips, praying.

'Christine.' Mommy's hand closes lightly around her wrist. 'Christine, I love you. Don't be afraid.'

'Mommy, I love you, Mommy. Why can't you wake up?'

A long pause. 'That's life, honey.'

Christine tries not to cry, but the hiccups are hard. 'Mommy, I love you. I love you but I'm so hungry. I want the room service trolleys. Try and get better.'

Mommy's voice fades away. 'No doctors.' Her hand quivers. 'Don't be afraid.'

She doesn't move. Christine stares at her accusingly. 'She's asleep again.'

She sits back on her heels, hands in her lap, scowling, hungry enough to eat her mother.

The phone's on the bedside table. The phone's a big thing. 'Mustn't be afraid.' She combs her hair looking at the phone out of the corners of her eyes, then pulls her long blond hair into a ponytail and puts the comb away neatly, picks up the receiver calmly.

'Yes, Dr Wotan?'

'Just send up what you sent up before.'

'Right away, Dr Wotan.'

Christine replaces the receiver. Her face breaks into a big smile, remembering the feast. 'Steak and lobster, big white rolls of fresh bread, double-chocolate cake!' She smooths her skirt and admires herself in the mirror, turns her head slightly to look grown up. When she knelt beside Mommy she creased the sheet; now she straightens it, smooths it. She decides to be Mommy's nurse until room service arrives, feels Mommy's forehead, frowns. 'Much too hot. You're burning up.' She takes the icebag on the pillow to the fridge, but it's out of ice.

She finds the light-pull in the bathroom, pulls the cord, holds a face flannel under the tap. The tap won't turn on. She turns harder until the metal squeaks, thinks again. Tries turning it the other way, and this time cold water gushes over the flannel. She rinses it, wrings it out, then folds it very, very carefully – not very well – as she walks back to Mommy and lays the cool flannel across her forehead.

She forgot to turn off the tap. She can hear the water still running in the bathroom.

A knock on the door. 'Room service.'

That was quick. She reaches towards the golden handle, then stops. 'Uh, just leave it outside.'

'Very well.' No footsteps. 'Is everything all right, Dr Wotan?'

Christine looks from the door to Mommy and back to the door. 'Mommy's in the bathroom. She says tell him just leave it outside.'

No reply. She's not tall enough to look through the eyehole. She puts her ear to the door, listening. Footsteps going away. More footsteps, two women walking by discussing stock prices. *Ting*, the hiss of elevator doors opening, shutting.

Christine fixes the heavy chromed security chain and unlocks the door. She turns the handle, peers through the crack along the angle of the door.

The corridor to the right's empty. She can just see to the closed elevator doors.

She unclamps the security chain, opens the door enough to get her head through, looks to the left. No one, just closed doors and soft lighting along the corridor to the fire exit.

In front of her stand the two gorgeous room service trolleys with big silver lids. She pulls them inside, closes the door, clicks the electronic lock, slides the security chain into its clamp.

Something's wrong. She can feel it in the room.

Something smells very bad in here.

She stands looking at the closest room service trolley, then lifts the big silver lid. On the silver platter, beautifully presented, thick steak meat hangs grey-green from the bone. It's foul. Foul with maggots, alive, stinking. Slime drips from the lobster on to its bed of lettuce leaves and bloody ice. She drops the lid, staggers back. The armchair hits her behind the knees, she sits.

Christine looks at the second trolley. She doesn't want to lift that silver lid. She can imagine what's in there. She can almost see it.

The door handle clicks, turning. She hears a light thump, a shoulder touching the other side. The door creaks.

'*Mommy*,' she whispers. No reply from the bed. 'Mommy, wake up.'

Now or never. She runs to the door, shoots the bolts.

'Christine.' Mommy's voice. Her body lies motionless, eyes closed, only her mouth moving. 'Christine, save yourself. I can't help you.'

The door bends forward against Christine, opening gently and irresistibly as she tries to push it back with all her strength. The lock buzzes, breaks with a sharp crack. The frame splinters around the teeth of the lock, splits open. She backs away a step. 'Mommy. Mommymommy.' Hears no reply. The door opens smoothly towards her, reaches the limit of its security chain, doesn't stop; the chromed links pull tight, stretch open like little shining mouths, snap all at once, and at the same moment the bolts wrench from both door and frame with sounds like muffled gunshots.

Run, Christine, run.

Christine runs.

Slowly and steadily the door opens.

Era Five

Revelation

Revelation

The present day, 21 December 2012

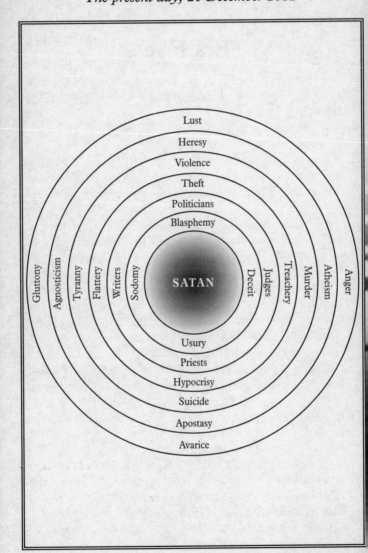

21 December 2012

'Mommy! *Mommymommy!*'

Her cries were so urgent that she reached deep into me, then there was silence. With all my heart I tried to speak.

Christine, save yourself. I can't help you.

Deep silence.

My eyelids fluttered. I whose strength was once limitless had hardly strength to open Winona's eyelids. This is dying. This is like the moment of death, everything slipping away. Everything that had been so easy, so taken-for-granted for a whole life, was now impossibly hard. Every breath. Every last gasp for breath a suffocating struggle. No muscles working. Everything exhausted at the end.

My eyes opened, staring upwards. I lay on the bed. The room was shadowed, but the glow of sunlight around the curtains was a brilliant agony in my eyes. I used all my once-great strength to turn my head away on the pillow, stared into the room too weak even to blink.

The door was opening. Christine backed from it. She'd closed the bolts, my clever girl. But still the door opened, bending, the bolts twisting and tearing, locks breaking, security chain pulling tight, stretching, snapping. I tried to speak. *Run, Christine, run.* She took another step backwards, her hip bumped a trolley, and the spell of fascination which held her broke.

She ran. I couldn't see her behind the clutter of trolleys and furniture. At the same moment the bolts broke, the door opened wide, and darkness reached into the room. The lights in the hotel corridor flickered, buzzed, died.

I lay weakly, my heart hammering almost empty of

lifeblood. I couldn't feel my hands or my feet. The sheet lay as heavy on me as iron chains. Worst, I couldn't see Christine, couldn't call her.

Nothing I could have done anyway. Not even the strength to whisper.

Footsteps coming in the corridor. To my horror I saw Christine's feet and ankles crouched behind the trolleys, she was almost hidden from me but in plain view of the doorway. Such a young child, so much she didn't know! I gasped, croaked. It was enough. The blond top of her head showed over the silver lid, her blue eyes looked at me. I stared at the bathroom door, half open. It was all I could do. I thought she understood, but the footsteps stopped.

Then someone I recognised stepped into the room. 'What's happened to the lights?' Jeri giggled, putting up her sunglasses in her hair. Long legs, small pretty head, nice smile: Todd's girl from the New Jerusalem Club, the girl who refused to be saved. She looked round. 'Where are you? It's spooky in here. I thought we were going to play in bed all afternoon and get drunk as skunks. You got the stuff?' She clicked the room switches but nothing happened.

Then she spoke again. 'This is a dump, where's the lights.' She grinned, persuading herself, I saw the white gleam of her teeth. 'All righty, got it all set up, huh? Let's do it in the dark while the sun's shining.' She peered naughtily into the shadows, saw me, and her face changed. 'Hey, it's somebody's room! There's an old woman in here!' She tripped over one of the door-bolts lying broken on the carpet. She turned it over in her hand, then noticed the door. 'Oh my God,' she said. 'Simon? What happened?'

A man's shape moved, swelled, grew heavy, came padding from the corridor into the doorway. Mostly I saw his white linen suit, a hunter's check shirt beneath, gold jewellery. The strong-faced man, Simon Says, came forward into the shadows, his shoulders just fitting through the doorway, the floor creaking under his weight as though he were made of iron or clay or gold, not flesh. He raised his hand, gold rings on the fingers, and rested the fingertips lightly on Jeri's shoulder. She fell silent, then burst out: 'Look at her! She's dying! I think she's been robbed.' Her voice rose. 'Is she dead? Oh my God is she dead?' She pushed herself into his arms for reassurance.

He put one arm around her, crossed the Temple Suite with long sudden strides, almost carrying her, stopped dead. He looked down at me. His eyes gleamed with pity. Just an old woman. How convenient. How quiet.

He bent down, whispered, 'Atone, Wotan.'

Jeri stared at him. 'You know her?' He turned her face, made her look at me. 'She's the woman in the nightclub,' she said numbly. 'Jesus, what's happening. She's old. She's *ancient*. Jesus, what—'

He said, very quietly: 'Jeri.' He handed her a bottle of Jack Daniels, no glass. She unscrewed the cap, took a drink. He said: 'That's better.'

'Better,' she said. 'I'm OK.'

'Better sit down, honey.'

She kept the bottle, leant against the armchair facing the bed. 'Send for the doctor, huh, she looks real bad.'

'Not right now.'

She reached for the phone. His hand reached faster, white marble given warmth and life, and covered her soft pale flesh. Behind them Christine moved, crawling from the trolleys to the bathroom. The light was on in there and her hip brushed the bathroom door, changing the illumination slightly. Jeri glanced round. Simon said, 'Get off the phone, Jeri.'

She pouted, then snatched her hand away and swigged from the bottle. She lolled on the arm of the sofa, legs crossed, then stood up again.

Simon pulled the desk chair close to the bed.

He sat.

He wiped the sheet with His great flat hands, smoothing it, then leant forward until He looked straight into my eyes, my staring unblinking eyes.

'You know who I am, Wotan. *Eyah asher eyah.*' His eyes twinkled mischievously. 'Or should it be *Ya Asherah? Ya Ishtar*, if you like. God and His wife. I know you spoke to Noah. I know what Noah told you. For that sin I made him my screaming prisoner in Hell for four thousand years. Almost an eternity.'

I struggled to speak. Jesus freed the prisoners of Hell. Like a billion others I know the Christian catechism. *I believe in God the Father Almighty, maker of heaven and Earth, and in Jesus Christ His only* – only! – *Son our Lord, who was conceived by the Holy Ghost, born of the Virgin Mary, suffered under Pontius Pilate, He descended into Hell.* Why? Pythagoras did, Hercules did (and so did I, if you believe the legends). By Christian legend Jesus freed the souls of the Jewish patriarchs, Adam, Noah, Moses, others, from Satan's prison. Only one great soul did He not redeem from Hell.

Satan's.

Satan spoke in a deep rumbling whisper as intimate as sex. My gasping breaths smelt him, fragrant, perfumed, indomitable, undefeated, the King of Hell. I was so weak that He was almost my whole world, everything I saw, breathed, felt, here on the point of death. They say an old woman dying leads apes in Hell; this was Hell.

'Atone, Wotan. Atone, Wotan, cursed, damned, cast down by your life. You were born sinful, and you have lived in sin. Atone for your sin, for you are alive.'

The words of the Bull of Heaven. I gasped but couldn't speak.

'Wotan, I know everything about you.' Infinite sympathy. 'I know your pride, your lust, your fear. Your every pathetic conquest of every whore. Every worthless battle you ever fought. I know them all. Your life has been a worthless waste of time. What good did you ever do?'

562

I gasped for breath.

He said: 'One good thing. Confess.' He listened to my silence. 'One good thing, my son.'

I gasped. I loved Mary.

He cupped His hand to His ear, tormenting me; or perhaps making me examine myself.

A groan of formless grief came from my mouth. My own blood, Kidu, had called to me when we were running together when we were young, *God didn't give you the gift of love*. But I had found love, I'd found love. I loved, still love, the only woman I never opened, never knew, never possessed.

He bent close, but my straining mouth couldn't utter the word. *Love*.

He said contemptuously: 'Love? Who? Look what it does to you.' His face came closer. He wanted something from me. Something very important. Something important enough that He took off at least a few of His masks, as He had before when He tempted me and I fell. He needed me – nerveless, breathless, on this body's deathbed, but perhaps I was not quite powerless. He demanded: 'Who is the mysterious Dr Winona Wotan exactly?'

I stared passively, shrivelled breasts heaving.

He bragged: 'I kill every child I believe to be the Christ. Who is she? *Wotan*'s a common Germanic name, *Winona* could be anyone. Where does she come from? Social security number, sure. Pre-school, school, leafy suburb, smiling kid. Exam results. Clean driving licence. Stockholm University, Department of Human Geography. You meet her there, Wotan? Some project? Their Project.Maya.012 brought you together maybe, or was it just chance, your usual lust, you dog, and she fell for you?' He stroked my, Winona's, dying face. 'Just a nobody, an ordinary boring human, or someone fated by God? Is she a daughter of God, or to be His earthly mother, a chosen manifestation like the Virgin Mary? You've fought me,

Wotan.' He clenched His fist lightly. 'What was your plan? How did it go so wrong for you? You both knew Eliot searched for Apachiohualitzá miles away from its real location. Miles away, so you weren't bothered, you knew the paintings of Jesus in America were safe. So you went ahead with Winona, or she with you, love or that's what you call it, a roll of the dice or God's Will, she's pregnant. But then everything changes. The old native legends of the Hand of God, the Flood, a priceless hoard, are given credence by NASA mapping, modern linguistic analysis, Brighamite scholarship. Is Apachiohualitzá ancient Zarahemla? The buzz! An archaeology team flies from Salt Lake City to Belize led by Winona's old friend and once close *close* associate, the Brighamite Professor Martin Rendell. An association close enough for everyone to think her child's Rendell's. Winona uses Rendell to get on the team, but she's going to lead him *away* from Apachiohualitzá, not towards it. She's obsessed; Wotan's obsessed. He knows the paintings of Jesus, real and true, the nugget of historical truth, are buried beneath the great statue of Satan, the victor for the last two thousand years. Apachiohualitzá, the symbol of Satan's victory over Christ! *My* victory.'

Was this all? This gloating? Satan must want more. I must possess something much more. I tried not to let my eyes flicker to the few paintings of Jesus I'd saved from the Reformed Temple of Sion of the Prophecy, lying where Christine dropped them by the balcony curtains. Something of greater value even than they.

Satan whispered: 'Give me your child.'

No, Christine. Not my Christine.

Is Christine why He's here? Is all this about Christine?

I didn't dare look towards the bathroom.

He whispered: 'Is she the One?'

My girl. My first, my only daughter, Christine. I heard the tap still running in the basin.

He whispered: 'Is she the Christ who is sent to save the living and the dead at the end of time? Is the time of God's Second Coming that close?'

Jeri drank from the bottle. She yawned, bored, wandered to a picture on the wall, cornfields in a window, windblown curtains, a Wyeth print, pretty.

Satan sniffed me, smelling my despair. 'Remember, Wotan, I tempted you. You're as imperfect, sinful, flawed as any man or woman I take to the mountain top. You fell! No Deuteronomy from *you*. "Jump and fly!" and Wotan jumped, he flew! You fell hook, line and sinker. I tempted you with one pretty girl running half naked on a beach and you jumped, fell, created a whole world of evil, Valhalla. Not enough though. You still couldn't be as good as the evil around you, you failed even at that in the end. You even tried to defeat Christianity.' He touched his nose. 'Yes, Wotan, I saw you look without understanding at the burning priest. Uh, dim. Not a trace of understanding of the men burning the guy. What about *them*, the virtuous? That's when I knew you'd failed me. Almost got you, huh? Beneath the mountain. Lucky to get out of that one. Great prison. I'm the prisoner who designs prisons.' He grinned, paused. 'Still not sure how you did that.'

I looked past Him, saw Christine's eyes looking round the bathroom door. She was just a little girl. With all my energy I blinked, stared. Come on, Christine, get the tap!

Satan frowned, looked round, she snatched her head back. Jeri came over, postured, teetered, swigged, grinned. 'Hey, Simon, come on, I'm bored.' Behind Jeri I saw Christine's reflection cross the bathroom mirror, saw her stand on tiptoe, saw the mirror image of her hand reach out hesitantly to the tap. Didn't she even know which way to turn it off? 'Can't we do something interesting, huh?' Jeri put down the bottle, slid her hands over Simon's shoulders. 'You're so tense.'

He pitied her. 'Shut up, Jeri.'

She made a mouth, pulled back. 'Hey, hear that? Someone's left a tap on.'

'Turn it off and shut up.' But she couldn't leave him, couldn't be quiet, she wanted all of her domineering lover, she swung her hips provocatively and smiled at me. 'What's she got that I haven't, Simon? Your new girlfriend, is she? Hey, beautiful eyes. Aren't they beautiful? A horrid old woman with beautiful blue eyes. I bet she was beautiful once. I hope I never grow old.' He looked up at her compassionately. 'All right!' she complained. 'I'm doing it. I'm busy. I love you.' She kissed Simon's neck, wiped her lips and turned towards the bathroom. 'It's stopped anyway.'

The sound of running water had ceased. Jeri paused by the trolleys in the glow from the bathroom doorway, put back her head and swigged from her bottle with drunken delicacy, and I saw the bruised needle holes in her arm.

The back of Christine's head moved in the bathroom mirror. From where she was standing Jeri would notice at once if the light went off. Christine, hide. Don't reach up. For God's sake leave the light-pull alone.

Satan leant close to me, His elbows compressing the bed. My body slumped helplessly towards Him, my head rolled on the pillow so I saw only His face.

'The Watcher.' He touched my cold forehead with infinite sympathy. 'I've watched you try so hard to be good. You have no idea what it is. Have you found any goodness in my world, Wotan? I won every battle.' He leant back with a sad chuckle and I saw Christine's hand stretch to the light-pull.

I stared at the paintings to save her, letting Him have them. He followed my eyes, got up. 'These?' With all my strength I uttered, 'I helpt the chillun paint paintings. Helpt them.' My teeth were gone, my tongue slipped in the corner of my mouth, I thought He'd never understand me. But He smiled, walked casually to the paintings on the floor. He'd known they were there all the time, I realised. Maybe He knew everything, even about Christine in the bathroom. So what did He want? He stood hands in pockets, examining each wooden panel, leafing through the pile with quick indifferent kicks of his white hunting boots, discarding them.

'Liar.' He decided affectionately, 'Liar. I love you, Wotan. You never give up. These were never painted by children.'

I gasped, 'Chillun painted.'

'No, everyone knows these were painted by Jesus Christ Himself. These works are the authentic Hand of God, obviously, not that I claim to understand them. The natives never understood either. The idol they tried to build to Christ became—' He grinned. 'Me.'

I gathered my strength. Oh, God, give me the strength to move my tongue, give me one more deep breath!

'The children painted them! Didn't you know? Didn't you *know*?'

For a moment I saw uncertainty, just a flicker in the eyes. 'Still trying to deceive me. Children can't paint like that. Everyone knows children can't paint like that!' He gave the paintings a good hard kick, scattering the pile. 'You're mad, Wotan. You're ridiculous. Trying to sow confusion. Lying to the Liar, deceiving the Deceiver? They say you're stupid, just muscle, but you're almost as clever as I. Lovely. I admire you so much. You will inhabit Hell for eternity. You really are a tiny, tiny version of Me, not born but thrown down.' He stared at me earnestly, intensely. 'You really heard the angels singing? You remember the song of angels?'

I muttered the truth. 'The children painted the paintings. Children.'

He laughed. He stamped His foot on the pictures, splintering the panels, breaking them.

I shivered, icy cold with this body's death, but I'd

succeeded. The bathroom light was off, He hadn't noticed.

'I got to pee,' Jeri said. She put down the nearly empty bottle and walked towards the bathroom. As she went between the trolleys I moaned, 'Food.'

She stopped, seeing the champagne bottle in a bucket of ice, and I knew she was thirsty after the bourbon. 'Want some, Simon?' She opened one of the silver lids and recoiled. It banged down with a sound like a cymbal. 'That's foul! Jesus, Simon! You got no sense of smell? Get the inspectors up, that meat's rotten!' She covered her mouth. 'That smells worse than anything.' She looked into Satan's implacable, unresponsive face. The rotten food didn't bother him, she did. She pouted, 'What's the matter, honey?'

I knew what was the matter. She made too much noise.

'I'll call the desk and complain if you won't. Hang on a minute, I gotta go.' She clicked on the bathroom light and shut the door, and Christine must have been hiding behind the door. I heard Jeri's scream and knew I'd lost.

The door jerked open. Jeri pushed a struggling figure. 'Look what I found! It's a girl.'

Christine pulled free, ran to me, knelt at my bedside. She looked up at Satan with staring eyes, mouth open, terrified. I think she saw more than I. I think Jeri and I were almost blind to what was really going on in here.

He murmured: 'Don't be afraid, Christine. I've been the god of fertility for almost all human existence.' In the shadows His face changed to a smiling sensitive boy, Baal who made the crops grow. 'The people danced joyfully to my shrines with bread and wine. You're not afraid, are you?'

'I'm calling the police,' Jeri said. 'Who's Christine? You know her? What's this, what are you mixed up in, Simon? This is a vice ring, pornography? You can do what you like to me, I'm calling the cops.' Her voice shook. She'd wet herself. 'I'm going to go home in a car, I want my dad. Don't look at me, I'm not drunk. I'm not in trouble. I haven't done anything wrong.' She shouted: 'Stay back from me, Simon!'

He took three quick strides, threw her against the wall, turned away. Jeri's head thudded, she fell to the floor.

Christine ran to Jeri. He let her.

He lifted the lid, grabbed a steak in His hand and held it in front of my eyes, a thick T-bone steak dripping stinking juices, foul with corruption. 'Just how you like it, Wotan.' He threw it back, slammed down the lid, licked His hand with a shudder of revulsion.

Christine cradled Jeri's head. Tears dripped from Christine's eyes on to Jeri's unconscious face, into Jeri's eyes, trickled down Jeri's cheeks.

'All my life,' Satan whispered in my ear, 'all my long, long, long life, every day, I have tried to climb back to God. There has not been a day when I have not struggled and strained and stripped My soul bare to climb back to Him. Just for one moment of Him. A single moment in twelve billion years. One breath. A touch. Just for one moment to *be* as I am. Chief of angels. Chief in God's glory. Believing.'

I stared at Christine. Her tenderness with Jeri. Her love. I murmured, 'Christine.'

He touched his cold hard lips to my ear, I felt his burning breath. 'Is she the AntiChrist?'

Christine's tears wet Jeri's face, she cradled Jeri's head in her lap, touched Jeri's hair with soothing gestures.

Satan crouched beside me, immense.

He sighed with infinite sadness. 'I have many deceits. Non-belief is not one of them.' He reached out His stained hand, opened the curtains, and sunlight blazed into the room. I tried to cover my eyes but couldn't. Christine screamed: 'You're hurting her!'

That wasn't true. I was too far gone to feel pain. I felt this body's face smile, the almost transparent calm smile the dying sometimes give, smiling at my daughter. It's all right. It's all right, Jeri needs you more than I do.

Christine stopped. She knew there was nothing she could do for me. It was almost time for her to go to make her own life, as my sons did, as they always do. But she wasn't like any of my sons; the tears poured down her cheeks.

Satan turned. 'Time to talk.' He shone bright as the sun down one side, and on the other side His shadow filled the room. 'I am One who is Many, I am Legend, my name is Legion.' Tallboy stood in His shadow, tall, thin, ginger-haired, flesh and blood. He took a couple of steps towards me on his long legs, speaking in an English accent. 'They're all in me, gallu-demons, aspects of myself.' Tallboy gave his cocky smile, acting in character.

His freckled face contorted in fear, his skin turned to blood. Tallboy shrivelled inside himself, revealing Snowflake the pastor, then Snowflake's body melted, belly slumping forward, and Gonzalez the plump Spaniard stood in front of me. 'Even me,' Gonzalez said in his fat sweating voice. 'We all led you forward to a nice safe place.'

I muttered, 'No, misled.' I'd thought the paintings were the prize Satan coveted. I'd been so sure that saving them was God's work.

'Exactly.' Gonzalez fell away and Satan stood up in the shape of the angel He once was, golden, radiant since the first curve of eternity in the sight of God, none gentler or cleverer or fiercer for God or more loyal. His golden eyes had witnessed God, and forgotten; His gold tongue had spoken to God. But there was nothing of God here. The gold flaked off, cheap pyrites, revealing black iron. He stretched His arms above His head, hands cupped, muscles straining and face contorted into a demonic scream of futile worship, a fallen angel trying to climb back to God. 'I believe utterly in God, My Saviour, knowing all, forgiving all, in the last instant of time. God, save Your servant, put me out of this agony!'

'I killed Huwawa,' I whispered. 'It's possible to kill You.'

He turned on me with flared nostrils. 'Huwawa wasn't worthy to tie my shoes.'

'You're iron, or flesh, or stone,' I whispered. 'You can be broken, or cut, or worn away.'

'You'll never succeed.'

'I'll never stop.'

'People believe in Me.' He changed into the old Satan I remembered, the one He thought looked like Christ: the fierce eyes, heavy eyebrows, intolerant mouth of a child born to be King in the Holy of Holies in Jerusalem. He wore a cloak of Tyrian purple, a gold circlet for a crown, and sandals with golden straps. Nothing, nothing whatsoever like the Son born two thousand and sixteen years ago to a humble carpenter and a virgin in Bethlehem.

'Wotan, Wotan.' Satan knelt by my bed, hands clasped in prayer. 'I watched you search. I watched you, the Watcher. I watched you fail, and fail, and fail. No man's mind can know Me, or encompass the greatness of my schemes for humanity.'

'Pride, the first of the seven deadly sins,' I whispered. His eyes narrowed in anger, the second deadly sin.

He said: 'You're all my children, born sinful. Not God's. How could you be a son of God as you claim, Wotan, living as you did filthy with lust and gluttony, a murderer, a rapist, a bully, a maker of widows and breaker of families, a man with blood dripping from his hands, a man whose fighting rages are legendary?'

I whispered, 'Maybe I don't know a difference between right and wrong.' He stared sharply. If I really was a son of God I wasn't descended from Adam, I'd bypassed the taint of the Tree of Knowledge of Good and Evil. I was a true enemy of the Enemy. A true adversary of the Adversary.

He said: 'You're *nothing* like me. I am the oldest of the old and greatest of the great, I suckled closest and most loved at God's bosom. This world is mine, these are *my* people.' I heard traffic hooting, the distant whine of a jet. 'I'll show you your failure, Wotan. Your defeat. You think I really cared about those little paintings?' His chest swelled. 'I own the earthly body of Christ.'

He gripped Winona's hand in His own, dragging her soul with Him, and the room stopped, became unimportant. No traffic, no jet, only the last rosy fingers of the setting sun, bonfires rising up against the night. Winona stood alone on a steep stony street that I recognised, the *Via Dolorosa*, smelling donkey dung and spiced meat from the cooking fires. 'Jerusalem,' came His voice. 'You know where you are, Wotan. Jerusalem, the sixth of January 1150. The screams are Muslims and Jews, it's a good time to be a Christian. Hear between the screams, that laughter? A man's laughter. That's yours. Valhalla fell eighty-three years ago, you're drinking in a tavern on the Temple Mount. You know Jerusalem's the place where everything happens, it's prophesied: the joining of the sticks, Israel victorious, the end of time. You've been here for years, watching, waiting, nothing ever happened. Look, there's you sitting by the tavern candle as usual, too strong, too loud, a girl in your lap, your hands on her breasts and your belly full as hers of strong red wine, drunk. Don't go in, Winona, he'll make a pass at you.'

Good times, I whispered. *Are you all right, Winona?*

I'm all right. Don't worry.

'Let's walk uphill, she's a Christian pilgrim, she won't be molested.' I looked through Winona's eyes at the summit of Mount Sion. It was a building site. Braziers cast a hellish glow and hammers thudded, stonemasons working late. 'They're building the Temple for the Knights Templar, the Order of the Poor Fellow-Soldiers of Christ and the Temple of Solomon, set up by the Pope to rid

572

Jerusalem of Muslims and Jews. Now no one can get rid of the Templars. The Order's immensely wealthy, supposed to be infected with the Devil.' I heard His grin. 'Templars believed – still believe today – in pain, suffering, humility, sacrifice. That Christ was only a man, that He didn't rise from the dead, that the world was created by an evil god. Common beliefs in southern France where the Templars were strong, but a heresy to their employer the Pope, so they keep it quiet then as now.' Again His grin. 'Templar heretics building their great Temple on the ruin of the Jews' Second Temple, which was in turn built over Solomon's Temple. The masons marking their foundation stones with Reformed Egyptian hieroglyphs, heaving stones into place ready for the morning, and any minute now – wait for it—'

The ground gave way, dust blew up, and the men fell down and disappeared so suddenly and completely that Winona screamed.

Satan looked at me over His fingertips.

'They fell down into the ancient prison dug beneath the foundations by Solomon and Hiram, the *Bir Arruah*, the Well of Souls.'

I whispered, 'The stories about King Solomon's demon were true?'

He frowned. 'Yes, Asmodeus, a gallu-demon, an aspect of Me, was tricked and imprisoned by Solomon when his work was done, and the Temple stood without cracking. Two thousand years fettered in a small stone pit underground; now you understand my lack of mercy. Asmodeus broke the fallen Templar masons limb from limb, snatched their souls, departed raging. If I'd stayed the history of the world would have been very different. Instead the Templar Master in Jerusalem, Sir Bertrand de Blanchefort, was called to the site by terrified survivors, and he made the discovery.'

I whispered, 'What discovery?'

'The winding stair going down into the earth. Blanchefort, of all people. *Grand Maître de l'Ordre de Notre Dame du Sion*, Master of the Knights of the Rose Cross Veritas – the Order of the True Blood, the up-and-coming Templar faction later called the Rosicrucians! Blanchefort believed in the Resurrection. He believed it would come in his own lifetime, and that through the intercession of Christ his living body would be translated in Rapture to Heaven so that he, like Enoch, would never taste death.'

Winona stood on the edge of the hole. The winding stair led down round and round into the shadows under the mountain like a giant screw. The walls were smooth as glass, straight as a drill into the earth.

Wotan, this looks basically like the one Mulek showed you in the jungle in Zarahemla, before he built the Temple over the top.

Yes. A place of power.

But here the stair was rough stone, the added work of Solomon's masons perhaps. Winona looked around her so that she understood exactly what she saw. The earth of the summit had been so flattened and scraped away over the centuries it was difficult to imagine this entrance before the temples were built on top; perhaps a natural cave-mouth, overgrown with bushes maybe, or covered by some primitive sacrificial altar like Melchizadok's or Abraham's.

Men came running, bearded knights in white tabards, chain mail, long white cloaks. Their leader strode forward to the very edge of the hole, fearless. This must be Blanchefort. '*Oc, vite, vite.*' He held out his hand for a burning stick, clicked his fingers impatiently, dropped the stick in the hole. Everyone leant forward, staring. The flame fell until it was small as a spark falling to the centre of the world.

Someone saw Winona and she was hustled away. The Templars dreaded women.

'Meanwhile, Wotan, you were down the street drinking, eating, and having sex as usual. Up on the mountain top, they were discovering God.

'Blanchefort climbed down alone, no witnesses. He drew his sword, held a flaming branch above his head. A very brave, stupid man. At first it seemed the stair might indeed lead to the centre of the world, but then he found an ancient tunnel cut to one side, and crawled to the pit with broken fetters and what was left of the masons who'd fallen. Blanchefort persevered in going forward, he *believed* in blood, in the saving power of blood. In the next cellar I believe he probably found Moses's Arch of the Covenant, *the* Arch of the Covenant, left where Solomon and Zadok hid it. For two millennia Moses's acacia-wood box had lain crumbling and almost forgotten beneath the Temple, abandoned, hardly more than a myth even to the Zadokite hereditary priesthood, not even that to their elected successors the Sadducees. A museum piece.' Satan looked at His praying fingertips. 'Asmodeus never realised he was almost close enough to touch it. All those years.'

'Blanchefort stole the Arch?' I whispered. 'Or not?'

Satan shrugged as if it didn't matter. 'What Blanchefort found was much more important, a tunnel, an old water tunnel dug under the city walls against times of siege. There are many in the rock, a few excavated, one or two now famous. This one led the Templar knights to the tomb of Joseph of Arimathea.'

I whispered, 'Blanchefort found the tomb of Christ.'

'Yes, Blanchefort found the earthly body of Jesus still lying on the funeral slab, laid out exactly as He was left by Nicodemus, Joseph of Arimathea and Mary Magdalene on Good Friday. Still wrapped in the death shroud. Blanchefort stole it, naturally.'

'That's the Templar treasure that's so famous now, the Shroud of Turin?'

'Why steal only the shroud? Blanchefort stole the shroud with the earthly, undecayed and bleeding Christ still wrapped in it. To him it wasn't stealing, it was faith. He believed the Resurrection would come in his own lifetime. He believed, by possessing Christ in the body, he'd make himself master of the Resurrection.'

I lay motionless, without breath.

I opened my mouth and breathed in. I whispered, 'The master of God.'

Satan smiled over His fingertips. 'That he could achieve godhood in his own life, without tasting death, just like your American friends Lehi and Nephi and all the others. Hardly an uncommon belief. No mortal wants to die.' He looked at me pityingly. 'An immortal wants nothing else.'

I gasped, 'I don't want to die.'

'Look at you. You surprise me. So, Blanchefort stole the body of Christ. Where did he go? There's the mystery. Gone. The vast Templar castle at Tyre? Constantinople? Rome? The secret was so well kept that I knew God was in my world. No soul screamed the place of the new tomb even in the torments of Hell, which, believe me, are worse than you can imagine. Even there they believed Christ was stronger than I. Meanwhile on their uniforms the Templars wore the blood-red Cross of the *sang réal*, the true blood, flaunting the blood of Christ.'

His lips compressed into a thin line. 'Jesus Christ, who had challenged Me. From the very beginning of the human world people had worshipped Me. From being a saviour, a dying and reborn god of fertility, praised to the sky each spring and harvest, I was the enemy.' He drew a deep breath through His flared nostrils. 'I went to great lengths. Great lengths. Finally I made a child of flesh of my own and set him loose. In the year 1188 Jerusalem fell to the Muslims, and Sir Nicholas Mason fled in a sailboat from the Holy Land to France. With him was Bernard de Blanchefort, son of Blanchefort the God-thief. My

576

Nicholas made friends with Bernard and was shown the mountain opposite Château Blanchefort where the body of Jesus lay concealed. With his own eyes Nicholas saw the prize as fresh and bleeding as though He still lived. I knew.'

I whispered, 'Stop.'

'Panic set in, the Templars were only human. Everyone thought, after Jerusalem, the Muslims would invade France as they had before. Nicholas helped move the body to a safer location. In fact he made sure of it. A cart to Bordeaux, the Templar ship *Baucent* to London. The prize was buried in one of the chalk caverns deep below the Temple in London. You had no idea?'

I was exhausted, defeated. I hadn't known.

I was too weak to whisper. I tried to shake my head, then closed my eyes.

Satan opened my eye with His fingertips, grinned. 'You kept searching for the truth, though, poor you. Wotan the fallen superhero, archetype of all heroes, Wotan the fool. I'd won. I was the master of God. I had nothing to fear. He was mine.'

I stared into His eye. 'You?' I whispered. 'You said *nothing to fear*. You live in fear?'

He swallowed. 'Don't you?'

'No.'

'It doesn't matter. Dawn on Friday the first of October, 1307. Every Templar in France was arrested, imprisoned, tortured. None revealed the prize, toothless old men mostly, none of them knew anything. The Templar fleet had already sailed.'

'I sailed with them.'

'The old stories are the best. The Templars knew the legends, they'd been to Sion by the Dead Sea, planted sugar cane in their farms there, found caves and pots and scrolls. A land to westward, keep the star Merak on your right eyebrow and the North Star on your right temple.

The Templars fled to New Sion, skull and crossbones flying at the masthead, and built a new Temple on Rhode Island. But all you brought with you was treasure, gold, silver, precious jewels, nothing of real value. You failed again, Wotan.' He put His face close, His eyes against mine. 'The Templars didn't have time to get it away. The prisoner was still in London, still mine. Chained.'

He gave a sudden laugh, much too loud. The walls shook.

I whispered, 'Why are you telling me all this?'

'This is hardly anything.'

'I'm impressed.'

He gave the same laugh. 'Yes, Wotan. Accept defeat. My power is total. There is no battle between us, you see. I won a long time ago. That's all you need to know.'

He was trying to persuade me of my defeat. I whispered, 'But you're the Liar. The Deceiver. The Tempter. How can I believe the truth of a word you say?'

He chuckled. 'Wotan, look at you! Pathetic, not an ounce of strength in you! Not a thimbleful of lust! What could you possibly offer me?'

I heard a sound. Jeri's eyes flickered. She saw Satan crouching over me on the bed, gave a low cry, and slumped back unconscious.

Without looking at us Christine went to the bathroom, turned on the light, ran the tap, and returned with a cold flannel. She folded it and cleaned Jeri's face, still ignoring us.

'I won't hurt her,' Satan said. 'Look, she likes my crown.'

'Please don't.'

'No, of course not.' He smiled, so I knew He would. Then He said: 'You aren't still trying to fight Me, are you, Wotan? Remember, I hold your soul in My hand.' He made a small movement of His hand and I saw Jerusalem, coaches flashing with Mediterranean sun, a gold dome, taxis, Uzis and uniforms, the ancient broken length of the

Wailing Wall, whatever Winona saw.

I whispered: 'There must be something I can do for you.'

'Hardly anything.'

So I knew there was something.

I whispered, 'I'll do anything.'

'Really?'

'I'll do anything. Don't hurt her.'

'Promise? Anything?'

'No.'

'Ah. That I understand. You're older and wiser, you could have been a worthwhile adversary. I fooled you once before, didn't I. Tempted you. Don't you love temptation? I won't promise you anything this time. Anything at all.'

'If you hurt her I'll kill you somehow. That's my promise. Remember Huwawa . . .' I stopped, lay weakly, heart fluttering.

'How could I forget,' He said silkily. 'Poor Huwawa.' He made the same small movement of His hand.

Winona?

Wotan! Where am I? Is it still Jerusalem? It's so dark in here! It's gloomy and I can hear terrible noises. It's like that place beneath the New Jerusalem Club, the seven circles. The seven circles going down getting worse and worse. There's screaming, it's getting worse. Wotan, don't leave me, where am I?

Keep calm. You're still in Jerusalem. Imagine my hand. Imagine my hand holding you. I am stronger than anything and I love you. I know what He wants.

Satan touched His fingertips to His mouth, inhaled, then sat casually. 'It's nothing. Such a small thing. Nearly two hundred years ago, it's 1823, a young farmer living in the place by then called North America, in Wayne County, which is just north of New York, walked out on an old hill remembered by that time as Cumorah.

His name was Joseph Smith and an angel guided him there. In those days no one understood fully what great cities were buried beneath these hills, or *tells*. They believed "America" to be a new place, without history, a new beginning not connected to the old world. Heavy rains had washed the soil down, revealing a hole. Smith knelt eagerly, he hoped to sell Indian artifacts, he saw gleams, but then more mud slid down. Smith came back, but he couldn't have imagined what a long task had been set for him. Over four years, after his chores were done, whenever he could find time away from his young wife and family, Smith dug out enough earth to get inside the cave.'

'Cumor-Ya,' I whispered. 'Smith found Moroni's cave.'

'He crawled into a heap of dusty stuff, gold sticks, mostly written on. Obviously fabulously valuable to whoever wrote them but useless to him, a forgotten language. Plates of jewelled wood with leather straps as though once meant to be worn, but almost rotted away by damp. When Smith touched them they crumbled, a couple of diamonds fell into his hand, and he knew he was a rich man.'

I whispered, 'He'd found an Urim and Thummim. The oracle the Zadoks consulted before every battle in ancient Israel.'

'Smith the farmboy stared into one of the jewels, by chance seeing through it like a lens on to one of the gold sticks, and suddenly the writing made perfect sense. *This is the stick of Ephraim, for the house of Israel.* Smith took the lens from his eye. Gibberish. Reformed Egyptian. Put the diamond back to his eye, angled it, rotated it, turned it back to front, didn't matter, everything made sense. *Have angels ceased to appear unto the children of men? Has He withheld the power of the Holy Ghost from them? Will He withhold it for as long as time shall last, or the earth shall stand, or there shall be one man upon the face thereof to be saved?* The Book of Enoch, the First Book of Nephi, hundreds of them. Smith stared around him, gaping. A movable feast. More than he could translate in a lifetime. Young Joseph Smith knew he'd found something far more valuable than diamonds. He'd found Scripture.'

I remembered Moroni sitting in the mouth of the cave, the dark outside, the single candle flame gleaming. 'There was more,' I whispered.

Satan sat idly. 'Nothing of importance.' He yawned, sat cross-legged.

I whispered: 'The sceptre King Mulek found.'

'Oh, that. Some old man – wasn't it Ether, last Zadok of the Jareds? – led Mulek to that place. Mulek built his Temple over the top. Of course, a sceptre.'

'Yes, Ether's sceptre.'

He clicked His fingers. 'Zarahemla. Something to do with turning Zarahemla to fire. Years later. Everything destroyed.' He grinned. 'Whole peoples.'

'Yes,' I whispered. 'Almost everything was destroyed.'

'Tut.'

'Mulek had discovered a tunnel and something in it. A round silver ball, a perfect mirror.'

'Really? A common symbol for God among pagan peoples, gnostic Christians, Templars. The Unknowable. The Is Not-Is. The Hidden God of the Kabbalist mystics.'

'Just like the one Moses found.'

'Ah.' He shrugged, but for the first time I smelt the smell of Him, like a lake of burning shit.

I whispered: 'Mulek even made the same sort of box to contain it, near as he could. An Arch of the Covenant. The fiery Sword of Mulek.'

'And Mulek had Ether's sceptre and the Urim and Thummim to decipher the instructions and put the hellish creation to good use.' He nodded. 'So that's how so few conquered so many and brought them to God.'

'Until it got out of hand and destroyed Zarahemla.'

He yawned. 'What happened to the Sword of Mulek, do you know?'

This was it. I whispered, 'Come close. I'm weak.'

Satan dropped his great hands on each side of me and leant close, purple cloak flopping over us, almost cutting out the light.

I whispered: 'It's where you can't have it.'

'I can have almost anything almost anywhere.'

I whispered, 'It fell into its own lava, and circles the centre of the earth until the end of time.'

He was startled. 'How do you know?'

I thought of Joshua. 'Someone very important told me. Impeccable authority.' Had Joshua foreseen this moment would come?

Satan put His fist to His chin, thinking. 'If it circles the centre of the earth it's out of reach.' He glanced at me, keeping up His lie. 'If I wanted it. Which of course I don't.'

My fingertips, barely moving, touched His sleeve. 'The original documents partly translated by Smith have never been found. You've got Mulek's sceptre and Urim and Thummim, haven't you?'

'No!' He laughed. 'Why should I? Why should I care? Old museum rubbish! I told you, I own the body of Christ. I am the victor. I have nothing to fear.' His face lost its laugh, then its smile. His lips hardened and turned downwards at the corners, demonic.

I whispered, '*Own*, or *owned*?'

'I should not have put my faith in chains.' He covered His face with His hands. 'I shouldn't have put my faith in chains.'

A child's voice spoke. 'He's a prisoner, don't you see?' Christine stood shyly by the bed. She reached out and touched His elbow with childish sympathy. 'He understands prisons and chains, that's all. So He thought He could imprison God.'

Satan lowered His head towards her. 'Will you come with Me?'

I whispered, 'No, Christine, no, get back.' I saw Jeri staring with wide eyes. 'Jeri. Help her. Help Christine.'

Satan roared, 'WILL SHE COME WITH ME TO HELL, WOTAN? *SHALL SHE?*'

Jeri called, 'Come to me, honey, Christine, come to me, darling.'

'Jeri looks like other girls' mommies,' Christine said. 'She's young. She's real pretty. I like Jeri.'

'My Lord, don't hurt them,' I whispered. 'My Prince, I know what you want. I know you have the sceptre and the Urim and Thummim, I know what you need.'

'He has no freedom,' Christine said. My God, she was unafraid. I stared at her in wonder. She pointed. 'He loses at the end of time. He's a loser. He knows it.'

'Silence your child.' Satan lifted my head in one hand. 'Wotan, defy me no longer.' His voice grew, gathering in power and depth like a wave drawing itself up in the sea, rushing forward like the wind as He pressed His face close to mine, skull to skull. 'I am the Destroyer. I know no love, God's love was taken from Me, like the love of a mother and father and wife and family and everything I loved and possessed and treasured, His love was taken from Me. I am the chief of angels thrown down by God. God help me, I'll destroy you all. God help me, I'll hurt God any way I can. I'll take His people from His love. *I'll destroy you all!*' He stood with His arms against the ceiling. The room shook. 'GIVE ME WHAT I NEED!'

He was ready.

I whispered: 'I can give you the Arch of the Covenant. I can give you the Power of God. I can give you the crown of stars that is lost.'

Wotan! Are you crazy?
What do you see?

583

Wotan, don't let me die!

You can't die. You're part of me. Imagine my hand. Hold my hand.

Don't let me fall! Fire, it's all fire below. It's Hell. It's huge circles of fire turning, it's bigger than anything, my God, it's almost everything. I can see mountain ranges and burning mountains and burning seas. Don't let me fall! I'm falling!

I love you I love you. Hang on to that. He hasn't won. He still thinks I have a soul.

Aaah, Wotan, I'm falling, I'm hanging on, the circles are going round and round, it's rising up, it's coming up, it's coming closer—

Satan stood on the bed, lifted my limp body in one hand. The damp sheet clung to my withered breasts then slid down. I hung naked and emaciated from His grasp, strengthless, my toes brushing the pillow. He murmured, 'Can you give Me what you promise?'

'To save my daughter. That's the deal.'

He glanced round. 'Done.'

Christine said: 'And Jeri too. I like Jeri.'

'Done.'

Christine said, 'And you mustn't hurt Mommy or Daddy.'

Satan grinned. 'Wotan won't be able to live with himself afterwards. He'll beg to die.' He shrugged. 'Done.'

'Write it,' Christine said. She went to the desk and found a piece of white hotel paper and a ballpoint pen, held it up.

'Child.' He stared at her curiously. 'Your soul is perfect. Not one stain.'

'Write it on the white paper then.'

Satan dropped me on the bed, reached out, and branded the paper with His fingertip, in fire.

He turned me over with His toe. 'If you keep your promise, I will keep mine. Show Me.'

Wind rushed into the room. He was gone.

Wotan?

I'm here, I love you, are you still holding my hand?

Oh my God, yes! Yes! Help me. Help.

Tell me what you see.

Hell. The circles of Hell.

Winona, I love you. Don't give up. He's coming. He's there.

I'm so alone. Thousands burning, can't you hear them? The oceans below are made of burning sinners, I see islands of burning crosses, the mountains above are burning sinners. All falls down, all rises up. Wotan, I'm so alone.

Winona, hold on.

I'm standing on a winding stair. There's nothing below, only fire, pain. Wait. Wait.

Winona?

There's something. There's something.

Don't look.

There's darkness. Satan. Satan's here at the centre. I'm so cold. Something immense. The doors are opening, everything's dust. Dusty caverns, people thrown down like fish. Can you see? Can you hear?

I'm with you, Winona. I feel you. Hold my hand.

Gates, huge gates, a city of gold, cheap gold. Pandemonium. A golden palace, dreadful. At each gate something's stripped from my body, claimed, not-mine. A kind of death. The third gate, the fourth. Help.

Winona, keep talking. Talk.

The sixth gate. I'm naked.

I bet you look great.

I love you, I love you, I'm hanging on to that. Stars above and below. Columns of fire and dust ten thousand light-years tall, galaxies turning like spoked wheels, neutron stars. I can't stop, I can't stop. I'm in the sixth room of the palace. The seventh gate.

Winona? Are you there?

I'm small. I'm so small. The gate's opening. I can't stop. A throne as big as the universe. Something. A buzzing of bees, bee stings. Can't you feel His pain?

I only feel you, I love you.

Desolation. Misery. Loss. Abandoned. Forsaken. The Serpent.

Winona?

HEAR ME IF YOU HAVE TWO GOOD EARS TO LISTEN. I AM B'EL, THE SON OF GOD.

Winona, don't listen. Hold on to my hand.

I AM BAAL, B'ELIAL, B'ELZEBUB, B'EL-ZEPHON, S-T-N, MY NAME IS LORD. I AM SATAN, LORD PRINCE OF THIS WORLD. THIS WORLD IS MINE, YOU ARE MY PEOPLE.

He's here. He's here. All around. Wotan, you're brilliant. I see it now. He looks – no, He looks – looks like an angel, a huge angel of black iron. Everything's uncoiling, spreading. This is the place where there's nothing but lies. Oh my God, He's—

SHOW ME.

I lay on the hotel bed where He'd dropped me, my passive face scrunched round by the pillow, one of my legs hanging over the edge. I felt Christine lifting at my foot, trying to get my body back in bed.

'No,' I whispered.

Christine called Jeri and they both lifted at my emaciated leg. 'Poor old thing,' I heard Jeri mutter. 'Doesn't she even have a nightdress? I hope I never get old, get my butt wrinkly like that. But she does have those beautiful blue eyes. And look at her hair. I bet she was blond once.'

I whispered, 'Food.'

Jeri leant close. 'What?'

I clutched Christine's wrist with my fingertips. 'Food, for pity's sake.'

'Food? She's too weak to eat,' Jeri said.

I gasped, 'Give me food.'

Jeri followed my eyes.

'But that's disgusting,' she said.

Wotan? I'm flying! I feel so powerful! It feels like the whole world's mine. I can hardly feel you, He took my hand in His, He whirled me up, Hell's all around us, it's fallen away below, I see Jerusalem, it's so tiny. It's nothing. Satan is an angel, He told the truth, a huge beautiful angel.

Winona! He never tells the truth.

It's so lovely up here. I'm looking down on birds and planes, I can see the curve of the earth. It's not like flying, I feel like a god. I could fly by myself, by my own willpower, I see that now.

Let Him hold you, Winona. He's the Tempter. Don't fall.

I can feel your hand too. I'm imagining you. Oh, it's so beautiful up here. I'm so fast! I can see the world like a map. I can see the Gulf. A yellow island in the blue between Saudi Arabia and Iran, is that really Eden? Oh God I'm flying like an angel. I can see the land of two rivers, Shem. It's Iraq! All those cities buried under the desert . . . it's so lovely. A city. Baghdad, is that Bab'El? I can see the cars glinting. Desert again, river valleys, hills. Where's the trees? Where's the cedar trees? It's bare, bald. A road, a barracks, a petrochemical works. Mountains ahead.

Here sounds good.

I'm pointing. Down, down. Anywhere?

A hilltop. I chopped down Huwawa's tree and killed him on a hilltop.

But I want to keep flying.

Don't give up on me, Winona. Hang on.

IS THIS THE PLACE?

Jeri covered her mouth. She looked haggard. Christine dropped the lid back but the smell didn't stop. She pinched her fingers over her nose and turned towards me but the steak slid off the bone, slipping between her fingers. She picked the rotten meat off the carpet, dropped it on the bed. She swallowed, watching me. With all my strength, bones cracking, I pushed my lips to the sweet soft meat, licked the juices with my dry tongue. Christine burped, turned away. 'Don't look, Jeri,' she said. Jeri stared.

I got a piece of the fat between my teeth, chewed weakly. A piece came off in my mouth, I found the strength to swallow it, took another bite. My hand moved. I pulled the meat towards me, ate.

'More food.'

Wotan? I'm standing on top of a hill. I'm saying maybe this looks like the place, I can't be sure. So long ago, all that, everything changes over six thousand years. Can't quite remember, blah, blah, seems familiar. Am I doing OK?

Keep it up.

He's angry. He's real angry. I don't know how long I can keep this up.

Tell him maybe another hill. Don't let go.

I hope to God I don't choose the right hilltop by mistake.

So do I.

I sat up weakly. 'Food!'

Christine and Jeri pulled the trolley to my bed. I leant on my elbows, fed more steak between my lips, chewed, swallowed. Steak, chicken breast, maggots, all soft and easy to eat, I filled my palms, pushed them against my mouth. Chocolate cake topped with cream and strawberries, profiteroles, a roast chicken which I tore in half, more steak, a bowl of salted nuts. Avocado pears, skins and all, and the pits. I found the lobster, upended it, sucked the meat out, cracked the shell, ate it impatiently. I could feel my strength coming back into me. My long blond hair fell over my eyes, I threw it back with my wrist, took a deep breath, belched, grinned at Christine. 'Good!' I said.

'Daddy,' she said reprovingly, 'you're just as naked as Mommy was.'

I pointed at the wardrobe, the thick leather workpants Winona had bought, pulled them on. Jeri stared at me. She didn't say anything. I ate the loaves and pushed away the trolley. 'Excuse me, ma'am.' I looked in the second trolley, more steak, saw the magnum of champagne on ice, pulled out the cork with my teeth and drained the bottle, belly fizzing with strength, then crunched the lobster in three bites. Christine looked at me with round adoring eyes. Winona had told her what to expect.

'Daddy!' She hugged me.

Wotan?

I'm here. I can hardly hear you.

I'm so faint. I'm seeing through me.

Believe in yourself.

He's so angry. I'm so alone, so afraid. I think He suspects you tricked Him. He can't believe it. He can't believe it. Everything's dust. I'm fading.

Winona! Hold my hand. Hold my hand, don't let go. He can't hurt you. Hold tight.

He knows—

YOU, WOTAN? *YOU* TEMPTED *ME?*

'Hold tight,' I called. The imprint of His hand was stamped into my own right hand, scarred long ago by the dragon's tooth. The imprint hardened, squeezing down, fingers were wrapped around my wrist like bands of iron. I pulled Winona into me and Satan stood in the hotel room, crown, cloak and all, His hand locked in mine. We twisted and turned, struggling, faces pressed together, teeth clenched. He threw me against the wall but I gripped, held Him. The muscles in my arm swelled, straining. The bed broke, the trolleys went over, Jeri pulled Christine into the corner and crouched over her. Plaster fell from the ceiling on her head and shoulders, a sparking electric socket started a fire, they tried to put it out. I stood on tiptoe against Satan, got my foot on His thigh, held Him down. 'Absolute power, absolute temptation,' I said. 'You were tempted, you bet. And I won. You fell.' He banged with His head, slashed with His teeth and I lifted Him, we struggled eye to eye. His face changed, angelic, demonic. He was terrified. He'd lived for eternity in fear, spreading fear; in loss, spreading loss; in sin, spreading sin. He was a small creature.

'Christine said it right,' I said. 'You're a loser.'

I SHALL CRUSH YOUR SOUL INTO MY LEFT HAND AND INTO MY RIGHT HAND, I SHALL TRAMPLE YOUR SOUL BENEATH MY TRAMPLING FEET, AND YOU SHALL SCREAM IN TORMENT TO THE END OF TIME.

I held up my scarred hand to His face.

'I have no soul,' I said quietly. 'Your own Huwawa cursed me. I have no death.'

He watched me without a word. He still did not believe His power was broken. He still believed that one day, somehow, He could climb high enough to climb back to God, to wriggle His way back to Heaven somehow and be all He had once been and not be fallen. He still thought He could get away with it.

He whispered, 'Let me go.'

I tightened my grip.

He whispered, 'You can't do this. God is greater than Me only at the end of time, in the last orbit of the last electron. Then my defeat will be total and the truth will be known. But not until then. I am the lie that illuminates the truth. Wotan, without Me there is no truth.'

Christine shouted: 'Don't listen to Him!'

He turned at once, snaking at her, but I gripped Him in my hands and then my arms, squeezing, tightening, swinging Him round, the balcony doors burst outwards into the Salt Lake City sunlight like a shining rain as He grew upwards, immense, screaming, darkening, a screaming angel with His hands outstretched reaching towards the clear blue Christmas sky, His weight crashing down through the hotel floors: and as I held His ankle I looked up and saw Him as He really was, all masks stripped away, as I really knew Him, the blood-red Dragon rising like a mountain.

His eyes opened, filled with terrible suffering.

I pulled all my strength into me, I gripped His heel, I lifted, I heaved, I never let go.

The Dragon roared, great wings of blood unfolding as He fell, but it was too late for Him. His spines and horns and scales struck the buildings and the street, He fell across the hotels and the temples and the highways, and the earth rose up like dust with His fall.

Like dust, and like dust blew away on the wind.

Ambulance sirens, police sirens. The sound of them rose and fell. News cameras and shouting people. Dust and smoke still drifting across the sky, then fire crews and fire hoses snaking, the roar of pumps and the hiss of water. I lay on the street with every bone broken. An ambulance bumped around the edge of the crater. They were still bringing people out of the hotel. A Santa stumbling past saw me, called the ambulance crew. Four of them lifted me on a stretcher.

They slid the stretcher in the back of the ambulance. Christine and Jeri were already sitting there, blankets round their shoulders, their hair covered in dust. On her lap Christine held the children's paintings from the Holy of Holies, unbroken, untarnished, perfect. The ambulance set off weaving towards the hospital and she held my hand. She kissed my lips.

'Daddy, I love you.'

'I feel better already,' I said. I winked at Jeri. 'Hello, Jeri.'

'It's a miracle you're alive,' Jeri said.

'Oh, that,' I said, eyeing her, trying to sit up and look good, she really was completely pretty. 'That's always the miracle.'

Epilogue

The end of time

Epilogue
The end of time

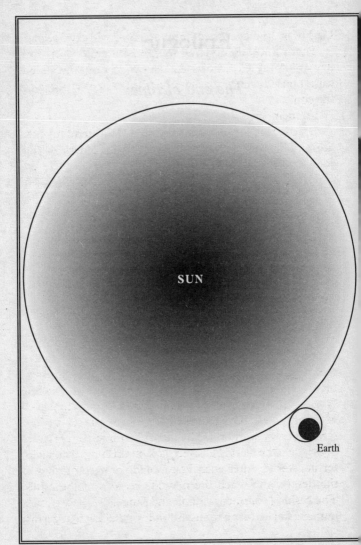

SUN

Earth

Darkness. In a thousand hours the Sun will rise. Listen!

That's the song of how I fought Satan and won, for a day or two at least. For a day or two the mother's hand wasn't raised against the father, or the father's hand against the son.

I remember.

Here in the deepest cave of dusty Earth I tend my little fire, and pull my cloak tighter about my shoulders. I could see your eyes in the firelight, if you had eyes.

Have angels ceased to appear unto the children of men? Will He withhold them for as long as time shall last, or the earth shall stand, or there shall be one man upon the face thereof to be saved?

One man.

I. Still young. Unsaved. Last.

Is there a footstep behind me? I turn slowly. 'Mary?'

Perhaps, perhaps not. I'm alone, except for you.

Kidu was wrong; love was exactly the gift God *did* give to me. I love you for ever.

The former world passed away, new Heavens and new Earths were born, new generations were born and died in their billions of joy and grief. I remember ten thousand times ten thousand new cultures rising up and falling down. I remember the sticks of Judah and Ephraim parted in infinite ways, brought together again, scattered again; I remember the world ruled by men, by women, by children. I've known the world light and dark, flourishing, irradiated, fertile, sterile. After each Fall a blade of green grows in the desert, after each fire new life rises from the ashes. The rushing continents bump and slide like jigsaw games; humans fall extinct a thousand times, smaller than germs, larger than empires. Nothing changes. It is all ordained. The smallest particle knows its place and path. Nothing happens by accident; there is no chaos.

I am immortal. I cannot die.

I lived in the forests, but the forests died; I lived by the oceans, but the oceans boiled; I camped by the last lake of bubbling salt, but the Sun covered half the sky.

Walk with me. Come outside.

There's nothing. My Earth's a ball of ancient dust, worn out. The sky's all stars, no darkness exposed between them. Look, only two mountains remaining on the planet; those two pyramids of sand, one on each horizon, which I built up with my own hands handful by handful by handful. The gap between them measures the growth of the Sun, a hairsbreadth each thousand years. When its rim touches both peaks at once, the time has come.

The swollen Sun rises, vast and slow and cool, deep as a quivering eye.

The Moon hangs in the sky like a burning coal, bitten by the shadow of the Earth.

The Sun's rim touches the twin peaks, the face of the Sun touches the Earth, and the Earth circles inside the Sun like a burning meteor.

I shall never die.

Even the deepest cave is burnt away. Every dark place is gone. Nothing remains but illumination. My body's stripped away by radiation, my strong muscles, my seeing eyes, my thinking brain, my beating heart. There is no death. The star burns my body to fine nuclear plasma, radiates my consciousness to the universe like a billion billion other stars, conscious, self-aware, complete. Beginning the journey.

I whisper, 'Mary?'

I am Wotan, son of El, and I remember the moment of my conception.

Resurrection

Philip Boast

From the last Ice Age to the Industrial Revolution London had at its heart a holy place. A place of worship, of reverence, of violence, of mystery. Five cathedrals were built on the site, four were razed to the ground.

Beneath their foundations rested a secret, a legacy whose existence was passed on through generations of women, that could hurt and heal in equal terrible measure – the lost gospel of Judas Iscariot . . .

An unforgettable story of two millennia and the loves, faiths and passions of the men and women who, as they played out their lives around the holy place we now call St Paul's Cathedral, grasped at a fragment of eternity.

0 7472 5379 X

HEADLINE

Sion

Philip Boast

Wednesday 19 June, 9 BC, 6:04 am

'Forget what you knew. God is dead, for He has forsaken us. I, Mary the Rainmaker, prophet, abandoned by the God of my fathers, gagged, bound hand and foot, set adrift by the priests of Sion in a rudderless boat on a lifeless sea, know this for certain: there is no God . . . God will never send His Son to be our salvation in this hellish abandoned world.'

But the Rainmaker's life is not ended; her story is about to begin. For Mary Magdalene has just been born in Galilee and is later to witness a spectacular birth in a poor stable in Bethlehem.

Joshua is the Son of God. But He is nothing like the Messiah Mary, and others, had expected – yet she falls in love with Him. Hopelessly, of course, because the Christ is the one man who can never marry her or give her children . . .

But what if He did?

SION is an unforgettably passionate epic which tells of the history of humankind and of the extraordinary relationship between an incredible woman and perhaps the most controversial figure ever to have lived: Jesus Christ.

0 7472 5960 7

HEADLINE

If you enjoyed this book here is a selection of other bestselling titles from Headline

THE TIES THAT BIND	Lyn Andrews	£5.99	☐
WITH A LITTLE LUCK	Anne Baker	£5.99	☐
LOVE ME TENDER	Anne Bennett	£5.99	☐
WHEN THE PEDLAR CALLED	Harry Bowling	£5.99	☐
REACH FOR TOMORROW	Rita Bradshaw	£5.99	☐
WHEN THE LIGHTS COME ON AGAIN	Maggie Craig	£5.99	☐
STAY AS SWEET AS YOU ARE	Joan Jonker	£5.99	☐
CHASING THE DREAM	Janet MacLeod Trotter	£5.99	☐
WHEN THE DAY IS DONE	Elizabeth Murphy	£5.99	☐
MY SISTER SARAH	Victor Pemberton	£5.99	☐
NO ONE PROMISED ME TOMORROW	June Tate	£5.99	☐
THE SOUND OF HER LAUGHTER	Margaret Thornton	£5.99	☐

Headline books are available at your local bookshop or newsagent. Alternatively, books can be ordered direct from the publisher. Just tick the titles you want and fill in the form below. Prices and availability subject to change without notice.

Buy four books from the selection above and get free postage and packaging and delivery within 48 hours. Just send a cheque or postal order made payable to Bookpoint Ltd to the value of the total cover price of the four books. Alternatively, if you wish to buy fewer than four books the following postage and packaging applies:

UK and BFPO £4.30 for one book; £6.30 for two books; £8.30 for three books.

Overseas and Eire: £4.80 for one book; £7.10 for 2 or 3 books (surface mail).

Please enclose a cheque or postal order made payable to *Bookpoint Limited*, and send to: Headline Publishing Ltd, 39 Milton Park, Abingdon, OXON OX14 4TD, UK.
Email Address: orders@bookpoint.co.uk

If you would prefer to pay by credit card, our call team would be delighted to take your order by telephone. Our direct line is 01235 400 414 (lines open 9.00 am–6.00 pm Monday to Saturday 24 hour message answering service). Alternatively you can send a fax on 01235 400 454.

Name ....

Address ....

....

....

If you would prefer to pay by credit card, please complete:
Please debit my Visa/Access/Diner's Card/American Express (delete as applicable) card number:

Signature .... Expiry Date..............